THE FIFTH COIN

Clydean O'Conner

Jacket Design by Mary Helen Preston

Library of Congress - United States Copyright
Control Number: TXU-335-130.
Effective Registration Date May 5, 2008

ISBN 978 098 1945 507

DEDICATION

This book is dedicated to people everywhere, who ever wondered whether the Bible is a metaphor, or if we are to accept every word as literal truth.

Did the Bishops, who participated in the Council of Nicea 350 years after Jesus' death, eliminate critical information? Did they only include books in the Bible to suit their own political ambitions and control over members?

You are invited to suspend belief and ask the question: What if everything we've been taught to believe in is wrong?

ACKNOWLEDGEMENTS

This book would not have been possible without the talent, knowledge, and time of friends who came to my aid when I needed it most. Rachel Korfman, Mark and Sue Potes, David Sadleir, Julianna Russo-Tryde, Cheryle O'Gara and Jeff Bissell. Without the help of Mary Helen Preston this book would have been consigned to the trash can because of my limited mastery of computer technology. There are no words to adequately express my thanks to everyone who gave unselfishly of their time and support.

CHAPTER ONE

Clouds, bruised with rain, cast a pall over a village so impoverished it had no name, no identifying spot on any map. Women hurried children indoors, out of the impending storm. Men turned back from the fields; once the rain began in earnest the ground would become a red, sticky ooze.

A fan suspended from the ceiling of what passed for a hotel room sliced through air so thick with humidity it hung like gauze. The artificial breeze created by shabby blades provided the only relief. Tugging at his collar, a man stepped into the down draft. The ragged uniform stuck to his shoulders and an annoying trickle of sweat slid down his face as he tried to wipe it away with a grimy sleeve.

Rain began to fall in torrents--with a force known only in the tropics.

Water cascaded off the roof as he closed the shutters against the storm.

The door opened and a man in a black cassock slipped inside; his eyes scanned the room. "We are alone?" His tone conveyed an expectation of betrayal.

"Si. There is no one here but you and me." Pointing an Israeli made machine-gun at the priest, Jeraldo Concertas moved with the quickness of a man on the run. He patted the cassock searching for weapons. "Bueno." It was a confirmation rather than an attempt at conversation.

"Only a fool would come armed." The Jesuit withdrew a pack of cigarettes from his tunic. No tremor divulged concern for safety as he cupped his hand to shield the lighter from the current of air stirred by the fan.

"My compadres in Mexico say you can be trusted." Wary eyes explored the priest's face for signs of deceit.

"Your friends are right. I'm here to assist your cause."

"I have known priests to lie." The Uzzi motioned toward the chairs surrounding the table below the fan. "If we are to form an alliance it must be struck quickly. Someone might recognize me and alert the police."

The chair's cane bottom was broken, and a multitude of scars climbed the legs. The priest chose to remain standing. He tapped the cigarette ash onto the floor--the gesture casual, a man in control of his emotions. "A Jesuit brother in Mexico said you need arms, ammunition and medical supplies."

"We always have need of these things. Why is the Church willing to supply them?" Picking up the pack of cigarettes the priest tossed onto the table Concertas helped himself, then squinted against the smoke.

"Suppression of the poor must be stopped! We want to aid the cause of justice--otherwise there is nothing ahead for your people but poverty and starvation." Smoke rings encircled the Jesuit's head; an aura of power enveloped the priest, then vanished as the fan continued its relentless circles--one blade endlessly chasing the other.

Beyond the shuttered window the storm smothered all light from the sky; activity in the streets ceased, as if people sensed something was coming.

"It has been so for many years. Why is the Church concerned for us now?"

"We have *always* been interested in the welfare of Latin America, but now we have a leader who is strong--a man who is willing to challenge injustice. Jesuits can once again fulfill our original calling."

"What do you want in exchange?" Suspicion made Concertas wary. He'd listened to other offers that vanished like cigarette smoke in the fan's wake.

"Just your friendship. We want you to be friends with the Church." The priest stubbed out the cigarette in the bottom of a rumpled soft drink can that served as an ashtray.

"Most of my men are devoted Catholics."

"And you?"

"I haven't been to mass since I was a child."

"That couldn't have been too long ago."

"The jungle turns a man old before his time." Smoldering eyes underscored a hardened stare. "It's difficult to believe friendship would be an adequate trade for supplies costing millions of pesos."

"Your rebellion will come to nothing without ammunition and

guns."

"I would sell my soul for what I need to wage my war."

"Your war?"

"Mine, and every man, woman and child who has ever been poor in Central America."

"I can help."

Jeraldo spat on the floor then wiped a mustache that drooped below the corners of his mouth with the back of his hand. Distrust made him cautious; behind bait there was always a trap. "I think there has to be more to this offer than a pledge of friendship."

"The Church will supply you with money and arms, but I'll need your word you won't betray the identity of your benefactors."

“And, if I do?"

The fan drew the smoke from Concertas' cigarette into a spiral. Tension thickened the air as each man evaluated the strengths and weaknesses of his adversary. Outside, the storm worsened. Lightning stair-stepped down out of the sky and rammed the ground a few yards away. The crash accompanying its descent sent a roar echoing through the room.

When the priest finally spoke, his words pierced the silence that had fallen between them. "The jungle is a hostile place. Unwary men are often swallowed up. People just seem to disappear. They march in with confidence but never return."

Sweat rolled down Jeraldo's face, but he didn't dare wipe away the cold trickle. His throat was dry; his pupils dilated as he struggled against the panic growing in the pit of his stomach.

The rain stopped as quickly as it began, and the heat turned oppressive so fast it was almost as if there had never been any relief at all. Concertas threw open the shutters, hoping to capture cooler air. He watched children playing in puddles, women reopening their stalls, men standing in clusters to discuss the damage. Perhaps he should shake the Jesuit's hand to confirm their agreement but when he turned the priest was gone.

Concertas grabbed the abandoned pack of cigarettes. The trembling which took possession of his hand disgusted him but there was nothing he could do to stop it. A shiver traced the path between his shoulder blades. Somehow, the priest managed to inspire a sense of terror. He was accustomed to dealing with creatures of the jungle, but this priest was more frightening than the reptiles that slithered through the forest or unseen predators lurking in the brush. Jeraldo Concertas couldn't suppress the feeling he'd just made a pact with the Devil.

Amariah straightened the folds of the shortened veil the sisters of her Order recently adopted. Searching for a confidence she didn't feel, Amariah tapped on Dame Angelica's office door in response to a rare summon. In the three years since she became a Benedictine nun, vows of obedience, poverty and chastity were as natural as breathing.

She knocked again. Her father opposed her choice of vocation. He resented everything about a way of life dedicated to a philosophy he couldn't embrace. As a psychiatric physician, electron microscopes, CAT scans and brain wave monitors were his gods! If something couldn't be measured, dissected, or probed, then it didn't deserve a place in his world. To lose his only child to such a chimerical belief was a blow.

The voice calling out was tense. "The door is open."

"You sent for me, Mother?" Amariah was both intimidated and confused.

"Sister Amariah, come in." Abbess Mother Angelica pointed at the chair on the other side of her well-worn desk. "Be seated. I must finish reading this memo before we begin our little chat."

Amariah's glance took in the conditions of the room: Sparse, functional, devoid of sentiment. Allowing her gaze to settle on the Abbess Mother's face, Amariah decided those were the qualities she would use to describe the woman whose concentration was riveted upon a sheaf of papers. Furrows framed a mouth compressed into an uncompromising line.

Lifting eyes that witnessed the tread of Hitler's armies, the creation of nuclear weapons and the footfalls of men on the moon. The Abbess brought her gaze to bear on the sister at the other side of her desk. "So, you've finished at Loyola. Have you considered your future?"

Caught off guard, Amariah was certain she'd made her desire to work with inner-city children quite clear. "I believe there's a copy of the Petition for Position in my file. I hoped to secure a teaching post here, at St. Anne."

"Yes--your petition is here." The Abbess' unflinching stare dashed

Amariah's hopes. "Sister, the request I am going to make will not be to your liking, but I don't need to remind you the Benedictine vows of obedience are not to be taken lightly."

Amariah's heart skipped a beat as she watched the Abbess push the file folder across the desk.

"Sister, the Vatican has summoned you to Rome."

The light in her eyes faded as Amariah strained forward. "Surely, there's been a mistake. They must have me confused with some other sister--someone in another Order."

"I sympathize with your doubt. Let me assure you, Sister Amariah, these orders concern you. It seems your gift of language was reported to the Father General by a Jesuit brother at Loyola."

The Abbess rose, hands clasped behind her back, and began to pace in front of the office's only window. Night took possession of San Francisco and the first pale stars hung against a dark winter sky. Her eyes fixed on the reflection of the apprehensive young woman. "Do you know much about this Father General, the man who leads the Jesuits?"

"Every Catholic knows about Father Simson! He's as famous as the Pope!"

"Our American brother has carved out quite a reputation for himself." The Abbess' voice was tinged with remoteness, as if her grip on control were tenuous at best. "You seem to know a great deal about the Father General." Brittleness claimed both her posture and tone of voice.

"No student at Loyola could escape Father Simson's influence. Many classes are still conducted by Jesuits--most of whom believe in his mission with passion."

"Yes, so it is rumored. Father Simson has a loyal following--a very loyal following." The Reverend Mother returned to the desk and reached for the file folder. "The Father General convinced our blessed Pope you are needed in Rome." Drawing the document into the penumbra of light cast by the desk lamp, the Papal seal flickered; it beckoned; it commanded.

As if reading the younger sister's thoughts, Dame Angelica's voice turned soft, caring. "Father Simson interrupted a busy schedule to assure me you are to be in Rome in ten days." Restlessly, her hand brushed across the papal seal, the motion brusque, the hostility taking up residency in her eyes conveyed the Abbess' distress. "Those are your orders--and it is your duty to obey."

"But!" The word hung in the air, then died on Amariah's lips like the last plaintive note in a sorrow-filled song. Obedience. It was the condition with which all those who chose a life of service to the Church had to contend. Those in authority decided the why and wherefore of a nun's existence. The servant went where called; served where service was needed. Lowering her head, Amariah struggled to hide her disappointment. "Yes, Mother."

Who ruled the Church now, the Abbess wondered? A feeling she didn't like made the muscles in her stomach tense and acid boiled up the back of her throat.

The Father General was the force that decided the fate of nations. He dictated the policies followed by millions of Catholics. If rumors coming from the Vatican about the 'Black Pope' were true, she feared this new horseman of the Apocalypse.

A man in a black cassock pressed himself beneath the foul-smelling cloth suspended from a rusty hook above his head. It might have served as an awning in more prosperous days, but nature destroyed its usefulness long ago. The street was filled with refuse discarded by countless human beings. Because the wharf was nearby, the smell of fish hung in the street like a rancid blanket.

As if attempting to soften the wretched conditions endured by its inhabitants, the setting sun cast red and gold streamers over the city. Father Ryan Evans shifted, seeking a comfortable position for coiled muscles ready to unleash in a preemptive strike. Scanning the crowd, he searched for a man wearing a yellow shirt with a red dragon on the sleeve.

A pebble bounced down the alley behind him. Turning, Father Evans strained to find the source. A flash of yellow caught his eye as a figure darted between a stack of boxes. Hands in his pockets, the priest strolled deeper into the shadow infested alley; a man confident of his abilities, one who relied on and trusted his instincts. As he strolled into the darkness between the two buildings, his fingers closed around the revolver concealed in his cassock pocket. If Cao Bang took him for a fool, the pirate would soon pay for his ignorance. The Jesuit kept moving--alert to danger.

"Go no further, priest. There are many of us here."

The voice came from a pool of shadow. Evan's eyes searched the gap between the buildings for other thieves. If they were there, he couldn't detect them over the stench clinging to the alley like an unpaid whore. Evans learned to distinguish the mainland Chinese by their smell. His eyes roved the pits of darkened doorways and crept along crates that looked like broken teeth as he sought the enemy. Finally, supercharged senses were satisfied the thief was alone. The Jesuit withdrew his hand from his pocket and spread his arms. "I come as a friend. You have nothing to fear."

"Friends I count on one hand—and you are not among them," a crackling voice shot back.

Now he knew where the man was hiding. "I hope to be a part of that hand one day. But trust and respect are earned. I don't expect you to offer them at our first meeting."

Sliding from behind a pile of garbage, a bone-thin man pressed deep into the shadows cast by decrepit buildings. The wind rose and surged inland from the harbor; it swept trash along the broken stones which paved the alley. "Words are cheap, priest, what do you have to offer?"

"Your people need goods. I have friends who can supply you with everything from tennis shoes to microwaves."

Hooded eyes seemed to flatten, and pockmarked skin folded into the semblance of a smile as the thief considered his options. "Why should I trust you?"

"Because I have what you need." Father Evans relaxed coiled muscles.

"I could disappear with your merchandise. Once in China there would be no way to trace me. A Caucasian priest can hardly question government officials about the activities of a known smuggler."

"One thing will keep you from betraying me."

"Oh?" Slipping his hand inside his shirt pocket, Cao Bang fished out a crumpled cigarette package. He was nervous and needed to calm nerve endings sounding an alarm. The match illuminated his face when Cao struck it, then returned to darkness as a cloud of expelled breath extinguished the flame.

In that second, Father Evans memorized the line of the man's jaw, the planes and angles of his cheekbones and nose, fragmented details--a mole, a scar. With an eidetic memory, he recorded the characteristics to identify a potential enemy. "Money from a single trip into the interior would be a one-time gain! You stand to reap a fortune from repeated journeys."

The alley filled with the aroma of tobacco. A trace of a smile lifted lips that were only a gash in a rock-hard face. Greed was the bait in this trap. With the relationship cemented by the prospect of wealth, Cao ground the cigarette beneath the heel of his sandal. "What do you want me to do?"

"Set up connection points throughout the interior. Make certain you have many layers between you and those transporting your merchandise. Nothing must lead to me."

"Priest, why are you doing this?

"Call it paving the way."

"What does that mean?"

"Let's just say when the day comes for the Sleeping Dragon to awaken, the Church will be ready to smooth the differences between the East and West."

"That doesn't tell me why you're willing to be involved in smuggling."

"Curiosity, Cao Bang, is a two-edged sword. It can clear the path of discovery, or it can smite the unwary. Control your curiosity so you will grow to a venerable old age and live to enjoy your newfound prosperity."

The thief leaned against a crate. He knew men like this. Chairman Mao's government was filled with them. Fanatics. Devoted to their ideals. Willing to die for their vision of a brave new world. Shrugging, he ignored the emotions laying claim on his bowels. The priest was willing to pay for his services and money took precedence over conviction. Let others have dreams of glory--he was only interested in what money could buy.

Still, the priest's eyes haunted him; he felt as if the Yellow River was sweeping him along. Many were killed trying to navigate it; the river belonged to the gods, not to man. There was another quality about the priest that frightened Cao. Something sinister lurked below the Jesuit's words. His mannerism implied military training. Years among the cut-throats which clogged Hong Kong's harbor fine-tuned Cao's instincts. Despite his cassock and cross, this priest was a killer! A predator's hungry eyes made Cao's flesh crawl and a pang of horror made it hard to think when the priest looked at him.

A trickle of light dribbled from a just risen moon. The alley became his Aceldama as he accepted the money: Cao Bang knew he just betrayed China.

The L1011 leveled off as it reached the cruising altitude which would take the load of passengers over the North Atlantic . . . the shortest way to

Rome. Like a shadow, the circumstances ahead cast a pall over Amariah's thoughts. She tried to concentrate on pictures of Roman ruins and the city's splendid churches, but a simple guidebook couldn't provide the kind of information she was seeking. Amariah wondered what it would be like to work in the Vatican library amid books dating back to the dawn of Christianity. How would it feel to sit beneath the frescoed ceilings painted by history's greatest artists--Raphael, Michelangelo, and Botticelli? As much as she looked forward to seeing the fountains created by Renaissance sculptors like Ligroin, Sollecito and Jan van Santen--Amariah was intimidated by the Father General's summon.

The Abbess' parting words ran through her thoughts like an annoying refrain.

'Father General Simson said you will translate documents in the Vatican's Secret Archive. The Archive is only opened for the Pope and his most trusted advisors. Thousands of documents have lain undisturbed for centuries. To shed light on matters locked away for generations might prove dangerous. Unintended consequences have the power to reshape history. I do not have good feelings about what the Father General is doing.'

Amariah retreated to the comfort of the rosary, hoping the Abbess Mother's concern was based on a fear of change, of the future--of growing old and being unable to adapt to anything new.

An ebony face topped a clerical collar so white it dazzled. Strong hands supported the man just released from a cramped, dark cell. The prisoner's eyes tried to focus on the collar, but they couldn't adjust to the sunlight. It hurt to walk. Years of imprisonment and torture reduced once proud muscles to worthless strips of meat, but he knew he'd walk again. He'd march against the whites who consigned his race to misery for generations.

A compassionate tone whispered in his ear, and he struggled to comply. There was a sense of urgency about the voice, a commanding tone that made him want to concentrate. Instinct sharpened by survival warned the sotto voice must be followed without question. If he wanted to live to fight another day the man, who supported his weight, was to be obeyed instantly, blindly.

A nod let the priest know he was understood. "I'll do the talking. Keep your head down. Don't look any of the guards in the eye. If you do, they'll see they haven't smothered your spirit and I won't be able to get you out of here."

Switching from a clipped, almost brutal tone of voice to the cultured speech of an Oxford graduate, the Jesuit's words speared the gatekeeper. "This man's release is in order. The Prime Minster of England confirmed his right to freedom. We will be on the next plane to London." Father Michael Sorenson shoved the documents at the guard. "His passport is stamped, and his visa processed. You won't have trouble with him again."

The jailer pressed against the filth-stained wall, seeking shelter from the priest. The kaffir was massive, and the black robes of the priesthood lent him a predatory aura. Piercing the grimy window overhead, a shaft of light found its way through the gloom and reflected off the cross in the middle of the priest's chest. The fearless expression occupying the Jesuit's face demanded respect and conveyed an authority which crushed any challenge.

Stepping back, the guard let the priestpass and the prisoner shuffled alongside him. In South Africa, black men couldn't be trusted, even if they were men of the cloth. But the papers were in order and the guard wasn't about to stop a man who acted like the furies of Hell would ride from that godless realm at his beckon.

The rumble of wheels locking into position announced the aircraft was on final approach. Amariah felt her heart quicken and her palms grow moist. What if she couldn't live up to the Pope's expectations? Stomach muscles tensing, Amariah tried to ignore the screech as the wheels slammed against the tarmac; her nerves as strained as the braking force the pilot applied to the aircraft. She was now in Rome.

The Father General was as good as his word, a priest held up a card bearing her name when she entered the terminal. When he caught sight of a Benedictine sister, he waved.

"Dame Amariah? Welcome to Rome!" The priest scooped up her overnight bag then touched her elbow, providing guidance. "Come with me. You've been cleared through customs. The Papal Seal carries great weight here. I know you're tired, but the Father General is anxious to meet you."

Amariah stared at the parapet above the baggage claim area. Like a fortress, the rotunda was surrounded by armed guards with weapons slung over their shoulders. A shiver tracked the path of her spine as Amariah realized how far she was from home.

The twenty-five kilometers between the Leonardo da Vinci airport and the outskirts of Rome was an ever-changing panorama of color. Spring would take up tenancy before long and rolling hills would soon don a mantel of bright flowers.

Streets grew congested as they pressed toward the heart of the ancient city. The Father General's limo slid through a tangle of cars down a street Amariah would consider impassible. It wasn't necessary to honk; both cars and pedestrians gave way to the vehicle bearing the insignia of the Black Pope.

The Leonine walls of the Vatican loomed through the windshield. Amariah lowered the passenger window to get a better view of the most famous church in Christendom. Its towering dome, brass-grilled doors and encircling colonnade sent a thrill through her body. The Egyptian obelisk served as the focal point for Bernini's pillars, symbolic of the Church's protective role in the lives of men. The eye of the beholder was drawn from the obelisk to the entrance of the basilica--and then beyond to the uppermost spire of Michelangelo's dome.

Slowing, the driver turned into the Porta Sant'Anna, the gate in the fortress wall which allowed vehicles access to the city.

"Sister, look," Father Montanegro gestured as they drew near the construction site. "Many are surprised at how much our Father General has done to modernize the Vatican. See those footings for the new museum? We needed to tear down a portion of the Museo Gregoriano de Profano, but time had taken its toll. The foundation was broken in too many places to be restored. Some of Rome's citizens were upset by how little we could save of the original room, but compromise was impossible."

Amariah stepped from the car and stared up at the three-story Pinacoteca. A weathered patina of pale pink marble offered warmth and the drape of white stone added as architectural embellishment reminded her of loops of icing on a wedding cake. Statues in recessed niches made Amariah feel as if many eyes watched her arrival.

"This way." The Jesuit gestured toward three flights of stairs. By the time they reached the top, Amariah's chest was heaving. Afraid she was going to make a miserable first impression, she struggled to find a degree of composure.

"Do you want to catch your breath before you meet the Father General? He's accustomed to receiving visitors who are so out of breath they can't talk. He says it gives him a decided advantage."

Straightening her wimple, Amariah tried to smooth the travel- creased habit but her efforts were futile. As ready as she would ever be to meet the most powerful man in the Catholic Church, Amariah nodded and stepped inside the office.

"Ah . . . Sister." With quick athletic grace, the Father General closed the gap between them. The black cassock strained against wide shoulders and strong biceps filled the sleeves of his robe as he reached for her hand. "I'm so pleased to meet you." His grip was too firm to be friendly; it controlled.

Simson was a medium-sized man although leanness gave an impression of height. Dark, curly hair framed black brows which arched across a field of fair skin. Although he was of English descent, the Jesuit's coloring betrayed a genetic code whose origins might have been rooted in Spain. Moody, tremulous eyes were framed by lashes so black they looked unnatural. The Father General's expression conveyed an intensity Amariah found disorienting. An angry glance from Andrew Simson could wilt the courage of even the most valiant.

Words felt cold and hard on her tongue. "Father, it is an honor to be of service to you and the Holy See." Managing a nod, she hoped would seem differential, Amariah felt a wrongness in the air.

To bring the nun's eyes level with his own, Simson cupped his hand beneath her chin and drew her head up. His words were warm and caring, every syllable and consonant gilded with compassion. "Be assured, Sister, the Church is grateful for your talent. Your work will contribute to the success of this undertaking."

Amariah's knees threatened to buckle. Perhaps jet lag was taking a toll because there was no logical explanation for sudden, turbulent feelings. Perhaps she was confusing fear with wonder.

Sympathy painted his words with broad strokes as the Father General guided their conversation. "Are your talents as marvelous as my friends at Loyola reported?"

His insistence demanded she put discomfort aside. "My skills were probably exaggerated."

The Father General's stare made her feel as if he could see through a self-deprecating response. Embarrassment made Amariah's cheeks turn crimson. "Indeed."

The sun tarried above the horizon and the blood-red stain reflected in Simson's eyes. "Did the Abbess Mother discover your gift of language?"

Amariah fussed with the wrinkles in her skirt, the flitting motion of her hand betraying nervousness. "The Reverend Mother used to comment on the ease with which I learned our Latin psalms. She said my tongue never faltered over the most complex liturgy. But it was really Father Carodine, one of my instructors at Loyola, who set me upon the path of language."

Dark lashes lowered a veil over his thoughts as the Jesuit considered how to respond. "I see, and how did he discover your talent?"

"He showed me a Greek manuscript and it seemed as though I had seen it before. When he explained the alphabet, it was like a light turned on. Somehow, I just knew what the phrases meant. Even obscure syntax was clear. Father Carodine encouraged me to study other languages."

"Languages of the New Testament?" "Those he knew."

"You read, write and speak Aramaic, Latin, Hebrew and Greek?" "And three dialects of Farsi."

"Have you ever wondered why you have this ability?"

"It doesn't seem like a skill because it came so easy."

"Have you ever thought about why it was simple for you?"

As his stare encompassed her again, Amariah decided why she found Father Simson's gaze so disquieting. His eyes reminded her of a snake--the lidless way a reptile stared down its prey always seemed frightening--as if the loathsome creature had the power to hypnotize its victim.

Amariah forced herself to inventory the contents of the sterile room rather than give in to the demanding stare. "My talents are natural, like walking or breathing. I don't think people with any kind of gift consider the reason. It just is, like the color of a person's eyes."

The stillness that lapsed between them ruptured when Father Simson cleared his throat. "I have to assume what you say is true. Still--having struggled so with Latin, I find your talent quite remarkable."

There was something in the way he took her measure, an underlying tone in his words Amariah couldn't quite decipher. The way he folded his arms across his chest made her defensive. As a psychiatrist, Richard Weatherby taught his daughter to decode the signals sent by one human being to another --but something beyond her frame of reference emanated from the most powerful man in Christendom.

A message tugged at the periphery of Amariah's consciousness. Clenched fists. The angle of his head. The direction his eyes traveled when Simson spoke. He was accustomed to wielding power. Andrew Simson was comfortable with authority. Yet a quality lurking beneath the careful patterning of his voice hung in the air like a delicate fragrance. His mannerisms, his emotion-stirring gestures gave Amariah the feeling she was watching a performance. There was something indefinable about this man. A shiver tracked her spine.

"So," he caressed each onyx bead in the rosary chain, "is the team settled in?" A veil lowered across Simson's eyes, obscuring his feelings, masking intent.

"All went well. Most are like children set loose in a candy store. The young nun, Sister Amariah, walked to the Aramaic section as if she studied there all her life."

"Watch this sister, make certain she does not get too far ahead of the others."

With a bow, Father Montanegro whispered, "I will be vigilant."

"We cannot use enough caution now that such brilliant scholars are in our midst." Father Simson's voice trailed away as his attention focused on the truck getting ready to pour a load of concrete into the foundation framework.

Lost in thought, the Father General forgot about the other priest. His dream was coming together in layers of concrete and steel. Before long the world would recognize his mission and begin to live the principles of Christianity. Fingering the lock of hair touching the clerical collar, Andrew Simson's thoughts turned toward a destiny both exhilarating and inspiring. Generations of men had access to the Secret Archive--but he was the one who stumbled across the document revealing how much treasure was buried in the catacombs beneath the Vatican. Early Princes of the Church were political figures. Spirituality lost in the struggle for power. Popes fought wars, gathered plunder, built palaces befitting the dwellings of earthly kings. Their spending infuriated Martin Luther and inspired the Reformation.

A long-forgotten document revealed the location of manuscripts written by the Sibyls and others considered heretics by the early Church. For hundreds of years, no one bothered to categorize the ten thousand unopened packets left to gather dust--until the hand of destiny placed him in charge of the Secret Archive.

Another newly discovered manuscript claimed items of antiquity buried in the catacombs would verify the existence of the man called Jesus. If the moldering parchment was authentic, Simson was confident he would find scrolls written by contemporaries of the Savior--perhaps a document penned by Christ himself! If he found such incontrovertible evidence--it would be easy to lead people back to the Church. He would be the one to implement the early bishop's strategy of universal conciliation. He would restore the Church to its former glory. The Catholic Church would resume its rightful place as the temporal executor of God's will! He would be hailed as the new Messiah, come again, to save mankind from its horrors. He would be the man to create the New Jerusalem. The glory that was Rome would rise again! The Holy City would be resurrected, and the world would follow the one who renewed hope for the future. The museum was only the first step in his plan of salvation. Simson turned from the window. "Status?"

"All units are in place."

"Have they initiated contact?"

"We are waiting for two more to report."

Satisfaction rippled across his face. "You have accomplished much."

"We have a loyal cadre of brothers."

"To your credit."

"Father, the credit belongs to you. You inspired their loyalty."

"Jesuits must breathe new life into the Society for we fight a dangerous war. The Church must regain its prominence and we Jesuits will resume our centuries-old role as Knights of God--protectors of our faith!"

Speculation about the existence of Jesus and the authority of the Catholic Church would be laid to rest. It was only a matter of time before he was accepted as the salvation of mankind. Andrew Simson knew his time was at hand.

CHAPTER TWO

Amariah stared at the Napoleon Hotel lobby. She marveled at the vaulted ceiling and towering archways that were such a part of old-world culture and lent the room so much architectural charm. Wheezing, a bellman hauled her bag up a wide flight of marble stairs, and struggled down a narrow, dim hallway. He ushered her into a room which did not match the opulence of the lobby.

As the bellman departed melancholy threatened. Amariah reached for the band on her right hand symbolizing her devotion to the ideals Christ--an action, which never failed to bring comfort and restore peace of mind. The Church called, and it was her duty to obey without question.

An insistent knock startled Amariah. She glanced at the dangling security chain before responding. "Who is it?"

"It's me--Uncle John! Your father wired me you were coming to Rome and asked me to look in on you as soon as you arrived!"

Amariah flung open the door and hurled herself into the arms of a man whose build belied his age. "You are such a welcome sight--I didn't know you were in Rome!"

How like her father to know when homesickness was likely to claim her feelings. How often did her father call just when she needed an encouraging word? And now, her father's best friend brightened the gloom of a lonely hotel room. Her adopted uncle's presence was a gift of love from devoted parents. Amariah led John Preston into the room and closed the door behind her.

"Daddy didn't tell me you were back in Europe."

"Amariah, your dinner table topics seldom include the wanderings of an international banker. I've been with the Weatherbys on far too many occasions to think you would discuss anything so trivial. World politics and religion are your normal bill of fare. How your mother put up with you and your father all these years, I'll never know. Dick called the other day to tell me when you were arriving and where you'd be spending your first night in Rome.

He said you'll be living in the dormitories at the Vatican after tonight."

"Yes, Father Montanegro is going to call for me in the morning."

"How about dinner? You're probably starved and before you enter the grandiose convent they've created for those of you working on this damned fool project, I'll treat you to a decent meal."

"I don't think things will be all that bad!" A smile exposed Amariah's dimples as she reached for the older man's hand. "This is such a wonderful surprise. I wasn't looking forward to dining all by myself."

"Amariah, I've always wanted to ask, but . . ."

"You want to know why I decided to become a nun. It's such an unfashionable thing to do in today's complex world."

"That's the crux of it."

"Uncle John, I don't know if I can explain. The moment I stepped inside the walls of St. Anne's I felt transported, as if by a miracle I was in the place I belonged."

"I've never felt the call of anything but a Dunn and Bradstreet rating, but it seems like you got caught up in this religious stuff when you were young and impressionable."

"I'm happy with what I'm doing, even if I can't explain it to your satisfaction."

"If you find contentment in your work then it doesn't behoove me, nor your father, to question your judgment. Few people are happy with their work these days, so I won't criticize your choice . . . even if I find the Church baffling."

"Thanks, Uncle John, if my Dad were half as tolerant it would be wonderful."

"He loves you."

"I know," Amariah hesitated, "but I really am happy. I love my life and I'm dedicated to my work."

"What does your mother think about your vocation?"

"She's always supported me."

"I know, but how does she feel about your chosen vocation?"

Her brow folded into a crease, then deepened. She didn't like to think about the disappointment she caused Elizabeth. If there was one person in the world she loved with all her heart it was her mother. "She looked forward to having grandchildren."

"I thought as much."

"I'm not certain she'll ever understand why I became a nun. I'm her daughter so she supports me--maybe that's the best I can expect."

"I give your mother a lot of credit." John Preston scratched his chin as he stared at the door, thinking about Amariah's childhood. "She was determined to let you lead your own life and not be overly influenced by your father."

A wistful note claimed Amariah's voice. "She made sure I didn't become one of Daddy's case studies. I think it was one of the few things she ever challenged him on."

"Honey, it was the only thing! She considered your birth a miracle and felt you were here to do something special with your life. Elizabeth wanted you to find your own way--not to become a reflection of your father."

"I think a life spent in service to others for the glory of God is very special."

Leaning against the rain-spattered window, the banker propped his chin in his hand. "Perhaps it is, Amariah, perhaps it is." He stared at the girl's reflection in the window and was taken back by the freshness of her beauty. It was like looking at the Amariah of childhood again. Lashes framed eyes as blue as summer sky and reddish-brown curls escaped beneath the travel weary wimple.

"Uncle John--why are you asking me this now?"

He exhaled, squared his shoulders, and took a deep breath before responding. "I wanted to know how firm your commitment is before you begin work at the Vatican. Dick told me you will be dealing with Andrew Simson."

A warning tremor stair-stepped through Amariah like a dash of lightning before a clap of thunder. She reached to switch the lamp on, grateful for the light which penetrated the storm inspired gloom gathering outside the window. The distraction gave her enough time to add conviction to her tone of voice. "I spoke with Father Simson just after I arrived."

"Sweetheart, you've been trained to observe human behavior by one damned fine psychiatrist--what was your first impression of the man?"

A chill as strong as the one she felt leaving Father Simson's office traced the path between her shoulder blades. The memory of the coldness in his eyes made her cautious, "He's dedicated to the new museum. We didn't speak of much other than the job in store for me."

"Amariah, we're not talking about his commitment--I want you to tell me about your impression of him."

Amariah dropped her gaze as she thought about their meeting. She struggled to give substance to intangible emotions as her eyes drifted along the molding--then drew upward toward the ceiling. "The Father General was distant, almost devoid of emotion. Were I the one spearheading such a revolutionary project, I would be excited. I'd probably express some anxiety about its success in the face of so much negative opinion, but I don't think dedication describes what I sensed," her glance focused--skewering the banker with the sudden illumination of awareness. "Determination, that's the word I'm looking for! The Father General is going to see this project through at all costs."

"I think you're more correct than you can imagine! I came to take you to dinner, but I also wanted to give you a couple of phone numbers, so you can reach me at any time."

"There's something else you want to say, but you're reluctant. Why?" Amariah studied the way her father's friend leaned into the space separating them, anxiousness the sole occupant of his features. The powerful shoulders that swung her into the air as a child remained strong; burly hands were curled into fists as if ready to take on the nearest contender. Yet, unaccountably, a feeling of helplessness radiated from a face weathered by time. Amariah noticed how much gray advanced through once chestnut-colored hair as a worried expression claimed his face.

"Don't trust this priest too much."

"Someone who leads the Church?' Defensiveness reshaped her eyes and the lines around her mouth became apparent as she compressed her lips. "I cannot believe a man, who has dedicated his entire life to the service of Church, would be untrustworthy!"

"Honey, please keep an open mind! There's something odd about his selection of a nun from a small Benedictine order in America. Surely there are hundreds of talented linguistic scholars available to him. Why you, Amariah, why you?"

Insecurity took ownership and her gaze wandered toward the darkened window, away from the banker's probing stare. "Father Simson said I was highly recommended by several priests at Loyola."

"What else did he say?"

"He asked if I'd ever thought about why I learned archaic languages with such ease."

"And?"

"I told him language skill was the dominant neurological pattern in a brain given to me by God. I can't explain it any more than that."

"Didn't you find his question a little strange?"

"I thought he was trying to make me comfortable, you know . . . Daddy's trick of getting someone to talk about themselves."

"Don't assume for one moment Andrew Simson would stoop to anything so cordial. No, Amariah, you can bet he had a motive. I don't want you to mention me to anyone on the museum team just yet. Simson may know I'm a long-time family friend, but if not--it's better left unsaid." Preston slapped his knee. "Let's go to dinner! Do you have to wear that dreary habit?"

Amariah turned to stare at her uncle. The banker smiled, and a teasing expression warmed his face. She laughed, John Preston always had the power to brighten her mood, so she took no offense at his remark.

"Yes, Uncle John, I must wear my habit and I don't find it dreary at all." She pulled a fresh robe from the closet and waved it in Preston's direction. "I spent considerable time and energy earning the right to wear this veil and robe. They are badges of honor!" Marching into the bathroom, she slammed the door in mock irritation.

A hard rain began to fall, sluicing down a many-paned window, distorting the world beyond, cloaking John Preston from eyes which might be lurking in the darkness. The banker withdrew into his thoughts. No matter what the Father General's reputation, no matter how the priest baffled the press, John Preston had an uneasy feeling about him. A sixth sense which resided in his bones told him the American priest would stop at nothing to achieve his mission.

Amariah studied the men and women brought together to unlock history's secrets as they took their seats in the main study room of the Vatican library. The conversation with her adopted uncle the night before kept rising in her thoughts. 'Amariah, why you?' The echo of John Preston's worried voice hammered in her ears. 'Why you, Amariah?' His question refused mercy; her temples pounded, her palms were moist as insecurity closed around her throat, constricted her chest, squeezing an already overwrought heart.

The scuffle of chairs as the scholars turned toward the back of the room heralded the arrival of the Father General. Amariah studied the Jesuit as he marched down the aisle between the tables and turned to face the group--feet apart, hands clasped behind his back like a general addressing his troops. Close-trimmed hair, crisp black cassock, ramrod straight posture, everything about him suggested a man unaccustomed to compromise.

Simson's voice echoed through the library as he began to address the hand-picked men and women. He knew what he needed to achieve--the critical path plotted with benchmarks established to measure progress. The scholars assembled in the library were the foot soldiers in Andrew Simson's battle plan; their skills would win his victories.

Conviction radiated from his eyes and his hands gripped a well-worn Bible, his knuckles as white as a scapular. Passion assaulted the scholars, incising any residue of doubt. The Father General drew away from the sanctuary provided by the lectern and closed in on the scholars. Sculpted brows framed eyes as cold as flint as he pounded one fist into the other--the sound echoed from architectural biers supporting a ceiling decorated with saints and angels by fifteenth century artists. "Our task is to enlighten the world! To convince people our Lord, Jesus Christ, laid the foundations of our faith before He ascended into heaven. 'Upon thou, Peter, shall I build my Church'. . . and the Church must endure at all costs."

Outside, the sky turned somber, and a blunt wind was growing sharp. The fading light surrounded the Father General in a soft aura. His voice shifted as he assumed the attitude of a loving father figure. "The Church is a sacred institution, ordained by the Son of God, to serve mankind's needs!" His hand swept over the scholar's heads, bestowing a blessing; "You will be responsible for helping humanity comprehend the role the Church played throughout history. Ladies and gentlemen--each of you in this room will act as midwives to the birth of the 'Second Coming'. You will be the new apostles to an ideology that will change mankind forever. Your hands will shape the philosophy, which will save our endangered planet and its ravaged peoples. You are here to restore the Kingdom of God on earth!"

Amariah trembled. Her palms grew moist with perspiration inspired by veneration. This was the first time she'd experienced the power of the Father General's oratory. His ability to enrapture crowds was legendary, but sitting in the emotion-charged room, held prisoner by his voice, captured by the impact of his personality gave her an appreciation for why the American priest had so much influence over others.

Suddenly, Simson's tone became casual, as if the man who'd spoken so eloquently only moments before vanished. "Since the world of biblical scholars is small, most of you are known to each other--so my introductions will be brief. Cormorant eyes roved toward a Franciscan priest, Father Gregory Lean. "Father Lean is an expert in Medieval History through the Renaissance. His knowledge of the early Church will validate the documents we find in the catacombs."

The friar's hunched shoulders made him look as if he had spent his entire life leaning over a pile of manuscripts. Bald, Father Lean's forehead seemed to go on forever. What little remained of his hair sprigged up like feathers over his ears and Amariah thought the tortoise shell glasses made him look like a drab species of barn owl. Despite his appearance, Amariah sensed the priest was a warm, caring man.

Next, the Father General gestured toward a sparse young man leaning on a centuries old glass case. "Leon Kaminski is an expert in Oriental languages. Professor Kaminski worked his way through several universities in Europe . . . Oxford, the Sorbonne, and the University of Bonn. He spent almost six years in villages in Afghanistan, Hindu Kush and Outer Mongolia, mastering languages rarely spoken in the Western world."

Simson's smile radiated warmth when he gestured toward Sister Magdalene, a Carmelite Sister, who wore metal braces on both legs. "Sister Magdalene will be responsible for designing the computer system to preserve data on thousands of historical items. She is already working on a program I have chosen to call "*Messiah*". When complete, this program will have the capacity to link to virtually every PC and main frame in the world. Through "*Messiah*" we will be able to communicate with every man, woman, and child on the planet with access to a computer in the blink of an eye. Think what it will mean to allow everyone to study the information we discover in the catacombs. Doubt will be laid to rest once and for all when the world can read the text of the Bible in its original form. Confusion suffered by mankind since the tower of Babel will be conquered at last because "*Messiah*" will translate every document in our data banks into every known written language in the world. Sister Magdalene is also working on a sound chip, which will enable those, who cannot read or write, to hear the text of the Bible as it was originally written. The barrier of language will finally be conquered here in the Vatican!"

Father Simson's eyes crawled slowly, inexorably, toward Amariah. "Dame Amariah, from the Benedictine Order of St. Anne's in San Francisco, just graduated from Loyola with a Master's Degree in New Testament languages. The Jesuit Fathers taught her to speak, read and write Aramaic, Farsi, Greek,

Hebrew and Latin. While this young Benedictine sister was still in graduate school, I was made aware of her outstanding grasp of language. Her teachers reported it was as if she'd spoken these ancient dialects all her life. It is second nature for Sister Amariah to read and write several forgotten tongues. In fact, her talent is so amazing my Jesuit brothers spent a great deal of time speculating on why she mastered these languages with such ease. It is as if she has come from the past, text in hand. Sister," soul-penetrating eyes studied the nun's embarrassed reaction, "you are a credit to this team."

A fierce blush turned her cheeks crimson. Glancing at the faces staring in her direction, Amariah wished everyone's attention would shift to Father Patrick Murphy, a Jesuit from the University of Dublin, the Father General just introduced. Faded red hair framed an equally faded, but still florid complexion. Short, squat, and barrel-chested, Amariah thought Father Murphy looked as if he would be more at home in a pub than a parish.

"Father Murphy will be authenticating records dating back to the time of Christ." Simson's voice rose to the ceiling, where it crashed against the golden seal of Pope Clement XIV set into the cleft between buttress and rafter. It radiated back to the scholars, a relentless tide engulfing a compliant audience. "Recent discoveries lead me to believe the three hundred bishops, who made up the first Council of Nicea, in 350 A.D. chose to leave out hundreds of documents in the Church's possession--our Holy Bible is probably ideologically imperfect. The responsibility for deciding if other doctrine should have been included will fall to Father Murphy."

Amariah recoiled when Cardinal David Woolsey acknowledged the Father General's introduction. British born, Italian educated, Woolsey clawed his way to the top of the Vatican hierarchy. She listened in earnest as he discussed his field of study--Church law and canon—distrust soon claimed her emotions. Woolsey's arrogance was unbecoming a prince of the Church. There was a cruel look in his eyes; a fire of uncontrolled pride was expressed in every mannerism. The way he spoke, the gestures used to punctuate his point of view revealed the Cardinal was a man unaccustomed to opposition.

"I am sworn to uphold the sacredness of our Holy Mother Church. Like parasites invading a host, erroneous ideologies attack our faith from all quarters. We, who hold positions of responsibility in the Church, have weathered similar storms over the centuries and it is my duty to ensure the Council of Cardinals finds clear passage through the sea of coming change. It is my hand that holds firm the rudder of direction. My leadership will guide the Church through these perilous times."

Amariah caught the flash of antagonism in Woolsey's eyes when his glance took in the Father General. These men battled for ecclesiastical supremacy and Amariah suspected their clashes were frequent.

A tall, slender woman, with bruised crescents above her cheeks, waved to the others after being introduced by Father Simson as Anna Romanov, a renowned historian. The pained expression in the woman's eyes, the way she squinted against the sun, the tremor in her hands, made Amariah wonder if she sought to diminish her sorrows with alcohol. From what did she need to hide? Like deceptive plumage, Amariah felt as if expensive clothing and jewelry were employed to distract casual observers from suffering. Imperious gestures, caustic remarks, the darting glance which refused to engage others, betrayed pain. The woman's emotions smoldered below a surface tenseness as taut as a violin string.

Amariah's attention was drawn to a man of East Indian descent, whose dusky skin was a stark contrast to the white collar around his neck. His clerical robe seemed out of place and somehow ill fitting. It would have been easier to accept him in the saffron robes of a Buddhist monk.

Simson's authority filled the library as he continued the introductions. "Mendicant Rava Prabhupada is an expert in Hindu lore. He graduated from the University of New Delhi and chaired the Department of Religion at that distinguished school for many years. Father Rava will authenticate the documents smuggled out of India and China by my early Jesuit brothers."

Pressing her hand over her mouth to suppress a smile, Amariah watched a short, fine-boned man stand in response to his introduction. Trying to make a barrel of his chest, the Englishman used the power of breath to make his voice commanding. He wielded his British accent like an actor on stage, pausing to give drama and impact to his words. Like many short men, Sir Duncan Davis used bluster and bravado to compensate for a lack of height. A Rhodes Scholar, he was too quick to inform the others his life was dedicated to studying man's psychological dependence on religion.

She sensed the British aristocrat ridiculed the faith of others because he lacked a belief of his own. His words rang like the clash of cymbals in Amariah's ears; she had to listen to such derisiveness from her father for years. Dandified clothing, perfect grooming, a manner a little too cock-sure to be convincing, added to Amariah's impression Duncan Davis was a man with limited self-esteem.

Jon Pierre LaPointe was introduced as an art expert on loan from the Louvre. Like many Frenchmen, LaPointe was thin and possessed a nose a shade too long for the rest of his face. It transformed otherwise handsome features into a sharp and angular appearance. Watery blue eyes betrayed hours of strain beneath fluorescent lights.

"Dr. LaPointe will be responsible for sorting the paintings, tapestries, vases and sculptures in chronological order. His most difficult assignment will be combining newly discovered works of arts with those in our existing museums."

Dark red hair swept back with combs gave Amariah the sensation Carole Phillips was as wild and untamed as a lioness. Dressed in knee-length shorts, the woman in her mid-forties was lean and fit. Freckles were scattered across the bridge of her nose and a deep tan on her arms and legs indicated the photojournalist spent a lot of time in the sun. Amariah was impressed to learn she conducted some of the photographic work on the Shroud of Turin. Carole was also a respected journalist with two Pulitzer Prizes for her work in Viet Nam and Afghanistan.

The Father General pivoted, retracing his steps down the center aisle. "Carole arrived in Viet Nam at the age of twenty-one with less than one hundred dollars in her pocket. She wasn't quite truthful about her previous experience and talked her way into areas forbidden to the press. Carole jumped with an Airborne unit behind enemy lines and was also wounded in action. This talented photographer will document the work on our world- altering project."

The law of opposite attraction told Amariah she was going to like this woman. It was with reluctance she pulled her attention away from the self-assured face and the aura of confidence so bold the American photographer viewed the stream of introductions with disinterest.

"Ladies and gentlemen, this is Mr. Jefferson Davis Brown." Father Simson nodded toward the handsome African American, who rose from his seat with the power and grace of a running back on the football field. "Mr. Brown distinguished himself in the field of carbon dating and the X-ray process used on the Dead Sea scrolls. His expertise is going to be heavily counted on as we try to place many of the artifacts in their proper chronological order."

Sitting stiff against the back of his chair, Klaus Von Friendberg looked every bit a reserved German skeptic when the Father General introduced him. "Professor Von Friendberg was the guiding force behind the restoration of the Summer Palace in Leningrad, which was almost destroyed during World War II. The people of the Soviet Union realized the palace was a national treasure and dedicated a vast amount of time, money, and energy to restoring the building to its former glory. The professor taught Russian craftsmen to use centuries old techniques. The palace was reborn under his devoted care. Cornices were gilded, ceilings repainted, tapestries repaired, parquet floors restored, and furniture renewed under his direction. Of special interest to me is how he combated damage created by the salt air and the devastating effects of snow and wind--because the palace was in shambles after the war. There is a great deal of moisture in the catacombs, and we have no idea in what condition we will find the items sequestered there. I am grateful, Doctor, you joined us."

Jean Paul Deveraux was introduced as a biblical archaeologist, who spent most of his life exploring the desert around the Dead Sea. Amariah decided she liked this gentle looking man. The desert held a preternatural fascination for her. The archaeologist's skin was the consistency of leather and years of squinting against the sun scored a permanent web of lines around deep set, gray-blue eyes.

Paul Grant's casual manner grated on Amariah's nerves. The MIT graduate in charge of determining the engineering requirements for various parts of the museum draped his leg over the arm of a priceless chair and swung his foot back and forth with an apparent lack of interest in his team's introductions. Prematurely gray hair gave a distinguished look to the engineer, a condition in which Amariah felt certain Grant took deep pleasure. The crisp pleat in his gray flannel trousers accentuated the clean lines of his dark blue blazer. A manicure, expensive Italian leather loafers buffed to a gleam, and gold cufflinks adorned him like a badge of rank.

Introductions concluded, Father Simson shuffled through a manila folder while he briefed the scholars on aspects of their historical undertaking. Amariah turned inward as she sorted through her first impressions about other members of the museum team.

Her gaze wandered, settling on the faces to which she naturally responded, avoiding those who were repelling. Her eyes traveled rows of books, painted columns, the frescoed ceiling, but she always returned to Andrew Simson face.

The man in black exuded authority; commitment; resolve. His tone of voice contained a tyrannizing quality. Amariah struggled against a feeling Andrew Simson had the power to convince others to follow him no matter what the consequence.

CHAPTER THREE

"Sorellas, Fratellos . . . pardona me, my English needs much improvement." Father Giuseppe Montanegro shielded his eyes against the sun as the group of scholars passed through opulent gardens surrounding the Casino of Pius IV. Dedicated to the care and upkeep of the Vatican, Father Montanegro was well versed in the history and lore of St. Peter's, the museums, library, and Apostolic Palace.

Amariah doubted she would ever grow accustomed to the grandeur of Renaissance architecture or the beauty of the gardens. Above the Casino's columned doorway angels of creamy marble balanced the crest of a medieval pope. Wreaths of stone laurel adorned pillars supporting the second story of the building created as a small but exquisite hideaway for the troubled Pope Pius IV.

Designed by Pirro Ligorio, the Casino's two buildings faced each other across an elliptical piazzale. An encircling chaplet of marble benches made it easy for visitors privileged enough to be allowed access to the gardens to admire the elaborate courtyard. A fountain, where water spewed from the mouths of dolphins with children riding on their backs, was the focal point of the courtyard. Slabs of softly hued marble joined in a geometric pattern paved an area surrounding the fountain. Statues peering down from niches created to enhance the beauty of this special, secluded place kept watchful eyes trained on the intruders.

"This is the path you will follow for many days to come. Father General Simson took many . . ." he hesitated, seeking the proper word, "wanted you to be comfortable with the walk from the dormitory to the laboratory!" A smile winged its way across his young, clean-shaven face. "My English will be better shortly, Father Simson promised this job will," he paused, his eyes going left to his ear as he searched for what he wanted to say, "cultivate my vocabulary! Come, I will show you the way."

Inwardly amused, Amariah remembered her own struggle with a new language. Words which fit together fluidly in English sounded absurd in another vernacular. Falling into step, she tried to keep her attention focused on the endless historical details Father Montanegro cited about existing museums and the new complex under construction. Her eyes strayed to the garden, where banks of jasmine sheltered emerging blue bearded iris, yellow daffodils, and apricot tulips. Winter had been mild, and the garden foretold promise of an early spring.

The day was sunny, the breeze gentle, as they strolled toward the Vatican Library. A massive wall built by Pope Leo V to protect the papal state could just be detected through tall Italian cypress trees planted to direct the eye toward rose beds and hedges of weeping wisteria rather than the imposing structure, which turned the Holy City into a fortress. Many popes were interested in horticulture and Father Montanegro pointed out rare forms of flora preserved for future generations with lavish care.

"The Holy Fathers tried to save beautiful things for mankind. Father Simson says if it not for our popes much art would be lost. Michelangelo would not have sculpted the *Pieta*, Raphael would not have designed the *Logetta*, nor painted any of his frescos, if our blessed popes had not championed their creation." The priest gestured toward the museums to prove his point. "Father Simson says the Church fed the artist and preserved their work for children of the future!"

Klaus Von Friendberg could not resist the challenge. "Isn't it also true, Father, gold for the ceiling in the Sala del Concistoro in the Apostolic Palace was provided by the Aztec treasure plundered by Pizzaro and Cortez?" Anger simmered beneath a passive expression as the priest answered.

"Signore, I don't understand your question."

Silence claimed the group as they headed toward the five-hundred-year-old building housing the apostolic library. Although the priest did not respond to the jibe, everyone sensed he understood the implication of Von Friedberg's question, if not the individual words.

Was the glory of the Vatican fashioned from greed and plunder? Had countless men and women lived in poverty to give what money they earned to the Church? Were early Popes men of God or were they mortals trapped in the web of human greed? Amariah wondered.

A disturbing feeling surfaced from deep within. Faint, it hovered past perception, beyond the range of knowing why the garden seemed so familiar. There was something about how fresh and sweet it smelled which lingered at the edge of memory. Something. Amariah forced herself to return her attention to Father Montanegro.

"Fathers, Sisters, before you a building magnifico--beyond the wonders of the world." Pointing toward freshly poured footings, the young priest directed their attention to the laboratory wing the experts would soon occupy.

Amariah watched workmen struggle through an ankle-deep mixture of cement, lime, and sand as they labored to smooth the concrete foundation. Movement was difficult, and they cursed the entangling web of steel mesh.

The architect, who designed this building, intended to make certain this structure could withstand the test of time and anything nature had to offer. With the money Father Simson was devoting to the museum, his showpiece was not going to be endangered by an accountant incapable of understanding his vision.

The tour over, the group made their way toward the Cortile della Biblioteca. Until the laboratory wing of the museum was complete Father Simson cleared space in a building containing the Vatican's vast collection of medieval books and manuscripts.

The Apostolic library was imposing; its construction a curious mixture of ponderous Baroque and more delicate elements ushered in by the Renaissance. Supporting arches, layered like tiers in a wedding cake, created the library's upper stories. As each succeeding pope tried to outdo past pope's splendor, the result radically altered Bramte's original design.

The courtyard surrounding the library soaked up the sun and earthen tiles lining the walkway radiated the welcoming warmth of spring. Doors, carved when Spanish galleons set sail for the New World, groaned in protest as Father Montanegro ushered scholars inside a building that charted the course of history.

"Come, come," he waved them onward, like a schoolmaster guiding children.

Amariah hesitated when she saw the Jesuit gesturing toward a flight of stairs facing the entrance. Braces on Sister Magdalene's legs forbid upward movement; surely Father Montanegro did not expect the frail nun to negotiate the library's upper floor until her computers were installed in the new museum? Slowing, Amariah decided to be at the sister's side if it were her misfortune to climb the stairs.

When she glanced over Sister Magdalene's head, Amariah found Leon Kaminski's gentle blue eyes looking at her. Reluctant to inhibit any of Sister Magdalene's proud determination, it was obvious he too was prepared to help her.

"No, Sorella, no. Stairs are not made to climb for you. Here, this way." Father Montanegro stabbed at a recessed button and a panel slid aside to reveal an enormous freight elevator. "Father Simson installed this only weeks ago. It descends into the lowest level of the catacombs. No matter what size of the artifacts we discover, this elevator is large enough to accommodate them with ease." Pride suffused the priest's olive colored skin with pink. "Tunnels are being excavated to connect the laboratory, the new museum and older buildings with the catacombs you will soon explore. This is the first elevator in the old museums, but others will come in time."

Father Murphy stepped inside to examine the control panel. Debate still raged throughout the clergy over installation of elevators in the historic buildings. Most members of the Council of Cardinals objected to a network of tunnels the Father General planned. The Council echoed popular sentiment that Simson was defiling history by adding modern conveniences to buildings designed by Bramte and Raphael.

With fierce determination, Father Simson insisted on connecting both the ancient and new museums with passageways which would honeycomb the hill beneath the Vatican. Once the tunnels were complete and elevators installed, equipment, supplies and archaeological treasures could be transferred from one building to another below the Vatican. Tourists would never see the army of technicians and scientists who staffed the museums. On the surface, the Vatican would appear calm and serene--a perfect Garden of Eden.

Father Murphy felt certain Andrew Simson was gifted with a special kind of insight. People were returning to the Church in droves. The Father General's methods might appear unconventional, but who was he to judge whether an elevator desecrated centuries old museums?

With a gallant gesture Father Montanegro reached for Sister Magdalene's hand. "Sorella Amariah, would you also come . . . Anna?"

Nodding, Amariah realized the young priest didn't want Sister Magdalene to think she was being singled out because of her handicap. "Of course, Father. Perhaps you can show me how to operate the elevator."

"Surely, surely. It is not a difficult matter."

Depressing buttons, Father Montanegro explained the elevator's high-tech engineering to the nuns and Anna Romanov. A huge hook welded onto a metal cable came shrieking out of the ceiling--stopping inches above Amariah's head as Father Montanegro jabbed at the controls.

"You see, we are equipped to move monumental artifacts with delicate care." The priest grinned at having startled the women. "The Father General thinks there are many large works of art stored beneath St. Peter's because the Church wanted to preserve creative gifts given to mankind by God. My English, it is better?"

"An angel could not have said it more eloquently, Father." Sister Magdalene crossed herself in blessing. "We are fortunate Father Simson is divinely guided and each of us should feel blessed to be a part of this project. I feel as if the presence of the Savior is at my elbow and I submit to His special, saving grace." The tiny African nun's face radiated the joy she felt at being a team member. Sister Magdalene was thrilled her years of schooling were finally going to be of service to the institution which rescued her from the torrid planes of Africa and a lifetime of privation and despair. If not for the missionary priests, who converted her mother and father Sister Magdalene knew she would be a crippled bush-woman, herding cattle and praying for rain. She owed everything to the Church--even the braces enabling her to walk were paid for by the effort of devoted sisters in the Carmelite Order. Her eyes frosted with a shimmery lens of tears; frail hands clasped her cherished crucifix and she stared upward toward a celestial stairway upon which archangels and the hosts of heaven assembled in a choir to sing the praises of Andrew Simson only Sister Magdalene was privileged to hear.

"So," long fingers stroked each onyx bead in the rosary chain, "are all the members of our little team settled in?" A veil lowered in Simson's eyes, masking intent.

"All went well." Not a trace of accent sullied Father Montenegro's English. "Most are like children, who have been set loose in an amusement park."

"Diplomacy and attention to detail will be required from here on in." Father Simson's voice trailed away when he noticed a cement truck pouring its load of concrete into the framework of the foundation. "I am so close."

Lost in thought, the Father General forgot the presence of the younger man. He was watching his dream come together in layers of concrete and steel. Soon, the world would recognize the truth of his mission. The Church would guide geo-political networks.

Andrew Simson's thoughts turned toward a destiny foretold by the Archive. Thousands of men had access to the Secret Archive over the centuries, but he was the one who discovered a document revealing the secrets of the catacombs. Notations in the margin, scrawled in Latin, described vaults filled with treasure.

Simson knew early Princes of the Church were worldly politicians. Spirituality lost to the struggle for power. Popes fought wars, gathered plunder, built palaces befitting the dwellings of earthly kings. Their unchecked spending infuriated Martin Luther and laid the foundation for the Reformation. This document also hinted at manuscripts written by the Sybils and others considered heretics by the Church. For centuries, no other cleric concerned himself with sorting ten thousand packets left to gather dust--until the hand of destiny placed him in charge of the Secret Archive.

The fragile parchment indicated the existence of a man called Jesus could be verified by evidence secreted away in the catacombs. Andrew Simson was convinced he would discover manuscripts written by contemporaries of the Savior. Perhaps something written by Christ himself was buried in centuries old tombs. He took a deep breath. It took courage to implement sweeping reform. The Holy City would be resurrected, and the world would gladly follow the one who gave them hope. The museum was the first step.

The whine of hinges drew his attention away from the window. Glancing at the door, he was surprised to find Father Montanegro slipped from the room--leaving him alone with his thoughts. Sister Josephina had a stack of papers in her hand.

"Forgive the intrusion Father, but the daily correspondence is ready for review." The large boned woman brought order to his cluttered desk as she gathered signed letters and discarded less important material.

"Sister, I appreciate the devoted care you lavish upon my correspondence. Without faithful followers like you, Jesuits would not have contributed so much to history. I suspect Tellihard de Chardin would have offered far less to mankind without the dedication of a faithful scribe. You are to be commended, Sister Josephina."

Flushing crimson, the nun was honored by such praise. "I live to serve you--and our cause."

"And you, dear Sister, are the force behind the Black Pope, as I am the power behind the Holy See."

The Augustinian nun bustled toward the door. "Father Wilson is waiting."

"Thank you for reminding me. Please, send him in."

Father Wilson paused at the door, wanting to be certain the faithful sister returned to her desk. "Father, you sent for me?"

"Yes, we have much to discuss." He reshuffled stacks of paper, briefly glancing at items marked 'urgent' with yellow squares of sticky paper Sister Josephina loved to use. "Status."

"All units are in place."

“Contact initiated?"

"Two more need to report, then we will move to ready status."

Locking his fingers, Simson allowed a smile of satisfaction to creep across his face. "You have much to be proud of."

"We have a loyal cadre of brothers."

"To your credit."

"Father, the credit belongs to you. You inspire their loyalty. Were it not for your leadership our brothers would not have undertaken this mission."

Eyes slightly out of focus, Simson's gaze drifted upward. "These are perilous times, and we must breathe new life into the Society of Jesus. We are lucky to have men with the courage to change world destiny. Father Ignatius de Loyola intended Jesuits to be the best. We will continue his tradition of entering the mind, heart, and soul of the people whom we intend to convert. The Church must regain its prominence and with Jesuits resuming the role of Knights of God--protectors of the faith!"

A shout from one of the workmen drew Simson's attention toward the garden. A man motioned the huge concrete truck away so the next one could back into position. The Father General stood at the window, absorbed by work going on below him. There would be storms to weather before his dream was realized. Centuries of speculation about the existence of a man called Jesus and the validity of the Church's authority must be laid to rest. It was only a matter of time before he was accepted as the salvation of mankind.

Dawn broke over the horizon. Amber streaks wrestled with a layer of clouds that tried to keep the sun from rising. A single shaft broke free, a lance directed at the door of St. Peter's. As if with a defined purpose, the beam streaked across the stratosphere, brushing across land masses on the blue planet, over hills and valley--to stream down the nave of the Christendom’s most holy church, toward an altar covered by sheets of gold. Dawn had, at last, fulfilled the promise of another day and the land began to warm beneath an eternal, gentle caress.

As the sun rose higher, above cloud cover, it compelled the shaft to leave the nave, pulling it toward the dome. Light found its way through slotted windows layered like strawberries in a torte. Saints, cherubim, angels of mercy . . . experienced a moment of illumination, then faded back into the mist of shadow. The dome was enveloped by darkness as gathering clouds smothered the sun's valiant effort. Rain splattered against blocks of polished travertine, which sheltered art works within St. Peter's. Single at first, then as clouds piled against each other, heavier drops foretold a coming storm.

Footsteps echoed across the nave. Electric bulbs flickered to life -- and St. Peter's was bathed in an artificial light which penetrated every corner. Glancing around, the timeworn cleric, who ministered to the needs of this building most of his life, decided St. Peter's was ready to receive its important visitors. He sighed. It was a pity the sun refused to shine--early morning light bathed the statues, a gilt covered ceiling, and the massive columns supporting the Baldacchino in an aura of spirituality. Cloaked by the warmth of the sun, St. Peter's bestowed peace upon a troubled mankind. The priest stood aside to let visitors pass through the brass grilled doors.

Amariah's breath caught in her throat. She had never seen anything so magnificent. The dome seemed to soar to the gates of heaven; the massive house of worship left her feeling insignificant as a human. Walking behind the group, Amariah tried to assimilate the beauty of a building which withstood political ravage. Towering arches supported the length of the nave.

Her eye followed the path to Bernini's Baldacchino, erected over the site where St. Peter was said to be buried. The design of the basilica provided a perfect setting for some of the greatest works of art known to man: the tomb of Leo XI, the *Pieta,* holy water stoops created by Francesco Moderati. Each rested in a protective niche created by a buttress.

Just being close to Michelangelo's *Pieta* gave Amariah goose flesh. Her eyes lingered on the statue of a mourning mother clutching the body she had once borne, watched grow to manhood, then seen slain. It was beyond comprehension to believe the grief etched in Mary's face was the result of one man's imagination. Michelangelo took a block of stone and turned it into something so life-like admirers expected to hear Mary's sobs, or, at the very least, see tears streaming down her cheeks. The feeling conveyed by Mary's hands wrenched the heart--one clenched her son's body close, the other stretched forth in an anguish which demanded why my child? Jesus' fingers, in contrast, lay limp against the folds of Mary's robe. No pulse throbbed through once vibrant arteries, no sound would ever again come from lightly parted lips; never again would his strong body walk, nor run, nor strain up a Galilean hillside.

Feeling as though she was compelled to go deeper into the nave, Amariah stared at the marble lion adorning the base of the tomb of Clement XIII. At rest, tendons and sinew waited beneath hide and hair--the power of a hunter brilliantly portrayed. Was the artist trying to convey a deeper meaning? Had the sculptor left behind clues to Clement's personality? Was he a man who used power wisely or did he savage his enemies?

Amariah was beginning to feel as if there was more to the Vatican and its treasures than people realized. History was created and buried beneath its forbidding walls. Drawing her attention back to the Baldacchino, she listened to Father Montenegro's recitation.

"Popes have been interred in the Sacre Grotte Vaticane for centuries. The Antonio da Sangallo was raised ten and a half feet to protect the church from dampness. This provided space for popes to build elaborate tombs. Father Simson's work in the Secret Archive revealed even more tunnels exist beyond existing catacomb walls." Father Montanegro expressed his admiration for the Jesuit leader as he continued, "Beyond the sacred grotto a cemetery rested on the hill of St. Peter's. Father Simson wanted nothing excavated until you were all gathered in Rome," he studied expectant faces, searching for loyalty, indifference, acceptance.

Incense drifted from both north and south transepts. Candles flickered in the corners of a church whose architectural form was patterned after a Greek cross. Lit by the faithful, tongues of flame glowed throughout the palace of worship, softening the countenances of statues in niches beside gigantic piers supporting the dome. The carved ceiling was crafted with such intricacy it was impossible for the eye to absorb its grandeur. Gold leaf over the coping acted like a mirror and reflected soft, flickering candlelight. The dome seemed to pulsate with a life of its own--as if it were a living, breathing entity. Precise geometric symmetry in the marble floor leads the faithful to the Baldacchino, a structure meant to bear witness to man's insignificance before God.

Everywhere she looked, Amariah was struck by the magnificence of Christianity's most famous church. Thebaroque influence of the Renaissance was evident in everything from the frolicking cherubim at the base of the holy-water font to the Cathedra Petri behind the twisted pillars of the Baldacchino. Bernini created an altar to enshrine a chair believed to have been sat upon by St. Peter himself. Four life-size statues held the sacred chair aloft to meet the rays of golden sunshine streaming down from heaven. Clouds covered with gold supported angels and cherubs, whose uplifted arms sang praises to the Lord.

Looking down the nave, Amariah realized it was the length of a football field! Reciting historical facts about St. Peter's with care, Father Montenegro's tone conveyed reverence for the building.

"St. Peter's is church of immense dimension. Michelangelo did not build the nave, but Carlo Maderno did a masterful job of joining two types of architecture to make them appear as one. See the bronze pillars created by Bernini? It took ten years for them to cool after they were cast because they are so large!

Amariah continued to gape at the workmanship of sculptors and artists, who crafted clay, metal, and wood into breathtaking beauty. Why did she hesitate to dedicate a mere two years to Father's Simson's project? She was standing before the efforts of men who dedicated their entire lives to the glory the Church. Bernini must have realized his work would make a lasting contribution to mankind to undertake the prodigious task of casting the pillars.

A flash of inspiration swept over Amariah as she neared the altar. Her work would also endure for generations to come. With the aid of technology, like computer-enhanced imagery and digitization, the documents she translated could be studied for centuries. Filled with humility, she bowed to the will of God. As she made the sign of the cross and gripped her rosary beads between clenched fingers, Amariah was determined to lay aside uneasy feelings about Father Simson.

He was a great man, dedicated to bringing the Church out of an era of abandonment. He wanted to rekindle interest in the word of God. If she didn't understand his methods, then perhaps they were beyond her ability to comprehend. Certainly, she was not qualified to judge Father Simson. He had to be inspired because so many people were returning to the Church!

It was hard to believe she was standing at the altar of St. Peter's. She was excited about receiving a papal blessing although Father Simson warned them the Pope's failing health would keep the mass brief. The Holy Father rose from his sick bed to say mass for the men and women, the priests, and nuns, who joined together to recover treasures buried beneath St. Peter's basilica.

A sound echoed from the south transept. When she caught sight of the man clad all in white, Amariah's face contorted with sympathy. The tall, pointed miter was too large for the sick man's head. Frail and weak, the Holy See displayed visible signs of a man battling cancer. Inching his way toward the altar, Pope Anastasius V clung to his golden crosier. As his staff struck the marble floor a hollow sound echoed throughout the basilica, the rattle of a death march. Amariah felt her heart constrict when she realized the gravity of the Pope's illness. Cancer had no master, it respected no one . . . be they saint or sinner. Determined to give his blessing to those who would be responsible for bringing renewed glory to the Church, the Pope inched toward the Baldacchino. Kneeling at the altar rail, the scholars paled to insignificance beneath St. Peter's dome and the struggles of a man who knew his time on earth was coming to an end.

Despite how far sound carried in the marble apse, the Pope's litany was barely discernible. The Holy Father used Latin verse and Amariah felt the ancient syntax heightened the pageantry of the ceremony. It lent solemnness other languages could only imitate to this sacred event.

Amariah was so humbled by her surroundings tears threatened. An image pushed its way through the mist. A kaleidoscope of impressions distorted the Pope's hand as he made the sign of the cross. Instead of the habits worn by the popes and priests of the modern Church, Amariah saw men in long dark cloaks with draping hoods which hid the faces of their wearers. The mass droned on--words striking her ears with the steady cadence of a funeral drum. St. Peter's lost its elegance, it was smaller, the coping without a covering layer of gold. Turning, the niche which should have sheltered the statue of Saint Veronica stood empty. Amariah felt dizzy and her mouth went dry. Nothing seemed real.

Outside, a severe thunderstorm waited on the horizon, a fadinglight cast a dusky mantle over the church.

'*I see but through a glass, darkly*', sounded in her ear and Amariah blinked, a futile defense against mist shrouded vision. St. Paul sounded as if he were close by, whispering. Incense caught in her nostrils--a heavy scent-- not like any she had ever smelled before.

A mixture of sandalwood and frankincense with a sprinkling of myrrh.

The gifts of the wise men. Her thoughts careened in a whole new direction.

Three men stood in a doorway, one of them--a man with dark skin--made her heart leap into her throat. His large, dark eyes pierced the core of her soul.

The image slipped away, and in its place, came another: *A coarse hood covered a monk's face. All she could see was a slash of skin which surrounded a spectral mouth. Lips, thin and parched, formed words she could not hear.*

A slowly moving mouth conveyed a warning, which registered on a deep, primitive level.

Amariah pressed her hands against her mouth to stifle a moan welling in her throat. Unbidden emotions threatened to overcome her ability to stay calm. Suddenly, a reassuring hand grasped her elbow as she started to sway. When the pall filling the nave began to retreat, Amariah turned to see who recognized her distress. Leon Kaminski stared at her with concern. Whispering in an effort not to disturb the mass, he asked if she was all right. Amariah nodded, the veil bobbed against her shoulders in a macabre dance. Grateful, she repressed the urge to faint, Amariah managed a tight smile.

The Pope's voice rasped throughout the transept, and she forced herself to pay attention to the remainder of the mass. Familiar litany seemed to restore her sense of wellbeing and Amariah followed the Pope in making the sign of the cross. The boy selected to play the part of the server hovered near, as if his youth and vitality could compensate for the old man's frailty.

"*In nomine Patris, et Filii, et Spiritus Sancti. Amen. Introibo ad altare Dei.*"

The altar boy's voice rang down the length of the apse in response as he played his part in a ceremony that crowned Charlemagne and sent crusaders to wrest Jerusalem from the Saracen.

"*Ad Deum qui laetificat juventutem meam.*"

The bony hand protruding from the embroidered vestment beckoned those gathered in the magnificent cathedral to follow the response. "*Judica me, Deus, et discerne causam meam de gente non-sancta: ab hominie iniquo et doloso erue me.*"

The Pope crossed his hands in front of his chest, a gesture meant to bestow peace and harmony upon mankind. He genuflected, and for a moment Amariah feared the Holy See didn't have the strength to rise. Labored breath rattled in his chest as he reached for the pyx and took the host. Old and tired, Anastasius V toiled on.

The altar boy continued, the tenor of a youthful voice rang loud and clear to disguise the Pope's weakness. "*Quia tu es, Deus, fortitudo mea: quare me repulisti, et quare tristis incendo, dum affligit me inimicus?*"

Although the Latin of some of the scholars was rusty, most followed the solemn ritual that had endured since the Council of Nicea organized a rag tag band of individual churches into a single governing body.

"*Emitte lucem tuam et veritatem tuam: ipsa me deduxerunt et adduxerunt in montem sanctum tuum, et in tabernacula tea.*"

The mass continued, Amariah was awed by the Pope's every word, his every motion. As the altar boy incensed the surrounding area she felt tears threaten again. It was the dream of every Catholic to be the recipient of a papal blessing. How grateful she should be for the opportunity to participate in a project, which would sanctify the authority of the Holy Mother Church.

Moving toward the altar railing with care, the Pope offered the host and wine to each of the scholars. Reaching to wash his fingers, he strained over the sacred words.

"Lavabos inter innocentes menus meas: et circumdabo alatre tuum, Demine: Tu audiam vocem laudis: et enarrem universa mirabilis tua."

To receive communion in this holy place from the hands of the Pope was more than Amariah ever dreamed possible. The sensation of light-headedness returned. Images from another time and place swam before her eyes again.

A black man dressed in an elaborate robe stepped toward her, his hand outstretched, beckoning, inviting her into his world. The richly embroidered robe faded-- replaced by the stark habit of a medieval monk. A hood was drawn over the priest's face. His features were indistinct, only his eyes were clear, and they glowed with frightening intensity. He, too, waved a bony hand in her direction, exhorting her to follow into the shadowy realm from whence he had come.

The feeling of familiarity about St. Peter's was clearly impossible. Amariah was not an international traveler, yet she felt as though she had traversed St. Peter's nave many times before.

Perhaps it was jet lag or fatigue. Amariah decided she would go to bed early instead of staying up to read the wealth of historical material at her disposal. She needed a clear head to accomplish the painstaking work ahead. Teeth clenched with resolution, Amariah returned her attention to the Pope. Kissing the altar, Pope Anastasius V raised his hands in blessing.

"*Te Deum.*"

"*Deo accelcius,*" all answered in response.

Slowly making his way across the transept again, Amariah felt a stab of sympathy for the old man. Every movement pained him, yet he fought to perform the duties of the papal office as if he were in the best of health.

A shudder coursed the length of her spine when Amariah caught sight of a man slipping behind the altar. A hand reached for the frail arm; ready to rescue the Vicar of Christ should he falter. Bending close to capture the hoarse whisper, long, atramentous robes eddied against the vestments of the most venerated man in the Catholic Church as the Father General helped the Pope.

"He loves this man."

Amariah's thoughts were at odds . . .

'No, this is a show.'

". . . Look at his face. There is sympathy in his eyes."

'An act, as if he were in a movie!'

". . . This cannot be! Father Simson is loved by many!"

'Is he really?'

Amariah closed her eyes and bowed her head. She wanted to press her hands against her ears to stop the internal argument. She had a job to do and then she was going home. Two years from now her life would resume its normal course and she would begin work with inner city children.

"Feeling better?"

Amariah turned. Compassion and sympathy undulated across Leon's expression in a tidal rhythm. There was an expression in his eyes; the way he rubbed the bridge of his nose before he spoke; how he observed people around him; the detached way he put distance between himself and others; so many of his characteristics seemed familiar. Maybe if she thought about Leon long enough she could decide who he reminded her of--perhaps a boy with whom she'd gone to school.

Amariah voiced a whispered question, "Do I know you from somewhere?"

"We've never met before." Leon found the grip on her elbow magnetic, and he was reluctant to break the current. It was easy to tell himself he was afraid Sister Amariah might have another dizzy spell as he tried to ignore the tingle in his fingers. "I would have remembered."

Amariah wrestled against the source of her confusion. "I do feel better now."

To put her at ease, Leon released her elbow and offered a smile of encouragement. "People always tell me I remind them of someone else. I must have a common face."

"No," Amariah shook her head, her eyes roved the contours of his cheekbones, the wide brow, the angular jaw, "there's more." Her voice faded, and the words seemed to come from outside herself, as if someone else were speaking. ". . . We've met before."

CHAPTER FOUR

Fan-shaped, the vault over the window on the east side of the library directed streams of light, which fell against an identical arch at the other side of the room. The sun rested against the horizon and diffused light bathed the library in the softening colors of magenta and rose. Angels hovered above the researchers, who toiled in silence below them. Pudgy cherubim seemed ready to flee a peril-filled world should one of the scholars look aloft. Shooting stars raced across a painted heaven--their planetary trajectory decreed by the artists laboring for the Church. History was made beneath the library's frescoed buttresses. Father Simson thought it fitting the dawn of a new era be born beneath the same mortar and stone.

Amariah's enthusiasm would not be restrained. Trembling, she caressed a tattered scroll. It was intimidating to know this document was written by a contemporary of the Savior! What had he been like, this unknown scribe? Warm flesh once toiled over this very scrap of leather; he must have had fears and woes, like an ordinary man. Had he dreamed his work would survive the centuries? Did this man of letters think of greatness? She could not get over the astonishment it fell to her to bring the ancient manuscript to the world's attention. Soon millions would acclaim the long- dead scholar.

Unrolling the scrap of leather with care, tears obscured faint brush strokes. The Aramaic alphabet beckoned across the corridor of time. When Amariah lifted the magnifying glass to her eye the sentence sprang to life.

"There it is," Amariah whispered to herself.

A voice intruded, "This will probably sound silly, but the first time I held a manuscript penned by Kublai Khan—it was like piercing a shroud separating me from the past. As I stared at text not seen by another human being for centuries, I could hardly catch my breath. I was humbled at being the first person to see it in hundreds of years." Kaminski leaned across her shoulder for a better look. "It's as if I realized--for the first time--how inconsequential *and* insignificant a single human can be." A blush seeped across his face and disappeared into his hairline. "You'll have to excuse me, I'm not usually so eloquent."

Relief loosened the lines winging across Amariah's brow. Leon put into words all the unacknowledged emotions that demanded recognition. She was awed by the random bit of leather consigned to oblivion by an unknown person for an equally unknown reason. Her heartbeat quickened as she drew the magnifying glass back to her eye.

Leon wanted to stop Amariah before she returned to work on the scroll. He interrupted with an explosion of words. "I know nothing about the languages of the Bible, please share with me what it says."

Enthralled by the prospect of discovery, he leaned forward, eager to know . . . anxiousness in his eyes as they flitted from the torn, decaying leather to her face and back again.

A feeling she couldn't place surfaced through the quicksand of the subconscious. An emotion consigned to the darkness of memory poked through the thinning edge of awareness, but she was afraid to give it recognition--and pushed it back beneath the surface.

"You'll have to be patient, Aramaic is difficult at best but when the text is so faint."

Kaminski gazed at the time-worn document. "This is an unusual language, quite unlike any I've ever studied."

"Yes," Amariah forgot about the rest of the world as she concentrated on the brush strokes. Here and there a word was clear, at other times the letters were indistinct. Drawing a note pad closer, Amariah tapped her pen against the table, the unconscious motion went unnoticed.

"The first word," Amariah turned the scroll toward Leon, "contains most of the letters for *father*, but I can't say for certain. Yes, look--the word is repeated here--the brush strokes are the same." Amariah's attention was riveted on the damaged scroll.

'Father, glad tidings.'

Words came in short bursts, punctuated by lengthy silences, as Amariah wrested with the syntax and vernacular of the ancient language.

'The man from Galilee passed the night in our home. He was wondrous . . . how is it we never heard a message such as his before?'

Amariah drew the scroll back in her direction. Her hand moved abstractly, lifting then dropping, she seemed to bequeath substance into the words taking shape on her lips before clothing them with sound.

Leon was fascinated at how Amariah turned Aramaic into English. The care she lavished on each syllable betrayed the depth of her passion for language.

'Father, the man says all is within our power to achieve. He says we have only to believe!'

Although her glance encompassed him, it was clear her thoughts were engaged in translation. "There's more, but the scroll is so damaged I can't make out the words. I'll have to put it on the light table and ask Dr. DiMetrie to work his magic. Marcello is the one who discovered how to darken ink without harming ancient paper, you know. I hope he has something that works on leather too." When her glance broke free of the scroll, Amariah was startled by the look on Kaminski's face--he stared at her in amazement, delighted to find someone who shared his fascination with documents linking mankind to the past.

Amariah stammered, "I need a cup of coffee."

"I think the sisters just brought a fresh pot." Leon watched the way Amariah's fingers hovered above the manuscript, as if she decoded the message by touch. "Stay here, I'll bring some."

Although midday, the sky was filled with smoke and dust. A ruptured gas line spewed fumes into the air, creating a noxious vapor as smothering as a blanket. Fire erupted and flames licked the side of one of the few buildings left standing--a smoky trail of destruction followed behind.

Silence reigned over the marketplace--then, one by one, screams filled the air. Where carefree, happy people once thronged the market--flattened stalls bore witness to the anguish beneath piles of rubble, smoking huts and felled palm trees. Cast about, like straw before a careless wind, cinderblocks were scattered across the square. An infant's wail sounded beneath a mound of debris. Frantic effort, supercharged by terror, propelled the priest toward the cry, praying he would reach the baby ahead of death.

"Father! Father!" A hysterical woman plucked at his sleeve, slowing his desperate movements. "You must come, my children--they are buried!"

"Anna, I will try to save them, but first we must rescue this infant. Help me!"

Joining in, the woman flung away brick, stone, and lumber with the strength of the insane. Timbers gave way, stones used in the foundation of the flattened house were tossed aside like pebbles. Reaching into the dark, the priest pulled the screaming infant into the light.

"Gracias, te Deo." Wiping his forehead with the back of his sleeve, Father Walton Mendez turned to survey the devastation. A once sleepy village at the heart of the Yucatan lay in shambles. He beckoned to the dazed woman making her way through the rubble toward the church. "Tia, Tia Maria! Care for this child. I must go with Anna--her family is trapped."

Trying to catch up with the frantic mother, the Jesuit leaped over the remains of what was once been a wall. "Anna! Wait! Don't start digging without me! After shocks may come soon."

As he spoke, the ground began to swell. What was perceived as firm and stable swelled like ocean waves. His inner ear lurched and Father Mendez felt his stomach rise to the back of his throat. Calling to Anna, he mouthed a warning but the roar accompanying the tremor drowned out his cry. The church bell tower began to sway, and the clappers banged against the huge iron bells--a fraction of a second before the tower collapsed.

A scream died on his lips as the priest watched the woman disappear beneath a shower of bricks. Another tremor came; this one flattened him against the ground like a leaf before a ferocious wind. Instinct warned him to protect his head. Rocks, tree limbs, palm fronds, all were missiles aimed at helpless targets. Man paled to insignificance before the force of nature. The Jesuit was filled with a mixture of awe and dread.

As suddenly as the earthquake began, the rumbling stopped, the waves ceased, and the earth settled back into its familiar contours. A silence as final as the grave descended over the village. Death seemed to have harvested every sound in the once thriving community. Those who might have survived the first shock surely succumbed to the second and third. Stumbling toward what was left of his church, Father Mendez tore the refectory door from its remaining hinge. Books had been tossed from shelves, clothing, canned goods, medical supplies lay scattered across the floor as if hurled by a demonic hand. Clawing, pulling, pushing away the remnants of a once comfortable dwelling, the Jesuit struggled toward his bed. Sheltered beneath a rope frame and down mattress was a short-wave radio. Dragging it into the center of the room, trembling hands fought to raise the antenna. Fumbling with the dials, Father Mendez searched for his link to the outside world.

"Come in. Station 03Q, this is an emergency! Station 03Q. Come in!" Leaning his forehead against the radio Father Mendez realized there was blood trickling down his face. No matter--he must reach Rome! The most powerful radio beacon in the free world awaited his regular transmission.

Checking his watch, he depressed the switch again. "Station 03Q, come in!"

An insistent buzz blared from the radio. Demanding the tremor in his hand to still, the Jesuit twisted the dial again. Finally, a familiar voice sounded from the speaker. "IL-0900, we read you. The seismic shock was recorded at the Academy. Cintalapa was the epicenter of a quake registering 7.2 on the Richter scale."

Shock numbed his body, his vocal cords froze, his vision cantilevered wildly as he gripped the edge of the bed for support.

"Brother," the voice from the box grew insistent, "have you assessed the damage?"

Training forced the Jesuit to collect his thoughts, to demand his body respond. "I haven't surveyed the village yet. As soon as the earth settled, I rushed to the radio."

"Help is on the way. Helicopters filled with medical supplies will leave Mexico City within the hour. Food is being loaded on trucks in Cancun. Depending on the damage, they could arrive in a day or two."

"What about manpower? I need help to search for survivors."

The supreme voice of authority floated across the haze of dust and smoke filling the rectory. "Our friends in El Salvador have been contacted. They've been ordered to reach Cintalapa as quickly as they can. You are to assess the damage and report back. I'll be waiting. Make contact again in an hour."

"Station 03Q, copy."

Frustration, then anger, ran through his body in shudders. The violence of his emotions left Father Mendez drained and exhausted. He would walk the village from one end to the other, so he could report with facts, not emotion. Struggling to his feet, the priest returned the radio to the security offered by his bed. The radio had to be protected--it was Cintalapa's only connection to the outside world. The sturdy dining table was broken in half, and he decided the pieces would provide additional shelter. Dragging the planks across the littered floor, the Jesuit heaved them over the bed frame.

Picking his way across the outer room, which served as both office and living quarters, Father Mendez gasped when he reached the door. The dust was beginning to settle--everything was leveled as far as he could see. Not a single building remained standing. Fires raged, smoke poured into the air and obliterated the sun. Gritting his teeth, knowing he had to provide strength to his flock, Father Mendez lurched down the path toward what was left of his beloved village.

Lower, mourning sounds as Death bore down on Cintalapa like an Apocalyptic Horseman punctuated high pitched, agonizing shrieks.

Amariah couldn't help herself, she was beginning to like Leon Kaminski. The way his light brown hair strayed across his forehead was endearing. When he glanced in her direction, her heart assumed a strange rhythm. Other than a few of the priests at Loyola, Amariah was unaccustomed to being with men her own age. Her feelings about Kaminski were new and strange.

She loved the room, which sheltered the library's contents, and dreaded each day that brought the laboratory closer to completion. Amariah knew she would hate being expelled from these beautiful surroundings. Marble floors, ornate moldings, manuscripts so old they predated Christianity, contributed to a sense of wellbeing she never expected to find in Rome. Amariah could not remember when she felt more at home. There were times it seemed like she was part of the library--as though she transformed into leather binding, or an angel in the frescoed ceiling. The papal librarians staring down from imposing portraits were no longer intimidating. No chalice, no altar, no shrine would ever do more to inspire reverence than this repository of learning.

Amariah massaged the base of her spine. Lost in thought, she huddled over the precious manuscripts . . . oblivious to everything until the ache could no longer be ignored. She stared at the barely visible pen strokes. The powdered charcoal, lampblack or soot was mixed with too much water to withstand the rigors of time. This document was written prior to the discovery of how to mix tree resin with ink so it would stick to papyrus, parchment, and leather. Leon enchanted her with bits of historical trivia like how clerics of the long-ago era learned to add iron oxides to ink to make it more durable. He was filled with obscure facts and anecdotes only a person with a passion for history would care about, let alone remember.

Amariah glanced across the room at the expert in Oriental languages. As she watched him labor their conversation of the night before replayed through her head.

'. . . The first Council of Nicea was comprised of over three hundred bishops. Sister--haven't you ever been frustrated by a committee?'

Amariah remembered how Leon warmed to his topic. Excitement propelled his hands and his voice rose to match the heat of their argument.

'The teachings of a man historians agreed to call Jesus Christ were passed down by word of mouth for nearly a hundred years! How much was accurate by the time someone got around to recording an account of Jesus' life? Constantine forced those first bishops to hammer out a doctrine, so it would be consistent throughout the entire Roman Empire. Do you think three hundred men could agree on anything? And yet, Sister Amariah, the foundation of your Church rests on the decisions made in that council. Did they ever teach you this? Did they tell you Emperor Constantine decided it was politically expedient to unify his kingdom under the banner of one faith rather than have it split by opposing political factions? No, all you were taught was a fable about the Emperor having a vision of Christ's name before he went into battle. Religious fantasy infuriates me!'

Like a leopard, he paced the floor, staking out a boundary, daring the faint of heart to enter his claimed domain; his movement a reflection of pent- up fury.

'And why do you think the Father General gathered us in Rome? Think about it, Amariah! I'll bet the further we go with this project, the more ludicrous we'll find the basis of your religion! What is Simson's purpose? Why are we here, Amariah? What are we really doing for the Father General?'

Amariah bristled. Her words pounded in her ears as she relived their conversation.

'We may, indeed, find concepts were excluded from early Church canon. Leon, what you fail to understand is religion comes from within . . . it's a matter of the heart, faith based on premise, not blind acceptance of ritual! I did not take my solemn vows because I was convinced every word written throughout the history of the Church was totally accurate! I did it because I believe in the basic goodness of mankind, in the decency of human beings. I want to help people and I felt the Church provided me with the best possible opportunity.'

Leon's words stung; his criticism wounded her more deeply than she cared to admit. Amariah knew she reacted with hostility because her father always made disparaging remarks about the belief she held dear. Certainly, she was not foolish enough to think the Church was flawless; some popes were little more than politicians and warrior princes . . . but her faith in the principles set forth by her Lord and Savior could not be shaken.

Her eyes were tired; she rubbed them and decided to rest a moment. Amariah let her gaze drift toward one of the glass cases beneath the library window. It sheltered a primitive piece of pottery that once contained a scribe's precious store of ink. The little pot was carbon dated to the time of Ahab, around 850 B.C. Almost intact, it was discovered near the Dead Sea. Every time she looked at it Amariah felt an emotion like a longing for home. Only a rough line was etched into the clay as decoration. Yet, there was something about the way the handle attached to the bowl, and how the fluted lid fit flush against the body that made Amariah feel like weeping. She wanted to touch the fragile clay, to run her hand along its sandy surface--but the glass was sealed and filled with nitro-furan gas to protect it from bacteria which might cause deterioration.

Nagging doubt surfaced again as Leon's ranting continued to ring in her ears. Not without effort, she finally managed to consign apprehension, insecurity and misgiving beneath the cast iron lid of her faith. She believed in the Church! It offered a sense of peace and emotional sanctuary. Life in the sisterhood was as natural as breathing. The responsibilities of the Order filled her with a sense of belonging. Perhaps she wasn't meant to be a part of the outside world. The Abby's cloistered walls provided a joy she wished everyone could experience. The Benedictine sisters taught the poor and provided food and shelter to the impoverished of San Francisco. Blacks, Orientals, children of Spanish descent, all found equality in her classroom. Her heart swelled to near bursting when she worked with little ones; the look in their eyes when they mastered the smallest task was the only reward she needed. Teaching gave her joy; service was how she honored God.

Amariah's eyes returned to the scroll. Translating tattered leather was not her calling! Trying to shake despondency, she forced herself to concentrate on the scrap of vellum beneath her hand. The children could wait--would have to wait--a mere two years. Someday, she'd tell her students what an honor it was to participate in the restoration of the Holy Mother Church. Someday . . . she would tell her students what it was like to have the Holy Father place the Eucharist on her tongue; how inspiring it was to study in the Vatican library; how wonderful to have played a part in bringing the message of Jesus to the hearts of mankind again. With that, her mood lifted, and Amariah felt renewed. Drawing the scroll closer, she reached for her glasses. Adjusting them, Amariah blinked at lines blurred by fatigue.

A voice called to her. It was so distinct, so clear, Amariah turned to see who spoke. The sun streamed through the tall windows, motes of dust danced down the rays that fell against the marble floor. No one stood behind her, yet it seemed as if someone had been standing over her shoulder reading the scroll. With a start, Amariah realized she was the only member of the team with enough knowledge of Aramaic to translate a document hundreds of years old!

She stared at the scroll. In clear, bell-like tones a voice read the message written by a contemporary of Christ. The voice did not hesitate, it flew over the ancient text, it claimed nouns and adjectives without hesitation, it filled the spaces Amariah left for further research.

". . . *If ye have faith, all things will be given, in their own time. Heaven does not move in days or nights; rather, time stands still beyond the veil of mind. I say unto you, faith will destroy obstacles as surely as if they were mountains, faith will put bread in your mouths and water in your well. Believing thusly, all things shall ye receive.*"

The voice ceased, and a deep, unnerving silence settled in Amariah's ears. Her eyes wandered over the message again. The translation offered by the voice was perfect and she rushed to record the words while they were still fresh in her mind. The text was *almost* the same as the verse recorded in the book of Matthew. Reaching for one of the reference Bibles she kept at hand, Amariah sought the verse as it had been recorded in the King James Version of the Protestant Bible.

". . . . *Jesus answered and said unto them, Verily I say unto you, if ye have faith, and doubt not, ye shall not only do this which is done to the fig tree, but also if you shall say unto the mountain, be thou removed, and be thou cast into the sea; it shall be done.*

And all things, whatsoever ye shall ask in prayer, believing, ye shall receive."

Tapping a pencil against her teeth, Amariah pondered the message. The passages were similar, yet the element of time was not mentioned in the King James Bible. Nor were there any references to food or drink. Her thoughts flowed and surged, each idea exploding into another--like nuclear fission. On the surface, the two passages were nearly the same, but . . . but, people were likely to dismiss the moving of mountains. But--if a person had the ability to remedy everyday problems through faith--interest in the subject would be greater! Why were the passages so close, yet so far apart? It seemed the author knew people wouldn't believe they could move mountains. The force generated by belief in oneself was easily dismissed if its purpose was to move mountains or wither a fig tree!

Amariah knew she would always be grateful to her father for teaching her not to be limited by fear and doubt. From childhood, he challenged her to seek new horizons, to guard against words like as *'can't'* or "*don't'*. The power of the mind was Richard Weatherby's passion. He spent hours working with his patients to make them realize *they limited themselves by what they thought they could or could not achieve.* Her father's inability to see that his views were also those of a man who lived two thousand years ago was her greatest burden. How many times had her father expressed the importance of bringing every desire--from the simple to the complex--into reality through the power of concentration? Her father called it positive affirmation; Catholics called it praying; St. Paul addressed the concept in his writings:

"*Whatsoever things are true, whatsoever things are honest, whatsoever things are just, whatsoever things are pure, whatsoever things are lovely, whatsoever things are of good report; if there be any virtue, and if there be any praise, think on these things.*"

Why didn't her father recognize the truth of Jesus' message? Why did Leon take such delight in pointing out the failings of the Church? Why couldn't both look beyond the organization? Why couldn't they accept a philosophy that survived despite the folly of man?

Premonition lay heavy against her thoughts like thunderclouds on the horizon. Richard Weatherby's words slipped into her consciousness and took ownership of the moment.

'*Amariah, anger is only fear disguised. Where you see anger, you find a person afraid. When you discover the reason for the fear you'll understand the situation*'.

Was her anger based on fear? Was she afraid her father and newfound friend might be right? Her head pounded, and her heart slammed against her ribs. Fear drove people to desperate measures. It reduced the stouthearted to crippling states of indecision.

A cloying sensation warned her she was desperately afraid--but the source of fear was illusive. It hung in the dark of her subconscious mind and refused identification. She stared at the scroll as if concentration alone would make the document yield its hidden meaning. Instinct warned the scroll contained a talismanic value, as if it were a charm to guard against misfortune. Mystery embraced her thoughts like a many-armed shadow. Her heartbeat increased its already rapid tempo and adrenaline poured through her veins-- but of what was she so afraid?

Amariah rose with the dawn. The window in her dormitory room faced east and she loved to watch the sun hover above the dome of St. Peter's.

Early hours offered inspiration. Vague words, so indefinable as the veil of night fell, were always crystal clear in the morning. Somehow the subconscious revealed what she sought--answers always came with dawn. Amariah reached for her coffee cup as the sun pushed back the steely grayness of dawn. As tender as a mother's caress, the orange-red glow stirred the land to life. She loved to watch the fiery disk crawl over the horizon, lifting itself above the Vatican, the small point of earth from which the Pope ruled the Catholic world.

As the garden warmed, songbirds welcomed the day with a chorus of caws and trills. Flowers opened, and the morning mist refracted a thousand scintillate rainbows. The earth reacted like a lover beneath the sun's embrace.

At the crunch of gravel, Amariah turned her attention toward the tranquility shattering sound. Surprised someone else was up and about at this hour, she leaned out the window to see who was walking up the path. Catching sight of the scarlet robes of Cardinal Woolsey, Amariah retreated into the safety of her room. She did not like this man. It was hard to remain impassive when he spoke to the members of the team in the pompous tone that was such a part of his character. As head of the College of Cardinals, he considered it his duty to monitor everyone else's work.

Striding across the garden near the casino of Pius IV, the Cardinal acted like a man on a mission. His steps were hurried, he glanced neither right nor left and kept his eyes trained on the path ahead. The gold, mauve and red of the sunrise went unnoticed; the Cardinal had no time to waste on nature. Craning her neck, Amariah kept Woolsey in sight until he turned the corner. He was probably heading toward Father Simson's office in the Pinacoteca--or perhaps he was on his way to an early morning inspection of the museum site.

The birds grew louder, and Amariah returned her gaze to the garden. Jogging along at a leisurely pace, Leon passed the casino. Sweat beaded his forehead and stains seeped beneath his arms.

Glancing upward at the open dormer window, Leon caught sight of Amariah in her bathrobe with her hair wet and fresh from a shower. She was so beautiful a ragged breath stuck in his throat. Instinct warned Amariah would be embarrassed if he acknowledged her presence. Undisguised by the robes and veil of the Benedictine habit, Leon could not get over how she looked. Even though her reddish-brown hair was short, a wisp of curl framed a complexion both warm and creamy. He always thought the wimple made her eyes luminous, but today, in the early morning sun, with freshly scrubbed skin and a blush on her cheeks--Amariah's eyes were startlingly azure. He turned and trotted back along the path hoping for another opportunity to see her without the religious clothing she cherished. He picked up his pace, but his heart beat a tattoo against his ribs that was far too rapid for the energy he was expending.

As he made a second lap around the rose garden he searched the window again. This time he was disappointed, sorely disappointed, for Amariah had retreated into the darkness of her apartment. Frustrated, Leon sprinted the final yards to his dormitory.

"I tell you, Andrew, I do not like what is happening here! You are trusting the girl with far too many documents." Woolsey's scarlet cap wagged back and forth as he shook his head and waved an admonishing finger in the direction of the Father General.

Dismissing the Cardinal with a laugh, Simson countered. "I have nothing to fear! Of far more concern is your meddling in matters that are not your responsibility." The harsh tone of Simson's voice was as unyielding as the line of his jaw.

"It is my duty to safeguard the principles of the Holy Mother Church! You have *not* spent your entire life studying canon like I have. I tell you, what is locked in the Secret Archive has been kept from the eyes of unbelievers for a reason! For centuries, our Popes knew better than to reveal certain information to mankind. People are meant to follow--they are like sheep!" The Cardinal puffed around the words, his breath still labored from the climb up the stairs.

A smile crept from the corners of Andrew Simson's mouth, but it lacked warmth and conveyed no sincerity. "My dear Cardinal, what you say is true. However, we are at the dawn of a new era. Even the most common man is no longer ignorant and superstitious. The poorest ghetto dweller has knowledge of such complex subjects as genetics and nuclear fission. Their counterpart only a few centuries ago would never dream of this kind of understanding. As for man being likened unto sheep, perhaps that's true. Every flock must have its shepherd, and, in this generation, the task has fallen to me."

Blood surged into Cardinal Woolsey's face, pounding against the veins in his neck, which stood purple against his vestments. Now shouting, Woolsey slammed his fist on the desk. "You are behaving like a madman! None of the documents you've shown me validates you are the new Messiah! That's *your* interpretation of a random passage! As guardian of the Church, I will not be a party to substantiating your foolish claim!"

Reptilian eyes turned toward Woolsey, rationality submerged, and something cold arose, something frighteningly inhuman took up residence in the Father General. "Bear in mind, brother, that's *exactly* why the Benedictine nun is translating those documents in the Secret Archive. Evidence will be unearthed to prove, beyond doubt, the validity of my calling. I must also ask you," an unreadable gaze settled on the crucifix at the center of his chest, then moved slowly to the Cardinal, "no, I must *warn* you, not to speak of this until I have gathered what I need. I do not need to remind you of this again?"

Woolsey vaulted out of the chair and backed toward the door. The gelatinous flesh beneath his chin trembled as he struggled to master repulsion. He'd misjudged Simson. As the head of the Council of Cardinals, he thought he exercised sufficient power to curb the Father General. The doorknob rattled when he tried to grip it; words failed him as he stared at a man, who feared no one--not even God.

"Cardinal, I should point out one other item of importance. As an ally I can be invaluable, as an enemy I will prove your undoing. Your choice is simple. Oppose me and lose what's left of your ecclesiastical power or align yourself with me and rise to further prominence. It is all before you . . . but you must decide in which corner you stand." With a wave, he ordered the perspiring man from the room.

The door slammed shut behind him, but Cardinal David Woolsey had no idea whether he retained the presence of mind to close it. Sweat drenched his robes; he pulled the three-cornered cap from his head to release the heat radiating from his scalp. His chest heaving, then falling, he felt incapable of drawing an adequate amount of air. A vise of pain closed around his stomach and forced him to seek the sanctuary of the stairs. The Cardinal reached to loosen his collar in a desperate attempt for air. Stress cut down the strongest body and David Woolsey knew he sacrificed his digestive tract to the temptations offered by rich living long ago.

The Father General's warning allowed no margin for error. He could follow in Simson's wake or oppose him--and commit political suicide. An image rose like a demon through the convoluted thoughts possessing his brain. Was this how Christ felt when the Devil took Him upon the mountain and offered the pleasures of the world? Woolsey knew he was far too human to order Simson to 'get behind' him as Jesus commanded Satan.

Squeezing his eyes tight to be rid of the recriminating image, he leaned his head against the marble balustrade. What was his life coming to? Was he to willingly sacrifice what integrity he had left to the ideals of a man whom he feared? Did he have a choice? A Roman Catholic Bishop was hardly prepared to embrace life in the outside world. He might enter a monastery in some remote corner of the world; perhaps he should become a Cistercian monk. Retreating from every aspect of secular life might be worth consideration. With a heavy sigh, he knew he was far too fond of food, good wine, and a comfortable bed to contemplate a life of deprivation. Desperation forced Woolsey to accept he lacked a real choice. An unholy alliance, their mutual disregard for each other--nay, their hatred--would bind them together because neither was willing to release his grip on power. David Woolsey pulled himself up and stumbled down the stairs.

A blood-red sun began to lower behind the horizon. The dust in the atmosphere hung suspended, like a layer of gauze. Land so bleak only a few hardy camphire bushes clung to existence stretched toward the distant line of mountains turned blue by nightfall. Soon, the desert would begin to cool and life forms, which called the most arid place on earth home, would slither from beneath the shelter of rocky outcroppings.

The length of cloth wound around his head left a narrow slit for the Arab's brooding eyes. The headdress hid the bottom half of his face, but his tone of voice was filled with suspicion. "Why would a Jesuit help us?"

"To bring peace to the Holy Land." The priest fondled the crucifix hanging at the center of his chest. "We share the same God, and our prophets are the prophets of Allah. It's time for the sons of Mohammed to set aside their feuds."

"Allah demands all infidels be put to death!" A hand begrimed with the dirt and dust of the desert tightened around the handle of the gun tucked into the waistband of his tunic.

"Allah's wish is for every man to worship the one, true God! The God of the Christians is called by another name, prayed to in a different manner, and sent a messenger called Jesus instead of one named Mohammed--but we all worship the same God. The priests of my Order wear black, your holy men wear white, but we both serve God and help His people."

What this priest suggested the holy ones would consider blasphemy. The Arab tried to hide the confusion that rose in his eyes by looking away. Twilight softened the desert of sand, alkaline flats and dry lake beds peppered with brutal spines of limestone as he surveyed his stark, primeval world. "I am no scholar, you would have to take up such matters with a Mussulman, who has studied the Koran. When *they* tell me to take an infidel to my breast, I will consider it. Until that time, priest, I trust you no more than a scorpion whose tail is loaded with poison."

Father Robert Norton smothered a retort. The cultural values of a nomadic people still living the way their ancestors did two thousand years ago was studied and committed to memory. He needed to speak plainly, taking care to use words the man could understand. Already distrusted, if he intimidated the Arab with lofty rhetoric his mission would be doomed to failure before it had a chance to begin. Spreading his hands palm upward on his knees in an attitude of openness and respect, the priest spoke softly. "You have no reason to trust me because I have not yet proven my worth to you. But I have well-placed friends, who will make certain your people receive just treatment."

"The English version of Justice?" The Arab lowered the concealing veil as the temperature on the valley floor began to drop with the sun lowering behind the mountains.

The priest studied the man at the other side of a pile of brush. He was as complex as the environment that spawned him. The desert offered a strange mixture of harsh conditions. Heat to sear the soul during the day; cold with the power to turn the bones brittle at night; a lack of moisture, which robbed the body of life-giving liquid and left a man to perish. "I understand you plan to keep the English hostages until your friends are released from jail in Israel."

A slow nod indicated the Arab agreed.

"Holding the hostages is one way to keep reporters interested in your political views, am I right?"

A second nod. "What have you to offer?" Releasing his finger from the trigger, the Arab's hostility began to cool like the desert floor now that nightfall staked its claim.

"I can help achieve your goals."

"How can an English priest help exiled Arabs regain their homeland?" "By making the press sympathetic to your cause."

Eyes narrowing, the Arab turned ugly, then hateful. Slamming his fist against his knee, fury ignited like sparks in the dry desert air. "We will regain our homeland! Allah defends the cause of the righteous!"

"In this case, Allah has nothing to do with it." Father Norton shifted his gaze to the horizon, now wrapped in deep purple. When the Jesuit glanced back, the Arab was caught off guard. An expression as immobilizing as the bite of a desert cobra froze the other man with fear, which gradually melted into begrudging respect.

"Take this proposal to Malek." The Jesuit's voice rose above the first stirrings of an evening breeze. "Tell him if he enters into negotiations to release the hostages, I can guarantee the press will speak favorably about a nation of people who have been oppressed since the Jews returned to Palestine. Jesuits have the power to wage a war for public opinion the likes of which the world has never seen. We have a spokesman who will champion your cause. He will raise a cry of outrage which will shake the foundation of the Israeli government. This man can regain the Arab's homeland."

"Who is this man?"

"I will not disclose his name until you present my offer to Malek and return with a commitment from him." The priest's voice lowered, and his eyes flattened at the edges. "Believe me, this man has dominion and authority unequaled by any president or king."

A sudden, fearful sense of foreboding ripped through the Arab's stomach with the fury of a well-aimed knife. He had to move, he had to act, and he could not allow the Jesuit to see his fear. "English, your story bores me!" Stalking away from the pit used to contain an open campfire, the Arab gathered more brush. "No one man can restore Palestine to its rightful owners! What you are suggesting is not only impossible, but it also strikes me as comic." He threw the armload of wood on the ground and squatted beside the pit. With a few practiced movements flames sprang to life--sending a shower of sparks into the blackness.

The priest was calm, coldly impassive. "Relay my offer to Malek. The man I speak of can supply you with arms. He also has an unending supply of money. What's more important, my friend, he also has the power of his convictions."

"Sister, please sit here." Amariah reached to clear away the notes littering the table beside her.

Gripping the edge of the table, braces clanking, Sister Magdalene lowered herself onto the chair. "I thought I should stop by and say hello. Perhaps I am being too assuming, but from the expression on your face I thought you could use a word of encouragement."

Amariah liked the shy, quiet nun. Sister Magdalene was often the topic of conversation around the coffeepot when the scholars took a break. A radiant personality masked an intellect equaled by few. The tiny sister had already designed a substantial portion of the program to control one of the world's largest computer systems. Only the massive electronic brains guiding the space shuttle and rockets of NASA, could match the complexity demanded by Father Simson's museum and a website, which would eventually link him to every computer in the world.

Closing one of her reference Bibles, Amariah decided to confide in the gentle, unpretentious woman. "There are times my work is discouraging. Just when I think I have unlocked the meaning of a difficult passage, something comes along to destroy all my linguistic theories. There are days I translate little more than a paragraph! At this rate, the entire museum will be built and furnished except the section devoted to biblical epoch scrolls. I fear I shall be at this very table, laboring over pieces of moldy leather for the rest of my life!"

Pearly teeth flashed against Sister Magdalene's dusky skin as she offered a sympathetic smile. "Dear, dear Sister, it is the same for all of us! I, too, have been laboring over the portion of the program to control the temperature in various rooms. It is a frustrating task because many articles of antiquity will require disparate environments. Father Simson wants the objects displayed according to their chronology. One end of the room may contain a marble statue, which will require a constant supply of cool, dry air. Then, according to the present placement diagram, beside the statue may be a painting so old the pigment in the paint is flaking from the canvas." The nun laughed--a merry, tinkling sound almost as fragile as the bones struggling to carry her where she wanted to go. "And the whole plan must be designed to be flexible because we have no way of knowing what will be discovered in the catacombs! Older works of art might need to be surrounded by a constant veil of moisture. So, you see, Sister, each of us grapples with the complexity and discouragement of our assigned tasks. You must not feel alone." Her hand slipped between Amariah's fingers. A gentle squeeze of reassurance made Amariah feel less troubled than she had in days.

"I know nothing about computers, but how can you create separate environments in the same room?"

The nun's face brightened. A special glow transformed her as she explained the museum's details. "Oh, it's simple. Pressurized air will create walls to separate the treasurers. Moisture will stay where needed and warmer temperatures won't be able to mingle with cooler air." Passion blazed from the sister's eyes as she talked about the museum. "I've never seen anything like Father Simson's plans! Sister, the museum is really the most magnificent undertaking of this century! One day his design will be compared to the dome of St. Peter's."

"Walls of air?" Amariah was astonished. "But won't these walls be disturbed by tourists? The complexity of your work leaves me feeling very ashamed. By comparison, the difficulties of translation seem insignificant. Father Simson is amazing--isn't he?"

Sister Magdalene's face turned from passive to devoted zeal. "The Father General has been sent by our Lord to reclaim the earthly kingship of the Church! His plans encompass the most minute detail. Should a visitor stray, an electronic beam will alert the Swiss Guards. If broken, a gate will drop into place to protect the artifacts. Father tells me I must design the program so the gate will fall from the ceiling to the floor milliseconds after the alarm current is severed. He does not want to take a chance on something happening to any of the museum's treasures. He fears a misguided soul might be compelled to desecrate another of work of art like the madman who attached the Pieta. I tell you, Sister, Father Simson speaks directly with God. He is surrounded by a host of angels."

"How is *Messiah* coming along?"

"That's one of the reasons I know Father Simson is divinely guided."

"Oh?"

"Yes," Sister Magdalene's eyes grew more luminous than usual, her breathing quickened as if she were running a race, "Paul Grant is expanding the speed with which the computer can transmit information. The Father General has thousands of pairs of fiber optic cables coming into the control room. He will be able to communicate with virtually every computer in the world at the same time!"

Amariah stared at the enraptured face. It made her feel ashamed of misgivings about the Father General.

"It has data uplinks, which can transmit binary messages to geo-stationary satellites in position around the globe. The Church is financing the product development of the telecommunication industry in the United States and Japan! His foresight is inconceivable! Why, he was responsible for funding the research that developed the Hubbell telescope . . . can you believe it, Sister?" The gentle nun thought Andrew Simson incapable of wrongdoing.

"I guess I don't understand why the Church would commit enormous sums of money to developing scientific projects when millions of children are going to bed hungry."

Sister Magdalene was shocked into silence. Her adoration of Andrew Simson kept her from thinking about the children of Africa, who still suffered deprivation and despair. Suddenly, a redeeming thought transformed her face into rapture again. "Father Simson says science will pave the way for a New World order. He says the scientists of today will be heralded as the saints of tomorrow because the power to eliminate mankind's suffering lies in technology!" She beamed a radiant smile at Amariah--as her momentary lack of faith in Andrew Simson was restored.

"I see," said Amariah wistfully, wishing she could share the tiny nun's feelings. Perhaps he was as virtuous as Sister Magdalene believed. Amariah wished the fire of faith could burn as brightly in her as it did in Sister Magdalene. She appeared to be in a state of ecstasy; her talents were serving the Church and a man she revered. There was no greater joy in the world than to serve--the devotion in the woman's eyes was unmistakable.

"Sister, your faith is inspiring. How wonderful it would be if all mankind had your burning testimony." Amariah studied the bowed head, the clasped hands, the look of peace and serenity in Sister Magdalene's eyes.

"I live to serve my Lord."

"And as it should be with everyone. Unfortunately, it seems as if there are those within every Order who place personal ambition before the good of the Church."

"Yes, some succumb to the frailties of being human." The nun leaned her chin in her hands. Eyes drifting downward, Sister Magdalene allowed her thoughts to turn inward, as if drawing upon an unseen source of inspiration for a response. "As women, words left behind by our Lord define the role we are to play. We are to serve without complaint, to place our own desires behind those of a husband and family. In our case, as brides of Christ, the Church dictates our role. I serve where called and rejoice in those callings. I dedicated my life to the Church and relinquished all personal longings. My life is no longer my own--it belongs to God. This assignment, though frustrating at times, gives me true pleasure."

Her braces struck the table as Sister Magdalene swung her feet forward. Straining, gritting her teeth against the effort it took to stand, Sister Magdalene concentrated on securing her balance. Legs stiff and slow to respond, the woman born on the plains of Africa shuffled away from the table with dignity. On impulse, she turned back to Amariah, her face radiant. "Had not our Lord seen fit to hinder the movement of my body, I might not have been led to develop the power of my mind. No greater honor could have befallen me than to be chosen for this project by Father Simson. There are times my prayers of thanksgiving must be disciplined so I do not become filled with the sin of pride. It is enough that I serve, I need no more . . . or I would do a disservice to the principles of womanhood." Sister Magdalene shuffled away in the slow gait demanded by the heavy metal braces.

'. . . Principles of womanhood'. The words pummeled Amariah. The scriptures were implicit about how a woman should behave. A woman was to subject herself to the men in her environment; to give herself completely to the needs of every human being other than herself. A woman was to have no regard for who *she* was! Amariah couldn't help but chafe beneath a dictum that required giving up all self-esteem.

Sister Magdalene didn't feel this way! Why was it so difficult for her to remain humble in the presence of the men of the Church? Amariah suspected it was because too many ecclesiastical princes retained an abundance of human failings to be given total, filial respect. They were just that: human! Why had Christian women been taught to be so subservient?

Amariah reached for the topical reference book she always kept at her side. Thumbing through the pages, she ran her finger down the index seeking the subject of 'women'. Scriptural reference went on for pages. What was she trying to find? Amariah hadn't a clue, but she searched on, looking up reference after reference. In Corinthians, she found a message attributed to the Apostle Paul . . .

> *"For a man, indeed ought not to cover his head, for as much as he is the image and glory of God; but the woman is the glory of the man.*
> *For the man is not of the woman, but the woman of the man.*
> *Neither was the man created for the woman; but the woman for the man."*

Amariah knew this was why religious women wore a veil, never allowing their hair to be exposed; a nun kept her hair cropped short to avoid the vanity and temptation long hair was thought to cause.

She read on.

> *"Let your women keep silence in the churches; for it is not permitted unto them to speak; but they are commanded to be under obedience, as also saith the law. And if they will learn anything, let them ask their husbands at home; for it is a shame for women to speak in the church."*

Why? Why had Paul demanded this? Amariah was working on a scroll, which appeared to be the recorded words of two prophetesses, Priscilla and Maximilla. From what she already translated, the women were followers of Montanus and his radical supporter, Tertullian. In vain, the bishops from neighboring villages practiced canonical exorcism on the women to stop their prophecies. Montanus, Tertullian, Prisiclla and Maximilla were excommunicated for trying to *substitute direct inspiration* for the authority of the Church! The text seemed to suggest these women were revered, their messages so inspiring someone decided to preserve them.

Turning the pages of the reference guide, Amariah ran her finger down the index until she reached the verse written by Paul to the Apostle Timothy.

"*For of this sort are they which creep into houses, and lead captive silly women laden with sins, led away with divers lusts.*"

It seemed like Paul thought women were the basis of man's corruption. But, if a man did not lust, could he be tempted? Amariah thought not!

The Apostle's view of women differed from the one expressed by Jesus. How many times did the Savior rescue women of low moral standing? Once, he'd even saved a harlot from being stoned. Amariah couldn't keep from dwelling on a passage she just translated. In it, Jesus was reported to chide the men so ready to stone a woman to death with the words:

"*. . . Any of you who hath not lain with this woman . . . let him cast the first stone.*"

Those words put a different light on the passage often quoted in sermons. It placed the burden of sin on the *man* for engaging in immoral activities with the woman in the first place! Amariah did not take her scroll to Cardinal Woolsey for confirmation. She wanted Jeff Brown to look at it first. If Jeff's scientific scrutiny dated the scroll at the time of Christ--*then* she would offer the manuscript to the Cardinal.

Staring at the Bible lying beneath her hand, Amariah's fingers tapped a discordant rhythm against the leather binding. Unfocused, her eyes drifted across the room as conflicting thoughts engaged in theological battle. It was Paul who said women were lesser in the sight of God than men. Paul demanded women be subservient . . . not Jesus!

A flash of light seared across Amariah's vision. Although she was facing the windows stretching toward the vaulted ceiling of the library, screened against her mind was a man with twisted shoulders. A hunch lifted his robe and the rest of his body seemed both awkward and strained. His head drooped unnaturally; the fire of hatred in his eyes contributed to a gruesome visage. The man's surroundings came into focus. It was a market square in an ancient city. Awnings offered a sheltering canopy of shade above the stalls of vendors, who screeched at passersby, hoping to attract attention to their wares. Debris passed between the hunchback's feet as a flurry of wind drove scraps of pomegranate rind, sheaves of wheat and the refuse from a hundred stalls down the street. In the distance, across the square, a group of women stood at the community well.

Amariah felt his emotional pain.

Giggles wafted toward the misshapen man on the rising breeze. Whispers passed behind screening hands--but the words did not need to be heard. He'd listened to disparaging remarks about his appearance all his life; the disfigured man knew them by heart. His thoughts were murderous, Amariah felt as if the man were speaking in her ear!

Women could be so cruel, their tongues so sharp, if only *they* had to bear the pain *they* inflicted upon poor, suffering, unfortunate men. No one comely ever cast glances at him other than those of pity, and he needed no one's pity! Even the whores, the women who sold themselves for paltry sums, looked the other way when he drew near. Women . . . how little regard he had for them!

Amariah blinked and the image disappeared. Glancing around, she assured herself she was still in the Vatican library. Portraits of Cardinal librarians stood guard over the cavernous room. Rounded arches supported grinning cherubim. Piles of papers and stacks of books rested against the walnut table at which she was seated. The only sound to break the silence was the rapid beating of her heart as it hammer-slammed against her rib cage. *How* and *why* had the image appeared? By what mysterious power did she divine the anguish of this man's thoughts? The clothing, the buildings, even the stalls of the vendors were how she imagined a street in Jerusalem might have looked two thousand years ago!

Amariah closed her eyes, and the image of the tortured man sprang at her again. His anger made her heart flutter. Hands clenched, she dug her fingernails into her palms and opened her eyes to make the image go away. The Aramaic alphabet went unseen as Amariah struggled to gain control.

Clouds boiled over the horizon, blocking out the sun. The librarian rushed to turn the light switches. Electric lamps blazed to life, flooding the room with artificial light. Amariah's mood plummeted as the first drops of rain clung to the window, hurled against the pane of glass by an angry wind. The day had turned as dark as her feelings; nature reflected her emotional despair.

CHAPTER FIVE

Father Laterano pushed the button, and the elevator began its descent down the shaft hollowed into the limestone. Two occupants watched layers of earth slip past as the cage lowered to the last level of the catacombs. Bits of pottery protruded from damp soil, lonely remnants of civilizations lost in the debris of countless generations.

When they reached the landing, the elevator bounced to a stop. A massive hook designed to hoist large objects swayed above their heads and Amariah felt threatened by the impersonal piece of steel. Folding back the accordion pleat gate, they stepped onto a platform chiseled from rock.

Amariah's rubbed the back of her arms searching for warmth and comfort. This far below the earth the temperature was a constant sixty-five degrees, but she felt chilled and claustrophobic.

"Come, the Father General is most anxious to have you see this area." Father Laterano gestured for Amariah to move ahead. Any other time, in any other place, the proffered hand would have seemed gallant. In the shadowy tunnel, illuminated by a string of dim bulbs, the action seemed demanding.

"I thought Father Prabhupada and Anna were going to meet us here." Despite vigorous rubbing her arms remained cold.

Like slashes of charcoal his eyebrows lifted; he seldom anticipated this woman's barrage of questions. "I'm sure they'll be here soon. Cardinal Woolsey is bringing them through the tunnels. We're going to meet at vault seventeen."

Lifting her skirt above the dust, Amariah nodded. "Lead the way." The tremor in her voice betrayed apprehension. Tunnels, caves, mine shafts, dark chambers released demons of imagination.

As she glanced over her shoulder, Amariah heaved a sigh of relief. Moisture seeping through porous limestone dust made the ground soft and the heels of her leather sandals left clear impressions. Fear of getting lost in the maze of tunnels made her grateful there was a way to retrace her path to the elevator.

The damp, musty smell associated with decay assailed her nostrils. Amariah coughed and pressed the corner of her veil beneath her nose.

"We're getting close to some newly opened crypts. Many bodies were sealed away from air and moisture until we broke into the burial chambers." Amariah fought against an impulse to turn back. As she crept through the dampness, her thoughts returned to a conversation with Andrew Simson.

'You'll be spending several hours every week in the catacombs with the archaeology team'.

'Why? I have nothing to contribute! I'm sure the construction team would find someone with my lack of experience a burden'.

'Sister, you sell yourself short. Dr. Devereaux is expecting you tomorrow'.

Every time Jean Paul Deveraux reported in the weekly staff meetings Amariah found herself on the edge of her chair. His stories about En Gedi, Massada and Qumram transported her back in time because he created such a vivid picture of the area around the Dead Sea. Images of barren mountains, cloistered communities, men, and women wearing white, sprang to her mind as clearly as if she were in the courtyard at Qumram.

A light bulb overhead drew Amariah's attention. Bobbing against the electrical wire, the light flicked on and off. A shower of rocks fell from the ceiling and a helpless cry escaped her lips.

The Jesuit touched her arm. "It's just a small tremor, we have them all the time. There's no danger of a cave-in. Limestone might be porous but we're standing inside a solid block of stone. We're quite safe."

Amariah swallowed hard, the rocks dribbled from a fissure overhead. Uncertain she could ever be underground with ease, Amariah fought for control. Logic dictated it was silly to fear being entombed, yet the walls pressed inward, crushing rational thought. Air was stale, fetid. Mustiness felt like a smothering blanket depriving her of oxygen.

At a bend in the corridor Father Laterano stopped. Amariah was so lost in thought she almost bumped into him. "Here we are, and I think I hear Cardinal Woolsey's voice!"

"I hate the catacombs!" Anna Romanov's voice rang down the passageway. "How people spend their entire lives underground is beyond me! Really, David, is it necessary for me to be here?" Anna stooped to enter the landing in front of vault seventeen. "Well, thank a merciful God, at least Sister Amariah here!" A brittle laugh bounced off the limestone but there was no joy in it, or humor. "From the look on your face, Sister, you are as delighted to be here as I am!" Searching her purse for a cigarette, the historian waved the pack in Father Laterano's direction. "Am I permitted to enjoy the one thing guaranteed to soothe my nerves?"

"I don't mind if it's agreeable to the others. A good deal of fresh air finds its way through the catacombs. There are remarkably strong air currents down here, so the smoke will soon dissipate."

Glancing at the small brown man whose robe was the same coloras his skin, the exquisitely dressed woman raised an eyebrow. "Rava?"

Bowing, the converted Hindu gave his permission. "Lady, I am happy to abide with your wish."

The Cardinal cast an annoyed glance in Anna's direction. She was such a bore; there were times she acted as if the royal family of Russia still existed, and she was a favorite child. Her granduncle, the Czar, all but ruined his country yet Anna behaved as if she had the power to order executions or destroy political ambitions. This silly woman marched through sacred halls of learning as though she were a man--a capable man! "If you must, go ahead. There's little I could do to dissuade you anyway."

"Your piousness does not intimidate me." She flicked the lid of the lighter with bravado.

The flame cast tumescent shadows across the faces of each person waiting outside vault seventeen. Father Rava's habit lost its modern lines. Folds of cloth hung unevenly--as if a poorly trained seamstress constructed the garment. Instead of being pulled away from her face in a smooth chignon, Anna's hair hung loose about her shoulders, a cloth covered her head. When the flame extinguished all faces assumed familiar contours and Amariah blinked, unsure of what she'd seen. Surely, the sudden burst of light and corresponding interplay of shadow distorted her vision.

Inhaling, Anna waved her cigarette at Father Laterano; the glowing ember an exclamation point that drew attention to her insecurities. "Well, let's get on with this! The faster we sort through the artifacts in this tomb the sooner we'll get back to fresh air and sunshine."

The clatter raised by several workmen reached the group as a wagon filled with hand tools, picks and shovels, burlap bags and wooden crates rolled along the uneven surface of the tunnel floor. Diesel powered generators, brought to the site earlier in the day, coughed to life as the foreman flicked a switch and the area filled with fumes. The tungsten filament in the construction lamps bathed the corridor in a glaring, yellow light.

"Ready?" Father Laterano motioned to the crew. "Take care, Father Simson believes this is going to be an important vault."

The workers spread out, two of them holding a saw to cut through mortar cementing the wall of earthen bricks. Removing bricks with care, each one was numbered and stacked in numerical order. Father Simson planned to recreate the vault for a display in the museum.

When enough bricks were removed so Father Laterano could peer inside he reached for the electric lantern in the foreman's hand. He turned to address the woman whose discomfort was increasingly apparent. "Anna, if the vault is empty we'll go back to the surface and leave the excavation work to the crew." Stooping, the Jesuit thrust the lantern inside and flicked the switch. Light flooded a chamber sealed since the days the Roman Emperor, Nero, forced Christians to hide in the catacombs. Father Laterano pushed his head and chest through the narrow opening.

"Merciful God!" His voice contained a mixture of awe and disbelief; his hand began to tremble with excitement as the lantern's beam of light carved a wide swath through the darkness. Discovery and a sense of the future made Philipe's heart pound.

"Father, what is it?" Curiosity prevailed over anxiety. When the priest did not move nor offer further explanation Anna became demanding. "For heaven's sake, what's in there?"

Free of the vault's spell, Father Laterano pulled his head out; a dusting of powder-fine mortar covered his face and shoulders. "A treasure! Treasure fills the vault!" Words rammed together, his tongue barely able keep up with the flow surging from an agitated brain. "It must have been a library! There's a table holding hundreds of manuscripts! It's unbelievable! Father Simson is going to be overwhelmed when I tell him what we've discovered. I must hurry back to get him. The rest of you, stay here! Watch the workmen. Let them dismantle the wall but no one is to enter until I return with Father Simson. He must be the first one into the vault!"

"So, Comrade, what do you think?"

"I don't trust him."

"Are you suspicious because of his words, or are your feelings the result of years of conditioning about the West?"

"I don't know. What I know for certain is the man's a zealot."

"Who among us is not?" Vassily watched his superior officer with concern.

The chair scraped against worn tile as the older man rose from his desk. Like most Russian men his belly turned heavy late in life. No longer strong, with the rigid flesh of youth, Balsahov Petrovich sighed as he thrust his thumbs beneath the wide leather belt girding his waist. Gone were days of savage struggle that left a man as hard and enduring as the land. Mother Russia. The *Rodina.* His brothers gave their lives to save Stalingrad. He sighed as he looked out the window of his office. One of the privileged, he enjoyed a view of Red Square. Bound by the vermilion walls of the Kremlin, the Moskva River, State History Museum and GUM, the department store, which was the pride of his government, Red Square represented his country's history; the heart and soul of Russia resided within these sixty-nine acres. Bricks spread in every direction like the thousands of souls who gave their lives to safeguard Russia's heritage. Red Square was huge; it was as vast as the territories which comprised his nation. This plot of land was the spiritual heart, and emotional center of Russia. Comrade citizens came from everywhere to visit Lenin's mausoleum, St. Basil's Cathedral, the Annunciation Cathedral, and the Assumption Cathedral--for these were the monuments of his people.

Much of his life was spent trying to bring Mother Russia out of a primitive agricultural age into an era of technology. Russia enjoyed more natural resources, more land, and almost more citizens, than any other country on earth. The mentality of his people was what he sought to change, and that was an unending struggle. Born on the land, their forefathers worked the same soil beneath the rule of Cossack, Czar and Communist. All Russians shared a mystical bond with the land which yielded their harvests. Industry was an alien concept, and it defied absorption into the minds of Russia's people. Mother Russia . . . could he guide her through the quagmire of shifting values presented by the twenty-first century? If he did not, his country would become a second-rate power and Russia deserved to be recognized as the best--supreme!

Petrovich stared at the onion-spired domes of St. Basil's. They were truly remarkable because the spires were built in the sixteenth century. Ornate and gaudy, the domes reflected the complex nature of his people. Their outer shell was still colorful despite enduring revolution, war, pillage, and plunder.

He loved the Kremlin and swore to preserve it. His mission was not unlike that of the Jesuit, both were dedicated to different sides of the same cause: influencing the Russian people. Petrovich turned away from the window.

The young man facing him still bore the hardness of youth. Vassily

Kharkov had not learned to compromise today for what might be gained tomorrow. Such was the relentless lesson of Mother Russia. Thousands died to preserve the future for the young man whose bright blue eyes studied him. "Vassily, watch this priest. Perhaps his plan will benefit us."

"But Comrade!" The young man exploded from his chair. The drab uniform strained against wide shoulders. In years gone by this young man would have tilled the land. "To align ourselves with the Catholic Church goes against everything we stand for!"

"Ah, Vassily, will you tell me what that is?"

"This priest represents decadent Western ideology! He thinks because he has money he can invade Russia and corrupt our way of life. By offering us trade agreements and an unlimited supply of grain, he believes we'll capitulate and allow him to open his churches. The man's ego is offensive!"

"Would you have our people go hungry again this winter? Have you read the agricultural reports? We've had too little rain again this year. Our present crop production cannot feed our millions!" Petrovich's knuckles turned white as he gripped the edge of a desk designed for utility, not beauty.

Eyes lowering, the younger soldier blushed. "I know we face another lean winter."

"Vassily, let me tell you one of the things I've learned in my years upon this earth! I've watched our people survive hardships undreamed of by most. Members of my own family starved to death. Yet, the *Rodina*, the Motherland, survived. Do you know why? Because our people understand the timelessness of the land. The Western mind prattles about the importance of scientific achievements, but we Russians . . . we understand only the land endures from generation to generation. Men who think themselves important might enjoy a moment of glory, but the land is the only thing to withstand the passing of succeeding generations. It is my duty to preserve and protect Russia for the future! What we have been offered is an opportunity to feed our people. The priest can provide enough grain to sustain us over several bad winters. We will take his offer --and meet his demands with caution. Vassily, we are being presented with an opportunity to preserve the future of Mother Russia!"

The young man shrank back, a look of uncompromising resolve took up residency in his superior's eyes. He'd seen it many times in the old guard who still held a tight grip on the reins of power. Coming up through the ranks as Communists, they didn't accept Western ideology. They seemed to think they could protect Russia by a display of force. Vassily knew continued exposure to the lifestyle of the West was a far greater threat than all the tanks and missiles

NATO had in its arsenal. The priest wanted far more than to open a few churches here and there. The man was like a trap door spider patiently spinning its web. Random lines would radiate outward. Then, slowly, they would begin to connect--one by one--until the web had the strength to snare the unwary. He didn't like the priest, he feared him. The long, black Jesuit robes could destroy all that had been built these past few decades--why didn't Petrovich recognize the danger?

"Carole, are you ready?" Andrew Simson couldn't hide his excitement.

"One more minute, Father! These pictures will assure I'm nominated for Photojournalist of the Year again. Let me take another light reading. I want everything to be perfect." Carole Phillips studied the chamber. Reflectors were in place, and she tested the batteries again to make certain the strobe lights were synchronized with the shutter speed. Blowing hair from her eyes, the woman concentrated on the setting. As one of the highest paid free-lance photographers in the world, Carole knew these pictures were going to record the archaeological find of the century! Perfectly preserved manuscripts were strewn around the room. Inkwells, styluses, quills, pots, even a few food bowls were scattered along a plank which once served as a desk. It almost seemed as if the scribe intended to come back but something prevented him from doing so. Anxiety made her test the flashes again. These photographs would earn a place in history alongside those taken in King Tut's tomb. Finally, she called out. "Father, I'm ready. Come to the entrance, I want to snap a few frames of you standing in the doorway."

He paused at the threshold--knowing he was stepping back in time. His heart hammered in his ears as blood shot through arteries and veins, accelerated by the force of adrenaline. Secrets to the past sequestered in this vault could validate his mission.

"Hold on! Don't move. There," the photographer pointed at the thick wooden slab, "keep your eyes on those manuscripts, I'm picking up a reflection in your pupils. The effect is quite magnificent!" The whine of the camera as it captured images was the only sound to break the graveyard stillness in a long-forgotten chamber. "Keep coming toward me, Father."

The click of the shutter echoed off limestone walls. The flash blurred the Father General's vision. Afraid he might step on something valuable, Simson held up his hand to shield his eyes from bright quartz lights.

"A moment, please, Carole. My eyes need to grow accustomed to the light."

Carole didn't like to use digital cameras when shooting in black and white. She reloaded one of her cameras, keeping an eye on the Father General a technique she'd learned in Viet Nam. The picture she took of a brooding General Westmoreland won her a Pulitzer for photojournalism. Her ability to snare unguarded moments was what made Carole Phillips the best in the business. Simson was so engrossed he didn't notice the photographer inched a camera slung around her neck up to her eye. She pressed deep into the sanctuary provided by the shadows beyond the glare. A thrill, half cold and half exultation throbbed through her body; she was going to leave the vault with some extraordinary photos. The camera never lied; images, good and bad, were quick-frozen for the world's inspection.

Floodlights bounced light along white limestone walls. Tungsten filaments struck silver reflecting umbrellas and refracted a diffused filter of yellow into the chamber. Dust particles hung in the air, making it seem as if the Father General was passing through a veil which separated man and time. Inching toward the table, Father Simson longed to pick up a manuscript--to begin sifting through these ancient records. His eye lingered on every document. This room would crown him the Savior of mankind. And Sister Amariah was going to help him establish his vision of a New Jerusalem. The Holy City, Jerusalem, rested on the land bridge traversed by conquering armies--Egyptian, Babylonian, Assyrian, Macedonia, Persian, Roman legions--would soon be the epicenter of the Catholic Church.

Out of the corner of his eye an object beckoned him. He freed it from the bond of time. His hand trembled when he picked up a silver object. Energy surged toward the synapses in his brain with fury. An ancient coin acted like a lightning rod; supercharged images flooded his thoughts--each one rolling over the other in a series of impressions so fast and so frightening he couldn't process the in-coming load of information. The sudden blaze of emotion which occupied the Father General's face was inexplicable.

From where she stood, Carole kept her finger on the shutter as Simson fondled an ancient coin. The expression she couldn't find words to describe changed his face as he stared at the object in the palm of his hand. It looked like the ghosts of memory rose to haunt him. Carole jammed another roll into the back of the camera and slammed the door, which protected the film from unwanted light. Swinging the Minolta back to her eye, she knew she was going to capture something vital. Everyone stepped aside as Andrew Simson rushed from the vault. Glancing neither right nor left, he raced down the tunnel toward the freight elevator.

The woman, whose I.D. badge read 'United Press International', waved her notebook--wanting to be the first to attract the Father General's attention.

"Father! Father Simson! Mona Desmond, UPI! We've heard rumors the archaeological team uncovered the greatest treasure-trove the world has seen since King Tut's tomb. Is it true?"

The light required for television cameras seemed absorbed by his Jesuit robe and the Father General radiated an almost surrealistic aura. No stranger to the microphone, he cleared his throat and waited for the reporters in the room to fall silent.

"Yes, Miss Desmond, we have." His fingers gripped the lectern; Simson was a man accustomed to controlling the mercurial moods of the press like a conductor leading an orchestra through Mozart's *Requiem Mass.*

"I understand there's a code assigned to newly opened graves, ah, Gerard Jones--Associated Press."

"Yes, this one is identified as vault seventeen."

"A number which will undoubtedly go down in history." New to the press corps, Gerard Jones stared at his notes rather than meet the Jesuit's gaze.

"More than you presently know."

"Father! Father, would you elaborate on that last remark?" An American network anchorman rose from his seat, intense light reflected off graying hair.

"Certainly. Time deteriorates all things—including information. These documents will bring about a renewed interest in the Church. Principles considered outdated by modern clerics will receive new and important perspectives. The authority of the Church will be upheld by information in vault seventeen."

"Father," UPI waved her notebook again, "sources from within the Vatican reported you found a document which led to the discovery of vault seventeen."

"When I first arrived at the Vatican, I was assigned the task of reorganizing documents in the Secret Archive. Records dating back to the time of St. Paul were set aside--their contents hidden. Some ten thousand documents, occupying a major part of fifty miles of shelving in the Archive, were never opened. I discovered a map of the catacombs and realized many items were stored beneath the Vatican, a record of which was lost through time. The new museum will display these treasures . . . despite criticism surrounding this project." Menacing eyes darted from face to face, spearing offenders who used their networks, newspapers, and magazines as a forum to oppose his plan. "I believe it is my responsibility to guide the Church through the difficulties of the twenty-first century. The righteousness of this sacred institution will soon be substantiated. Areas of theological mystery will be explained when these documents are translated."

"You seem very sure of that, Father." The network anchorman stood firm against Simson's visual challenge.

A normally brooding, handsome face assumed an enlightened, compassionate expression as he focused on the anchorman. "I am John, I am. In His day, the Savior was rebuked by men much like yourself. They scoffed, they criticized, they challenged His conviction and belief." A gasp rippled across the room. "It is important to remember *His* views are those which have endured the test of time. Is there a contemporary of Jesus about whom history recorded greatness? No! Pilot, Caiaphas, Herod Antipas, even Caesar paled to insignificance. Their mark on history is the role they played in *His* life. They are nothing but names to those of us who populated intervening centuries." Pointing at the offending reporter, Simson's voice rose. "I tell you, John, as Jesus warned the doubters of his day, God chooses the greats of a generation . . . not man! My role in history will be validated to the satisfaction of a disbelieving world!" His eyes seemed to blaze like a napalm fire; reporters stood transfixed as they tried to process the complex chain of logic, reminding them sinners were always punished by God. "While you shrivel back into the dust from whence you came."

Black robes swirling, the Father General stalked across the platform, righteous anger apparent in every movement. Shoulders taut, eyes boring through those with the courage to meet his glance, Andrew Simson exuded such authority reporters let him pass without a single delaying question. The door slammed shut but television cameras continued to roll. Reporters clutched their microphones as if they were lifelines tethered to a rescuing ship.

Finally, from the back of the room, the expressionless voice of an ABC news commentator broke the cumbrous silence. ". . . Ladies and gentlemen, Father General Andrew Simson, just left the room."

Carole Phillips reached for her fourth cigarette; three still smoldered in the ashtray. The red light in the darkroom cast phantasmal shadows along its whitewashed walls. She'd grown accustomed to the spectral images that floated in and out of her peripheral vision but vanished the moment she turned her head. Unaccountably, it seemed as if the spectral images came more often in Rome. Perhaps the ghosts of history were restless in the Vatican; the tortured souls of evil churchmen seeking forgiveness.

Photos were clipped to a length of cord suspended from the ceiling and chemicals dripped from sheets of photo paper into developing pans below. Carole studied the wet prints. She preferred the contrast of black and shades of gray against the intense white of well-lit objects. In the tradition of Ansel Adams, Carole felt contrast heightened perception. But she never expected to capture an expression like the one staring from the wet print. Nestled against his palm, Father Simson gazed at a coin with an emotion Carole could only describe as longing. No priceless gem or work of art, the coin had little value other than historical significance. Carole sucked the cigarette again. Cameras never lied. The Father General would probably be powerless to explain the expression on his face. There was a quality in his eyes that was dark, frightening, hypnotic. Stubbing out the butt, she was mystified by her feelings. After all, she owed her next Photographer of the Year award to Simson. He hand-picked her to record the project which would take its place in the annals of history!

She studied Simson's eyes some more; it was like looking into the eyes of a Viet Cong executioner. Haughty defiance. Above humanity. Even if they were butchers. Insane passion if she had to give his expression a name. There was something unreal about the man--devotion tinged with madness. A tap on the door brought Carole off the counter, her feet thudding against the floor.

Father Laterano called out. "Miss Phillips?

The tap came again, this time she couldn't ignore it.

"Have you developed the film yet? Father Simson is anxious to see your pictures."

"Hang on!" Reaching to unfasten the sheets of photographic paper, Carole shoved them into an open safe. She spun the dial, her heart racing. Why didn't she want Simson to see them? Instinct prevented her from reopening the safe. "Wait one more second and it will be okay to open the door. Bear with me!" Carole emptied the solution trays, dumping smelly chemicals down the drain. Wiping her hands, Carole slid back the bolt and opened the door. "Come in, Father. Look at these but remember they're just proofs. There's a couple I want to scan and retouch some of the bright spots--you know, artistic stuff."

The black cassock was consumed in the darkroom's red light and Father Laterano's face seemed to hover above his body. A phantom's mouth formed his words. "I know nothing about photography, but I admire your work." Stepping closer for a better look at the pictures of Father Simson, the priest sucked his breath. The tungsten filaments starred the Father General's jet-black eyes. Dust particles trapped by the reflecting umbrellas created a halo around Simson's head. The other members of the archaeological team hovered above Father Simson's shoulder, floating disembodied. Behind the priest, slightly apart from the group of anxious onlookers, the face of Sister Amariah was framed by her white wimple and veil--a ministering angel.

"The way the light surrounds his head makes the Father General appear divine! This is magnificent, he seems like a modern-day saint."

Carole studied the picture with a critical eye. Smoke from the endless chain of cigarettes that never left her hand curled around her head, making her squint. “He looks more like a fury to me," she whispered.

CHAPTER SIX

Jefferson Davis Brown was a tall man with the shoulders of a weightlifter. Brooding eyes stared out a rain-streaked window. He glanced at his watch--its hands moved too slowly. Returning his attention to the window, the African American decided the weather reflected his mood. Both sisters should have been here by now. Why the Father General decided Sisters Amariah and Magdalene needed to be present during the testing of a few pieces of papyrus was beyond comprehension.

Rome disagreed with him. He was tired of the rain and sick of Simson's project. It withered his insides, it gave him a feeling he was an accomplice to something inhuman--like ship captains who filled their cargo holds with frightened natives and sold other human beings into slavery. Father Simson gave him the willies; the long, black Jesuit robes reminded him too much of his childhood in the south. Klan members still rode through his nightmares; hooded faces screaming obscenities at a small boy who wanted nothing more than to get home after school. Flapping robes against the bodies of rearing horses was an image he couldn't scrub from memory. If it hadn't been for his stout-hearted mother, Jeff knew he would've given up trudging along a lonely dirt road from the schoolhouse to a one-room shack the Brown family called home.

Outside, a clap shook the windowpane just behind the lightning that cracked like a whip across the sky above Rome. This kind of storm covered the noise which might have alerted his family to the Klan's approach. Trying to shake the gloom claiming his emotions, Jeff struggled to hold back searing memories which always accompanied fierce storms.

The door opened, and Jeff turned, grateful to be rescued from looming depression. When Amariah entered the room, she was awestruck by the vast assortment of equipment.

"By all that is holy," Sister Magdalene's voice contained wonder as she shuffled between cabinets filled with blinking lights. Twenty metal boxes, resembling microwave ovens, housed digital read-out displays linked to a mainframe tucked against one wall. Green fielded monitors glowed like one-eyed Cyclopes. Other screens displayed charts, graphs and bars, test tubes and racks of bottles labeled with chemical glyphs lined glass-fronted cabinets. A row of stainless-steel sinks bordered the other side of the lab and three refrigerators large enough to store a side of beef stood side by side. At the end of the lab, aluminum shutters protected a bay window overlooking an open-air courtyard in the middle of the museum complex. Her eyes returned to the black American with a Ph.D. in physics. "You have enough equipment to launch men to Mars!"

A hearty laugh dissolved the layer of tension, "The Father General has certainly outdone himself. You are looking at some of the most sophisticated equipment in the world. The risk of shipping artifacts to universities and laboratories scattered across the globe for authentication was eliminated when he outfitted this lab. Father Simson prepared for the future! Are you sisters ready to begin?"

Amariah nodded too amazed to say anything. What could she possibly offer such a respected scientist? Few scientists had more credentials than Jeff Brown. Amariah glanced sidelong at his broad shoulders as he lifted a tray of cultures from an oven. She'd heard stories about how football and scholarships paid his way through college. Like many African Americans, Jeff knew he needed to work harder and longer to prove himself than most of his white counterparts. Even after rising to eminence in the field of carbon dating, his demeanor broadcast the injustice served up by racial prejudice.

"Do you know anything about carbon dating, Sisters?"

A shake of her head sent Amariah's veil swirling. Sister Magdalene was not afraid to voice her ignorance. "Mr. Brown, I can tell you all about bytes and megabytes and gigabytes. I can sing the praises of complex database and statistical analysis programs. In your American schools, I learned a language spoken by computers. The complex path of logic demanded by a computer is as familiar to me as the Most Holy Rosary of the Blessed Virgin Mary. The Sacred Heart sisters saw to it I received a marvelous education, but your area of science is as much a mystery to me as the trans-substantiation of the body of Christ!"

Amariah couldn't repress the smile that made her cheeks dimple. From the twinkle behind his soul-dark eyes, Jeff Brown found Sister Magdalene's response amusing too. Intuitively, Amariah sensed humor might be the chink in the scientist's emotional armor, so she chimed in, "Conjugating verbs somehow pales to insignificance before the technology in this lab and the intelligence required to run it. In fact, Mr. Brown, I sometimes feel as antiquated as the dusty artifacts over which I labor. Men have walked on the moon, the space shuttle will soon launch men toward Mars, medical technology replaces the human heart--and I worry over whether some ancient scribe was using past or present tense!" Amariah shrugged and an engaging smile revealed sincere admiration.

Handsome white teeth stood in stark contrast to his dark skin as Jefferson Brown exploded with laughter. Dabbing at the tears suddenly filling his eyes, he surrendered. "Sisters, welcome to my lab." Grasping Sister Magdalene around the waist, he lifted her onto a chair as if she were a delicate sparrow, "Please, call me Jeff. I'll give you a rundown on what I'm doing as we go along. Carbon dating requires a lot of mathematical equations, but I don't want to bore you with technical jargon."

Gesturing toward a digital read-out, words filled the lab as Jeff began to explain the work he loved. "Sister Amariah, sit right here so you can witness the wonder of modern technology at work."

Perching atop a stool, which didn't look sturdy enough to support his linebacker frame, Dr. Brown slipped his hands into a device that looked like a pair of thick rubber gloves. "From here, I control the robotic arms inside this sealed chamber." A metal shield retreated and behind glass reinforced with wire mesh, Amariah could see two manuscripts on top of a stainless-steel pillar in the center of a room so barren she knew it was sterile.

"We take elaborate precautions with this material. The room is free of bacteria or mold, which might hasten the decay of papyrus or leather. Most of what we found in vault seventeen was in good condition because the room was unusually dry for a subterranean chamber. Devereaux told me the walls were sealed with the same kind of plaster the Essenes used to waterproof the caves in which the Dead Sea Scrolls were discovered. When Devereaux starts talking about the Essenes, you can't shut him up."

Jeff Brown glanced at the nuns, who listened with rapt attention. "Jean Paul is in vault seventeen now, scraping away some plaster so we can test it to see if it's comprised of the same material Essenes used. He's pretty fired up. I guess he hopes to prove his theory about Jesus being an Essene."

Sister Magdalene shook her head. "He is certainly controversial. No one has ever been able to prove a connection between the Dead Sea sect and our Savior."

"I quit going to Sunday school as soon as I was old enough to outrun my Mama, so I can't offer an opinion. But I've worked on enough projects to recognize the look in a man's eyes when he thinks he's on the edge of discovery. Dr. Devereaux thinks Sister Amariah is going to do some mighty important verb conjugation in days to come!" A smile warmed Jeff Brown's face as he glanced at the younger nun, whose hands were wrapped around her knees, her face a study in concentration.

Jeff watched the digital display flip over, then reached to adjust a knob before he continued. "If I lose you in the scientific stuff--stop me. I tend to forget not everyone knows, or cares, about half-life and radium output." Flexing his fingers inside the rubber gloves, the robotic hands mimicked his motion. "I'm going to pick up the scanner and pass it over each of the scrolls. "Sister," he nodded his head in Amariah's direction, "will you please record the sequence of numbers as they register on that digital display? I'm going to measure the amount of carbon-14 remaining in both the papyrus and the leather."

"What will that tell you?" Sister Magdalene lifted herself off the stool and pressed her fragile body against the glass as if to help guide the metal fingers toward the delicate remnants of scholarship.

"How long ago these were written. I established a fairly accurate date on a funeral boat unearthed in Egypt a few years ago and we'll use those numbers as a basis for comparison. Wood holds a half-life about as well as charcoal. I once got to work on a project that tested the ashes from a campfire dating back to prehistoric times."

"Upper Paleolithic, right?" Amariah was pleased she remembered reading an article about the discovery which thrust Jeff Brown into the scholastic limelight.

"Yes, how did you know?" A smile warmed his face.

"Your picture was in every magazine in the country for weeks. I think you even made the cover of *People*, didn't you?" Amariah teased.

"Sister, please, no scientist worth his supposition would admit it!"

"The Father General seems to welcome the attention of the press."

"Father Simson gets more publicity than a movie star." Jeff couldn't suppress the sarcasm in his voice.

Sister Magdalene's braces struck the tile below the window when she turned, her voice filled with rebuke. "Father Simson has been chosen by God. He is directed by Divine sources and if we don't understand how the Almighty moves, it is because we are mere mortals!"

Amariah leaned against the stool, her arms across her ribcage in an attitude of defense. Concentrating on the scrolls rather than the quick retreat into scientific explanation offered by the embarrassed scientist, Amariah knew she should have stopped the conversation when it turned to Father Simson.

Sister Magdalene worshiped him . . . why couldn't she?

Numbers on the digital display flickered as the probe roved over a scrap of torn papyrus and a fragment of tattered leather. Red numbers blinked, changing from red to black, the strobe of light pulsing in time with Amariah's heartbeat.

Her thoughts strayed--when the Father General rushed from vault seventeen, Amariah wondered if she was the only one to catch a glimpse of the coin in his hand. His face was enigmatic, but she didn't notice the message conveyed by hunched shoulders or the way he shielded the coin.

A chill marched down her spine. His eyes contained an unbalanced expression, as though he couldn't see the group of people crowded into the corridor. He seemed to be reliving a scenario screened against his inner mind. As if his persona--the very thing that made him Andrew Simson--was no longer in residence.

Numbers continued to flash as she watched the steady flick with an unblinking stare.

Amariah tried to analyze her reaction when she stepped inside the chamber. A room, perhaps twenty feet long, was hollowed into the limestone. Plaster walls still bore trowel marks made when some long dead craftsman applied his finishing touches. One wall was lined with shelves, the wood showed almost no signs of decay, as if erected only days ago instead of centuries before. Strewn around the room, hundreds of scrolls littered the floor.

The screen changed from red to black and back with the rhythmic beat of a metronome.

The feeling that welled up from somewhere deep inside was all too easy to recall, even now. As if passing through the gossamer barrier of time, she felt separated from the rest of mankind forever when she stepped across the threshold of vault seventeen. Amariah looked at the room with physical eyes, but the mechanisms of the subconscious altered the chamber in subtle, yet astounding ways. Shelves were stacked with bundles of manuscripts and a candle burned at the edge of one scribe's desk. Two men, deep in conversation, spoke in hushed tones.

Shock must have registered on her face because Father Rava followed her out of vault seventeen when she fled into the corridor. 'Sister, are you ill?'

The conversation played against her ear drums every time she allowed her thoughts to stray to the encounter.

'I don't know what happened. I guess my eyes were playing tricks on me. The shelves were suddenly filled with manuscripts and two monks were conversing in the corner-- but that's impossible!'

A gentle hand reached for her arm to lead her away from the blinding lights, the press of anxious people and the smell of the generator's diesel fumes.

'Can you describe what you saw?'

Rava's tone of voice was so compassionate repressed emotion came tumbling out in a rush.

'Father, ever since I began work on these manuscripts images have been springing up before my eyes. I see monks wearing the kind of habits that haven't been in use since the Middle Ages! I feel as though I am stepping through a portal moving me back in time. I have no idea what triggers the images and feelings so real they're hard to deny!'

The plea died on her lips and Amariah remembered lowering her head, so the priest wouldn't see the tears of confusion and frustration.

The digital display continued to flick as the recording head in the robotic arm swept over the surface of the scroll—seeking telltale signs of radiation. It counted upward at a steady pace. Numbers glowed briefly, then the screen went black, replaced by the next set of numbers which cast a red glow on unblinking eyes taking no notice of the change.

'Sister, dear, in my country, great sages claim to have the power to travel through the past while living in the present. It is said the mind contains unlimited memory--that we all have ability to discover levels of awareness which are, perhaps, beyond our present ability to understand. You may be one of those gifted enough to connect with another place and time. Far more exists in our world than most people want to admit. We are hampered by the dictates of a science that seeks to reduce all subjects to commonly accepted units of measurement. Yet the power of the mind defies the very rules science tries to implement! Your gift is simply not yet understood by the Western world'.

The whir and hum of the computer, warmth radiating from an oven baking a variety of bacteria, a storm steadily worsening beyond the laboratory window lacked meaning for Amariah as she stared at the digital display like it would soon reveal mysteries of the universe.

Was she catching a glimpse of the past? Amariah shook her head, her temples pounded at the thought of something so vast, so redoubtably complex. Perhaps she was searching for a way to rationalize the thoughts invading her mind and challenging the structure of belief since her arrival in Rome!

"Malek, for the love of Allah, listen to me! What the priest offers us could change the course of our struggle! What are a few hostages compared to press coverage, the goods and arms we would receive in exchange?"

A heel lashed out at the dying ember of the fire, a motion as lightning quick as the black desert cobra striking prey. "I do not trust this priest. He is trying to take over our minds, win us with his words. What does he really want?" The checkered cloth wound around his head was suddenly stifling and he yanked off the only protection an Arab had from a hostile sun. "If we give up the hostages what assurance do we have the British will not retaliate?

"What assurance do we have now? We play a dangerous game of cat and mouse, my brother."

Eyes webbed by deeply scored lines glared across the fire. The women had cleared away the meal and council members leaned against pillows, which provided the only comfort in a Bedouin's tent. "Another player in the game compounds the odds."

Kammal reached across the fire, wrapping the handle of the metal teapot in the folds of his robe. He seemed absorbed by the task of refilling his cup. A dark, bitter liquid streamed into a cup stained by years of use.

Heat made a man languid. Energy spent in haste was energy wasted in the desert. His people learned to live in harmony with the conditions demanded by unyielding terrain and a hostile sun. Foreigners were never prepared for the rigors of the life of a nomadic Arab. Yet the priest adapted to these hardships during the weeks he spent with them. The robe he wore was that of Bedouin man, except for the all-absorbing color. Despite the heat and a blistering sun, he refused to adopt the cooler, lighter clothing of the Arab.

Reflecting, Kammal sipped his tea. This priest insisted his god and Allah were one. He said radical sects were using the words of Mohammed wrongly. The priest believed Mohammed was a great prophet, a man sent by God to the dwellers of the desert. It was time for all true believers to live in peace. Mohammed wanted that; it was the extreme factions who taught the prophet demanded all infidels perish beneath the sword of righteousness. Kammal could barely read and could not write the fancy flowing script of the desert--its graceful letters swept across paper like wind-sculpted sand dunes pushed across a barren landscape. He wasn't smart enough, nor did he have enough education to debate with the priest, but somehow--Father Norton's words rang true.

Despite his religious calling, Kammal sensed the priest displayed the mind of a warrior. He offered too many comments about strategic location for their camp to doubt his military training. From where had he come? And where did he disappear to in the night? The priest was as stealthy as the treacherous jackals who plagued the flocks of the Bedouin.

Kammal lifted his eyes to men sharing the hospitality of his tent. "We will strike a favorable bargain with the British using the hostages to gain our ends."

A hiss of steam followed the gob of saliva Malek spat into the fire. "This priest will counsel peace and I counsel death to all who oppose Allah's will."

Kammal studied the tea leaves at the bottom of his cup. "Malek, what is Allah's will?"

"To put to death all who do not believe in the one true God!"

"Ah, yes. And, my friend, how often do you read the Koran?"

"I cannot read, you know that!"

"Then, from where you get this information?"

Angered, Malek pushed away from the pillows and began to pace. "Kammal, your courage is that of an old woman. You blind our men with your words instead of exhorting them to action!"

"But Malek, I do not understand. If you cannot read the words of our beloved prophet, how do you know what he said?"

Stopping, his robe eddied around scuffed leather boots. "Our Holy Men read the words and tell us what they mean."

Kammal tipped his head back, draining the cup, but his eyes never left those of his tribal leader. Finally, the cup empty, he tossed it aside. "Do you think perhaps it is the Mussulman and the priest who need to talk? Perhaps it is they who need to spar with words, to duel with each other over whose philosophy is right? We are poor, simple men, uneducated and unworthy to debate the meaning of Allah's intentions. What I do know," the conflicting emotions of fear and courage chased across his expression, "is we have an opportunity to bring guns and ammunition into this camp. I might see my oldest son for the first time in five long years if he is released from prison in exchange for our hostages. I am willing to give the British back their reporters if it benefits me to do so. The life of an infidel is of no consequence to me. But I do care about the welfare of the people living in this camp."

Eyes on the tent flap, Kammal watched the others depart. Most were angry, thinking his counsel weak. There was much to gain by aligning with the priest. Kammal knew he must convince Malek to cooperate with the Jesuit. He wanted his son back! Breathing deeply, Kammal filled his lungs with pure desert air. His eyes strayed to the blaze of color painting the sky majestic shades of orange and scarlet as the sun lowered--before abandoning the desert to the indigo of night. He wanted his son to be free of the fetid air in the British prison. Kammal wanted him to roam the sand dunes of his childhood home again. The priest spoke the truth--Kammal could feel it. The Jesuit could free his son!

"Ah, Sister, do come in." Andrew Simson pushed away from the desk in the center of the sparsely furnished room. "Thank you for coming."

Amariah took his extended hand. The Father General's grip was firm, befitting a man secure in his position of authority. As he motioned her toward the bench beneath the window, his voice assumed the warm, comforting tone of a concerned advisor.

"Sister Amariah, I wanted to speak to you about the importance of the work you will begin in the next few days. The scrolls in your keeping might be some of the most valuable pieces of historical evidence ever discovered. The cloak of historical responsibility has fallen on your shoulders." He paused, giving her an opportunity to comment.

The armor of skepticism restrained her tongue. Most people offered up their innermost secrets because they felt compelled to fill long, uncomfortable silences. Her stomach muscles twisted, and her diaphragm fought for air as she waited for him to continue.

Assessing the girl's posture, Simson knew she was testing him. Her father's training was revealed in her composure. He straightened, the cassock straining against a body as taut as a crouching panther. "Do you understand how much the significance of your area of expertise has increased since the discovery of vault seventeen?" The question demanded a response.

"The importance of the documents in the chamber will only be determined with time." Amariah kept her voice even, fighting against uncertainty.

"Indeed, Sister, indeed. You will have access to a network of computers linked to the data banks of a thousand universities scattered around the world."

"Yes," Amariah's eyes drifted to the garden below the Pinacoteca, "Sister Magdalene spent a lot of time training me on your program these past few days. I fear she had an appalling task."

"Quite the contrary. Sister Magdalene tells me you mastered the program with ease; that your fingers act as though they are guided when you touch the keys."

"It is Sister Magdalene, who operates the system as though she were born to it. The only skill I possess is the ability to remember the sequence of keystrokes which allow me to operate the program. I can't get over how easy it is to access information on the Dead Sea Scrolls in Jerusalem through the Internet. It is a modern-day miracle to have reference material at my immediate disposal which would take months to research before the Internet evolved to its present state. "

"Perhaps Sister Magdalene's program will be the Church's contribution to the twenty-first century, and it will establish world-wide dominion."

Amariah turned from the window, her eyes accusing. She clutched the rosary beads in her pocket as doubt spilled, unchecked. "Do you plan to have the Church's dominion supplant the role of traditional government? Will your authority take precedent over kingships dating back centuries? Are you above the law of nations?"

Simson arched his back as his fists coiled against his thighs. He did not expect her challenge. "The Lord command the Church to feed His sheep, and so we shall."

"I'm not certain the Savior would counsel us to exercise dominion over the world! Were I you," Amariah thrust her chin forward in an air of defiance, "I would tread lightly with those who do not share our faith."

The Father General sprang from his chair and began to pace the room like a tiger who just missed its kill. His fury engulfed Amariah like a tsunami. "And I, like St. Paul, put no stock in the counsel of women! You should refrain from speaking on subjects which are none of your concern. Your talents do not lend themselves to international matters."

Simson checked his outburst. Damn this woman, why did she throw him off balance? He halted and took a deep, calming breath. "Devote your time and energy to translating the work awaiting you. History will be rewritten once you finish this task."

"Father," The delicate mechanism of Amariah's mind jolted as a sudden foreknowing pried open the gate of the subconscious. "You expect me to find something--don't you?"

A web of red lines traced an intricate pattern against the whites of Simson's eyes. His arteries throbbed against the clerical collar and his hand wrapped his crucifix in a crushing embrace as he whispered, "Throughout the ages Jesuits hid scores of documents in the Secret Archive to shield the information from profane eyes. Illiterate masses were not prepared to receive the true doctrine of Jesus Christ! But I plan to restore the Holy Mother Church to the greatness intended by our Lord. An age of enlightenment so great it will be referred to as the 'Second Coming' by future generations is within our grasp."

Amariah was desperate to escape the supercharged atmosphere. Simson frightened her. How could an educated man think he had the ability to unify such a diverse world? Her hand rested on the doorknob as she stopped to look back at him. "I will translate these scrolls, Father, for humanity deserves to know their contents. As you say, their message could help many who require spiritual direction. You may be hailed as the new Messiah, but you can never measure up to our Savior because," her words dropped like iron balls raining down on concrete, "you are just an ordinary man."

Andrew Simson stared at the closed door. New aspects of the Sister's character were revealed every day; he hadn't counted on such a streak of independence. He assumed she would follow him blindly. The girl was not so intimidated by his position that she would do his bidding without question. She could not be allowed to interfere with his project. He was a man of destiny! Sister Amariah was wrong! He was not an ordinary man! His mission, his calling, his view of the future was inspired by forces beyond the normal ken of this world.

Amariah hovered over the magnifying glass. Adjusting the overhead light, her eyes strained to read faded ink. She shivered, then wrapped her arms around her ribs and slumped forward, seeking the warmth of her own body. Her new lab was kept at a constant sixty-five degrees; warm enough for humans, yet cold enough to retard the growth of bacteria which could deteriorate the manuscripts.

Light from the fluorescent tube overhead flooded the Formica workstation. Amariah glanced at her hands. At least the rubber gloves helped keep her fingers warm. The top of her head began to itch, and she rubbed the surgical cap, which replaced her veil and wimple. Somehow, she felt exposed without the religious clothing she wore—making her feel without protection from the harsh realities of the outside world. The habit provided a defense mechanism she hadn't recognized until now. More and more, Amariah realized how sheltered she was from coarse and unsavory conditions because people respected a nun's robe and veil.

A knock on the window intruded. Glancing up, a smile lifted her drawn features. Kaminski stood in the hallway, awaiting permission to enter the electronically sealed room. Amariah depressed the switch beneath her worktable and a buzz heralded his entrance.

"You'd think this is a top-secret military installation. I had to show my badge before I was even allowed access to this floor." Kaminski sauntered toward the white Formica counters lining one side of the room. "Do you feel like you're locked in a prison?"

"At times. The library was more hospitable, and I find this," Amariah held up a gloved hand, "disturbing. But this room made me discover things about myself I never knew."

Leon drew his fingers across the counter's gleaming surface knowing he wouldn't find a trace of dust. "I'm surprised to hear you say that. You seem so self-assured."

Amariah laughed and her melancholy lifted. "Quite the contrary! There are far more character traits that give me grief than those about which I feel confident."

Kaminski's smile was slow, and his eyes crackled with the fire of amusement as he spoke. "I want to hear about your voyage of self-discovery. Share with me, Sister, and I shall confess the harbingers of evil which crowd the confines of my soul."

"You sound like Dostoevski. Does grimness plague your thoughts often?"

"Sister, this place is growing on my nerves like the fungus the Father General seeks to avoid in these frigid laboratories. What deep, dark secrets have you uncovered?" Hopping on the counter, Kaminski leaned against the wall. "I suppose I'm not allowed to smoke in here?"

Amariah nodded, "I didn't know you smoked."

"I don't--you see, my confession has begun, and it wasn't even my turn."

Since moving into the lab, Amariah hadn't spent much time with Leon and she missed his easy banter, the way he made her laugh, and the wry humor he brought to heated conversations.

"Amariah, what's on your mind? I was at the window for some time before I knocked, your thoughts were far away, and I gather they were not entirely pleasant."

Stripping the glove from her hand, Amariah felt the cold against her skin. It was a welcome sensation. There were times she felt as if translation sprang to life at her touch as much as from information stored in her brain.

"I don't like this room. It makes me feel though I'm segregated from the rest of the world. And that's something I've discovered I don't like."

"You finally figured out you've been sheltered from the muck and mire most people face?"

Her eyes flashed, defiant. "I didn't say that!"

"You didn't have to! Amariah, you've had to contend with very few of life's realities. You went from being cared for by your father to being cared for by your Order. You've never worried about shelter, food or the needs of a family."

Amariah's glance dropped as she searched her memory. "It's strange, but I never realized it until now."

"What made you think about it?"

"This." Amariah lifted the hem of the surgical gown. "I didn't understand how much my religious clothing shielded me."

"Don't you think that's part of the intent? Didn't it ever occur to you, religious robes have a sobering effect on people?"

Comprehension darted across Amariah's face. "I never thought about it before. The history of our Order is filled with stories about Abbess Mothers, who died rather than violate the tradition of our habit. The veil and wimple are as sacred to a Benedictine sister as the stole, amice and surplice are to any priest. We're taught to revere our clothing."

Leon continued, his tone on edge. "That's the problem with religion! People follow without question. You're taught to memorize convenient answers! God forbid you entertained a thought which ran contrary to established tradition."

"The Church would never have lasted as long as it has without structure."

"Exactly what it needed was constant reform! Amariah, don't you see? In a world living with the threat of nuclear holocaust, exploding populations, political leaders who think nothing of throwing thousands of men into pointless, bloody conflict--where does the Church fit? Trite solutions pulled from ancient text do not satisfy the needs of our modern society." He slid from the counter, pacing the room in restless, elongated steps.

Amariah voiced a limp protest. "That's why we're here! Father Simson believes we'll restore mankind's faith in the Church. He's convinced we'll find evidence of Christ's wish for the Church to provide guidelines for humanity to follow." Amariah's eyes brimmed with tears refusing to be suppressed. She desperately wanted to believe her own protest.

When Leon's voice bounced off the tiled walls, it was brittle and cold. "The Father General seeks to validate his mission! The last thing on his mind is the good of mankind."

"You heard?"

Simson leaned his head against the high back of his office chair. "We must keep close watch over the meetings of Kaminski and Sister Amariah. Were it not for his command of oblique languages the man would not be a part of this endeavor."

"The two of them will create opportunities to exchange views." Father Montanegro gazed at the workmen, lunch pails in hand, as they headed toward the gate. Quitting time had been pushed back further and further as Father Simson ordered hurried construction deadlines.

Drawing the DVD closer, the Father General examined the date scrawled on the label, happy he had the foresight to install a concealed camera in each lab. "I want to watch this again. I may have missed something—a tone of voice, inflection, something to indicate what's going on between the nun and Kaminski. I'll call you when I'm finished."

"As you wish." Father Montanegro bowed and left the room.

Within the hour, night would take possession of Rome and the fading shadows of twilight thickened over the expression on Andrew Simson's face. Pressing play, the voices of Sister Amariah and Leon Kaminski filled his office as he adjusted the volume. Unsure of what he was seeking, Simson let the recording play all the way to the end. It surprised him to hear Sister Amariah spring to his defense. Only a blind man would not see how she shrank from him or notice how quickly she terminated their conversations.

Kaminski was becoming far too vocal. His questions would spread doubt like an epidemic. Amariah's voice floated from the speakers. Anxiety lay beneath her supportive words. She was beginning to question her own faith in the Church, and he never considered that a possibility. The girl's growing attachment to Kaminski was another unknown factor. Furious, he withdrew the DVD from the computer, determined to put a stop to their meetings!

Silently checking the row of grenade launchers one last time, Sean admired his handiwork. Six pipes, three-quarters of an inch in diameter and thirty-six inches long, leaned against a low stone wall. One end was threaded to accept a smaller diameter of pipe. A shotgun shell inside was jammed against a rubber washer. The firing pin, consisting of an ordinary nail, would strike against the shell forcing the homemade bomb high into the air. A smaller dowel fit just inside the pipe. A liter bottle filled with gasoline and soap was securely taped to the dowel; a length of rag wedged between the dowel and the neck of the bottle. Sean flipped the lighter open and inched along the ground, setting the line of rags on fire. Satisfied each torch was burning, he yanked out the narrow strip of aluminum foil separating primitive but efficient firing pins. Like rockets, the dowels left the pipes hammered into the ground. Crude weapons hurtled toward a group of Protestants just leaving church. Bottles shattered on impact, splashing gasoline across the square. The flaming strip of fabric ignited first one pool of spreading liquid--then another. People's clothing caught fire and in a matter of seconds the area in front of the church became a sea of flames. One bottle struck a man and his entire body disappeared into the flames, his hands and feet flapping grotesquely. Screams tore from throats of the dying, the injured struggled to flee. Blood seeped across centuries old paving stones, a tide of red, anguish, pain and confusion following in its wake.

Wanting to assure himself the task was completed with maximum efficiency, Sean O'Flannery surveyed the carnage. Four were dead, possibly six. Two others sustained burns that would surely see them expire before morning. A quick glance in both directions confirmed his position was still undetected. He would have to hurry. A raging fire would bring the police all too soon. A child began to wail, its screams a counterpoint of terror as the church burst into flames with a roar as the last round of home-made rockets exploded against the roof.

Jumping over rickety fences separating the yards of working-class dwellings, Sean twisted and turned through rain washed streets. Doubling back, then countering by going forward again, he left a trail so broken it would be impossible for police dogs to follow when the remains of the rockets were discovered. As soon as he was certain no one was following, Sean stepped into a darkened alley and hunkered down to watch the entrance of the pub on the opposite side of the street.

Several men from the neighborhood ducked inside, their bawdy voices calling to one another over the misty rain which began to fall. As the drops gathered intensity, O'Flannery pulled the collar of his jacket over his ears and rushed across the street.

The tavern was filled with smoke, but Sean threaded his way through the tables with ease, his destination familiar. No one hailed the gaunt figure as he headed toward a table in the rear. Choosing a corner draped in shadow, he lurched into a chair, his back secure against the wall. Rain dripped from the jockey cap on his head onto the table, but he seemed not to notice as eyes swept the room. Without being summoned, a barmaid placed a pint of ale in front of him and she didn't bother to wait for payment. Scuttling back across the inn, the barmaid seemed anxious to be away from the table and pockmarked man. If the tavern owner told her to give this stranger a pint, she wasn't going to ask any questions. It never registered on her limited capabilities the number of men, such as the one in the corner, were increasing of late.

Most of the early evening crowd had already thinned out. Regulars were local workmen whose job required them to be up at the crack of dawn; to work in the shipyards or on trawlers plying the North Sea in search of fish.

The brim of his cap tugged down until it almost touched his nose, Sean's eyes grew heavy. The warmth of the fire, the ale, and the letdown after the adrenaline high he always experienced when he inflicted his rage on bastards who caused his people such endless suffering, left him spent and drowsy.

The tavern door opened, and a figure clad in black slipped inside. Above the trench coat, a clerical collar identified a priest.

"Evenin' Father." The barmaid offered a clumsy curtsey. "You'll be havin' a brew?"

"Tea, lass, if you please. The night is turning ugly, and I've lost souls yet to comfort."

The priest strolled toward the back of the room and took a seat at a table near the fire. Crackling logs would muffle the words he spoke to the man hulking in the corner. The girl busied herself making tea, unaware of the conversation taking place across the room.

Hands stretched toward the warmth of the fire, the priest's lips barely moving. "Good-work, lad. It's all over the TV news. Nine dead, including several children."

"Fewer to contend with in the future."

"The fire will get some fine press. Nothing stirs the hearts of the bleedin' liberal like the death of children. I've always wondered why it's easy to condone the slaughter of grown men while the mere mention of a child's passing, or the suffering of an animal, can make the most stouthearted seethe with indignation. Pity for the innocent, perhaps."

The conversation ceased as the thick-legged girl padded toward the table, her weight shifting from side to side as she plowed steadfastly toward her destination.

"Ah, lass, you'd warm the heart of our blessed Savior with your kindness." The priest shoved some coins in her direction. "A stiff spot of tea and I'll be back out into the weather. A soul is near to departing this world, I'm afraid."

The girl quickly crossed herself and lumbered back toward the bar. "Father, what'll ya' be havin' me do next?"

"Lay low for a few weeks. I'll contact you when I have another job worked out. No point in jeopardizing your talents by exposing you to the law too frequently."

An angry hiss expelled from beneath the leather cap. "I'll not get caught. I've had too much trainin'."

"Even more reason to make certain you don't end up in a cell or beneath a marker. I've no intention of losing my star pupil." The Jesuit longed to take his hat off and wipe the perspiration from his forehead, but caution warned the shock of white through carrot red hair would provide the barmaid with something easy to remember. Tipping his mug, he quaffed the remaining tea. "Keep to your flat, I'll get a message to you later."

Amariah leaned her forehead against the warm casing of the lamp suspended above the workstation. Her eyes burned, and her vision was blurry. Glancing at the clock, she was determined to work at least another hour.

Now that she was familiar with Sister Magdalene's program, Amariah found it amazing to have a dictionary with millions of cross-referenced word combinations at her fingertips. She could work at ten times her normal speed. She tapped in the words *son of man.* The hard drive emitted a whirring noise, and its one red eye began to blink, signaling the beginning of its search. The screen filled with references on how many times the phrase "son of man" was used in the New Testament. Twenty-six times Matthew, Mark, Luke, or John called the Savior the *son of man.* Apostles described the *son of man* coming from the clouds of heaven or sitting on the throne of Judgement at the right hand of God; they said Jesus identified *himself* as the *son of man.* Yet he was portrayed as having super-human powers, the dispenser of everlasting life.

Her eyes turned toward the scroll lying so innocently on the workstation. It contained a message, which shed an entirely different light on the phrase. According to a newly discovered document, *son of man* meant Christ was a normal human being! The idea was so foreign Amariah decided she'd made a mistake in translation. Tapping a command key, the screen dissolved, and the monitor filled with another set of words. Amariah moved the cursor down the row slowly, seeking proof she was mistaken.

The muscles in the back of her neck were tense and her head began to pound. Nothing in the thousands of words she could access because of Sister Magdalene's program linking her to universities, linguistic centers, museums, and other scholars around the world indicated she was mistaken! *Son of man* was a transliteration of the Aramaic phrase meaning *'my father's son'*. The words shouted at her across the corridors of time. This witness to the ministry of Christ, whomever it was that laid the quill against this tattered scrap of leather, said Jesus called himself a *son of man* to prevent his followers from attaching any God-like characteristics to his person.

'I say unto you that I am no more than a man. Any of you can do all that I do and more. For it is within the power of every man to fulfill the promise of the Lord. It is you who shut yourself way, hiding from the pure light of day, you who deny yourself this power. It is man who feels himself unworthy to become a member of the legion of God. All may do as I do, speak as I speak, heal as I heal. . . for I am nothing more than my father's son.'

Amariah's stomach muscles wrenched, and all the air seemed to spill from her lungs. This passage was the opposite of everything she'd ever been taught. So mystical was the Catholic concept of Jesus it defied anyone's ability to put it into words. Heated debates over how the union of God the Father with the Son and the Holy Spirit was accomplished had raged since Constantine demanded early Christian bishops unify their churches. Determined to understand the concept, Amariah poured over the works of St. Thomas Aquinas and other leaders of the newly formed Church. She finally gave up, deciding she was not smart enough to understand such a spiritual concept. Now, in view of what lay beneath her gloved hand, Amariah wondered if these bishops understood what they were writing about--or had they merely wanted to sound inspired! Was Church cannon the ramblings of men who wanted others to think they alone were worthy of comprehending the complexities of the Divine?

Son of man . . . the words acted like a battering ram against her ears. After hours of internal argument, Amariah decided to take her notes to Cardinal Woolsey. Once the obligatory conference with the Cardinal was over, she intended to turn the scroll over to Jeff Brown. Its mystery might be resolved if the age could be confirmed. If a contemporary of Christ did not write the scroll, it was probably nothing more than someone's opinion of what Jesus might have meant! Amariah was beginning to wonder if the entire Christian religion was based entirely on opinion! Certainly, St. Paul did more to bring the teachings of Christ to life than any other leader. As an educated man, he left behind many letters; documents said to have been written by his own hand. But Paul was not a contemporary of Jesus, in fact, he never met the Savior! Jesus had been dead thirty years by the time Paul converted to Christianity. How much was distorted by word of mouth over three decades? Were Paul's letters his feelings about those things he only heard repeated?

Amariah stared at the computer screen, the on-off key beneath her trembling hand. How many more disturbing revelations were contained in the scrolls locked in her laboratory safe? Her fingers were numbed with cold as she stripped off the surgical gloves and threw them at the trash-can.

"Cardinal, Sister Amariah is here."

"Send her in, Brother Pasqual, send her in." Pressing his stomach, Cardinal Woolsey tried to suppress a belch. His digestion was far from normal anymore. Heartburn seemed to plague him day and night. The Vatican physician warned of the onset of ulcers--and with just cause! Simson's cursed project was taking its toll. Not only did he despise the Father General, he was also concerned about what would happen to his position should Simson's house of cards collapse.

Sick with worry, he spent most of his waking hours trying not to get too closely aligned with the Father General's politics. Simson was pressing him more all the time; his threats were no longer veiled--they were implicit! He kneaded the area below his breastbone as if touch could make the pain go away.

"Cardinal Woolsey, are you ill?" Amariah stood at the other side of the desk, hesitancy taking up residency in her voice.

"Sister Amariah, do sit down. If you are asking after my health, it's been miserable of late. I seem predisposed to chronic indigestion. I'm afraid I'm growing too old for the pleasures of pasta and wine." A grim smile settled over his face as he waved her into the chair at the other side of his enormous teak desk.

Amariah wasn't certain whether the Cardinal's sour expression had to do with his physical condition or if his face betrayed a lack of regard for her. Perching gingerly at the edge of the chair, Amariah pushed a sheaf of notes toward a man she neither liked nor trusted. "Cardinal, I wondered if I could take a few moments of your time to discuss the ramifications this translation might have on Church doctrine."

One eyebrow arched skyward, doubt spread like ink across features bloated with fat. How impertinent of this woman to think her work might affect canons which had withstood the test of time. "Sister, I know you're sincere, but the importance of your work has been overstated."

Smarting at his rebuke, Amariah decoded the message for the disbelieving Cardinal. Thankful she'd brought along references to validate her findings, she tried to keep from smiling at the Cardinal's growing astonishment.

Woolsey felt the blood drain from his face as the Benedictine nun finished. Feeling as if he'd been immobilized by curare, David Woolsey was beginning to wonder why he chose the Church as a career--and he saw his vocation as a career rather than a spiritual calling. As the nun unrolled the scroll, he studied pen strokes with the power to unravel a lifetime of study. Fire shot up the back of his throat. Blast this woman and Simson. He was not going to have his entire career ruined by a posturing nun! He'd worked too hard to establish himself as an authority on Church doctrine. This, this-- slip of a girl-- was chipping away at the very foundation of the Christianity! Eyes round with anger, Woolsey raised his gaze to meet the girl's open expression.

Innocence radiated from her face; the nun was earnestly seeking an answer to the dilemma posed by this manuscript. He suddenly realized she was still in possession of her faith! Cardinal David Woolsey hoped he was mistaken. The nun was an accomplished scholar! She should have shed the trappings of faith long ago. Yet when he looked at eyes as blue as cornflowers, Woolsey recognized the fire of belief; Sister Amariah still believed the Church was a Holy institution.

"My dear . . ." he kept his tone condescending. Perhaps he could discourage further investigation if he made her feel foolish, "If the meaning of *son of man* has been misinterpreted throughout the history of Christianity, we might face a schism in doctrine. Are you quite sure of this translation?"

Amariah nodded, trying to ignore the degrading tone of voice; she used irritation to suppress tears of humiliation. Amariah clasped her rosary beads and buried trembling hands beneath the folds of her habit.

"Well, then, I must think on the implications." The horn-rimmed glasses required for reading slipped to the bottom of his nose. Pushing them back, the Cardinal gestured toward the scroll. "May I look at it?"

Pressing against the condemning scrap of leather by the corner, Amariah pushed it across the desk toward Woolsey.

"I'm not an Aramaic scholar but I can make out a few words here and there. The scroll seems to have suffered from the onslaught of time. How did you manage to read ink so faded?" He thrust the manuscript beneath the hard bar of light cast by the desk lamp.

"Computer enhancement--Dimitri Marcello photographed it with infrared film at a high shutter speed. What he produces after the image is digitized is remarkable." Handing over a copy of the computer enhanced message, she went on. "This is an exact translation."

Unwilling to admit he barely understood the process, Woolsey nodded. "I see. I believe there is only one course of action open to me at this point. I shall go to the Holy Father and seek his opinion on the matter."

"Is Pope Anastasius well enough for an audience?"

"The Pope and I are old, personal friends. Although he is gravely ill, there is nothing of greater concern to him than the stewardship of the Church. He takes the responsibilities of being the Vicar of Christ seriously . . . he always has. I will talk to his nurses. They can advise me of when he is likely to be lucid. When he is heavily sedated they say he often talks with the Savior. The Pope pauses, as if he were listening to another person. There are times the nurses are quite frightened by what they hear."

Amariah's eyes flicked over Woolsey's heavy frame as she assessed his sincerity. "Has anyone thought to record what the Holy Father says?"

Unnerved, the Cardinal squirmed against the chair. "Wisdom from a man under the influence of morphine? I think not, Sister, and you tread close to blasphemy to suggest such a thing."

Amariah compressed her lips, there was no point in arguing with Woolsey, his mind was as closed as a rusty trap. From her experience in the nursing wards at St. Anne's, Amariah knew patients removed from worldly cares often muttered statements of great relevance. She reached for the scroll. "I'll return this to my safe."

"No, I want to show it to the Pope. After I meet with the Holy Father I'll send it back to you. Be warned, however, it may take several days before he feels up to speaking with me. Leave this in my hands, my dear, and--don't worry about a thing."

As Amariah reached the foot of the stairs, she glanced back toward the door which shielded Cardinal Woolsey from museum guests and the large staff it took to maintain the building and its treasures.

She was worried . . . desperately so. Instead of feeling relieved by the Cardinal's promise instinct warned of impending doom. Amariah whispered a fervent prayer for Pope Anastasius' health as she headed out the door into the sun-drenched garden.

A cricket chirping in the garden below her dormitory window was a welcome sound. From her vantage-point, the last pale rays of a setting sun caressed the upper circle of the stones in St. Peter's dome making it seem like a golden coronet.

Clouds gathered on the horizon and in the distance, lightning threw bright streaks across the land, carrying the promise rain before long. As a distant clap of thunder reached Amariah's ears she turned toward the north— greeted by the smell of moisture borne on an increasing wind.

In daylight, the Vatican gardens boasted an array of flowering shrubs and trees rivaling the palette of any artist. Rose bushes, profuse with blossoms, painted a backdrop of purple, red and orange so vibrant the gardens seemed surreal.

At night, in the cold silver of moonlight, the gardens assumed a different personality. Cheeriness of day disappeared and in its place, came the shadows which obliterated all color. As night approached on darkening wings, birds called to one another, a final trill to mark the close of day. A shiver traced a fractured path between her shoulder blades as Amariah stared into the gathering darkness. Had a legion of ghosts begun to tramp beneath her bedroom window, in truth, she would not have been surprised. It was easy to imagine troubled souls of early Christians, whose bones lay beneath the papal city, had been deprived of a lasting peace. They seemed to take possession of the garden at night, lonely, calling out to anyone who could hear their desperate cries.

Amariah reached for the window, drawing it closed against the cool night air and frightening thoughts she couldn't contain. A long hot bath was the remedy for tired muscles, aching bones and a mind consumed by worry.

Testing the water pouring from the tap into the tub, Amariah allowed her thoughts to drift while the room filled with stream. As the storm grew closer, humidity made the air in the tile-covered room murky. She forgot to turn off the lamp on the study table; the door was ajar, so she switched off the bathroom light. Her favorite CD playing in the background contributed tranquility—waves surging against a sandy beach. Stirred by a howling wind, the ocean seemed to have a life of its own as the echo of steady surf pounded against ceramic tile in the bathroom. Amariah slipped off an old terry cloth robe and stepped into the tub. Gliding beneath the water, she didn't stop until her nose and eyes were the only parts of her body not submerged. Soothing, comforting, Amariah batted at the water until waves conformed to the sound of a tumultuous ocean. Filtered by a yellow shade, the study lamp threw weak beams of light through the steam. Waves pounded, the warm water soothed, and Amariah released her troubled thoughts.

She was conscious of neither time nor her body as the stress of the day peeled away like the layers in an exotic dancer's veils. The tempo of the tape changed, and the ocean grew peaceful. Gulls called, surf lapped against a sandy beach and Amariah felt her troubles vanish.

Staring at the reflected gleam of the study lamp in the faucet without really seeing, she was nowhere . . . yet everywhere. She thought but didn't think.

Peripheral vision captured movement in the shadows. Accustomed to motion at the corner of her eye, Amariah didn't bother to turn. Nothing was ever there. She continued slapping at the water in an abstract motion . . . waves beat on, and ocean sounds filled the bathroom.

Again, movement slipped along the far rim of her vision. This time, it seemed as if a swirl of cloth demanded attention. Slowly, Amariah turned her head. Suspended in mist, a tall man in a black robe beckoned. With a startled scream, Amariah sat bolt upright. Water surged against the tub and spilled onto the floor. Grabbing her robe, Amariah tipped over the stool which held her CD player. Soothing sounds screeched to a halt and a hush so heavy it was almost palpable stole through the bathroom as Amariah's foot found the cold tile floor.

The vision faded when she located the switch and flooded the apartment with light. No one stood in the sitting room, yet Amariah could not slow panicked heartbeats slamming against her ribs. Gasping for breath, she stumbled toward the outer door. The dead bolt was in place, no one entered there. Her eyes flew to the window, had she remembered to drop the latch? Lightning flashed against the windowpane illuminating the room in a haze of silvery blue. Her heart throbbed even faster as her gaze settled on the locked window.

Amariah searched for a towel to wrap around her hair. Her imagination was working overtime--perhaps the ghostly image was the result of too many hours hovering over manuscripts written by men, who had been dead for centuries. Maybe stress was taking a greater toll than she realized. There were times she felt overwhelmed by her responsibilities. A hallucination, that's all. A simple trick of light and shadow filtering through steam.

Feeling better, Amariah slipped inside a long cotton night gown. She was tired, more tired than she wanted to admit. It might be good to call Father Laterano and tell him she wasn't feeling well. Maybe she'd stay in bed tomorrow and review some of the research she hadn't taken the time to read. Thoughts focused on what she would read if she allowed herself such a simple luxury, Amariah drifted off to sleep.

The red, glowing numbers on the digital alarm clock were the first thing she saw when her eyes flew open at the sound of her name. It was 1:20 a.m. A man's voice, firm and deep called to her.

'Amariah'. It came again. *'Amariah'*.

It took Amariah a few seconds to decide where she was; that her father was not calling her from the coziness of her bed beneath the dormer windows of her childhood home. She was not in San Francisco, and it was not time for another day of school. It was now 1:25 a.m. -- *and she was in Rome!* The voice called again.

'Amariah . . . I am with you . . . have no fear'.

Her eyes searched the room. Flashes of lightning cast many armed shadows against dormitory walls, but no one lurked in the corners. Then, out of the darkness, she sensed, rather than saw, a man. Eyes burning from lack of moisture refused to focus--yet she could feel a presence.

'Amariah . . . I am here'.

A blinding arc filled the room with an electric blue-whiteness. Amariah tossed back the covers and went to the window. Her eyes were playing tricks on her again; she was straining them too much lately. A clap of thunder rattled the windowpane, rain pummeled the glass, a tree branch thudded against the window. Another bolt of lightning stair stepped down through the sky, striking the tallest tree in the garden. Flames shot into the air, coloring dormitory walls an ugly shade of crimson. As Amariah stared into the garden, a figure ran from the revealing light of the fire to the safety of shadow.

Frantic sampietrini poured from their apartments. Researchers and technicians awakened by the storm rushed to join the Vatican residents in extinguishing the fire before it spread. The man, who pressed his body deep into an alcove of Pope Leo's fortress wall, was hidden. An inner sense of knowing warned Amariah he had been standing beneath her window. But, to what purpose?

The figure moved away from the wall, retreating into the garden until he was swallowed by shadows and rain drenching the Vatican. A chill closed around Amariah's heart. Things were happening over which she had no control. She clutched at her robe, desperate for its comforting warmth.

The voice sounded behind her.

'I will protect you.'

She whirled. The lightning ceased, and her room was wrapped in folds of darkness. An image lumbered closer, but Amariah had nowhere to go. The demon of fear could swallow her alive or she could stand and fight for her sanity. "Who are you?" The challenge resounded throughout the room and Amariah was surprised at the determination in her voice.

Convoy-like, wagons stretched to the horizon. A thousand miles of flat, miserable swamp still had to be crossed before they got anywhere near the border. Sun beat down on the backs of cattle and men alike. No breeze cooled the stifling land, no clouds sheltered them from a blistering sun. Water in barrels strapped to the wagons tasted rancid; yet both soldier and cattle were grateful when the man leading the column ordered a halt. Groaning, infantrymen sought relief in the shade of a few flat-topped Acacia trees--the only life form bearding a forsaken plain.

Flies swarmed over pest-ridden cattle and men swatted at insects they knew wouldn't go away. The march north from their base of operations in Cangamba, across woodland and scrub, was proving interminable. Wagons and cattle slowed their advance, but it was impossible for any army to live off this land. Like early Romans, the rebel army of Angola had to carry supplies with them. The earth turned to dust beneath the cattle's feet as the temperature rose.

Loto knew they had to push on; according to his map they were nearing the Chicapa River. Water barrels could be replenished, cattle would fill their bellies and his men could cool off in the river. Squinting up at the sun, Loto judged the time. Perhaps if they hurried they could reach the river by sunset. They might be able to rest for a day or two before pushing on to the border--and certain encounter with the soldiers of Kanga-Kanga. That power monger would stop at nothing to make the proud, rebel princes bow before him. Their civil war had already lasted thirteen long, bloodstained years. Signs of peace had come and gone, but Kanga-Kanga was not to be trusted. Loto got to his feet, waving his men to follow suit. He watched the priest sling the automatic rifle over his shoulder and push himself up off the ground. The Christian was as tired as the rest of them. Setting a brisk pace, Loto glanced back at the column only once and the expression in the priest's eyes disquieted him.

He expected the fair-haired white man to give up long before now. Loto thought the priest would turn back or at least asked to ride in a wagon. The uniform he wore, the long black robe, was now gray from the dust and grime of their journey. When the ground turned muddy, as it always did after brief squalls, he simply tucked the hem of his robe into his pants waistband. Leather boots, well suited for a long march, strangely, did not seem out of character on this priest. Father Ruger Stein marched relentlessly onward. He shared their meager supply of food and drank the foul water like the rest of the soldiers, but Loto never heard a single word of complaint. The white man spoke their language as if he was born on the high savannahs. Loto couldn't get over how strange it seemed for a man with blue eyes and golden hair to mouth the words of his ancestors. Loto didn't understand why the priest was here, but it wasn't his concern.

Besides a backpack filled with supplies for their journey, the priest carried a weatherproof box. Loto suspected it contained a radio. Every night, just after sunset, the priest disappeared into the bush. He said he was going to offer prayers of thanksgiving to his god for surviving another day's journey. The priest's god lived in a stone house, behind a golden altar. Loto had been inside the strange god's house--once. He didn't like it. The priest's god hung from a cross, anguish etched in his features. The white man's god did not smile, nor dance. He only suffered. Loto liked the god of the air, the god of the earth and the god of the animals. They were happy gods; they brought prosperity to his people.

Glancing over his shoulder again, Loto reassured himself the priest was keeping pace. The man in black was his responsibility. Loto would be happy to see Tshikapa and turn the whole confusing matter over to him. Tshikapa was educated, he had been to the white man's schools in Kenya. Tshikapa was waiting for the priest. They had many important things to discuss. Loto lengthened his stride.

"Mind if I sit down?" Leon lowered a tray filled with biscuits and bacon on the table. A mug filled with steaming coffee seemed perilously close to the edge.

With a nod of permission, Amariah kept her eyes averted. Dark circles, which marked the passage of many sleepless nights, left bruised crescents across the top of her cheeks. The hand clutching her coffee cup trembled noticeably.

"Amariah, are you ill? You look as if you've seen a ghost."

What little color was left in her cheeks drained away, leaving her skin so white it melted into the wimple. She lowered the cup toward the table but lost her grip on the handle and coffee spilled over the rim.

Leon reached for some paper napkins, mopping the coffee up before it reached the edge of the table and spilled onto Amariah's habit. It struck him as odd she didn't try to assist with the clean-up operation or joke about being clumsy. "Amariah?"

No response came from lips Leon noticed were cracked and peeling. It looked like she had been chewing her lower lip for quite some time. He reached to take the half-empty cup from her hand, his fingers lingering a second longer than necessary. "I'll get you more coffee--then I think we need to talk."

Staring after him, Amariah was only vaguely aware of what Leon said. He waited in line, impatient to reach the coffee urn which served all scholars and technicians in the cafeteria. Once back at her table, he straddled the bench. Without saying a word, he reached to butter a biscuit, then spread it with a layer of raspberry jam. Pushing the plate in her direction, his voice took on an authoritative tone. "Eat this, you'll feel better." He paused, a smile of memory tinged his expression. "I'm beginning to sound like my grandmother. Her antidote to every ailment was something to eat. I suppose it was a result of all the years she spent trying to keep her family from starving. The difficulties of my life seem insignificant when I think about the life she led."

Leon shot Amariah a glance, the biscuit was in her mouth, and she chewed it without recognition of what she was doing.

"I don't think I've told you much about Lillian Kaminski, have I?"

No flicker of interest gave Leon any indication his words registered but he felt the need to draw Amariah's thoughts away from the crisis upon which she was so inwardly focused.

"Her story is right out of a movie. My grandfather was a Polish army officer, and he knew Hitler was planning to invade Russia. He decided to get his family to England before the war worsened. Unfortunately, he was murdered by Nazi sympathizers just weeks before Hitler launched Barbarosa."

Studying folded hands, the bowed head, her vacant stare, Leon knew Amariah wasn't listening to a word he said but he continued, hoping to spark interest.

"With little more than the clothes on their backs my grandmother walked all the way across Poland with five little kids. My aunt was about seven at the time and my mother was just a baby. My newly widowed grandmother succeeded in getting her children out of Poland just as Hitler's army swept across the country. Because my grandfather had connections with some British generals, she made it to England and took a job as an interpreter. I think I inherited my gift of language from her."

There was still little response, the biscuit left on the plate, half eaten, the coffee in her cup grown cold. Leon forged ahead, watching for a reaction, something to tell him he'd broken through the wall barricading her thoughts.

"The stories Allied generals used to tell about my grandmother were really something. They respected for her ability to predict what the Germans were going to do next. She became a legend in intelligence circles. One-night Winston Churchill called on my grandmother. She was the one who decoded the message about Coventry, and Churchill wanted to make sure she had no doubts about what was going to happen. My grandmother said she'd never forget the suffering in his voice as long as she lived."

Amariah's head lifted, she was looking at him, but was still imprisoned by desolate thoughts. Leon pressed on, hoping his story would erode the emotional dam behind which she retreated.

"Churchill was a man in anguish. From what I've been told, my grandmother offered him comfort and bolstered the courage to make the most painful decision of his career. She said a leader always bore crushing responsibilities. Her message to him was to accept sacrifice as a part of life. Her husband gave his life to save his wife and children. She gave up friends and family to insure her children's freedom. If Churchill ordered the evacuation of Coventry, the Germans would know their code was broken. Coventry's sacrifice was something the Prime Minister had to live with the rest of his life."

Drawing a knife through the jam, Amariah created an abstract pattern, but she nodded, aware of what Leon said.

He switched to a topic he felt would ignite Amariah's interest. "Grandma's experiences always made the Bible story about the 'widow's mite' seem like more than a parable. I know it's supposed to make people remember the true value of a gift, but I always wondered if Jesus wasn't really talking about a *'widow's might'*. It seems to me a woman with a family to support and protect all by herself is a powerful phenomenon which merits study."

Leon paused. Amariah was staring at him; the blank, emotionless expression gave way to curiosity. "Is this a true story or are you just trying to get my attention?"

"Sister, no words can express the admiration I feel for my grandmother. She got my aunts and uncles through conditions where greater men would have faltered. Whenever we try to do something for her, she brushes us aside by saying our achievements are her reward. When the Father General asked me to work on this project, I thought Lillian was going to burst with pride. I accepted this assignment because I knew it meant a lot to her.

"She got five children through the German lines?" Amariah's eyes reflected the emotion of an experience she realized must have been filled with panic and terror.

"Lillian took on the most awesome fighting machine known to man and lived to tell the tale."

"How?"

"Most of her youth was spent in the countryside around Warsaw because her father was a farmer. She grew up hunting and fishing in the hills with her brothers. The rural parts of Poland were as familiar to her as the back of her hand. She hid her children in abandoned farmhouses and ate off the land. Sometimes a relative would run the risk of sheltering them for a night or two. When they reached France, my grandmother was stealing linen off clothes lines to wrap her children's feet with because their shoes were little more than pieces of shredded leather."

"She must have been incredibly frightened."

Leon dropped his gaze, the older he got the more he realized what hardships his grandmother endured. "Her turmoil was horrendous because my grandfather knew about Hitler's plans for the Jews and the families of Poland's political leaders. Lillian decided she would rather have her children die in the open, attempting escape, than have them end up in a death camp."

"How awful." Amariah's chest began to rise and fall as the impact of Lillian Kaminski's story hit a responsive nerve. "Hearing about your grandmother makes me feel guilty." A feeble attempt at a smile collapsed the moment she stopped struggling to maintain it.

"Amariah," Leon's eyes brimmed with sympathy. "I didn't tell you about Lillian to make you feel bad. I just wanted you to realize people can achieve the impossible once they set their minds to it."

Amariah nodded then let her gaze wander over the room while she tried to sort out the conflict in her thoughts. "I feel like I'm not myself—like I'm outside myself, watching." Her voice lowered to an inaudible whisper. "Watching, watching and wondering if there's any way to hold back the darkness."

"Tell me why you're so afraid."

"It seems so foolish when daylight comes. Perhaps it's nothing more than a dream." Amariah's fingers began to toy with the rim of the cup; she watched the pattern trailed by her fingerprints on the ceramic surface. "It's probably nothing."

"Amariah, there are times in everyone's life when they have to act with courage--when they are forced to take dread in hand and cast off the chains of fear which bind them to security. My grandmother possessed that kind of courage. She left everything she knew behind and sought refuge in a foreign land. She wanted her children to be free and she paid a staggering price in terms of personal sacrifice. But my grandmother has no regrets! She faces each day with a clear conscience because she did the best she could under brutal circumstances."

Her gaze shifted to the window framing a clear blue sky free of clouds, but Amariah felt the rope of fear tie a knot around her vocal cords. The words came out hoarse and sharp. "I think we're all going to need that brand of courage in the very near future."

CHAPTER SEVEN

"Sister . . . Sister Amariah!" A rap drew Amariah's attention away from the manuscript over which she was laboring. Her hand paused above the keyboard, her train of thought disrupted by the insistent knocking.

"Unlock the door," Anna Romanov pointed toward the men near her elbow, "we're raging at one another and you're the only person, who can settle this issue!" Eyebrows, plucked and penciled into a perfect arch, jetted upward as Anna waited permission to enter the sterile lab.

Amariah depressed a button releasing the magnetically sealed door. Waving the trio of researchers into her lab, she tugged at the edge of the surgical cap to make sure her hair was tucked beneath it.

"I told you the Sister would allow us to disturb her work." Brown eyes swung in Amariah's direction; Anna's haughty expression always softened in the Benedictine sister's presence. "I'm going to start calling you Amariah. Sister reminds me too much of the dreary convents I spent my childhood in. The mere mention of the word makes me think of all the nuns who beat me into submission with a ruler! My knuckles were raw from six to sixteen." Anna waved a cigarette in Amariah's direction. "It's all settled. I'm Anna and you're Amariah--and from today forward we shall be best friends!"

Pushing a glass petri dish toward falling ash, Amariah tried to keep the amusement she felt out of her voice. "Anna, would you put the cigarette out? Father Simson insists the labs remain free of smoke. He fears it will damage magnetic tapes or our scrolls."

"Nonsense! Andrew is just being a tyrant. It pleases him to punish those of us who have human weaknesses! He loves behaving as if he were an avenging prophet straight out of the Old Testament. He can be dreary with little or no provocation. Nevertheless," she ground the stub into the small glass container meant to grow cultures in which placed on the counter in front of her, "Andrew is not a man to be challenged."

Amariah was surprised to find someone intimidated her new friend.

Just talking about the Father General seemed to repress her spirit.

"Well," Anna's glance fell on sheets of parchment lying beside the computer, "I'll bet you wonder what brought three furies riding out of hell into your laboratory! Jon Pierre and I were having coffee in the lounge when Duncan dropped by. We were discussing vault seventeen and suddenly we found ourselves involved in a debate threatening to turn violent! Since you are the only person who can read the documents in the vault we decided you should be the one to cast the deciding vote--which I know will be in my favor!"

"Anna, you're such a bore!" Duncan Davis plopped onto one of the stainless-steel chairs in the sterile room; this debate could last all night and he planned to be as comfortable as possible.

"I'm only boring when you know I'm right! It's your way of getting out of an argument you can't win. It drives you nuts because you think I'm a silly, frivolous woman, yet I have both the education and the intelligence to destroy your theories about religion! Lord, Duncan, the only way I could stay out of my father's house was to be in school! I haven't spent my entire life swilling gin. There are a billion or so neurons in my brain which still function!"

Although her words were laced with sarcasm, Amariah knew Anna revealed the reason she drank so much. She carried the burden of a father she both feared and adored. Amariah was certain Anna achieved phenomenal success as a historian to prove her value to a parent who had little interest in her.

"Mon Dieu!" LaPointe drew his finger down the length of his nose. "I've never encountered two people who engage in a contest of wills like the two of you! We are interrupting the Sister enough as it is! Why not put our question to the lady and then excuse ourselves? Do we not have enough work to occupy our hours? Must we burden Sister Amariah with a waste of her time as well?"

The combatants ceased bickering. Anna leaned against the counter as Jon Pierre paced the room.

"Sister," the art expert rifled his thinning hair with both hands, "we find ourselves on the horns of a weighty theological dilemma. Duncan prides himself on understanding the emotional needs of mankind."

"Man created God out of feelings of inadequacy and insecurity. There is no God--so what created man?" The veins in Sir Davis' neck throbbed; his blood pressure reflected his agitation.

"Please, Duncan, allow me to finish. Sister Amariah has no idea why you are so distressed."

Settling back against the hard chair, Davis crossed his arms over his chest; defiance written in his eyes.

Jon Pierre cleared his throat with a lot of noise as if sound could enforce a thready truce. "As I was saying, dear Sister, each of us holds a conflicting view about the significance of the sacrament. Anna thinks a person is literally transformed by consuming the bread and wine. I believe it is an act of faith . . ."

"It's a ritual borrowed from barbarians!" Duncan slammed his fist against his knee, fury making his body taut. "I don't care if you think Jesus instituted the ceremony at something you so fondly call the 'Last Supper'. If such a thing did happen, the words . . .'eat of my flesh and drink of my blood' were put there by a bunch of fools trying to convert savages to a loose form of Christianity!"

"No! You're wrong!" Anna hurled away from the counter. Expensive leather sandals rapped against the tiled floor as she stalked back and forth. "The nineteenth Ecumenical Council, the Council of Trent, determined bread and wine, by a mystical power we do not understand, changes into the body and blood of Christ. Human beings must become one with the Savior, and the sacrament is the method which brings the union about!"

Duncan shot back, his voice loud with anger. "In 1545 A.D. men were superstitious pagans! Your precious sacramental rite is nothing more than the cannibalistic practice of consuming one's enemies! The process is not transcendent--it is a carryover from the barbarian tradition of eating the brain, liver and heart of a conquered enemy or a revered leader! By eating flesh, the consuming party thought they either gained the strength of their enemies or assumed the attributes of the person they admired! Anna, you're celebrating a cannibalistic ritual!"

"I am not! You'll never convince me the sacrament is anything less than a powerful rite which elevates the soul through the union of God and man." Nostrils flared, Anna Romanov stormed toward the British aristocrat, waving her finger in his face. "I will not have you parading nonsense before the press!"

LaPointe held up a silencing hand. "Sister, see why this debate has been raging for hours? I don't think bread and wine literally turn into flesh and blood, no matter how enigmatic the process, but I do believe in spiritual transformation. I've watched artists operate from a region of the mind that defies analysis. It's as if they are transported away from the body. I don't know how to describe it, but they seem more a part of the brush and pallet than the hand. Perhaps the sacrament accelerates this phenomenon in the mind of a believer. But a cannibalistic rite? I cannot accept this concept either. Sister, please, enlighten us with your thoughts on this subject."

Amariah blushed as expectant eyes demanded an answer from her. "I've never heard the sacrament compared to cannibalism, but Sir Davis' theory is well grounded. It was common among the early Church fathers to absorb as many local customs as possible. They adapted Christianity to fit the prevailing culture. Anna, as a historian you know this to be true. A classic example of this assimilation process is the date on which we celebrate Jesus' birthday."

Amariah walked to the laboratory window overlooking the garden. She watched an ancient sampietrini prune rose bushes with loving care while she collected her thoughts. Finally, she turned back to face both friends and disbeliever. "According to the book of Matthew, lambs were being born when Mary gave birth to Jesus--but sheep only bear their young in the spring. It only stands to reason the season of his birth as we celebrate it is wrong. During St. Paul's time Mithraism, the cult which worshipped the sun, was the dominant religion of the Roman Empire. This god's birthday was celebrated on the 25th of December. It was a holy day and throughout Rome thousands flocked to the Mithranic temples. It's possible Paul thought the same date should be an important Christian celebration. The creation of a holy day, which just happened to fall on a competing deity's day of celebration, might help win converts."

Stainless steel chair legs scraped against the tile floor. "So, the issue is settled. Settled!" Duncan Davis grinned like a cat that snared its prey.

"I do have one other opinion, if you'll allow me to offer it, Sir Duncan." Amariah tapped the computer keyboard to save the work just logged into the translation file.

"Let's hear it!" Davis was jubilant, gloating with triumph.

"It might be best to explain some of my background first. My father is one of the leading psychiatrists in America and we have debated the issue of religion all my life. He feels much the same as you, Sir Duncan. To him, faith is a 'fix' for the wretched conditions in which most human beings find themselves. Marx's belief that religion is an opiate for the masses is a philosophy he supports. So, I'm well versed in your point of view."

Amariah studied the British religious psychologist. He sat with his legs spread apart, his arms protecting his chest. Like her father, this man would be quick to dismiss her reasoning process.

"Because my father argued with me on every point of faith I cared to raise, I studied the 'mysteries' in greater depth than most people. As an educated person living in the twentieth century, I realize bread is not literally turned into flesh and wine into blood."

"See! I told you it was a crazy concept, Anna. How can a woman, who has been schooled in the finest universities in Europe, embrace such an outmoded, unfounded, superstitious doctrine?" Duncan flapped his arms as thickset legs propelled him across the lab in a few strong strides. Pointing to the mainframe sealed behind the glass doors across the hall, Davis waved his finger at the panel of lights and display meters. "We are at the threshold of tomorrow! Religion has no place in the twenty-first century. Man has come of age at last. We possess superior reasoning power--and reason cannot accept, nor condone--any form of religion! Your foolish belief system is going to vanish into the dust these next few years."

"No!" Anna's eyes flashed, "No it won't, of that I am certain! Why do you think we're all gathered here? Father Simson will stem the tide of disbelief. He's going to restore the Church to its rightful place of prominence in the world." Color rose in Anna's checks and her fingernails tapped the countertop in a harsh, static rhythm.

The way she defended the Father General made Amariah wonder about Anna's feelings for Father Simpson. History was scored with tales of women in love with men devoted to religious life. It was almost as though unavailability lured certain women into an emotional maze from which there was no exit.

Amariah hesitated before stepping into the ring with hostile contenders. "Duncan, as you so aptly put it, we are at the edge of an age of discovery the likes of which may never come again. We stand at the threshold of the universe; we're about to cross-distances only dreamed possible in the realm of science fiction. We perform miracles of modern medicine which restore the dead to life. Yet, regardless of our intellectual sophistication, we still cannot answer a question that has plagued mankind since we first began to reason." Amariah slammed the flat of her hand against the countertop shocking the others into obeisant silence. "We still wonder why we are here, to what purpose we have been born! To my knowledge, no answer to this question has satisfied even the most primitive among us. We long to reach for the stars because by exploring the universe we hope to discover we are not alone--that there is a structured scheme to our existence--a greater force is interested in our well-being and seeks to guide us!"

Pupils dilated with emotion, Amariah's gaze swept over the people huddled against the counter, astonished by her outburst.

"And yet, all we need to do is look to ourselves to know the answer."

She held up her hand, moving her fingers back and forth in a deliberate, slow fashion. "Consider the wonders of the human body. When it functions, it is a miracle of creation beyond comprehension! When it fails misery and suffering, often unimaginable, result. How can anyone think something as complex as a human being, or as balanced as the earth's eco-system, could be the result of random accident? The miracle we refer to as 'nature' is but a reflection of God!"

Amariah sagged against the counter, her hands gripping the Formica as though she feared like ancient sailors who set forth to explore the ocean, she might slip off the edge of the known world. "If we, as individuals, misconstrued theological doctrine, it is because we are human. If our minds are too undeveloped to understand messages from a Higher Power who is at fault . . . man or God? Or, have time and circumstance distorted this information? The foundation of Christianity was laid at a time when mankind was in a primitive state. The people of Jesus' day were victims of their physical world as much as we are today. To them, something as unseen and complex as the functions of the mind were beyond comprehension. Perhaps the Holy Fathers of the early Church were trying to come up with a rite which was a physical expression of a force neither seen nor heard. Jesus said God exists inside every man! What better way to get the idea across than the consumption of two things which made up the fabric of life in their society--bread and wine! Sacrament is a symbol, a ritual to help man realize God is inside us. Universal Intelligence exists in our bodies--it sets our digestive juices in action, transforms the sustaining power of bread and wine into energy, then converts this force into motions which sustain our life on earth."

She paused, taking a moment to look at each man directly, then her gaze settled on Anna. "An intelligence beyond our ability to comprehend called our world into being. This vast, superior knowledge set into motion the events which shaped our world, and it resides within every man, woman and child who ever existed since the dawn of time."

Reaching to pat the scrolls, she continued. "The more evidence I find in these ancient documents, the more I realize there is a central, unifying message contained in Christianity. Perhaps the Church hasn't always acted out of the most noble reasons. Maybe there were those who guided the Church down a path which was not entirely spiritual." Amariah paused, as if sensing she was drawing upon an inner understanding using faith as a translator--a Rosetta Stone for the human mind. "For me, the Church is a caretaker. Some popes have been better than others, but the Church has guided mankind through troubled times. Hopefully, Father Simson will lead the world through another transition into a more peaceful era. Duncan, your criticisms are like many handed down through the ages. Your vision is limited to the literal, the factual, rather than being expanded by acceptance of a force within. On one hand, science is too caught up in the physical to examine an ethereal solution which cannot be measured. On the other hand, theologians are so busy interpreting classical metaphors contained in the Bible on a physical level they overlook the timelessness of the message! If a person believes they are transformed by consuming the Eucharist, then I think they really are! We have a need to affirm our faith and accept religion's faults and weaknesses with a loving heart."

Amariah's eyes radiated the power of conviction. Duncan stared at her, his shoulders hunched, his expression a kaleidoscope of conflicting emotions. On her part, Anna stood stock still, transfixed by the complex chain of logic the nun forged with a single connecting link . . . faith! LaPointe stared at the blank field on the computer screen; his hands thrust deep in his pockets.

Finally, Sir Davis shuffled back to the chair to collect his laptop. His feet scuffed the tiles as he walked, as if he hadn't the energy to lift them. Turning back to Amariah, he struggled to give substance to churning thoughts. "Sister, I wish to God I had your faith. The world could be transformed in the blink of an eye if everyone saw things as you do. Perhaps," his gaze strayed toward the computer room, where slender cabinets contained compressed knowledge of the past four thousand years on thin silver discs, "that's what being transformed means. Maybe we must come to terms with the boundaries of our faith before our time on earth is at an end. On my part, my dear, dear Sister, I have suffered too many crises which left me bereft of ministering belief. I, like countless others, am a wandering soul . . . wanting to believe, yet lacking the courage to defend a scientifically unsupported position. You see, Sister, to speak as you just did takes courage. You are one of those rare individuals who can honestly say you believe in God. Of even more importance, your faith is so intense it has the power to sway the undecided."

Amariah watched Sir Davis leave. Mystified, Anna and LaPointe's gaze followed the psychologist out of the lab and down the hallway. Amariah's expression crumbled. Courage? She possessed no special brand of courage. Her words were a limited reflection of her feelings about God. Had her friends not asked, she would never have volunteered her viewpoint. Sir Davis was wrong. She was not special. Not a rare individual. She was a common, ordinary nun.

"Klaus? What do *you* make of this?" Leon jammed his eye back against the scanner.

"I don't know, that's why I summoned you. After all, my friend, you're the Oriental language expert! I merely put these things back together again--like Humpty Dumpty after his fall." The clipped German accent spoiled an attempt at humor.

"It'll take a few hours on the computer to see if I can figure this out, but what I'm picking out leaves me astounded!" Leon leaned back, away from the scanner. "From the look on your face, I gather you realize what's here."

"I figured out a few phrases." Von Friendberg stretched across the desk, reaching for his pipe and foil lined pouch of tobacco which were never far away. Tapping shredded leaves into the bowl, he struck a match, and the smell of apples filled the room.

"Where did you get this?" Like a magnet, the scroll drew Leon back and he fit his eye against the rubber pillow cushioning the tube of stainless-steel.

"Vault seventeen." Klaus waited for the other man's reaction.

Leon's head shot up, astonishment, doubt and dismay undulated across his face in ripples. "That's impossible! I got a list of contents the other day. There was no mention of any Hindu or Tibetan scrolls."

"I'm quite aware of that." Rising, Klaus strolled to the safe in the corner of the room. He spun the dial several times and the tumblers locked in place with the certainty borne of repeated practice. The door swung open, and his arm disappeared inside as he retrieved two wooden boxes. "These weren't on the inventory because no one is quite sure what they represent." Reaching the workstation, Klaus removed the lid of the ancient box with caution because it looked like it might disintegrate beneath even the most delicate touch.

Leon strained to get a better view, his curiosity fanned by Klaus' deliberate movements. Inside the box, pieces of parchment lay in a jumbled heap. They were charred, as if exposed to fire.

"Father Simson didn't think I could piece any of this together but," Klaus' eyes brimmed with amusement, "he's unaccustomed to dealing with the German obsession with precision. It was a challenge that could not go unmet!"

"You put this together from the scraps in those boxes? That's remarkable!"

"To the untrained, yes. To someone who's spent years matching up fragments it was an exercise in degrees of difficulty. Once I discovered a layer of cloth was used to wrap the documents, it was simpler to separate the pieces."

Leon looked amazed. "I've always hated puzzles."

The pipe billowed smoke and an aromatic cloud floated across the room. "Translation has to be quite similar."

Leon watched the smoke dissipate. "I thought Simson discouraged smoking in the labs."

"If the man wants my expertise he also gets my vices."

Amused by the German's disdain for the Father General's rules, Leon leaned closer to the computer screen. "So how did you get this clear enough to read?"

"The sack of Rome probably had something to do with their charred condition. I'm not a historian, but I'd be willing to bet when the armies of Roman Emperor Charles V besieged the Vatican, burning everything in their path, someone rushed these documents to vault seventeen. The vault is only a stone's throw from the secret passageway connecting the Vatican to the Castel Sant'Angelo, the way by which the pope escaped King Charles' army. Whomever hid these documents must have been aware of the vault's significance."

"Who else has seen this?" Leon glanced at the words that seemed to leap off the document.

"Just you and me. Jeff has been too busy with some of Sister Amariah's scrolls to check back with me. Once he photographs a document and feeds the information into the computer, his work is done. Like most of us, he is content to focus on his aspect of the project. The actual translation is of little interest to him."

"I'd like to work on this before we say anything to Woolsey or Simson."

"My feelings exactly."

Leon engaged Von Friendberg's glance, the German's honesty was disconcerting.

Reading the look in the other man's eyes, Klaus decided Leon deserved an explanation. "There's a smell to Simson's undertaking, something akin to three-day old fish. If, for even one moment, I thought Simson was sincere I'd put my heart and soul into this project. But he has motives which are so ulterior they stink to high heaven." He waved his hands through the cloud of smoke settling over his head like a shroud. "A man of the cloth should not have such worldly intentions."

Leon didn't know whether to agree or protest. Klaus' features disappeared behind another puff of smoke and his expression was quickly veiled.

"I swept the lab for surveillance equipment. I suspect Sister Amariah's lab has also been bugged." He grinned at Leon's disbelief.

"You think Father Simson is listening in on Amariah's conversations?"

"I'm reasonably certain of it."

"Why?"

"I think she might present a potential threat to Father Simson's plans--whatever they are."

Leon felt as though he was given more information than he could process. The analytical side of his nature longed to take Klaus' statements apart, to study the words individually, to analyze their portent, but he found himself floundering in doubt. "How could she do that?"

"That's the question of the day."

"This scroll caught me by surprise. I've never been comfortable with Simson, and I can't work up the enthusiasm for this project the others claim to have."

"You also care about Sister Amariah."

Leon flushed crimson from the top of his collar to the roots of his hair. "She's bright and we've had some spirited conversations."

"It's your growing attachment to her, which makes me feel I can trust you with what I'm about to say."

Leon nodded at Klaus to continue but his thoughts were a million miles away. Was there more to his feelings for Sister Amariah than the passion they shared for language?

"You see," Klaus patted the computer console, "these are fountains of information once you decode the secrets of their programs. After watching Sister Amariah in several of our staff meetings I got curious about her background. I couldn't imagine why Father Simson chose someone so trusting, so guileless, to be his Bible languages expert. It kept running through my mind there had to be countless others who could have just as easily done the job. He patted the monitor, "So I decided to access records of major universities offering a higher degree in New Testament languages. After weeks of searching, I developed a list of about fifty language experts. As someone who's dedicated his adult life to piecing together random bits of information, I started looking for the determining factors in Sister Amariah's selection--that's when it finally dawned on me."

Klaus pulled out the center drawer in his desk, rummaged through its contents and finally thrust a crumpled piece of paper in Leon's direction. "Sister Amariah is a dedicated Benedictine nun. She entered the Order straight out of the American high school system, so she was eighteen when she chose the Church as a vocation. Years of maturation into adulthood were spent under the direct influence of the Church. None of the other people on this list had those qualifications."

Leon's eyes scanned the names followed by their degrees. "I'm not following you."

Klaus shifted his weight against the chair, welcoming an opportunity to confide in Leon, "This is conjecture, but I think Simson wanted a thoroughly indoctrinated Catholic translating what might be some history shattering documents. Think about it," he pushed forward, closing the distance to Leon; intensity radiating in the way he leaned across the desk, how he rubbed his brow, an earnest expression deepening the lines in his face, "if you were certain you'd find damning evidence to the organization you desperately wanted to lead, would you involve someone who didn't share your point of view? What if--and this is a big if, I'll grant you--but what if the person translating this information had a grudge against the Catholic Church? Would they be as likely to interpret the information as favorably as a person who dedicated their life to the institution?" A smile of satisfaction stole across his face as Klaus pulled the pipe from his lips. Leon was churning the information. "Simson wants the world to see things from his perspective, so he chose someone dedicated to the Church, someone, who lives its belief system to the marrow of her bones--Sister Amariah."

Leon began to pace. He rubbed his chin, the motion as probing as his thoughts. "Then it stands to reason her laboratory might be bugged. Simson would want to make certain she didn't discover something to endanger his plans."

"Correct! Simson is like other power mongers who've plagued mankind throughout history! I have no quarrel with Christianity, I think a good man tried hard to make a bunch of barbarians think kindly about their neighbors. There's no doubt in my mind, however, should Jesus return to earth today his fate would be repeated. We don't want to confront the ugly, superstitious, barbaric inclinations that lie deep within all of us."

Leon fought against the words imploding through his brain. The logical side of his nature resisted what was bubbling up from some unknown, unfathomable realm of understanding. The words came at him again and they hammered in his ears. It was impossible; yet Leon sensed Amariah's language gift was a two-edged sword. "What do you think Simpson might do?"

"Try spending more time with her to gain her confidence. That way, if you find out she's uncovered information Simson might not want made public, you'll be able to help her."

"What are you suggesting?"

"We need to figure out a way to get her out of Rome in a hurry." Like the wind whipping off a glacier, the frigid expression on Von Friendberg's face conveyed conviction. "I could be wrong about the whole situation, but I think it wise to formulate a plan . . . merely as a precaution."

Leaning against a storage cabinet in the corner, Leon felt trapped, his thoughts raged and surged as he considered the consequences of what might happen if the information on the scanner was made public. His grandfather must have been just as panicked when he discovered what the Nazis had in store for Poland.

Klaus gestured toward the computer. "When I've finished, I'll burn a copy of the DVD for you. Translate all the information, then we'll discuss it more. We may look back on this and think the words 'potentially explosive' were short sighted!"

The telephone jangled, disturbing Amariah's tranquility. She found the hours of twilight soothing. It was relaxing to watch the sun paint the travertine blocks in the dome with a blend of orange, gold, and scarlet. At dusk, the Vatican was transformed from the busy hub of Catholicism to a silent sepulcher as grand as any built to honor the gods of ancient Egypt. Stillness lowered over buildings and gardens as if the inhabitants of Vatican City turned to stone with the coming of night.

The ring was insistent. Amariah uncrossed her legs, forsaking the comfortable position in which she had been studying, and reached for the phone.

"Hello?"

"Hi, honey! How are you?"

"Uncle John, how nice to hear your voice. You must've been busy these past few weeks. I called your office a couple of times, but your secretary said you were tied up in meetings."

"I know, and I apologize. Ordinarily, you are to be put through immediately but there've been some high-level meetings going on I just couldn't break out of."

"I gathered as much."

"How's the world treating you?"

"Just fine. I'm working hard on the Aramaic documents found in vault seventeen. You've read about them, haven't you?"

"Sweetheart, anyone in the western world who isn't criminally insane knows about your discovery. You can't pick up a newspaper or magazine without seeing Simson's face. In fact, your name has been mentioned several times."

"My name? Who knows I exist?"

"United Press International, *Newsweek*, *Time*, CBS, CNN, Fox News and the independent news services, to name a few. Simson called you as 'his modern-day link with the past'."

"He did?"

"Sweetheart, you've been out of touch with the rest of the world."

"I suppose that's true."

"How about dinner? Can you leave your moldering manuscripts for a few hours and join me next week?"

"Uncle John, I'm not a prisoner here."

“Sometimes I wonder."

A stilted laugh reached through the receiver. "Ah . . . Uncle John, would you mind if I invited someone else along? I've made friends with someone I think you'd like."

"Dinner with two pious people of the cloth should offer an evening of devoted contemplation."

"He isn't Catholic."

"Not a priest?"

"No."

"Then by all means bring him along. My prospects for an enjoyable dinner are suddenly much brighter."

Amariah couldn't keep irritation out of her voice. "Really, Uncle John, you make it sound as if I tie you to a chair and force you to listen to scripture reading every time we get together."

"Darling, you know how I feel about your religion. I respect you, I offer you my full support . . . but trust me, no rope exists to secure a full evening of scripture recitation!"

Amariah laughed despite her annoyance. "You win, I'll stop pouting. Name the time and date--Leon and I will be there."

Amariah smoothed the folds of her habit before putting the super-starched napkin in her lap. It felt good to be wearing her Benedictine robes instead of sterile clothing required in the lab. Smiling, her gaze took in her adopted uncle and Leon Kaminski. As both men warmed to one another and she listened to their conversation, Amariah knew they were kindred spirits.

"I tell you, Leon," the banker relaxed against a chair covered in expensive damask, "there's more to the link between those two Italian bankers and the American Archbishop than the Vatican wants outsiders to know. Their deals upset the world banking system to a degree few will ever understand. The Vatican's bank, or the Institute for Works of Religion, needs a thorough overhauling. Vast sums of money are channeled through the organization, but no one is responsible for the way funds are disbursed. I'm certain the Institute couldn't withstand the kind of audit a big ten accounting firm would give it. There's something going on. A banker's nose can smell a sour deal eighty-two ledger sheets away."

"I agree," Leon lifted his wine glass, the rim a sudden point of fascination, "although I know nothing about sophisticated finance or banking scams, the Archbishop and the Father General have too many connections to be above suspicion."

"From what I'm hearing bandied about in boardrooms all over Europe, information is surfacing which points to the Vatican backed sale of arms to some third world countries."

"Oh, Uncle John!" Amariah sat her wineglass down with such force its contents spilled on to the tablecloth. "Now this is where I really must draw the line! It's out of the question to think the Vatican has anything to do with supplying guns--to anyone. The Church serves as the spiritual caretaker of mankind. It does not provide a method of slaughter!"

"Well, sweetheart, remember this! When Stalin jested about how many 'divisions has the Pope?' he was speaking of the modern papacy. At any time prior to 1870, the response could have been a list of various infantry and armor units. The *Santissimo Padre*--the Holy Father--as a purely spiritual figure, one who wields influence solely through moral force, is a relatively recent development." John Preston was growing annoyed. Why couldn't Amariah see the truth about the Church? Why was she so willing to be deceived? Certainly, her faith put blinders on much of her logic, but sometimes her righteous indignation about Catholicism drove him to distraction!

"I think your Uncle's right, Amariah. Simson is like the warrior pope, Julian II. Were it feasible, I'm sure the Father General would relish command of an army!"

"Gentlemen, if you'll excuse me," the legs of her chair scraped against the marble floor as she pushed away from the table, "I need to visit the ladies room."

Both men watched Amariah storm across the room, unspoken concern for her welfare the glue which bonded them together. John Preston was uncertain how much he should confide in Leon but when he turned to look at him, doubt vanished.

"Leon, you spend a lot of time with Amariah, don't you? Could you get to her quickly if necessary?" The banker hesitated, studying the complex folds of his napkin.

Leon could tell Amariah's uncle was having trouble finding a way to open a difficult subject, so he guided their conversation along a different line. "You said something about the Vatican financing the sale of arms to third world countries. Do you know that for a fact, or is it speculation?"

"I know it for a fact. I wish I didn't." Preston glanced around the room, studying the faces of people close enough to overhear their conversation; he'd learned to be a cautious man.

"Such matters would be closely guarded secrets. How could anyone uncover an incriminating tie?"

"International banking is governed by strict rules of procedure."

"Meaning?" Leon bent closer, Amariah's uncle was whispering.

"Computers, my dear boy, have the power to unravel any secret--no matter how well guarded. The right passwords gain access to an impenetrable system. Did you know the Great Wall of China was never breached? Yet the Mongol hordes managed to invade China on three separate occasions." His words accelerated once he realized he intended to tell this young man what he had discovered. "Do you know how? It's so simple, the Mongols bribed the gatekeepers! And I bribed a computer programmer. Well, I didn't do it myself, but I caused it to happen."

"Sir, I'm afraid I don't understand. I can hack my way through most computer programs, but when it comes to the complexities of inter-national banking, I'm in the dark." Leon reached for his half-empty glass, but the wine tasted sour on his tongue. Fear clutched his stomach; Leon knew he had started down a path which disappeared into the fog of deceit and uncertainty.

"Banking has been reduced to a series of electronic digits. Via satellite, one bank wires another to transfer or deposit sums of money between different accounts."

"I see." Leon was listening intently.

"The Swiss have been moving large sums of currency to rebels in El Salvador and a lot more money has been pouring into the Slavic countries."

"I thought Swiss accounts were confidential. I was under the impression bankers never knew the identity of their patrons."

"That's true, Leon." He signaled the waiter to bring another bottle of wine. Waiting, John remained silent until the waiter moved out of hearing range, then continued. "When you have access to as many computers as I do, it isn't difficult to match incoming transfers to those that are outgoing. I've been monitoring all the transfers leaving the Institute for the Works of Religion. Then, I watch for similar amounts leaving banks to which the Vatican made the original deposit. Simson is a crafty bastard, I'll give him that! I once followed a deposit of over a hundred thousand dollars all the way around the world before it finally ended up in El Salvador. Twelve different banks and twenty different accounts were involved by the time the arms sale was concluded."

"Can you be absolutely certain the money is buying munitions?"

"You mean, can I prove the Church is aiding rebel forces around the world by providing the means to annihilate their fellow man?" Preston's eyes reflected a primitive sense of foreboding, but his expression registered more than that--it was filled with a superstitious fear announcing something sinister. "No, I do not have a bill of sale and I have not had a personal conversation with an arms dealer, nor anyone affiliated with the underworld. I just have this," he tapped the side of his nose, "I can smell a rotten transaction across three continents. I hate the fact my best friend's only child is involved with this Jesuit, and I can't help but wonder why."

"I know. The German art restoration expert, Klaus Von Friendberg, figured it out."

Preston felt his closely held emotions collapse like a house of cards in a windstorm. "Really?"

Leon repeated the essence of Von Friendberg's discovery and when he finished, Leon addressed the banker in a questioning tone. "Mr. Preston, there's still one thing I don't understand."

Rubbing his hand across the day-old stubble on his chin, the banker was stricken by a premonition he lacked a desire to examine but he nodded at Leon to proceed.

"Where is the Church getting all this money?"

A sad smile twisted the edges of John Preston's compressed lips. "Son, the Church is the wealthiest institution on earth. It owns banks, blocks of stock, mutual funds, industries, and ranches. The Catholic Church has the most widely diversified portfolios in the history of investment. I'll let you in on a little secret. For some months now, the price of gold has been depressed."

"I remember hearing a news commentator saying a lot of gold was suddenly showing up on the market, but what's that go to do with the Church's wealth?" Leon felt as if the flow of time was suspended, as though he were struggling to cross the mire of a slow-moving dream.

"I'll tell you where I think the gold is coming from--the Vatican treasury! For centuries, adoring faithful sent a fortune in precious gems and gold to Rome every time a local priest was ordained a bishop. The treasury is so valuable its worth can't be estimated. I think Simson is selling off some of the lesser items. He's probably melting gold rings, cups, and crucifixes, into ingots and fencing individual gems. There's actually no limit to what he can lay his hands on--if he needed money."

The waiter came forward with a new bottle of wine, but the banker waved him away. "No, bring the bill. We've had a wonderful dinner, but we'll be leaving now." Beneath a hastily expelled breath Preston voiced concern, "Your friend's story makes perfect sense. He's right about why Amariah was selected. I can feel it!"

Amariah paused when she noticed how deeply her Uncle and Leon were engaged in conversation. Dimples furrowed both cheeks as she crossed the room, irritation forgotten. "Don't let me interrupt you two. From over there," she motioned toward the hallway leading to the bathroom, "it looked as if you were hatching a plot to save the world."

"Oh? Well, it was nothing quite like that." Leon tried to keep the mood light but the brooding expression in John Preston's eyes told him it was going to be an impossible task.

"This young man is extremely bright, Amariah--I hope you listen to his advice. He's got a handle on the situation in the Vatican, and by God, I'm grateful he's close by." Rubbing his eyes against the weariness of a long and eventful day, John didn't see the ripple of reaction crossing Amariah's face. As they waited for the bill, Preston asked politely, "What do you hear from your mom and dad?"

"I got a letter from Mother just the other day. She said Daddy's practice is keeping him so busy he doesn't have much time to stir up trouble. She's accepted a position on the Board of Directors at St. Anne's. The orphanage is trying to cope with the influx of refugees from Central America right now. God bless her, mother is campaigning for contributions day and night. She may regret I'll never have children, but she's found a marvelous way to fill the void." Amariah tried to smile but the attempt was completely in vain. She knew her mother looked forward to grandchildren.

"I'll give Richard a call tomorrow. He'll be grateful to know you're in such capable hands. Tell you what, why don't I find a taxi and you kids can drop me off at my hotel."

Leon jumped to his feet, "Mr. Preston, I'll get the cab. You stay and visit with Amariah."

As Leon disappeared into the darkness of the foyer beyond the restaurant, John reached to pat Amariah's hand. "I feel much better knowing that boy is around. He thinks a lot of you."

Amariah felt herself go scarlet, her mouth turned to sand and a response refused to take shape on her tongue. Finally, she managed to stammer, "Everyone on the archaeological team gets along well together."

A flood of relief swept over Amariah when Leon waved from the doorway. She was afraid her uncle was going to launch into a lecture or worse, start to dispense advice. As they bundled into the taxi, Leon's shoulder pressed against her sleeve. Amariah asked her uncle to roll down the window because she was warm. As the cooling breeze caught the folds of her veil, weariness took unchallenged possession of her body. Too many things were happening simultaneously; she was emotionally and intellectually worn out. A lurch as the taxi fell into a pothole thrust Leon's knee against her leg. The cooler air rushing through the window could not account for the chill which raced from her scalp to her feet. Amariah sensed she was on the brink of an emotional quagmire, which was going to rip her world apart.

"I trust you understood what I said." The tone of voice the Father General used on Cardinal Woolsey was harsh, sharp, and grating.

Casting furtive glances around the room the Cardinal recognized he was cornered with no place to hide. The sky outside tall windows of the Pinacoteca were fast losing light. Fallen leaves were swept along the pavers in the courtyard, driven by the breath of a northern wind, but Cardinal Woolsey sensed the chill he felt was more from the premonition of dread crawling up the base of his spine than the temperature outside.

"Really, Andrew, how can it be done? We cannot just erase evidence! Your billion-dollar computer program has far too many safeguards. Perhaps over zealousness will betray you yet." Fear eroded bravado; his bowels ground against each other sending jolts of fire searing through his body. The amount of acid pouring through the ulcerated hole in his stomach increased with each passing day. No medicine could dispel the effects of constant worry. Like an animal with its foot caught in a snare, Woolsey felt there was no way to escape the Jesuit.

"Cardinal, you must find a way. All traces of the scroll have to be eliminated," words hissed between his teeth, his eyes darted from the Cardinal to the damning scrap of leather lying on his desk. "The girl is right--this scroll could destroy the theology upon which Christianity is founded. Dr. Brown ran the document through a battery of tests and authenticated its age. The document was written when Jesus lived. If the manuscript is, as Sister Amariah believes, an authentic record of the message of the Savior then Christianity will have to undergo a complete shift in doctrine. If, and I repeat if, Jesus denied his divinity we must make certain the public never learns of the scroll's existence."

Light from the desk lamp starred Simson's jet-black pupils, his eyes blazed with an unquenchable fire. "Damn it, Woolsey, what do you think will happen if every man believes he has the power to create his own destiny?"

"There would be no need for the likes of us." His red robes lost their brilliance as the sun disappeared below the horizon. The room was draped in shadow, but neither man took note of the approaching darkness.

Simson's voice was so cold it crackled like shifting plates of ice. "Your authority and influence will evaporate! You will have no one to lead, the world will not bow at your passing . . ."

"And what of you, Andrew? What of you? You wield far more power over others than I."

"I do not revel in the badge of office. My authority is for the greater glory of the Church! Personal gain is not my motive . . . however much it may be yours."

"It was not so in the beginning, but power is a narcotic." Woolsey's double chins dipped against his scarlet robe--a vibrant symbol of higher office. His skullcap slipped forward, disturbing carefully arranged locks of curly hair. "What must I do to prevent this scroll from being seen by anyone else?"

"Access the computer file. Erase all record of this manuscript in the document log."

"Who knows how to do it?"

"Father Wilson."

"Ah, yes. I had forgotten."

"You see, Cardinal? There is always a solution when brilliant minds begin to seek. Father Wilson believes in my mission with a zeal second only to my own."

A hand swollen with an accumulation of fat, the result of rich living, reached for the piece of animal hide, denuded of hair, and softened with lime when the Savior's feet tread the hillsides of Galilee. "Do you really intend to destroy this? Why not put it back? Find another vault, another subterranean chamber, where it will be safe for centuries to come."

"No." An implacable veil obscured the Father General's expression; his feelings were unreadable; his voice assumed a flat, monotonous tone. "It must be destroyed. Otherwise, we run the risk of discovery--a chance I do not intend to take."

Turning it over in his hand, Woolsey stroked the time-marred sheet of vellum. "Still, it seems a sin to deliberately wipe out a link to the past."

"A link with the power to destroy my plans for the future."

The chair screeched as Woolsey pushed away from the desk, his weight caused streaks on the polished floor beneath its legs. "And your future is to be considered above everything else! Your jaundiced view of religion is all the world will ever know."

"The vision of great men has always shaped the destiny of mankind."

Rising, the Cardinal felt older, as if his bones were no longer strong enough to support his weight. "Do as you will, but I'll have no part in it. Have Wilson delete the records! Have him get rid of the scroll! I may be an accessory to the foulness you've unleashed but I will not set my hand to this desultory act." Shuffling toward the door, he flung it open in a final act of defiance. "You have my silence, Andrew, but my respect will forever be withheld."

Simson watched the Cardinal depart. The pettiness of subordinates never concerned him. Small minds dwelled on small matters. Few men had the scope of vision to understand what he was placing in motion. Perhaps it would be better to reassign the Cardinal to some provincial post. Somewhere he would pose no threat. Satisfaction crept into his eyes as the Father General reached for the phone; a smile of self-assurance slipped into place; the hand of God guided his actions!

Amariah peeked her head around the door, a note of trepidation in her voice. "Sister Josephina? Do you have a moment? I have a question I'd like to ask." Cautious not to move any further, Amariah waited for permission to enter.

A stern expression conveyed the other sister's irritation at being interrupted. There were far too many tasks to be completed to stop for idle chatter. "I do not have much time to spare, Sister, but if it's urgent."

"Oh, it is! Cardinal Woolsey doesn't have a manuscript I was working on. I thought perhaps you could help me locate it."

"There's a record log for every document and artifact and who on the team worked on it. I keep track of all entries myself! What are you searching for?" Fingers flying over the keyboard, Sister Josephina accessed one screen after another. "Aramaic texts?"

"Vault Seventeen." Amariah tried to follow the whirling screens as Sister Josephina probed deep into the heart of the computer.

"All documents are checked out to you. Look," she turned the monitor in Amariah's direction. Holding her finger against the arrow key, a flashing bar of light scrolled down the list, "every item has an identity number, a language code, and a probable date of origin. The only thing missing is the actual translation which, of course, is in your hands. We have a photographic replica stored in the computer's memory banks against the day when the scrolls will completely deteriorate."

"Amazing." Amariah studied thick brows, the long, angular face, the muddy color of the nun's eyes which defied definition. The sister was, at best, homely and her personality contributed to a demeanor just as unbecoming. Perhaps she had spiritual gifts, which gave her an inner beauty not apparent on the surface.

Words sharp and brief, her tone announced Sister Josephina resented the waste of time. "You see," she pointed at the screen, "the only items I show checked out of the vault are those in the Aramaic language--and you have them all."

"How many are there?"

A hollow series of clicks filled the room as the nun tapped the cursor. "Nine. There are nine scrolls listed in this section."

"Ten were delivered to me. Are you certain of the quantity?"

"Computers are seldom wrong." Annoyed, Sister Josephina drew erect and expelled a long, hissing breath. "I'll run through the files again if that will satisfy you."

"Ten scrolls were delivered to me. I entered them in my log."

"My records indicate there were only nine Aramaic scrolls in vault seventeen. Perhaps you counted incorrectly. Now, if you'll excuse me, Sister, I must get back to work. Father Simson is expecting these cost estimates before the end of the day and I assured him they would be ready."

Amariah lifted the skirt of her habit to hurry. As she twisted her way through the corridors, she began to fish through her bag for the keys to her lab. Thoroughly frustrated, she stabbed the lock several times before the key fit the tumbler. Without stopping to change into sterile surgical garb, Amariah rushed into the room. Dropping her bag and notebook into the chair beside the desk, she depressed the 'on' button. A whining noise as the program booted up bounced off tile covered walls. The monitor blazed to life as Amariah searched a plastic box on her desk for the back-up zip drive containing a record of her files. Her hand shook as she fit the zip drive into the port. Where was it? The cursor flashed down the directory. Locating the code assigned to the scrolls, a bar of light slid down the list, its speed controlled by the pressure of her finger. One. Two. Three. Four. Five. Six. Seven. Eight. Nine. Nine!

The explosion in her veins as adrenaline shot through her blood stream made Amariah feel as if her heart was going to burst. Only nine scrolls were listed . . . yet ten were placed in her keeping.

All traces of the document she gave to Cardinal Woolsey had vanished. Bytes of information held in place by a magnetic force could easily be erased. Losing information stored magnetically in a computer was always a nightmare, but this loss was deliberate!

Someone eliminated all traces of the tenth scroll! Amariah fumed. She couldn't very well accuse one of the most respected members of the curia of committing a wanton act of destruction. Woolsey would deny her story with the arch of an eyebrow. Who would believe her? The Cardinal served the Church for the greater part of his life; he was a man known and respected by half the world. Why would anyone believe the ramblings of an obscure Benedictine nun?

Slamming her hand against the desk, Amariah raged. What could she do? Whom could she tell? In the wake of the rush of adrenaline, exhaustion claimed her body. She leaned her head in her hands, hurt, angry, frustrated, and depressed. Slowly, like ground water filling a well, Amariah lifted her head. Her heart slammed against her chest with the force of hammer blows. If the questions she'd posed to the Cardinal about the text were invalid, then there would have been no need to destroy all traces of its existence. Someone was afraid of its message! If Jesus said He was nothing more than a son of man, the document promised everyone could do the things He did and more! Her mind reeled and cavorted like a Dervish dancer. What if Jesus had been an ordinary man?

"This is the first installment." A manila envelope slid across the cheap table in a motel catering to budget minded tourists.

"What do you want me to do with it?"

"Buy television time."

"Then what?"

"Once you get into the State House of Representatives we'll make sure you get local coverage."

"I see you've got this all thought out. From the House of Representatives on to the State Senate?"

"You've acquitted yourself well throughout your district."

"A district which happens to be populated by union members."

"You're a strong union man."

"Without the union, I'd still be shoveling coal."

"Unions without leadership are nothing--and you've displayed a talent for getting men to follow you."

"I've never done more than what was right for the people I work with and my neighbors."

"Still, we'd like to see you take your leadership ability higher." The black sleeve of the Jesuit's robe brushed against the scratched Formica tabletop as the priest pushed the envelope closer.

"How high might that be?"

"It depends on how well you do these next few years. After the State Legislature, you should plan to run for Lieutenant Governor."

"Then Governor?"

"I don't see why not and don't consider national government out of the question."

A low whistle cleaved the silence which descended over the room. "That's into big bucks! I don't have that kind of money and neither do the people I represent. My district is made up of men struggling to provide for their families. A lot of women are trying to bring up three and four kids on their own. They don't have money to contribute to a political campaign--and I wouldn't feel right asking for a donation."

The sun was beginning to set, and sprinklers came on outside. A pleasant tinkling sound filled the room as drops of water hit tree leaves and dribbled on to the porch. A lark trilled and in the distance a dog yapped at a passing car. Suburbia was calling another day to a close on a far more pleasant note than the inner city where Will Marshall dwelled. Laying his hand on the envelope, the priest kept his tone of voice casual. "You won't have to."

"Man, when I was a kid unloading trucks, I learned there ain't nothin' in this world that's free. What do you want in exchange for all this money?"

"We want you to support the First Amendment."

"What?"

"We want people in office who believe all men should be free to worship as they choose. We want the freedom of religious choice to be protected. The current trend is a shift away from organized religion but that will change in the future. Until then--we need strong men holding the reins of government."

"I don't know. It's too good to be true. I've never trusted bait sitting in the open. There's sure to be a trap somewhere!"

"Run for the State House of Representatives. After a term in the House, if you don't like it, or if you think we're asking too much for our support--quit."

"Just like that?"

"Just like that. The Society of Jesus honors its commitments."

"Well, I guess it can't hurt to try."

"The people from your district will be glad you did. You're a fine politician, worthy of our support."

There was a degree of timidity in the way he reached for the envelope, almost as if he expected the earth to open and swallow him before he could capture his good fortune. True, money was an answer to his prayers, but there was something about the priest that made Will uncomfortable. Maybe it was his robes; the clergy of his church never looked so forbidding. Maybe it was the color of the priest's skin. No matter how many of his brothers in the union were white, there was still a distrust between the races buried so deep it would never be rooted out. He'd taken too many beatings when he first joined the union to ever trust whites completely. A trembling hand touched the envelope filled with money. To think the Catholic Church was supporting a common black man bordered on the unbelievable.

Quietly taking her place at a table beneath a ceiling covered with paintings of various saints, Amariah made herself comfortable. She was delighted Father Simson instituted the practice of a weekly staff meeting. It gave her a chance to become familiar with other areas of work in progress as well as providing a reason to be in the Vatican library.

She loved everything about the room, from the checkered pattern of the inlaid marble floor to portraits of saints, to frescos decorated with a hundred cherubim on the arched buttresses supporting the domed ceiling. Even column bases were decorated by Renaissance masters and considered priceless works of art. The richness of the library was unimaginable; her eye met by a symphony of color everywhere it traveled. Carefully placed floodlights made cupolas etched with gilded trim radiate rainbows of gold and amber. Glass encased tables held manuscripts dating back to the earliest days of the Church. History poured from every nook and cranny; artifacts set out for display pre-dated Christ by centuries. And yet, Amariah felt as comfortable in this room as she did in the living room of her San Francisco home. It was as if she'd taken a step back in time, into a mysterious, but hauntingly familiar world.

As Father Simson entered the room all banter ceased. Beneath his arm, several manila folders labeled with colored tabs indicated an agenda the staff meeting would follow. "Ladies, gentlemen. Sisters, Brethren. Work is proceeding smoothly. You are all to be commended." An amazingly genuine smile spread across his normally forbidding features. "I've just come from a meeting with the press. They are anxious to interview many of you on an individual basis. Right now, however, I must discourage such activity. Official statements are issued each week and I don't want the public confused with opinions, which might deviate from official Vatican policy." Formidable eyes swept the room; when he was certain his wishes were understood, he spread the folders on the table in front of him.

"Let's get on with this week's agenda. Sister Josephina, please pass out copies."

A model of efficiency, the nun held neatly typed sheets, awaiting the Father General's command. As she walked between the tables, sturdy shoes struck the marble floor and the harsh sound carried throughout the vast room as a cumbersome silence descended over the scholars.

A file with a brown label slapped against the lectern and Father Simson began the staff meeting on an unusual note. "Fathers Murphy and Lean have come across some surprising information. Rather than do injustice to the subject, I'll let them enlighten you." Gathering his robes, the leader of the Jesuits lowered himself into a nearby chair, allowing the other priests to take charge of the meeting.

Faded red hair, shot through with streaks of gray, capped a frame gone soft over the years, but Father Patrick Murphy still possessed a strong measure of masculine authority. His hands were the hands of a fighter--worn and misshapen knuckles hinted at the struggle to exist in a harsh environment when he was young. Clearing his throat, a low, rumbling voice rolled over the room like the fog coming in over the moors. His words had the soft, lyrical sound of Dublin in them, and a vocabulary that, to Amariah, bespoke a childhood spent in the streets.

"This is not my doin'. What hand I had in it was far too little to be makin' me out a partner in history! Father Lean will give you the background you'll be needin'."

Unaccustomed to be the focus of attention, Father Gregory Lean peered over the wire rim of his glasses--no longer clinging to hope his friend would explain their findings.

Amariah could tell by the dismay on Father Lean's face dust-laden manuals defined the boundaries of his comfort zone. Speaking to a group of people was something the friar was not called upon to do often and Amariah sympathized with his distress. A twinkle of amusement in Father Murphy's eyes, half-hidden beneath an over cropping of bushy brows, betrayed his maneuvering. Father Pat manipulated the Franciscan friar into addressing the other scholars.

A palsy-like tremor made the papers in Father Lean's handshake as he stood. "This is something I do not often do, so bear with me if I start to wander. It is a failing of mine, and I tend to forget others are not as passionate about Gregorian chants and medieval history as I am!"

A ripple of laughter went around the room and Father Lean drew courage from the response of his peers; heartened his fellow scholars understood how easy it was to be absorbed by one's own area of expertise.

To Amariah, the brown robe seemed much too large for the little man who wore it with the disdain the man of God had for worldly fashion. The hood fell in layers against his shoulders, as if he'd borrowed it from a larger brother. Pushing his glasses back along the bridge of his nose, a high, reedy voice gave life to the historical drama he and Father Murphy had been caught up in for the past several weeks.

Amariah cupped her chin in her hands and gazed at the friar with wide-eyed attention, lending unconscious support to someone she had grown to adore.

"It was thought, until now, that the *Oxyrhynchus Hymn* was the oldest known piece of ecclesiastical music. Written about 300 A.D. what remains of the hymn revolves around praise of the Holy Trinity. It was penned in a Greek alphabetical motion, and we think the author was probably a Greek- speaking Christian residing in Egypt. It mayseem odd, in view of our present perspective, but music was frowned upon by the early Church."

Amariah inched her chair beneath the table in an unconscious effort to get closer to Father Lean. This scrap of history was fascinating; she loved hearing about the ramifications of ecclesiastical actions just now coming to light.

"A prejudice against hymns was expressed in the earliest years of the Church's existence. It arose over the abhorrence early fathers had to the introduction of anything other than biblical commentary in the liturgy. It was feared music might be a vehicle for heretics to propagate errors of faith. Remember, the Church was struggling to gain a foothold in a pagan world."

Pale, watery eyes turned in Father Murphy's direction seeking approval and support. "We discovered a sheet of papyrus, dating back to the time of Christ. Dr. DiMetrie conducted exhaustive photo and X-ray tests on the scroll, and we are certain it is an authentic document of the era. Another of our good friends, Dr. Devereaux, lent his support to our theory and as you all know, Dr. Devereaux spent a good portion of his life in Judea searching for information to validate the existence of our Savior for the 'Doubting Thomases' of this world."

Father Lean tugged at the neck of his robe, the excitement of talking about their discovery was making him warm. "The score is written in what musicologists call *iambic dimetres.* For those of you with as little musical background as myself, that means it has one short beat followed by three long ones. A rhythm St. Augustine feared was '*bewitching*'.

Amariah raised her hand with hesitation; she didn't want to stop the friar but burning curiosity demanded clarification. Granting permission for her to speak, Father Lean reached for a glass of water, welcoming the interruption.

"Reverend Father, why was music banned from the Church?"

"Ah, lass," black robes stirring, the Irish Jesuit rose, "you're not alone in wonderin' that! Never forget, lass, humanity was still in the fearful grip of the Dark Ages . . . a time when ignorance and superstition reigned supreme! The Church, along with its holy champions, was little more than a pagan institution. Regardless of the danger the flame of Christianity never faltered. At last, the Age of Enlightenment blossomed an' men began to question. As men of science searched for answers the Renaissance burst into full flower."

He stopped to scratch the side of his nose. After a moment's contemplation, Father Murphy continued. "Both good and bad came along with this new-found pursuit. Popes had a great deal o' political power, but they lusted after complete control. And power is paid for by coin of the realm. Taxes, tithes, indulgences--both popes and bishops searched for ways to get money to fund their passions. Were it not for the desire Pope Julius had to leave a lastin' mark on the world we would not have St. Peter's basilica and Luther might not have converted half the world to Protestantism!"

Amariah smiled, she liked this bandy-legged Irishman. He saw the Church for what it was and had a clear view of what he wanted to help it become.

Blue eyes glazed with the joy of discovery, Father Murphy suddenly realized the attention of everyone in the library was riveted on him. Church history was a topic most people found frightfully dull. He'd learned to content himself with his own ideas about why the structure and doctrine of the Church evolved the way it did. Few were willing to listen to theories they considered outdated and unworthy of their time. Yet here he was surrounded by men and women who shared his love of history! This group hung on his every word, and he found himself enjoying the limelight.

"In 589 A.D., the Council of Toledo instituted laws against dancin' during service. The activity was too pagan. At the Council of Glasgow, in 747 A.D. bishops declared it unlawful for a priest to adopt an effeminate pronunciation of the liturgy--after the manner of poets. Priests were also forbidden to imitate actors because it might draw attention away from the sacredness of the liturgy--spoken in a language a dwindlin' number of people understood. The Council of Trent laid a death knell to music in 1562. From that point only, the mass could be set to music and then in a form tha'd make anyone weep. Christian music lost its joyful spirit, it became solemn, a dirge."

The priest reached for a small box tied with a wide piece of string. Fumbling, arthritic fingers labored to perform the sample task. Frowning with concentration, Father Murphy finally got the strand of cord untied. Pulling on a pair of white cotton gloves he lifted apiece of papyrus about ten inches wide and a foot long out of a time worn wooden box. The pounded reed was brittle, and edges of the scroll had been worn away by time.

His eyes caressed the ancient paper. An excitement he hadn't felt in years surged through his body as adrenaline accelerated the pump of his heart; his mind seized upon the potential outcome of this discovery with fanatic zeal. "Here we have," his gaze hesitated on each face a fraction of a second as he measured each man and woman's reaction, "somethin' that could change the history of music in the Church in the 'twinkling of an eye'. According to experts, this piece bears a strong relationship to gospel music celebrated by black Americans! It is joyful! Its melody boasts a rhythm unheard of in our worship since the Council of Trent. We know it was performed in the early churches, because a notation on the back gave the priest instructions on how and when to insert it into the liturgy. It appears the stand taken on music by the bishops in the fifteenth-century had nothin' to do with the principles of the foundin' Christian fathers."

The Father General arose from his chair and interrupted the old priest. "Father Murphy, thank you for sharing this information with us but we have more exciting news today." His robe undulated above expensive leather loafers as Father Simson began to pace. "Jon LaPointe has discovered another important piece of sculpture."

A sweep of his hand in the direction of the art expert diverted everyone's attention. Clothes rumpled and grimed with dirt evidenced a recent exit from the catacombs. Amariah watched LaPointe dust off his trousers and shirt. A voice quavering with elation filled the library. "We've just uncovered a piece which is most certainly the work of Michelangelo! It was thought the *Pieta* was the only work of art the master ever signed but this statue also bears his name!" His fingers drew to his lips, and he kissed them emotionally, a Gaelic gesture of awe and respect. "I took a few digital photos before leaving the excavation site to attend this meeting. The floor of the vault above the one where the statue was discovered has been deteriorating for years and the statue was covered with debris. Here," he passed the prints around the room, "you can see why I am so excited I can't catch my breath!"

Amariah reached for the picture thrust in her direction. As she brought it close a preternatural chill invaded her body like the killer fog that smothered the first-born sons of Egypt. Shock, then veneration, then a feeling of familiarity so strong it left her weak and disoriented, pounded her body.

The picture in her hand, if created by Michelangelo, was surely his greatest work of art. To Amariah, there could be no doubt the artist captured the essence of Jesus--the grown man--who became the Messiah. His hand was raised over his head, a whip clenched in his fingers. Anger filled his eyes; the muscles in his jaw clenched with fury as he lashed a cringing moneychanger huddled beneath his feet. This man had passion, this man knew rage! Jesus was portrayed as a man caught in the grip of fury. Sinews in his wrist, the muscles flexing beneath the coarse weave of his robe left no doubt as to his physical strength. Long hair cascaded in a tumble around his shoulders and a full, rich beard rimmed his face. Strong and proud, his features were those of a handsome man distorted by wrath. This was a man, a real man, a human being who knew suffering, resentment, and anger. How had an artist working with a piece of stone captured these emotions?

Amariah thought back to her initial impression of the *Pieta.* How had Michelangelo turned marble into the soft folds of Mary's gown? How had he changed something hard and lifeless into an object so filled with anguish it claimed the beholder?

Fighting to suppress tears the picture compelled her to shed, Amariah drew the colored square closer, searching out its details. A voice--the same voice that came in the night--whispered in her ear.

"He knew him . . . he was there."

She turned, knowing no one was standing beside her. Yet the voice was so real, so filled with compassion, she expected to find an earnest face pressed close to her cheek.

The expression, the stance, the body language, everything about this piece of sculpture would make one think Michelangelo witnessed Jesus' attack on the temple defilers. Amariah could feel the Master's ire. Rage called out across the centuries, indignation with fools, who conducted business on the steps of a structure he considered sacred, radiated from the image on the paper. What would it be like to be in the same room with the magnificent statue? Tears spilled and rolled down her cheeks, but Amariah didn't know she was crying.

A gentle hand touched her shoulder, "Sister, I too was so moved I cried as I brushed away the dirt from the statue's face. No one can look upon this work of art and escape its emotion, its compelling message. That such a masterpiece was lost and forgotten is criminal."

The Frenchman turned toward the Father General, his hand still resting on Amariah's shoulder, an act meant to comfort, to sustain. "I think Father Simson's work in the Secret Archive has given him more insight than he's led us to believe."

Black eyes surveyed the assembled scholars from a face as hard and unyielding as the marble in the statue. Expressionless, Simson's features conveyed neither admission nor denial. "The inquisitiveness of lesser men is the reason access to the Archive was denied for the past five hundred years. Records were in a sad state when I took over the task of reorganization. In one section of shelving, I discovered over ten thousand packets which had never been examined. It was from these I learned many lies lay buried in the catacombs beneath St. Peter's. What those items are, what the chambers contain, how much is sealed away," he paused, skewering each person with a glance which held no compassion for the folly of mankind, "I have no more idea than the rest of you."

Amariah studied the Jesuit. His voice was soft and his expression neutral; the man knew the image he wanted to project. Such theatrics probably accounted for his spectacular success with the press. Still, the habit he had of scraping his thumbnail up and down the crucifix betrayed inner tension. A tic near the spot where his jaws came together was just visible beneath closely shaved skin--another indication Andrew Simson wrestled with unknown devils. Perhaps the most revealing action was the way his other hand gripped the file folders on the table. So fierce was his grasp, the knuckles were drained of color. Had she not been taught to observe signals the body beamed like a transatlantic beacon, Amariah might have accepted his remarks as true. But the way the Father General's eyes flicked up and to his right neurologically revealed his lie. Simson knew what the research team was going to discover.

Amariah's glance returned to the face staring up at her from the photograph. The vault containing the statue was poorly lit, the picture dim. The hypnotic eyes of the statue beckoned her into the past. They called to her across the chasm of time and a now familiar voice sounded in her ear.

"You knew him too!"

Amariah thrust the key in the lab lock. When the tumblers didn't release immediately she jiggled the key with irritation. Finally, the door opened, and she stormed across the room, frustration evident in the length of her stride. Plopping the book bag on her workstation, she leaned over the computer console and began pressing buttons. One by one, the hard drive, monitor, printer, and modem sprang to life with an electronic whir. A draft of warmer air from the hallway wrapped around her ankles alerting Amariah she did not shut the door. Still agitated, she gave the door a kick. Deciding it would do her no good to begin work until her temper cooled, and Amariah crossed to the window.

The dome of St. Peter's towered over the Vatican in majestic glory. The noon day sun bathed it in a radiant halo. Shouts from workmen sounded in the distance over the call of birds roosting in cypress trees sprinkled throughout the garden. The tranquil scene mocked the turbulence of her mood. Amariah clenched her fist, crumpling a sheet of paper. Klaus showed her how to search back-up files in the mainframe. Although someone erased most of the evidence, one small detail was overlooked. Data contained on a redundant support file matched what she originally inputted into her laptop--the damning printout was wadded in her hand.

Amariah marched to the laboratory safe and spun its dial. Until now, she'd thought her documents well protected. Amariah hoped her knowledge of Aramaic was sufficiently better than most to foil all but a skilled thief. Surely, few people would figure out a combination was derived from the number value assigned to letters in a language spoken by Jesus.

To make certain the scrolls were not tampered with Amariah took a fireproof metal box to the workstation. Lifting its lid, her heartbeat joyously as she counted the contents. Why they made her so emotional was shrouded in mystery. Two of the scrolls had never been unrolled. Amariah made up her mind to spend the rest of the morning looking over their contents and make an outline of the message. Distrust colored everything she did now. If something happened, at least she would have an idea of what a scribe in that distant day thought important enough to record.

Absently, Amariah reached to tuck a lock of hair beneath the surgical cap, then drew on thin latex gloves. Setting the scrolls on the sterile counter, she reached for a pair of tweezers. With care, she grasped ancient paper at the corner and gently tugged. It was painstaking work; fibrous material had to be separated one layer at a time. Intense concentration on the scrolls soon blotted out the rest of the world.

The persistent ache in her back was annoying and she flexed her arms over her head. Twisting and turning, Amariah tried to relax back muscles which cramped after long hours hunched over the workstation. Despite fatigue, the last scroll beckoned her. For some reason, she'd put it aside although she'd been drawn to it from the first.

She reached for a scalpel resting in the stainless-steel rack. Slicing the remnant of cord binding the document together, Amariah wielded the surgical instrument with dexterity. As she unrolled sheets of vellum with the edge of the scalpel, she was surprised to find another scroll adhered to the animal skin. The other document was thick and heavy, a crude form of paper.

One centimeter at a time, she separated the layers. As she probed deeper the more excited Amariah became. The writing was still legible. Letters were written in a bold, heavy hand--almost as if the author wanted to make certain it could be read far into the future. When the remaining section finally separated, Amariah found herself looking at two very different documents.

The scraped animal skin scroll was written in Aramaic; the message on the sheet of lumpy paper was in Latin. Amariah's mind raced as she tried to decode them simultaneously, her eyes flitting back and forth. Deciding it was impossible to work on both at the same time, she turned her attention to the message penned in Latin.

"Dear One,

I am an ordained Jesuit priest by the name of Adamus. Only recently have I returned from the desert of Egypt. Seven years did I labor in that foreign kingdom, a country so strange it would take many days to record the wonders I have seen and the ways of the people I grew to respect. But their story is for another time. This day, my hand is set to another, more tragic circumstance. I leave this record behind in the hope someone--in whose heart the spirit of our Lord and Savior is strong--will discover this record. I suspect my days will be ended shortly, for the knowledge gained in my travels will cost my life. But, if that is the price for protecting the truth . . . so be it. I give up my life gladly, like the Redeemer before me, our Lord Jesus Christ. Hold this written message to a candle flame and a map will appear. Follow its path through the catacombs to where I have secreted a cache of documents. I pray the finder of this message will have the courage to see this circumstance through to the end. The world deserves to know how wrong they have been . . . how wrong I have been.

Adamus, the Society of Jesus
Year of our Lord, 1601 Rome"

Amariah held the parchment against the window. Although faint, lines appeared on the other side of the paper. Turning the sheet in her hand, she studied it closer. The lines appeared to be the same on both sides. It was almost as if something was inside the paper. Amariah's heart leaped to her throat. Of course! That's why the paper was so thick--it was sandwiched around a map. Rushing to the workstation, Amariah reached for the scalpel again. Inserting the blade into the edge of the paper she worked it back and forth with caution.

Slowly, painstakingly, Amariah slipped the scalpel back and forth, ever deeper. She moved the blade a fraction of an inch at a time--afraid she might cut too deep and damage the map. Resistance against the scalpel suddenly lessened; Amariah knew she penetrated the core. Using the blade to pry upward, she lifted the surfaces apart--to reveal a centuries old map.

Nestled in a cradle of high rag content paper was a thin sheet of parchment. Waiting for her hand to stop trembling, Amariah coaxed the map away from its place of rest. Its lines were dark and clear; the map was perfectly preserved. It didn't take long to decide it was a map of the papal state as it probably existed in the early sixteenth century. Boundary lines were different, but the position of St. Peter's basilica to the Castel San Angelo ran true. Landmarks were well defined; compass points clearly marked. The map indicated how many levels of catacombs lay beneath the Vatican.

Counting, Amariah was astonished to discover the archaeological team had not yet reached the lowest crypts. If the map was accurate, there were two more levels. Adrenaline surged through her bloodstream making Amariah feel lightheaded. From the discussion in the weekly staff meetings, Father Simson didn't think it necessary to search further.

Amariah could hardly wait to disclose this startling news at the next meeting! Settling back against the chair, a premonition filtered from the many chambered recess of her mind. Should she even mention the map? What had the medieval priest been so terrified of that he hid the cache of documents? She read the letter again. Due to recent events, it might be prudent not to let anyone know about it. Maybe she'd wait and see what course of action Simson took. For now, Amariah knew she didn't trust Woolsey.

Two could play this game. Amariah slid the computer keyboard across the desk. Settling in front of the terminal, she tapped in the code which brought up the document log. Without a moment's hesitation, she erased all traces of scroll nine. Then, using the notes she took as Klaus moved from one screen to another, Amariah accessed the mainframe. A few whirring noises and several rapid blinks of the red light on the hard drive and Amariah was in. Her fingers raced over the keyboard--screens were brought up and dissolved as she moved through the program toward her intended target. Passwords provided by Klaus were as accurate as the German himself. She had complete access to the Father General's secret programs. After deleting all records of the ninth scroll, Amariah leaned back; no magnetic cairns would mark the document's worldly sojourn. As far as the world would ever know, only eight documents in Aramaic occupied a place on the shelves in vault seventeen. Now that the task was complete Amariah wondered why Klaus was in possession of the program's passwords and why he'd taught her to use them without hesitation. Reflecting on the sequence of events, Klaus never even asked her why she wanted to know how to bypass network access.

Thankful she'd chosen this morning to bring a fresh can of coffee to the lab, Amariah emptied its contents into another container. Wiping the metal skin free of grounds, she stuffed the scroll and map inside and ran her thumb around the plastic lid, sealing it tight. Perhaps her caffeine addition would serve a useful purpose after all.

"What do you mean?" Simson's tumultuous eyes were wide with anger, his arteries pulsated against the collar of his cassock.

"I came to tell you as soon as I discovered the problem! We're no longer receiving a picture from Sister Amariah's lab. Apparently," Father Wilson studied the floor beneath his shoe--afraid to be engulfed by the caldron of wrath radiating from his superior's expression, "the camera failed twenty-four hours ago."

"Anything could have transpired in that length of time."

The rasp of his thumbnail as it scraped along the uneven surface of his gold crucifix echoed the hammering of Philip Wilson's heart. "Yes, I'm afraid it could have. We know Sister Amariah has been spending long hours in the lab."

"Did any audio pick up?"

"Only the sound of bags tossed into the chair, the scraping of stool against the floor, the whine of the computer--normal sounds associated with a research lab."

"Damn!" The Father General's fist tightened around the crucifix in a strangling embrace. "Can we get the camera repaired?"

"The sister has been staying in the lab until early morning."

"Can it appear the work of a cleaning crew?"

"Not where the camera is located. It would be too obvious."

"Do you know what caused the failure?"

"The cameras transmit radio signals. Equipment in the basement of the Pontifical Academy of Science translates their signal into pixels which are then broadcast on a monitor. All we've been receiving from the camera in her lab is static. The screen is filled with 'snow'."

"How did this happen?"

Father Wilson shrugged his shoulders. "It could have been anything from a bad electronic circuit to computer error. We simply won't know until we remove it from the lab." He hesitated, his head low, he found it impossible to endure the Father General's disappointed stare. "Once we have it dismantled, it could be several weeks before it's fixed and back in place. All laboratory cameras are advanced prototypes--the CIA doesn't even have them. Replacement parts simply don't exist."

Simson's eyes wandered to the window of his sparsely furnished office. "Pressure the manufacturer to repair it without delay. A new camera must be installed immediately. Until then," the abrasive sound created as his thumbnail sought the recessed hollows of the golden cross struck nerve endings in auditory channels of his brain like the screech of fingernails drawn down a blackboard, "we'll have to rely on observation and audio. Increase surveillance on Sister Amariah. Make certain someone is in the computer room across from her lab at all times."

Anger spent over a situation he was powerless to control, Andrew Simson pulled his fingers through the curling hair at the nape of his neck. "Were I a mystical man, Father Wilson, I might be tempted to wonder if this sudden turn of events was an obstacle placed in my path by a greater power." A twisted smile drew his tightly compressed lips downward, "This challenge will be met--I shall prevail!"

"Father Sorenson, there's a message for you from White Hall." The secretary smiled her brightest at the Jesuit who just entered the office. "The Prime Minister is anxious for you to return his call."

"What else awaits me?" Reaching for a stack of messages in the tray, Father Sorenson shuffled pieces of pink paper. "Only local calls?"

"No messages from the continent today."

"Perhaps no news is good news." He crossed the foyer, heading toward his office. "Susan, don't ring through any calls just yet. I need a few hours to catch up on this." He waved the stack of correspondence in his hand. "If it gets late, go on home. I'll dictate tomorrow."

"Buzz me if you decide to take more incoming calls. Since your picture appeared in the *Times* people are desperate to reach you. It seems as though you have the power to solve everyone's problem!"

Father Sorenson pushed aside his office door and wearily flicked on the light. The trip was long, the debriefing session longer and the interview with the press stretched across eternity. But Gwelo's picture appeared in papers all over the globe. It would signal the underground he did not bargain falsely. Dropping his overcoat into the chair, the priest laid his briefcase on top--where it could be seen--just to be safe. Gwelo's life history rested in an inexpensive leather case. Tomorrow he planned to call several news sources and leak the information Gwelo revealed during his plane trip back to London.

The poor man still could hardly believe he was not going to be returned to solitary confinement in that pesthole of a prison. For twenty years Gwelo called a four-by-eight cell home with rats as his only companions. His children grew to adulthood and had children of their own now. Gwelo missed the entire course of their lives, but he remained true to what he believed. His story needed to reach the world. The man was a hero in every sense of the word. Had his skin not been black, had he not been born in a land ruled by the whites---he might have become a great statesman.

Sinking into a worn chair, Father Sorenson swiveled toward the window. Fog was rolling in and a fine mist haloed streetlamps as they sprang to life. The distinctive dampness of London was welcome after the dust and heat of the plains of Africa. Inhaling deeply, Father Sorenson decided he was glad to be back.

Tomorrow was time enough to set journalistic wheels in motion. Two or three well-placed stories could make the news cycle. Interest in Gwelo's cause would ignite idealists. Revolutions were triggered over lesser events. He would see to it the story that reached the press was sorrowful enough to stir a worldwide sense of injustice. His brothers in South Africa would know he was as good as his word.

The fog turned to steady drizzle as the priest's gaze fixed on the penumbra of gray light cast by the streetlamp. How many nights had he spent beneath such lamps as a child? Alone on the street, unwanted. The vision of rain-blackened streets fluttered up from memory. Garbage scows plied the murky water of the Thames--piled high with the refuse of humanity. The stench still haunted him. Cold and shivering, an orphaned child of black descent had neither coat nor shoes to ward off the chill of winter. His stomach often rumbled, hunger his only companion. Checking the tide of self-pity, Father Sorenson forced himself to turn the focus of his interior journey. The Father General counseled his soldiers of God to guard the contents of their thoughts. Never were they to dwell on despair--only on what must be accomplished in the future. Never the disappointments of the past . . . always the future . . . always what was to come. His hand reached for the crucifix suspended from the chain around his neck. Comfort always followed. What might his life have been like had his Catholic mentor not rescued him from the streets? He didn't know what the old priest saw in him that was worthy of such unflagging devotion, but he knew he would be eternally grateful.

He'd borrowed the priest's name, but the Jesuit didn't seem to mind. It was the only thing he could think of to honor his teacher--nay, his savior. He owed the education that allowed him entry into every level of London's social fabric to the older Jesuit. It was the aged Father Sorenson who was responsible for the phone calls of Prime Ministers! It was he who polished a child's mind and taught a street urchin the ins and outs of the political arena.

The young Father Sorenson brushed a particle of dust from his cassock. Everything that mattered stemmed from the priesthood. Everything he hoped to become was for the glory of the Order. The Jesuit brothers saved him from an anonymous life in the putrid squalor of London's slums.

Reaching to wipe away the single tear, which refused to be brought under control, the new Father Sorenson turned his thoughts to Rome. He owed his life to the Church; he was determined to carry out his part of Father Simson's mission.

The world's populace would soon know the true circumstances of Gwelo's story. It was the history of the bondage of his race--all wrapped up in the events of one man's life. But sell papers it would, and after a period of adjustment, Gwelo would meet with certain members of the press. Exclusive interviews would be granted. All he had to do was follow Father Simson's carefully constructed plan. In a few weeks, mankind would pay homage to Gwelo, and the Jesuits who engineered his rescue. Pressure could then be put on the South African government to release other political prisoners--men who would gladly support the aims of the Church.

Father Sorenson knew he was destined to wield influence on the apartheid nation whose political leadership hated him because of the color of his skin.

Gwelo would never see the high savannahs of his native country again. He would never hear the yip of the jackal, nor watch birds of prey swoop low at sunset. He would not feel the scorching sun beating on black shoulders still broad enough to command considerable respect. His captors never quenched the fires of Gwelo's indomitable spirit! Had he lived in another age he might have gained recognition as a great warrior chief. The spear and shield would have been his weapons, the loincloth his uniform.

Sorenson knew he owed it to his race to succeed . . . just as he owed it to the Church to fulfill his calling. Rubbing the ache behind his ear the priest closed his eyes in weariness. Father Simson never noticed the color of his skin. Only the color of his cassock mattered to the leader of the Jesuits. Father Sorenson acquitted himself well during the years of training and he was proud of being one of the forty-four men hand-picked by Andrew Simson. They were the men who would return the church to its former glory. They were the men selected to uphold the ideals of Ignatius Loyola. Forty- four men would rekindle the message of Jesus. They were the core of the Society of Jesus; they were the new messengers . . . they were the new Apostles of God!

Leon joined Klaus beside a display case that was crafted when men worked without the precision of power tools. Enclosed beneath the glass was a priceless manuscript dating back to the time of the Pharaohs. Hieroglyphics were as unfathomable to Leon as the languages Amariah could read and write. Beneath the twin-barreled archways of the library, Leon drifted toward another costly table inlaid with lapis, mother of pearl and onyx--appearing interested in the design. The baroque style of the legs twisted upward, supporting a priceless vase resting casually on the table's surface. Etruscan, the cobalt blue favored by that distant civilization, contrasted perfectly with its gleaming gold trim. The library overwhelmed even the most jaded with its opulent beauty.

"Did everything go well the other night?" Leon traced his finger along the intricate pattern inlaid in the table--he stopped short of touching the vase--

afraid he might dislodge it from the carved ivory base.

"Yes, it was a fairly simple matter." Klaus motioned the other man toward another of the glass cases beneath the library's tall windows. A particularly ancient Bible rested against a velvet cloth. "Once I discovered the cameras were all operated by a radio signal it was easy to send it a signal to turn. As soon as the lens focused on the window, I opened the door with Sister Amariah's missing key."

"The camera isn't operational anymore?"

"I don't think it will ever work again. And, if the invoice records stored in the computer are correct, there are no replacement parts. It seems the Father General purchased some very experimental equipment."

Leon nodded, glancing out a window overlooking the Cortile del Belvedere; it was deceptively peaceful in the Holy City. Few would ever imagine the true nature of the operation being conducted behind St. Peter's basilica--if what John Preston believed was true.

"Do you think it's safe to tell Sister Amariah what we've done?"

Squinting against the light, the German considered the question for a moment. His chest rose as he drew in a deep breath of air; then his rib cage slowly lowered as he released it with a hiss. "I think we'd best wait until we gather stronger evidence. The only thing we know now is vast amounts of money were transferred out of the Vatican bank and the Father General purchased some technologically advanced surveillance equipment. If asked, I'll bet Simson has a plausible explanation for both situations. Have you given any thought as to how we might get Amariah out of Rome in a hurry--if the need arises?"

"No, I haven't. I don't like Simson, I don't trust him--but to think a man of the Church is up to what John Preston is accusing him of . . ."

The German bent closer, examining hand-drawn letters, the exact up and down strokes penned by an unknown monk in the Middle Ages. "Leon, give me your estimate of probability."

Wariness narrowed Leon's eyes and deepened the frown lines in his forehead. The German possessed the knack of throwing him off kilter. "Probability of what?"

"Here's a piece of history which has always fascinated me." He tapped the glass case lightly, "This Bible, and all literature produced prior to the invention of the printing press, was copied by hand. What are the odds you could take a lengthy document and reproduce it exactly? How good do you think your penmanship is and your ability to translate? Do you think you could labor from sunup until sundown and still make exact pen strokes at the end of the day? Especially if you were sitting on a hard stool in an unheated stone cell and your only source of light was a tallow candle! What's your estimate of the likelihood of error?"

Leon examined the Bible closer. The elaborate swirls and penmanship were works of art. But accurate? Leon glanced at the German. "I think the ratio for error was high."

"And yet the foundation of Christian worship is based on a literal interpretation of every word recorded in this book. Scientific examination has been applied to every subject under the sun--but the Bible alone was shielded from scrutiny. We measured the heavens and explored the depths of the sea with astonishing accuracy . . . yet we feel duty bound to turn a blind eye to a document which should undergo the painstaking evaluation of every scientific discipline. We've been taught to ignore the ecclesiastical madness that has taken place since Constantine forced Christianity to fit the mold of Roman government! Why? Why! If you'd like to hear it--I'll be glad to offer my conclusion."

Nodding, Leon encouraged his friend to go on, intuition warned what he learned was going to alter his concept of Christianity.

"It can be summed up in one word . . . control! As man progressed out of the Dark Ages into the Age of Enlightenment, he began to question physical matters. In the book of Joshua, the Bible states the sun stood still. That's where they got the notion the sun went around the earth. You may think this was silly, and perhaps by today's standards it was, but Copernicus put his life in jeopardy when he declared the earth revolved around the sun! Copernicus was excommunicated for his heretical theories; his work was confiscated, and he was sent into exile. A few years later a chap by the name of Galileo took the art of measuring to new heights. He proved the earth moved around the sun! The Church was on a collision course with scientific evidence. The Pope tried to appeal to Galileo by telling him such newfound knowledge could not be sprung on an unsuspecting populace. The illiterate, peasant mind was simply not prepared for such revolutionary concepts. Remember, the people of the day were taught to accept every word in the Bible on a literal basis. Galileo, however, was a man of conviction. He stood toe to toe with the Pope and said if the Church didn't admit the truth to the faithful, he was going to use the newly developed printing press to spread his ideas all over Europe. The Pope retaliated by excommunicating Galileo, but science gained a foothold in a world which had been the exclusive domain of the Church. Why, you're asking yourself, were Galileo's conclusions so harmful? The Church was also the government of the time. If the faithful learned the Church was wrong for the past fifteen hundred years, the Pope would lose control over his subjects. And loss of control meant economic destruction for the politically powerful institution."

Klaus blew a mote of dust from the glass case, then buffed it with his jacket sleeve. He leaned closer, appearing to examine the Bible with intense interest. "We're facing the same situation Galileo experienced five hundred years ago. The clergy is still afraid of what might happen to their control over millions if the Bible undergoes intense scientific investigation. Congregations are manipulated by the most potent weapon in the arsenal of human psychology . . . fear! Preachers scream, and shout God punishes offenders. Televangelists warn the doubter's soul will rot in hell for eons and the curious are brought to heel. Organized religion puts blinders on rational thought and clouds the mind with a veil of emotion." Tapping the glass with his finger, Klaus emphasized his point. The noise drew the attention of the Swiss Guard who motioned him away from the priceless manuscript. Klaus acknowledged the guard with a respectful nod and stepped back.

"Leon, the bottom line for the clergy is control over the faithful. Lose control and you lose revenue! It's that simple. Wars are fought for economic reasons--not for matters of religious ideology or principles of justice, no matter what idealistic dreamers imply. Simson is preparing to put economic control of entire nations in his hands. He's using a universal weapon called the Catholic Church."

Staggered by the plausibility of Klaus' words, his fingers absently traced a cabinet's gilded coping, his gaze strayed past a painting of St. Jerome adorning the pillar in the center of the room--but he didn't notice the beautifully draped robe, the full beard of the robust saint, nor the children playing at his feet, as he wrestled with the enormity of his thoughts.

The expression on Leon's face reflected the turmoil of his emotions; his gray eyes assumed a glassy look, like circles of polished steel. When he finally spoke, his words contained a note of expectancy, knowing if he ignored the sensation seeping through his thoughts it would be at his own peril. "The logical side of my brain wants to resist what you're saying. Facts and figures keep flitting in and out of my head to prove you wrong. What you've said puts a torch to everything in which I've been taught to believe. It's difficult to come to grips with, but Klaus," Leon pressed his hand over his abdomen in the area just beneath the sternum," . . . I feel in the pit of my stomach what you say is true. I can't explain why I know you're right, but I've never been more certain of anything in my life!"

Amariah awoke with a start. Had she been screaming? Her chest still heaved with the emotion of the nightmare. Or had it been a nightmare? In truth, she couldn't remember what she was dreaming--only the ghosts of fear still owned her emotions. A glance at the clock assured her it was still the middle of the night . . . 1:01 a.m. Six hours of sleep stretched ahead of her as she tried to remember what terror elicited such a strong response. When her body began to cool, Amariah reached for the covers and drew them beneath her chin. Thoroughly awake, she stared at the clock--trying to remember what she'd encountered in the dream to bring on the sense of horror.

The moon disappeared behind a cloud, leaving a phosphorescent outline of silver. Night pressed against the glass as surely as if it were a demon summoned from the great beyond; a creeping form of sleep slowly, but firmly, retreated. Amariah pushed the pillow beneath her head, searching for a more comfortable position. She turned over, then back again. The clock now read 2:10 a.m. Flattening her back against the mattress, Amariah began the relaxing countdown her father taught her years ago. Envisioning a cloud of blue light around her ankles, she slowly drew it upward, over her legs, to her thighs, encircling her abdomen. Amariah tried to concentrate; there was therapeutic value in quieting the mind's anxiety, perhaps she could overtake the thief of sleep. She deepened her breathing; the blue cloud raised, pulled upward by her inner vision. As she forced light to cocoon her rib cage, Amariah slowed her breathing, taking deeper breaths and holding them to a predetermined count.

One. Two. Three.

Amariah focused on the numbers and soothing visualization.

One. Two. Three.

The cloud drew upward and surrounded her head. Then, like her father instructed a million times before, she envisioned a change of color in the imaginary mist. The cloud lost its soothing, pastel tones and transformed into a shimmering field of white.

One. Two. Three.

It was so bright she could hardly focus on the resplendent glory. With the change in color, Amariah felt as if she were no longer a prisoner in her body.

One. Two. Three.

Freed from the cares of the physical world, she seemed to float--to hover somewhere in a distant sphere. Totally relaxed, she was no longer aware of the room, the bed, and the cushioning pillow. Deep in an altered state, it was easier to disregard demands of the body. Here, as her brain wave pattern widened into an alpha state, Amariah felt free.

A voice called to her from across the expanse of her inner universe. She was not asleep--she was very much awake--only relaxed and feeling tranquil. Amariah kept her breathing slow, her state of mind calm. Curiosity outweighed fear of the faceless voice and so she waited. Opening her eyes, Amariah surveyed the room. Lights guarding the construction site stayed on all night. They cast a sodium yellow glow through the drapes drawn across the window. Her glance traveled toward the wall near the bathroom. Its flat, white surface reflected diffused outside light. Eyes out of focus, Amariah kept her gaze trained on the wall. She blinked, hoping to relieve the burning sensation. In the second it took her eyelids to flutter, the medieval priest appeared.

A hand stretched forward but the rest of his body melted into shadow. The moon slipped from behind an obscuring cloud, a silver white beam of light pierced the curtains, revealing a visage with blazing eyes; Adamus' unyielding stare was sharp and probing. Wind blew withered leaves against the window and over the roof. Her steady breathing was amplified by the unnatural silence engulfing the room.

'You must find the hidden vault. You have the map.'

A heightened sense of serenity pervaded Amariah's spirit. "Is it lower?"

'You must go further.'

The figure blurred, its robes melted into the darkness as the moon slipped behind a bank of clouds--only the searing eyes remained distinct.

"The Father General doesn't intend to dig deeper. He doesn't think there are deeper levels in the catacombs."

'You must convince him.'

"How?" Amariah knew she had to remain calm, or anxiousness would lift her to the state of waking consciousness. "It will cost thousands of dollars to dig deeper . . . do I tell him about the map?"

'Find a way. You must convince him. Everything depends on you.'

His eyes radiated a feeling of intensity that was super-normal; an urgent, frantic sense of purpose overwhelmed her. "I am just a nun. What can I say to be convincing?" Despite concentrated effort, Amariah felt the altered state of mind slipping away as her thoughts centered on the difficulty of convincing Andrew Simson to explore further.

Sharp eyes glowed with the radiance of a thousand suns, as the priest conveyed his final message. '*Trust your feelings--you have more knowledge than you know. Have faith. You will be guided.*'

It took Amariah a few moments to realize the glittering eyes had faded away and she was staring at a blank wall.

Have faith. You will be guided. Wasn't this the essence of Jesus's message? Didn't he try to convince his followers they had the power to perform miracles, if they believed? One thing was clear to Amariah, the lower levels of the catacombs had to be reached. An incredible secret was locked away in the chamber indicated on a map drawn four hundred years ago. Deep in her soul, Amariah sensed she was being drawn into a vortex of predestined events. The past beckoned . . . crooking its bony finger like the Pale Horseman of the Apocalypse who rode the horse called Death.

Chairs scraped as everyone drew to attention. The Father General strode into the room, the aura conveyed by his black robe was commanding and purposeful. Amariah glanced at the portraits of the papal librarians, who acted as guardians over the treasures in this room; today their countenances seemed as forbidding as the Father General.

The smell of decaying leather reached her nostrils--a comforting scent, like the aroma of fresh baked cookies from her mother's oven, it transported her to happier memories of hours spent in other libraries. The stacks of books towering overhead offered shelter to those seated at the tables below. The library was a bastion of learning, which withstood the ravages of both time and man.

Amariah studied the paintings of the librarians. What was it like to be the keeper of documents created by authors who long ago turned to dust? It must have been a staggering burden to be responsible for preserving knowledge for the generations ahead. The same responsibility had fallen to her--she was the guardian of information hidden by a frightened Jesuit in the sixteenth century. She had to convince Simson to dig deeper -- but how? Amariah hadn't a clue what she could say without revealing the existence of the map.

"This has been a week filled with important work." File folders slapped against the table as the Father General drew everyone's attention to him. "Everything is proceeding, the museum is finally taking on form." His hand waved at the window. "The foundation has been laid, girders are in place and before long marble walls will encase the outer shell. The museum is finally coming to life."

Amariah thought she detected moisture in the Father General's eyes. How strange an inanimate object could elicit such deep emotion in a man ruled by logic; a man who considered human emotion a defect.

"You've all taken time to look at the sculpture?" The question was rhetorical, but stormy eyes swept the room, measuring the depth of conviction.

Raising her hand, Amariah found herself standing. Despite the timidness in her voice, her question was not lost in the cavernous room. "Father, will we search out deeper levels?"

Simson stared at the trembling nun. She seldom said a word during the staff meetings. Amariah appeared to enjoy listening to others, but she always seemed reluctant to speak before her peers. Sensing he would have to tread cautiously, or the girl would retreat into silence, the Father General kept his tone of voice considerate. "We've no evidence to make us think there might be more chambers further beneath St. Peter's."

Unable to meet the Father General's challenging gaze, Amariah studied her fingers as they twisted her rosary beads in a spiral. "Do you have evidence to make you believe there are not more levels?"

"In truth, I do not. However, the expense makes me question the wisdom of proceeding when I cannot be reasonably assured of the outcome." The Father General reached for his crucifix. What was the girl getting at? "We have uncovered a wealth of documentation dating back to the time of Christ. Art hidden by the early popes stretches from the developmental stages of the Grecian culture all the way through the Renaissance. If there are other levels, would what we uncover be of greater value? Is it worth the cost?"

Amariah's head snapped up, her eyes filled with preternatural fire. Shoulders straightening, she faced the Jesuit squarely, her voice strong and clear. "What if there is another masterpiece of Michelangelo's work buried in a lower chamber? What if there are more works by Raphael, Botticelli or Signorelli hidden away? Can we afford not to discover another *Laocoon* or *Belvedere Torso*? Would you have mankind deprived of the likes of another *St. Jerome*? What if DiVinci painted another *Last Supper*? Would you deny Christians another view of Jesus through the eyes of Michelangelo? What if there is a Laughing Jesus, a Jesus sorrowing for the suffering of humanity hidden deeper beneath the Vatican? Father, if there is even a slight possibility something else exists--we owe it to the millions of faithful Christians to continue the excavation. Does an archaeologist ever know what he will find? We go on faith, experience . . . and lastly, evidence. The *'Angry Jesus'* is evidence enough we should push on. The archaeological team might turn up nothing . . . but at least we would know for certain nothing else exists! Wouldn't stopping now defeat the purpose for which we are here? You decided to unlock the secrets of the Archive--you decreed the time was at hand to rekindle the importance of Christianity in the hearts of man! Can you afford to stop the dig? Would you leave your mission incomplete?"

Amariah stopped to take a breath; her hands were moist, and she self-consciously wiped them against the skirt of her habit as she wondered from where the sudden burst of courage and beseeching words had come.

The other scholars sat in silence. Nervous coughs were muffled beneath restless hands. Eyes darted from one face to another. Leon was astounded; he had no idea Amariah would challenge the Father General so openly. He tried to catch Von Friendberg's attention, wondering how his friend felt about her outburst.

The German was also surprised; his expression reflected a complex array of emotions which ranged from awe and admiration to outright fear. Klaus fought the impulse to stand and cheer!

A tide of emotion sweeping across the room engulfed the Father General as technicians, researchers, historians, and scholars nodded their heads and whispered to each other.

The Father General cleared his throat and appeared to be considering his response with care. "Sister, your eloquence is moving, deeply moving. I will review the operating budget and if there are any funds available we will proceed." Turbulent eyes whisked up and down the nun's slender frame. Her passion was an example of the strength he knew was buried deep in her subconscious. The nun would have to be handled with care lest he lose control of what he worked so hard to create.

Anna pushed her chair back; the sharp, grating sound echoed off the vaulted ceiling. A slow, measured glance took in the group of scholars. Bringing her hands up she began to clap. One-by-one, scholars and technicians rose to their feet, lending support to Amariah's stirring oration and the Father General's decision.

The sound carried throughout the miles of corridors in the library. It drifted downstairs and out windows. Gardeners tending plants and flowers looked up. Birds scattered from their nests, alarmed by the sudden noise. Even cats, which called the Vatican home, paused in their cleaning efforts. Pink tongues stopped halfway along raised paws and slanted yellow eyes turned toward the library. Applause filled the Belvedere Courtyard. It rippled over buildings whose foundations were laid by hand--before impersonal technology replaced the craftsman--finally to reach the Apostolic Palace. From his bed, despite the drug-induced malaise, Pope Anastasius smiled. A voice so weak it couldn't be heard by the nurses slipped between lips which were parched and cracked. "You see, Adamus, I told you she could do it. This Sister will light the way for His return."

It was late. The sun had set hours ago, and Amariah's hands were stiff from the wintry conditions in the lab. Deciding it would do no good to push her body beyond its natural level of endurance, she shut down the computer and began to gather up her notes. Leaning forward, then back, she worked to relieve the strain of sitting in one position for hours. A spin of the dial on the safe insured her work was locked away from those nameless, faceless persons she had come to dread.

She longed to shed the surgical gown and trousers she wore while working in the lab. With a start, Amariah realized she was so homesick for St. Anne's it was almost a physical ache. To dispel longing, she tried to rationalize away the gloom with thoughts of how well her work was going. If no more scrolls were discovered perhaps she'd be back in the classroom at St. Anne's within six months. Somehow, the thought made her feel more down hearted than ever. Isolation in the lab was becoming a strain. She hungered for the companionship of children; the look in their eyes which announced intelligence would lift them out of poverty; the merriment only a child's voice could convey.

Amariah forced thoughts of home to remain locked away as she slammed the door on pleasant memories. It would do no good to brood. Glancing at the clock, Amariah wondered if the cafeteria was still open. The lab coffeepot was dry, and she had not taken the time to brew more. She decided to stop by the dining hall to see if there was one last cup to enjoy.

Lights were on in cafeteria and several people lounged around a few tables. Pushing open the door, Amariah headed for the serving line. Father Simson spared no cost in providing physical comforts for staff members. Bread puddings, cake, pies, and sweet rolls rested beneath glass cases.

"Is the coffee fresh?" Amariah smiled at the rotund sister who ran the cafeteria. The woman rose at dawn and labored all day to create luscious wonders for the museum team. "Sister Felicity, do you ever rest?"

A laugh greeted Amariah as pudgy fingers pushed a cup of black coffee in her direction. "I live to serve Father Simson. His wishes are my wishes. My talents are not those of scholars but if I make your sojourn here more comfortable, then I too have contributed to something which will endure for generations."

"Sister, you're marvelous. I think I'll cap off an evening of work with some bread pudding. I fear I've become as addicted to it as I am to coffee!"

Amariah took her cup and bowl and headed toward a table. As she cast about for a comfortable place to sit, Amariah's glance settled on Anna Romanov. She looked so fragile, so forlorn, Amariah's heart seemed to skip a beat.

"May I join you?"

"Sure, but my companionship may be dreary this evening."

Amariah took a sip of coffee. Anna's head drooped, her mouth was turned down, and the expression in Anna's eyes betrayed emotional strain. Amariah tried to draw the historian out.

"How is your work going? We've had little time to visit these past few weeks."

"I think Andrew ran a slave galley in a past life. The way he drives us--he might as well have a whip over our heads!"

"I never suspected you believe in reincarnation." Amariah kept her eyes trained on the other woman as she chopped the pudding into pieces.

"I can't say that I do. My friends explored past lives and discussed their findings with me. If I had any strong impressions I might be willing to investigate it further, but one thing holds me back."

"What's that?"

"I've had far too much misery in this life! Why would I want to discover I've been an ignored child or an abandoned lover in other lives as well? Rejection is too unpleasant to find out you've experienced it in other lifetimes as well as this one."

Amariah toyed with the custard, separating it from the bread flavored with cinnamon and nutmeg. "I sensed a great deal of unhappiness in you the first time we met."

Anna leaned back, assessing the nun. From the right side of her brain, a wellspring of emotion percolated to the surface. The dam of reticence broke and an overwhelming urge to confide in someone instinct told her could be trusted allowed the hurt, insecurity, and longing, to come tumbling out.

"My father harbors a lot of guilt over being related to Russian royalty. Nicholas and Alexandria were his aunt and uncle. My grandfather urged the Czar to change his ways but when it became apparent a revolution was close at hand, he secretly transported his wealth to France before the collapse of the ruling aristocracy. Instead of appreciating his father's foresight allowed them to escape exile in Siberia, my father feels guilty about living a life of luxury in Paris. I sometimes think he's trying to atone for the sins of the Czar."

"But that's foolish!" Amariah's spoon stopped halfway to her mouth. She put the pudding back in the bowl, her appetite gone. "None of us can be responsible for the stupidity or brilliance of our ancestors. I certainly can't take pride in the fact my great-great-uncle rounded the Cape of Good Hope. I may have a few adventuring genes on my DNA spiral, but the loss of half his crew in his endeavor is not my burden."

Anna's expression was still bleak. "The best psychiatrists in Europe have been telling my father the same thing for years. He seems driven to punish himself for something which took place two generations ago. He seems consumed with guilt—but I can't figure out why."

"From what I understand, the eastern philosophy of karma warns of reaping the pain of negative actions in a lifetime to come. Anna," Amariah engaged the other woman with an open, frank expression, "has your father made a lot of money?"

"Oh yes, he took my grandfather's fortune and tripled it several times over. It seems every investment returns to him ten-fold."

"Some people are ashamed of wealth. Part of their psyche feels unworthy to be the recipient of good fortune. Unconsciously, they don't feel right about enjoying the bounty of life."

Anna reached for her cigarette case as a reflex action. "A privileged life has been a burden to me. I always felt guilty about not struggling like other students, but I could never participate in the carefree life of the jet-set crowd either. So, I remained in school, gathering degree after degree."

Amariah studied the cup. "Doing penance? The classroom might have been your private hell. Professors wield the power of life and death in that environment and seldom grant favors--even to the rich. You had to earn your degrees, didn't you? Was it the one thing that could only be purchased by your effort?"

"Merciful God," the ripple of reality transformed Anna's expression from one of confusion to understanding. "Sister, you have put into focus a muddy past. My father's wealth paid for my apartment and provided my living expenses. He spent thousands of dollars on tuition, but I wrote my thesis, I earned each of my degrees by the sweat of my brow!"

"Perhaps you were trying to send him a message."

"Our communication was usually limited to the sums in my bank account."

"Maybe you were trying to tell him you could earn your own way in life."

"That's an interesting thought." Anna began to toy with the layer of paint at the edge of a manicured fingernail. "Amariah . . . this has been an enlightening discussion. Since we're talking, and you seem to possess such profound insight, perhaps I could ask another question?"

Luminous eyes enhanced by eyeliner and shadow emphasized the woman's emotional pain.

"I don't have any real wisdom, I listened to my father's lectures all my life."

"You have differences of opinion with your father?"

Amariah laughed, "There were times my mother threatened to call the United Nations to negotiate a peace treaty. He bitterly opposed my becoming a nun."

"At least you knew he cared about what you did with your life. The only demonstration of concern I received from my father was his signature on the bottom of a check." Her gaze settled on the table's Formica surface. "Offer me an opinion about this dilemma." Anna traced a pattern in the liquid left by the coffee cup with the tip of her finger. "Why is it I fixate on unavailable men? I'll be frank--if a man isn't married I don't find him attractive."

Now it was Amariah's turn to study the table. What did her father always say about a woman's attraction to a married man? Did Anna want an honest response? Was she seeking a solution or was she making conversation? "It seems as if you're following a pattern established very early in life."

"A pattern?"

"Yes. Your father was emotionally unavailable so subconsciously you selected men who either couldn't or wouldn't commit to you. Whether we realize it or not we follow patterns inputted into our psyche from birth."

Anna was choking on her emotions, like a drowning woman, and she gasped for air. "I guess a priest would be ultimately unavailable, wouldn't he?"

Her anguish crashed against Amariah with the force of an explosion. The frustration and bitterness of a barren emotional life engulfed Anna--she was suffocated by sorrow. Reaching across the table, Amariah laid her hand on top of frigid manicured finger; tension constricted the flow of warming blood. "I suspected your feelings about Father Simson ran deep."

"Is it obvious?"

"I've been taught to observe people since I was a little girl." Amariah's voice was filled with sympathy.

"So," Anna engaged Amariah with a forthright stare, "what am I to do?"

"Recognition of a problem is the first step. Acceptance of the situation and a desire to change is the solution."

"Like an alcoholic?"

"Yes. Each of us has our own weaknesses. Coming to terms with them is difficult."

"Sister, you seem so self-assured, so confident, you must not have any problems."

Amariah took a sip of luke-warm coffee, but the temperature went unnoticed. "I'm as insecure as anyone else. I know I have traits that need changing."

"Like what?" Anna tipped her head closer, she couldn't imagine the nun possessing any weakness.

"My passion about what I believe makes others feel insecure."

"You rendered everyone speechless in the staff meeting and reduced Duncan Davis to mortal status after challenging his lack of belief the other day."

"I didn't mean to do that! Duncan treasured his viewpoint--it's what makes him feel important. Because my beliefs rest comfortably on my shoulders does not mean others are prepared to carry the same burden."

"Andrew would oppose such sentiment."

Amariah studied the bowl, the pudding now soggy, its contents stirred beyond recognition. "He makes me feel uncomfortable most of the time."

"Andrew makes everyone uncomfortable. It's part of his charm. He glowers with righteous indignation, he parades spiritual vengeance with the zeal of a newly come Elijah!"

"He's convinced he has a special purpose."

"Even those of us who lack your training sense it."

"Anna," Amariah's voice was flat; it was difficult to voice her growing concern. "Sometimes I wonder about his motives. On the surface, his plan seems noble but I'm beginning to wonder about his true intent."

The coffee cup stopped mid-way to her lips. "As a historian, I've studied the character traits of world leaders. They all share a common thread. Leaders tend to possess a gift of genius which can tread close to madness. Perhaps that's the quality which lifts a man above the commonplace. The person, who convinces others to follow, must have a powerful personality. They seem to radiate a sense of personal destiny."

"The Father General certainly fits the profile."

Drawing a scarlet tipped nail across the table, Anna studied the nun. "Sister, since we're being candid, I've another secret to confess. I can't say why I feel moved to reveal it because I haven't told anyone else about what I overheard."

"Oh?" The fear in the other woman's expression aroused Amariah's curiosity.

"Have you heard about the 'forty-four'?"

Amariah shook her head. "I don't think so."

"I happened to be waiting to see the Father General last week. Sister Josephina stepped into the copy room and Andrew's office door was ajar." The manicured hand waved through the air. "I sound like a silly schoolgirl with a crush, but I edged close enough to hear what was being said yet stayed far enough away to make it look like I was admiring the garden if Sister Josephina returned. What I overheard has had me in turmoil ever since."

A frown creased her brow and the lines of worry webbing her eyes deepened as Amariah spoke. "When did this happen?"

"Yesterday. I haven't been able to get Andrew's conversation out of my head."

"What you overheard had something to do with forty-four? Forty- four what?"

"Andrew has a select group of Jesuits scattered throughout the world who are carrying out his political ambitions."

"That sounds somewhat Machiavellian!"

"Sister, I fear it is." Anna Romanov's expression conveyed sincerity. "From what I gathered, the Father General has forty-four men acting as advisors to rebellious political factions."

Amariah wrapped her fingers around the cold cup to disguise the tremor controlling her hand. "Perhaps you misinterpreted what Father Simson said."

Anna's eyes flashed left, level with her ear; the heiress was drawing on the memory of what she'd heard. "He said . . .' my men are all in place. Now it begins. Lines of influence have been laid, like the foundation of the museum. Russia. Angola. Mexico. Central America'." When her gaze returned to Amariah's face, Anna's eyes were glazed with apprehension. "There's even a priest who brokers influence for the Father General in America. Amariah, it wasn't so much what he said as how he said it! His tone of voice was so cold, so emotionless, like a moving glacier, its momentum crushing everything in its path."

"Anna, I don't think you overheard anything out of the ordinary. The Jesuit Order has members in every corner of the world. I can't tell you I like Andrew Simson, but I don't believe a man, who has dedicated his life to the Church, has intentions other than the spread of Christianity."

The metal disc on top of the building that housed the Vatican radio station began to move. Slowly, it followed a predetermined arc until it faced east. The dish tilted, its beacon pointing at an orbiting communications satellite. A static hum filled the garden as the technicians in the building below the disc began to transmit.

An ocean away, Father Walton Mendez twisted the dials on his radio. Checking his watch, he waited for the message from Rome to interrupt crackling, snapping sounds which smothered noise from the plaza. Men and material reached Cintalapa several days ago. The dead were buried—the injured evacuated to Cancun by helicopter. The task of rebuilding would begin as soon as roads were cleared.

Rubbing his eyes, the priest stared at his only means of communication with the men who offered guidance and direction. As he waited for the radio to come to life, Father Mendez concentrated on the many things which still needed to be accomplished. Clearing the well was most important. Everyone in the village had been living off what they collected from leaves in the jungle and what could be gathered in pots during afternoon showers.

Father Mendez knew the power of focused thought. The Father General taught him how to maintain mental discipline under trying circumstances. A smile tugged at the corners of a kind-hearted, generous mouth. How well they'd been trained! Concentrate on success . . . never let failure enter your mind . . . success . . . always success!

A sound from the radio drew his gaze away from a flattened market stand in front of the church. He reached for the handset, ready to transmit. A voice he knew well floated from the metal box. "IL-19. Come in. IL-19, this is Center. Come in."

Father Mendez depressed the button with his thumb. "Center, this is IL-19. Over."

"Situation report." The voice commanded, it didn't request.

"Medical supplies reached us by helicopter. The dead have been laid to rest, the wounded evacuated."

"Damage estimate." Clipped, the voice spit words in a military tone.

"Destruction total. The only thing left standing in Cintalapa is the rectory and north tower of the church."

"Road condition."

"Severe damage to both north and south access. It will take a week to reach Tenhuantepec, perhaps longer to get to Minatital."

"Supply lines south must be reestablished. Our brother in Nicaragua is expecting a major effort soon. Once material reaches the Salvadorian border, Father Bagaces will see it reaches the right hands."

"Understood. Is Guatemala secure?"

"As much as it can be."

"I will begin work on the roads tomorrow. With only a few able--bodied men it may be slow going."

"Make it one of your first priorities."

"It will be."

"Clear the airstrip for transport planes before you do anything else. You will begin to receive aid from the Catholic Relief Foundation shortly."

"What kind of aid?"

"Blankets, clothing, food. The Foundation is mobilizing rapidly and will reach you in a matter of days. Red Cross wanted to provide more aid, but we advised them the Church has the situation well in hand."

"Those things are badly needed but of more importance is the manpower to help rebuild homes, schools and roads."

"It would be best to do without intervention. We do not want your influence among the people weakened."

Father Mendez stared at the hand clutching the microphone. His fingers were cut, and blisters worn searching for the dead left his palms sore and bleeding. The cassock he wore was begrimed with mud and blood--he had not changed since the first shockwave jolted Cintalapa. Somewhere along the way, his stole and maniple were lost, and he was forced to bury the dead without the benefit of proper ritual. The thatch of dark, curly hair went uncombed, and dust turned him gray. Yet the earthquake thrust him into a position of authority which might have taken a generation to earn under normal conditions.

He was so preoccupied with the tragic results of the devastation he hadn't considered potential political ramifications; the dawn of awakening overtook the horror of the past few days in an intuitive blaze. Walton Mendez understood. These were simple people, they would return his care with undivided loyalty. The earthquake provided him with an avenue of leadership which would never be disputed. God moved in mysterious ways. A few months from now, he would be firmly established as the benevolent father figure in Cintalapa . . . the gateway to Central America.

"Serendipity, haven't you ever heard of the effect?"

"Klaus, you never cease to amaze me. I come to you with a piece of information I can hardly believe, and you engage in a game of verbal Scrabble!"

Leon gestured at the German with a sheaf of notes clutched in his fist.

"Serendipity means the faculty of finding valuable or agreeable things not sought for. In this case, neither one of us expected to find this."

Throwing himself in the chair across the desk from the art restoration expert, Leon tossed the yellow papers at Klaus. "You said you knew a word or two of Hindi. How much did you make out of the scroll you gave me to translate?"

"I got as far as the name. That's when I decided to involve you."

"Then you don't know what I've been working on?"

Von Friendberg reached for his pipe. After a few moments of tamping and toying, the smell of apples mixed with sulfur filled the air as smoke drifted toward the ventilation screen. His hand whipped back and forth to extinguish the match. "The name was enough to alarm me. I knew I needed the help of an expert." Dropping the match into the ashtray, he reached for Leon's notes. "You kept this secret, I trust."

"We'll decide what to do once you read what the scroll contains. I'm still so shocked my decision-making capabilities aren't working at full capacity."

Spreading the notes across his desk, Klaus adjusted his glasses and clamped his teeth around the pipe. A cloud of smoke bellowing from the bowl cast a veil over his expression. His eyes scanned hand-written lines on yellow sheets of paper. "Are you quite certain of this translation?"

"My friend, I have access to practically every word of every written language in the entire world. If there is a phrase that's been mistranslated, it's only because no record was ever left behind. Every line on those pages is absolutely accurate."

Von Friendberg returned a worried glance to the papers lying beneath his hand. The pipe hung limp in his mouth, the tobacco ignored. Klaus began to read in an oddly raspy voice, uncharacteristic emotion forced elongated spaces in his words, as if he sought objectivity which remained elusive.

'There passed among us a woman called Amariah and with her was the boy-child who will assume the role of the new Messiah. Their stay was for many phases of the moon, and the boy came of age amongst us. He learned our ways. Our wise men taught him to heal; to read the contents of another's thoughts; to ease pain and offer comfort. The boy was truly gifted. As for the woman, his teacher, it was her second journey to our land. When she returned it was with this special a young man. A woman of power, of much learning, her talents paled like the moon before the sun when compared to the new teacher of the ages. The cycle of life

continues like a prayer wheel turning before the wind. Always, the return, always reaping the harvest of seeds sown in another season. This new Messiah will light the light within the hearts of those who suffer'.

Klaus leaned back in the chair and busied himself relighting the pipe. "If this document is taken at face value, instead of being rationalized away as mere coincidence, the message certainly points to the writer's belief in the cycle of rebirth. You realize the subject is forbidden in Christianity."

"I always thought reincarnation was a machination of the Oriental mind. "Leon pointed to the yellow sheets of paper, "but finding the name 'Amariah' in the scroll caught me off guard. You're right--it's probably a case of serendipity. Amariah told me her mother named her after the heroine in a novel. The Aramaic translation means 'Promised by God', so the Benedictine sisters allowed her to keep the earthly name when she took her vows. Something I would like to explore deeper is the possibility Jesus spent his so called 'lost years' in Egypt and the Orient. As far as I know, there's no hard evidence regarding the events of his childhood. The Bible chronicles his birth, there is a brief mention of an event, which took place in the Jerusalem temple when he was twelve, and then no record of his life until he began to preach at the age of thirty."

"Biblical scholars will tell you it was traditional for a young man to carry on his father's trade."

"The essence of Jesus' message challenged tradition! I don't think it's beyond the realm of possibility to think he might have studied in the Egyptian mystery schools—they were still active when he was young." The prospect of discovery made Leon anxious; he rubbed the bridge of his nose while troublesome thoughts receded--making room for wonder.

". . . With a woman called Amariah." Klaus stared at the yellow papers, the name flashed at him like a neon light.

"It could be coincidence, like you said." Leaning forward to gather up his notes, Leon examined his friend. "The name is probably one of those quirky things that just happens."

Klaus studied the younger man. As a companion of age, Klaus experienced a burning desire to probe the mysterious, to wrest an explanation from the imponderables of life. "I wonder if it really is coincidence. I'm beginning to wonder a great many things . . . especially about a woman called Amariah."

CHAPTER EIGHT

"Here . . . dig where this tunnel ends." Amariah pointed down a passageway cloaked in darkness.

"But Sister." The workman began to protest but was silenced by a glance from the foreman.

Waving, the man in charge of the excavation crew motioned construction lamps closer. The generators used to power tungsten-filtered lamps were cumbersome and the tunnel's rough floor made moving them awkward.

When the generators coughed to life a cloud of diesel belched into the confined corridor. Amariah waved at noxious fumes as the lamps flooded the tunnel with yellow light.

Mendicant Prabhupada pressed closer to Amariah. "Sister, are you certain of your feelings?"

Amariah peered down the tunnel's length, straining to see beyond where it disappeared into yawing blackness. "Father, I've never been more certain of anything in my life."

A bow bespoke the gentle mannerisms of his East Indian upbringing. "In my country, feelings are highly respected. Indian culture has practiced mental arts for generations. We understand the mind acquires information in many ways. If you feel certain, it is with good reason."

Amariah had to convince Father Simson to extend the excavations north and south, following the layout of St. Peter's transepts. The cross assumed tremendous importance by the time Constantine made Christianity the official religion of the Roman Empire. Part of her argument was early Christians would have connected gravesites in the shape of a cross because of its spiritual significance.

"Sister, I got here as soon as I could. I wanted to be with you when workers broke through the wall regardless of how I hate being in these wretched corridors!" Anna fished in her purse and withdrew a handkerchief, which she flapped in front of her face. "These fumes are awful! Can't somebody get a fan down here?" Her look was so accusing the foreman blanched.

"I don't think they've had time to move all their equipment to this level yet." Amariah sounded apologetic as she tried to explain the reason for the smell.

"Rubbish! These men should have everything in place. Your guidance has been uncanny since you convinced Andrew to continue excavating. There are times your self-deprecating manner is frustrating to someone who's truly insecure!" Anna lit a cigarette and smoke cast a hazy filter down the length of the tunnel.

"I think I've hit a hollow spot!" A workman turned, his eyes squinted against the brightness.

"Hold up! Don't strike another blow." Taking the hammer and chisel the foreman tapped the tool up and down mortared bricks listening for a change in pitch. "The wall thins here," his hand moved in an oval, "A few hammer blows will crumble this section."

He placed the chisel point in the center of a scored area. Powerful strikes created a fissure which traced an erratic path to the floor. Metal clashing against brick reverberated down the tunnel. With one last strike, the chisel and foreman's hand disappeared.

"It's hollow!" His face pressed against the opening, the foreman motioned the crew of laborers to inch the lights closer. "Sister, come here!"

Amariah rushed forward propelled by an excitement which made her heart feel as if it were going to burst the bondage of her ribs. She thrust her face into the opening and glanced back at the foreman, "How long will it take you to break an opening big enough for me to get through?"

"Stand back, Sister. I can do it with three strikes." Years of experience in the marble quarries of northern Italy taught him to begin with the new fissure. Quick blows, lightning fast, reduced the wall to a pile of rubble.

Amariah couldn't believe the sight that met her eyes. A network of tunnels stretched beyond the false wall. Every burial chamber appeared undisturbed and looked as though they might be more elaborate than the ones the team just finished excavating. Marble copings bearing the inscription of Greek and Roman names rested above the physical remains of their owners. Amariah stepped over the rubble, compelled into a vortex drawing her back through time. Knowing she was the first to walk between these rows of mausoleums since frightened Christians tried to escape the wrath of their Roman oppressors,

Amariah was humbled. The flashlight in her hand swept a curved swath of light across the marble crypts. *Marcus Quintarius, Thaddius Linvaul, Octavian the Decturian.* These names lingered at the edge of consciousness. Names that made her feel as if she should be able to recall their owner's faces! An inexplicable force charged the air. Amariah felt as if the bodies in those ancient tombs were calling to her--drawing her into a world she didn't understand.

Andrew Simson inserted the key in his desk drawer and yanked it open. Satisfied the object from vault seventeen still rested amid a litter of pencils and paper clips, he eased the drawer closed. Impulse made him open it again and he reached to withdraw the coin from its protective box. It had become a habit of late to rub his fingers along the raised outline of the tree or the crossed swords on the opposite side when he was thinking through a problem. In a vague way, he felt comforted as he caressed the coin. Stormy, chaotic thoughts, ideas which refused to focus, coalesced when he rubbed the coin. What mysterious message did the symbols convey? The work of an artist, tree roots intertwined with cabalistic glyphs. Branches reached overhead toward the sun, a star containing the thirteen mystical points of initiation and a waning moon. Swords on the opposite side always drew his attention. Locked in eternal combat, their wide blades were inscribed with curious symbols. Above these *sica*, short, curved swords, the face of an angry sun scowled out of radiant beams of light. The Egyptian symbol for eternity rested behind the swords and a lizard appeared desperate to flee from the field of conflict. One thing was certain, he was attracted to the coin with a passion he couldn't explain.

At a tap on the door, Simson returned the coin to its customary resting place. Locking the drawer, he called out. "Come in!"

Father Laterano slipped inside the Father General's office and closed the door behind him. "Father, I brought the documents you requested."

"Good. They will provide me with interesting reading. I only wish my knowledge of Greek were as strong as my Latin. Had I Sister Amariah's talents, I might have undertaken this section of the project myself."

"While I do not dispute the nun's ability, think what the world would have missed had you chosen a life of obscurity as a simple scholar! We are at the dawn of a new era--an era made possible by your leadership."

The Father General's appraising glance studied the other priest. One day, Philipe Laterano would lead the forty-four. The youthful Jesuit was his shining star--the one who would follow in his footsteps. "I want to show you something." He pointed to a tattered piece of leather. "According to what I've deciphered from this scroll, it was copied from a much older document written in Greek. The original scroll's journey from Judea is fascinating. Why it was moved from its original place of authorship to an obscure Benedictine monastery in Rumania, close to the Yugoslavian border, remains shrouded in mystery. What we do know is this manuscript surfaced at the beginning of the second century. To escape the barbarian hordes sweeping down out of the steppes, monks rushed their entire library to Monte Cassino, a newly established headquarters of their Order. As you can see," he lifted another piece of soiled, creased paper, "we are also in possession of a copy of a scroll brought from Ethiopia by a priest named Cosma de Koros. He was the first European to translate Coptic into Latin. Here," he thrust a document at Laterano, "tell me what you make of this."

Reaching into the breast pocket of his cassock, Father Laterano withdrew reading glasses. Adjusting them several times, his eyes traveled the lines of faded ink.

Andrew Simson watched with satisfaction as color drained from Laterano's face. The hand holding the fragile piece of parchment began to tremble. Finally, the priest removed his glasses and whispered through stiff lips. "My memory for Latin must be fading. I can hardly believe what this says."

"I'm certain it's accurate."

"Tradition would lead us to believe Jesus remained in Nazareth with his father. It would have been highly unusual for a son to leave an apprenticeship with his father." His voice failed. Clearing his throat, the priest tried again. "I cannot believe the Messiah was entrusted to the care of a . . ." the word refused to take shape on his lips.

Dropping his feet from the desk, the Father General stalked to the window, graying shadows of twilight turning his visage stony. "You can't believe a boy of twelve could possibly have studied in the Egyptian mystery schools in the company of a woman?" A caustic laugh crashed against the walls. "And what's more, my Jesuit brother, you cannot accept the enormity of the name? Have I judged your thoughts correctly?"

"How long have you known about this?" Trembling hands refused to still and Father Laterano buried them in the folds of his cassock.

"When I began my search for a language expert, Sister Amariah's name leaped from the list of candidates."

"Coincidence." Laterano's mind fought to come to terms with what he just read.

"Coincidence, perhaps, but look at this." Simson shoved another fragment of parchment in the bewildered priest's direction.

Laterano's gaze finally lifted. Shock, fear, horror--rippled across his expression like the wake of a boat passing through still water. "I can't believe this!"

"Believe it! I traced the message all the way back through the original records of the Council of Nicea. With this single statement, the bishops separated Christianity from the rest of the world's great religions."

Father Laterano's eyes jerked across the parchment as he scanned the words again.

'Let him who should embrace the doctrine of the subsequent wonderful return of the soul to earth, again and again, let him be called an anathema.'

"With that simple statement, the concept of reincarnation was stricken from official theology of the Christian Church. All reference to the subject was taken out of the compilation of texts we think of as the Bible. Reincarnation was a commonly accepted doctrine throughout the early Church and perceived as an anathema by those first bishops." The Father General returned to his chair and lowered himself slowly, deliberately. With amusement, he watched as the face of the man seated at the other side of his desk lost its hostility and embraced confusion.

"There's more to what you're telling me, isn't there?"

"I thought you would make the connection by now." His fingers steepled over the crucifix on his chest as he waited for Philipe to collect his thoughts.

"Father, do you accept the doctrine of reincarnation?"

"The literal translation of the word reincarnation from the Greek means 'to live again'. The literal translation of the word resurrection from ancient Greek means 'to live again'. Does the soul enter a new body—or die with the old one?"

"You're giving me an option--should I choose to exercise it."

A smile peeled away from strong, white teeth. "You know me too well."

The look in Andrew Simson's eyes was one Philipe would never forget. The Father General knew something the rest of the world did not. He had the capacity to understand theology on a far deeper level than most people. Slowly, prior information imparted by the leader of the Jesuit Order surfaced from embedded memory. Random comments replayed through his mind, turning his emotions to quicksand.

'The girl speaks ancient languages like she lived in the past.'
'The nun possesses an understanding of history, which defies conventional knowledge.'
'Leave Sister Amariah alone, she knows the layout of the catacombs."
'Her grasp of how the early Christians lived and worshipped is beyond our comprehension.'

The smile tipping the corners of the Father General's mouth was tinged with a mixture of amusement and scorn. He was reliving the dilemma faced by the fifteenth-century popes as they grappled with how to handle the scientific discoveries of Galileo and Copernicus. No one in pursuit of salvation dared question sacred writings. For two thousand years Christians were taught mankind had only one opportunity to live a life worthy enough to enter heaven. Galileo proved the Bible wrong. The sun did not revolve around the earth. Andrew Simson was in possession of equally revolutionary information--the soul returned to earth--perhaps countless times!

The laughter which filled the Father General's office was as cold and unyielding as the graves of martyred Christians. "So, my dear brother, how do we inform millions of faithful Christians the beliefs of other religions are correct, and this information was withheld from them for the past fifteen hundred years? The energy force of the soul reenters the earth plane in another body—perhaps countless times."

"Father Norton? Brian Newcome . . . BBC."

A tall man extended his hand toward the dark-haired priest. He'd heard the Jesuit spent a lot of time in the desert, confirmed by the skin on his nose and forehead which was peeling, the result of many hours in the sun. Bronzed skin framed eyes as clear and blue as the waters of the Mediterranean. "I came as soon as I got your message."

"Yes," the priest smiled, but it was not a warm, welcoming smile; it was a smile of intent. "I'm pleased you decided to take me up on the invitation to come to Lebanon. Others in the press corps did not."

Glancing around a shabby airport lined with crates serving as counters for customs agents, who queried arriving and departing passengers, the newscaster met the stare of young men with dark, angry eyes holding rifles against their chests. He blanched at the hatred smoldering in every expression. "I'm a little nervous, it's always open season on journalists in an Arab nation. I'm a chap with little heart for adventure."

The British journalist cast a sidelong glance at the priest who strode through the airport undaunted by murderous looks hurled in his direction. "I've friends in government who assured me if anyone could make this rag-tag lot of desert nomads behave it was the Jesuit, Robert Norton."

"Effusive praise is seldom deserved." The priest acknowledged the salute of a soldier as they passed. "When you learn to appreciate their cultural values, the Arabs are a tolerable lot. They're like children, argumentative, hostile, and greedy. But according to their code, most are men of honor. The man I'm taking you to see, Malek, is a character straight out of the Bible. He's fascinating when you get to know him. There are times I think I'm talking to Abraham, Moses, or Mohammed. The desert is a cruel environment, and it bred a race of harsh men. Their culture is based on survival of the fittest--the weak and sick soon die. Those who are feeble cannot survive the sun, the lifeless conditions of an arid land, and the bitterness of the wind. To understand, you must live in the tents of the Arab, ride their camels, eat their food. Perhaps then, you are fit to pass judgment on their traditions."

The weight of his suitcase and tape recorder made it difficult to keep pace with the priest's rapid stride; Newcome was so enthralled with the conversation he didn't want to miss a single word. "You admire these people?"

"I've learned to. You see, the West's problem is we think we are right about everything, so we refuse to consider another point of view. If a culture does not meet our technological or ideological standards we write it off as an unworthy of the effort to understand. These people may be living under primitive conditions but who's to say that's bad? They don't have to worry about over-crowding in the cities nor the destructive behavior of rebellious adolescents. Their children won't die in automobile accidents, nor will they succumb to the evils of alcohol and drugs. Racial conflict doesn't exist because if you profess a belief in Allah then you're automatically accepted. Skin color doesn't matter when you worship the one true God."

They reached the outer doors and stepped into the blast furnace of the sun. Shielding his eyes, the reporter scanned the landscape. Beirut bore deep scars of political unrest. Bombed out buildings stood against the horizon like blackened effigies--stark reminders of troubled times. The number of armed soldiers milling around raised the hair on the back of Newcome's neck.

Waving down a beat-up taxi, the priest stepped off a broken curb. "We'll take this journey in several stages. I promised Malek his desert hiding place would remain secure."

"I intend to play by your rules." The journalist loosened his tie and unbuttoned the shirt collar. Heat was growing oppressive, and the temperature was going to soar as the sun rose higher.

Noticing the journalist's discomfort, Father Norton tried not to laugh. "I hope you brought light weight clothing. Where we're going will be hotter than this."

Paul Grant stifled a yawn. Sir Duncan Davis was going on at length about the reason people need religion. He flicked a piece of worrisome lint from the jacket he'd just purchased in one of the delightful shops near the Spanish Steps. Coming to the Vatican achieved wonders for his wardrobe. Despite the boredom of being trapped in gab sessions like this one, the job had not turned out to be all that disagreeable. As the museum began to take shape, his area of expertise was called upon more frequently. It was surprising to find the Father General provided him with more up-to-date equipment than he left behind at MIT. And this project was going to look impressive on his resume when he applied for a job with IBM, Apple or maybe even Microsoft. Paul Grant figured he could write his own ticket when he returned home. He suddenly realized Duncan Davis was speaking to him and he swung his head in the other man's direction.

"Grant, you're an educated, intelligent man. Why do you think people need religion?"

"Frankly, Duncan, I've never thought about it. I don't go to church now and when I was a child the subject was seldom discussed. Religion was never important."

Apparently, he was not going to inspire argumentative conversation with the engineer, so Duncan addressed the art expert. "Jon Pierre, give us your thoughts."

"It boils down to the human need to belong. From the time man drew erect, he hunted the savannas in packs--clinging together for survival. Women tended community hearths and saw to the welfare of all children assuring survival of our species. We long for companionship and the need to belong to a group, a tribe if you will, is a large part of our psychological make- up. Man is, after all, a complex social animal."

"Agreed!" Davis loved to debate, and it looked like he'd found a willing partner in LaPointe.

"But it goes beyond that. People are afraid of the unknown. If any theology earned my support, it would be a dualistic concept--like the Zoroastrian or Manichean sects practiced. That is, a good spirit and an evil spirit battling for supremacy over control of man's soul," Jon Pierre added.

"Did you know Christianity is a redress of the Manichean philosophy? Nature and history do not agree with the human concept of good and bad. Rather, both nature and the passage of time define good as that which survives, and bad as that which surrenders. The universe is impartial; it has no prejudice in favor of Christ and an equal amount of indifference toward Hitler! Religion offers man a degree of comfort to face what they didn't understand. We seek others who believe as we do, think as we do, act as we do. We're all looking for moral justification." Duncan's glance took in the others, satisfied his point was being considered.

"Isn't that what culture's all about?" Paul Grant began to take an interest in the conversation. Duncan had a passionate way about him--the knack of drawing out everyone's most soul-searching thoughts.

"Of course!" Sir Davis slapped his thigh. "We cling together to prove our 'all-rightness' to ourselves and each other. We've developed inflexible rules for the game of human survival. We must live in the 'right' section of town, our children must go to the 'right' schools, our wives must belong to the 'right' bridge club, and it's helpful if we attend the 'right' church and pay our dues to the 'right' country club. Right, of course, depends on which area of town you happen to live in!"

"I never thought of it that way before." Grant glanced at the trousers it took him hours to select with a degree of self-consciousness. He remembered wondering, as he'd studied himself in the mirror, if they would look 'right' with the jacket he intended to purchase. He had to admit there was an element of truth in what Sir Duncan was saying. He attended the 'right' school . . . selected a field of study which was the most up and coming. He'd even gone so far as to date girls from the 'right' sorority. His wife's bloodlines stretched all the way back to the Revolutionary War. Abruptly, the engineer decided it was time for him to leave--he didn't like the direction his thoughts were taking. He'd spent a lot of time, money and effort getting where he wanted to be. It was right for him and that was all that mattered. "Well, gentlemen, this has been enlightening--as always--but I have an appointment at the lab. A Japanese computer firm wants to sell the Father General some equipment and I've got to analyze the bid before I make a recommendation." Touching his finger to his brow, Grant saluted the other men.

"I think I struck a nerve." Sir Davis watched Grant sander through the cafeteria's double doors.

"It would seem you have." LaPointe studied the American engineer as he strolled down the hallway.

Drifting back to his subject, Davis turned a questioning eye toward LaPointe. "Do you know the character traits of an obsessive personality?"

"Good lord no! That's not my field. Do you know the amount of pigment the Renaissance masters used in their paint?"

"Touché, my friend, touché! I had a conversation with Simson which left me feeling perplexed."

"Oh?" LaPointe sipped coffee from his cup and made a sour face. It suddenly seemed bitter.

"I've spent the better part of my life studying human behavior and the need we have for religion, but there's a quality about him that bothers me."

"He's a fanatic. As a child, I remember seeing Hitler's troops march through Paris. Although I was too young to remember much else about Nazi soldiers there was a look in their eyes I can recall to this day. Maybe it was superiority--they were so sure of themselves, so certain they were smarter, better, physically peerless--you could see it in their body language. They acted as though they were empowered with special abilities because Hitler personally chose them. Their importance promised to transcend mortality."

"A messianic complex?"

"That might be an appropriate term."

"Simson thinks he's something special--do you think he is?"

"The man has a rare combination of qualities. Certainly, he can convince others of the importance of what he's doing. Look at us! All of us are here working like madmen. He's got the unique quantitative factor of personal charm, brilliance, and leadership. With those characteristics, the weak are obliged to follow. I think he has hypnotic power over lesser men."

"Like Hitler?"

"And Alexander the Great, Napoleon, FDR, and practically every other leader throughout history! I'd wager a week's work even the likes of

Genghis Khan could exhort ordinary men to follow his dreams of glory."

"Perhaps that's what I find so disquieting about him." Davis lifted his glasses and began to rub an irritated area on the bridge of his nose. "I don't believe a word of his religious rubbish and yet I devote long hours to this project. I'm a reasonable, intelligent man--but I follow the Father General like a piece of flotsam trapped in the wake of a boat. I seem powerless to stop what I consciously consider an irrational activity!" The rubbing stopped, and his eyes focused on the French art expert. "Makes stimulating conversation though, doesn't it?"

"The entire world is going to be discussing the Father General soon. I suspect he's going to impact society more than any of us presently realize. I'll bet a lot of us become slaves to his directives. What's even more frightening--I'm afraid we'll do so willingly!"

"Gentlemen, welcome to the home of an Arab sheik." Malek bowed low and swept his hand toward the pile of cushions in the middle of the tent. His robe swirled around leather boots scuffed from walking across terrain so forbidding it scared the souls of those who dared call it home.

Brian Newcome glanced around the tent. Thick goat-hair felt offered a surprising amount of shelter from sweltering heat. Taking his cue from the priest, Newcome sat on a cushion and laid his tape recorder nearby. Malek and the priest were chatting in Arabic and Brian allowed his natural curiosity to record the details of the people and surroundings.

This Arab was probably wealthy by a nomad's standards because his encampment spread clear across the sandy wadi protected by ridges of bleak, dun colored limestone. If he had to hazard a guess, Newcome thought at least a thousand villagers dwelled in this sea of tents. A permanent well was built around a meager spring, and in the distance, he'd noticed several large herds of grazing goats. A beat-up brass kettle rested over the coals of a fire in the center of the tent, but oddly enough, it didn't seem to contribute much heat to the enclosure. Perhaps it was too hot to matter.

The conversation switched to English and Newcome turned his attention to the men lounging against plump, goat-hair filled cushions.

"My Christian brother tells me you can be counted on to report our situation fairly."

Brian nodded. "Father Norton told me many things about you. He says you are an honorable man."

Dipping his head in acknowledgment of the praise, Malek chose his words with care. "The wealth of American Jews darkens the picture of us painted by the press. We are portrayed as barbarians, troublemakers, religious fanatics. My Jesuit friend," he patted the hem of the priest's cassock, "tells me the great holy man in Rome would like to see all this changed."

"Are you referring to the Pope?" Brian's brows knitted, he seldom paid attention to the comings and goings of Roman clergy.

Father Norton intervened. "Malek is speaking of the Jesuit Father General. Andrew Simson has assumed many of the Pope's responsibilities of late. Unfortunately, Pope Anastasius is dying of terminal cancer."

"Oh yes, I remember now. He's the chap in charge of the new museum at the Vatican, right?"

"That's the achievement for which he's received the most recognition, but Father Simson has other inspiring qualities, which will bring about world peace."

Brian Newcome had covered news stories all over the globe. He was one of the few journalists to accompany rebel factions in Afghanistan as they fought against the Russians. He'd reported stories about Sinn Fein blood baths and Red Brigade slaughters. He'd seen the look in a man's eyes when he was caught up in idealistic causes. The expression on the priest's face reminded him of the time he'd sat in a cell in Belfast with Sean O'Flannery. An hour with a cold-blooded killer blinded by fanatic belief produced the best article he'd ever written. But Brian promised himself he'd never get that close to a zealot again. Now, as he stared across the tent at the Catholic priest, he realized he was about to repeat the experience. A trickle of sweat rolled down the path between his shoulder blades.

"Newsman," Malek withdrew the kettle from the fire and poured boiling water into the three cups on a tray which had been placed close to his feet by a veiled woman, "what will you tell the world if I allow you to interview my people?"

"I can't honestly say. Other members of the press accuse me of being too emotional--but straight journalism never conveys what I feel. From experience, I've learned to take notes to make certain everyone's name is spelled correctly, then I sit back and observe. When I'm ready to write, I turn on my computer and stare at the screen. Words bubble up from an interior wellspring and my impressions are transformed into words to convey my experience. I'm sorry I can't tell you the content of my article, Malek, but I'm being honest. If you think I can't do your story justice, then I've come a long way for nothing."

The Arab passed cups to the priest and reporter. He appeared more concerned with sharing the hospitality of his tent than what Newcome said. Finally, cups accepted, he returned his attention to the sweating journalist. "Remember this, newsman, treat our desert kindly. Do not berate the sun, sand, or the lack of your green English beauty. Take care to paint a sympathetic picture of our world--wadis so alkaline they support no life, dunes which shift when the wind rises, mountains so cruel none can scale their summits. These things are all part of the Arab world. Make the English world respect our primitive way of life like Arabs respect dry lakes, which can take a man's life with ease. We cherish our world of umber, ocher, and gray as much as the English love their pastel country. Speak fairly of my people. Those who survive the brutality of the desert are not soft--our way of life does not allow a man to become fat or arrogant. Do not forget, English, we have lived by ourselves for centuries. Report this to your people: The feud between Arab and Jew goes back to the time of Abraham. Hagar and her son, Ishmael, were cast out of Abraham's tent by a jealous wife. This desperate woman was forced into an inhospitable land with a young son to care for. So, you see, newsman, the way of the Arab has always been hard. We are scorned by industrial powers because we're nomads living in tents. We've eked out a living on a land no one else wanted--only to have it taken away from us! English, there are reasons for our anger. Our sustenance is our belief in Allah, and his servant, the Prophet Mohammed. He alone cared about a scurrilous lot of desert dwellers. I will allow you to interview your compatriots--to determine they are not being mistreated or tortured. They may not like the heat or the goat meat--but then neither does the Arab! Remember my words . . . English, record them well."

Brian Newcome was moved, profoundly moved. There were more reasons for the regard the Jesuit had for the Arab leader than he'd suspected. Maybe a person had to live with the Arab to understand why they acted as they did. Maybe that was the basis of all greater understanding! Perhaps it was time to change how the rest of the world perceived the followers of Mohammed.

Newcome forgot about his horror of fanaticism. Peace, brotherhood, understanding; they'd just been hollow rhetoric until today. After a week with Robert Norton, Newcome realized his point of view had shifted. Somehow, the power of the Jesuit's personality softened his inherited prejudice about people of color. Maybe it was because he wanted to share the priest's faith in a better world.

Amariah held her breath and tried to slow the anxious beating of her heart. Pressed deep into shadow, she waited for the Swiss Guard to complete his rounds. A full moon would rise soon, so she would have to hurry across the courtyard. The skirt of her habit was clenched in one hand and the other cradled a small bag as she rushed toward the library entrance. Turning the knob, Amariah breathed a sigh of relief as the door swung open; caretakers had not yet sealed the library against technicians and scholars. Cautiously, she slipped inside and crossed the outer vestibule. Her hand reached forward, searching for the panel concealing the elevator from wandering tourists. As an oak veneer panel slid back, she tugged on the wire mesh gate. Slowly, cautiously, Amariah slid it open--hoping to avoid any sound to betray her presence to the people in the nearest research room.

As the elevator lowered through layers of earth to the deepest level of the catacombs, Amariah mentally reviewed the sketch of passageways drawn on a centuries-old map. She committed it to memory, afraid to risk taking the map from its hiding place in her apartment in case she was discovered in the tunnels below the library.

The elevator jolted to a stop. Deciding it might betray her presence if she left the elevator in the catacombs, she pushed the button to make it return to the library lobby. If all went well it wouldn't take long to find Adamus' cache of documents. Choosing not to dwell on what would happen if she were discovered, she lunged into the darkness.

Amariah groped the wall as she made her way deeper into the newly excavated catacombs. Algae formed a slimy film on an ancient retaining wall built with sun-hardened bricks. The joining mortar wept an accumulation of filth as old as the medieval fortress far above her.

Grateful she remembered to put fresh batteries in the lantern, Amariah swept the corridor ahead with an intruding slash of light. Ears straining, eyes searching, she struggled to remember faint lines sketched on a scrap of paper during the Dark Ages. Now that she was in the tunnel, Amariah found herself becoming disoriented. The reality of where she was and what she was doing hammered at her senses--making every drop of water sound like the footfalls of a predator, every whisper of air the breathing of unseen foe.

The echo of footsteps sounded from somewhere further down the tunnel. Amariah froze; the shiver that tracked the path of her spine plucked at a primeval cord of fear. She'd counted on no one else being in the newly discovered passageways so late at night. Fumbling for the switch, Amariah rushed to extinguish the lantern.

Voices were growing distinct. Running her hands along the wall, searching for an alcove deep enough to hide in, Amariah fought against the disgust threatening to overcome her as the slime and ooze of a thousand years slipped beneath her trembling fingers.

The voices were coming closer. A niche just wide enough to slip inside opened beneath her probing hand and Amariah pressed herself into a narrow antechamber. Reeking of mildew and mold, stagnant air assailed her nostrils. There was nowhere else to hide; and she dare not risk discovery.

Holding her breath, trying not to move, to dislodge anything to betray her presence, Amariah bit her lip to stifle the scream trying to rise in the back of her throat. A sewer rat's sludge coated hair slid across the top of her foot as an enormous rodent sniffed at her sandal. A hairless tail which followed the creature through abysmal, disgusting pools of sewage flowing beneath the city streets slithered across her toes. A resultant trail of slime caused frantic nerve endings to send a firestorm of messages to her brain. Instinct as primitive as the dawn of time warned Amariah not to push the rat away. A screech of alarm would alert the men coming down the tunnel. She could not, would not, betray the existence of a message left behind by a long- forgotten medieval monk.

She forced herself to think of other things--to keep her concentration focused on anything but the rat and the voices drawing closer. Adamus risked his life to trace the lines on a scrap of parchment. Amariah pressed her hand against her mouth—suppressing an urge to vomit as the rat's poking paws worked to pull her foot away from the sandal.

Think of something else! Anything! Amariah tried to turn her attention away from the rat's teeth gnawing on the sandal's leather sole.

Was Adamus sane? Or did he suffer from ecclesiastical madness, a disorder common among early Jesuits. His last words were pleading, their simple logic so convincing, Amariah had to trust the content. His fear reached her like a spotlight shed across a deep, dusky gloom. Adamus jeopardized his vocation and perhaps his life to hide a message the Church didn't want the world to discover.

The rat pulled its bloated body on top of her foot and stood on its hind feet. A front paw braced against her leg, it stretched to sniff at the rosary beads suspended from the strip of cord at her waist.

How was it possible to understand the thoughts, feelings and emotions of a priest who lived in the sixteenth century?

Concentrate! Concentrate on something--anything!

The wet, slobbering sound the rat made as it began to chew at the leather tassel on the end of her belt made Amariah sick.

Think!

She wanted to scream--to strike at paws toying with her rosary beads, making them sway back and forth; the rhythm causing her stomach lurch.

How was it possible to hold a scrap of parchment in her hand and know the depths of a dead priest's anguish? How? How? Yet the betrayed Jesuit reached across the centuries and compelled her to explore this passage beneath the Vatican.

Amariah forced herself to concentrate on Adamus; his words; his mission. She couldn't dwell on the long, yellow teeth which began to gnaw the cord holding her rosary beads together. She had to think about the Adamus, about the control he was exerting over her actions; the power transcending the grave; the force which compelled her into this dangerous situation.

Adamus was here--She could feel him!

Guiding . . . directing . . . providing her with the courage to keep silent--to resist feelings of repulsion and disgust the rat aroused.

The voices were now abreast of the alcove in which she was hiding. A beam of light forced aside deep shadows entombing the length of the tunnel. It crept across ancient bricks, over lines of decaying mortar. The light searched, it probed the corridor, it had the power to reveal her hidingplace.

As the voices and beam of light faded into the distance, Amariah allowed her breathing to deepen. Then she kicked the rat. A shriek of alarm bounced off the walls. Annoyed, but persistent, the rat returned to Amariah's foot--intent upon severing the leather tassel dangling from her rosary beads. Reaching the lantern switch with her thumb, Amariah pointed it at thesound of visceral gnawing. A blinding arc suddenly filled the alcove's dark interior. Wide yellow eyes hastened to narrow against the intrusion. Trapped in the brilliant incandescent glow, the rat pressed its sewage caked body further into the corner in a desperate effort to be rid of the menace.

Amariah inched back into the main corridor. She brushed the hallway with the revealing beam, then inched further down the tunnel, listening for voices.

Suddenly, the tunnel split. Which direction should she go, right or left? Concentrating, Amariah tried to recall lines mapped out by the long-dead Jesuit.

Certainty took possession of her body.

As if Adamus were guiding every footfall, leading her down a causeway forgotten through time, a force she didn't understand directed her to turn left. Just as quickly she knew it was important to stop. Ahead, her eyes settled on a line of mortared bricks; a massive wall supported the floor of a mausoleum above it.

Another sensation swept through her emotions. It was a feeling of familiarity so overpowering it dispelled all doubt and fear. There was a slight depression in the wall which attracted her attention; a single row of bricks drew her eye. Warmth seemed to flow toward her outstretched hand--the closer she got to the wall, the stronger the sensation became.

Without thinking, Amariah reached for the bag slung over her shoulder. Propping the lantern against the wall so a wide arc of light flooded an area just above her head, she withdrew a metal nail file brought from America. Its gray surface glittered as tiny specks of shattered diamonds reflected lantern light.

Guided, reaching toward a specific brick, Amariah pushed the point into the mortar. Sawing, drawing the nail file back and forth, she watched with astonishment as the mixture of lime and sand crumbled. The brick loosened. Oblivious to the pain running all the way to her elbow as she jammed the file into the mortar with the heel of her hand, Amariah worked to dislodge another brick. Her hand thrust into a cavity behind the wall when the bricks tumbled to the floor.

Amariah reached for her lantern. A square niche had been prepared with care. Trowel marks etched into plaster used to seal out moisture were still evident. A wooden box rested in the center of the niche, and she reached to withdraw it. Elaborate markings decorated a hand-carved lid. A tree stretched leafy branches toward a sun, moon, and a star with thirteen intersecting points. Tree roots pierced the earth and stopped just above a pool of troubled water. Entwined into the roots were symbols Amariah had never seen before. Heart hammering, head pounding from the adrenaline surging through her body, Amariah lifted the lid. Inscribed on the other side were two swords, linked in constant combat. Amariah suddenly felt so faint she had to lean against the wall.

Images on the silver coin.

Six scrolls, once tied with cord lay at the bottom of the box.

Her mind whirled as she tried to keep focused on the task at hand. The scrolls were ancient, she must use care, so they didn't crumble when she moved the box; one jarring slip could damage ancient paper. Glancing at her bag, Amariah dumped its contents. Note pads, pencils, a tube of much used lip balm, a disposable camera, a leather wallet containing a few liras and her passport spilled across the tunnel floor. Glad her habit skirt had deep pockets, Amariah thrust items of importance into the folds of dark cotton. Note pads and pencils could be replaced; medicated cream meant to soothe chapped lips should have been discarded long ago. These she pushed into the secret chamber, wondering if another team of archaeologist would discover them someday, hundreds of years from now, and wonder what purpose they served.

On impulse, she stooped to pick up the camera and switched on the flash. Instinct told her this moment, this place, must be recorded for history. As the last flash extinguished, Amariah scuffed at the floor with her foot, spreading powdery traces of decayed mortar in all directions. The team would explore this tunnel in a matter of days. By then, hopefully, moisture seeping down the rocks would obliterate all evidence of her handiwork.

Picking up the lantern, Amariah tiptoed back down the corridor. Once again, she was overwhelmed by the eerie impression Adamus was leading the way, her footsteps certain, her direction one of purpose--the route back to the library clear in her mind.

Amariah's heart hammer-slammed against her ribs and her lungs swelled with joy as fresh air wafted down to greet her through the elevator shaft ahead. Peering around the bend in the passageway, she checked to make certain the elevator landing was empty. The bag containing a box filled with Adamus' documents clutched beneath her arm, Amariah rushed across the landing and jammed her finger against the control button, urging the elevator to hurry. From somewhere overhead she heard the gears begin to grind. It seemed to take forever for the empty elevator to carry her out of hell. Amariah checked an imagination running wild. The pitch-blackness, musty air, fear of being caught with Adamus' scrolls were claiming her emotions.

Time collapsed, and moments stretched into hours as the elevator made its way back to the library foyer. When the cage reached its destination, its counterweight slammed home with a dull metallic thud. Silence lowered over the library landing like a hen settling on her chicks. Lights were still on in the research rooms and Amariah heaved a sigh of relief when she realized how her sense of time had distorted--she'd been in the catacombs less than an hour instead of the eternity it seemed. Deciding it would be foolish to wait, she slid back the heavy gate. The resulting screech made her wince. Voices came from the research rooms--someone was headed in her direction. Amariah threw herself across the foyer to the outer doors and ran down the steps into the garden. As she reached the path leading to her dormitory, Amariah forced herself to slow down. Should anyone take notice of her, it had to look as though she was returning from the library after an evening of research.

The recently installed dead bolt slammed home as Amariah sealed the door of her apartment against intruders. Rushing to her desk, she cleared away the accumulation of scholarly litter--papers, pens, notes, dusty books which hadn't been the object of a researcher's scrutiny for years. As she thrust her hands into the bag Amariah's heartbeat lost its rhythmic pattern and excitement made it flutter. Gently blowing way the dust of centuries, Amariah lifted the lid. She pulled the study lamp closer, its diffused light caressed writing consigned to darkness before Michelangelo painted the Sistine Chapel. Drawing a manuscript out of the box, she laid it against the desk and began to unroll it.

Adamus took care to ensure the sheets of parchment were preserved from moisture by wrapping them in folds of oil-soaked leather. How had he kept rats away? Then she remembered the ingenious way monks protected manuscripts from the rodent population, which was the scourge of Medieval Europe. Adamus must have dipped these papers in a solution of arsenic before he penned his message.

There it was! Letters precisely formed, the way medieval clerics were taught to write. But what was the message?

Reaching for the old toothbrush she kept in her desk, Amariah tried to remove some dirt. Pen strokes were there but they weren't clear enough to read. Drawing bristles over the parchment, Amariah stopped--fearing it might scratch away traces of ancient ink. The camera case drew her attention. A rubber bulb used to clean her assortment of lenses would work better. Squeezing the fat bulge of rubber, air brushed across parchment created by pounding strips of linen into pulp. Slowly, the words became distinct.

The mustache tracing a doubtful path along his upper lip took Cao Bang years to cultivate. Despite constant care, patches of skin continued to show through wisps of hair. Shoulder length tresses were greasy, as if he had not bothered to wash his hair for many days. Bodily purification was unimportant to Bang unless he planned to spend the night with Lily. She demanded he smell like the flower that bore her name--or she refused her charms. Cao leaned forward, tapping the priest on the knee with a grime encrusted finger.

"You have much to be pleased with! Connections in Guiyang, and Guizhou have been established. So too Changsha, Kunming and even Chengdu in Sichuan. I have men exploring outposts as far north as Zhengzhou and Taiyuan. The work goes well." Cao Bang pressed against soiled cushions; a smile caused his eyes to disappear beneath the layer of fat which protected the sight of his ancestors before Genghis Khan rode the steppes on shaggy Mongol ponies.

A tremor of disgust ran through Father Evans as he drew away from the filthy fingernail and knuckle. Hazel eyes, the color of the Yellow River when it flowed to the sea in spring, made Cao uncomfortable. The priest's irises were the color the river took on when the water was glutted with silt and sand trapped in the melting snow of the mountains standing guard over China.

Ryan Evans allowed his gaze to wander out the window of the shallow craft. The stink of rotting fish and garbage thrown overboard by the teeming hordes, which lived on tiny boats in the Hong Kong harbor, hovered above the water. Putrefying slime--was how the priest had come to think of these water dwellers. There were children, who had never walked on land, living on boats used to ferry goods and produce to Hong Kong. Their poverty was unspeakable.

Waterways were jammed with thousands of shallow draft craft. Some were still ferried the old way; men of the family standing on a high keel, sweeping the water with a single massive oar. Others relied on diesel engines--their fumes adding to the peculiar waterfront odor.

It was no wonder Cao Bang operated beyond the law. Only the foolhardy braved the flotsam of humanity which called the harbor home. The waterfront had its own code of ethics--its own set of laws--defying civilian authority.

Father Evan's eyes narrowed as he returned his attention to the greasy little man. "When do we move our goods?" His voice was icy, his distaste for the way Cao Bang lived reflected in how he refused to lean against filthy cushions provided for his comfort.

"Ah! The impatience of the white man never ceases to amaze me. In China, my friend," Cao Bang's eyes disappeared behind the layer of fat as he exposed stained and jagged teeth, "one must have unlimited patience." Cao doubled up with laughter. His finger pointed at the begrimed window of the airless cabin toward boats crowded together in the harbor. A sharp wind began to blow in from the sea and the bump and thump of wooden keels knocking together as waves began to swell muffled his words. "I rule out there! Your cassock means nothing in my world, priest. It might even get you killed!"

Ryan Evans was not intimidated. His movements were almost imperceptible as he straightened his shoulders. Muscles tensed, the habit strained against a barrel-like rib cage; the white clerical collar seemed to strangle a neck as thick as a bull's. Then, like a cobra, the priest struck--his forearm pinning the smaller man against the bulkhead.

The Oriental's breath was putrid, and Father Evans had to fight the urge to avert his face. This waterfront vermin would consider aversion to such a rancid smell a sign of weakness. Lowering his face to within inches of the smuggler's flat features, the priest kept his voice one low, emotionless, monotonous tone. "Cross me and you will not live to rue the folly of your actions." The priest pushed against the other man's windpipe, cutting off his air supply. As Cao Bang struggled, Father Evans pressed against his throat with greater pressure. "I represent a power an illiterate thief wouldn't begin to understand. But, Cao, trust the words I speak."

Like an alien in a movie nightmare, the voice echoed through the cabin.

"You fail . . . you die." The priest pressed harder.

Cao fought for air, his vision grew dim around the edges. All he could see was the hazel-colored eyes flecked with green. A yellow ring circled the priest's pupils; it seemed to grow and wane with the throbbing in his head as Cao's brain cried out for oxygen. His windpipe was being crushed by the priest's forearm and he was growing dizzy.

It took Cao a few moments to realize the priest had relaxed his grip. The dimness began to clear; and the long black Jesuit robes came into focus again. Massaging his throat, Cao swallowed several times. But the eyes remained merciless. A cold chill ran down his spine. Cao Bang was frightened.

Amariah's hands were thrust deep into the pockets of her habit. It rained during the afternoon and flowers, grass and shrubs were spangled with droplets reflecting the evening light. She loved this spot in the garden and hoped her peace of mind would be restored as she strolled along the walkways--between the rarest plants on earth, through trees which had grown on these hillsides since Marco Polo returned from his first trip to Cathay. She stopped, taking a newly opened rosebud in her hand. The green, protective shield of leaves had recently parted to reveal the delicate color of lilac. Amariah couldn't remember seeing anything more perfect in her entire life. How was it, she wondered, people had the ability to ignore the divine perfection of nature? How could they rape forests or strip the land of its minerals leaving it naked . . . like the bleached bones of an animal trapped beneath a predatory sun?

Her mind whirled. Since translating Adamus' scroll, her thoughts traveled in circles, as if trapped in a vortex from which there was no escape. The words haunted her; the message shouted at her from across the haze of time. Adamus called to her in a declaration he wrote in the hope it would be discovered somewhere in the future, *'when men are better able to understand.'* Her thoughts struggled with the memory of a message contained in one of the scrolls.

'. . . Christianity has not destroyed paganism, rather, it adopted the symbolism and ideology of other cultures. The Greek mind, although dying, impressed its philosophy upon the theology and liturgy of the Church. The Greek language, having reigned supreme over philosophy since Alexander conquered the known world, became the vehicle of Christian literature and ritual. Greek mysteries were incorporated into the Mass, along with the concept of a virgin birth. From Egypt came the ideas of a divine trinity, the Last Judgment, and the personal immortality of reward and punishment. From Egypt, too, came the adoration of the Mother and Child, and the mystic theosophy that contributed to Neoplatonism and Gnosticism, both of which swallowed the Christian Creed. In Egypt, the monastic orders of Christianity found their origins. From Phrygia came the worship of the Great Mother; from Syria the resurrection drama of Adonis; from Thrace the cult of Dionysus, which gave the world a dying and saving god. From Persia came the millennium, the 'final conflagration', and the dualism of Satan and God. We borrowed from the cult of Mithra a ritual so closely resembling the Eucharist sacrifice of the Mass early bishops charged the Devil with inventing these similarities to mislead frail, uneducated minds. But I say unto the person who reads these words in a future I cannot begin to imagine, Christianity is the last great creation of the ancient, pagan world!'

Unbelieving, Amariah spent hours in the library researching each of Adamus' claims. To her astonishment it was just as the Medieval priest revealed. Anthony of Egypt was the desert mystic after whom St. Benedict, St. Augustine and other twelfth century monks patterned their monastic rule. By accident, she stumbled across a passage in ancient Greek claiming Anthony's group of followers, who lived on the banks of Lake Moaris in Egypt, were Essenes! She had yet to take her findings to Dr. Deveraux, even though she knew he would be overjoyed at the discovery of a link to the mysterious group who lived on the shores of the Dead Sea.

The cult of Mithra had also undergone her scrutiny. Just as Adamus stated, the so-called pagan religion believed in a virgin mother, a child of divine origins and the sacrificial rite of consumption through which mortals were united with the magic of their gods.

Most Christian ritual was borrowed from pagan religions so distrusted by these early bishops! It stood to reason the Church was afraid followers might return to paganism because they borrowed so freely from its ritual and tradition. Yet the bishops claimed Christianity, alone, was the link to God! The Church conquered by absorption and a comparison of philosophies was the last thing clerics wanted to encourage in the Church's struggle for supremacy. How better to ward off the danger of discovery than by making its members fear other sects? Branding other cults as devil worshipers, or cursed by God, assured control. *One Church, one Bishop*, was the cry of the orthodox. What the clergy perceived as threatening was labeled heresy and crushed. All records of opposing sects were burned; eliminated; never to be worried about again.

Amariah's thoughts wandered. Looking up she realized she'd sauntered through the gardens past the Casino of Pius IV and was headed toward the Pontifical Ethiopian College. On her right, the enormous gothic building housing the Vatican radio station thrust against the sky. Its tiled roof and massive gray walls gave beholders the impression they were looking at a fortress.

The door opened, and Father Simson stepped onto the wide staircase. The look in his eyes betrayed no surprise at finding her on the walk. "Sister? What brings you so deep into the Vatican garden?"

"I often stroll here. I find it comforting to be close to nature."

Simson joined Amariah, "Father Montanegro says you rise at dawn to be in the gardens as the sun comes up."

"I had no idea my comings and goings were so closely monitored."

A hiss of displeasure caught on his tongue as the Father General struggled to suppress a retort. He had to guard against this woman; she'd proven far too clever at seeing the intent behind his words. "Nothing unkind was meant, I assure you. The Vatican is a small place and those of us who reside here are accustomed to knowing about all that transpires. The *sampietrini*, the permanent residents within our walls, are a close-knit group. They talk. Father Montanegro is a great favorite among them. Your wanderings are observed by many." He waved back toward the building. "It takes a staff of four hundred administrators, broadcasters, secretaries and technicians just to keep our radio station running. Most employees are ordinary citizens of Rome. A condescending expression softened the planes and angles of his features, "What has you so troubled? You appeared far away just now."

Amariah didn't like the way he leaned into her personal space, there was something about how he lowered his shoulders that reminded her of a hawk diving toward prey. Perhaps it was his height she found intimidating, but as the black robes drew closer, she backed toward the edge of the walk. "I didn't realize my thoughts were so transparent they could be discerned from inside the building."

Trapped, Simson knew he had to disclose he'd been observing her stroll through the garden. "I noticed you quite some time ago. It was plain you had a great deal on your mind from the way you stared down at the path. Your direction seemed taken at random."

A breeze gusted, and the edge of the veil lifted off her shoulders. Unconsciously, Amariah shifted her weight, planting her feet squarely to face him. "It just seems odd the Father General of the Jesuit Order would spend valuable time watching the wanderings of a simple Benedictine nun," she challenged.

Muscles in his jaw twitched as he reached for his crucifix. Fingers tightening around the rough gold surface, Simson's body grew as rigid as his hand clutched the symbol for which thousands had perished. "I am responsible for the welfare of everyone laboring on this great project. My concern for you is the same as it is for everyone else working in the Vatican. It is my sacred duty as the Chief Deputy of the Vicar of Christ to monitor the activities of each member on our scientific team. Too much stress placed upon one individual has the potential to weaken the entire project. Believe me, Sister, I understand the difficulty of your work. If I am being too harsh, if I am pushing any of you beyond endurance, then I must correct the situation. I wear the yoke of office with concern. If I am guilty of treading harshly, I must make amends. One of my greatest faults is thinking others share my passionate vision of the future. I get so caught up in what I'm doing, my actions can be oppressive. As Father Laterano is so fond of pointing out, my conviction is intimidating. Sister, my concern for your welfare is genuine."

If his body language had not betrayed his words, Amariah might have believed him. It would be so easy to confess her fears, so relieving to give voice to the chipping away of a faith turned as brittle as ice.

The power and authority of the priesthood was engrained in her thinking. Resisting the Father General was like swimming against the tide. Amariah gritted her teeth and stood straighter, as if her rigid stance could protect the sanctuary of her mind.

"All of us have been working hard to keep up with the schedule for the opening of the museum. You taxed our capabilities, but we've been fortified by your eloquence. Most of us share your dream, Father. We long for a suffering humanity to know the relief of Jesus' words. For truly, can one who really comprehends the importance of His calling doubt Jesus was sent to earth with a message so powerful it can calm a troubled heart? Would we not all lay sorrow aside and rejoice in the most trying circumstance if we understood the true meaning of His words? Would grief and despair be eliminated if we could grasp what it was He wanted us to know? Have His words, His mission, the acts of His daily life been recorded rightly--or, has humanity been misled?" Amariah spun on her heel and fled into the garden, leaving the Jesuit standing with his hand on his hip and his lips parted, a last rejoinder unspoken. As the nun's habit disappeared into the folds of protective shrubbery, Andrew Simson sensed he dared not follow. Her words reverberated inside his skull like rockets on the Fourth of July. " . . . *Have His words, His mission, the acts of His daily life been recorded rightly or has humanity been misled?'*

Simson's fingernail grated down the cross suspended from its golden chain. Sister Amariah's words continued to ricochet through his brain. He was unaware of the sunset bathing the dome of St. Peter's with streaks of copper. He didn't hear birds cooing as they settled for the night; he was unaware of scampering sounds cats made as they prepared for nocturnal hunting; the tightening in his stomach as he dwelled on the sister was the only sensation of which Andrew Simson was aware.

"Leon, lad, thank you for coming." John Preston rose and stretched his hand over the table in greeting. "I'm sorry I couldn't give you more notice, but my schedule has been more hectic than usual."

"There are few times I wouldn't be available, Mr. Preston. Besides," a lopsided grin showered the older man with warmth, "it's nice to be away from the Vatican. Since our last meeting I find myself looking over my shoulder and watching the lights in Amariah's lab to make certain she's there."

"You've been able to keep an eye on her?" The banker lifted the menu and pretended to examine its contents. John Preston was a frequent customer and the waiter scurried forward at his beckon. After ordering, Preston glanced around the room before resuming their conversation. "I think I've stumbled on to something that might be important." He shoved a folded piece of paper across the table.

Leon appeared to study the crease in the napkin while his eye traveled down the series of numbers and dates that peeped beneath the linen. "What do these figures mean?"

"The numbers represent the accounts used by the Vatican Bank in various parts of the world. See the digits that begin with the same sequence?"

Nodding, Leon felt his scalp tingle with a premonitory warning.

"Those accounts belong to banks in Switzerland. The rest are scattered around the world. It's easy for a banker to recognize them because all financial institutions are required to have a unique identification code."

"Why?"

"The age of electronics! We send a signal from New York to a satellite orbiting the earth. The signal hits it and bounces down to Paris. In a matter of moments, we electronically transfer vast sums of money from one country to another."

"What do the dates represent?" Leon reached for the wineglass filled by the solicitous waiter.

"That's the piece of the puzzle I've been searching for, my boy." The banker's blue eyes turned dark and stormy; he was so astonished by his discovery he had to reveal it to someone who was also concerned about Amariah's welfare. "I've been watching the newspapers. The dates you see listed beneath those numbers," he gestured toward the list, "correspond with terrorist activity in the country of an individual bank. Now the interesting part of this scenario is the bank deposits match the amounts of money moved out of the Vatican a few weeks prior to the outbreak of violence. Simson is no dummy. He shifts money from bank to bank around the globe, but once it reaches its destination, terrorist activity occurs within a few weeks. I found something else that might make the hair on the back of your neck stand straight."

Fingers tightening around the stem of the wineglass, Leon's expression turned wintry. "I'm afraid to ask."

"If anything should happen to me, I want you to make sure this information isn't lost." Taking a gulp of wine, Preston motioned the waiter to refill their glasses before he continued. "If there's one thing I've discovered in my years on this earth--it's when you start searching, you usually find what you're looking for. Several of my banking colleagues were with me at our club the other night. A few too many glasses of fine Italian wine got them playing the 'I know more important people than you do' game. Well, one thing led to another and one of them let slip the biggest arms dealers in Europe was on the Board of Directors for the United Catholic Relief Agency--a guy by the name of Aquion San De Giovanni."

Leon stared at the other man. "That could be gossip!"

"I wish it were. I checked with a few of my associates in New York. The CIA has been trying to get the goods on this guy for years. It seems he's so smooth they can't pin anything concrete on him, but they know he's the key figure in a big underworld operation."

"I find it hard to believe the CIA is powerless to stop him!"

"Leon, the man is a respected citizen in Rome and a big supporter of

Andrew Simson. He's been honored for his good works around the globe. Whatever the disaster, the relief agency he chairs is the first on the spot--arranging for food and medical supplies to reach the victims of both natural and man-made holocausts. You may not know this, but he was the one who paid for bone marrow specialists in America to fly to Russia to help treat the victims of Chernobyl! The man's connections percolate through the highest levels of government around the world. There's talk he's going to be nominated for a Nobel Peace Prize. Our boys are treading cautiously on this one. A slip could make us look as foolish as the Bay of Pigs incident. San De Giovanni is arranging for tons of supplies to reach the people hit by the earthquake in El Salvador. Personally, I'm willing to bet my General Motors stock that guns and munitions are being smuggled into Mexico in the middle of sacks of grain. Leon, look at this from a logical perspective. The Yucatan is the perfect supply depot for the rest of Central America! The United States is beefing up aid to the rebel forces in Nicaragua--so the Sandinistas will need more weaponry. El Salvador is ready to explode, and we can't afford to let our influence in Panama slip through our fingers. These countries could be up for political grabs at any time. And you want to hear something interesting? There is a Jesuit priest who's with each group of insurgents."

"Oh, come on John! If Catholics got involved in politics in Central America, the influence of the Church could topple the balance of power!" Leon's glance flitted from face to face around the room as he wondered whether anyone else was close enough to overhear them.

Preston lowered his voice. "That's exactly what I'm talking about! Every one of those rebel factions has an in-house priest . . . a Jesuit, who's influential in their decision- making process!"

John Preston reached for the ice bucket, pretending to examine the label on the wine bottle. In a tone of voice as cold as the breath of Death, he continued. "There are a number of priests scattered all over the world, who are gaining a prominent voice in political issues. One brought a black man out of prison in South Africa the other day."

"I saw something on television about him! A man named Gwelo--a political activist the government of South Africa locked away for thirty years!"

"That's the one. Besides those in Mexico and Central America, there's a priest in Ireland who appears to be keeping the IRA in check. I've also heard rumors concerning a priest living with a renegade band of Shiites. I think they're all taking orders from the Father General."

"The priests are Jesuits?" Leon began to toy with the remainder of the pasta on his plate. Somehow the noodles bathed in a rich oil and garlic sauce were no longer appealing.

"Yes! I can't quite put my finger on the heart of the matter, but I'm going to do some more investigation. Something strange is going on all over the world and instinct tells me the lines of influence lead straight to Rome."

"Lines of influence? John, I'm a Hindu language expert not a political science major."

"Politics is a series of trade-offs. You vote for my project, and I'll vote for yours. Together we gang up on someone whose ideas we don't like at all! National or international, politics is one big effort to broker influence."

"Amariah and I had a pretty heated debate about that the other day."

"She was raised on controversy!"

"I told her taking the Bible literally was a like worshipping the Democratic National platform. Several hundred years after Christ, Constantine brought together three hundred of the most politically powerful bishops in the Church. Together, they hammered out an acceptable party platform which we call Christianity. Who knows what got traded off in the process? Deal making certainly took place back then too. The early Church was rocked by horrendous theological battles! For years, pontifical princes fought over whose concept of 'consubstantiation' or the power of the 'word', *logos*, was going to provide the theological foundation of the Church. The lengths to which those bishops went to imprint their viewpoint on Christianity was nothing short of political intrigue."

Rubbing his chin, Leon stared at the candle flickering in the centerpiece while he gathered his thoughts. "Amariah told me about an interesting bit of history. According to her, a bishop by the name of Priscillian, from the city of Avila, was a man who believed in the influence the stars had over mankind. Apparently, astrology was a widely accepted philosophy for the first five hundred years after Jesus' death. There was a lot of bickering going on between the Gnostics, Manicheans and a group of Christians who became known as Priscillians. The theology of these groups was radically opposed to official philosophy. Most bishops were hostile toward these loosely structured organizations because they were gaining a larger following than official Catholicism! The controversy boiled down to control over a growing number of people! Although Priscillian died about 385 A.D., his followers continued to increase. Finally, Pope Gregory the Great labeled Gnostics, Manicheans and Priscillians heretics. He issued an ultimatum, which said if you believed in the influence of the stars--you would be condemned to the everlasting fires of hell. With that, in 565 A.D. Pope Gregory deleted references to astrology from what we now regard as the Bible! That's how they did things in those days. If you didn't like what someone else believed, you confiscated their records and burned them! End of story! If you destroyed all mention of their beliefs, you never had to worry about opposing viewpoints again because contrary thought was consigned to oblivion! What we have left is, at best, a highly edited version of the truth. Truth, I have come to realize, is whatever the bishop with the most political influence wanted it to be!"

"Merciful God." The veins in John Preston's neck bulged over his collar and he reached to loosen his tie. "Simson is doing the same thing! Why can't Amariah see it?"

"Mr. Preston, I wish I had an answer. I think she is teetering on the brink of having her faith destroyed. She devoted years of her life to a single viewpoint and a unique way of life. Shedding the trappings of her faith is an enormous step. Her belief in God is so strong she can stir the most cynical among us. Amariah makes members of our group feel as if we can expect to see Jesus walking down the hallway at any given moment. The passion of her oratory when she gets of the subject of belief is overpowering and it's backed up by extraordinary intelligence. I would pit her reasoning ability against anyone else and yet there is a child-like simplicity about her faith in God that makes me feel inadequate."

"I know. She makes me feel as if she knew Jesus."

The color drained from Leon's face. The fork in his hand clattered against the china plate.

"Leon! What is it lad? You look as if you've seen a ghost." Reaching for the ice bucket, Preston splashed more wine into the glass and pushed it in Kaminski's direction. "Here, you need a drink."

"Mr. Preston, why did you say that?"

"Say what?"

"Why did you say you thought Amariah knew Jesus?"

"I don't know. It's just a feeling. She has a way of making sense out of incomprehensible passages in the Bible and I've heard her relate parables to children. She makes the simplest story seem more profound than the theory of relativity! Maybe it's the faraway look she gets in her eyes when she speaks of the Judea of two thousand years ago. Why do you ask?"

"We're discussing a concept some people will never accept."

"And others will think I'm crazy to suggest there's more to the Father General's plans than is apparent on the surface."

"Sir, I feel compelled to tell you what Klaus and I uncovered the other day."

John Preston's eyes grew rounder as Leon explained the tidings recorded on the Tibetan scroll. "That's about the damnedest thing I ever heard! Amariah's name is unusual but to have it turn up in some archaic manuscript dealing with the whereabouts of Jesus' lost years has to be coincidence!"

"Do you think reincarnation is possible?" Leon leaned aside allowing the waiter to remove dishes and empty glasses. Despite being hungry when he arrived at the restaurant most of his meal went untouched.

"Leon, I was born and raised in an Irish Catholic home. That left no room for independent reasoning. In my mother's house, we accepted conventional Catholic wisdom without question. As I grew older, and became more educated, I left that world behind because I realized there was far too much for which Catholics had no answer. Having tragedy and suffering be 'God's will', or one of 'God's mysteries', didn't satisfy the logic demanded by my DNA. It seemed like a cop-out. Business became my Eucharist, Wall Street my mass. I turned away from religion and concentrated my energies on what I felt had substance. EBIDA became my Holy Creed. These last few years caused me to reevaluate my position--perhaps because I'm getting old. Now, I wonder what's going to happen on the other side of the veil called Death. I can't accept the Catholic belief in heaven and purgatory, but I'm not convinced the Protestant version is any better. Let alone the Hindu belief of a return to earth multiple times in many variations? Truthfully, I just don't know. On the surface of things returning to another life seems like an experience I don't want to repeat but I've read enough about karma to find the concept intriguing. Do any of us ever know? All we have is faith there is an existence beyond the grave. But I'll tell you what—I'd like to believe in reincarnation! I'd like to think I'll get a chance to right some wrongs of this life. I'd like to believe Colombian drug lords are going to live a life of privation and despair somewhere in their future. I want to believe good people, who receive no emotional or monetary reward for their selfless endeavors, will enjoy better circumstances in a life to come. But do I believe it? Leon, I don't know."

As the two men stood waiting on the curb for a taxi, heavy silence fell between them. It was not an uneasy sort of quiet, each man simply retreated into a realm of thought that could not be shared. The streets were still, they stayed at the restaurant so long the other diners had long since departed.

Hands thrust deep into the pockets of his over coat, John Preston didn't notice the headlights that swung into the street. He remained unaware of the sound of an engine gunned to life as it hurtled down the street in his direction.

Leon looked up; it took forever to realize the taxi rushing in their direction didn't intend to stop. The bump and crunch of the wheel rim as it impacted against the curb echoed across the paving stones lining the streets in this ancient part of Rome. The cacophony of sound bounced against sides of buildings crammed together like spectators in a stadium. A canopy meant to protect diners from inclement weather buckled beneath the impact of a taxi careening out of control. The tear of canvas, screaming protest of metal fasteners ripped from supporting framework added to a moment of terror--quick frozen in time. Leon hurled himself against the older man, knocking him to the ground--just out of reach of tires screeching across cobblestone. The whoosh of breath as both men collided against the walk added to a symphony of terror.

Leon fought his way back to reality. The moment passed in such slow motion he saw the deliberate look in the driver's eyes as he aimed the taxi in their direction. Rolling over on one elbow, Leon reached to shake the banker. "John! John! Are you hurt?"

The voice that reached his ear was disembodied, it sounded as if it were coming from someone other than the man he had grown to admire and respect.

"I'm okay. Winded, bruised and battered, but I think my coat took most of the abuse."

Neighbors, restaurant employees, passers-by began to gather. They gestured at the retreating taillights.

John Preston sat up, inhaling deeply. "Son, are you injured?"

"I'm fine." Leon struggled to his feet and offered the banker his hand. "In my younger days, I might have seen that coming. Thanks." He began to brush the dirt from the elbow of his overcoat, then realized it was shredded beyond repair. "Leon?"

Still shocked by what happened, Leon turned glassy eyes in the banker's direction.

"That was no accident! I haven't been as careful as I thought. The taxi was headed straight for us. If it hadn't been for your quick reaction we'd both be on a coroner's slab now."

Fear became the prism which focused Leon's stare. "Are you sure?"

"I've never been more certain of anything in my entire life. That taxi intended to kill us, or at least me. "He reached into the deep pocket of his overcoat. "Here, take this. Hide it somewhere. Better yet, mail it to your mother. Tell her to put it in a safety deposit box in a bank in London. I know a man there who can be trusted. If anything happens to me, get this information to Philip Clarke in the CIA at Langley. He'll know what to do. This conspiracy is dangerous, and its unholy alliance of fanatics has to be disbanded."

"Subterfuge is way out of my league!"

"Son, you get this scrap of paper somewhere it will be safe. There will come a time everything will have to be pieced together and this information will help." Preston forced the piece of paper into Leon's hand. "Get it to your mother, tell her to put in a safety deposit box in Peter Grave's bank. He'll take care of it for me."

"John, maybe you should tell me more about this alliance."

"I'm not going to--for your own wellbeing."

As the banker shoved past the crowd of curious onlookers and disappeared into the cloaking shadows cast by buildings standing footing to footing, wall to wall, Leon sensed a siren's song of danger was drawing him closer to a precipice from which there was no turning back. Leon felt as if the Four Horsemen of the Apocalypse were galloping full speed through the streets of Rome.

"Oh, Anna, I can't accept this!" Amariah turned a leather box between her hands. Opening it, she gasped at the quilted velvet lining.

"I found it in a shop by the Spanish Steps. It caught my eye and I thought it would be perfect to hold your scrolls. The padding will keep them from being damaged."

Amariah's eyes glittered with both joy and frustration. "I can't take this--it must have cost a fortune!"

"Nothing I can't afford, I assure you." Anna began to dig through her purse for her cigarette case, embarrassed Amariah found such a small gift so overwhelming.

"Anna, one of the hardest things about being a nun is there's no way to reciprocate the generosity of others." Amariah ran her fingers along the interior. Tiny brass buttons secured puffs of velvet to the box. She admired the design tooled into the leather stretched over the wooden frame. The craftsman used unique colors of dye to create a woodland scene. Amariah was so taken back by both the expensive box and the warm-hearted gesture she didn't stop Anna from lighting her cigarette.

"Sister, you've given me the gift of understanding. You taught me how to recognize emotional patterns established in my childhood and comprehension is far more priceless than gems or gold. Sister Amariah, you can't imagine how awful it's been to chase men who didn't want me. I never realized I was pursuing my father through the tapestry of ever-changing lovers who've drifted in and out of my life."

Anna stubbed out the cigarette. Her eyes followed the trail of smoke drifting toward the vent. When she finally spoke, words came in breathy interludes, as if verbal expression made her relive memories which brought tears to her eyes and a lump to her throat. "I think I'll be able to handle relationships better in the future. The box is just a token of what I'd like to give you. You can ask anything of me but poverty or chastity!" A genuine laugh filled the lab as Anna's spirits lifted.

"Advice seems such a poor exchange for your generosity." Amariah turned a gentle gaze toward the woman, who stood with her back to the window, allowing the sun to cast a shawl of warmth across her shoulders.

Sunlight caught in strands of dark hair swept back from her face with bejeweled combs. Red highlights blazed through the mass of curls like sparks of a dying campfire and few lines scored a complexion as silken as any fine fabric.

"Advice seems insignificant because you see it as words connected here and there by adjectives and conjunctions. But" a restless hand waved through the air and the clatter of bracelet charms echoed against the lab's ceramic tile walls, "your advice was a lifeline to a woman drowning in a sea of emotional chaos. I could never do anything to please my father. He threw a fit when I told him I wanted to become a business major. He refused to let me to follow in his footsteps. He didn't believe women had any place in the board room."

"Well," Amariah watched Anna beneath lowered lashes, "thankfully, things are changing.

"Where did we get the notion, women weren't good for anything other than providing the needs of men and tending to the snotty noses of little children?"

Amariah scolded, "I don't think our role has been all that bad! Children are their own reward."

"Perhaps." Anna smoothed a crease in her jeans and tucked the hem into expensive leather boots. "I still think men are afraid of a woman with intelligence and ability."

"Christian perception of a woman's place in the world came from St. Paul. He was a hunchback, and he probably didn't like women. Jesus, however, held women in high regard."

"St. Paul was deformed?"

"Severely."

"No wonder! I'll bet no woman ever fell in love with him and he harbored a grudge."

Amariah smiled at Anna's impertinence. "Isn't it strange we think the founding fathers of Christianity were devoid of ordinary human failings?"

"If what you say is true, millions of women haven't explored their full potential because one-man experienced rejection two thousand years ago! And Shakespeare said 'hell hath no fury like a woman scored'."

Drawing a stool closer, Amariah perched on top and rested her chin in her hands. "Since the subject has arisen, I'd feel I can confide in you. Please don't think I'm crazy . . . it is so alarming I haven't been able to speak of the experience to anyone."

Anna leaned closer, her eyes grew luminous, her jaw slackened, and the new cigarette went unlit as Amariah talked about the image she'd seen of a man with twisted shoulders. She explained how the women in the street laughed and whispered behind their hands about the unfortunate man. Amariah's eyes drifted as she drew upon the kinesthetic memory as fresh in her mind as the day it occurred. "It was a bazaar in Jerusalem. The image was so clear--the colors in striped awnings were so vibrant it seemed like I was there! Clouds looked like the sails of galleons scudding across an ocean. I could smell lamb roasting in open braziers and pungent pomegranates so ripe they'd burst. Figs were purple . . . olives tangy with brine made the glands under my tongue tighten. I could hear the women's laughter. They were cruel, and the man was hurt and angry. I could feel his pain and I felt sorry for him." Amariah shook her head, the surgical cap came loose exposing auburn, curly hair. "I can't get the impression out of my mind."

"Do you believe it's possible to have the memory of a past life locked up inside the brain?"

Eyes as blue as spring cornflowers lifted and focused on the other woman. Tears seeped from the corner of her eyes. "Anna, I don't know.

Concepts I believed inviolate are now stratified with doubt. Ideologies which seemed so secure, only days ago, are now riddled with other truths. Did I witness Paul's suffering? Was the image a memory? Or did I tap into another dimension in time? The only thing I know for certain is Christianity needs to be reexamined. What we've been taught to believe may not be true at all!"

A single line of tears followed the pull of gravity down Amariah's cheek. Anger, doubt, fear, jostled her emotions like subway riders anxious to get home. Only Amariah didn't know where 'home' was anymore!

Father Medland elbowed his way into the far corner of the crowded room and pressed himself into shadows spread by television lights. Photographers and reporters were jammed against the podium, all vying for Will Marshall's attention.

As the gaunt, black man stepped up to the microphone, a hush of anticipation lowered overanxious reporters. Clearing his throat, Marshall tapped the microphone a couple of times to confirm the equipment was working. "Ladies and gentlemen," a deep voice belied the man's stature, "I want to thank all of you for attending our news conference today. This announcement is mighty important to me. I will officially enter the race for the House seat at the end of the week. Constituents from the area I represented the past four years urged me to run for the House of Representatives. As an elected city official, I brought improvements to my district, which earned the respect of my party. My agenda will be based on the following plan of action. If elected, I'll do everything I can to improve the literacy rate all over the state. As most of you know, the campaign waged in my neighborhood improved the reading and math skills of most children a full grade level. If chosen as your Representative, I will fight against drugs and crime the same way I did in the section of town where I live. Drug related crime and drug use is down in my neighborhood. And last, but not least on my list of priority measures, is the continued education of union members forced out of their present jobs by the installation of high-tech equipment."

Will Marshall took a deep breath and reached to loosen his tie. Unaccustomed to the bright lights required by television cameras, he was hot and uncomfortable. He was a modest man who figured people would vote for him because they liked what he had to say. He didn't think his constituents were the sort of folks who cared whether he was wearing a jacket or had his shirt collar unbuttoned. "I come from a working-class neighborhood, and I take pride in that fact. My children attend public schools and my wife shops at the local market. What happens in my neighborhood concerns me. I don't want to fear for my wife and daughters when I'm not home. I want my girls to ride their bicycles on the sidewalks--they shouldn't be afraid to play with their dolls on the stoop in front of our home. My wife shouldn't have to worry about running to the market for a gallon of milk after dark. If elected I promise to bring methods, which have cleaned up what used to be the most undesirable neighborhood in Detroit, to the entire State."

The microphone began to emit a piercing wail and Will covered it with his hand. He allowed a political aide to adjust the dials on the equipment before returning to his speech. "The bums are gone--productive men now fill our streets. Drug dealers have disappeared, and men have a look of pride in their eyes again because they have meaningful work. I plan to restore a sense of satisfaction to the life of the working man. I want a man, who works with his hands, to stand straight and tall for there's no shame in earning an honest living! In my neighborhood," his voice began to quaver. Will gripped the lectern to regain his composure. He cleared his throat, beginning again. "My daughters feel secure in our neighborhood for the first time in years. I want the sons and daughters of everyone in this room to enjoy their youth! Our children have been robbed of their childhood and to me that's a serious crime."

The strong hands of a man who labored in automotive factories gripped the edge of the lectern. Will Marshall hunched over the podium, his mouth inches from the microphone. The sound of his voice carried out the hall and into the street. It echoed against buildings which had once been lifeless shells--the afterbirth of a dying industrial city. He convinced computer companies, manufacturers of lady's lingerie and an Oriental tennis shoe entrepreneur to take a chance on a worn-out section of Detroit. Once empty buildings now boasted the happy sounds of workers calling to each other over the whine of equipment and the blare of street traffic. Lights which had been extinguished for years blazed anew.

Will Marshall's eyes glowed with conviction. He believed in America and the American way of life. He wanted his fellow countrymen to walk with their heads held high; to regain their faith in a tarnished political system. Will wanted to restore the pride a man had in being an American, the way it was generations ago. He could do it, he'd already proved it on a small scale.

Questions exploded from the floor.

"Mr. Marshall, just how did you improve the literacy rate of the children in your district?" The woman reporter heard stories pouring out of one of the poorest areas in Detroit, but she doubted their validity.

"I went to the mothers of impoverished, illiterate children and enlisted their help. Several welfare workers and educators convinced me if we were ever going to improve the plight of those children, we had to teach their mothers to read first. As most of you know, women in my district out number men three to one. In-home fathers are a rarity. I explained to these desperate women if they wanted a better life for their kids, it had to begin at home. We worked nights, weekends, lunch hours, but we taught those mothers to read. We taught them to sit at night with a book in their lap and ignore the television set--even if it was blasting away in the corner. We taught our mothers to lead by example! It's been an uphill battle and it's taken hours of devoted struggle. But the mothers in my area are tough . . . they've had to be to survive. They're tired of the crime and vice which robbed them of their sons and daughters. They banded together and test scores in neighborhood schools prove beyond doubt how successful they've been."

The woman reporter looked down a nose too long for the rest of her face. "I've heard about the test scores, but I have difficulty believing the scores are the result of teaching mothers to read!"

Will Marshall stepped in front of the lectern. He leaned against the block of polished oak, crossing his arms over his chest. "Lady, let me tell you something. I don't care what you believe! My neighborhood is proud of its children again and I'd be willing to bet you can't say that about where you live!"

Another man shot forward, microphone in hand. "Mr. Marshall, I'm sure television audiences around the country would be interested in knowing what you did to cure the drug epidemic where you live. After all, the district you represented was the worst drug using area in the country!"

Leaning down, Marshall drew close to his audience. "I can sum it up in a word. Pride! The young men in my district take pride in themselves again. When you have no hope for the future, when you live in squalor and you haven't a chance in hell that things will ever get better, mister, it's easy to douse your misery with a heavy dose of drugs. Cocaine, crack, heroin, make life seem a little rosier for one moment. And, mister, sometimes those fleeting seconds are all my people ever had! I helped restore their pride. I found them jobs and together we cleaned up the project slums. We hauled the garbage out of the streets and painted over graffiti on the walls. Our children saw men going to work for the first time in years instead of standing around on the street corner selling drugs and swapping lies! Families started staying together longer and the basic social unit of life experienced a revival in our neighborhoods. Women respect their men folk again."

The woman with the oversized nose pushed her glasses back. "Mr. Marshall, you sound like a sexist. I don't think the women of this country will think highly of that remark."

"Lady, let me tell you again. What you think of me, or what anyone else's opinion of me happens to be, is of little or no consequence. I know what's happened to my people. Hell, I'm not advocating women stay home and have babies! I'm just saying for the first time in years the men in my district have a reason to hold their heads up high. You see, self-respect is like a stone thrown into a pond--it ripples outward. A man with pride is likely to treat his family better. Wives aren't abused, and children grow up in a male/female environment. It's not natural for a kid to develop under the influence of only one sex."

"Oh, come on, Mr. Marshall! That's antiquated thinking! Today, many single parents are doing a fantastic job of raising children by themselves." The woman's shoulders drew erect, she was offended by the politician's tone.

"All I'm saying is children have a better chance of getting along with their peers throughout the remainder of their life if they've had a chance to grow up in a home with two parents. God created males and females for an important reason. There's not a man on this earth who can bear a child and a woman needs the man's help with conception. I think God intended men and women to share the child-rearing process. I'll tell you another thing, the women in my district should be commended for the job they've done with their kids. But they would've had it a whole lot easier if there'd been a man around the house. A father's presence is not to be taken lightly."

"Are you now putting this issue in the hands of God?"

From the defiant look in her eyes, Will Marshall's words hit home. "No, lady, I'm not. I'm the one living in my neighborhood and I am responsible for its condition. If I want a better life for my children, then I'd best be prepared to get off my lazy duff, turn off the television and get busy. God is not responsible for the filth in my street . . . I am! Nothing of consequence has ever been achieved by a person too lazy to get involved. Oh, I've heard a lot of criticism about my methods, but I'd like to challenge you . . . or anyone else . . . to come up with something better. I'd like to see you sit on a filthy couch teaching a child to read and kick away a rat. I'd like to invite you down to my district and offer your services to the indigent. I'd like you to hold some drug addict's head while he pukes all over your shoes! Lady, when you're prepared to work as hard as the people in my district have, then you come back--and we'll listen to you talk about what you think we should do!"

The reporter turned and fled the room, her Coach bag flapping against her gray flannel skirt. Carefully applied makeup began to smudge as tears of humiliation seeped beneath her lashes.

A slow smile crossed Father Medland's face. He'd watched Will

Marshall in action before. The union leader came up the hard way. Years of experience in the factories and tough streets of Detroit taught him valuable lessons. The rich, the pampered, the elite of society melted like butter over the flame of Will Marshall's indignation. Reporters were cautious about asking Will biased questions. All too often they were hoisted aloft on their own cynical petards!

Will's fierce gaze traveled across the room. It stopped, suddenly, as he focused on the shadowy form of the priest, who stood in the darkness beside the door. The Jesuit raised his hand in salute. A reporter called out, drawing Will's attention away from the priest. When he glanced back, the Jesuit was gone--he slipped from the assembly hall into the cover of night.

Amariah pulled the study lamp closer, searching for better light. The sun had been down for several hours, and the cooler temperatures of autumn were changing Rome's appearance. Reaching for the quilt at the foot of her bed, she drew it over her shoulders. Translating Adamus' letters was slow because she was afraid of taking the scrolls to her lab. Forced to rely on manuals and hard copies of reference material, Amariah spent a lot of time sifting through pages of text.

Some of Adamus' message dealt with topics about which she'd never heard. As inconspicuously as possible, she searched the library for books dealing with a group of women prophetesses called Sibylline. Modern dictionaries cited the Sibyls as any one of several prophetesses, usually accepted as ten in number, who lived in widely separate parts of the ancient world. Amariah discovered numerous references to the works of the Cumaen Sibyl. Early Christians relied on her prophecies to substantiate the role of the Messiah. Several of the revered women foretold the coming of an exalted teacher and predicted dire consequences for all who failed to heed His words. The message of the Delphic Sibyl was incorporated into the *Dies irae* of Thomas of Celano and was sung at Requiem Masses until the time of the Second Vatican Council. Her words called to Amariah.

The day of wrath, that dreadful day
Shall the world in ashes lay,
As David and the Sibyl say.

The Sibyls' influence was so widely accepted Michelangelo painted portraits of the women between Old Testament prophets on the ceiling of the Sistine Chapel. Each woman held a book to her breast conveying an attitude of protection. Had the artist tried to portray the important knowledge these women possessed? Did he know about the Cumaen Sibyl's visit to Rome with a bundle of nine prophetic books? Had he heard the story that three scrolls were buried for safekeeping in the temple of Jove, where they were consulted at specific intervals? Was Michelangelo aware the women's prophecies foretold of revolution, the appearances of barbarian armies and the deaths of leading politicians? Did he know these holy priestesses divided the history of the world into ages, one of which would be a golden age introduced by the new Messiah? Why were these women so feared by Church authorities?

Amariah discovered several manuscripts quoting two women, Priscilla and Maximilla, who fell into religious trances. Members of the early Church accepted their words as guides by which to live. Women played an important part in the formation of the Church! Despite Paul's aversion to women, the Sibyls wielded tremendous influence in the Catholic Church until the Protestant Reformation.

Amariah wedged her foot against the desk drawer and stared at the wall. She was gnawing on a pencil when a tap at the door roused her from the quandary of her thoughts.

"Sister Amariah, come out, come out, wherever you are!" Leon's banter halted the moment she opened the apartment door.

"What have you been doing? From the expression on your face, it looks like you've been wrestling with the Devil!" He forced a bright smile as he entered her living quarters; his tone of voice was so lighthearted it sounded contrived. "You've been locked up in here for days and I thought I'd come by and make us both a fresh cup of coffee. I know where you keep it." He walked to the cupboard and reached for the coffee can.

Amariah bolted upright. Snatching the tin from his hands, she reached for a foil bag of gourmet coffee in the small refrigerator beneath the cupboard. "My mother sent me a new kind of coffee. It's flavored with vanilla and vacuum-packed. See?" She held out a silver package for his inspection.

Leon stared at the can clutched against her ribs. From her reaction, he was sure it contained something more important than coffee. "What have you been working on?"

"Why do you ask?"

"Your uncle believes there's a theosophical plot boiling in Rome and for some strange reason Klaus feels you might be at the center of the controversy."

Amariah tried to keep the coffeepot from rattling against the faucet as she filled it with water. "Uncle John has a way of seeing goblins lurking in shadows cast by a midday sun!"

"The more your Uncle talks, the more he makes sense."

A look she hoped would pass for nonchalance altered Amariah's tense features. "I'm sorry if I've been cross, I'm just tired."

"Simson has been pushing all of us to the limits of our endurance." Leon decided it was pointless to prolong the conversation. Amariah was not going to take him into her confidence. His hand rested against the doorknob moment as he offered a final statement of support, "I just want you to know when you need a friend--I'm right here."

Amariah's elbows banged against the desk, and she rested her head in her hands after Leon closed the door. What was happening to her? What was happening to her faith in the institution she believed in so strongly? Confused, she withdrew the manuscript from the coffee can and read it again. Perhaps she'd missed something, maybe the portent would change if she looked at it with a fresh eye.

To the one who reads this message,

Caesar hoped to reform mankind by changing their institutions. Christ tried to remake those institutions and lessen the need for laws by changing man from within.

I discovered records in a Coptic monastery, deep in the Egyptian desert, where Jesus taught mental powers were not intellectual. He did not depend on learning---nor formal knowledge. Jesus derived his abilities from the keenness of perception, intensity of feeling, and singleness of purpose.

His personality was so strong he had the power to influence people through the force a confident spirit can wield over an impressionable mind.

This also, have I discovered. Judea gave Christianity its ethics, Greece gave it theology and Rome its organization. Christianity absorbed a dozen rival faiths. The Church took over many religious customs and forms, which were common in the days before Christianity became the religion of the State. A fledgling clergy borrowed the stole and vestments of pagan priests. The use of incense and holy water in purification ceremonies came from the ancient Egyptians. The burning of candles and the use of an everlasting flame before the altar was commonplace in other faiths long before the advent of Christianity. The worship of saints, the architecture of the basilica, the law of Rome as a basis for canon law, the title of Pontifex Maximus for the Supreme Pontiff, and, in the fourth century, the Latin language--in which I write these words--became the noble and enduring vehicle for all Catholic ritual . . . all borrowed from Rome! But none of these rites began with Christianity! Bishops, rather than Roman prefects, became the source of order and the seat of power in cities. Archbishops supplanted provincial governors. The Synod of Bishops did away with the need for a territorial assembly. The Roman Church followed in the footsteps of the Roman State! It conquered the provinces, beautified the capital, and established discipline and unity from frontier to frontier. Rome died in giving birth to the Church . . . the Church matured by inheriting and accepting the governing responsibilities of Rome.

None of this, my dear reader, had anything at all to do with the holy words spoken by our Redeemer. The Church took His words, His deeds, the actions of His life, and used them as a weapon against the ignorant! Just as the emperors before them, the men who led the Church sought to establish enduring power. That power, alas, has been secured by robbing men of their freedom of choice. They rule through fear, by manipulation, by keeping people in darkness.

It will be up to you, dear reader, to bring the truth to the world. You must enlighten a suffering humanity, you must set their minds and hearts free. It will fall to you, oh noble one, it will fall to you. You have returned to fulfill the prophecies of the Sibyls.

Amariah stared at the piece of paper fashioned from pulverized flax stalks. It was like she could hear the dead priest's voice reading the words in her ear. She could see Adamus sitting at his writing desk, a tallow candle burning low, rushing to complete his message. She could feel his head pounding, his back aching; she could sense the coldness in the stone cell he called his own. Knuckles and fingers swollen and red, Adamus struggled to keep a tight grip on the quill pen. Ink stained his fingers and the cloth he used to absorb the excess rested at the corner of his desk. Amariah's hips ached as if she were the priest who sat upon the hard, wooden stool. She felt the iciness in his feet and suffered a dripping nose—it seemed like the memories of the medieval Jesuit were stored inside her head. His voice echoed through her mind as frequently as her own!

Amariah pushed away from the desk and stood beside the window. Although she lacked a way to explain the agonizing emotions, Amariah knew the voice from the past was calling to her . . . urging her to right the wrongs of countless men!

But how? She leaned her head against the windowpane, its coolness welcome against her burning cheek. Was it her duty to bring Adamus' message to a disbelieving world? How could she oppose the Father General, the might and power of the Catholic Church?

The voice whispered in her ear.

'Amariah, fear not—the way will find you.'

Colonel Balsahov Petrovich put his hand against the window frame. Below the warehouse at the water's edge, an ocean-going cargo ship was moored in its berth. Long vacuum hoses disgorged grain sucked from the hold into the bins mounted on railroad cars. The spur line skirting the dock fed into a larger railway line--the life support system of his people.

He watched the men working to unload the ship. Grain for his people would be transported to mills across the country. A sigh of relief lifted his shoulders. Younger men did not understand. It was from a grain mill in Stalingrad that he and his friends withstood a thousand German soldiers. They'd fought block by block, building by building. But it was the hand-to-hand fighting of men pitted against each other in savage combat, which left Petrovich so emotionally scared.

He hadn't known, until then, how terrible humans could be. In the end, over a million of his countrymen died in Stalingrad during that horrible winter. Countless soldiers gave their lives to preserve the Motherland; thousands of women and children starved to death as Stalin burned everything in Hitler's path. His own wife and children were among the first to perish.

It could never happen again! If it was the last thing he did--he would see to it the Russian people never went hungry again--even if it meant an alliance with the priest. What did a few churches matter compared to the lives of his people? His job was to preserve Mother Russia--for the generations to follow. That was all that mattered. The priest, and those like him, would come and go. Who could have guessed Stalin would become a pariah amongst his own people?

Conditions changed. Time eroded all things. His gaze drifted from the waterfront. Trees were beginning to dot the horizon again. Americans did not know what it was like to have everything in their homeland destroyed. It had taken forty years to renew the landscape. There were places grass still refused to grow--the soil polluted by the aftermath of war. It was a relentless struggle to survive those bitter, starving years. There was no time, no money, no energy to devote to beautifying the land. Russia had once been a fertile plain filled with trees, bushes, and tall grasses. All of it was consumed by the flames of war. Nothing was left. Nothing. His people did not want to see war come again, at least not the older generation. Stalin's paranoia was giving ground to a more moderate type of man--the madness permeating the government was gradually disappearing.

Petrovich felt tears sting his eyes as he thought about the mill, now preserved as a monument to the men and women who fought and died to save Russia. He was proud of a tradition which started after the war. On the day of their wedding, couples placed flowers at battle sites all over the city. Brides and grooms paid homage to those who preserved the land for them--and the children of the future.

Young men didn't understand. Their war was Afghanistan . . . fought on foreign soil. They did not see their homeland mutilated, ripped apart by men bent on its destruction. They couldn't comprehend the upheaval of the heart when war was waged on the soil of the Motherland--the *Rodina.* Petrovich prayed his deal with the priest would preserve the future of every young man and woman in Russia.

Vassily Kharkov pressed into a cleft of shadow. From this vantage point he could observe the church entrance and he counted the men and women entering a dilapidated building. Candles flickered around the altar for the first time in memory. At first just old women came. Toothless crones in dark coats, shapeless babushkas on their heads, knelt beside pews worn by age and splintered with neglect. A priest wearing a tall black headpiece waved an incensor up and down. His movements were jerky, as if he scarcely remembered how to perform the Mass. Kharkov was dismayed to see several younger people collecting in the street. At first, they came in ones and twos, then larger groups headed for the pine door standing ajar; a welcoming light fell across the bank of snow brushed from sagging wooden steps.

Within an hour the church was filled and from somewhere deep inside the scratchy, wheezy sound of an organ, whose pipes were rusty from lack of use belched the strains of music Vassily had never heard before.

Pressing his cheek against the cold bricks in the building, Kharkov held his breath when he caught sight of a Jesuit hurrying up the street. The priest paused at the door, making the sign of the cross before he entered. Light faded as the door shut, the harshness of weather held at bay for a moment.

Vassily felt his emotions plummet. It had begun. The priest put in motion what he feared might bring the Russian Politburo to its knees. It started in the villages--with local, impoverished churches. How long would it take to spread to the cities, across frozen tundra, all the way to Siberia? How long before the Roman Catholic Church held all his people in its spell? Vassily was afraid. He was more afraid of this priest than his father was of Stalin. The priest was insidious. At least Stalin never hid his methods—he ruled by clear brute force. He took what he wanted and discarded the rest; he toppled adversaries with the same methodical ruthlessness he used to fell a tree.

This priest's influence was seeping through his land, spreading Catholicism like a spider spinning its web. On the surface, the web looked fragile, too frail to pose a threat. But, like an unsuspecting insect lured into the center of the spider's web, Kharkov feared his people were going to prove just as vulnerable as the insect and the priest as deadly as the waiting spider

Sean O'Flannery crawled from the darkness and crossed a shadow swaddled street to a dilapidated warehouse. With a glance over his shoulder, he pulled lock picks from his pocket and set to work opening a padlock securing the door. Within seconds, he was inside. He waited, settling himself on a pile of crates. Not too much time elapsed before he heard footsteps. The door opened a few inches and the priest slipped inside.

"Sean?"

"Over here, Father." A square of red cellophane was taped over the torch lens, and it winked to life when his thumb depressed the switch.

"Did anyone see you?"

"Father, suren' you know better than that."

The priest nodded, then looked around. "Come over here with that light."

A beam of red traced a narrow swath between crates stacked several layers high. Father Patrick Youghai passed down corridors of merchandise without hesitation and stopped before some large boxes in the middle of the warehouse.

"You can take the cover off the torch now. No light will get through those windows."

Narrow openings near the roof were meant to offer more ventilation than light and Sean nodded in agreement as he stripped away the plastic. The torchlight revealed the name *Cox* stenciled on the side in bold black letters.

The priest reached inside his cassock and pulled out a box cutter.

Plunging his hand into spiral Styrofoam pellets he withdrew a model car.

"Toys? Father, have you lost your mind!"

"Toys, and no," his smile reflected annoyance rather than mirth, "my mind is intact." The other hand disappeared into pellets, which screeched as pieces of air-filled plastic rubbed against each other. Locating the object of his search, Father Youghai retrieved another small box. Through clear cellophane panels Sean saw a steering wheel. Opening the container, the priest asked, "Know what this is, lad?" The car began to whiz around the concrete floor, spinning in circles as the Jesuit twisted the steering wheel on the control box.

"It's a fuel powered remote control car. Did you drag me here for an early Christmas?" The tension in Sean's voice was clear as he shifted his weight from one foot to the other. "You know, monsignor, I don't mind exposing myself to the law for a good enough reason, but if you want me to hijack a load of toys for the orphanage, you've got another think coming."

The car halted as the priest placed the signal box on the floor. "Do you know what else a remote-control car can do?" The rancorous tone silenced the thug. The priest reached back into the crate and withdrew another car. "The fuel consumed by this car, mixed with the right amount of ammonia, is more powerful than military TNT. And a shipment of children's toys is hardly going to arouse suspicion in customs, now is it?"

The dawn of awakening filtered through Sean's limited brain. He studied the box on the floor with new interest. "You mean these can be turned into bombs?"

"Sean, you've been complaining about primitive weapons. These toys just thrust you into the age of electronic warfare."

"Father, I don't know nothin' about that sort of stuff." Sean knew he couldn't comprehend complicated circuitry or schematic designs.

"Don't worry," the lips peeled back in an atavistic smile, "I'll teach you. All we need are a few items from the local apothecary! A couple of nine-volt batteries, some electrical wire and this," he pulled a tiny bulb from the car's headlight, "will serve as our detonator."

Television cameras panned the ceiling of the Sistine Chapel. Below, Margaret Anderson paced back and forth in front of the altar, mentally rehearsing her questions, again. If this interview came off well, it could catapult her into a network anchor job, or at the very least, a co-host position on a major morning news show. Biting her thumbnail, the tall blond went over the questions one more time as a technician and cameraman asked her to stand still for a few minutes while they took a light reading.

Her long hair was swept back, held secure by a black velvet bow. The suit she chose to wear was classic charcoal and a checkered silk blouse, frothed with lace at the neckline, softened the chaste lines of the jacket. Chewing her bottom lip, Margaret had to remind herself to stop, or she'd ruin her makeup. She began to pace the length of the chapel, from the entry door to the altar grille.

Margaret was oblivious to the chapel's famous frescos. The ceiling was in the last stages of a cleaning process, which had taken almost twelve years to complete. The colors, turned somber beneath repeated applications of lacquer, sprang to life again. The prophet Ezekiel's scarlet robe contrasted sharply with the vibrant shades of green, which marked the eviction of Adam and Eve from the Garden of Eden. Vivid splotches of yellow colored the snake wrapped around the forbidden Tree of Knowledge and a garden boasting blossoms of pink, violet, and red. Margaret didn't notice the Sibyls, who guarded their esoteric books, but the prophetess' eyes seemed to follow her as she paced up and down the most famous chapel in Christendom. Erythraen, Lybian, Persian, Delphic, and the wrinkled face of the Cumaen Sibyl challenged the authority of the prophets of the Old Testament, who sat beside them, and offered protection to the woman in the chapel below. The prophets of Michelangelo's masterpiece looked haunted, brooding; by contrast each Sibyl conveyed an attitude of inner peace. But Margaret had no time to admire the setting, she was indifferent that the interview was taking place in a room considered sacred by millions of Christians.

Nor did she take note of the frightened eyes looming from the fresco at the end of the room, the writhing bodies struggling to escape the consuming fires of hell. The *Last Judgment* was considered by many to be Michelangelo's finest work. She never glanced at the Savior's uplifted hand as he sought to redeem the souls of a sinful humanity. The muscles, sinew and tendons of the Renaissance master's Jesus conveyed a man of power and grace.

Margaret Anderson's single worry was whether she could hold her own with Andrew Simson. Glossed lips framed the researched questions . . . again and again and again. Father Simson's could make mincemeat out of veteran anchormen, but Margaret clung to the hope she would be treated kindly.

"Miss Anderson?" The voice rang across the chapel, the acoustics adding to its power.

Whirling, Margaret tried to manage a smile as the man in a black robe bore down on her. In a brave attempt to exude confidence, Margaret felt herself pressing backward until her foot struck one of the cables snaking across the floor. Instinct warned if she seemed intimidated the Jesuit would tear her to shreds, like the martyred Christians entombed beneath the chapel. "Father!" She rushed forward, the heel of her shoe catching on another power cable.

In a single stride, Andrew Simson was at her side, his hand grasping her elbow for support. "Miss Anderson, it would do the world no good for you to come to an end in the Sistine Chapel. Please, be cautious of those things. They contain enough amperage to kill a person twice your size!"

Disentangling the heel of her shoe, Margaret straightened. "Thank you, Father." As her eyes lifted, and she came face to face with the man who ruled the Catholic world, her cheeks flamed with blush which started deep in her blouse and ended at her hairline. No one warned her about the Father General's brooding, handsome looks. Margaret was disappointed when he released her elbow and found herself reluctant to shift her gaze. His eyes were magnetic, as though the Father General had the power to light each dark crevice in the folds of her struggling ego.

"Are we all set?"

His voice carried her to the gates of heaven and for the first time since entering the chapel, Margaret looked aloft. The panel which met her glance was the extended finger of God as he reached to bequeath life into His creation, Adam. A chill made Margaret tremble. It had been years since she'd gone to church, but she felt as if being in this place, with this man, fostered a sense of overpowering spirituality. It was as if, at the touch of Andrew Simson's hand, her life had been permutated. Suddenly, Margaret felt like she'd been selected to fulfill a mission she didn't understand. It seemed destiny summoned her from obscurity.

Meek, her voice lost its range and came out like a timid whisper. "The crew will need to set the lights once we are in place. Where do you want me to stand?"

Leaning his head back, Simson studied the ceiling for a moment before he turned toward the *Last Judgment.* "Who is in charge?"

"Jeff Lyons is our director, the man with the ponytail."

"Ah! Jeff, would you come here for a moment?"

Andrew Simson bent over the director using his body to influence the smaller man. Gesturing at the fresco in the background Lyons smiled, then nodded, in obvious agreement with the Father General's suggestion.

Lights set, cameras in position, Margaret Anderson struck a casual pose as the director cued her to begin.

"For those in the television audience, who might not know the Jesuit Father General, I'd like to introduce Andrew Simson . . . an American by birth."

The camera panned the chapel as the crew moved closer to the black robed priest. A warm smile crossed the Father General's face as his head dipped in acknowledgment of the introduction.

"Father, this is an unprecedented first, allowing us to tape this interview beneath the acclaimed works of Michelangelo."

The camera zoomed in on the ceiling, moving from the Drunkenness of Noah to a tight shot of the face of God as he called forth Eve.

"The announcement we are here to make is worthy of the most spectacular setting ever created by man. You see, Margaret," the Jesuit reached for the cross in the center of his chest, "the early fathers of the Church felt art was a direct link to God. The creativity required by sculpture and painting was a way of praising the remarkable power granted to the individual by God. Truly, the genius of Raphael and Michelangelo bears testimony to the Force which set our universe in motion."

"Well, certainly, no greater works of art exist than in this room. But then, the Vatican houses the most extensive art collection in the world, doesn't it?" Margaret's pale gray eyes seemed to freeze, as if the focus of her gaze would be forever fastened on the Father General's intriguing face.

"The Church has acted as a caretaker of art for mankind--preserving articles of antiquity, manuscripts, paintings, sculptures and holy relics. What we are here to unveil tonight will prove the Church followed the right course throughout history. There are those," the cameraman zoomed in on eyes so dark the iris and pupil were one, "who criticized the cost of the new museum. But within moments those who have seen my vision as folly, will be silenced. Margaret," the priest reached for her hand, "if you follow me, you will be the first to view what the archaeological team found beneath the Vatican."

Andrew Simson drew the reporter toward the opening in the grille, the man with the camera on his shoulder followed close behind. The Father General's touch sent electric fire throughout Margaret's nervous system. The cameraman zoomed in for a tight shot as he braced his back against the grille. Simson slipped through the altar rail pulling the awe-struck woman after him.

"Margaret, if you would be so good as to pull on this rope."

Placing the cord in her palm, Simson smiled, one of his truly compassionate smiles . . . and Margaret felt all objectivity melt beneath the flame of his personality.

"Go ahead. Pull!"

Obedient, the American journalist pulled on the cord; in truth, she could no more have resisted the Father General's command than she could silence the beating of her heart. A cry escaped her lips, but she was unaware of the plaintive, mewling sound. Stunned by the sight that met her gaze, Margaret felt hot tears begin to well. "I never," her voice crackled with emotion, her tongue would not shape the words she wanted; she halted, hesitated, stumbling over sounds she had given voice to a million times, "seen anything so beautiful in my life. I feel as if I should fall to my knees in worship. And, Father," gray eyes jerked toward the Jesuit, "I am not a religious person."

Andrew Simson put his arm around her shoulders. "Everyone is religious in their heart, although most don't realize it. I, too, was as moved by this statue as you. The archeological team authenticated the name inscribed at the base of the statue," the camera lens closed in on the letters chiseled in stone. "The *Angry Jesus*, as we've chosen to call this statue, was sculpted by Michelangelo."

The cameraman returned the focus of the eye-like lens to Andrew Simson's face as he approached the statue with reverence. "I decided to unveil this magnificent work of art because the world is suffering so much right now. It's time to accept the principles for which our Savior lived and died. He brought a message of love and understanding, He taught us to cherish our fellow man; to be mindful of their needs. Yet, He too felt anger at finding his Father's house defiled by those who sought profit from service to the soul. But the world is at the dawn of a new era."

The camera's lens swept up, taking in the muscular, upraised arm, whose fist clenched a whip.

"It is time to disregard political boundaries. We must throw off the yoke of territorial bondage, we must come together to save children imperiled by a strife-torn world."

The camera's revealing eye closed the distance to Jesus' face, whose features were contorted by rage.

"We must live together in unity and harmony--it is time for the lion to lie down with the lamb. All men are brothers, the time is at hand for men to put war and prejudice behind them."

It was the eyes of the marble statue that conveyed unrestrained emotion. They burned, they simmered, they demanded retribution for a sin so reprehensible Jesus struck out in anger.

"People must band together to stop the plunder of our planet--for we share one small speck in the universe as it hurtles through a vast, unspeakable void. We are at the threshold of change. We must learn to respect differences in the cultural heritage of our neighbors, while sharing a common bond of humanity."

Margaret was enthralled by the authority of the Father General's words. A wellspring of unfamiliar emotion had been tapped and it radiated outward from the center of her being. Her eyes glowed with jubilation as she clasped the Jesuit's hand between her own, her face transformed by the rapture of a true believer.

The voice rolling toward the sound boom was low and commanding. The towering vault of the ceiling amplified his words, a compelling voice reverberated down the length of the Sistine Chapel. The Father General became the personal representative of the God who stretched forth a single finger to bestow life to an awaiting Adam. "The Prince of Peace asks only that you learn to love your fellow man. Put personal consideration aside and embrace the cause of brotherhood!"

The angle of the camera began to slide up the central panel in the *Last Judgment* toward the illuminated hand of the redeeming Christ. At the last moment, the director gave the signal to pull back, a small viewing screen at his elbow projecting the camera's wider angle. A tearful woman was seen clutching the hand of a loving, caring priest. The *Angry Jesus*, who rebuked greedy merchants, served as a backdrop to the words thundering from the Father General.

"We must stop the annihilation of other human beings because they do not share our views. We must learn to live in peace, accepting our brothers for their differences and glorifying their uniqueness. Christians must begin to live the lessons offered by the Savior. The time for change is at hand . . . we must unite to save our planet and its people . . . we must.

CHAPTER NINE

Sean's tongue protruded from the corner of his mouth as he concentrated on the task at hand. With a lady's nail file, he caressed the top of the toy car's headlight to expose a hole in its fragile glass shell. Reaching for a rolled paper cone, he filled the bulb with gunpowder. When a switch on the remote-control device was activated electric current would surge through the filament and ignite the gunpowder. In turn, the gunpowder would detonate a blasting cap made from common acetone and hydrogen peroxide tamped into an empty shell casing. It required patience to teach Sean how to mix the chemicals. Pipe bombs filled with fuel which powered toy cars was powerful. Sean and the priest tested these new weapons several times. Their remote control activated a servo in the car's control mechanism, powered by a nine-volt battery. The pipe would fragment into a thousand deadly pieces; its tiny battery, servo and switch blown apart with such force no one could ever trace the bomb to its creators.

Actual explosives would be placed a good distance from the detonator. The only limit to how far away Sean could be from British soldiers and wealthy Protestants was the range of the signal on the remote controller. They predetermined the radio signal worked best at two hundred meters. If the signal had a clear path to the detonator, he could hide anywhere . . . in an abandoned building, behind a haystack, in a church!

But Sean O'Flannery knew he would never settle for concealment. He wanted to watch soldiers and British aristocrats get blown apart. The sight of shattered limbs and blood spilling in all directions gave him as much pleasure as a woman's charms . . . perhaps more. He liked to watch his tormentor's anguish.

He hurried to complete the current set of pipe bombs; Father Youghai would be here soon. The priest wanted to give his handiwork one last inspection. The creak of wooden stair outside his shabby apartment notified Sean the Jesuit had arrived.

Once inside the room, Father Youghai stripped a stocking cap from his carrot red hair with its identifying white stripe. Tossing the neck scarf into a nearby chair, he peeled off his coat and gloves. As his eyes drifted across the table a harsh expression brought on by responsibility and the elements softened. "Excellent work, lad! You've accomplished more than I thought you could."

Sean glowed under the praise; it was not often the priest spoke to him so warmly. "It makes me feel good to know we're going to strike with such vengeance. Father, where did you learn to make bombs like this?"

"Oh," the priest hovered over the worktable, inspecting wires wrapped around battery terminals, "someone showed me. It seemed like a good thing to remember."

"I see." Sean watched with fascination as the black-clad Jesuit tested the electric line and checked the rotor's movement to make sure it made positive contact. "You've a genius for this stuff, lad! This is as good a bomb as could be built by the Brits!"

Sean sat back in the chair and began to massage his neck. He was stiff from hours of bending over the table, deep in concentration. "I'm ready to blow every stinking one of them clean out of Ireland."

"Patience, lad, patience." Patrick Youghai drifted toward a window begrimed with the soot of industry.

"Patience! Always you tell me to be patient! Father, I don't want to wait any longer. The bastards robbed me of me mother. Twarn't nothing wrong with her but she was kilt by overwork! One o' them bloody soldiers, he ruined my sister. She ain't been right in the head since 'ter rape. Father I want to kill 'em all!"

"I know, Sean, I know. But a great man counseled me on the strength of patience. You see, lad, there was a time in my life when I felt as you do now. I wanted to bring my hand in an act of vengeance so great it would force the British from our land. But this man, the important one I'm talking about, convinced me the war in Ireland could only be won by erosion. Did you know wind and rain are more destructive than all the bombs ever created by man? Water can wear down anything, given time. Wind can tear apart the most formidable mountain. You know how? One grain of sand at a time! Relentless abrasion can reduce a mountain to rubble before an ever-blowing wind. And, Sean, that's what we've got to become. Relentless! You and I will move like the wind. We must be nowhere, yet everywhere! And one soldier at a time, one sniveling Protestant at a time, we'll erode the strangle hold the British have on Northern Ireland. Our war is one of attrition. The battle for supremacy will be counted in years, not days, my boy. We need not concern ourselves with a major battle. No, we'll slip in quietly and blow up as many of them as we can, then disappear just like the wind and the rain."

"The distinguished man I'm speaking of will eventually rise to glory. Ireland will be Catholic again, a haven for the working man. Wealthy sots who think our churches beneath their dignity, will take the money earned by the sweat of the Irish and slither back to England. It will be a great and glorious day for both the Catholic Church and Ireland."

"Father . . ." Sean's eyes were bright as he stroked the wires, the servo, and gunpowder ready to fill the next light bulb. He was stirred by the Jesuit's words. "Who is this man? When is he going to wrest control of Northern Ireland away from the bloody British?"

"Ah, lad, the man of whom I speak is the torrent of the wind; he is the man whose mere word can move mountains. He is the most exalted man on earth. When he is done all will be one. So great will be his power kings, princes, and statesmen will bow at his passing. This man has been sent to us by God!"

"Who, Father, who are you talking about?"

Eyes as blue as the sea surrounding his native Ireland shone beneath auburn lashes. A look of zeal transformed a melancholy countenance, and the Jesuit took on an expression of glorious wonder. "Who, lad? Of whom do I speak? Why, Sean, I am talking about the new Messiah!"

A cold tremor traced its way down the length of Sean O'Flannery's spine. Grave walking, that's what his old grandmother called the chill that could not be accounted for by temperature. The toothless crone terrorized him with tales of ghosts who rode the peat bogs late at night. And sure, if he didn't feel as if 'ter haints that were so much a part of his Irish heritage had, indeed, just walked across his last place of rest

The low, marshy swamps left behind, Loto was relieved to feel the hard earth of rocky mountain passes beneath his military boots. The air was cooler, the water less fetid away from the plains. Rain fell, but the ground didn't turn to mush beneath the caisson wheels. Loto was happy to be back in his country again. He didn't like the lowlands--the wild beasts that roamed the night and the swarms of insects, which flayed a man's flesh, tried his soul. Air in the flat lands was different too; it reeked with decay as marshes rotted beneath the sun. It wouldn't be long before they reached the Kwango River separating his tribal territory from Zaire. Loto suppressed a bitter laugh. No one respected native boundaries in their rush to carve up Africa. No one ever considered the needs of nomadic peoples who followed migrating herds since the dawn of time. No, the big chiefs, the men who spoke the white man's tongue, they never worried about hardships artificial boundaries imposed. Borders created from pieces of cardboard fastened to sign posts were supposed to frighten his people into abandoning game trails. Didn't their white masters realize starvation was more fearful?

Loto watched his men prepare the evening camp. Soldiers were posted; rocket launchers dug into the ground--the way Father Stein taught them. More soldiers combed the surrounding countryside for wood. It had been a dry summer and good firewood was easy to find. For the first time in days his men could enjoy a hot meal. At the snap of a twig, Loto whirled--rifle in hand.

The priest held his hands up, palms out. "It's only me, Loto."

"Ummghf." Loto grunted at the man and waved his gun barrel in the direction of the campsite, granting passage.

Patting the large black man on the shoulder, the priest was understanding, familiar with the hardships of a long march. "Loto, friend . . . come sit by the fire. I've got some leftover C-rations, probably World War II issue, but they're edible. Come, I'll share them with you."

Despite the disheveled appearance the priest acquired during their long journey, he still projected a commanding dignity. Loto learned to respect this white man. He knew how to live off the land. He wasn't afraid to smear his skin with foul smelling, rancid butter to ward off attacks of hungry insects. He slept on the ground, he ate what they could gather and kill--just like the rest of the men. And never did the white man utter a word of complaint, even when his skin blistered and peeled beneath the tropical sun. The priest carried his share of the burden too. When the wagons got mired in the mud, his was the first shoulder pressed against the wheel. His hands were blistered from hauling barrels of water up steep embankments from the river's edge. He shared his food and dispensed medical supplies to all the men. Were it not for the medicines he carried in his pack, the expedition might have succumbed to malaria in mosquito-infested marshes or dysentery caused by drinking from streams.

Loto hunkered down near the fire. Dark, luminous eyes watched the priest with interest as he dug through his rucksack. Fishing around, Father Stein withdrew several cans of food.

"Ah! Fit for royalty. Do you prefer tuna fish packed in water with garden peas or roast beef and gravy?" Ruger Stein's hair had bleached to the color of oat straw and the skin that wrinkled around his icy blue eyes when he smiled was as brown as the bark of a tree.

"Loto doesn't know what those are." A hand the color of polished ebony reached for a can.

"Rumor has it there's been another tribal massacre to the east."

To spruce up his cassock, the priest slapped at his sleeves and continued down the sides of his body. Dust flew, but his activity did little to remove the grime of weeks on the trail.

"Drums say much." Loto stirred the coals with a stick and propped his tin of food on top of rocks encircling the fire.

"Loto, do drums really talk? I don't understand their message."

"Fast beat bad coming. Storm brewing, take cover. Low, slow beat, people coming . . . sometimes strangers, sometimes not. Happy, tapping sound means news worth rejoicing will reach village soon." Loto watched a huge burnt orange sun begin to set beyond the mountain ridge far to the west.

"What about the sounds the drums make when your shamans, your medicine men, communicate with each other? What are they like? I've heard talk about how the bones of dead men rattle and how restless the animals become when the drums of the shaman throb."

The liquid quality of Loto's black eyes contrasted with the whites turned phosphorescent by a slowly rising moon. Nostrils flared, the bushman conveyed his fear like a horse spooked by unexpected movement. He pushed the food tin closer to the fire with the point of the stick, absorbed by the difficulty the task presented. Mumbling, his voice was barely distinguishable above the cracking and popping of dry twigs in and his words lingered on his lips an unusual length of time. "Loto know nothing about those drums."

"I see." Father Stein sat cross-legged; he shifted his weight to get comfortable. "A long time ago, before I came to serve God, I lived in a faraway land called Viet Nam. I used to live with some people much like the people of your tribe. They called themselves Montagnards. They communicated with other villages by pounding on hollow logs. Their method covered greater distances than the two-way radio I carried. I found it interesting they knew about our comings and goings sooner than we did." The priest rummaged through his pack again, searching for a can opener. "I got to know some of their chiefs because I stayed with them many phases of the moon."

Loto squirmed beneath the hardened stare engaging him from across the campfire. Long shadows cast by the flames threw spectral patterns over the white man's face. A red reflection trapped in the priest's eyes reminded Loto of a panther stalking prey. The Jesuit's dark robe made him blend into the shadows and his face appeared to float above the fire. Loto knew his uneasiness was borne of the law of survival; it was pure, raw instinct that made him shiver.

"The Montagnards taught me their 'sound talk' and I wondered if it was like yours." Father Stein tossed another branch on the fire and a shower of sparks flew into the air.

"What did you do in that far away land?" Loto studied the priest's confident gestures, the way he engaged another man directly, how he could spear someone with a glance that was murderous.

"I was a soldier before I turned to God."

Ebony colored lips split, revealing teeth perfectly aligned and so white they glowed in the moonlight. "Loto knew that!"

"Despite my present calling, it's difficult to hide what others call a 'military bearing'. But war had sickened my spirit and warped my soul. A man, whom I will revere to the end of my days, saved me from certain self-destruction. He gave me hope and a reason to go on living. He made me understand self-inflicted wounds were my way of showing how sorry I was for the pain I caused many others. He convinced me by serving God all would be forgiven." A branch crumbled, and sparks flew in the air--like phantoms cavorting through the darkness.

Loto blinked. "White man, tell me true . . . what is this God you worship? What place has He in the world? Why do you make Him live in cramped dwellings you build in His name?"

"Oh, Loto my friend, my God is the god over all the deities you worship! My God causes the wind god to blow. He is the force that pushes the river god to the sea. My God creates the clouds and makes rain fall on the earth mother's breast. My God rules the lions in the jungles and all the great beasts that roam the land and oceans. My God is the supreme God, Loto. He is the highest of the high. My God is everywhere and nowhere. He does not live in those cramped houses, that is a place for those of us who worship Him to gather. No, Loto, my God is all seeing, all knowing!"

"This man you worship, does he serve the same God?"

"I do not worship Andrew Simson, I honor him. And, yes, he introduced me to God. He was the one who taught me how to have faith--he was the one who convinced me God could enter my heart and free it from suffering. Andrew Simson put my hand in God's and placed my feet on the path of righteousness. I owe Andrew Simson everything, he changed my life."

"He is big a chief?"

"The biggest. Soon, very soon, Loto, he will be the chief ruler of all lands. He will tell us what it is we must do to earn salvation in the world to come."

Loto finished eating the last of the roast beef and gravy. Tossing the can onto the smoldering embers of the fire, he assessed the priest. Despite the combat boots, green army fatigues, and rounds of ammunition slung over his shoulder, Loto was still a primitive man. He'd been taught the mechanics of modern weaponry, but he still believed unseen spirits controlled the forces of nature. Loto shivered, suddenly afraid. If this black robed man served a God who was over the gods of the river, the trees, the antelope, the lion, the plains, and mountains of his land, then Loto knew the world with which he was familiar was going to end. The priest meant to impose his God upon all the peoples of Africa. The priest said his God was supreme. Loto worried about what this would mean for his people, but right now he needed to meet Tshikapa.

It would be improper for the greatest warrior in his nation not to be greeted with respect and Loto tried to hurry to the riverbank.

A broad smile split Tshikapa's dusky face when he caught sight of his old friend. Lifting his paddle in salute, he put more force behind his efforts. Loto splashed into the waist high water as the canoe got closer. He helped Tshikapa drag the boat ashore, then turned to clasp the other man's hand in greeting. In another day and age Loto would have laid his spear and shield at Tshikapa's feet as a sign of respect.

"Brother! I'm glad you're here! Our journey has been long. I am happy you are here to take charge of the men. Their complaints are as worrisome as the insects that hound me."

"Loto, old friend. Men on the march have little else to occupy their thoughts but what is difficult about the journey and the hardships they have been asked to endure. Still, they came. They followed you across half of Africa to join me. I commend you for that!"

Smiling, Loto stared at the ground, unable to respond to the compliment bestowed by a man he honored as a great chief.

"The priest. Is he with you?"

Eyes as murky as the river at night swept the horizon. "He's here."

"Has he said much?"

Loto shook his head. He was uncomfortable talking to the priest and tried not to engage him in conversation.

Sensing his friend's discomfort, Tshikapa slapped Loto's shoulder. "Well, let's you and I get to camp. We've much to do these next few days if we are to take on Kanga-Kanga's warriors."

As the two men strode into camp the men, who had been lolling about their fires, sprang to attention. Tshikapa commanded respect and these soldiers were eager to show him how well trained they were; how much better they were than the last time he saw them. Still men of the bush, it was hard to contain their excitement and before long they broke ranks and rushed to Tshikapa's side. Their leader had time for each man, he spoke words of encouragement, asked after families, and made the soldiers feel as if his mission would fail without their personal support.

Leaning against a wagon wheel, the priest watched the gathering from afar. He didn't intrude on Tshikapa's reunion with his men, so the soldiers wouldn't resent sharing their leader's attention. Finally, Tshikapa caught sight of the shock of golden hair. He pushed away from his men, making his way toward the black robe turned gray by miles of travel through an inhospitable land.

"Father Stein, I was told you would be here." Tshikapa extended his hand, white man's fashion.

Ruger Stein matched the firm grip with equal pressure. As if testing one another, the handshake lasted a moment longer than required by social custom. Ice blue eyes locked with dark-brown eyes and a look passed between them which measured the other's sincerity.

"Your superior sends his greeting and hopes all is well." Tshikapa did not need to offer a name.

On his part, the American priest nodded. He knew he was being measured.

"Loto, do we have tea?"

"I'll put water on to boil."

Soldiers settled themselves a discreet distance from the two men of power, who were deep in conversation, as they waited for tea.

Finally, Loto brought two cups and poured a cloudy liquid from a travel marred kettle. Tshikapa lifted the cup to his lips. Looking over the rim he dismissed Loto by means of mental communication. He had serious business to talk over with the priest. Pleasantries concluded, Tshikapa turned questioning eyes in the Jesuit's direction.

"Priest, why are you here?"

Rubbing the corner of his eye with his finger to remove a particle of dust, Father Ruger Stein prepared to answer the question he knew was certain to come. After a pause which seemed to stretch forever, he retrieved the cup from the rock on which it rested. He'd never acquired a taste for tea, coffee was more to his liking. He took a long draught and swallowed. Finally, he lifted eyes radiating inner pain. "Tshikapa, I hope you will be patient with me. To explain why I share the campfire of your soldiers I must tell you about the life I've lived."

Tshikapa nodded, settling on his haunches. He had all the time in the world.

"When I was hardly more than a boy, about the age your young men are inducted into the rites of manhood, my country went to war. I know you're an educated man, that you attended the finest schools in Europe, so I don't need to explain about Viet Nam. I was drafted into the army and shipped to a foreign country I'd never even heard of to serve in a war no one would let us win. Somewhere along the way I discovered I was good at killing. A man, who proves superior at such a task, gets a lot of special training during war. The army taught me ways of being even more efficient. The more they taught me, the better I got. I turned into a ruthless, mindless machine. Nothing and no one got in my way. I learned to live off the land and wage war with my enemies on their terms. I earned a reputation among my peers and my adversaries. For a time, I lived with a band of people not unlike your own. Primitive by Western standards, they were a compassionate, caring group, who lived the spirit of my God better than most Christians."

Ruger Stein squinted at the fire. Lines around his eyes and mouth turned sorrowful as he searched for words to make Tshikapa understand. "I killed with speed and profound accuracy. I was so good they let me reenlist for several tours of duty. By then, the war was everything to me--I had become a ruthless warrior! I lived and breathed the calling of my craft. I learned to traverse jungles with greater stealth than the Viet Cong. 'No Blood' became my call sign because my superiors said I had ice water in my veins."

Stopping, the priest let his eyes follow a hawk as it glided on a current of land-warmed air. He reached for his cup, the tea grown cold, but the liquid felt soothing on the back of a parched throat. Memories were painful, even now. He hated thinking about his experiences, but he had to make this man trust him. Returning his gaze to the black man sitting across the fire, the Jesuit continued.

"When the war was over, like most other soldiers, I went home. Only when I got there--nothing was waiting for me. The very thing for which I was trained had no value. Killing was the only skill I possessed--a skill shunned by the civilized world! I drifted around the country, with no place to go and nothing to do. You see, I'd grown accustomed to the feeling a man gets when faced with extraordinary danger day after day. I don't need to explain how powerful, how desirable, that sensation can be. I got into scrapes with the law. You can't train a man to wage war for five years and expect him to suddenly stop."

The priest reached into his cassock pocket and flicked out a knife. Tshikapa tensed, then watched with amazement as the Jesuit scraped the dirt beneath his fingernails with the blade tip.

"While I was in jail a priest started coming to see me and we got on friendly terms. You see, I had no one else to talk to. He explained his beliefs and gave me some books to read. For the first time in my life, I began to accept the existence of a Higher Power. After all the death I'd seen, the maimed bodies, blown up humanity--I didn't have much faith in a godwho'd allow that kind of terror to be unleashed on an unsuspecting world. But this priest got me to see life from a different vantage point. I won't bore you with the details of my conversion, but that man gave my life meaning again. He convinced me life's real battle was waged for the soul and this fight was far more brutal than the ones I'd fought in 'Nam."

Tshikapa unfolded his legs, this man believed in his god. He reached for a stick and began drawing patterns in the dirt. "I accept your story because I know about your war in Viet Nam. It was a favorite subject of my college professors, and the conflict was debated in my political science classes. Your story rings true--I've heard versions of the same from other men. But, priest, that doesn't explain why you are in my country. Why did you trek across thousands of miles of wasteland? Why did you endure the hardships of travel in Africa? Why have you chosen to support my cause?"

"Because you respect the mission of the Church." Father Ruger Stein drew erect; devotion to Andrew Simson's purpose filled him with pride and conviction. "Throughout history the Jesuit Order has supported men of vision, men who were sympathetic to our goals. Through you, the Church can reach the people of Africa. I can help you conquer your enemies. I will supply you with the means to fight a modern war and train your men to use complex weaponry. And, when it's over, the Church will count on you to keep a proper peace. People will thrive beneath your benevolent rule. After peace is established the Jesuits will go among the tribes of Africa and teach them the ways of the Christian God."

Loto walked up behind them, years as a stalker of lions and game made his presence go unnoticed. Both men started when he spoke. "The priest says his god is a bigger god. He says his god is the chief of the river god, the god of the wind--better than all the gods of our people. Is this true, Tshikapa?"

Tshikapa's eyes roved the horizon of a land he loved. It was a brutal environment and centuries of living in harmony with nature produced a hardy people. Good people. People who deserved to live without fear; people who deserved to have food in their bellies; people whose children were worthy of a future. He watched a hawk dive toward unseen prey. A lizard scurried from beneath a lifeless looking bush and rushed across the sunbaked earth to the cooling shade offered by an outcropping of rock. In the distance, the reeds growing in clusters along the river's edge moved with the current--a lazy, rhythmic movement--slow and hypnotic.

The killing had to stop. Thousands had been exterminated, thousands more left to starve on a land which no longer had any hope of sustaining them. The blood baths had to end. Children had to have an opportunity to grow strong again. Crops had to have a chance to flourish. Peace had to be won . . . but at what price?

Tshikapa listened to the Christian missionaries many times before. They were a hard, grim people, who wanted to obliterate the gods of his tribe. At least the priests, who wore the long black robes, were realists. They were not idealistic dreamers. They knew what it took to gain and hold power.

The people of Africa needed surcease from struggle. They needed to rest. His eyes took in the posture of the priest as he waited for an answer; he was a confident man. But what was it going to cost his people if he agreed to work with the Jesuits?

A baleful sun hid behind a narrow filigree of clouds, casting a shadow over the landscape. Somewhere in the distance a jackal howled, and Tshikapa turned his head in its direction. High in the sky several vultures were circling over a carcass hidden by a dense stand of brush. The law of survival ruled the high savannahs of Africa. Only the strong lived from one day to another. The weak were carrion for scavengers. Tshikapa hoped his country would not become a rotting carcass fought over by scavenging countries. A dim thought pushed up from the deep layers of consciousness--would he be a match for this blond-haired, blue-eyed priest? Could he accept the help of the Catholic Church and still preserve the cultural heritage of Africa?

Tshikapa's gaze turned toward the men who followed Loto across the length of Angola. They were so trusting. They marched a thousand miles, carrying weapons of war to engage the enemy . . . for him.

He must fulfill his responsibilities to the people of Angola, nay, to all Africa. Somehow, he had to find the means to allow his people return to their traditional ways of life. They did not belong in the modern world. They were simple men, men who hunted lions and herded cattle. Tshikapa knew it was critical to preserve the tribes of Africa. Taking a deep breath, he turned back to Loto.

The proud man waited, as if sensing his question required his leader to think very hard.

"Loto, my friend, the great Christian, Jesus, told his followers . . . 'in my Father's house there are many mansions'. I think he meant there was room for all ways of thought, all forms of worship. For whom is to say the Christian God does not assume the form of the Gods of the African people? Wouldn't God understand all men are different? Wouldn't God try to come to people in a way they understood? The Christian world has forgotten nature; they do not care about plundering the planet created for them by their God. Africans live at the breast of mother earth and dwell beneath a ceiling of stars. We listen to the God of the Wind when He speaks because our houses do not keep Him out. The God of the Rain washes our dusty faces, and the God of the Sun causes our crops to grow. Perhaps it is not a superior God the Christians worship, perhaps it is the same God wearing different clothes."

Returning his concentration to the jackal as it struggled to frighten the vultures away from its kill, Tshikapa wondered who the jackal was and who was the vulture between himself and the priest. Saying a silent prayer to the gods he had known from childhood, he asked for their help. He beseeched them to provide him with the strength to fight off the scavengers threatening to tear Africa apart.

Black robes swirling, Andrew Simson left the library after previewing the interview with Margaret Anderson for everyone involved in the museum project. Amariah's nervous glance took in the rest of the team. Faces mirrored varying degrees of shock; everyone was obviously moved by the Father General's speech. Many scholars on the team did not agree with Simson's methods, but there was little doubt even his most severe critics were going to be silenced after the interview aired.

The library began to clear--normal chatter between technicians and the archaeological team was subdued. It seemed as if the Father General's words lingered in the air and demanded a reverent hush from normally bright, sociable personalities.

Amariah's thoughts turned toward other leaders with the power to sway. Martin Luther King stirred the conscience of a nation with his oratory. His famous *'I had a dream'* speech was responsible for the civil rights movement which changed the direction of America. President Kennedy's challenge to *'ask not what your country can do for you, but what you can do for your country'* forged a new spirit of social responsibility in an entire generation. Churchill's ability to mobilize his country's resistance was due to his ability to draw upon the emotional resources of his countrymen. It gave her a chill to think about the Prime Minister as he praised the pilots who kept the superior force of the Luftwaffe at bay during the Battle of Britain. *'Never in the field of human conflict was so much owed to so few by so many'.*

Amariah knew with just as much certainty that tomorrow Andrew Simson's speech exhorting the unity of man would take its place in history. She had to give the devil his due; the Jesuit knew how to evoke an emotional response. Margaret Anderson provided the perfect counterpoint to his strength of purpose. Her elegance stood in stark contrast to the simple robes of the priesthood. His choice ofsettings could not have been more spectacular than if Cecil B. DeMille designed a movie set for the occasion. The camera's sweep from Simson's blazing black eyes to the hand of Christ was so dramatic she felt inspired! And his oratory! His words stirred her to the depths of her soul! Margaret's tears, the way she clasped his hand, the look of adoration as she absorbed the magnitude of his message was how Andrew Simson was going to impact an unsuspecting world.

Amariah glanced at Leon, he too appeared reluctant to leave the library. When Anna noticed Amariah remained seated, she crossed the room and dropped into the chair beside her. "What do you make of the interview, Sister?"

Smiling, Amariah reached to stop Anna before she could light the cigarette she'd retrieved from her purse.

"Oh, I'm so shaken I forgot we can't smoke in here. Thanks," a grateful smile beamed at Amariah. "Andrew would have killed me!"

"I've become fond of you, and I'd hate to see the Father General make you the target of another of his scathing lectures." Amariah stopped talking as Leon approached.

"Ladies, I can't tell you when I've felt more emotionally drained. The man in that video made me want to stand and cheer! I felt as though I should take to the streets and embrace the first person I saw. He really moved me."

"May I join this pensive group?"

All three heads swung in the direction of the East Indian priest--Father Prabhupada stood quietly, awaiting permission to be seated.

As Anna beckoned him forward, light streaming through the library windows refracted through the diamond rings she wore and hundreds of scintillate rainbows danced around the table. "Father Rava, I, for one, would welcome your opinion. You see the world from an enlightened perspective. Nothing ever seems to disturb you. It is as if you peer through the silken veil of insight."

"Your words of praise are kind, if unfounded. It is simply that I have learned to contain my thoughts unless asked for them. Men of color are not welcome in the white man's world; their thoughts and opinions are seldom solicited." He studied the dark hands folded in his lap.

"And more is the pity for that!" Diamonds shot more sparks of fire around the library when Anna waved her hands. "Father, whether you realize it or not women fall into the same category. I've been fighting self-righteous, white-male superiority for years! Frankly, there's not a subject which makes me angrier! If one's skin tones are not vapidly pale or if you happen to have mammary glands . . . then it's obvious! The brain does not function under the influence of pigment or gender. I must have a cigarette. Can we adjourn to a bench in the garden?"

Amariah regretted leaving the library, book stacks and manuscripts made her feel protected--as if knowledge was an impenetrable shield--the means by which iniquity could be vanquished!

As they stepped from the library into brilliant sunshine, Anna shaded her eyes. "Let's sit in the courtyard at the Casino! I think it is the loveliest place on earth."

As they settled themselves on the benches surrounding a fountain on which stone children rode water-spewing dolphins, Amariah wondered anew at the grandeur and passion the popes had for architecture. The facade of bias relief statues, drapery of laurel carved from marble, an infinite wealth of detail overwhelmed the human eye. Cypress and palm trees flanking the courtyard thrust obelisks of green against an azure sky--a more beautiful setting had never been conceived by the mind of one man for the pleasure of another.

Anna lit her cigarette, a cloud of smoke turning her features hazy as she expelled air from her lungs with nervous force. "How does he think he can do it? How can one man unite a world torn by civil strife and national hatreds dating back centuries?"

Father Prabhupada turned thoughtful. His hands gripped the edge of the marble bench as he rocked back and forth. His body bobbed, the rhythmic motion hypnotic, while he pondered the question. His gaze traveled to the fountain, then beyond to the tree lined horizon pierced by St. Peter's towering dome. "Religious leaders have always shared a common dream of uniting mankind. About six hundred years after the death of our Savior, Mohammed set about unifying the tribes of the desert. His successors did a remarkable job of fulfilling Mohammed's goals. Nearly twenty percent of the world's population adheres to the code of ethics defined by Islam. Six hundred years prior to the birth of the Nazarene we worship, Gautma Buddha brought his enlightened beliefs to the world. A thousand years before Jesus walked the earth Zarathustra recorded a system to live by in the Zend Avesta. Each great mystic wanted to unite, by faith, a strife-torn humanity. Ten thousand years before Jesus, the Vedas of my people were written. Of course, it is difficult to know what is original and what has been added over that vast expanse of time, but scholars think one verse survived intact . . . *Ekam Sat Vipra Bahuda Vadanti.* When translated the phrase means: *that which exists is one; sages call it by different names.* If, at the dawn of recorded time, men recognized the core of one universal truth--should not we, an advanced society, heed the call of unity? This may sound shocking to cultures which have not been taught to accept the return of the soul, but I've wonder if all great teachers were the same intelligence . . . returned to enlighten inhabitants of earth again and again. I think perhaps Zarathustra, Buddha, Lord Krishna, Confucius, Jesus, and Mohammed, were all the same soul, come back to teach mankind how to live. For you see, my beloved friends, the same thread of truth runs through each philosophy--modified, perhaps, to suit the needs of the time and the culture to which the Ascended One came."

The little monk seemed swallowed up by the folds of his robe as he continued to rock back and forth. His listeners inched closer--trying to capture his every word; afraid they might miss a vowel or consonant carried away by a breeze which harried small funnels of fallen rose petals. Mediterranean pines began to sough as the wind enlivened the needles. Clouds started to bunch against each other, blocking warming rays of the sun. The hem of Anna's silk shirt fluttered, and its flapping noise threatened to drown out the monk's words. With a gesture of exasperation, she gathered the folds of material close to her chest and pressed forward, listening with every fiber of her being.

"I find no fault with the doctrine of reincarnation. Our lord Jesus asked his disciples who men thought he might be, and they responded by saying some believed he was Elias returned to earth, others thought perhaps he was Moses or John the Baptist. Another time, the disciples asked Jesus why the scribes thought it necessary for Elias to precede him. Jesus answered them saying Elias had come but they did not recognize him. I think our Lord was speaking of the return of the soul to earth repeated times." A darkening bank of clouds seemed to unlock a door through which cooler, brisker breezes swept into the world.

"Forgive me for digressing from the topic of our discussion. You asked what I thought of Father Simson. I believe all men of vision share a dream of unifying the world beneath one banner. Alexander conquered what was known of the world in his time, Genghis Khan swept out of Mongolia, spreading a new culture in his wake. All great leaders sought to imprint their views upon the minds of other men. Perhaps we are watching history repeat itself. Who is to say, maybe the Father General is the soul of Alexander or Genghis Khan returned to try again."

"Or Hitler about to unleash his madness on the world once more?" Kaminski's tone of voice was raspy. The marble amphitheater intensified the sound, and he was shocked he allowed himself to verbalize his thoughts. "There are rumors Hitler exchanged priceless works of art his armies plundered from museums across Europe in exchange for his life. Some say he only died recently after living out the remainder of his life in the Vatican--as an obscure Jesuit priest."

"Father, do you think that's right?" Anna was disturbed, their conversation was deviating from the tenets of a faith in which she'd been taught to believe in without question.

"Child, who is to say what is right or wrong? Have we learned nothing else from history? Only five hundred years ago if cows sickened and dogs died a woman, any woman, was labeled a witch. It was considered an act of mercy to burn her alive. People believed the flames would purge her sin and the smoke would carry her aloft to heaven. And, why only women? Why were men spared this cruel fate? One hundred years ago it was accepted as fact if a man traveled in a vehicle going faster than a hundred miles an hour, his immortal soul would be forced from his body. Yet today we send men toward the stars with such acceleration it boggles the mind. Reality changes with the times and who can say for certain what reality is? For the people of India, the teachings of Krishna and Buddha are the only reality they need. The nomadic tribes of the deserts prefer the exacting God brought to them by their prophet, Mohammed. Many of us accept the wisdom of the Nazarene, Jesus. Religious myths mirror the culture of the people who believe in them."

Amariah's voice could barely be heard above the scurrying leaves blowing about the courtyard. "Father, why are you a Christian?"

"Oh, child, that is a complicated story. Suffice it to say I've traveled and studied with many men of high religious standards. For me, the laws of Krishna and Buddha seem too archaic. They did not fulfill the longing of my need to understand the incredible force which guides and directs the modern world. For a primitive mind, one not fettered by the changing informationof a technological society, perhaps Buddhism and Hinduism provide the answer. But

I have been thrust into the scientific world where hard data and instruments probing the depths of the universe and the interior of the atom are the religious icons of our time. Gods and goddesses of the Hindus, and the Buddhist belief in 'nothingness' do not fit into the scientific complexities of the culture in which I find myself. Not that their philosophy and code of ethics are unsound--no, it was simply those modes of thought did not quench my eternal need to know. My lord, Jesus, on the other hand, offered keys of wisdom more reasonable to me. Most of His message has been lost or distorted, but if one searches, significant phrases leave pertinent clues. I believe our Lord was trying to teach us the way to find harmony with the Guiding Force of the universe was by turning inward. '*The kingdom of God is within*', He counseled, but we do not comprehend. The human mind must deal with the physical world, so we took a message which defies the senses and tried to explain it in terms we could understand. You see, we all suffer the barrier of language. The only means by which we can describe the very thing beyond explanation are words associated with sight, sound, touch, taste, and smell. We cannot force any of those words into a box and yet man feels compelled to try. The role of the Messiah had nothing to do with the yoke of oppression forced upon the Jews by the Romans. It had everything to do with escaping limitations. Primitive minds of the era simply misunderstood. Then, down through the ages, the Church assumed the dimensions of a political, not a spiritual, force. Slowly, the tidings of our Master became distorted to suit the ends of those who sought control over mankind. Today, we are experiencing a resurgence of a need to turn inward. I feel we are on the threshold of the Second Coming, foretold by the Master of the Ages."

"Father Simson sees himself as the new Messiah." Leon's words were as acidic as the fear that burned a hole in his stomach.

"I know." Father Prabhupada kept his gaze fastened on the ground. He didn't look at the clouds obscuring the rays of the sun, nor did he notice a sudden drop in temperature. He didn't hear gusting wind as it blew life into dry, dead leaves, only to withdraw its support so they fell against the ground again, limp, and lifeless. The voice coming from folds of soft brown cloth was so quiet it was almost lost to the heavy sigh of nature. "I know."

Leon stood, jamming his fists in his pockets. "Father, you don't believe Andrew Simson is the new Messiah! The man is consumed by ambition. He might well be Genghis Khan, Alexander the Great and Hitler all rolled into one! Only he's got something they didn't have. Simson has the means to communicate with every person on earth. He can reach out through television and the internet to enter the hearts of men, women and children everywhere!"

Cao Bang stared out a window overlooking the crowded harbor. The first slender fingers of dawn caressed the horizon, but the waterfront still slept, and boats rocked peacefully as the tide began to turn. Drumming his knuckles against the windowsill with irritation, he strained to hear the wheeze of the hydrofoil fans used by giant boats which plied the river from Canton. Hopefully, his sister's son would arrive from the interior on the next ferry. Cao sent for him over a week ago but the boy experienced trouble getting out of the mainland. The priest's plans were too ambitious for any one man to implement, and instinct warned Cao he dared not fail.

He probably wouldn't recognize the boy--he hadn't seen him in years. Family ties were still revered in China despite changes demanded by the Cultural Revolution, so Cao knew he could count on Fuchsine Hu. There was little opportunity for a young man in China and Cao knew he was offering Fuchsine a chance to make something of himself!

Turning toward the waterfront as a sea breeze began to freshen, Cao's thoughts drifted to Garden Lily. If the boy didn't show up soon he planned to leave a message with the old hag who shared this part of the harbor with him. Lily was an impatient woman. Although he provided a lavish apartment, expensive clothing, and the services of a maid, she whined and complained when Cao was unable to take her to fashionable restaurants or on shopping sprees.

Lily was beautiful--she loved to display her long, silky hair, skin the rich color of mellowed ivory and a body created by the gods to pleasure a man. Cao felt the familiar warmth of longing between his legs. Where was that boy? His sister promised Fuchsine would be on the first ferry! Glancing down at the cheap watch on his wrist, Cao's impatience increased. Just thinking about Lily made the blood pound in his veins and his manhood rise. One side of his head began to ache with the pressure that accompanied desire. Fifteen more minutes, he would wait just fifteen more minutes!

Cao rubbed his hand over his chin, satisfied it was as smooth as the satin sheets on Lily's bed. Stepping back, he surveyed himself in the bathroom mirror. Fresh from a bath, his hair smelled of almonds because he rubbed the scented oil Lily favored into his scalp. His teeth gleamed, and his breath was fresh with cloves. Cao recognized he was not a handsome man. Even for a Chinese, he was not tall, but his flesh had not turned mushy with age-- although Cao realized all too well his looks would never have captured Lily's attention. His teeth were crooked and the sparse mustache gracing his upper lip did little to camouflage them. Patting his stomach, Cao decided he was ready to present himself to his lover. It hadn't taken long to learn he dare not approach her bed unless he washed away the stink of the harbor.

Living as she did, in a modern apartment complex in the fashionable section of Hong Kong, Lily was not exposed to the sordid side of life. And--she'd been clear--unless Cao supported her mode of living she would find another lover. Cao tried to keep his jealousy in check. Every time he considered the possibility of some other man's hands touching the sensuous mounds of flesh which made up Lily's lush, firm buttocks, he felt his stomach twist. No matter what the cost, Cao knew he would continue Lily's upkeep.

He opened her bedroom door. Although the sun was well over the horizon, Lily had drawn thick, dark drapes over the windows to afford a few more hours of uninterrupted sleep. She hadn't expected Cao to arrive so early.

Sliding his hands beneath the elastic of his shorts, Cao removed them. A faint light seeping beneath the curtains silhouetted Lily's sleeping form. Long, dark hair trailed across the sheets, like the wake behind a boat. The aroma of jasmine reached his nostrils as Cao fondled her hair. God, this woman always smelled so good!

He lifted her sheet and slipped between folds of satin. The fabric felt cool against his skin. Reaching for Lily, he allowed his hand to linger on the softness of her shoulder before he traced the swell of her hips. Lily rolled on her back, not awake, yet aware of his touch. One small breast was outlined by the light. Coaxed by Cao's stroke, her nipple hardened. His hand traveled the valley between the soft cones of her breasts, then followed her stomach to the patch of hair between her legs. Lily wanted to shave her pubic area, as was the custom of women in her trade, but Cao insisted she let it grow. He liked to entwine his fingers in strands of hair which reminded him of feathers. Burying his fingers in the curls, Cao probed the warmth beneath.

Opening one eye, Lily greeted him. "You are here early! Had I known, I would have been waiting properly."

"I wanted to surprise you."

Lily smiled, revealing small regular teeth that reminded him of pearls. "You did, but I would have had tea waiting, scented myself with perfume and strewn the sheets with flowers."

Cao's mouth went dry as he felt the wetness seeping from inside her body. He could barely hear what she was saying over the rapid pounding of his heart as she snuggled closer. The warmth of her skin electrified his senses as she pressed against the length of his thigh. Beneath her touch it seemed as if his manhood had a life all its own. It was as if the rod of flesh existed apart from the rest of his body, unmalleable, needing to be satisfied in a way which compelled the rest of him--his body, his mind, his soul--to follow.

Bending to kiss the upturned lips awaiting him, he felt her breath against his face as she whispered. "Did you bring Lily something? A present could warm my passions to even greater heights."

It was a lesson he'd learned early in their relationship. If he wanted to enjoy the most endearing of her charms, there was a price to pay. The higher the cost of his gift, the more intriguing the present, the greater his pleasure. But Lily was so erotic, so passionate Cao didn't care. Money didn't matter compared to what he received in return. No woman ever made him feel the way Lily did; she could transport him to the gates of heaven as she brought him to the edge, then slowed to prolong his rapture again and again. Lily knew how to excite every nerve ending in his body and she set his skin on fire with the delicious wetness of her tongue, the gentle pressure of her fingertips. Yet she had the strength to push and shove, to buck and rear in a way that drove him wild.

Gems were a small exchange for the release she always brought. In truth, had Cao not established the lucrative relationship with the priest, he would have found another way to keep her. Lily was more addictive than opium and the residue of her talent didn't cloud the mind the next morning--like alcohol. Lily kept his heart racing and his mind spinning. He hated the hours they were apart. And Lilysold her charms to no one else--that was the bargain they struck. Lily's cost was high, but Cao had never experienced the delight she brought when she wrapped her mouth around his cock, or sucked and toyed with his nipples, or plunged her hot, wet cleft down on his manhood--engulfing him in ecstasy.

"I have a present for you." He reached for the velvet box on the stand beside the bed.

Sitting up to inspect her gift, the sheets fell away from her inviting buds of breasts. Upturned nipples beckoned him, and a shudder of anticipation left goosebumps on Lily's arms. "Oh!" A cry of delight escaped the lips Cao loved to wander down the length of his body when she withdrew a strand of diamonds on golden chain. "Cao, this will look beautiful with the red silk dress you bought me!"

"You see, Lily," he took the diamonds and fastened the chain around her neck; a pendant with a full carat in the middle hung suspended between her breasts, "I wanted to adorn the mounds that excite me so." Desire turned Cao so stiff he thought his manhood would burst the moment he entered Lily.

"These blossoms bring you pleasure?" Lily brought her nipples within inches of Cao's face. Tracing the tip of his nose with one taut button of flesh, her voice teased him. "How is it these small buds bring satisfaction to a man of the world?" Throwing her leg across his chest, Lily slid down his body, leaving a warm, moist trail along his stomach. With her tongue, she licked his navel and then sucked each of his testicles so gently Cao thought he was being caressed by a hummingbird.

"They give me much joy." Cao's voice came from so deep in his chest, Lily couldn't distinguish the words. He reached around her waist, throwing her back against the bed. "You are my garden of earthly delights." He penetrated, then thrust. Lily turned her hips upward, greeting him, wrapping her legs around his back, welcoming him into her body. The sound that escaped his lips was the moan of a rutting animal. It filled the room and echoed against the walls. For Cao, nothing existed but the fire consuming his flesh. The heat in his loins burned an upward path to his brain. It exploded there in colors as intense as the fireworks invented in China when Mandarin lords owned hundreds of concubines.

Cao fell against the pillow, his chest heaving as he fought for air. Lily straddled her lover and swung the diamond necklace with its dazzling pendant before Cao's eyes. The sun was almost overhead, and a shaft of light pierced a crack in the curtains. It struck a facet in the diamond and filled the room with a thousand prismed rainbows. "Cao," Lily bent to kiss him, "this is beautiful, and Lily always pays her debts. Are you ready for more of the carnal delights found in my garden? There are hidden places your manhood has not yet explored."

"Lily, I do not think it possible to begin the journey again so soon."

The warmth of her tongue tickled his ear as she whispered. "Lily can do wondrous things to revive a soldier weak from battle."

As she began a slow descent down his chest Cao gasped with pleasure as she applied gentle pressure to his nipples with her teeth. Hot, wet lips sucked the flesh of his belly, and caressed the inside of his thighs. No matter what it cost, no matter what the priest asked, Cao knew he would do whatever the Jesuit wanted. He would never give up Lily! He would keep the priest happy, and in turn, Lily would provide him with hours of erotic pleasure.

The warmth of her mouth as she sucked his cock into the back of her throat brought a flash of red before his eyes. No matter what it took . . . he would find a way to keep the voluptuous Lily!

Amariah glanced at the clock on the wall above the desk. It read 2:10 a.m. She'd been working on Adamus' scroll for several hours. Satisfied it was complete at last, Amariah checked her notes one more time. The syntax, and verb tense of Greek and Latin made the passage difficult, but she continued the battle throughout the evening and into the early hours of morning.

Rubbing her eyes, she tried to clear her vision. She tapped the pencil against the sheaf of papers, she was certain--the message was correct. Had she left anything out? Her eyes wandered to the notebook again.

Adamus referred to Christ's words in Luke 13:3, "*I tell you, no, but unless you repent, you will all likewise perish.*" Translated from Aramaic, the language spoken by Jesus, the verb *metanoeo* meant to repent, as far as most theologians were concerned. But Adamus was clear . . . the word meant more than being sorry for past actions; it meant a complete change of mind. According to Adamus, the meaning of repentance was distorted by the early bishops to gain control over the uneducated. The literal translation of *metanoeo* was *'to turn your mind around'*.

Reaching for the scroll, she unrolled it for the hundredth time. The words leaped at her, its message seared to the core of her being. It seemed as if Adamus was whispering in her ear.

To the one who reads this message,

Peace be unto the troubled portion of your mind, for by the time you find this missive there is no way to predict the circumstances in which the world will find itself. The era in which this scroll is discovered will be a time of dramatic change. I pray its message will bring peace to worried hearts, pour the oil of atonement on ravaged souls, and put the most learned mind at rest.

The words of the Master have been preserved by a few desert mystics, who never knew him, men who never had the privilege of hearing his voice or meeting the Messenger! These souls, locked away behind their desert strongholds, saved the truth of His mission for the generations to come. So important were His words, that they tunneled deep into their cherished mountains and created chambers inside the earth. In tall jars, they stored His glad tidings until a time it would be safe to reveal them to mankind again.

Here is but a portion of what this secret Brotherhood allowed me to read, and I copied down:

'I tell you, unless a man changeth the way of the thoughts in his heart, he will perish. For as a man thinketh, so is he. His thoughts can light his world or consign it to darkness. The Kingdom of God is at hand, but it does not rule the world you see, no, rather, it rules the 'heart' and can only be discerned by turning within. Render unto Caesar that which is Caesar's for when a man's heart is guided by right thinking, the conditions of government do not matter. No man can be a

slave when his mind is free; no man can be a master when enslaved by thoughts of darkness. Caesar cannot rule the soul! He cannot govern the mind of any man! Turn inward, seek the goodness within you, strip from thine self all that is untrue, unkind, or deceitful. For I tell you truly, such is the path of a Master. The things that I do, and more, ye also can do through the power of belief. It is all that really matters. If you believe in me, then accept the truth of my message. God is within the hearts of every man, woman, and child. When you find the Kingdom within, the circumstances of life are of little consequence. First, turn your mind around, then all the wonderful conditions of life will follow!'

Amariah sat back with a sigh, her head hurt. As if the veil of deception had been torn from her eyes, she saw the truth for the first time in her life. The process of abandoning concepts cherished by Church dogma made her body ache. Like a surgically removed tumor, Amariah felt the foundation of her faith being cut away. The evidence was so staggering it was impossible to ignore. Everywhere she turned, she seemed to stumble across material which pointed to the manipulation of biblical text to suit the politics of those early bishops. She was beginning to think Leon was right. To accept the Bible verbatim was like believing the platform of the Republicans and Democrats was divinely inspired and should be considered a holy document! Those original three hundred men were as politically motivated as the members of the House and Senate. They all had a personal agenda and compromise was required to hammer out a platform suitable to all three hundred!

If this manuscript was authentic the concept of repentance would have to undergo a complete change. Jesus didn't ask sinners to mourn past actions, he counseled them to stop their present way of thinking, to change their activities, to forge ahead in a new, positive direction. *'Turn you mind around'*. The words refused to leave her thoughts, like a broken record they went around and around. *'Turn your mind around'*. It was so simple. *'As a man thinketh in his heart, so is he'*.

Richard Weatherby recorded case histories where the impossible happened because a person had faith in themselves and believed they could achieve their goal. He counseled Amariah to guard her thoughts, to be aware of the destructive power of negative thinking. How often had she heard him say, *'Tell a man he can do something, have faith in his ability to achieve . . . and he'll make it happen!'*.

The words on the parchment came into focus again. It seemed like her father paraphrased the epistle Adamus claimed to have found on his journey into the Egyptian desert. Wasn't the author of the text implying it was up to the individual to determine the condition of their life? Perhaps that was why the Savior's message was so threatening to the men of his day. Wasn't he telling them to quit blaming others for what happened to them? Was he divulging a master secret . . . think right and the world was right, no matter what the situation?

Amariah cradled her head in her arms, she was tired. Working on Father Simson's project all day and staying up half the night to translate the words left behind by the sixteenth-century Jesuit was taking a toll.

Perhaps it was the by-product of fatigue, but she longed to tell someone about her discovery. Maybe feelings she had about the Church would clear if she talked about them. Reviewing names of potential listeners, Amariah quickly eliminated John Preston--he'd want her to go to the press with the story. Amariah wished her father shared her passion for religion. He would be the perfect person with whom to discuss her feelings. Her dad had a talent for putting fractured thoughts in order. Suddenly, Amariah lifted her head. Leon's face flashed through her thoughts, and she felt a weight lift from her shoulders. She knew she could trust Leon Kaminski.

Fuchsine Hu slipped into the cramped cabin and looked around. The Hong Kong harbor was not unlike other ports hugging the Pearl River. In China, all ports looked alike. People thronged busy waterways in shallow draft crafts which reminded him of water skippers; the noise, the refuse, the smell of fish clung to the river and the inhabitants who called it home. Other than the slender stalagmites of concrete and glass, which thrust against the sky, Hong Kong looked like Ziaolan, Rongqu, Guillin or Yangshuo.

Glancing around the hot, airless room, Fuchsine wondered if it would anger his uncle if he opened shutters closed tight against a cooling breeze. Deciding it would be better not to take an action which might offend Cao Bang, Fuchsine slumped against the bulkhead. It had been a long and tiring journey down the Gui River to the Pearl. The trip took several days longer to reach Canton than anticipated. There were patrol boats plying the waters of the Pearl between Canton and Hong Kong. Traveling without proper papers Fuchsine knew, if apprehended, would mean an untimely end or years rotting forgotten and abandoned in some hellhole jail. Caution delayed him longer than desirable, but he thought it would please his uncle to err on the side of discretion rather than act out of impatience. He had to prove himself to his uncle. Cao Bang was a man whose temper needed to be respected--if half the stories he'd heard were true.

Eyes drooping, Fuchsine gave in to the weariness screaming at him from every muscle in his body. He leaned his head against his arms; the lapping of the water against the hull soon lulled him to sleep.

Cao watched the slothful piece of humanity he assumed was his sister's son for a moment before he unleashed a kick at the young man's thigh. "Hiyah! What are you doing sleeping in my cabin?" Cao voice was piercing, as if truly offended he'd found the young man asleep.

Nonplused, Fuchsine lifted his head. A smile spread across an uncommonly handsome face. Jet black and straight, the way his hair lay against his head made Fuchsine look as if it had been shampooed and trimmed only hours ago. Fuchsine was large boned and muscular, he looked as if he'd walked many miles behind water buffalos which tilled the rice patties of his homeland. "Uncle, I am Fuchsine Hu, my mother sent me to be of service to you." Rising, Fuchsine bowed, anxious to appear respectful.

"Did your mother say why I sent for you?"

"Honored Uncle, my mother said to reach you as fast as I could by any means it took. She warned me to be cautious and to avoid all patrol boats. I do not think she knows why you wanted me to come to Hong Kong--only that it was a privilege to honor her illustrious brother with my service. You are a powerful man because when I asked a lowly harbor dweller where I might find you, their eyes glassed over with fright before they pointed the way to your junk. A child said you left quite some time ago--he did not think you would return before sundown--that is why you found me asleep."

"Much is known to these boat people. Remember this fact, it might keep you from harm in days to come. Over a quarter of a million people dwell in this harbor. Their way of life is unusual, and they embrace a code of ethics all their own. If you learn to dwell peacefully among them your life can provide an infinite number of rewards. Cross them," Cao's eyes narrowed to slits, "and you will suffer a horrible end!" The glitter in Cao's eyes was inspired by menace. "Have I made myself clear?"

Fuchsine drew to his full height, he was head and shoulders taller than his uncle. "Uncle," Fuchsine lowered his eyes, "I am here to serve you. My family is poor, the land they work is worn out from centuries of use. More nights than not they go to bed hungry. It is my wish to please you because by doing so their suffering will be lessened. You have a reputation among our family as a man whose temper can be sharp, but you are said to have a kind and generous nature toward those who please you. I will work hard to assure your generosity."

A burst of laughter bounced off the wall that once boasted a coat of paint. Cao slapped the young man on the shoulder. "Honestly spoken, nephew! Had you said anything else I would sense you could not be trusted. Men are always honest if it is to their advantage!"

Familiarity ceased as suddenly as it had begun. Cao stormed across the cabin and threw open the shutters. Gesturing, he pointed toward the skyline holding back the bank of gray-black thunderheads on the horizon. "There is a fortune to be made out there as long as we are smart enough to avoid the suspicion of authorities. You've been in the mainland all your life--I'm counting on you to know who we can bribe and who we can trust to take our goods up rivers into China."

"Uncle," Fuchsine's arms remained at his side; his body stiff and straight, an attitude of military respect, "may I know what it is we are to do?"

Turning from the window, Cao Bang searched the lad's expression for a sign to betray deceit. He was still young, Fuchsine had not yet been jaded by the pleasures life had to offer. He probably had not taken to the pipe yet and perhaps he knew nothing more than the occasional charms of a peasant girl. The boy was an idealist, he would tell by the clear, straightforward look in his eyes. He knew the lad was not prying by asking, rather, he was expressing honest curiosity about what lay ahead. Instinct, and years among the most cutthroat people on earth, taught Cao never to tell anyone anything they didn't need to know.

"You will be moving goods into every province in China." Cao laughed, the cold, mirthless laugh of man with a heart turned to stone by a lust for profit. "We have powerful allies dedicated to making sure China undergoes a bloodless revolution. Fuchsine, you've much to learn about human nature. Never forget people are greedy. Feed that greed and you can control the destiny of nations!"

Leaning against the bulwark, a veil lowered in Fuchsine's eyes. His expression changed as emotion gripped him, then turned his face unreadable. Cao noticed but was caught up in his own self-importance. He didn't see the way his nephew's fingers curled into a fist, nor how stiff his shoulders became. Cao still basked in the memory of Lily. So many physical releases soothed a normally paranoid nature. He was too relaxed to pay attention to the flat stare hardening his nephew's expression. Cao was on the threshold of gaining everything life had to offer and anticipation of greater bliss obscured the warning signals being broadcast by his nephew.

"Klaus, you can't be serious!" Leon's eyes narrowed as his expression changed to reflect preternatural dread.

"I've never been more earnest about anything in my life." The German shoved a map in front of his fellow scholar. "You've got to give this consideration!"

"I'll grant you the plan has merit, but it also contains elements of political intrigue!"

"Truth is often stranger than fiction! What do you think the driver of that taxi was doing . . . taking a random pass at two men, who just happened to be standing in front of a certain restaurant on a nearly deserted street? Leon," Klaus' eyes assumed a glare that was slate cold and hard, "whether you want to accept it or not, it was an attempt on your life! I'd be willing to wager a fair amount of money someone in the restaurant passed along a message. You said Preston is a frequent patron and the two of you stayed until most of the other guests departed. It was a perfect opportunity--and someone took it."

"But attempted murder?"

"Why?" Klaus disappeared behind a cloud of smoke as he drew on the pipe, his frustration evident.

"I grew up in the free world and I've lived my entire life in a society which abhors murder. I've spent a lot of years in remote corners of the world learning to speak the languages of other men. In my line of work, I haven't been exposed to politics or intrigue. I have trouble coming to terms with a deliberate effort to harm another human being."

"I see!" The restoration expert tapped an aluminum tin of tobacco against his desk with a rapid, staccato beat, the noise a counter point to the irritation in his voice. "You think everyone is basically good?"

"I guess you could say that. Villains create excitement in stories. The coarser side of mankind is an abstract concept to me."

"My dear young friend, you'd best come to terms with it in a hurry because a perfidious force is loose in this world. My keen sense of order detected something more despicable than either of us ever thought possible. I was quite young when the war began, but I've listened to my relatives. In fact, an uncle of mine was a guard at Hitler's private bunker. He saw Der Fuhrer every day. The stories I've heard about the changes occurring in Hitler might be unbelievable except for one thing."

Leon studied the other man. There was a hardness in Klaus' expression which conveyed an uncompromising nature. The 'sense of order' about which Klaus often remarked was more than a way of life with him, it was a consuming passion. Every detail of life had to fit, events must assume a logical pattern. This character trait was beyond a passion for restoring great works of art; it devoured him. Leon realized the German's idealism verged on fanaticism. Was Klaus seeing circumstances as they were, or was he taking abstract details and weaving them into a distorted tapestry of assumption and self-deceit?

Eyes so cold they were the color of the Arctic Sea in winter stared across the desk. "I used to watch my uncle's expression change when he spoke of Adolph Hitler. You see, he shared the man's dream. He believed the German race was superior to the rest of the world. He was certain his country was destined to rule the entire planet because their methods were better than any system devised by other cultures. My uncle thought the Third Reich would last a thousand years. He would have laid down his life for Der Fuhrer because Hitler gave him something in which he could truly believe. Leon, I've studied this phenomenon. When you provide hope, when you promise a man an opportunity for a better life, when you tell him he's better than anyone else--he changes. My uncle learned he was not any more unique than the Americans, Brits, or Russians. He was just an ordinary man, and in the end, the hero he worshipped turned out to be a common madman. My uncle abhorred the thought of being average. He wanted to rule! He needed to be better than everyone else! He lived out the rest of his life a prisoner of the past."

"So, how does your uncle's experience effect our present situation, Klaus? I know you too well to think you'd share your family history with me for the sake of conversation." As he watched Klaus tamp tobacco into the bowl of his pipe, he could see the same kind of fixation in his friend's eyes.

"Leon, my fear comes from somewhere so deep inside it defies rational explanation. I might sound like a lunatic, but I can no longer contain my misgivings about Simson. Hitler's madness thrust the world into chaos. It affected entire nations and cost the lives of millions! I don't want the experience repeated in my lifetime and I'm starting to think it might."

"Don't you think we've learned anything from war?" Leon's fingers curled into a fist, his stomach muscles tensed. A burden was lowered across his shoulders as the enormity of Klaus' concerns penetrated his emotional defenses.

"I don't think we've learned a damned thing! When a charismatic man is consumed by a concept, he has the power to sway the most rational mind. Like tuning forks, we will start to share a common resonance. It's as though a negative force contains the power to dominate everything good and honest."

The harshness of the German's words seemed to press Leon into the chair rungs. "That's really cynical."

Klaus closed his eyes when he opened them the gaze which bored through Leon was enigmatic. "I've read dozens of accounts about flashes of inspiration. Einstein said the theory of relativity came to him like 'a bolt out of the blue'. Edison told of how the concept for the electric light bulb woke him from a dream in 'a blinding arc of light'. Alexander Graham Bell related he was inspired with the idea for the telephone 'in an instantaneous spark of knowingness'."

Leon stared at the other man, waiting for a connection to be revealed.

"My friend, sitting here, just now, with my eyes closed, a zig zag of light flashed across my thoughts and behind it came the answer I've been seeking. For weeks, I've sensed the power coming from the Vatican has nothing to do with saving souls. Father Simson's idealism just didn't ring true. His vision for humanity appears righteous, holy if you will, on the surface. But there's an undercurrent of malfeasance to his mission. He'll force the world to submit to his ideology, if necessary. He plans to be the one to lead the masses toward his dream of a united world. You see, Simson is going to use the Church to dominate a global political structure. He's going to appeal to billions of believers through their emotions--he'll offer everything they lack. If it's political freedom, he'll be the man to assure their human rights. If they're deprived of the material things in life, he'll be the one to open the doors to trade, so goods can reach heretofore inaccessible regions. Leon, Simson has set in motion a master plan. You and I, the other members of the team, the museum, are all part of it. His plans are far more encompassing than I ever thought possible! And, my friend, I fear Simson will stop at nothing to ensure his strategy succeeds."

The picture coming from the television set illuminated the corner of the room. Drawing his chair closer, using the remote control, he adjusted the volume. He replayed the interview with Father Walton Mendez a hundred times since it was broadcast several weeks ago. Whenever his spirits faltered he watched the incredible exchange. With the saga of human drama, his zeal soared. A single half-hour segment made more converts, brought more donations, than any of his other efforts. Smiling, he leaned back into the padded chair. Margaret Anderson didn't know he arranged an interview with Father Mendez. His instincts were correct, she proved to be the perfect standard bearer--so open, so honest, so guileless, so naive.

Margaret jumped at the chance to fly to Mexico with the first planes carrying food and supplies from the Catholic Relief Agency. Her popularity in America soared after the landmark interview in the Sistine Chapel. Her wholesome looks, mane of blond hair, and wide-set clear gray eyes reminded people of a by-gone era when dreams of the girl next door were achievable. The impassioned expression filling her face, when she turned toward the camera, made her a champion of the American public.

When the camera closed in on her anxious face, focused on hair slicked back and secured with a colored scarf, Margaret looked like a tourist out for a mid-afternoon stroll in a sleepy village. A safari shirt stretched over generous breasts and the legs protruding from linen shorts could have belonged to a fashion model.

Holding the microphone close to her lips, Margaret began by introducing Walton Mendez, a Jesuit priest, who had done so much to relieve the suffering of people hardest hit by the earthquake.

"Father, where were you when the quake struck?" Margaret reached to pull a wisp of hair from her eyes.

"In my office, preparing for afternoon mass."

The microphone pulled back in her direction. "Do you remember your first thoughts?"

Father Mendez's eyes strayed to the tree-rimmed horizon, a ripple of anguish brought on by memory crossed his face. "When I heard the explosion caused by ruptured gas tanks at the filling station, I thought we were under attack. Seconds later buildings surrounding the marketplace toppled off their foundations and bricks came crashing into the square. Cintalapa seemed to shudder beneath the impact of a hundred mortar rounds."

Panning the village, the camera's sweep took in scattered bricks and beams littering the area, where vendors once brought goods to market. "As you can see," Margaret's voice explained the destruction to the viewing audience, "nothing in Cintalapa is left standing but the church. "Father, what happened then?" The camera zoomed in on Margaret's stricken expression as she relived the disaster with Father Mendez.

"Severe aftershocks hit us within minutes of the original quake. I thought I'd never be able to regain my feet. The vestry floor swelled like the waves of the ocean."

"It must have been awful," Margaret's eyes grew moist as currents of emotion swept through her body.

"Finally, when I could stand up, I ran outside. Devastation was total. The village was as quiet as death, not a sound came from any direction. A jungle is usually alive with the hum of insects, hundreds of birds jabbering, and occasionally, the scream of a jaguar. But for a minute, I thought I might be the only person in Cintalapa to survive the earthquake. Then, the screams began. The dying called for absolution and injured cried for help. Margaret, as I stumbled down the steps to a marketplace reduced to a pile of smoking rubble," the cameraman turned toward the area that was once a thriving center of commerce, "I faced a fear so shattering it paralyzed me. Everywhere I turned," the camera made a slow arc from the left side of the village to the edge of the jungle, "nothing was left standing."

"Father, these people are so poor . . . how can they possibly rebuild their homes, their lives?"

The Jesuit forked his hand through his hair. For a moment he said nothing, then he cleared his throat in a valiant effort to control the timbre of his voice. Father Mendez swallowed hard and reached beneath his cassock for a rumpled handkerchief. He pressed the cloth against his eyes as he gathered the composure to go on. "Margaret, these people live in unspeakable poverty. They have no resources. It isn't a matter of calling your insurance agent and waiting for a check so you can restore your home. They have nothing . . . absolutely nothing!" A voice choked with emotion muffled his words. "I'd like to ask you and the crew to come with me--leave the camera running so the world can bear witness to the plight of these people."

The priest, Margaret, and her crew of three, threaded their way down a narrow path cleared through rubble. The lane disappeared as Father Walton Mendez pushed giant elephant ear ferns out of his way. They barely pierced the curtain of vegetation when Margaret put her hand over her nose--an awful odor was coming from up ahead.

"What is that smell?"

A cameraman coughed, then gagged and another reached to flip the lens cap down, but Father Mendez pushed his hand away. "No! Keep filming! I want everyone to understand what happened here!"

Gray eyes bulged with shock when Margaret saw the bodies lying in a tangled heap at the bottom of a deep pit. Many were bloated beyond recognition; in other's the flesh had melted to reveal slashes of bone, where powdered lime hastened decomposition. Margaret pressed her hand against her mouth, fighting the acid line of vomit climbing the back of her throat. Finally, the smell was so overpowering, the sound of thousands of flies crawling over open mouths and across eyes, which no longer saw the sky, became so loud, she couldn't control the urge. Running to the side of the road, the shaken woman vomited until there was nothing left in her stomach . . . not even bile.

Mendez forced the camera in Margaret's direction, his glare warned what would happen if the cameraman stopped filming. Dry heaves racked her body although nothing was left in her stomach. The priest cradled her waist as if she were a child. He passed his handkerchief beneath her chin and wiped away spittle clinging to her cheeks. Margaret began to sob and buried her face in the priest's shoulder. His body shielded her from the grotesque grave and hands that were a mass of blisters stroked the back of her head to comfort, the soothing action of a compassionate parent with a distraught child.

"Oh, Father." The words were hoarse; they launched up her throat and spewed out in a hollow, despairing, mournful cry. "I didn't know!"

Kissing the top of her head with tenderness, the priest led Margaret away. His gestures extended mercy, but his eyes mirrored the horror endured by the people of Cintalapa.

Later that evening the cameras rolled again. Candles dispelled an early darkness and what remained of the vestry was draped in a curtain of weak light. The priest extended Margaret Anderson a cup of wine. Few bottles were spared the destruction of the earthquake, but Walton Mendez knew the woman needed to be soothed by alcohol.

Putting the cup down after a long, slow drink, Margaret faced the priest. "Father, I've never felt so helpless in my life. Tell me what I can do to relieve the suffering I saw today. I can't bring back the lives of those who bear the indignity of a common grave, but perhaps there's something I can do for their families. Tell me, all you have to do is ask--and I will move heaven and earth to see help reach these people!"

"Margaret, from the time the initial shockwave hit, I began some soul-searching the likes of which I've never been inspired to do before. I realized, as I walked through the devastation of Cintalapa, my life had been turned in a new direction. I decided right then and there," the camera narrowed its focus, zooming in on the brown-black eyes reflecting the candle's sputtering flame, "that I was going to dedicate my heart and soul to restoring these villager's fragmented lives."

The Jesuit reached for a crucifix made from polished wood. "When you pull a body from a pile of rubble, and that body turns out to be a little girl, who celebrated her first communion at your altar rail only weeks before, something happens to your spirit. Margaret, I've stood waist high in bodies in that burial pit, only they aren't just bodies to me. They were friends, people who'd become my family. Nature can be far crueler than anything envisioned by man--but I realized a greater good could come from Cintalapa's destruction."

Margaret's expression was outraged with disbelief. The cameraman moved back, eager to capture her reaction. "Greater good! Father, how can you suggest such a thing? These people lost families, they have no homes-- they face disease and starvation! There's no way to bring a father back to a grieving family, no way to restore a dead child to its parents! Father, I'm sorry . . . but I can't see anything positive coming from this!"

An arm streaked with sweat and stained with dirt and blood shot across the table as Walton Mendez grabbed Margaret Anderson's hand. "If this interview touches the heart of just one man, if one person looks in their mirror and decides to help the victims of Cintalapa, then my life has not been in vain. My people need food, they need clothing, they need building materials to restore their homes. We have a desperate need for manpower to clear our roads, to reestablish contact with the outside world. Margaret," the camera closed tight on the tormented priest, "I am appealing to the decency in every man. I'm asking people to send whatever they can spare to their fellow human beings in Cintalapa. Mankind must realize we share this endangered planet. We can no longer honor tribal boundaries, we cannot think people who are from other cultures unworthy of our charity. We are all brothers! We must care for each other if our planet is to survive! The people of Cintalapa might be the residents of San Francisco or Chicago a few days from now. I ask the citizens of the world to accept the survivors of Cintalapa into their hearts *because we are our brother's keepers!"*

The office door opened, and the Father General reached to switch off his television set. Father Walton's interview inspired an instant and overwhelming response. "So, what is the report on today's activities?"

A smile of satisfaction crossed Father Wilson's face. "We had to close the bank at noon today. Donations were pouring in so fast we couldn't keep up. Volunteers are coming in to work on the computer terminals overnight so by morning we should be back to normal again."

"What was the last figure?" Andrew Simson drew his lips away from a dazzling array of teeth; it was a voracious smile, a predator accustomed to snaring prey.

"Twenty million dollars and like I said, we were too busy to take a count today."

Stroking the crucifix at the center of his chest, Andrew Simson turned thoughtful. "These television interviews exceeded my wildest expectations."

"Father," the other Jesuit's voice was filled with a mixture of wonder and foreboding, "you inspired Father Mendez."

Simson stared at the blackened television screen. "The segment showing Margaret vomiting into the bushes was particularly compelling." His thumbnail rasped down the cross. "Half the world was moved by her reaction."

Eyes darker and colder than the far side of the moon turned to the window. Night had fallen, and residents of the Vatican were preparing for sleep. His thoughts were silent, he did not wish to share them with Father Wilson quite yet. 'I took men who were homeless, with nothing to live for and made them a part of my dream. A convicted killer, an assassin, a military genius without a war, an orphan . . . all forty-four only needed something to believe in.'

Father Patrick Murphy bowed at the rail beneath the pillars of Bernini's Baldacchino and lowered himself to his knees--his fingers slipping along his treasured rosary beads. His whole life had been dedicated to the Church--consecrated to the glory of God. Father Murphy's shoulders heaved, and his head sank against his chest. He hoped here, in God's house, an answer would come. Squinting his eyes tight, trying to close out the noise of the tourists come to pay homage to the greatness of St. Peter's, Patrick Murphy recited a prayer.

"*Grant to Your people, we beseech You O Lord, to avoid every contamination of the Devil, and, with pure minds, to follow You, the only God. Through our Lord, Amen.*"

Surely, he and Father Lean were wrong. His finger grasped at the next bead, clutching the round onyx as if the stone could provide a miraculous answer.

"*We beseech You, O Lord, that Your healing mercy may uphold our weakness, so that what of itself is falling into ruin may be restored by Your Clemency. Through our Lord, Amen.*"

How could he have been blind to something so obvious? Why hadn't he seen this before? Why did Father Lean have to point it out? Were they falling under the spell of Satan? What was happening? Was he losing his mind? His stomach rumbled, it had been two days since he'd eaten, hoping an answer would come through fasting and prayer. The next bead rolled beneath his finger as he continued the litany memorized across the span of forty years.

"*Grant, we beseech you, O Lord, to Your suppliant children, that, as they abstain from bodily food, they may likewise refrain their minds from vice. Through our Lord, Amen.*"

Father Lean seemed so certain, and the evidence *was* compelling. Prayer. The answer was prayer. It had to come. Had not the Savior promised if the penitent asked, they would receive? If the searcher sought, they would find? Patrick Murphy felt like hammering against the gates of heaven. God had to provide an answer. The answer he was searching for! The answer to explain something he didn't want to face . . . couldn't face! The next rosary bead felt cold and heavy, almost as heavy as his heart.

"*Almighty and merciful God, in Your bounty, graciously defend us from all that is hurtful; that, free in mind and body, we may with ready mind carry out the things that are Yours. Through our Lord, Amen.*"

The sound of the brass doors as they closed out both tourists and the night reverberated up the nave. Last rays of a waning sun threaded through the western windows at the base of Michelangelo's dome. Its gilded ribs trapped the fading light and reflected an aura of gold on figures of Christ, the Virgin, St. John the Baptist, St. Paul, the Apostles, and angels. A final, piercing spear of light reflected upward, headed for the painting of God in the uppermost spire of the dome.

Craning his neck, Father Murphy could just make out the distant figure. God appeared amid the clouds, his hand stretched forth in benediction. The magnificent dome, gilded coffering, elaborate paintings, and the words of Christ recorded in mosaic tiles on a background of gold conferred temporal authority upon the popes: "*Tue es Petrus et super hanc petram aedificabo ecclesiam meam et tibi dabo claves regni caleborum.*" Upon thou, Peter, I shall build my Church.

A sudden spasm brought him up short. His heart quivered, sending shooting pains down his arm. Taking a deep breath, Patrick Murphy waited. The jolt finally stopped its downward journey. His heart resumed a normal, steady rhythm. His pacemaker needed to be checked. He would go to the infirmary tomorrow. Hopefully, it wouldn't have to be replaced again so soon.

Gripping the altar rail with determination, Father Murphy pushed to his feet. The course of history would be altered forever if he and Father Lean made this discovery known. Was it right? Was it right to change the way mankind had believed for a thousand years? Was it right to rip the world asunder? Patrick Murphy's gait was slow, his movements that of a haggard man.

His shoulders sagged, and his head drooped when he realized his prayers had not been answered beneath the magnificent dome. As he made his way down the nave toward the doors opening into the square protected by the colonnade, he sighed again--a heavy expulsion of breath in a troubled man. He felt abandoned; alone; as if God had forsaken him after a lifetime of faithful service.

CHAPTER TEN

"Is the camera set? Sound recording? Testing . . . one . . . two . . . three. Everything working? What? You want me to move left? How far? Okay? The newsman wiped his palms against his pants; afraid perspiration would make the microphone slip from his hand.

"We're going live in thirty seconds. Stay on your mark. You're centered between the fire and rescue team. No matter what happens in the background, don't move Len." The cameraman's hand formed a hollow square, indicating the box of space in which he wanted the newsman to stand.

"Okay. Give me a count."

The soundman thrust four fingers in the air and began the countdown to the broadcast which would be flashed around the world via satellite communication links. "Four. Three. Two. One. We're live."

"Ladies and gentlemen, we're on the air, live from Belfast. Behind me is the largest apartment building in the Protestant section of the city. It is now engulfed in flame despite valiant efforts by fire fighters on the scene. As of this moment, it's feared hundreds are dead. According to reliable sources, fire swept through an apartment building in a matter of minutes and several interior walls collapsed shortly after the first explosion was reported. There seems little doubt *the fire was not accidental.* Witnesses said flames broke out in several areas of the building at the same time and blasts shook the entire structure before fire erupted. We have with us a man who was standing across the street when the first explosion occurred. Sir, can you tell us what you saw?"

The microphone swung toward an elderly man and without thinking he backed away. The reporter glimpsed the cameraman's frantic gesturing, and he drew the apprehensive man closer. "In your own words, sir, what happened?"

Squinting against the glare of the television lights, a gnarled hand rubbed the day-old gray stubble on his chin. "I cain't rightly tell yer. Twarn't no ordinary gas main rupture, I reckoned tha' much fer sure. I served in 'ter war, yer see, and I knows tae sound of high-grade explosives when I hears 'em. This 'ere blast was set, went off the way we used 'ter blow the German's out of their bunkers. 'Twas the IRA at it again."

The microphone returned to the reporter's chin. "So, you're a war veteran?"

"Suren' enough. Served in the big one. Hit Sword Beach with Monty, I did. Marched across 'alf of Europe right behind him! Now that were a soldier's soldier." Warming to the reporter, the old veteran became less intimidated by the camera and crew.

"Based on your experience, you feel the fire was deliberately set?"

"Like I tol' yer, that were no gas main what went. Bubber, that were a charge of plastic explosive or a whole lot of TNT. Yer sees, 'tis the way the sound 'its 'ter ear that makes 'ter difference. We used to could tell how big 'ter bombs 'ter German's was throwin' at us by 'ter sound they made comin' in. We'd 'uddle together and 'ang on to our 'elmuts and call out to each other . . . 'two 'undred kilos in that one, blimey! Or 'itler must be runnin' out of powder, that one was more likely a 'undred kilos. Once yer get familiar with 'ter blokes, yer can tell what they're tossin' at yer."

"I see, you think this explosion was caused by high grade ammunition?"

The old man reached for his cap and pulled it off his head. Grimy fingers ran along the brim for a minute and camera lights reflected against a shiny scalp which long ago lost its covering of hair. Eyes that seemed watery at first turned cleared as they stared into the camera. "Sonny, I lost a lot of friends fightin' 'ter Germans and I lived through battles I shoulda been kilt in. It's been some years, but 'ter memories . . . theys fresh in me mind. I knows an explosion when I hears it, and that there buildin' took several 'its. I ain't seen nothin' like it since 'ter war."

Both men turned as a rescue crew shouted at them to clear the way. Men rushed by with a stretcher clutched in desperate hands, bleak expressions drained faces of every emotion save shock and fear. Blood-soaked sheets did little to disguise the battered remains of a young boy. The roar of flames grew louder as the building collapsed. Wails from mothers who couldn't find their children mingled with the screams of burn victims. Hoses ran in every direction as firemen labored to extinguish an inferno.

The old man's voice was hushed, his words swallowed by the cacophony of horror as fierce and as frightening as Dante's Hell. "It's like relivin' the Blitz. I 'oped I'd never see such 'ideousness again in me lifetime."

Turning, the newsman pulled his microphone away from the old man and opened his mouth to speak.

A shock wave from another explosion roared down the street, knocking bystanders, firemen and the wounded off their feet. Fighting to hold on to his equipment, the cameraman collided with the pavement but managed to keep the building in frame. The awkward angle of the lens focused on more sky than building as he struggled upright.

The reporter pushed himself off the street, his cheek bloody from the impact of gravel mashing sensitive skin. Chest heaving, fighting for air, he tried to marshal his thoughts and continue reporting events that seemed to be transpiring at the speed of light. The weary old solider pulled on the reporter's coat and gestured down the street.

"Blimey! Look there's another one blown to smithereens."

Motioning for the cameraman to follow, the reporter rushed toward another building where people were pouring from doorways and jumping from windows. Billowing balls of flame hurled down the side of the brick structure and spread across the pavement. Screams were drowned by a second blast which tossed the men about as if they were dried leaves scattered before the wind.

A wail drew the newsman's attention as a woman waved her infant in the air five stories above him. "Catch her! God, please save my baby!"

Before he had time to think, the infant came hurtling toward him. Throwing the microphone aside, the reporter made a desperate lunge. The impetus of the baby hitting his chest knocked the wind from him and dropped him to his knees. The baby's cry penetrated thoughts frozen by shock. Looking back at the window, he raised his hand, a signal the child survived the fall. A wall of flame lowered over the window and extinguished the mother's scream before it reached him.

The camera continued to broadcast the scene to a communications satellite high in the stratosphere although its operator laid it aside and rushed to help his partner.

Searing pain stabbed the reporter's chest; a rib or two was probably broken. His lungs screamed for air and a veil of black threatened as they hurried to escape the rain of burning debris; the infant in his arms screamed and screamed and screamed. When they reached the sheltering arch of a nearby doorway, the reporter sank to his knees. He tried to soothe the baby, but its cries refused to be stilled. The cameraman retrieved his equipment and the newsman beckoned him closer. The microphone was lost but both men were sure the audio equipment on the camera would pick up his voice over the holocaust going on around them.

Coughing out words despite the pain in his chest, the newsman forced himself to relate what was happening for the rest of the world.

"Ladies and gentlemen," he stopped, a spasm drained his lungs of air; he wheezed out the words as he gasped for breath, "a second apartment complex in Belfast just burst into flame. I don't know if we captured how a desperate mother tossed her child form the window of a fifth-floor apartment, but it is an experience I'll never forget." Another cough seemed to shred his lungs and his silence found its way around the world. Collapsing against the wall, he swallowed several times then strained to continue. "Within moments after flinging her child to safety, the mother disappeared in the flames which consumed her apartment. If this attack was perpetrated by a terrorist . . . " his Adam's Apple bobbed as he fought against a rising tide of emotion, "I cannot understand how someone can inflict horror upon defenseless women and children. Although we don't know the cause of the fire, I can tell you this for certain--people here are victims of senseless destruction. Children lost their parents tonight--and parents have been robbed of their children. What kind of men would do such a thing?"

Tears coursed a path through the smoke, grime and coagulated blood gathered on his cheeks. Without realizing he was doing so, the reporter pulled the wailing baby beneath his chin. He rubbed the top of the tiny girl's head with the side of his face, his tears dampening a soft cap of hair. "What kind of man would deprive an infant of its mother? What kind of beast unleashes such horror on the innocent, the unsuspecting?"

In a voice subdued by the stranglehold of emotion, the reporter choked out his last few words. "I'll tell you one thing, I'm going to find the devil who robbed this baby of her future! If it's the last thing I ever do, I'll track the bastard down! I'm making a solemn promise to this child . . . I'll find the murderer responsible for taking her mother away." The words were a primordial scream, a voice turned inhuman by rage. "I'll find you--I'll hunt you down if it's the last thing I ever do!"

The cameraman laid his equipment aside, but he didn't shut it off. He offered a supporting arm to his friend, and they limped off in search of medical aid. The world watched in horror as the signal sent to a communications satellite overhead bore silent witness to the carnage. More explosions jolted the street as another apartment building burst into flame. Screams of the dying, the cries of the wounded traversed the planet.

Men and women in Denmark sat before their television sets on comfortable couches and wept at the scene which turned their living rooms into a battleground. Mothers in England clutched their children, grateful, yet ashamed of their gratitude; their young were not lost to a madness no one seemed to understand. In America, New Zealand and Australia, shocked faces could not turn away from devastation so frightening it seemed like the Apocalypse had finally come.

For weeks, the last words of the newsman as he clutched the wailing infant were repeated on newscasts around the world. The Prime Minister of England put the IRA on notice they crossed a fatal line. England was at war again. The killing would be stopped if it took an all-out assault on the IRA. The Crown would shelter Protestants in Northern Ireland.

IRA leaders sent frantic messages to anyone who would listen. Theirs was not the hand that ignited the torch, which, seemingly, blew Ireland apart. They did not carry war to children! They were not responsible for the lives of the innocent. Their war was with the soldiers who inhabited a land that did not belong to them.

Sean O'Flannery listened to the news reports with satisfaction. Both sides were going insane. Soon, like hungry jackals, they would tear each other apart over a worthless carcass. The British and IRA were dull-witted fools who allowed themselves to be manipulated by a superior mind. It was working just like the priest said it would. Sean knew he'd have to lie low for a while, but he could still enjoy film clips of the fire on the telly. It was just as thrilling to watch it for the hundredth time as it was the first.

The glow cast by the screen in the corner of the room threw a lens of color over Sean O'Flannery's pockmarked face. Sean was glad he'd decided to steal the color TV. The blackness of his pupils reflected the red from the fire broadcast over the airwaves. The colors were vibrant, alive, and dancing. It was all working according to the priest's plan!

"Cardinal?" Amariah closed the door behind her, softly.

"Ah, Sister, do come in. It's been some time since we had the pleasure of a chat. I fear Father Simson has everyone chasing their tails of late." David Woolsey lowered his glasses, staring at the nun, who sat poised at the edge of the chair as if ready to take flight. "What can I do for you?"

Amariah chewed at her lower lip and began to twist the rosary beads around her fingers. "I would like permission to do some research in the Secret Archive."

An eyebrow arched then the muscles protecting his eyes closed into a scowl. "Sister, I had no idea your area of work involved the Archive."

"There are passages I've run across I would like an opportunity to research."

"Such as?" He picked up a pencil and began to tap it against his teeth.

"I'm interested in early Jesuit missionaries, the ones who traveled to remote places--like the monasteries of Tibet, India--and Egypt."

"That portion of history does not concern you. What on earth does the translation of the ancient languages of Hebrew, Aramaic, Greek and Coptic have in common with Jesuit missionaries?"

"Well," Amariah studied the rosary beads in her hands; "a document I've been working on refers to an early Jesuit who brought a number of Coptic manuscripts from Egypt. Father Simson said an adequate codex was never developed for keeping track of records stored in the Archive, but I seem to have an ability to locate obscure text."

"Sister, I hate to disappoint you but there is no reason for you to invade the Archive."

"You opened it for other scholars! I should think the significance of this project would permit me an opportunity to see if I can find what I'm seeking."

"Tell me what that might be?" Woolsey was growing more impatient with each passing moment, but he realized his frustration was only a masquerade for fear. A rivulet of sweat passed between his shoulder blades as he struggled to discourage the nun.

"I'll know it when I see it."

"Ah," he steepled his fingers over a ponderous layer of fat shielding his stomach, "your power of intuition is at play here?" His fist slammed the desk causing a canister filled with pencils and pens to rattle. "Would you have me defy holy Church canon? Only the most serious researchers are allowed an opportunity to enter a sacred place, which shielded the world from the profane, the damned!"

Amariah's head whipped up. "Are you forbidding me? The frontiers of our faith are being challenged from every direction. Can you afford not to let me search for what might beproof our Lord really existed? Would you be the one to deny me an opportunity to find evidence that Jesus walked the earth, talked with his disciples--that he ate, drank, and slept beneath the stars? All we have is hearsay about his life. We cannot say for certain He ever existed. Cardinal, I may be on the trail of evidence, which could prove once and for all, that Jesus Christ was an actual historical figure!"

Woolsey shoved away from the desk, an angry expression turned his face a mottled shade of scarlet. Pulling a set of keys from beneath the folds of his tunic, he glared at the woman who seemed to best him so easily. "I will give you four hours--no more. This is far longer than we normally allow scholars access to the Archive. Grab some notepads and pencils. Once you are inside I shall lock the door behind you. And" a furious expression burned in his eyes, "when I come back for you . . . you will leave willingly . . . and not ask to return!"

Knowing it was pointless to protest, Amariah nodded. Stuffing the pad and pencils he gestured at into her bag, Amariah followed the Cardinal out the door.

Woolsey's pace was fast for a man of his size, and she had to hurry to keep up. They stomped down seldom-used hallways in the library, up stairwells which seldom felt the tread of a human foot and finally stopped before an oak door. Heavy metal hinges, crafted in an era when copper was forged by hammer and fire, held wide planks secure. Shoving a key into an ancient lock, David Woolsey fumbled a few times before time-worn tumblers clicked into place with a sharp sound that mocked the hush in the corridor.

The door opened, the timbers screaming a protest their rest had been disturbed! Amariah stepped into a room sealed against intruders for centuries. Light from overhead fixtures switched on by motion detectors fell against leather bindings yellowed by time. Motes of dust wrapped the room in a gauzy haze. Amariah felt as if she were stepping into another world when she crossed the threshold. Metal shelves were utilitarian, and the room lacked the artistic elements like the Vatican library. A layer of dust clung to her fingers as Amariah reached to clear a space on the cluttered desk beneath a long window.

Woolsey's voice was petulant, angry, demanding immediate attention. "I'll be back in four hours. Put everything back where you found it and don't touch the codex. The Father General has done a great deal of work in here--nothing must be disturbed."

"Did Father Simson arrange the Archive chronologically rather than by subject or author?"

Woolsey snorted out a derisive laugh. "Sister, some packets in this room are so old the hand that penned them has long since been lost to time. Three-quarters of what you see here was written by men history has long forgotten."

"The work of women does not deserve a place in the Archive?"

"I'll not dignify your silly remark with an answer."

The door slammed shut and Amariah turned back to the desk. The Archive was a haunting place . . . a secret bastion of knowledge which stood fortress-like against the assault of ignorance. Blood surged through her arteries and veins; excitement made her hands tremble as she reached into her purse for paper and pencils. Just standing in a room filled with so much information was exhilarating. It was like exploring an uncharted cave or being the first to travel down a river that had never been navigated. Surely explorers of every age thrilled at the prospect of discovery, whether they were charting the universe or probing a dark and distant past.

Amariah placed a notepad on the desk and began to search for the codex. She blew dust from a ledger containing Andrew Simson's document log. As she scanned the pages, Amariah was surprised at the number of entries.

On impulse, she laid the ledger aside. Walking to shelving running parallel to the window, she reached her hand over her head and swept the air in front of dusty manuscripts, as if the books and scrolls could impart the information she sought. As she walked between rows of shelving, Amariah rotated her hands back and forth, scanning them like a radar antenna.

She stopped. Removing a scroll which seemed appealing from a shelf at eye level, she tugged against the cord securing it. Words penned in Latin read like simple verse.

A woman called by an ancient name will return from out of the past
This woman will stand alone amid a nation of men whose badge of office is red and black
Men whose dreadful reign cannot be allowed to last
She will wage a desperate battle with this nation of men
She will tell the world of their inequity and shout against their sin
This woman will return armed with the knowledge of her student's ways
She alone has the power to end the reign of their wicked days
Her vows she will forsake because she'll find them false
But her life will not have been lived in vain
Through her, the influence of these despicable men shall wane

Cumaen, the Sibyl

Amariah flinched when she recognized the signature. Historians believed all recorded works of the Sibyls were destroyed in a fire which consumed most of Rome during Nero's reign. If this document was authentic, it was a piece of history which deserved immediate attention. She couldn't help but wonder about the woman the Sibyl described. It was clear the prophetess thought this woman would be involved in a terrible conflict.

Returning to the desk, Amariah laid the piece of pumice smoothed animal skin aside and checked Simson's notations in the codex. It appeared the Father General gathered all the information that could be traced to the time of Christ and put them in one location. Her glance took in row after row of shelves--he hadn't indicated where the documents of the period were stored. She decided to walk the length of the room again, then turned and paced the perimeter. Where had Simson put them? Amariah traced her fingertips across packets sealed in wax with the stamp of the pope in office at the time; along book bindings whose leather was moldy with decay; over stacked rolls of papyrus turned brittle with age. She walked, then turned and walked in the opposite direction, her hand extended toward the shelving. Refusing to glance at her watch, Amariah tried to ignore concern about minutes that were ticking away; Cardinal Woolsey would return to the Archive all too soon.

On the fifth row, halfway into the center of the room, Amariah found her eyes drawn to one shelf. She reached for a small book which seemed to beckon to her. The content was written in Hebrew, and judging from the condition of its binding, it might have been penned near the time of Christ. Amariah took another manuscript from the shelf, then another, and with a quick glance confirmed their content. Her hands grew moist, and her heart began to race. She had stumbled across the location of the New Testament era documents! At the back of the shelf, a packet was wedged between the metal frame and wall. She tugged it lose with gentle pressure. Holding the manuscript close, she scanned the text.

Dear Ones,

Behold, the Light of the world is here. We are sending Him to Egypt to study with men who have different knowledge. Men who preserved the wisdom of an ancient civilization so distant it has been buried beneath the weight of time.

I, Elias, High Priest of the Essenes, have committed the new Messiah of the ages unto the care of my most beloved student, a woman called Amariah. This one has out distanced all the men of her day.

She returned to earth to prepare the Messiah for his mission. Now I can rest. I leave the future to the woman called Amariah.

Elias, High Priest, of the line of Aaron

Her vision turned purple, a haze of black draped the room and the floor dropped away. Clutching the shelf, she labored to steady the trembling which took unchallenged possession of her body. Molten lava burned upward from her stomach, and she covered her eyes to keep back the tears. Coincidence. Mere coincidence! She quickly scanned the other document she took from the shelf.

I, Iraenous, Supreme Bishop of the newly created Church, lay my hand upon this paper to justify the meaning of my actions, for mankind must know why I have acted thusly. Heretics are threatening to destroy what I have labored to create! Lesser men criticized me, and I dealt with them harshly. The Gnostics of Egypt had to be silenced, for their beliefs are dangerous. They claim each man should be allowed to reach God by their own path; to be free to find salvation by individual means. This idea endangers the order and structure of the Church.

Mankind is weak! They need strong leaders to exhort them to righteousness. Few have the strength to follow the dictates of their conscience. Anarchy would reign supreme if everyone did their own bidding! No, the Gnostics must be crushed, or their ideology will weaken the foundation of Church authority. As in heaven, so must it be on earth! One God rules the heavens, and one Bishop must rule the earth!

The Priscillians are a menacing lot. They would have mankind believe the stars guide and influence man's destiny. Men will become confused if they learn to trust in forces other than the Church. Loyalties cannot be divided! Priscillian must be eliminated! His followers run to ground, his works destroyed. And the Sibyls. Alas, they grow too powerful. Men seek their advice instead of turning to the Bishops for guidance! They must be stopped--for they are only women! God does not speak through them! They must be silenced forever! The keys of authority were passed from our Lord and Savior to Peter, the founder of the Church. Their influence must be crushed!

The Church will replace Caesar's legions as the final authority over mankind. I am the new Caesar, and I will stamp out all who oppose my reign! I will bring a new order to the world, I will rule as the temporal authority of God! I, and I alone, will be the sovereign Bishop of this world. Other influences must be wiped from the face of the earth, or they will challenge the authority of one bishop to rule! I have set in motion plans to be rid of the heretics. There can be only one leader . . . and I will be the Roman Bishop of the Catholic Church!

Irenaeus, Bishop of Rome 357 A.D.

Amariah's fingers drummed against the desktop. Penned in his own hand was an admission of how Irenaeus shaped the Church. He achieved his objective by destroying opposing points of view! He saw himself as another Caesar, and like Caesar, he craved power. To what lengths had he gone? What truths did he sacrifice in his crusade to reign supreme? What schools of thought did he wipe out in his bid forpower?

The Gnostics were an aesthetic group who built their monasteries in a remote part of the Egyptian desert. Yet Irenaeus did his best to obliterate evidence of their existence. She knew little about Priscillians. The Sibyls were so important to Michelangelo he placed them between the prophets of the Old

Testament on the ceiling of the Sistine Chapel. She was unaware these women played a role in the formation of the Church. Amariah's thoughts began to spin.

Shading her eyes against the light streaming through the window over the desk, Amariah stared at three pieces of history. Each one could damage the foundation upon which the Church was built. The throb at her temples increased and Amariah massaged the area in front of her ears. The significance of what she uncovered raged like the approach of thunder. Amariah stared at these documents; if this information were made public--the world would never be the same again. What should she do? Her eyes traced the pattern in the wooden floor until the planks disappeared beneath the metal shelves; a solution surfaced in her troubled thoughts; a lifeline thrown into the sea of emotional chaos.

In fifteen minutes, the Cardinal's key would be rattling in the lock. Grabbing the Bible, she raced to the shelf. Had it been lying on its side or was it upright? Amariah stood on tiptoe, hoping a telltale shape would be outlined by a layer of dust. Not quite tall enough to see the top shelf, Amariah pulled the back of her skirt through her legs, tucked the hem into the waistband and climbed the bookcase. The Bible had been lying on its side. Amariah wiped the leather covering with the sleeve of her habit then wondered if paranoia had overcome logic, but for some reason, she knew she had to remove her fingerprints from the binding. Hopefully, enough dust would settle over the next few days to make it appear the ancient Bible was never disturbed.

Rushing back to the desk, Amariah rummaged through her purse, seeking a way to hide these documents. Scattering the contents of her bag across the desk, she sifted through an accumulation of personal and scholarly items. Her hand rested on *St. Joseph's Daily Missal*, the book she carried to mass every morning and from which she recited her evening prayers. The Missal was as much a part of her daily life as her coffee cup. Everyone was accustomed to seeing it flung across the top of piles of notes or withdrawn from her purse as she hunted for some other item. The entire research team knew she carried it with her every day!

Would the documents fit inside? Could they be slipped between the pages of the Missal? Amariah reached for the scraps of parchment and leather. Trying to steady the hand that shook aged papers with the rattle of a gourdsman in a mariachi band, she slid them between worn pages. After replacing the contents of her bag, Amariah decided if Woolsey asked to search her purse nothing would look out of place. She straightened the desk and replaced the document log, the manuscripts and reference works just as they were when she entered the room.

When the key turned in the lock and Amariah grabbed the codex. Only her breathing broke the silence like waves breaking against an unyielding shore. She needed to appear casual, as if the last few hours were spent in disappointing study.

The door opened, and the Cardinal's red robes preceded him into the room. "Well, Sister, I trust you spent the afternoon productively?"

"I'm somewhat disappointed. It's impossible to trace beyond the point where the Father General stopped his organization process. I would love to spend the rest of my life in this room because there's so much knowledge here. Think what might be in store for the rest of the world if we could translate and classify all the documents which have been lost within these walls for the past five hundred years. Perhaps when the museum is built, and the artifacts are in place, the Father General will allow me to continue where he left off." Amariah brushed at the wrinkles in her skirt, an abstract motion--an action intended to keep her hands from wandering to the bag lying on the desk. She fought against an impulse to shove past the Cardinal; to escape into the garden with damning evidence. Instead, she engaged in pleasant conversation. "It could take a lifetime to index all these documents. It's nothing short of a miracle the Father General got as far as he did!" Reaching for her bag, Amariah slid the strap over her shoulder. "Cardinal, would you ask the Father General if I might extend my stay in Rome? I am fascinated by what this room could offer mankind."

"You didn't find what you were seeking?"

"No, I was being naïve. I didn't realize the magnitude of the volume of documents here." Her eyes skimmed books pre-dating the invention of the printing press by centuries. "It would take years to trace through this maze of manuscripts. I spent most of the afternoon studying the codex. If granted the time, I could extend the limits of the Father General's work and I would like that opportunity." Amariah's fingers wrapped around the purse strap, her knuckles turning white beneath the pressure.

"Perhaps I can bring it up at some point. For the moment, Andrew is so occupied with the task of opening the museum he cannot be disturbed. If you will allow me to say so," his red robes swelled as he expanded his chest with an indignant breath, "I tried to tell you a search through the Archive would prove fruitless."

"Well, I had to hope. A scholar is like a Jack Russell Terrier. We latch on to random threads of information and can't let go until the missing piece of the puzzle is put in place." A forced but dazzling smile beamed in the Cardinal's direction. "Please intercede in my behalf--once the museum is open."

A raspy voice spat out words as if the Cardinal found them distasteful.

"We'll see what the future holds."

Woolsey led Amariah into the hall and locked the door. "Your time would have been better spent in the research lab or the library. You've created a fuss over nothing!"

Her arm pressed against the bag in an attitude of defense, Amariah responded sweetly, "Cardinal, I wouldn't trade an afternoon in the Archive for any other experience in the world."

"You what?" Andrew Simson launched his lean, athletic body across the room.

"She asked permission! What was I to do?" The Cardinal pushed deeper into his chair, seeking escape from the wrath direct at him with intensity of a heat-seeking missile.

"Why didn't you stall her until you talked to me?" Pacing, the black robes swirled around polished leather boots, the flow of cloth as menacing as the unnerving directness of his words.

"I am head of the Council of Cardinals! The Archive is my responsibility. Don't you think it might have aroused the nun's suspicion if I picked up the phone and asked your permission for her to enter? Why wouldn't I have the authority to open the door?" Woolsey's fingers were growing slippery with sweat as he gripped the chair arm; desperate to salvage what was left of his dignity and the last vestige of his ecclesiastical power.

Eyes radiating animal fury swerved in the Cardinal's direction. "What did she say?"

"She wasn't able to get any further than you did. She spent most of the time studying your codex. She also asked permission to work in the Archive after the museum opens. She was intrigued by what it might contain."

The thumbnail traced a relentless path down the crucifix. "Did you search her bag?"

"Really Andrew, what would I say?" His tone of voice rose an octave higher as fear speared his bowels. "Excuse me, Sister, you might be a thief and I'm going to search your purse? You've taken the vows of a Benedictine nun, but we suspect you might be on to something which could upset the Father General's plans!" His voice became a ululant shriek. "Would you have had me say that Andrew . . . would you?"

The hiss that escaped the Father General's lips was venomous. "If you're not the man to fill the responsibilities as the head of the College of Cardinals, then I suggest you retire someplace more to your liking. Somewhere it's peaceful, where you do not have to suffer the rigors demanded by the Vatican."

David Woolsey felt the blood in his veins turn cold. The face that scorned him was menacing; the doom transmitted by its expression was almost palpable. With dread, David Woolsey sensed his days were numbered. Somehow, some way, Andrew Simson was going to best him.

The cyclopean disc rotated slowly, its signal pointing toward the satellite hovering above the continent Columbus stumbled across in his quest to find the riches of India. Dawn caressed the horizon with pink fingers and like a lover, the sun fondled the earth, warming it, arousing the world to a new day. Inside walls which housed the Vatican broadcast station, Father Wilson tapped in a new set of coordinates. The antenna swung a few degrees, then halted. A priest waved toward a soundproof booth and flipped a series of switches which made the console look like a Christmas tree festooned with lights.

Fingers springing forward as he marked the countdown, Father Wilson smiled at the man who shuffled his notes in front of the microphone. Father Simson conducted a monthly broadcast to the Jesuits laboring in the vineyards of the Lord. A red light began to flash, and he signaled the Father General to begin.

His voice reverberated from waffled acoustic tiles as eyes as black as midnight scanned the papers in his hand. "Brothers, I am addressing the chosen of this world." Andrew Simson reached for his crucifix, "Were he here, Ignatius Loyola would be pleased with the words of our brother in Mexico when he inspired thousands to cast off spiritual lethargy. Father Loyola began his mission with only *seven* men, whom he sent into the world as representatives of the word of God. These defenders of the faith crossed the Himalayas and made the perilous journey to the Americas."

He shuffled his notes and glanced up at the clocks in the control room indicating the time in other parts of the world. "These brothers met occasionally to exchange news. When they returned to the distant lands in which they labored for the glory of God, lines of communication were established so they could relay messages to one another. In the Americas, natives traveled jungle trails with handwritten accounts of their travails. Throughout Tibet, India and China--along trade routes traveled by caravans since the days when our Lord walked the earth--messengers reached Rome with letters from these early defenders of the faith."

The Father General glanced at the clocks again. All over the world his men would be checking their watches. He slowed his delivery. The set of coordinates linking them with the communications satellite had to be spoken at the right moment.

"Soon after he began his missionary efforts, Father Loyola gathered unto him *nineteen* more dedicated brothers. They, too, went into the world."

Eyes fixed on the clock, the Father General cleared his throat, as if overcome by his message; another signal the forty-four were trained to recognize. The second hand swept up the face of the clock and he began again.

"Our brother in Mexico, who has been doing such a valiant job alone, will be joined by *seven* more Jesuits, who are on the way to assist him. Brothers," Andrew Simson's hand closed around the microphone, his knuckles bleaching white, "we are in the last days and each of you will bear witness to the glory of the Second Coming! Each of you have been selected to carry its banner. You've been chosen to prepare the way for the glory to come. Take heart, Brothers, the Kingdom of God is at hand!"

Walton Mendez shut down his two-way radio. He understood: 7-1- 9-7, the coordinates to program into his geo-position locator. As small as a pocket pager, it transmitted a signal to a satellite high in the stratosphere. With this sophisticated tracking device, the Father General could determine the exact location of his men any time, any place. Andrew Simson was nowhere--yet everywhere.

Glancing at his watch, the Jesuit decided he could go back to sleep. No one else would be up for some time. There was nothing to do until the workmen rose at sunrise. He lay back against the pillow, but his mind refused to rest.

Father Jorge Bagaces could now begin the journey north. The trails they cleared needed to remain unobtrusive yet be wide enough to carry supplies and weaponry through miles of jungle. Reliable men, dedicated to revolutionary ideals, would hack a road out of rain forest which remained virtually unchanged since the disappearance of the dinosaurs. Despite himself, the priest felt his heartbeat quicken. It was going to feel good to sleep in the open again, to enjoy the backbreaking work of forging supply lines, and he looked forward to the weeks ahead.

Hopefully, Jeraldo Concertas would remain in check while he was gone. With ammunition, weapons, food and clothing, Concertas' ego might gain the upper hand. The man was troublesome; he listened to the Father General's advice less and less with each passing day.

"Father?" A delicate voice whispered from the hallway.

Securing the locator in the shatterproof container, the priest shoved the box beneath the bed, then reached to rumple the sheets and blankets before opening the door. "Amalita, what are you doing here?"

"I couldn't sleep, and I noticed the light coming from under your door. I thought perhaps you were lonely." The girl's haunted expression was enhanced in large, earthen colored eyes by the reflection of the flame from the single candle on the table.

"A priest is never alone, Amalita, God is always with me."

"I prefer the company of flesh and blood." Long lashes lowered against cheeks the color of honey.

The girl was standing so close the warmth of her body reached Father' Bagaces' naked hands and feet like the heat from an open fire. "Amalita, you must return to Jeraldo. If he awakens and finds you missing another unfortunate incident might occur. There are times you provoke his wrath. A dutiful wife should not arouse the ire of her husband."

Lips full and swollen drew into a sensuous pout. "There is no excuse for beating me."

"No, my child, there is no excuse. But, please, hurry back to your room before he awakens. After I say morning mass we will talk about your situation."

"Only if you promise, Father."

"I promise. We will have many hours during which we can talk tomorrow."

"Then I will leave, but I shall be waiting for you in the chapel of the

Casa Grande."

"All right. Go now, quickly!"

Father Bagaces closed the door and leaned his forehead against the cool wood. The woman's demands upon his time and attention would have to cease. If only he didn't need her to report the comings and goings of a man he didn't trust.

"Carole? Carole? Are you in there?" Amariah kept up an insistent knocking.

The photographer flung the door open, then stepped back to let Amariah inside. "Lord, honey, you look like you've seen a ghost. Come on in, I'll fix some coffee. I think I might have something stronger . . . alcohol is the weakness of journalists, you know."

Amariah glanced around the lab but didn't really see the piles of photographic paper or seem to notice the odor of developing chemicals. Perching at the edge of the stool Carole pointed at, Amariah clamped her arm over the bag beneath her elbow.

"Honey, what's the matter? You might as well tell me because I'll get it out of you sooner or later. You can't come waltzing in here looking like you just escaped from a living nightmare and tell me you were after a cup of coffee!" Carole filled the pot with water and scooped rich brown grounds into the filter. A smell that reminded Amariah of home wafted through the room as the water began to trickle through the grounds and into the pot.

"Carole . . . " Amariah stopped, cleared her throat, and then tried to start again. "I really don't know why I'm here. Maybe," she began to fidget with the shoulder strap of the bag, "I made a mistake in stopping by." Lips trembling, Amariah stared at the floor to keep the other woman from noticing the tears gathering in her eyes. Amariah pressed her hand over her mouth to still the quiver threatening her lower lip. "But" her eyes lifted--and tears began to spill down her cheeks, "but I feel I can trust you."

"Here," Carole handed her a cup of steaming coffee, "take a couple of swallows and then start from the beginning. Sister, I liked you from the first time we met. You have a sincerity and genuineness I lost somewhere around Da Nang--but I recognize it in others--and I certainly admire it in you." Carole plopped down in the desk chair. Wiping her hands against the worn-out military uniform she liked to wear around the lab, she stared at the distraught nun.

"What's wrong?"

Amariah cast a nervous glance at the door. A degree of communication passed between them that was so strong it was eerie. Carole walked across the room and threw the dead bolt home with a slam. "Now, we won't be disturbed. If it takes fifteen pots of coffee and all night, I'm going to get to the bottom of your troubles." Her glance measured Amariah's hunched body. She was so upset the hand clutching the coffee cup could barely keep it close to her lips.

Carole engaged in comfortable chatter, hoping to offer Amariah assurance she'd done the right thing. "I was one of the last civilians out of Saigon when it fell. You might remember one or two of my pictures. I got some shots of Vietnamese civilians, scared out of their wits by the rapid withdrawal of American troops, trying to escape the country by hanging on to the skids of helicopters evacuating American personnel from the embassy. I got out by the skin of my teeth one step ahead of the NVA. I'm pretty resourceful when I have to be--why don't you tell me what you're so worried about."

The enormous ashtray looked as if it couldn't hold another butt and the air in the office adjacent to her darkroom had turned hazy. The coffeepot was filled and drained several times during the last few hours. Carole opened a small refrigerator beneath the countertop and withdrew a couple of sandwiches as she thought over the nun's story. "I always keep food in here. There are times I work late, and I don't have a chance to get to the cafeteria before it closes. It's a journalistic habit because you never know for sure where your next meal might be coming from--if you're fortunate enough to get one at all. Here!" She tossed a sandwich in Amariah's direction. "Your story is about the damnedest thing I've ever heard!"

Slowly, Carole peeled away the cellophane wrapper and slung her legs beneath the desk. She began to chew in a slow, deliberate fashion--as if she wasn't hungry but needed time to ponder the details of Amariah's astounding revelation.

Amariah's shoulders were hunched, she was tired, so tired all she wanted to do was sleep for the rest of her life. The sandwich went untouched, her appetite lost to misery. "You don't believe me, do you?"

"Sister, you have to understand a few things about reporters. We're trained to be cynics. If you don't doubt the sun is going to come up in the east in the morning, then you won't make it in my line of work. Journalists are the loudest, crudest, most logical bunch of hard-hearted bastards on earth. I know, because I'm one of them, and I'm on speaking terms with every reporter who's ever covered a major event from here to the North Pole and back. I'm a lone wolf and I don't team up with big news services--but I'm good enough that major publications hire me to cover different stories--even though my primary talent is taking pictures." Smoke from another cigarette began to curl past her eyes, forcing Carole to assume a protective squint. "Honey, I learned a long time ago . . . cameras don't lie, they just bend light. You can re-touch the hell out of an image, but cameras don't conjure up what isn't there!"

Swinging long legs from under the desk, Carole crossed the room and slid back a cabinet door. With the cigarette still dangling from her lips, she spun the dial on a safe. Reaching inside, she withdrew a stack of photos, "Sister I believe every word of your story, and these will show you why."

Carole thrust the pictures she took of Andrew Simson in vault seventeen at Amariah. "No one has seen these, but we *are* exchanging secrets. If you think I'm safe enough to be trusted with what you've got in that bag, I'll let you look at these."

Amariah stiffened as she flipped pieces of glossy photographic paper back and forth. Finally, she reached for the lamp on Carole's desk and drew it closer. "Carole, you're a great photographer--can you explain where this came from? How did that light get around his head? Did it pick up on the film because of the dust in the chamber? Are we looking through dust particles toward construction lamps?"

"Sister, I don't have any experience to draw on to provide a logical explanation. All I know is looking at these makes me feel like I'm looking at a psychopath."

Amariah examined the pictures again. Her palms began to sweat; unconsciously, she wiped them against her habit as if trying to be rid of something awful, something slimy. "Carole," the words were sharp and hollow and contained a nervous quality, "the Father General looks like an apparition out of my worst nightmare. The way the light surrounds him makes him appear almost super-human. He always made me feel uneasy but looking at him now, like this, it's almost like he's guided by some strange power." She stopped, glancing up at the photographer.

Cupping her hand over the end of another cigarette, Carole screwed her eyes against the lighter's flame. "Like the Devil?"

"Something like that." Almost beyond her will, Amariah's eyes were drawn back to the photographs lying beneath her hand.

"Sister, let me tell you a story. I was the only woman journalist who covered a battle in Viet Nam. You may not remember the news reports, you couldn't have been much more than a kid when the incident took place. For me," Carole stared through the filter of smoke toward an undetermined point near the ceiling, "it will remain one of those haunting incidents that changes the course of a person's life. For some insane reason, the brass in Saigon decided a remote promontory should be a primary military objective. The boys from Airborne were told to keep on assaulting a little mound of earth until they took it. Eleven times they went up what came to be known as Hamburger Hill and hundreds of kids died in the effort. NVA soldiers were holed up in deep trenches--they had a machine gun nest that was virtually impregnable, but our boys were ordered up that hill again and again." Her hand dropped and the wisp of smoke from the smoldering ash between her fingers rotated in spirals.

"I spent seven days in Hell. I know the look that surfaces in a man's eyes when he's seen too much and suffered too greatly. A kind of veil comes down, something which lets you know the mind's grasp on reality is tenuous--in fact, it's fragile." Carole ground out the stub of her cigarette, her motions frustrated and angry. "Too many boys died trying to take a worthless piece of real estate and I'm still bitter. I vowed if I ever got a chance to stick it to the political theorists of the world--the insane pricks who cause such senseless slaughter--I'd do it with a vengeance."

Amariah watched the other woman. She changed--transformed from a reserved, quiet photographer, to a rigid person furious with conviction. "Carole, I don't remember a lot about the war, only what I've seen on television, or read--so I'm not sure I understand."

Eyes shifting from the ashtray that had been the focal point of her bitterness, Carole's expression was livid. "Well, Sister, I'll try to make myself clear. Andrew Simson is as demented as those bastards who sent fifty thousand innocent kids to their death in a stupid, senseless war! He wouldn't hesitate to expend many more lives over a useless piece of land if it happened to be in the way of his ideological campaign. The pious Father General wouldn't think twice about sending men to their deaths if it meant gaining political control. Simson is ruthless, drunk on power, believing his authority is divinely inspired. As far as I'm concerned, it's the most dangerous thing that can happen to a man."

Carole turned toward the window, her anger spent; in its place, sorrow weighed her shoulders forward and drew down the corners of her mouth. Her eyes had the same look of suffering as those of the anguished mother, who clasped her dead son's body close, in Michelangelo's *Pieta.*

"Honey, whatever it takes, all you have to do is tell me what I can do to help you. I don't know what you've got in that bag of yours, but I'll bet it's probably evidence that would make the Father General mighty uncomfortable."

Amariah fought to keep her expression from revealing how alarmed she really was. "Am I all that transparent?"

"To a reporter." Carole smiled--a sad smile, but one which tried to convey reassurance. "What can I do? How can I help you?"

"Hide these for me." Amariah reached into her bag and withdrew the manuscripts she smuggled out of the Archive.

Pulling back leather wrappings, Caroled peered inside at age-frayed documents.

Amariah pointed at the pieces of yellowed parchment. "Two are written in an archaic form of Greek, the other is in a form of Latin used by the early Church."

A shallow nod dipped in the nun's direction. "I think I'll take an added precaution."

"What?" Amariah watched as the photographer gingerly unfolded creases which were centuries old.

"I'm going to photograph each of these. I'll develop and print them here in the lab, but I think we need to mail a few sets to a couple of other people."

"Who can I trust?"

"We'll think about that for a few days. I send a lot of pouches to my publisher in New York. His firm is compiling a book commemorating the opening of the museum. David Stone is a good man, he can be trusted to safeguard an envelope for me."

"I've been corresponding with the Abbess Mother. I could ask the same thing of her. The pictures would be safe at St. Anne's."

"Come back the day after tomorrow. I'll have the film developed and we can figure out a plan then. We're both too tired right now. People make foolish decisions when they're exhausted."

Carole shuffled the documents between the other pictures on her desk then placed the stack in the laboratory safe with reverence. "They'll be secure here. No one knows the combination, but you can memorize it in case you need access to them if I'm not here." Carole scribbled a set of numbers and passed the paper to Amariah.

A sensation so sharp it felt like fingernails raking across her soul enfolded Amariah as she studied the numbers. "Carole, the combination has some sort of significance, doesn't it?"

Surprised by Amariah's intuitiveness, Carole reached for the last cigarette in the package, crumpled the wrapper and threw it toward the trashcan. "Yes, it does."

Amariah repeated the numbers several times, staring at the floor as she placed the combination securely in memory.

Crossing the room to the wastebasket, Carole stooped down and began retrieving cigarette packets which missed the container. "In Nam, hills were given military codes corresponding to their elevation."

Amariah stared at the journalist; a glimpse of what was coming was daunting. The realization that she knew what the photographer was going to say was overpowering.

Carole Phillips reached to take the paper from the nun's hand and touched it to the end of her cigarette. As it caught fire, curled, and blackened, the woman's face became as hard as heat-tempered steel. "Honey, that series of numbers is the elevation of Hamburger Hill."

CHAPTER ELEVEN

"Ruger, brother, how have you been?" Father Michael Sorenson embraced his fellow Jesuit.

"Well, Michael, and you? It's been months since we've had the pleasure of each other's company." Steely blue eyes beamed genuine affection from a tanned face. Ruger Stein embraced the black man again--to the astonishment of Tshikapa's soldiers. "I sorely miss our classes together in Rome. You and I," his voice lowered, then turned wistful, "were such good partners at debate." He clapped his friend's shoulder and motioned him toward the campfire. "I've kept track of your comings and goings. Even in the bush we heard about your exploits."

"And you make me laugh! Exploits! Ever the sarcasm, eh Ruger?" "Well, my brother, whether you realize it or not your daring in South Africa earned you quite a reputation. Not many men would have the courage to walk into the white man's jail and demand the release of their most celebrated prisoner."

"I had papers from Her Majesty demanding Gwelo be released into her personal custody. I did nothing more than expedite the Father General's plan. The real work was executed by Father Simson."

"Michael, Michael . . . I know what it took for you to enter that prison. Surely you must have wondered if you'd ever leave those walls."

A smile slashed across skin as black as his friend's skin was white. Luminous eyes took the measure of a man he trusted; someone he called a friend. "And you, Ruger, know me much too well. I confess there were moments I thought I was about to join our Savior. In truth, I never expected to win Gwelo's freedom."

Father Stein passed the other priest a cup of tea. "Drink this, it is surprisingly refreshing. The locals concocted this mixture to keep away insects. It also provides instant stimulation--their answer to caffeine, I suppose."

Sorenson took the cup, smiling. "I'm glad to see you again."

"And I you." An expression of genuine pleasure softened his sunburned features. "I'm to smuggle you into South Africa?"

"Yes, I'm going to work in the mines."

A low whistle split the air and a few of Tshikapa's warriors turned in their direction. Waving, Father Stein assured the men everything was in order before he returned to the conversation. "Is that safe?"

"The Father General thinks it's the only way to achieve our mission. You've got a man here who can teach me both Afrikaans and Xhosa?"

"Sure. Loto speaks those languages, as well as Zulu and Sesotho. He's a good man, one I've come to trust."

"Can he guide me across the border?"

"Loto could walk up on a sleeping lion, pull hair from its mane and live to tell the tale. He can get you across, but I'm not confident we'll be able to extract you."

"The Father General developed a plan for my escape."

"Why is he risking a valuable man in a country where you are despised for the color of your skin?"

Sorenson swirled the remains of his tea against the cup. Leaves and ground up bits of bark left an interesting pattern and the priest's dark eyes studied the soggy heap for a few moments as if trying to divine an answer. "Do you believe in fate, Ruger?"

"Deep down, I think most of us hold a secret belief in destiny."

"Well, I've thought about it a lot. It seems more than coincidental that I--out of all the slum kids in London--was rescued by a Jesuit priest. A man who gave me a wonderful education and, more importantly, faith in myself. He brought me to the attention of another man, one who instilled true meaning in my life. I feel as if I've been selected by destiny to do what no other man has ever done before."

"Michael, I know you well enough to have a great deal of admiration for the way you've handled the circumstances of your life. We both had a lot to overcome before we were chosen as one of the Father General's elect. Perhaps each of us was picked for reasons we don't quite understand. Your task involved public recognition while I've led men, who are little more than savages, through an unspeakable wilderness. I've trained them for battle, and we will wage a desperate war in a few weeks' time. I'm proud of these men and I feel as if I have justified Father Simson's faith in me."

"It seems as though we were both rescued from tawdry lives for a larger purpose. Ruger, it's possible I'll never see you again--and I wanted to tell you how much your friendship has meant to me these past few years."

"All of us, all forty-four, have a special bond--a bond which will never be broken." A strong hand, as brown as the husk of a nut, reached to clasp fingers far darker by contrast. "Tell me, Michael, why are you going back?"

"Because I'm the only one who can achieve Father Simson's plan."

"I've been out in the bush for months, what is it you intend to do?" Ruger Stein peered over the rim of his cup, his eyes seemed even bluer now that the sun had bleached his hair white and turned his face the color of coffee mixed with milk.

"I'm going to unite mine workers and exhort them to rebel against whites who have power over them."

The cup dangled from Father Stein's fingers, a few remaining drops of tea stained hard, stony ground. "Praise be to Jesus."

"I'm the only black man among the forty-four."

"Michael, you can't blend in with impoverished people who live in the horror of a South African ghetto! You're educated! That fact cannot be hidden!" Worry drew a web of lines between Father Stein's eyes and his mouth.

"Given a few weeks with your man, Loto, I'm confident I will pass for an Afrikaan. I'll mingle in the streets until I'm comfortable with the language and mannerisms of the people."

"You have papers?"

Michael Sorenson allowed himself a genuine smile. "Have you ever known the Father General to leave a stone unturned, a thread dangling, an 'i' undotted or a 't' uncrossed?"

Ruger laughed, "I guess I've been away from Andrew so long I've forgotten about his thoroughness. However well he's prepared you, be careful my friend. South Africa is a powder keg, and it won't take much to ignite it. If you pull it off, if you get the keffers to stand fast against their oppressors--you could be the torch which sets the country aflame. It's been a long time coming and those poor souls need relief. They've suffered long enough." Reaching out to pat his friend's knee, the dazzling white of Ruger Stein's teeth presented a sharp contrast when he grinned. "I might be sitting next to a future saint!"

"It's a bit unusual, but I suppose with proper implementation it can be done."

"Without anyone knowing about it?"

"That'll be the tricky part. This place is swarming with engineers and technicians. There's also that plucky little nun who's working on the *Messiah's* programming. She's quite brilliant. Too bad private industry didn't snap her up when she was at Cal-Tech."

"Several corporations tried."

"I've never understood the predilection some people have toward a life of privation."

"It's a lifestyle not many would choose."

Paul Grant stroked the sharp crease in his flannel trousers as he studied the Father General. He knew the man was cold, but he never suspected this degree of ruthlessness. A shiver tracked the path of his spine; the hair on his arms and on the back of his hands stood erect as a premonitory tingle pushed a warning through his body. A trail of perspiration trickled down the side of his rib cage, turning his linen shirt soggy, as the engineer spoke. "With the proper equipment, I'm sure I can do it. What I don't understand is--why?"

"I have my reasons."

"If I'm going to be involved in this you owe me the dignity of an answer."

Eyebrows, like the hulking back of a jackal, arched upward. The Father General's face trailed phantoms of annoyance across his expression. "Perhaps you're right." Andrew Simson shuffled through a pile of papers, selected one, and handed it across the desk. "Here is where the explosive charges will be placed. A munitions expert will take care of this detail. I want you to devise a system of sequential controls to be activated from a single workstation." He reached behind him to pat the disk drive on his laptop, "Then you'll teach me to run the program. What I want," his hand moved toward the crucifix, "is to be able to destroy the museum within a few keystrokes."

The sound of Simson's fingernail on the crucifix sent cold waves of dread down Paul Grant's spine. "It's possible . . . but why would you want to?"

The head of the Jesuits crossed his office to the window overlooking the new museum construction site. His eyes wandered along concrete pillars and steel reinforcing beams designed to withstand a 9.5 earthquake.

Paul noticed the storm of emotion sweeping across the Father General's normally imperturbable features. A black mood settled over him; his shoulders hunched forward, the hands clasped behind his back were pressed together so hard his fingertips were turning red. The arteries in his neck bulging over his clerical collar looked ready to burst. Grant decided it was the word he would use to describe Andrew Simson--the man was ready to burst!

Whipping around, Father Simson faced the engineer squarely. "You must swear never to reveal what I'm about to tell you."

"I'm reliable." Grant squirmed against his chair. The wooden rungs seemed harder than they did a moment ago. His temperature raised to the point the crease in his pants wilted into nothing.

"Your word is good, but I'm prepared to make you an attractive offer in return for your service to the Church."

Wiping his hands against his jacket pocket, Paul Grant couldn't contain his nervousness. It seemed as if all his clothing had turned limp and shapeless by sweat.

"A position on the Board of Directors at Microsoft will be waiting for you once you've completed this assignment. Your achievements will be lauded by the press, and you'll return home rich--and famous. Your salary will be in the top six figures, and you'll have unlimited perks. A generous stock option also accompanies this offer. I'm sure you understand the prestige such a position offers you and your family."

Paul Grant felt his throat go dry, his hands froze against his legs. Nervousness vanished, replaced by shock. This was beyond his wildest expectations! The Vatican project was going be a strong selling point on his resume, but he never considered the possibility the Church would secure a position for him once the job was over. The Father General's offer was an unexpected turn of events!

"I assure you the position is legitimate. If you'd like to have it in writing before you begin work on this assignment, I'll be happy to have Bill Gates finalize the agreement." Eyes glittering, Andrew Simson knew he just secured the engineer's services.

Paul's tongue felt as if it were no longer a part of his body, words got stuck in his mouth and refused to take shape on his lips. "I'll take your word for it."

"Business is business. Gates will email you a letter of intent." The fish was hooked, the bait swallowed; the museum could be blown apart at the touch of his hand.

"I still don't understand why you'd destroy the very thing you've worked so hard to create. It's inconceivable to me you might want the building to come down around the 'Angry Jesus', or any of the other pieces of history you've discovered in the catacombs."

"Paul," the priest lowered his voice; he assumed the supplicating tone used to instruct a child in catechism, "much of what we've discovered must not fall into the wrong hands. Misinterpreted, misrepresented, the information could pose a threat to the future of the Church. My hope is to rekindle an interest in Christianity with documents and artifacts we've discovered . . . but we walk a precarious line. Our present civilization is so complex, so technical, the organization established in the Middle Ages does not appeal to a modern mind. In bringing the Church abreast of the times, many have mistaken my intentions. They blaspheme my mission and mock what I am endeavoring to accomplish. If those who oppose me possessed the information we've unearthed, they could wield a formidable sword against me. Much like the Savior, my own words would be the nails thrust through my flesh, my accomplishments the spear which pierces my side. Lesser minds cannot begin to comprehend my role in history, and I must protect this endeavor--at all costs. I am prepared to see my work destroyed rather than have it defiled by people who do not have the intelligence to grasp my vision."

"I see." The look in Simson's eyes was one the engineer had never seen in another human being. Paul Grant wanted to escape the room; he felt as if he had been thrown into a pit of vipers. The image of thousands of reptiles tangled together flashed before eyes. Getting up from the chair, Grant reached for the plans. "I'll get to work on this right away."

"Good. The letter of agreement will be in your hands by the end of the week."

Fleeing discomfort that was palpable, Grant hurried out of Simson's office. Nearly running, he vaulted down the stairs of the three-story building constructed to house paintings collected by early popes. As cooler air generated by a freshly watered expanse of lawn caressed his face, Paul Grant's body began to shake. Perspiration evaporated leaving him chilled. Arms crossed over his chest, hugging his body, seeking internal warmth, the American computer design engineer had never been colder in his life.

Autumn arrived in Rome overnight. Tree leaves lost the bright, glistening green of summer. Flowers no longer blossomed, and the air was filled with fewer fragrances. But Paul Grant didn't notice of any of the subtle changes to indicate the earth was continuing its cosmic rotation around the sun. He didn't see a basking cat, nor the fountain making a tinkling sound in the Vatican garden. Grant didn't know he took the wrong turn and instead of returning to the dormitory he was walking in the direction of the library. He didn't glance at the gardener preparing the flower beds for winter; nor did he see how carefully the craftsmen were restoring a crumbling section of the Gregoriano de Profano.

His mind raced back and forth between the sequence Andrew Simson was asking him to create and the lure of the future. His thoughts bounced between a sense of outrage and the seduction of riches. How could he be part of a scheme to ruin priceless relics at the flick of a switch? How could he turn down a position on the Board of Directors of the largest software company in the world? He would enter the domain of the rich and powerful. A private jet, company cars, an expensive house, prestige--all would be his!

Nothing would probably come of Andrew Simson's plan. More than likely, it was one of those fail-safe measures like the government used. Yes! His mind latched on to the thought with the zeal of a convert. The United States was honeycombed with missile silos loaded with nuclear warheads. A contingency measure--that was exactly what Andrew Simson was doing! The best defense was a strong offense. Hadn't he heard the phrase a million times? Wasn't the Father General just thinking ahead? Certainly! Andrew Simson developed a plan based on a worst-case scenario--like the military. Grant breathed deeper, his shoulders straightening. He rushed back through the gardens toward his dormitory. He hoped his wife was home. She would be astounded when he told her to start shopping for a new house. He might even ship a fancy Italian sports car back to the States--knowing he would be able to afford one!

Amariah drummed her fingers against her coffee cup. If she was translating Adamus' scrolls correctly, there had been a lot of alteration to the *Beatitudes*. She stared at paper so old the edges were yellowed and crumbled at her touch. The words were translated correctly! Verb syntax, nouns, subject matter was all impeccably correct--but when the words were linked together the content was startlingly different!

Almost as if Adamus were in the room, the message thundered through her head. Words sprang from the paper, challenging what she'd been taught to believe.

"And there followed him great multitudes of people from Galilee, and from Decapolis, and from Jerusalem, and from Judea, and from beyond the Jordan River.

Seeing the multitudes, he went up onto a high promontory, from where all who were gathered below could hear him speak. When he was set the disciples came unto him and said . . . 'Jesus, tell these people the way it is in heaven'. And Jesus opened his mouth to speak. 'I say unto you that the poor have not learned to open themselves to the power of the voice within, for the riches of the kingdom of heaven are available to all who dwell on the earth. Those who are meek, who do not understand the power of the wellspring within, are pressed upon by the strong of this earth. But, I say unto you, the meekest of men can turn away the aggressor without a sword or a shield. Within is the power to disarm any adversary, any foe . . . and he who wields this power shall inherit the earth. The merciful are those who understand the kingdom within for they know justice is meted out in full measure. He who kills shall experience a taking of his life in a life to come. He who steals shall be stolen from. The wise man extends mercy for there is no escape from justice. The man who remains pure in heart, despite all difficulties, is the man who will look upon the face of God and know peace of mind. The faithful will call unto their earthly kingdom untold riches through understanding. Those who work without ceasing to offer their neighbors the message of love will be known as peacemakers and will be called to the right hand of God; for no greater thing can a man do than he sooth the anguish of his neighbor. Turn your heart and thoughts away from those who persecute you--when you do the slings and arrows that would smite you fall short of the mark. Nothing--not Caesar, not soldiers, not the Levites in the temples--can destroy peace of mind when you know God is within. I do not come in a bolt of lightning, nor as a voice from within a storm; I do not come to vanquish soldiers nor to smite thine enemies. I come to awaken the voice within! I do not come to preach in the temples, for they are only pillars of stone, and their priests mock the word of God! I come to tell you the meaning of the Law, because your hearts are hard, and you have forgotten how to listen to the voice within. You looked to the priests for answers to your suffering, you think by placing money or sacrifice upon the altar in the temple courtyard a hand will issue forth from a cloud and you will be raised up from your troubles. All a man need ever do is silence his mind and listen! God whispers in every ear! Be silent so that you may hear! The priests would have you believe God speaks only to them, but you have closed your heart against God so that he cannot speak to you! You are the ones with ears made of stone! Everyone can be a priest or a prophet when they silence anxious thoughts and turn inward. The voice that speaks inside the mind cannot be heard when the heart is troubled. The heart must be at peace and the mind restful . . . then, and only then, will you hear God!"

Amariah couldn't get over it! The text was written in the first person, present tense--as though Jesus was speaking. This passage was a far cry from what was contained in the King James version of the *Beatitudes*. Had Christ exhorted His followers to turn away from the priests and the temple? Was He admonishing them to find a silent corner to communicate directly with God?

The foundation of her belief was crumbling. She could feel the bricks of theology falling all around her. The dawn of awakening demanded she accept the cornerstones of Christianity were based on pagan ritual more than the words of a wandering Rabbi. If this text was accurate, if it could be dated to the time of Christ, then it meant the *Beatitudes* were deliberately changed.

Was Jesus validating reincarnation when He told His followers they would reap the harvest of actions sown in this life? Had he been talking about a return to earth rather than heavenly reward?

The Church wanted followers to believe there was only one chance to earn salvation. Resurrection offered the clergy control. Control and money. Jesus seemed to be warning His followers about those very conditions. Had nothing changed? Control and money.

Amariah was beginning to wonder if her father was right. Was religion such a powerful narcotic a person couldn't sort truth from a fabric of lies?

Tears began to slide down her cheeks. Amariah grappled with the realization the Church had deceived her. An unsuspecting faithful were led astray while the Church plundered pockets and pilfered goodness from the soul. Humanity had been robbed, not only of worldly goods, but of self- respect. How many gave up their lives for an ideal that tarnished and blackened when exposed to historical evidence? As she stared at the stained parchment, Amariah realized the philosophy she once thought absolute was built on shifting sand--and the tide was going out beneath her feet.

Anna checked her reflection in the window near stairs leading to the Pinacoteca entrance. Every hair was in place and the red silk jumpsuit complement her figure. Adjusting a rope of pearls draped between her breasts, Anna found her hands perspiring. She checked to make certain her notes were in order. Andrew hated wasting time and Anna spent hours rehearsing what she would say.

"Hello there." Anna slipped inside the Father General's office.

Sister Josephina's eyebrows shot upward at the sight of the flame red jumpsuit and cascade of dark hair. "Father is on the phone."

"I'll wait." Dropping her eel skin briefcase beside the chair. Anna struggled to appear calm.

"It might be some time--he's speaking to the committee chairman who selects candidates for the Nobel Peace Prize."

"Really?" To quell her nervousness, Anna decided it would be better to talk than search for a cigarette. "Is Andrew going to be nominated?"

"I can't say." The nun stiffened as she turned back to her computer keyboard. The way her fingers jabbed at the keys communicated a disapproval she dared not voice.

Ignored, Anna turned her attention to the museum site. A tall steel outer structure was in place. Windows were now installed, and they smoldered with the fire of a fading sun. Struggling to keep her mind off the coming interview, Anna craned her neck to watch workmen at the far end of the building. She tapped her fingers against the windowsill, drawing an annoyed glance from Sister Josephina.

Simson called out. "Anna?"

Glancing at Sister Josephina's horsy face, she tried to summon a smile.

"Half an hour . . . no longer! The Father has a busy schedule to keep." The nun's jaw was inflexible as if she hated to allow such a frivolous woman to enter the Father General's office.

The door shut as Andrew Simson laid the phone in its cradle. He smiled a smile usually reserved for television cameras. "Anna, please sit down. I'm pleased you stopped by. Sister said you had news of importance."

Emotion riddled eyes flashed in his direction. "I thought I should discuss this with you before our staff meeting." She retrieved a stack of papers from her briefcase. "The controversy about cleaning the Sistine Chapel can finally be put to rest."

The Father General settled back, leaning his chin on the heel of his hand. "We spent a fortune to prove conclusively previous restoration attempts used animal glues which collected dust and dirt. It's a pity there are still those who refuse to accept our findings."

"I think I've found something to silence your critics once and for all. This is a letter penned by Michelangelo himself."

"Where did you unearth this?"

"Klaus convinced me there was something we didn't know about the technique used by Raphael and Michelangelo."

"What did Klaus have you looking for?"

"A secret ingredient--a chemical compound added to their pigment to make paint adhere better to wet plaster."

"Did you find a record of this mysterious substance?"

"No, but if these letters are authentic, I stumbled across something more significant."

His gaze wandered across the photocopied pages. "Where are the originals?"

"Jeff Brown has them--he's going to conduct an atomic spectrograph analysis test. We also have a handwriting analyst comparing these letters against samples we're certain were penned by Michelangelo."

"Offer me a conclusion based on your superior knowledge of history." Andrew Simson wrapped his crucifix in its long, slender chain.

Anna crossed her legs. "If these prove valid, they could change the way we perceive Renaissance art and religion. Remember how amazed Father Lean was at finding a piece of music dating back to the time of Christ? He's certain St. Augustine deliberately changed the original tone of music used in the early Church. He said religious music took a dramatic shift away from sounds which were uplifting, gay, joyous, because Augustine felt the beat was 'bewitching'."

"I remember." His thumbnail began the long, irritating descent down the side of the cross.

"Well, if these documents are original, they prove Michelangelo intended the chapel to be a jubilant, colorful work celebrating the creation of man. According to this document, he believed religion should offer some of the happiest moments in a person's life. He wanted people to rejoice when they looked at his paintings, he hoped they'd feel a surge of love when they saw the face of God! Andrew, Michelangelo wanted people to celebrate the gift of life--like when it was bestowed on Adam."

Anna drew a deep breath before rushing on. She couldn't tell what Andrew was thinking, his expression was as uncharted as deep recesses in space, "Michelangelo was trying to tell us we should be uplifted by religion . . . not fear it! For some reason, we've gotten off track. We lost the original intent of

Christianity. We got muddled along the way and you've got to set things right!" She lunged across the desk, covering his strong hand with her fine-boned fingers. "I know you are the man to do it."

Her eyes blazed with passion as her fingers strayed down the back of the Father General's hand, her movement deliberate, caressing.

Simson didn't disentangle his fingers and Anna reached across the desk with her other hand, enclosing the fist hovering above his desk. "Andrew, you are a man among men. You can have anything you desire--power, glory, honor and . . . women."

The voice which reached her ears sounded hollow and metallic, as if the Father General were speaking through a pipe. "Anna, I am not interested in earthly matters."

Undaunted, Anna donned a pouting expression which melted the hearts of other men. "I'm certain you could find time if the reward were great enough to warrant it."

Simson withdrew his hand and stormed around the desk--stopping inches from Anna's upturned face. Hands that were strong, virile, and masculine, grabbed her shoulders and shook her so hard the hair whipped around her shoulders.

"You fool! You are a silly, stupid fool! Do you think fleeting physical pleasure could tempt me away from my destiny? Do you think I would risk all I have set in motion to satisfy mere lust? Are you so naive as to think I can be manipulated by pouting lips and a wanton expression? Anna, you are not the first woman to try to entice me away from the vows of a Jesuit, but I will never compromise my mission!"

Anna wrenched away. "You're nothing more than an actor!"

The Father General assumed a mask displaying an element of pity. "Anna, you're overwrought."

Anna heard her voice rise until her words tumbled out in a hysterical shriek. "How can you be so callous?"

"A priest must submerge personal desire for the greater good of humanity." Simson backed away, one step at a time, deliberately, increasing the gap between them. Reaching for her briefcase, his gesture was cold and curt. "Your offer is touching. I'm certain our Lord, Jesus, refused many women in His day, but some men cannot be tempted by the momentary delights a woman can provide."

Anna kept her expression cool and detached until she reached the Casino of Pius IV. Then, flopping down on a bench, she allowed tears to flow. Being ushered out of an office was an experience she suffered many times.

Her father never had time for her either.

Indifference was more humiliating than rejection and an emotional storm began to brew. The mascara applied so carefully only hours before left tracks down her cheeks as tears coursed through her makeup. A dam broke and emotions she kept guarded for years came perking to the surface. She was not going to be ignored anymore!

"Mr. Preston, your call to San Francisco has gone through. Richard Weatherby is on line two."

"Thanks, Louisa." The banker depressed a lighted button. "Dick, how are you?"

"John, I'm fine! There's nothing quite like being awakened by an overseas operator! Now that you've got my adrenaline flowing is something wrong with my daughter?"

"Dick--calm down. Things are fine in Rome, for the moment anyway. I'm sorry I called you at this hour, but I wanted to talk to you before our offices filled up with people and phone lines got jammed. An hour from now it will be impossible to get a call in or out of Italy because people are phoning in donations to the Vatican Bank at an unprecedented rate."

Richard Weatherby drew a long, hesitant breath--a frustrated sound crossed the ocean to Rome. "I've been following the situation on the news."

"Dick?" Preston lowered his voice, uncertain of whether anyone was listening outside his office door. "Is Liz in the room?"

"She just went to put on a pot of coffee. Want me to get her on the line?"

"No! I've got something to tell you and I want to get it out quick. I'm sending you a packet by courier. It's coming to your office--registered as diplomatic mail. Your signature is still on record with the State Department."

"John, you've used me as a drop before. I know what to do."

"This time it's different, my friend."

"From your tone of voice, I gather you're worried. Can you tell me, is this line secure?"

"It was swept before I placed the call. Unless the Father General has come up with some technology the rest of the world doesn't know about, our conversation is not being recorded."

"Simson? John, are you sure Amariah is okay?"

John Preston reached for a pencil and began to draw concentric circles which grew increasingly constricted on the note pad beneath his hand. "I can't go into details over the phone, but I've uncovered incriminating financial evidence about the Father General."

With a hiss of anger, Richard exploded, "I knew she shouldn't have gone! I argued with Amariah for hours--trying to convince her to turn down the assignment."

"Dick, we don't have time to waste on recrimination. When you get the packet put it in a safety deposit box in Edward Jordan's bank. You remember him?"

"Sure, we've had drinks at the bar in the St. Francis several times."

"He can be trusted. Make sure the box is double keyed. You keep one and tell Jordan I want him to keep the other."

"Okay." Richard Weatherby's words slammed together like cars on a suddenly braked train; clipped punctuation betrayed his tension. "What's in the packet? I think I have a right to know what's going on!"

"You're right, Dick." The note pad now contained deep, dark strokes crossing the circles in harsh lines. "The packet contains a list of account numbers I think might have been used to launder huge sums of money through the Vatican Bank. There's also a roster of safety deposit boxes in banks in Paris, London, Rome, and Madrid. Data about each account could shatter the existing political structure of several countries and plunge their fragile economic system into chaos--if I'm right about what's going on in Rome. If something happens to me, get that packet into the hands of Lucas Owens at the State Department. He'll know what to do."

"Jesus, John . . . this sounds more dangerous than anything you've been involved in before."

A sigh stuck halfway up John Preston's throat. His mouth was as dry as old cotton and he desperately wanted a drink. "It is."

"Does this have anything to do with Amariah?"

The words were challenging, the anger so clear in his voice, Preston could almost see his friend sitting on the side of his bed, gripping the phone so tightly his knuckles stood white against a tennis-tanned hand. "Dick, this is going to sound mystical, and you pride yourself on being analytical--but, I've got a feeling so strong I can't describe it. Somehow, some way, your daughter has the potential to destroy the empire Andrew Simson is building. Dick, that may sound crazy, but you asked."

"Your voice tells me you believe she might be in danger." Richard Weatherby's emotions were boiling like a desert sandstorm and a swirling wall of fear obliterated rational thought. He went to stand at the window; the sun balanced on the horizon like an acrobat on a tightrope.

Preston sighed, "My fear is not just for myself, nor for Amariah. Dick, I'm afraid of what is happening all over the world. You've seen the Simson interview in the Sistine Chapel. He uses the press like a virtuoso in command of a Stradivarius. My God, he nearly made a convert out of me! People are flocking to him in droves because he penetrates their emotions. The man is probably the most charismatic leader since Hitler. Add to that the need people have to belong, their innate desire for purpose in their lives--and the result is a political weapon with the power to dominate entire nations!" Preston was sweating, and he reached for a tissue to wipe his brow.

Fog began to shroud streets below the hill on which the Weatherby home was built. From his vantage point, Richard felt as though he were encased in a mist separating him from a world in which he no longer belonged. Streaks of sunlight forced probing fingers through the fog and the atmosphere turned shimmery. "Do you think Simson has any idea Amariah might pose a threat to him?"

"Dick, two men working on the museum project with Amariah, Klaus Von Friendberg and Leon Kaminski, stumbled across a document referring *to a woman called Amariah* who took Jesus to Egypt after the incident in the temple when he was twelve. They think the scroll accounts for at least part of Jesus' lost years. If they found something like that, I'll bet Simson has documents of the same nature in his possession." The note pad beneath his hand was a mass of ugly black circles and scouring lines. "I'm beginning to think it's beyond the realm of coincidence your daughter is a Catholic nun who just happens to be fluent in the languages spoken during Jesus' lifetime. Dick why would the Vatican reach halfway around the world to a Benedictine Order in San Francisco and snatch a young woman who just happens to have the name Amariah?"

The voice coming across the phone line was strangled and flat. "A name I'd never even heard of--a name Liz insisted on—it means promised by God."

His pencil snapped beneath the pressure exerted by a tension-racked hand. "Dick, this may sound demented to a practicing psychiatrist, but do you give reincarnation any credence?"

"I'm seeing more evidence in my practice all the time. Situations, unexplained by the present, are spilling from my patients. John, I'm not certain I believe in God--or a Universal Force, or the existence of a Superior Being--let alone that a human being returns to earth to inhabit another body! The consequences of such a belief are nearly insurmountable." Richard lapsed into silence as he grappled with issues as alien to his way of thinking as ceremonial voodoo. All he knew for certain was he wanted his daughter back in San Francisco. Now!

"I'm beginning to rethink many of the concepts I've held since childhood."

"John," he refused to dwell on anything other than his daughter's safety, "what about Amariah?"

"I'm going to give your phone number to Leon Kaminski. The boy is as fine a young man as I've ever met. He's watching over her, although she's scarcely aware of it. Amariah is in good hands. If you hear from him, for God's sake do what he asks without question."

The sun was beginning to burn away the fog and Richard Weatherby could just make out the streets below his home. Trees were losing the bright green of summer and a gust of chilly morning air swept scraps of paper and a volley of fallen pine needles down the ribbon of asphalt. His spine stiffened, and his knees locked as if to support the anguish of his cry. "When is Amariah going to wake up to what's happening? Why is she so blind to all this?"

John took a deep breath and tossed pieces of the shattered pencil into a wastebasket beneath the desk. "Dick, when she does realize what's happening . . . I pity her. She truly believes in goodness--in the integrity of all human beings. She lives the message left behind by a man called Jesus. Amariah has a charity in her heart that's close to sainthood. When the foundation of her belief is shattered," he drew another breath, a sound which pealed like a warning clap of thunder, "I hope her sanity doesn't snap. I've seen it happen before. Without the support of a philosophy they believed in for so long--some people lose the will to live."

In an instant, the world turned dirty for Richard Weatherby. Streets below his home lost their charm, their sun-drenched California beauty. The piercing wail of a siren as an ambulance rushed another victim of society to a nearby hospital demolished the silence of a sleeping neighborhood. A lone, hungry dog overturned a metal trashcan and sent it rolling down the hill. The irritating rattle reached every nerve in his body like a slow, agonizing fingernail dragged across a blackboard. "What can I do?"

"As hard as this may be, all you can do for now is wait. Be ready if Leon asks for help. And Richard," he paused, hoping to find words to sustain his friend, "Amariah will find her way--she has to."

The phone line went dead, and Richard Weatherby replaced the receiver in its cradle. A stiff wind had come up and it was pushing in another bank of fog from the ocean. Huge, sulfur-yellow clouds lowered across the city--obliterating everything from view. Turning from the window, he stared at his rumpled bed. The clock radio went off and music blasted through the room. It was time to take a shower, shave, to move through the morning ritual he had performed a thousand times before. Below, his wife was making breakfast; the clank-bang of kitchen drawers being opened and closed carried up the stairwell. The fortress-like condition of his home seemed less secure than it had only moments before.

A whine drew his attention. From the doorway, the Rottweiler made his presence known. In three bounds, the dog crossed the bedroom and jumped up beside him. The stub, which was all that remained of his tail, wagged.

"You know she's in trouble, don't you?"

Uncanny intelligence filled the dog's wide, round eyes. As he reached to scratch its massive head, the Rott pushed forward, a soundless signal he wanted the area beneath his collar to receive Richard's attention. A paw capable of tearing up flowerbeds and shrubs jabbed at his owner's leg. He had stopped scratching. Looking at the brown eyes rolled in his direction, Richard wondered anew at the characteristics of this dog. There were times he stared at the phone, only to have Amariah call a few moments later. The enormous brute would pace the yard before her arrival. Richard learned to respect the animal's body language, which served as Morse code, foretelling Amariah's comings and goings.

A rumble came from somewhere deep inside Damascus' chest and the ridge of hair between his shoulders stood erect. Richard stroked the length of the dog's back. "There's nothing we can do!" He inched closer to the edge of the bed. Damascus moved closer placing a paw against his master's hand. Keen eyes scanned Richard's face and a throaty whine pleaded with him to do something. "Damascus, there's nothing we can do."

He patted the dog, trying to give and find comfort. An unusual name for a dog, Damascus, but his daughter insisted on it the moment she laid eyes on the eight-week-old bundle offur and fat.

A low, mournful wail bruised the silence that descended over the room. Richard Weatherby returned his attention to the dog. Like a portent of impending doom, Damascus seemed to be issuing a warning.

The animal moaned again. The sound speared his body and sent a wave of cold throughout his nervous system. In his heart of hearts, Richard Weatherby knew the identity of his daughter had nothing to do with her parents, the life they created for her, the education she had gained, nor the Church to which she belonged. Pure, raw instinct warned Amariah was here to achieve something unimaginable.

CHAPTER TWELVE

Malek watched the sky as the sun prepared to drop behind a distant line of mountains. His sky--the desert sky--was a thing of beauty to behold. Purples and blues chased a spectrum of orange and red trailing behind the sun. Shadows threaded with violet softened the brutal ridges and deep wadis cut into limestone by sun, wind, and occasional violent rain. Sunset was a peaceful time of day in the desert. Animals were settling in for the night as silent, dutiful women cleared away remnants of an evening meal. Stillness lowered over the desolate, forbidding landscape like a blanket drawn over the shoulder. Here and there an insect chirped beneath a leafless bush clinging to life in the waterless terrain. Malek thought he detected the shift of sand beneath a desert cobra as it sought the stored warmth below a rocky outcrop.

The harshness of this land bred a cruel and exacting culture. Everything was meted out in measure and Allah's great messenger, the prophet Mohammed, gave his people strict laws to obey without question. Everything about their way of life had its origin in the Koran. For the Arab, the values of the Koran--spelled out in static simplicity--was sufficient.

"Malek, may I join you?"

Turning, the Arab chieftain watched the priest's robe swirl, then die--as if the fabric had a life of its own. "Of course. Sit, we will enjoy a last cup of tea as the sun rests for the night."

Robert Norton eased himself down on a spine of rocks. High above wadis slicing through the desert floor, the view was uninterrupted for miles in every direction. A sigh escaped the normally reserved Jesuit.

"What troubles you, priest?"

"Malek, I've come to love this inhospitable land. I will value the time I've spent here more than any other experience of my life." He turned to watch the older man. "You've taught me a great deal these past few weeks. Someday, I hope the world will accept the Arab nations for what they are. You have a great deal to offer."

Malek reached for a stone then cast it into a deep ravine. "Priest, what could you have learned in the tent of a nomadic Arab? We are not learned scholars. We have no scientific knowledge to present to a world caught up in technological madness."

"No, Malek, you have none of those things." Robert Norton returned his gaze to the west falling sun and squinted against the last fiery streamers dusting the horizon. "What I learned from you and your people is of far more value than camcorders and DVD players, or missile silos, or tanks and guns. From you, my friend, I've become conscious of the beauty of this land. From the Arab, I learned to honor the earth as a living, breathing being. I no longer take survival for granted for a single cup of water can be a life-or-death matter in the desert. The rich foods I once thought so tempting will never grace my table again for the Arab taught me to appreciate far simpler fare. Now, when I look at the sun casting its majestic tapestry across the sky--I find glory. I may never again hear the bleating of a newborn lamb, but I will carry the memory of the miracle of life in my heart forever. To watch the first feeble efforts of a kid to stand on wobbly legs taught me each of God's creatures must contend with the difficult conditions of life. Malek, it is easy to forget what is important when you are surrounded by the hustle and bustle of city life. At night, stars are hidden--lost in the sky--consigned to oblivion by the light pollution of society. We are isolated from nature--we do not hear the cry of the lamb, nor the call of quail running for cover. No matter where I go from here," he gestured toward the broad expanse of land stretching toward a distant horizon, "I will always be grateful for my time in the desert."

Eyes reddened and rimmed with a ring of dust skewered the Jesuit. It was a cold, relentless stare that flickered, then softened. "I never expected to hear such words of praise from you, English."

"I mean them, Malek, I sincerely mean them. When I return to Rome I'm going to make sure members of the press hear your story. You've been given a reputation you don't deserve, and I'd like to rectify the situation."

"No one will listen." Malek turned his face back toward the horizon. In the east, a canopy of stars began to sparkle against contusive colors heralding the advance of night.

"I think I know a way to make them listen." The priest picked up a stone and began to toss it in the air, catching it deftly, then throwing it again.

A snort conveyed Malek's disbelief.

"If you release your prisoners I guarantee your cause will make headlines around the world. There are men with powerful connections who will listen to what you have to say and treat you fairly, I promise."

"How can you make such a promise?" Malek traced a pattern in the dirt with his boot.

"Public opinion, whether we like it or not, can topple governments and sway those who make political decisions. It's high time people were made aware of what you are trying to do."

"Priest, tell me what you think that is."

"You want to wander the desert in search of pasture for your flocks. You want to be able to worship Allah like your forefathers. You have no desire to be a part of the twentieth century, despite your vast reservoirs of oil. You think your people should be allowed to live the way they have for the past four thousand years--without outside influences pressuring you to change. When you felt the encroachment of modern society, you fought back . . . with the only weapons you knew would strike sufficient fear into the Anglo heart. You, and your followers, turned to terrorism and manipulation of oil prices to attain your ends."

Breaking a twig off a nearby camphor bush, Malek began to clean his teeth. Finally, a stream of tea-laden saliva shot across the desert floor, leaving an ugly brown path. "Priest, you've learned much from the desert."

"Malek, release the hostages to me and I assure you . . . you will be left in peace."

"How can you make such a guarantee, Jesuit? English promises turn as rancid as goat butter left too long in the sun."

"There's nothing I can say to make you believe the press will listen to your story, but you have my word for it. The man I represent wields more power than any king or president. His bidding is carried out in every corner of the world."

"Who is this man?"

"Andrew Simson, the Jesuit Father General. He sent me here, to come to an understanding of what it was you needed so he could ensure your desires were met."

"Why would he do that?"

"Because he wants to abolish strife. He wants mankind to live without conflict. Malek, he too worships Allah! He calls Allah by another name, but his allegiance is to the One, true God of the Muslim. We may pray in different temples, our ceremonies are different, but we share the same God! He wants you to follow the traditions of your ancestors. He knows how important it is for you to maintain your tribal boundaries. The Father General thinks you should be free to honor the customs and ritual of the Arab . . . he wants you to live without the pressures of a modern world. Let me restore the hostages to their homeland, and I give you a solemn promise--you will be left in peace forever."

The sky turned to black velvet and a million stars shimmered like diamonds. Behind him, campfires were lit to protect his people from brutal cold which settled over the desert when the sun vanished below the mountains. Dry twigs showered the air with fiery sparks as Malek's people fed the flames of warming fires. The noise and red glow offered a line of defense against predators roaming the desert, hidden by the cloak of night.

Malek knew he was a simple man. He knew how to find water where none would suspect the presence of a life-giving spring. He knew how to track an antelope across terrain so rocky no trail was left behind. Malek fought his enemies and could wield a sword as passionately as a younger man. At night, when stars took their place in the heavens, he could chart his way across the desert with the skill of a modern navigator. Yet he knew in his heart civilization posed a threat to his people. Children clamored for televisions and village parents hounded him to permit their little ones to go to school, to learn to read and write. These things troubled Malek. His skills were not the skills his grandchildren would need to survive. They would have to know how to read complex agreements; their wars would be waged with words, not weapons. He feared pressure on the Arab to adapt to a modern world could not be stopped.

Despite the odds, despite probability of failure, Malek knew he had to buy time for his people. They were too simple to be thrust into a world ruled by technology. They could not adapt quickly to rules of a society which lived compressed in many little houses. His children would rebel, and his men would turn violent. Malek realized he had to make a pact with this priest. He had to buy the Arab tribes time--even if it turned out to be years instead of the generations the priest promised. He had to bring his followers abreast of technology slowly, in stages.

Light from the fire made the lines in Malek's weathered face seem deeper and the reflection from the campfire captured against his cornea made the Bedouin look frighteningly inhuman.

"All right, priest. I'll give you the journalists in exchange for tribal boundaries which must be guaranteed. I will chain my dogs of war. I will call them in and forbid more terrorist activity. I will force my brothers to lessen the impact of oil prices on the rest of the world--but you must fulfill your part of the bargain, or I will loose their savage fury on the industrial powers again. Before Allah, that is my promise."

Amariah laid aside the glasses she wore more and more, to rub the bridge of her nose and flesh behind her ears. Her head ached; her eyes refused to focus on another line of print. Manuals turned blurry and she gave in to fatigue. Lying against the desktop, she cradled her head in her arms. It would feel good to close her eyes for a moment, and then she'd resume work again.

A breeze brushed the back of her neck, as if someone passed behind her, but Amariah was too tired to raise her head. Regardless of her promise to return to work quickly, she drifted off to sleep.

The voice called to her again through the fog of a troubled dream. She no longer feared the voice; she came to welcome it; to be guided by it.

Amariah turned her head, seeking comfort in the cushion of her arm. A breeze stirred the hair on the back of her neck which escaped beneath the surgical cap required in the lab. This time, Amariah sensed something. Leaving deep sleep, she floated upward. The voiced called to her.

'Amariah'.

"Yes?" She spoke, without knowing she was speaking.

'There is one more thing you must seek out'.

"I cannot return to the Archive, Woolsey won't let me."

'You must find it'.

"Is it in the catacombs? Should I go there again?"

'Follow your instincts, you will find it'.

"I don't know what that means! You must show me, I'll never find it any other way."

'Follow your feelings. Logic can lead down false paths. Emotion cannot be blinded. Turn within, listen to your inner voice. You will be guided'.

"I don't know how! I don't know how!" Amariah awakened as her fist hit the desk. Fully alert, she sat up and wiped away the trail of saliva running down her cheek. She was dreaming again. Adamus often came to her in dreams. Adamus had been demanding her to look further; more information would surface if she followed her instincts. The medieval priest's words rolled across her thoughts with the force of a hundred cannons. *'Follow your feelings. You will be guided'*.

Amariah reached to shut down her computer. She was tired and needed some uninterrupted sleep. As she went about the lab, turning off switches, emptying the coffee pot, straightening notes and reference books, the words sing-songed through her brain. *'Follow your feelings. You will be guided'*. What she wanted more than anything just now was a bowl of bread pudding! Deciding to give in to the impulse for a late-night snack, Amariah locked up the laboratory and headed for the cafeteria. A quick glance at her watch assured her Sister Felicity would still be on duty. The older nun was a wonderful person and Amariah felt guilty about not spending more time with her.

Leaning her shoulder against the double doors, Amariah pushed her way into the cafeteria. She waved across the room to the roly-poly sister, laid an armload of books on the table and dropped her bag beside them. Free of her burden, Amariah strolled along the baked goods counter, wondering if she should give up her passion for pudding in favor of a new dessert. No, the pudding was always good, and Amariah smiled brightly at the sister.

"I stopped by for a nightcap! A few bites of your pudding and I'm headed for bed."

Sister Felicity slid a bowl across the top of the counter, "The circles beneath your eyes betray you. You may smile, my dear, but your eyes do not lie. The window of the soul tells no false tales! Perhaps you should take a few days to enjoy the wonders of Rome. It is a pity you haven't taken time to see the coliseum or any of our churches."

"I plan to, once my work is done."

"My child, even God rested on the seventh day. Should man do less? Enjoy Rome, it has much to offer."

Amariah laughed, dimples appearing in both cheeks as she took the proffered bowl and spoon. "I'll tell the Father General you said so!"

Turning toward the tables, Amariah spotted an aged sampietrini sipping a cup of tea in the corner. "Eduardo, may I join you?"

"Ah, dear lady, come sit beside me." He beamed a smile of welcome at the one person who always had time for him.

"How goes it?" Amariah reached around the old man's thin shoulders and gave him an affectionate hug.

"Well, lady, well. Have you seen the news lately?"

Amariah slipped a spoon beneath the custard layer to spice laden bread. "No, I must confess I haven't. My time has been spent in the lab or library. The world could be at war, and I wouldn't know it!" She brought the spoon to her mouth. "What's happening in the land beyond the Vatican?"

"Oh, lady, the most glorious news is right here." The gnarled hand, which labored a lifetime for the glory of the Church, clutched his mug.

"Really?" Amariah knew Eduardo was lonely; he outlived most of his friends and much of his family. The nuns, priests, and civilians, who helped run the complex ecclesiastical structure, were all he had left.

"Yes!" A flame kindled in eyes turned red and rheumy with age. "Tomorrow scaffolding in the Sistine Chapel comes down and visitors will be able to view the completed restoration project."

"I didn't know work was complete."

"I know about these things first because it's my job to clean up after the experts. I make sure trash is swept from the floor, coffee cups removed from scaffolding . . . that sort of thing."

Amariah studied the old man; his eyes glowed with pride. "You must be excited about seeing the scaffolding removed and the chapel restored to its former glory."

"Yes and no."

"What do you mean?" Amariah pushed what remained of the pudding around the dish.

"The scaffolding allowed me a chance to see the master's work firsthand. Often, after crews are gone for the night, I take the elevator up to get close to the greatest masterpiece ever created. I can touch the faces of the Sibyls and prophets. A lifetime could be dedicated to studying the fresco and still not absorb the intricacies of Michelangelo's work."

"It must be wonderful to be close enough to see his brush strokes."

"Lady, his paintings are holy to me." Standing, Eduardo reached for her hand. "Come, I will share this with you for you have been kind to an old man whose mind often wanders."

Through the gardens, between the walls of the Cotrile della Sentinella, along the cloistered walkway of the Cortile Borgia, down the courtyard of the Pappagallo, they made their way to a seldom used entrance to the chapel.

Eduardo fished ancient keys from his pocket, opened the door and ushered Amariah inside. Stepping into a long, narrow room, she was surprised by the extent of scaffolding. Electric cords dangled everywhere, and computer equipment used to document every brush stroke, every spot of flaking paint, every detail of the master's work--had yet to be removed.

"Come. Up we go." With skill and agility belying his age, the sampietrini scuttled toward a tiny elevator which hoisted equipment and researchers aloft. The scissors lift raised the platform toward a vault in the ceiling towering sixty-five feet above the floor. Gone were gloomy, dark colors once thought to be indicative of the artist's emotional psychology. Instead, brilliant oranges, lemon yellows, deep magenta, greens, both dark and bright--a veritable rainbow of color radiated from the ceiling fresco. Amariah's eyes grew round as awe and reverence took command of her features.

"It is magnificent, no?"

"Eduardo," tears brimmed, "I feel as if I am truly in the presence of God." Amariah walked the length of the scaffolding. Starting with a panel portraying God creating the sun and stars, her admiration increased with every step she took. The panel depicting God with His fingertip extended toward Adam took her breath away. She reached out, then withdrew her hand--as if not worthy to touch the hand of God. Divine influence upon the physical body was evident in the soft folds of flesh gracing Eve's body as she stepped away from Adam's side. The garden scene, where Eve was tempted by the serpent, was a tapestry of vivid color. Noah's sacrifice, the flood and drunkenness of Noah displayed a genius which belonged to Michelangelo alone. She moved closer to the edge, drawn to the Sibyls and prophets. Each woman held a book clasped close to her breast, shielding information contained within. Prophets sat in various poses, distracted by inner thoughts. The lunettes of King Solomon with his parents, the family of King Rehoboam, and King Asa alongside his children, were wonders of light and shadow. These scenes were fitted into architectural buttresses; yet each told a unique story and bore testimony to the artist's ingenuity. Now that the colors were revealed in their true glory, it seemed as if the ceiling had a life of its own. Each character in the fresco was so life-like, so real, so human-- Amariah almost expected to see them take a breath or speak at any moment. She retraced her steps along the scaffolding and stopped just below the hand of God stretching toward Adam.

The fingers of Adam and God outstretched--not quite touching--moved her in a way she had never experienced before. She reached forward again, still reluctant to place her fingertips against the painting.

Eduardo whispered from the shadows. "Lady, go ahead. You will never have an opportunity to be this close to the master's work again.

Michelangelo knew something the rest of the world does not."

Her thoughts whirled; was the chapel a code? Had Michelangelo left an encrypted message for a time when the world was ready to understand?

Two Sibyls seemed to stare at her with questioning eyes--as if asking her if she understood!

What was the message? Compelled to touch God's hand, a flash of light momentarily blinded her. She closed her eyes, then looked at the painting again. If she held her fingers together they filled the space between God and Adam's outstretched hand. She stared at both hands which were a wonder of composition and form. Muscles swelled the palms, tendons traced the path of extended wrists, and the subtle blend of color brought out each detail reflected a superior knowledge of anatomy. As if guided, she pressed her fingertips into the empty space.

Making the connection between Adam and God, Amariah suddenly knew what the artist wanted to convey.

Michelangelo depicted the story of creation recorded in the Bible, but the look on every face in the fresco conveyed another meaning. They were people involved in the battle for survival, but they were not unhappy, fearful souls! Eve, as she accepted the apple from the serpent, did not seem to dread the Sword of Justice. Amariah realized people in the fresco did not fear God!

Her eyes sought the Sibyls. They held their books in a protective embrace, as if trying to shield their knowledge from eyes blinded by false logic. Prophets stared out at the world--in challenge.

Books. Hidden. Secret Archive. Her thoughts came in fragmented pieces. She had to go back. Something else was in the Archive; something else was hidden in the repository.

Turning to the old man, who clung to the edge of the scaffolding his head bowed in an attitude of devotion, Amariah whispered. "Do you have a key to the Archive?"

"I do."

"Will you let me in?"

"Yes."

"Will you keep my presence a secret?"

Eduardo's face expressed resolve. "Lady, I saw it in your eyes--you know what the master was trying to say. He left mankind a message!"

"Have you seen this?" Vassily Kharkov's face was crimson with anger. "Did you permit this to happen?" He threw a DVD across the desk at his superior. "Old man, your mind has dimmed with age! You are no longer the strong, the virile specimen of Soviet youth who fought to save the homeland. Your heart, your head and your stomach have gone soft! You may think you saved Russia by negotiating for grain through this priest--but I'll tell you the cold, ugly truth. He waved an admonishing finger in Balsahov Petrovich's direction. "You doomed Russia to take-over by a foreign power. Only it won't be the imperial capitalists you feared so much in your youth--no, it will be the influence of the Catholic Church that will seduce our people away from their loyalty to Mother Russia! Their hearts will be hardened against our leadership. Instead, they will follow the priests in Rome. And Balsahov, let me tell you something else," he was out of breath with anger, "I'm far more frightened of the man masquerading in black robes than I am of nuclear warheads which lie beyond the Urals. This priest's influence is insidious! His power cannot be checked with military devices of our own. Instead, he creeps into people's minds and toys with their emotions. Petrovich, this man is a cancer! He begins as a single cell, then quickly multiples. And you," his face contorted as he shouted at the older officer, "you brought this menace--this disease--to Russia!"

Balsahov Petrovich stared at his hands. Kharkov was right. Age made them tremor and his knuckles were swollen with arthritis. His eyes had dimmed so much he wasn't sure he could even hit the outer edge of a target anymore; he knew his bones would no longer endure miles of forced marches, nor the brittle cold of winter maneuvers. Had his mind gone soft as well? Had he betrayed his people? Balsahov shoulders shuddered as he grappled with the realization. "I saw the interview last night."

Noticing how hunched with humility the shoulders were, which once carried the burdens of a starving nation, Vassily softened. "Balsahov, I know you thought you were doing the right thing. Perhaps if I lived through the winter at Stalingrad--had I watched my family starve to death --had I seen most of my comrades die, one by one--perhaps I might have done the same thing."

Eyes lifting, the old soldier, who survived Hitler and Stalin's purges, searched Kharkov's expression for a sign to betray insincerity. Vassily stood ramrod straight, like a good soldier, but his eyes were filled with an odd mixture of sorrow and compassion. Tall and square, this young man was the epitome of Russian virtue. He spoke his mind yet remained loyal to orders dispensed by superiors. "What can I do?" Balsahov thrust his chair back, the springs screeching against his weight.

"Perhaps we can learn about the priest's intentions. I would like to have Dr. Rubtsovsky offer his opinion."

"Rubtsovsky?"

"Many think him radical and his ideas bizarre, but the man has insight into the workings of the human mind."

"You've talked to him?"

"Several times."

"Is he as insane as others in the Kremlin believe?"

"He is just as sane as either one of us."

"I don't know, Vassily, I don't know. Involving a man such as Rubtsovsky might prove our undoing."

"I think Russia is worth the risk."

Petrovich turned to gaze out the office window. Winter would soon descend on his land. It was neither men nor machines that saved the Motherland from invasion--it was weather. Twice, freezing cold and blizzard conditions stanched attack by invaders. Winter defeated both Napoleon and Hitler; nature took the best technology had to offer and reduced it to insignificance. Clouds turned slate gray with moisture promised snow. All too soon Red Square would don winter's majestic mantle. The domes of St. Basils would be crowned with a layer of white which would sparkle like a blanket of diamonds. "Can we afford the risk?"

"Do we have a choice?"

"Arrange a meeting."

"He's waiting for us now."

Eyebrows, turned gray by the passage of years, lifted.

"He's going to analyze the recording and offer an opinion." Vassily held his breath, uncertain how Petrovich would react.

The old man leaned forward, grasping the edge of his desk to ease the strain of standing. "Let's go."

The white tile corridor gleamed; a scrubwoman placed mops and buckets in the closet as two men passed. After the war, when living conditions were the bleakest, she went to her father's friend and pleaded for a job. Balsahov Petrovich put her to work cleaning the floors of an office building the military occupied. Grateful, she worked long, hard hours to make certain walls and floors were scrupulously clean. She emptied wastebaskets and dusted the desks of the mighty for decades. But today, the expression on Comrade Petrovich's face worried her. Even during the dark days of Stalin's madness, she never saw the old general so disturbed. He nodded, acknowledging a shared past. The cleaning woman reached to tighten the triangular piece of cloth flattening her hair against her head. Discreetly, she watched to see which elevator the two men entered. The middle. They were descending to the tunnels which honeycombed the area beneath Red Square--concrete bunkers built to withstand the force of a nuclear blast. This was where leaders of the Kremlin would retreat if an invasion of the homeland occurred. The war room was down there. The world beneath the Kremlin was a frightening one, filled with shadows and rumor. She fervently hoped Comrade Petrovich made the return trip . . . some never did.

Lights in the lab dimmed as three men settled down to watch a replay of the interview with the Jesuit, Stephen Andropov. Across eleven-time zones, throughout the length and breadth of Russia, millions saw and heard the priest.

A television set blazed through the darkened room, casting translucent pools of color on white tiles lining the laboratory walls. Rubtsovsky rested his bearded chin against his hand as he studied the Jesuit.

Donetsk Millerovo, patterning his broadcast style after the anchormen of the West, began with a penetrating look at the camera. "So, Father Andropov, with a name like this your ancestry must be Russian."

A warm, almost tender smile spread across features of an immaculate man. His hair was closely trimmed and the dark, flowing robes of the Jesuit Order hugged a strongly masculine body. "My grandparents immigrated to the United States just after World War I."

"Your Russian is fluent, was our language spoken in your home as a child?" He looked from the priest to the camera, above which a red light glowed.

"Our heritage was treasured. Russian was spoken in our home, and I went to a Russian-Orthodox church every Saturday to learn to read and write our language. Our priest was from Moscow, and he owned many pictures of St. Basil's, the cathedrals of the Annunciation, the Archangel, the Assumption, and the Twelve Apostles. He loved Russian architecture and the magnificent wall paintings in each of these churches. Photographs of the Iconostases by Rublev and Theophanes dominated our classroom. When he spoke, our teacher's eyes glazed over, as if he returned to the churches of the Kremlin when he recited stories about his native land. All of us knew Father Andreovich hungered to go home. My parents said the Motherland never leaves the soul of one who had the good fortune to be born in Russia. It's as though the land imprints upon the hearts of its people."

The newscaster was taken back, his expression registered surprise. "I never expected to hear such words from an American priest."

The boyish smile came again; something happened in the priest's eyes. A shift; movement like the fall of colored rocks in a kaleidoscope. His fingers began to toy with the arm of the chair. "Preconceived attitudes are what keeps people of this world apart. Boundaries exist in the mind, not on land. I happened to be born in a capitalistic country, so you assume I don't respect the homeland of my forefathers. But I am as moved by the spires of St. Basil's as my father was, and his father before him. The snow sparkling on barren tree limbs is as great a beauty to my eye as it was to my grandmother—whose heart never left Russia."

Adjusting his tie, the interviewer appeared to have trouble swallowing. "I confess, respect for our homeland is something I never thought possible from an American. In Russia, we've been led to believe your countrymen hate us--that you are bent on our destruction."

Glancing at the cameras, the priest found the winking red light and looked directly into the lens. "Perhaps some Americans were--perhaps some still are. But we all share a shrinking planet, and we must strive to overcome misconceptions about other cultures. We must learn to view other men as our neighbors, not as a race of aliens threatening to destroy our homes and families.

Certainly, our people enjoy a broader viewpoint than we have in the past. The fact I am sitting here, interviewing you on a television broadcast, which will be beamed across eleven-time zones, is a measure of our government's effort to implement change." The newscaster sat back in his chair smugly satisfied with his response.

"I agree. Your Premier is to be lauded for his political ideals. I sincerely believe he wants to safeguard our planet for future generations."

"Indeed. Do you think your country will be open to the withdrawal of men and equipment from the NATO installations along our border?"

"I cannot speak for America--my allegiance is to the Jesuit Order in Rome." The priest smiled again, his eyes never leaving the interviewer's face. "I do not represent the government of the United States. I can only convey our Jesuit Father General's hope for the future."

The newsman reached for the knot of his tie again and adjusted it several times as if it suddenly grew tighter. "Many of my countrymen do not know who Andrew Simson is. Could you enlighten them, Father?"

"Andrew Simson is the elected head of the Jesuit Order. Periodically, our Order calls Jesuits together from all parts of the world to attend a General Assembly. Before those gathered in the last meeting, Father Simson took a solemn vow. He promised to dedicate his life to restoring peace to our strife-torn world. He committed the power of his office to ensuring future generations had an earth to inherit. He warned us the madness of the past must stop. He said mankind must learn to live together peacefully, and respect one another's culture. It was the Jesuits who arranged for grain to be shipped to Russia to feed your millions through the coming winter. We interceded with our American President to expedite wheat shipments and negotiated a fair price with farmers in America's heartland. Andrew Simson is determined to bring world hunger to an end."

"Father Andropov, you are conducting a mass in St. Paul's today--for the first time in fifty years."

"An historic event, for which I want to convey my personal thanks, as well as those of the entire Church, to your Premier."

"We'll be covering the event live in Moscow and the rest of the Russian Federation will see portions of the mass broadcast on our next news program."

"Another blessing for which I am eternally grateful."

"Father, do you have a message you would like to impart to all the peoples of Russia?"

"Yes, this message is actually from the Father General." The priest reached into the pocket of his cassock to withdraw his glasses and a folded piece of paper. Donning dark frames, his stunning good looks made the Jesuit seem more like a movie star dressed for a role than a man on a mission from God.

He cleared his throat, shifted his gaze to the paper, then lifted eyes so penetrating they blazed like candles lit against the darkness. "To the people of the Russian Federation: We must come together to save our planet while there is still time. I am appealing to each of you to support leaders who understand the folly of war. The men of Lithuania, Latvia, Estonia, Kirghizia, Armenia, the Ukraine and Georgia, have been cut down by the sword of senseless conflict." The priest delivered sincerity; he leaned forward-- conveying urgency. "We must come together! We must work out our differences in a peaceful fashion. We must vanquish hunger and disease, for they are the true enemy. I send you the message of our Lord and Savior, Jesus of Nazareth. He said to love your enemies. I ask you to make your enemies your friends. Let us live together in peace, let us save our plundered planet, our ravaged societies for the children of the future . . . "

Vassily turned the volume down and glanced at the doctor of parapsychology. "Doctor Rubtsovsky, what did you think of the priest's speech? More precisely, what do you think of the man?"

The sparse, bird-like scientist took off his glasses. Composing an answer, he pulled on a beard hiding deep pockmarks. Replacing his glasses, he took the measure of these two men, who called for an analysis neither was prepared to accept.

"Gentlemen, I know why you summoned me to examine this video. You want me to present you with an answer to the dilemma you face. You want me to expose this priest's weakness."

Both officers of the Red Army exchanged surprised glances, a fact that did not go unnoticed by a man who had dedicated his life to the study of human perception. "We are looking for an analysis of his character," Petrovich finally said.

"Do either of you know what it is I really do?" He searched their faces, seeking telltale signs of honesty.

Petrovich shrugged his shoulders and wagged his head. "No, doctor, I have not the slightest idea what black arts you practice."

"But you know my reputation?"

The old soldier felt defensive; this scientist made him feel inferior. Gruffly, he drew erect. "Many things are said of you--probably out of ignorance and fear."

Rubtsovsky relaxed; the senior army officer was not going to be the problem he anticipated. Thick glasses magnified his eyes and gave the scientist a strange appearance. He turned his gaze toward the younger of the two men. "And you, Kharkov, what do you think of my work?"

"Well," Vassily had an open, eager expression on his face, "I'm fascinated by what I've heard about your experiments. Military implications aside, if you have attained any degree of success in expanding the potential of the human mind, then I think the rest of us should get out of your way and allow you to proceed!"

He was in the presence of men who were willing to put notions of reality aside; men who would listen. "Thank you. Based on what you just said, I will offer you information about this priest."

He reached for the remote control and depressed the button to restart the DVD. Rubtsovsky froze a frame. A bony finger stabbed at the screen. "This man is remembering. His eyes move to the left at the level of his left ear. Gentlemen, this priest has been programmed. He learned this impassioned oratory and his gestures are carefully choreographed."

Vassily knelt in front of the television. Rubtsovsky moved back a few frames. "How can you tell this?"

"The eyes indicate the pathway by which the brain sorts incoming information."

The young soldier stared hard at the television as he tried to assimilate unfamiliar information. Balsahov joined them. "I grasp the purpose of the 'pathway' as you term it, but what significance does it have in this situation?"

'The military mind of the general must have all concepts reduced to black and white. He wants to see the plan laid out, arrows sweeping across the map to point the way'. The doctor did not voice his thoughts; he'd learned to keep his own counsel years ago.

"This man is highly trained. Our own operatives do not undergo the intensive mental programming this priest experienced. His actions, his voice inflection, the delivery of his speech was rehearsed a thousand times. No actor has ever been more thoroughly coached to achieve an emotional response from his audience."

Both soldiers stared at the set, watching the Jesuit's movements without the benefit of sound.

Rubtsovsky kept the DVD playing at slow speed as he spoke to Andropov. "See how he shifts his weight? He leans forward, communicating urgency to punctuate his words. See how his eyes follow the camera? At no time does he allow his attention to waver. This priest projects his passion. Emotion is like an epidemic--easily spread."

Suddenly the set turned black as the scientist jammed his finger against the power button. "Gentlemen, let me explain what this means. Can I offer you something to drink?"

Vodka made Vassily feel like his body turned to fluid, but Petrovich's system was far more tolerant. The older man's mind was still alert, hanging on every word the doctor uttered. If half of what the scientist said was true, the world was in far more trouble than he originally suspected.

Vodka loosened Rubtsovsky's tongue, "All human beings respond to the language of the body. The brain can intercept the slightest message conveyed by a gesture and turn it into a flight or fight response. We are unaware of why we react to others, but we always react."

Petrovich drained the remaining vodka from his glass. He wasn't sure he wanted to think about events which violated the boundaries of logic. "I learned to rely on my feelings to determine who I could trust and who I could not."

The little man hit his fist on the table and sent the glasses flying. "We all have feelings, intuitive knowledge, that if heeded, could improve our lives. I teach students to pay attention to subtle impressions the brain broadcasts and how to understand symbiology unique to their subconscious mind. Once they understand the brain's language, they learn to rely on information in dreams, feelings, the impulsive thoughts so fleeting they leave no memory trail!" Rubtsovsky tapped his fingers against the side of his head. "The complex machine inside our skulls is a computer with unlimited capacity for storage and retrieval! There are those who scoff at me . . . but I can go inside another mind and withdraw information as if I were a computer connected to other networks via a modem. Gentlemen, let me warn you about this man!"

Rubtsovsky turned the television on again and kept his finger depressed on the forward button until he found the frame he wanted. Although alcohol effected his muscles, the scientist's eyes blazed with clarity and intelligence. "Look at him," his fingers circled the priest's face, "look at this man's eyes-- he was trained by someone with a superior understanding of human emotions. And he is not alone. These men go without being questioned, their motives above suspicion."

Vassily Kharkov lurched against the chair he was sitting in; a screech echoed through the lab as metal legs scuttled across ceramic tile. A glance at his superior officer told him he understood Rubtsovsky's prophecy. Petrovich leaned forward; straining to capture the scientist's every word.

"Russia is in grave danger from this man," Rubtsovsky's hand moved in circles, searching, seeking information. "Watch him, watch him day and night. He means to destroy everything we hold dear. He incites minorities; he exhorts them to rebel against us; he seeks to foster the economic collapse of our country. Gentlemen, if you wish the Russian Federation to continue, do not allow this priest to fulfill his mission!"

Wire Service Report Bulletin. All Line Service Subscribers: a0401dwBC-Vatican-Bjt=1st add, 750-1000 ASSOCIATED PRESS WIRE SERVICE REPORT

According to a recent survey conducted by this news service, attendance at Catholic churches throughout the world has increased, in some areas by as much as sixty percent. Parish priests are speaking to overflow crowds when not long-ago Sunday morning services were limited to an older generation. The message coming from the pulpit is broader in scope than has been expressed by Catholic theology in the past. Sermons based on unity, brotherhood and a coming together of all nations to save our planet from industrial plunder, predominate. There appears to be a grass-roots movement toward a return to basic values: compassion for our fellow man, aversion to greed, and opening one's inner-self to brotherly love.

Another phenomenon indicative of the move away from the "me first" culture is being reflected in cable content throughout the United States and Europe. The interview conducted in the partially restored Sistine Chapel between the American journalist, Margaret Anderson, and Father Andrew Simson has been downloaded by millions and millions more purchased DVDs of the interview. The distributor is rushing to ship an additional ten million copies to retailers around the world to fill an unprecedented demand by viewing audiences.

Psychologists are at a loss to explain the impact the Father General of the Jesuits has on people everywhere. Most experts agree, Father Simson has reawakened a sense of moral values and, overall, his influence has been positive. Political forecasters are predicting Andrew Simson will be the single most powerful man in the world by the turn of the century if this trend continues.

Ticket sales for the opening of the new museum at the Vatican are in such demand people could, conceivably, wait two years for admission. Ticket scalping, while strictly forbidden by the Vatican, has reached outrageous dimensions as citizens everywhere vie to be among the first to see the recently discovered masterpiece by Michelangelo, the *Angry Jesus.*

Work on the museum should be completed shortly and the job of placing newly discovered artifacts will begin the moment the architectural firm turns the building over to museum officials. According to an unnamed spokesman within the Vatican, the display of documents, art and artifacts will have no precedent. For now, secrecy shrouds the contents and the team of scientists, researchers and art restoration experts working on the project are unavailable for comment.

Fuchsine smiled. Things were going well; even Cao Bang was beginning to show him respect. He sat in the airless cabin wishing the priest would hurry. Once his progress was reported and he conveyed the Jesuit's message to Cao, he could board a sampan and work his way up the Gui River. Fuchsine knew he would feel much better once he was on the river again, where the air was fresh, where his heartbeat was in time with the river's current.

A shadow fell across the louvers concealing thousands of tiny boats which plied congested waterways. Uneasiness, more instinctual than intellectual, made Fuchsine reach for a knife hidden beneath his belt. Tense, he watched the door handle dip downward. Dark clothing blended into the shadows of a cramped cabin, and he waited, a panther ready to spring should the opening door reveal anyone other than the priest.

Ryan Evans had to duck his head to step inside. He opened the door slowly, giving his eyes a chance to adjust to the shallow light. Deliberate movement also allowed the man on the other side of the cabin an opportunity to identify him. "Fuchsine?"

"Here." The powerfully built Oriental moved from ghostly shadows which hung in the corners like ravaged scarecrows.

"Brother." The Jesuit extended his hand and firmly clasped the other man's wrist.

"We haven't much time."

"These people are accustomed to my comings and goings."

"Still, the fewer our contacts, the better."

"Provide me with a report." The priest drew a chair away from a splintered table and sat down. Relaxing, he allowed his mind to record each detail the other man offered. Father Evans knew his power of recall was the reason he was selected to fill this position by the Father General.

Fuchsine flopped against another battered chair, placed his hands against his thighs and took a deep breath. Closing his eyes, he visualized the course of the river. "Bases have been set up along the Gui all the way to the Hunan Province. The Pearl becomes inaccessible when you reach Guagdong, but we penetrated the interior as deeply as the mountainous terrain permits. I have not gone north to the Min. My connections are better in the southeast and I thought it wise to secure this area first."

The priest nodded, his hands relaxed, his chest lifting as he breathed deeply. "It is wise to secure your base of operation before moving further. It is too hard to protect supply lines extended over vast distances. "

"The freighter will drop anchor four miles out to sea. Ocean going junks will transport goods into the harbor. From there, sampans will come in twos and threes to take on board manageable amounts of cargo. It is dangerous for them ride too low in the water. Not only would they be more likely to draw the attention of patrol boats, but should the wind arise, we might lose more than we would gain."

"Good. Good." The priest began to rock back and forth, in time with the beat of his heart.

"Sampans will mingle with normal river traffic and sometime during the night their journey to China will begin. Within thirty days we should have our supply lanes secure. Officials have been promised goods they never dared dream of, and they will allow merchandise into their areas."

The priest's body assumed its normal posture as he turned away from the relaxed, reflective, all absorbing mental state. "The first freighter will be here at the end of the month. Will you be ready?"

"With certainty."

Rising, the Jesuit thrust his hand across the table. Both men clasped each other's wrists for a long moment. Ryan Evans finally broke the spell, "It is good to see you again. How do you want me to send word of the ship's coordinates?"

"It might be easier if I come to you."

"On the mountain?"

"I am less noticeable than a Caucasian priest! Dressed thusly, I blend in and can slip through the streets without drawing attention to myself."

"I'll have the information by the end of next week."

"Until then . . .."

The Jesuit clasped Fuchsine Hu's shoulder warmly. "Until then my brother."

Will Marshall sat at the kitchen table. His wife was clearing away the remains of a breakfast meeting with steadfast supporters. He stared at the sheaf of papers lying on the table, massaged the muscles in his lower back, then reached for his coffee cup. Draining it, he glanced across the counter at the woman he still found as exciting and beautiful as the day they married.

"Got more coffee?"

"I'll put some on."

The kitchen was old, as was the house, but he wouldn't have traded it for any place in Detroit. Too many precious memories resided in the scarred wood cabinets. A table, which should have been replaced years ago, still supported elbows of elected officials as they wrestled with the weight of political decisions. Besides, he didn't want his people to think he'd grown uppity. He refused to move, and he wasn't going to make many outward improvements to his place either; he was determined to remain a common man. Will didn't want to lose contact with the values he'd fought to retain over the years. This neighborhood, this house, served as a constant reminder.

The smell of coffee perking filled the room. He rose from the table and went to stand behind his wife. The dishwasher was loaded, and the mess cleared away.

"Do you know how much I love you?" His arms encircled her waist.

"Well, Will . . ." she turned in his arms to face him, "I know I'm an awfully good maid!"

Laughing, he nuzzled her ear. Humor was a trait he prized in his wife. No matter how lofty he thought himself, JoAnne was always there to remind him of his feet of clay. She helped him keep his grip on reality firm. The phone jangled, disturbing their infrequent interlude. He let it ring, continuing to kiss her neck.

"Will, it might be important." She gently pushed him toward the insistent instrument. "It's okay, over the years I've grown accustomed to coming second!" His wife smiled, letting Will know she was proud of him. Although her words were mocking, she was not.

He reached for the receiver. "Will Marshall . . .."

"Will." The voice needed no introduction. "I called to congratulate you on winning your election. We were very impressed with the way you handled the press corps throughout the campaign."

"I just spoke honestly and expressed my views the best I could." His fingers gripped the receiver. Somehow, he never welcomed these calls.

"Nevertheless, we wanted you to know your brilliance did not go unnoticed."

"I'd hardly call myself brilliant--a working man, a man who has remained true to values of working-class people--but brilliant? Hardly!"

A laugh that wasn't very warm echoed through the receiver. "I wanted to touch base with you--that's all. Is there anything you need right now?"

"No. The campaign contribution was a decisive factor. All that TV time did a lot of good." He tried to remain polite, but non-committal. He didn't feel right, for a reason he couldn't quite put his finger on.

"There's an issue coming up in the State Senate in a few months we'd like you to spearhead. We think it will help your political career and it would certainly be in our best interest to sway votes."

Will's stomach muscles tightened, he hadn't expected to be asked for anything so soon. "What's that?"

"As you know, Conservative Christians have been lobbying to modify laws guaranteeing religious freedom."

"Yes." A bead of perspiration rolled down the side Will Marshall's head.

"The laws protecting religious liberty of the people of the United States should never be altered. Freedom is what makes America strong. We want you to speak out in favor of the right to free speech and individual belief."

Will relaxed his grip on the receiver and glanced at his wife. She had gone back to wiping down the countertop and wasn't listening to his conversation. "I already believe in that!"

"You'll probably be surprised at the resistance you're going to encounter. There are a growing number of revivalist preachers, who want to legislate morality, but we feel it interferes with personal liberty."

"Somehow, I thought you'd want it the other way around."

"Will, the man who leads my Order wants everyone to be free. He feels all people should have the freedom to choose how they want to worship and what they want to believe. He's convinced inherent goodness resides in all mankind. Religious beliefs can't be legislated. Morality has to come from within . . . it can't be mandated by inflexible laws."

Will sagged against the counter. Why had he been so worried about aligning himself with this priest? Because he wasn't a Catholic himself? Because he was Black? Obviously, these Jesuits had good intentions for everyone. They respected the right of an individual to choose . . . he'd been watching news reports coming from the Vatican closely. Andrew Simson seemed to be a living testament to the philosophy of Jesus Christ. The voice that spoke into the receiver was firm, filled with conviction. "You can count on me."

"I knew we could."

Pope Anastasius labored to reach the buzzer installed beside his bed. The nursing sister rushed in the door at the sound which alerted her to the Pope's needs. With effort, he gave voice to the thought which awakened him from a drug-induced sleep. "Send for Father Simson."

Within the hour, the Father General stepped into the room. He knelt beside the bed and lifted the frail hand, now devoid of softening flesh, to his lips--kissing the ring of office. "I came as soon as I could. Your Holiness, what can I do for you? You have only to ask."

Drawing his lips back in a parody of a smile, the Pope's expression was spectral. Skin hung in folds around his skull, cancer turned his body into the horror imagined only in nightmares. "I want to see the Benedictine nun, Sister Amariah."

Black brows drew together as apprehension flitted through Andrew Simson's eyes. "Father, are you well enough for visitors?" How had the Pope learned about the girl? How did he know her name? There were times Anastasius didn't recognize his closest associates--men who served him for over forty years.

"I already asked Sister Ellena to send for her. I wanted you to know she is coming at my request."

"Father, it wasn't necessary to involve your nurse. I would have seen to it Sister Amariah got your message."

A hand, which was nothing more than skin clinging lifelessly to bone, rose from the covers—a skeletal finger pointed at the man kneeling beside his bed. "My son, she already has my message. I asked her to come tomorrow, after the medication has time to take effect but before it clouds my thoughts."

"Holy Father, why do you feel it important to tax your strength?"

The drug induced veil normally clouding Pope Anastasius' eyes lifted, and it shocked Simson to be the recipient of such a probing stare. The Pope's voice rang through his private apartment as if he'd returned to the strength of his youth. For years he led the Church with vigor, considering himself the earthly shepherd of tormented souls and he strove to relieve mankind's suffering. "Andrew, there are matters in this world that do not concern you. Take warning, my son, do not let pride supersede the mission of our Savior. I am warning you--your intellectual gifts might prove your undoing. You direct the political force of nations, and that pleases you. Always remember," the finger thrust at the Jesuit was wielded with surprising force, "God rules the earth . . . not man! I did not call you here just to tell you I was going to speak with Sister Amariah. I wanted to give you this warning. God will not be mocked! He sees all. He knows all! The workings of your soul are clear to Him! Do not consign yourself to eternal damnation! Do not! I raised you to this position because I saw an Inner Light in you. Has power corrupted your thoughts? Has lust for control turned the goodness I once saw in your soul to depravity? You will be stopped, Andrew . . . I give you fair warning: God will not be mocked!"

A spasm of coughing silenced the Pope. Sister Ellena rushed into the room to check on solution dripping into an IV taped to the back of the Pope's wrist, increasing the supply of morphine. Gentle pressure on his hand encouraged the Father General to leave. "The Holy Father should rest now."

Andrew Simson allowed himself to be ushered out of the parlor, but his eyes never left the Pope. His body was stripped of muscle and nerve endings no longer responded to command, yet the expression in his eyes was lucid, in control. The Pope knew. But how? How had he learned of his plans? How did he known what was happening to the Church? News broadcasts were forbidden in the papal apartments, at his direction. There was no way the old man could know--yet he knew--he knew what was happening around the world.

CHAPTER THIRTEEN

The nurse quietly closed the door behind her. Amariah was alone with the Pope in an elegant salon in the Apostolic Palace, which had been converted into a sterile, unsociable room. A high mechanical bed was surrounded by equipment designed to sustain life far beyond the will of the patient. Pulsating, a monitor followed the Pope's respiration rate and heartbeat with blips on a green screen. The movement was slow, then erratic, not the normal ebb and flow of a healthy man. Bottles of solution hung above his bed and tubes carrying life-giving liquids entered the backs of hands turned raw by surgical tape. His wrists and arms were bruised, the result of needles penetrating veins collapsed beneath the torture of a hundred painful insertions.

Amariah moved closer, the Pope looked as if he were asleep. She crossed the room on tiptoe and knelt beside his bed. With reverence, she lifted a battered hand and drew the ring, the seal of hierarchical office, to her lips.

Anastasius' eyes opened and he tried to smile but his mouth was too dry, his lips cracked and swollen. "Ah, Sister, thank you for coming to visit a tired, sick, old man."

"Your Holiness." Words stuck in her throat. What was she to do? Deny illness had ravaged his body almost beyond recognition? His skull was devoid of hair; chemotherapy robbed him of a dignity ingrained by culture. His skin hung in folds, flaky and gray.

Gesturing at the mechanism, which lowered and lifted the bed, he asked, "Would you elevate my head? We have much to speak of and it's easier for me to talk if I am upright."

Amariah depressed a button, and a whirling noise filled the room as the bed tilted.

"That's better." A smile came again, it was debilitated but had courage. He reached for her hand. "You are wondering why I sent for you."

Dipping her head, Amariah managed a timid nod. The Pope

squeezed her hand, the pressure gentle; he was capable of no more. To Amariah his feeble gesture conveyed such warmth and clemency, tears filled her eyes. Closing her fingers around his hand, she experienced a sensation so loving it startled her. Despite the ravages of illness, Pope Anastasius was still a compassionate, sympathetic man.

"Forgive me if my voice grows weak. There are moments when I find unexpected words upon my lips. My nurses believe it is the effect of morphine, but I know different. My Lord and Savior sits with me, and we discuss an iniquitous world."

Amariah tried to hide her surprise. She could not imagine Jesus sitting where she was now, holding a dying man's hand, offering encouragement, contemplating the events of a life of promise and frustration, discussing the foibles and frailties of being human.

Out of the corner of his eye, Anastasius saw the nun's reaction. "Dear, dear Sister, what I am about to tell you is quite true. I ask that you listen with an open mind--try to keep doubt from destroying the value of what I have to say. There is precious little time until the medication takes over and my mind becomes so shrouded I cannot hold a lucid conversation. Just hold my hand and indulge the ramblings of an old man."

Scooting her chair closer, Amariah shifted her weight and rested her arm against the protective rail. She owed it to the Pope to concentrate on what he had to say. He had increased aid to the poor, inspired the faithful with his gentle, benevolent messages, and stirred the conscience of Christianity during his papal reign. That he wanted to speak to her was a miracle and she was determined to give the Pope her complete attention.

Anastasius reached for the glass on the tray at his bedside with a trembling hand. Saying a silent prayer for his voice to hold out until he shared the information which came to him when he was calm, at rest from savage pain; he sipped some water and then began. "To understand what I am about to divulge, I must explain the Church from a historical perspective. Five hundred years before the birth of our Savior, Pythagoras decided God caused all things to come into being. Since God was also Truth, he reasoned the closer a man came to truth, the closer he came to God. So, he decided man could approach God three ways: geometry, music and astronomy."

The Pope was amused by the expression on the nun's face. She thought his mind was already wandering but the sweet sister was determined to remain attentive. She radiated doubt. She didn't understand how music, mathematics and astronomy were a pathway to find God!

Swallowing several times, he tried to moisten the inside of his mouth with another sip of water, so his tongue could lay hold of words he needed to utter. "In geometry, we have rules of logic and assumptions we accept without proof! Music provides us with vibrations which can lead to rapture. Astronomy is the study of the order of the elements in our universe. Do you see why Pythagoras thought if man studied rules of logic, was inspired by music, and applied the order of elements in their lives, then they could come closer to the Divine Being?"

Closing his eyes, the Pope drew a deep, struggling breath. He was already growing weary. It was a fight to keep his train of thought focused, but he had to--it was his responsibility to communicate the message to her. "About the time of Pythagoras another mystery school was gaining prominence in Egypt. At the Hermetic School initiates were taught how to focus their mind upon a desire. Students learned a special form of prayer, which fulfilled the person's wants and desires."

The tape on the back of the Pope's hand was a constant source of irritation. He withdrew his other hand from Amariah's loving grasp and began to rub the offending area although the nurses warned him not to do so a thousand times. "As word spread of the ability of certain priests to bring about anything they desired, something tragic happened. These priests succumbed to pride and arrogance. They taught new students only part of the process--keeping real power in their hands."

His throat was raspy, and a quavering hand struggled with the water glass. Amariah stretched across the bed to assist the dying Pope. He swallowed slowly, allowing the liquid to sooth devastating dryness--damage inflicted by radiation men of science promised would keep the cancer at bay. Stopping to rest, Anastasius closed his eyes, praying for the strength to impart a message he wasn't certain the girl could accept.

"As Christianity became organized it tried to follow rituals established by Pythagoras and the Hermetic Schools. Prayer became an invocation and Christians were taught to include five separate steps in prayer! First, they were to repent of all wrongdoing. Then they were to ask for what they wanted. The next step was to have faith God would answer their petition. The last step was to accept, through faith, their prayer would be answered." The Pope turned his head toward Amariah. He wanted to watch the girl's reaction. He wanted a sign, a glimmer in her eyes to tell him his job was done-- his mission on earth completed--so he could lay aside bodily cares and go home.

"Doubt that their desires would become a reality through such a simple five-step process ruined everything. Doubt was playing havoc with early Christianity. Finally, Church fathers settled on a solution! They instructed people to leave praying to the priests! Contact with God would be done for mankind--relieving people of the burden of doubt. The Church took over what was the jurisdiction of the individual. People willingly transferred all responsibility to their priest!"

He studied the girl. She was leaning forward, listening to what he said. Her mind was sorting and sifting, categorizing, and selecting, discarding and ignoring, as she struggled to understand. Anastasius knew Amariah was unprepared for what he was going to say next. He reached for her hand again, enclosing it in a shallow grip. The I.V. needle pierced deeper into his flesh, sending pain up the length of his arm, but he felt compelled to offer all the assurance at his disposal.

"Amariah, Christ chastised the priests of His day for interceding between God and His people. He told His followers God dwelled within the heart of every man. He said the *'kingdom of God is within'*. He warned people they couldn't find salvation in a temple, nor could they purchase it with offerings. Jesus instructed the Disciples to listen to the still, small voice that sounded from the heart. My dear, do you know what He was really saying?"

The wimple undulated around her shoulders as she shook her head. Amariah knew what the Pope's words meant, but he was conveying a concept which was totally alien to Christian theology.

"What He told them, my dear, was they did not need a church! To prove His point, He preached in fields among flocks and shepherds. He wandered the hillsides, calling nature a sacred place of worship. He drew his followers away from the temples, away from the activity of priests, and told them to listen to the God within for guidance and direction!"

His hand waved through the air; tubes carrying pain deadening narcotics, saline, and a liquid so rich in nutrients it prolonged life, swayed back and forth--expressing his agitation. "And where are we today? Back where we started two thousand years ago! We worship in temples and try to purchase salvation. Modern Christianity is just the opposite of what Jesus taught! We have come full circle. Our priests are no better than the jealous, petty, self-seeking Levities who controlled the Sanhedrin in Christ's time."

His eyes focused--gone was the mist of morphine and in its place, came a force so radiant it compelled Amariah to listen with every fiber of her being.

"Jesus understood this was going to happen. That's why He spoke so often of a Second Coming. He knew His message would be distorted, used, manipulated by men who wanted to control others!"

A dry, hacking cough silenced the Pope. When the spasm ended,

Anastasius was quiet; his physical reserves were dwindling. He had to tell Amariah! His Lord and Savior was counting on him! He had to convince this girl, he had to make her accept the truth!

Forcing words around a tongue which seemed too thick for his mouth, the Pope began again. "Lady, He comes to me in dreams. He speaks in my ear, and He parts the veil of doubt with the clarity of His words. He has shown me the errors of the past. As I have lain here, a prisoner of the body, my mind has been free to evaluate many Christian traditions. With worldly pressures removed from my shoulders, I can view religion from a new perspective. I know where the Church went wrong--and why. We have another opportunity . . . mankind has been given a second chance."

Claw-like fingers wrapped around the girl's hand, holding her fast. How was she going to react? Would she accept what he was going to say? Would she?

"Amariah, you are here to restore His message."

The room began to spin; fog swooped out of nowhere and filled the air. At the center of this haze, the Pope's face remained clear, undistorted. Burning eyes conveyed sincerity. His mouth moved and the voice that filled the room was like the Levites of old, calling the faithful with a blast of the shofar.

"Your mind will guide you. You have only to jar open the door of consciousness. You taught Him, you see. You took Him to study in the temples in Egypt and with the Masters in the East. You brought Him back, a mature, noble young man. You were His inspiration, His mentor, His teacher. To you, He confided His doubts, you helped Him through the dark night of His humanity. You have come from the past to reawaken the still, small voice within every man. Your purpose in this life is to rekindle the Light which has nearly been extinguished. You must fan that flame, Amariah! You must ignite the spark lying dormant in humanity. If you do not . . . if you do not assume this responsibility, mankind will be plunged into a Dark Age at the hands of the Evil One."

A shroud lowered over the Pope's eyes as morphine shut down the lucid channels in his brain. Amariah saw a rational man slip away, and in his place came the ramblings of a man confined to an illness ravaged body. Laying his hand against the sheet, Amariah backed away from his bedside. She was aware of movement, she knew she was walking along a flower lined pathway, knew she stopped in the courtyard of Pius IV's Casino; but in another dimension of her mind, she was still at Anastasius' bedside, and his voice hammered in her ears.

Modesty demanded she deny personal acquaintance with Jesus. Were it true, she would know more, she would be smarter, braver, brighter, move loving, less likely to find flaw in other humans!

She would be special!

She would have gifts and powers!

She would not be a simple Benedictine nun from San Francisco!

Amariah knew she was an ordinary woman.

The Pope was suffering from a drug-induced delirium, his brain affected by chemotherapy and radiation.

Logic appeased, Amariah fled the garden but deep in her mind a spark ignited. Feelings she could not repress were beginning to firestorm through her brain. The lid of the subconscious was being pried open. On an unconscious level, Amariah knew she became a different person.

A blood red sun set hours ago, and a troublesome moon chose to hide behind a band of clouds. Leaves scurried across the courtyard, pushed by a stiffening breeze which grew colder. A slow shuffle of footsteps was percussive in contrast to the silence enveloping the courtyard. Shoes as ancient as the man himself slapped against paving stones in front of the library, announcing Eduardo's approach.

Glancing at the windows above her, Amariah wondered if she was doing the right thing by sneaking into the Archive. Yet she felt compelled to climb the stairs, to slip inside and wander rows of manuscripts and documents. Something was in there and it was waiting for her. The last light in the Braccio Nuovo extinguished--the forbidden room on the library's uppermost floor. Amariah checked her watch. The library, the museums, and art galleries would empty in the next few minutes. Eduardo wanted to wait another hour before entering the Archive to make certain no one was around.

Finally, the old man gestured at her from the far side of the courtyard. She followed him through corridors draped with limp shadows, beneath columned porticos, along tiled walkways which endured the tread of sandals for six hundred years. They climbed a set of stairs Amariah felt certain was not the normal route of tourists and scholars. Eduardo led Amariah through hallways as familiar as the time worn face that stared back at him from the mirror every morning.

"Lady," Eduardo's voice was a croak, "I will wait beside the door. It is said ghosts of past Popes haunt the Archive. I will stand guard against phantoms whose souls are too troubled to rest. Go," he made a shooing motion with his hands, "I'll wait for you."

Amariah nodded. Eduardo turned the key in a brass lock forged when knights rode abroad on magnificent chargers and ladies anxiously awaited the return of their Crusaders.

A shadow moved across the floor and slid up the stacks as the moon followed its course across the heavens. A man in a black robe seemed suspended in the darkness. Amariah could not tell where the man began, and shadow ended. "Adamus?"

'*Come . . . follow me*'.

Amariah moved away from the doorway. "Adamus, where are we going?"

'*Follow me*'.

Several twists and turns led her to the heart of the Archive. Only the palest slivers of moonlight gained access to the heart of the room. Her eyes hungered for light, then she realized she was being guided by sensation rather than sight.

'*Stop*'.

Amariah stood stock still, before she could turn to see the face that drove her onward, a black robed arm guided her hand--not by touch, but a preternatural, alien power propelled her fingers toward a single leather binding.

'*In here. You will find it*'.

Amariah balanced the manuscript as she took it from the shelf. Cradling sheaves of parchment against shelving with the curvature of her hip, Amariah sought a better grip. When she was confident she wouldn't drop the ancient parchment, she turned—but nothing met her anxious glance other than the damp night air.

"Adamus?"

No answer came. The logical side of Amariah's brain pitted itself against the hemisphere which controlled emotion. The image had evaporated, and it was now difficult to believe she had been guided to this specific document. Retracing her steps, her heart fandangoed as she wrestled with uncertainty. What would she find? What did the dusty manuscript contain?

Flipping the pages, Amariah tried to determine what was so important about the medieval manuscript. Penned in Latin, flowing handwriting was difficult to read in the cloud-dappled moonlight. Suddenly, her attention riveted on the date at the top of the page. Forcing herself to slow down, she looked closer. The text appeared to be a log of some kind--a record of the proceedings at the Council of Trent! The date corresponded to the critical event which brought the Church out of the Renaissance and into the era of Reformation.

Now she was sure. Whoever maintained this log recorded the names of the bishops who spent ten years of their lives in solemn debate about Church principles. The log documented the minutes of various meetings which took place during the Council of Trent. On second thought, it read more like a narrative. A diary perhaps. On closer examination, Amariah decided that was exactly what lay beneath her hand . . . the diary of the recording scribe who witnessed events triggered by Martin Luther's rage. A few more minutes of examination revealed the unknown cleric was not pleased by what was happening. Her head ached, her eyes throbbed as she tried to read in the light offered by the moon--she had to know why Adamus led her to this book!

Scanning a randomly selected page, Amariah felt her pulse begin to race.

". . . *I grow weary of these wretched proceedings. The princes of the Church are viperous lechers. They grovel in one another's presence yet exhibit acts of unchristian-like behavior behind each other's back. And this, this is perhaps the final straw. It rankles my soul to witness what they have done!*

"*Our Lord and Savior was not an impoverished preacher. Yet the Bishops want poverty to seem noble. Their comfort depends upon the contributions made by people whose very existence is in constant jeopardy. Should the faithful decide not to share what little they have with the priests--they might have to earn their keep by the sweat of their brows, by the labor of their backs! What they have done is reprehensible. They portray Jesus of Nazareth as a destitute Rabbi who wandered the hills of Judea begging for sustenance. What they edited out, what they have changed beyond recognition, is how our beloved Savior met His needs. He requested the heavens to supply Him, and through the power of faith, feasts were spread at His feet and His followers were sustained.*

"*Oh, this, and more, have they changed. I want to punish the bishops for what they are doing. This is a world of abundance, Jesus showed us the lie of limitation when he fed the multitude with a single basket of loaves and fishes. He called forth sustenance and the people heard Him in their hearts! They shared with their neighbors and none on the hillside went hungry.*

"Our Lord, Jesus, admonished His followers to listen to His message with the Inner Ear; to see His glory with the Inner Eye; to feel His presence. He said man's thought was the force that shaped the destiny of our world.

"And our Lord and Savior warned the Second Coming was inward. He said it came like a thief in the night and stole into the hearts of the faithful. It called to one man, and his companion, who plowed the same field, heard it not. Two maids spinning at looms in the same room--one would feel its force, the other would sense nothing at all.

"I am tired, and I must stop for the night. If only my thoughts would cease as readily as my hand. For truly, though the candle burns low and flickers, my mind rages against the actions of self-serving men. I weep for the future, I cry out against the injustice done to the legions of men and women yet to come. Perhaps, perhaps, the Second Coming refers to a generation of men and women who will rise against the wrongs perpetrated by these Princes of Darkness!"

Amariah closed the book. Glancing up at the window, she was surprised to see the first streaks of gray announcing a false dawn. The moon settled beneath the horizon long ago; she managed to read a document whose pen strokes were faint, the pages worn--as if the scribe had thumbed through them a thousand times. Her eyes burned, her head felt as if it were a powder keg, ready to explode.

Tapping against the door, Amariah heard Eduardo scuffle forward at her summons. The keys rasped against the ancient lock before the door finally swung open.

"Lady." He offered her a hand gnarled and twisted with arthritis. Amariah managed a tentative smile. "We must hurry, no one can know I have taken this book."

"You found what you were seeking?"

"That and more, old friend, that and more."

"Lady, I must tell you something."

Amariah hesitated on the threshold; there was a timorous quality in the caretaker's voice she had never heard before.

He beckoned her closer, then whispered--the muted dialog of two conspirators. "You know, don't you? I can see it in your eyes. You went into the Archive a girl and emerged a woman awakening to her destiny. Something has changed in you. Lady, your body reveals a new force flowing in your veins. You know, don't you?"

"Eduardo," Amariah placed her hand on an arm that had long ago given up the firmness of youth. Her chin came up, her eyes filled with anger and betrayal, "I know we've been lied to. We've been taught to put our faith and trust in men who barter falsely. The words of our Savior have been manipulated to suit the political ambitions of the princes of the Church. People must know, they must be told--we have been lied to!"

He smiled, and the lines in his face vanished; haggardness and pallor replaced by energy and strength. The hand which lifted to the side of his head no longer tremored and the fingers tapping against his temple were firm. "Listen to the words which resound in your head, my lady, you will be guided. *He* will light your way. Come. We must hurry. No one can find you here-- we must safeguard your secret treasure."

Leon tapped his knuckles against the laboratory door and waited impatiently to be buzzed through. Klaus reached for the switch which severed an electromagnetic lock. There was a look in the German's eyes, a mischievous gleam which made Leon wonder what the restoration expert had been doing.

"Ah, Leon. Come in and shut the door. The Father General is giving me a devilish time about smoking. He says I'm going to pollute the air filters and cause the main frame to malfunction." A billowing cloud of smoke obscured his face. "I keep the door closed so the smoke doesn't get into the hallway. That' much I'll concede--but if Simson wants me in this lab he'll have to endure my habit."

Leon strolled across the room; removing some papers and a stack of books from the wide windowsill where he settled with his back to the sun. Sitting in the sun made him feel connected to nature the same way working with a document penned by human hands in the days when Genghis Khan stormed across the steppes on the backs of shaggy Mongol ponies made him feel like a part of the past. "What's going on? I haven't seen you for days--I wondered if you left Rome."

"I did."

"I suspected as much."

"I flew to Leningrad to see an old friend of mine. I wanted to check on how the Summer Palace, *Petrodvorets,* was holding up against salt air and the Russian winter. We took every precaution with our restoration efforts, but I decided to see for myself if those techniques could be applied to frescos in Rome. There's a tapestry I'm concerned about that's in the same condition as the one in the Czarina's bedroom."

"Why didn't you tell me you were leaving?"

"I didn't have time. Comrade Petrovich only had one day to spare so I caught the first flight to Leningrad."

"I see." Leon placed his foot on the windowsill and rested his chin on his knee. Arms clasped around his shin, he studied his friend. "So . . . how's the palace doing?"

"You'd have to see the Summer Palace to believe it. Some buildings Peter the Great commissioned are every bit as opulent as the papal apartments. Most of *Petrodvorets* is in excellent condition but the restoration work is less than twenty-five years old."

"I thought Leningrad was founded in the seventeenth century."

"During the war, the palace was virtually destroyed and what a tourist admires today is the effort of thousands of modern-day artists and craftsmen, who were taught techniques used during Peter the Great's territorial expansion. The palace overlooks a series of fountains and pools which extend all the way to the Gulf of Finland. Most of the marble was still in decent condition despite German efforts to sabotage the palace. They had the grounds rigged with land mines so when the Russians soldiers over ran fortifications they'd trip wires rigged to blow up the palace, gardens, and fountains. Fortunately, someone spotted the devices, and the palace was spared complete destruction."

Leon squinted as he turned his head to gaze out the window; he watched a cat licking its paws in the garden below. "Klaus, you're not the kind of person who would stop in the middle of a project to check on a tapestry or how the woodwork is faring on a job you completed years ago."

Klaus' eyes traveled upward, a melancholy expression settled across his features. "I get homesick for *Petrodvorets.* There's something about the palace that enchants me. As strange as this might seem, I feel as though I was with Peter the Great when he laid the foundation of *Petrodvorets.* Everything is so familiar--the gardens, the fountains, the layout of the palace. There are times," his eyes glazed over, and his voice thickened, "when I felt as if the Czar was at my elbow. It's as if he couldn't bear the destruction of his beloved retreat and returned to oversee its restoration. You're quite right about one thing-- checking restoration progress was just an excuse."

"Who's the Russian you went to see?" Leon stretched upward, like the cat in the garden, flexing his back, twisting his head in a wide arc.

"Balsahov Petrovich. He talked me into taking on palace project after the war. It was nothing more than a burned-out shell."

"He must have been happy to see you."

"We've become friends."

Watching the German begin tamping fresh tobacco into the bowl of his pipe, Leon sensed more had taken place on Klaus' visit to Russia than he was ready to reveal. "Klaus, I'm worried about how we're going to get Amariah out of Rome."

"I've been considering a few possibilities." A trail of fragrant smoke rose toward the ceiling, wafted toward the air ducts, finally, inexorably, to be sucked into the filtration system.

"Are you going to tell me?"

"I'm thinking about involving Anna."

"She's been depressed lately. Do you think she's reliable?"

"Despite the difference in their personalities, Anna and Amariah are good friends."

Leon stared at his shoelace, then began to the retie the bow. "When should we spring this on Amariah?"

"When I hear from Petrovich.

"What's he got to do with it?"

"That old man survived Hitler, Stalin and Khrushchev and he's got connections in a lot of places. He can secure travel documents, false passports--things people need when they're on the run."

"Klaus, what are in God's name are you planning?"

Klaus reached over to the computer terminal and tapped in a command. The printer sprang to life, its sound filling the room as Klaus met, then held, the other man's eyes for a moment that lasted an eternity--the single decisive moment when one person knows for sure they can trust another. "As soon as Petrovich tells me the documents are ready, I'll fill in all the spaces. Right now, I think it's better if only one of us knows the details of our escape."

"I've been wondering how to tell Amariah what we've discovered. I'm not certain she's going to accept our hypothesis."

Tearing the paper from the printer, Klaus studied the series of dots which revealed a grander, cohesive design. "I think she's going to approach you."

Leon's eyes darted around the room as if searching for something to confirm Klaus' feelings. "What makes you think that?"

The computer report fluttered to the desktop, abandoned and forgotten. "I've been watching her during the staff meetings. Her eyes follow you. She studies your movements and analyzes your every word. I'm positive Amariah has uncovered something on her own and she's trying to decide whether to trust you."

"She's never said anything."

"Watch her in this afternoon's meeting. She flinches every time Simson comes near. The anxiety in her expression lessens when her glance settles on you. Be prepared, my friend, that girl is going to ask you for help soon."

"Father, I have the list you asked me to prepare."

Drawing off his glasses, Andrew Simson beckoned the younger Jesuit into the office. "How many names did you come up with?"

"About thirty." Father Wilson passed a piece of paper across the desk and sat down.

Scanning the handwritten list, the Father General frowned a few times, picked up his pen and made a notation in the margin beside two of the names. "Remove these. The others are well chosen. As usual, you have done an excellent job."

Crossing his legs, Father Wilson tried to be casual. "Thank you, but it wasn't difficult to determine your most outspoken critics."

"All forms of media are represented?"

"As you requested."

"Do we have adequate television coverage?" The comment was rhetorical rather than questioning. Andrew Simson settled deeper into his chair and began to toy with the crucifix--his thumbnail rubbing against the intricate pattern in the design.

"All networks in the United States will be there along with CNN, Fox News, MSNBC. The Russians are even sending a news crew. A Dutch group will cover European countries. BBC will be represented by a couple of anchors. And, of course, we've got the usual number of Italian critics to contend with."

A harsh rasp continued to pierce the silence which filled the room. "Newspapers?"

"We'll get global coverage. Twelve papers are sending their top reporters and primary news services will feed the story to subscribers."

"Excellent. Periodicals?"

"*Time, Newsweek, People and USA Today* from the United States. You said to keep the coverage limited to the most influential, so I was selective about European magazines."

"Good." The Father General returned his attention to the list. "Has the press conference been announced?"

"Yes. We'll clear the nave in St. Peter's. The picture will be placed directly in front of the Baldacchino. The light through the dome is excellent at two in the afternoon. Reporters covering the event will be allowed direct access to the painting."

"It will be veiled prior to my announcement?"

"Yes, Father, a cord will be placed nearby so you can reveal it at the proper moment." Father Jacob Wilson couldn't suppress the smile that found its way to his lips. A newly discovered painting by Michelangelo was going to silence the Father General's critics. Detractors of the museum project would be forced to admit their criticism was unfounded once they saw the latest example of the master's work.

"Is Carole Phillips prepared to cover the reporter's reaction to the painting when it's unveiled?" A gleam of pleasure surfaced; but Simson's eyes contained no warmth, no compassion for his fellow man, they were avaricious.

"She'll be there."

Candor was replaced with compassion. "You have done well Jacob, you are a credit to this project."

Father Michael Sorenson gripped a handrail welded to the dashboard of the Jeep as Loto hit another rut. He lurched sideways and struggled to regain his balance before he was ejected from the vehicle. The trip south was proving interminable, and he felt certain road conditions were going to cause permanent damage to his kidneys. The Jeep lunged again, and Father Sorenson's body plunged in the other direction. He gripped the roll cage, which served as the passenger's only protection if the vehicle overturned.

The sun was directly overhead. It was hot on the savannas and the priest longed to drink from the canteen strapped to his waist. Another pothole bounced Father Sorenson out of his seat; it would be useless to try to wet the back of his throat although it felt as dry and dusty as the road that stretched ahead of them. Perhaps when they stopped for their noonday meal he would offer to drive. Sorenson knew he couldn't do any worse than Loto; but least he could cling to the steering wheel.

After what seemed like an eternity, Loto pointed to a scraggly tree which was the lone occupant of the vast horizon. "We stop."

"Good! I need to get out of this Jeep!"

It didn't take long for the bushman to gather an armload of twigs. He stacked it carefully, pushing bits of yellowed grass into openings between the branches. Then, with a shiny lighter, he lit a fire. Placing a battered kettle over the flames, Loto prepared water for tea.

Father Sorenson rummaged through his rucksack, extracting packets of dried meat and a couple of cans of fruit. Both men fell silent, consumed by the effort of preparing their meal.

When the last morsel of food was devoured, Loto reached to fill the priest's cup with tea. "Drink this--bitter but keeps sickness away."

Swilling a sludge of leaves and bits of bark around the bottom of his cup, Loto turned pensive. He had been dwelling on the Jesuit and finally gathered the courage to speak. "Priest, tell me about this god of yours and the big chief who represents him."

"Gladly, Loto. What is it you'd like to know?"

"Father Stein, he say this chief priest a good man, but Father Stein, he is white. You black man. You tell Loto true."

"Loto, Father General Andrew Simson is a man whose every movement is guided by God. I speak to you as a black man, a black man who rose out of wretched poverty. I owe everything I am to Andrew Simson. For you see, Loto, the Father General never took notice of the color of my skin. He was only interested in my ability. He gave me an education and sent me into the world as his personal representative. He always treated me with the respect accorded a loyal and faithful companion."

Loto shook his head. Dust from their journey showered in all directions as he slapped at the sleeve of his desert camouflage shirt. "Father Stein, he tell me your god is over the god of the animals, the forest and the river. Is this true?"

"Yes, my friend, it is very true. The God I serve, the great God, is the God over the earth and all its inhabitants." Sorenson smiled, revealing a row of perfect white teeth. He was trying hard to keep his explanation simple; he knew Loto didn't have the capacity to understand complex theology.

"Then, priest, tell me this. Why didn't we know about your god before? Why did white men bring the knowledge of this god with them? Is he only the white man's god? If he truly is the God over all, wouldn't he have talked to the dwellers on the African plains too? Wouldn't he also have told us of his existence? Do white men think they are so much better than their black brothers this god speaks only to them? Did the white man create this better god? I've seen your churches. Windows of colored glass line the walls and an altar of gold stands in the back. Your god's servants adorn themselves in robes grander than the feathered capes worn by our medicine men. The god of the rain can't go in your churches. The god of the wind can't blow through your closed doors. Priest, I think you have been blinded. You were raised in a white man's world, and you think their ways are better. But I tell you something true . . . I not so sure."

Tossing the remaining twigs on the fire, Michael Sorenson sent a shower of sparks into the air. The land of his progenitors was beautiful. Primitive, harsh, cruel, but the glory of its landscapes, the majesty of its rivers and mountains could melt the heart of any who were indifferent. It was easy to understand why nature's simple gods were appealing to the man across the campfire. There was no pollution on the wide savannahs to separate man from the glory of the stars; there were no fences to keep him from walking the earth and feeling the soil beneath his feet.

It was important for all men to worship the same way, to understand why they were on earth. Confusion had to be conquered. Sorenson glanced across the fire at the man who'd spent his entire life on the plains of Africa. A thought clicked into place with the sureness of a rifle bolt slamming home. Loto just provided him with the means to ensure the Christian God commanded a place in the heart of every man, woman, and child in Africa.

A gloved hand reached to withdraw a set of coveralls from the locker.

An embroidered logo on the chest pocket identified the wearer as an employee of the local telephone company. Checking the toolbox at his side, the man reviewed its contents. Nothing could be left to chance; he would only have two hours to place plastic explosives and connect the detonators.

He closed the locker door, scrunched a cloth cap on his head, drew the uniform collar toward his ears, and walked out of the building toward a van waiting for him in the moonlight flecked parking lot.

Taking the stairs three at a time, the man in the coveralls rushed to the basement. Massive boilers which operated heating and cooling systems were to his immediate left. Overhead, pipes ran in every direction. Conduit for electric wires spread beneath the floor of the new museum like arteries in the human body. The hum of equipment covered the sound of crepe-soled shoes squishing against a concrete floor.

The man in the uniform knew where he was going. He headed for the furthest corner of the building and cautiously opened the door which led to another stairwell. Listening, he satisfied himself no one was coming. Opening the bag at his feet he withdrew several large hex head bolts. He reached behind the metal stair frame and unscrewed one of the fasteners which held the structure together. Inserting a plastic-coated washer between the framework and the bolt head, he reached for a ratchet to torque it down. Stringing electrical wire from one bolt to another, he took care to conceal the wire beneath the lip of the girder. It took less than an hour to insert the bolts, which had been hollowed out and filled with C-4 explosive. The detonator fit into the bolt head. Sandwiched between micro-thin layers of plastic, the washer's metal core provided the conduit for the electrical charge. At his command, current would surge along the hidden wire, summoning detonators to life. High-grade military explosive would gut both stairwells in seconds, rendering them impassable. It would be impossible for firemen to reach the building's basement.

Using economy of motion, honed by years of training, the man set more charges beneath boilers which heated the building. He ran a strip of plastic explosive, disguised like weather stripping, along the inside edge of the metal boxes protecting electrical transformers. Beneath the explosive cord, a thin wire snaked around more detonators. The wire which would herald the destruction of the museum disappeared into thousands of others bound together in massive feeder cables which served as the life support system to the building.

The velocity of the explosion would send the transformer through the concrete ceiling above--an ordinary piece of equipment turned into a weapon at the hand of a master. As gloved hands snapped the lid of the toolbox shut, he took a moment to survey his handiwork. Trained eyes checked to make certain no loops of wire were exposed, no equipment slightly out of alignment--

everything concealed, his work would go undetected. The Father General's plans were protected. Like men lost in battle, everything had strategic value. The museum was expendable; to a Jesuit, the end always justified the means.

Scar tissue beneath his gloves ached--it had been a long time since he'd been responsible for such a task. It felt good to know they hadn't completely robbed him of his ability. They might have reduced the effectiveness of a body trained as a weapon of war--but his memory was intact, and it served the Father General!

"Randolph Publishing. May I help you?"

"Carole Phillips calling for Jack Price."

"I'll connect you with his office, one moment."

Carole lit a cigarette while she waited, impatient to conclude the coming conversation.

"Mr. Price's office."

"Hi, Connie--this is Carole. Is the grouch in?"

"Carole, it's been a while since we heard from you! Mr. Price was going to call you this morning, but he got tied up in a production meeting. Hang on, I'll get him on the line."

"Carole, honey, how the hell've you been?" A strong, masculine voice boomed from the phone into Carole's ear. She could never convince Jack it was no longer necessary to shout on a trans-Atlantic call.

"Fine, Jack. I'm just fine. Uh, Jack, I wanted to brief you on some pictures before I sent them over. I got a couple of incredible shots of Andrew Simson revealing what he calls the "Learning Jesus" to the press the other day."

"I saw it on the news." Jack Price rose from his desk. It was time to head for the gym. He was getting antsy, and he reached for the bag stashed inside the credenza behind his desk. Cradling the phone on his shoulder, he began rummaging through the contents, checking to make sure his wife packed all the items he needed for his workout. "The piece was certainly dramatic."

Carole drew down on the cigarette, studied the glowing ember for a long moment, and then tapped the ashes into a glass dish on the desktop. "There's one photo which captured something I can't put into words. Jack, I feel as if I'm witnessing a drama, set against a current backdrop, but the pivotal element, the characters, the situation, were forged in another time and place."

The publisher pulled his shoes from his bag and looked to see if there were two pairs of socks tucked in the corner. Satisfied his wife paid attention to his request, he returned his attention to the voice at the other end of the line. "Carole, what are you talking about?"

"Something is going on in Rome and its coming from a level of consciousness beyond my understanding. It's like nothing I've ever encountered before. Simson previewed Michelangelo's masterpiece for the members of the museum team prior to the press conference. I've become friends with a young Benedictine nun working on his project and I took a picture of her standing in front of the painting. In my day, I've captured some remarkable moments, but this one, well, it shakes me to the core of my being."

"Carole, honey, you aren't turning esoteric on me, are you?" Jack Price put the bag aside. "Don't tell me you're getting caught up in a bunch of religious Voo Doo! The characteristic that makes you the best photographer in the business is your cold, analytical eye. You can spot the flaw in a situation and freeze-frame time for the inspection of the rest of the world. Lose that special capability, honey, and you'll lose the quality which makes you better than any other photo-journalist in the world."

Jamming her cigarette against the ashtray, Carole crushed it out with the same force she ground out the words. "Yeah . . . maybe." She reached for an eight by ten color photograph and drew it beneath the desk lamp. Depressing the on switch, a cold, white bar of light flooded the glossy paper. Sister Amariah was reaching out to touch the face of a young boy in the painting. Carole's intrusive eye spotted the resemblance between the Benedictine nun and the woman painted by Michelangelo several hundred years before. On canvas, the woman with electric blue eyes hovered over a chart displaying geometric planes and angles, which rested beneath her hand. She studied the young boy's face, as if trying to determine if he understood.

Light filtering through dome windows towering above the Baldacchino, spangled the air surrounding Amariah. Like the hand of God reaching out to Adam, Amariah's fingertips reached for the painting, but she seemed reluctant to touch the face of the *Learning Jesus*. A film of tears in Amariah's eyes refracted harsh light from the camera's strobe, turning them turquoise.

Michelangelo portrayed the *Learning Jesus* with colors which lent a magical quality to his expression. Eyes as blue as those of his teacher radiated curiosity. A cascade of brown hair, shot through with warming streaks of red, tumbled around the boy's wide shoulders. Although his youthful features still retained a symmetrical softness, his jaw was firm and angular, his cheeks high and pronounced, his nose straight, his chin split by a soft cleft. But the observer's gaze always returned to the young boy's eyes, as demanded by a master artist. Sadness lurked at the edge of his expression, like he knew too much for his age; like an awareness of events to come caused him to mature too fast. The hand holding a stylus was comprised of sturdy bones and strong sinew. The arm extending from his homespun robe was already heavily muscled; evidence the boy worked at a demanding trade; he spent few hours of his day in idealistic dreaming.

Reverence, love, the look of longing was so deep on Amariah's face it couldn't be expressed in words, but it was captured in the photograph. It was unusual to use color film, Carole's preference was black and white; contrast, delicate shadow and texture was more in keeping with her photographic style. The wimple framing Amariah's face matched the drape of cloth which covered the hair of the woman in the painting. A special bond between a beloved teacher expanding the horizons of a cherished student was tenderly captured by Michelangelo.

"Jack, reserve judgment until you get a look at these pictures. I wish I could explain my feelings about Simson's project, but I've got to trust my instincts on this. Even if my behavior seems irrational on the surface of things --I'm asking you to trust me!"

"Carole," Jack gripped the receiver. He'd never heard his star photographer talk like this before, "The photographs you've already sent are remarkable and the copy accompanying the pictures won't need much editing. It's your best work to date! Try not to get caught up in the mystery of religion. It can befoul the best mind."

The mouthpiece on the phone disappeared behind a cloud as Carole exhaled smoke from another cigarette in one, short burst. "Jack, try to put your Eastern establishment, white male ego behind you for a second, okay? Look at the picture and analyze your emotional reaction to it."

"Okay, honey, if that's what you want. Anything for you, you know that. Just keep your stuff coming."

"Jack, will you do me a great big favor?"

"You're not going to ask me to go to church and pray, are you? I haven't done that sort of thing since puberty."

"No, I wouldn't ask you to violate all the rancorous, pre-conceived barriers you hide behind. I want you to put a packet of photographs in one of those metal containers you use to store negatives and write Sister Amariah's name on the label. Keep the box in your fire-proof vault."

"Okay." The sun continued its relentless march across the sky. His trainer was going to wonder where he was, but suddenly, the workout lost all significance.

"There's no point in trying to explain the situation to you now. I'm coming to New York to review the galleys sometime soon. We'll talk then."

Alarmed, Jack nearly shouted into the phone. "Carole, I haven't heard such an empty tone in your voice since you bailed out of Saigon. You had me scared to death when I got your call from the Lexington, asking me to wire money to Manila. You sounded so low, so desperate. For God's sake, Carole, there were tears in your voice back then and I'm hearing them again now!"

Carole couldn't keep her eyes off the photograph of Amariah. It was haunting; something ethereal clawed at her mind, something was trying to pry open the gates of memory. She sensed, recognized, remembered; Carole felt as if she witnessed the scene in the painting, just as it took place, in the dusty hills of Judea when Caesar's legions tramped the roads which were the glory of Rome. Somehow, someway, the painting unlocked the vault of the past.

"Saigon was a low point in my life. Jack . . . I'm talking about some inexplicable feelings--not the comfort zone of logic."

"Honey, are you okay? Do you need anything? I don't want to lose the best god damned journalist of the century!"

"Jack, I'm fine." Carole couldn't come to terms with the look on Amariah's face. There was a shift in her expression, which transformed the girl from a normal human into a being so spiritual, so in tune with the divine aspect of her nature--she didn't look real anymore. A chill zigzagged back and forth between Carole's shoulder blades. "I'll talk to you when I get to New York."

Jack Price stared at the phone in his hand. A sizzle, like bacon frying, burst from the phone as the connection severed. Carole Phillips had been in combat situations more times than many career soldiers. She'd covered wars in Beirut, Nicaragua, and El Salvador. She'd taken prize-winning photos of Sinn Fein massacres and brutal British retaliations. She was no stranger to the ugliness of life. Yet, despite every situation Carole ever faced, Jack Price had never heard this element of fear in her voice before--not even after getting out of Viet Nam with only the clothes on her back and the film in her camera. This was a Carole Phillips he didn't know. She was frightened; her terror was transmitted across oceans and continents via a communication satellite.

As the sun closed in on the horizon, the publisher forgot all about his appointment at the gym.

CHAPTER FOURTEEN

"I dunna know, Gregory, I just dunna know anymore." Father Patrick Murphy walked with his hands clasped behind his back, eyes fastened on the rain scrubbed walkway, his thoughts as sodden as the clouds. Upset, the priest slipped into the brogue of his youth spoken by the tough men and women who labored to wrest crops from Ireland's thin soil.

"Pat, we've got to resolve this! We daren't tarry. Either we forge ahead and bring this document to the attention of other members of the team, or we consign it to the oblivion of the Archive. Our choice is simple. As a historian, returning this document to the Archive is unthinkable! If the hierarchy of the Church has been wrong--the world deserves to know! Ignorance is a sin! I would fear for my immortal soul if I buried the truth!" Friar Gregory Lean watched his friend from the corner of his eye.

Father Murphy surveyed the garden with weary, bloodshot eyes; it had been days since he'd gotten more than a few hours of sleep. "Even this devastating?"

Friar Lean pointed to the Casino of Pius IV. "Let us sit in the sun while it lasts, brother." When they reached the chaplet of benches Friar Lean glanced at the sky, wondering when the weather was going to turn. He patted the bench. "Sit, Pat, while we ponder our dilemma."

Father Murphy was in turmoil. He studied the marble floor and watched the fountain dolphins. The beauty of the Casino courtyard did little to soothe his troubled heart. "Are yae thinkin' it's accurate?"

"I've no reason to think otherwise."

"Gregory, I'm troubled by what this is gunna' mean to the Church."

"I think we'd be guilty of malfeasance if we don't bring it to light. Let's consider this from a historical perspective--what we possess is a document, which looks like an agreement between Pope Leo X and Martin Luther. It appears Luther agreed to modify his theory of the '*potential of belief*' in exchange for his life. On his part, the Pope conceded not to burn Luther at the stake for heresy."

"It's not that part I'm worrin' aboot! I'm thinkin' aboot the notion of grace--and the responsibility the Church has ta' assume for barterin' Luther out of his concept."

Shaking his head, Friar Lean studied clouds scudding across the sky. "It appears Luther agreed to modify his concept that a righteous man didn't need to partake in the seven rituals deemed necessary for a Catholic to enter heaven! Our document contains Luther's declaration that Lowera person need only profess a faith in God to be saved. Luther seemed to be saying emphasis on ritual was supplanted by faith!"

Patrick Murphy massaged the area of his chest where the pacemaker was implanted. The spot beneath his ribs ached more all the time. "This topic is suren' to be as hotly debated in clerical circles today as it were when Luther nailed his protest to the church door in Wettenburg! Are we no closer to understandin' tae true message of ter' Bible than we were several hundred years ago?"

Pulling his glasses off, Friar Lean cleaned them with the edge of his robe as he considered his friend's question. "I'm beginning to think Luther was right!"

A look of alarm swept across the Jesuit's florid features. "Don't be puttin' personal feelings in ta' this, Gregory! You must be objective and keep a proper historical perspective."

"I know, old friend, I know." Father Lean focused on Patrick Murphy's hand--a hand which gripped the bench, as if afraid the world would tilt, and he'd fall into the Unknown. Age had deposited flecks of brown across tendons and sinew, which once held the reins of doctrine firmly. "According to this, Luther was certain when man allowed faith in a Higher Power to guide and direct their lives, they didn't require rituals to enter heavn!"

"Aye, and what oor little document seems to be sayin' is when someone listens to the voice of inspiration, they dunna need the Church to guide them!"

"What surprises me is Luther signed the agreement."

"It saved his life! William Tyndall was burned at the stake for translatin' Luther's German Bible into English."

Clouds were beginning to bunch against each other, and the sky was fast turning to a dull, scarred-up chrome color. A shiver made the small, bookish man tremble. "Tyndall is another problem we've yet to resolve. The King James version of the Bible is nothing more than a revision of Tyndall's translation of Luther's work--by a group of forty English bishops! Protestants regard their Bible as a more reliable, more sacred rendition of the word of God. They look at the Catholic Bible with scorn. Yet, I wonder what most Protestants would say if they knew Tyndall added his own commentary and feelings to his translation? His romantic style of writing accounts for many discrepancies between the two Bibles."

"Which passages are you referrin' to?" The ache behind his pacemaker was growing more insistent. Patrick Murphy made a silent promise to himself to stop by the infirmary in the morning and have the doctor check the mechanics of the apparatus.

"For instance, the sixth chapter of Matthew . . . where Christ teaches his followers the importance of faith."

"Matthew six, verses twenty-five through twenty-nine, I'm knowin' the verse well. '*Consider the lilies of the field, how they grow; they toil not, neither do they spin: And yet I say unto you, that even Solomon in all his glory was not arrayed like one of these*'."

"That passage was created by Tyndall! It wasn't a part of the original Greek text from which the Catholic Bible was translated! In fact, this whole section of the Book of Matthew is suspect in light of some of our recently discovered documents."

"I canna believe Tyndall was so audacious as to take it upon himself to incorporate his own thoughts into the holy writ of the Bible!"

"Well, for whatever reason, that's exactly what he did!" Clouds obscured the sun, and the earth grew as cold as if another ice age were sweeping down from a frozen north. The dark underbelly of a cloud bank overhead looked ominous, and rain threatened to pummel the land soon. Gregory Lean pulled the earth-brown habit beneath his chin and drew its hood snug against his head to ward off the increasing tempo of the wind. "I've had a thought, and in the not-so-distant past, I might have been burned at the stake for entertaining such a notion."

"Don't spare me now! I've heard too much to have you stop! Go on, tell me what thoughts the Devil ha' put in yer mind. 'Tis sure and certain Satan must be behind this awful business."

Father Lean searched for proper words. The difficulty of giving his thoughts substance made them shatter like glass under a hammer's impact. "I wonder if Tyndall was a contemporary of Jesus, reborn in a later age. Passages we know he added to the original text fit so well I can't help but speculate about how a man, who lived fifteen hundred years after the time of our Savior, could make his sentences fit with such perfect harmony we've only just discovered they were not part of the original text!"

"Are you suggestin' William Tyndall was reincarnated?" Astonishment bleached Patrick Murphy's face of color and constricted the gigantic, faltering muscle of his heart.

"Remember, Pat, another of our discoveries concerns how and why the word 'reincarnation' was stricken from the Bible by the bishops at the Council of Nicea. With one sweeping statement: '*Let him whosoever should believe in the subsequent wonderful return of the soul again and again, let him be called an anathema*', Christian doctrine was forever altered. The bishops substituted the word resurrection, with its one life only interpretation, for the word reincarnation, which according to this translation means the 'subsequent wonderful return of the soul'. This is entirely conjecture, but I can't help but wonder if the early bishops thought they could better control their followers if Church doctrine taught Christians had but a single lifetime in which to earn a place in heaven? Patrick, think about the political climate of the day. If this concept was struck from the Bible, then reincarnation must have been widely accepted in Christ's time. Certainly, there are passages in the Bible which could lead one to think Jesus believed the soul returned to earth many times in different bodies. How else can you explain why he asked the disciples whom they thought he had been before . . . '*Who do men say that I am?*'."

Rain began to spatter the courtyard. Large drops threw splotches of ugly, mottled gray across polished marble. Hoping motion would relieve mounting distress, Father Murphy rubbed the center of his rib cage. "Gregory, I dunna know what to believe anymore! I thought I was an expert--and I was, based on information provided by an authority I considered sacred. My field is shifting. The more I explore, the more I uncover, the more I am faced with the possibility the foundation upon which I based my belief--the history I've been taught to accept without question--may be honeycombed with error and distortion."

"And outright lies?"

The vise around his heart twisted another notch. Patrick Murphy knew Church doctrine was being assaulted as surely as if a column of Roman soldiers were advancing up a hill with a battering ram. Could he participate in the destruction of what he'd sworn to uphold? The word that escaped between compressed lips was the equivalent of a hiss. "Perhaps."

Father Ryan Evans turned his head, straining to capture the direction of the shuffle outside the hotel room door. With his back pressed against the wall, he withdrew a revolver from beneath his cassock. Holding his breath, he waited. The doorknob turned; the person on the other side was testing the strength of the lock.

A light tap came. The Jesuit whispered. "Who?"

"Fuchsine."

The priest released the lock but kept the security chain in place. Pressing his eye against the narrow slit as he cracked the door, he made certain the man matched the voice. Stepping back, he opened the door with such force it acted like a vacuum, sucking Fuchsine into the room.

"You got here sooner than I expected." The priest laid the Colt-45 Combat Commander on the table in front of the couch.

"I have much to report. If you don't mind, I'd like to wash before we settle into business. It seems like I'm never rid of the stink of the harbor."

"We'll talk while you wash up." A smile warmed a countenance normally preoccupied and dour.

Fuchsine ran the water until steam filled the bathroom. Standing beneath hot water, he luxuriated in the feel of grime dissolving. Reaching for soap provided for guests of the grand hotel, Fuchsine gloried in the fragrance of roses which greeted him as he lathered soap through his hair. The square of terry cloth, turned hot and soapy, felt good against his lean, well-muscled body. Fuchsine wanted to remain in this small room forever--cleansing away the sins of a society in which he was forced to dwell.

Ryan Evans' voice called from the parlor of the luxurious suite. "What have you to report?"

"Many, many things. Of utmost importance is how smoothly the operation is going. Our supply routes are firmly established. As it turns out, Cao knows all the right people. I'm astonished at the value most villagers place on stereos, tee shirts, Levis and portable televisions. It's as if a small slice of heaven has been provided."

"They follow you?"

"Like adoring sheep."

"What of Cao?" The sun hovered above the horizon, as if reluctant to leave inhabitants of the earth to the darkness crowding the eastern sky.

Humidity, the haze of pollution caused by thousands of human beings living in tight confinement, turned the sun into a sodium yellow sphere hanging low over the island, a giant sword of Damocles--ready to smite the unworthy.

"He spends most of his time smoking opium and lying in bed with Lily." Fuchsine reached for a towel and rubbed it briskly against hair so black it refracted the light coming through the bathroom window like sun on an oil slick.

"The man's debauchery is well known, it's part of the reason he was chosen."

"The lure of the pipe is a curse without precedence." Fuchsine rubbed the rest of his body fiercely, anger betrayed in the rough movement. "Opium ruined the most glorious civilization ever known. Chairman Mao was a necessary evil because he transformed a society which allowed opium to become part of its culture. Without him, China might never have cast aside the drug-induced yoke of oppression clouding the minds of my people. Such a waste--to think what might have been achieved if we had not succumbed to the poppy. Now--we are ready to assume our place as a major power. We are a strong, proud people--a race not afraid of work. China is ready to hold her head up high again. We will soon influence other nations and impact an awaiting world!"

The Jesuit glanced at the gun lying on the table, its black metal barrel reflected the mustard-colored rays of a dying sun. "And you, Fuchsine, you will be at the vanguard of leadership."

Fuchsine entered the room, his hands over his head as he slicked back his hair with a cheap pocket comb. "The Sleeping Dragon is about to awaken!" Fuchsine slid the closet door aside and reached for his cassock. Slipping it on, he quickly secured the buttons down the front--then reached for the crucifix and drew it over his head. "I'm ready."

"Our congregation awaits us. Andrew Simson will be hailed as the savior of China, the man who brought its people into an era of freedom and economic prosperity. And you, brother, are one of his chosen!"

Wire Service Report Bulletin. All Line Service Subscribers: BC-Angola, Bjt, 980 ASSOCIATED PRESS WIRE SERVICE REPORT

Reports are scattered and have taken time to reach the capital of this third-world country. Kanga-Kanga was killed, and his forces crushed, in what has been termed by many, the most decisive battle ever-waged in modern times.

This despotic ruler, who had a complete strangle hold on central Africa, was toppled by vastly inferior forces under the leadership of a man named Tshikapa. In a statement broadcast throughout Africa over a powerful short-wave radio, Tshikapa praised his men, saying they waged a war of attrition. Using hit and run tactics against Kanga-Kanga's supply lines the huge army was crippled.

Further reports indicate Kanga-Kanga's headless body was thrown into the Lubilash River, where it was consumed by crocodiles. His generals were lined up on the shore and forced to watch the carnivorous reptiles devour their leader's body. Tshikapa issued a statement to the effect that members of the opposing army would be detained in prison camps for an extended period. The purpose of this, it is reported, is to indoctrinate Kanga-Kanga's soldiers into a new way of thinking. Tshikapa plans to involve them in the restructuring of Africa.

The rebel leader has been quoted as saying, ". . . the time of killing must end. The tribes of Africa will now learn to live together in peace. Tribal chieftains will concern themselves with the survival of their people, instead of waging war against neighbors. Hunger and disease are our true enemies. We must unite to conquer epidemics which are the true scourge of our land."

Tshikapa pledged sweeping political and educational reforms to help Africa survive the jump into the twentieth century. He hinted several European, American, and Japanese automakers indicated their willingness to establish manufacturing plants on Africa's plains. This will provide employment to the thousands who've followed migrating herds since the dawn of time. World leadership awaits Tshikapa's plans with interest. Many government officials are openly skeptical about his ability to bring stone-age tribes into the age of technology. Opinion is varied as to whether he has enough power to unite the tribes of Africa and breathe the life of industrialization into a decaying continent.

For the first time since the Pharaohs unified the upper and lower Nile, there is a sense of cohesiveness spreading throughout Africa. People living on desolate savannahs, in steaming jungles, along massive river basins, are feeling the stirring of peace for the first time.

Rumors persist regarding the role a Jesuit priest played in Tshikapa's victory. No one knows if such a person exists, but stories about a man wearing a long black robe continue to filter out of Africa.

John Preston was sweating as he ran up the flight of stairs leading from the subway. The drop went smoothly--the courier would take the next flight over the polar ice cap and Richard Weatherby would be in possession of a manila envelope sometime tomorrow. The most damning evidence he'd ever discovered, over the course of his career as an undercover operative for the CIA, had just been dispatched back to the States. Incontrovertible proof the Father General used his position to finance subversives; broker power and shuttle governmental institutions like pawns on a chessboard would soon reach Washington. Andrew Simson's hypocrisy reached such appalling dimensions it was beyond the rational thought of ordinary men. Jesuits had been selling off the Sacristy treasure for months. The money supplied rebel forces in third world counties with the means to purchase weapons, explosives, and other military supplies. The Catholic Church is waging a political war, rather than pitting its priesthood against Satan in the battle for man's immortal soul. Instead, the so-called soldiers of God took to the field of conflict to secure arenas of interest. Wire transfers, codes, digits, information reduced to a blip on a magnetic tape wove a tale of intrigue and deception the likes of which vanished with the Borgias. Simson was tampering with governments, bartering influence, and usurping power with cunning and avarice. But the Father General's reign would soon crumble! A foundation built on lies and manipulation could not withstand the scrutiny which would be brought to bear on the Jesuit Order. Amariah Weatherby could go home to San Francisco. With any luck at all, she'd give up the Church and marry Leon--the boy was damned likable.

On the sidewalk, John Preston was grateful to be away from the stale subway air. He breathed deeply, feeling more confident and clear-headed than he had in days. He felt renewed; maybe it was time to retire from government service. There were plenty of good years left--he could still devote productive time to private enterprise.

Traffic showed no signs of lessening, but the banker wasn't in a hurry. His thoughts were focused on going back to San Francisco, settling down, buying a house--maybe across the street from Dick and Liz. A new condo development was being built close to them. Perhaps he'd even get married. He'd never wanted to subject a wife and family to the pressures of the life of an intelligence agent before--but if he put all that behind him--maybe, just maybe.

A warm sun was shining, the blare of traffic lost its normal discordant sound and struck his ears with a primitive kind of melody--basal, throbbing, sensual. Swirling cars cast a kaleidoscope of colors through the streets, the madcap shouts of tourists and shoppers, the wonderful contrasts which made Rome such a unique city suddenly became enlivening. He took another deep breath of air, relieved his mission was about to end. Perhaps he played a part in preserving peace in his time.

A man dressed in a stained trench coat lurched through the crowd. A frayed collar was pulled beneath his chin and a worn fedora rode low over his ears. He seemed to be hurrying toward a predetermined destination although his gaze never left the sidewalk. Glancing neither right nor left, the man shouldered his way through people standing on the corner waiting for the light to turn.

Something struck the middle of his back. Peripherally, John Preston saw a fellow pedestrian fall against him, and he turned, prepared to offer a protest. A hand propelled the off-balance banker into oncoming traffic before he had time to react. The last thing John Preston saw was the shiny hood ornament and grill of a bright red car thundering down the street toward him.

SAN FRANCISCO CHRONICLE - The body of international banker John Preston was met by a host of mourners at the San Francisco airport today. The financial community on two continents grieved over the loss of what some called the finest banking analyst in the world. Preston was in Rome to firm up trade agreements between countries of the European Community. John Preston made his mark in banking early in life when, as a young man, he pressed for free trade between the European Common Market and United States.

In what is being regarded as a freak traffic accident, Preston sustained a mortal blow to the head when he apparently lost his balance in the jostling crowd of people leaving the subway station. The driver of the car was not cited. A police investigation determined the accident was unavoidable. John Preston left no surviving relatives.

Amariah laid the article her parents e-mailed to her aside. Tears of grief flowed from an inexhaustible well; she had blown her nose until her upper lip was raw. Uncle John might not have had a wife or children, but hundreds of friends met his body when it returned to San Francisco.

Watching the coffin disappear into the cargo hold of the huge airplane, which took her uncle home was an agonizing experience. Had it not been for the comfort of Leon's protective arm, Amariah would not have had the strength to handle the difficulties of shipping body from one country to another.

Swollen eyes returned to the window. A miserable drizzle saturated Rome, the sky wept huge drops, which turned the entire landscape ugly and muddy. Her heart was as filled with grief as the rain gutters laden with torrents of dirty brown water. The phone rang, its piercing alarm-like sound startled her.

"Hi, honey. We just got back from the cemetery. Your mother and I wanted to know how you're doing."

"I'm as fine as I can be Daddy, under the circumstances."

"Amariah, I want you to come home. I want you to get on the next plane out of Rome!" Richard Weatherby could no longer suppress the anxiety he felt, an angry tone crowded out his normally neutral voice. Seeing the body of his best friend lying in a coffin took a toll on his emotions. His last conversation with John kept running through his mind with the recurring beat of funeral drums.

"Darling?" Elizabeth took the phone out of her husband's hand. "John's death has been a terrible shock. The museum is nearly ready to open, isn't it?"

"Yes, Mom, it is. Finishing touches are being put on displays right now." Amariah's voice was raw with grief. She couldn't imagine what her world was going to be like without her beloved Uncle John.

"Is there really any reason for you to stay?"

"Father Simson wanted us to be present at the dedication ceremony. Other than that, I'm just wrapping up a few things here and there."

The sweetest sound in the world reached across landmasses and oceans to comfort Amariah. It was the cherished voice which soothed her to sleep, the one that always dispelled childish fears. "Darling, come home. We need to mourn John together. Our grief won't begin to heal until we've cried it all out. We need to get the photo album and look at pictures of him in happier times. We must remember him as he was--a wonderful, generous man."

Tears began to stream again as Amariah thought about the man who always showed up on her birthday, and how a Christmas never went by without a special present for her under the tree--even when he was out of the country. "Okay, Mom. I'll finish here as soon as I can."

Her father came back on the line. "Amariah, the last time I spoke with John he was concerned about your safety."

Amariah wrestled with a nervous laugh. "Oh, Daddy, you know Uncle John always saw ghosts and goblins everywhere! I'll be fine."

"All the same, I want you to take care. I'm on a global satellite cell phone system now. I called to give you the number."

"Daddy! You hate cell phones! Why on earth have you given in now?"

Richard stared at the small object in his hand. It looked so harmless, yet it had the power to carry a message which might mean life or death. "It seemed like something I needed to do. John didn't like what is taking place in Rome. He admired the young man who helped you get his body home. John said you could trust him."

Amariah pressed the phone receiver against her chin. Would the tears never stop? She fought against emotions tightening a corrosive band around her heart. It would make her parents feel worse if they knew how badly she was taking his death.

"Please come home now!" Smashing his fist against the kitchen counter, Richard ignored the shocked look on his wife's face.

In the hallway, the Rottweiler lowered on his haunches. He twisted his massive head, as if assimilating his master's angry words. Slowly, forcefully, a low rumble crawled up this throat from inside the wide chest cavity. It grew louder, the predatory, primordial sound of an animal whose genetic code was imprinted with a lust for battle. The hair stood erect on the ridge of his spine as the dog began to pace.

The growl carried across oceans and continents via a communication satellite orbiting the earth. The primeval bark reached every nerve ending in Amariah's body--Damascus felt her pain. "Kiss Damascus for me, Daddy. And" she thought about the arm that reached out to shelter her, the hand which guided her toward the diary in the Archive . . . please try to understand, I'm in good hands."

Richard Weatherby could only stare at thephone which suddenly went dead. A menacing sound filled the kitchen as the Rott growled in his master's direction. "Come here you fool. My daughter says I should kiss that big ugly head of yours!"

Damascus crossed the room in two great, loping strides. He stood on his hind legs, pressing his front paws against Richard's shoulders. An enormous, lolling tongue fell from the side of his mouth and dark eyes tried their utmost to convey a message. Dropping to the floor with a thud, the Rott marched back to the hallway. Turning, the dog looked over his shoulder, as if waiting for Richard to follow him out the door as if he expected his master to march at his side all the way to Rome!

Richard replaced the phone in its cradle. For a moment, he watched the dog pace, then went to let him out into the yard. As he stepped onto the patio, Richard looked up into a dull sky streaked with clouds as swollen as his emotions. "Dear God in heaven," he addressed the vast space stretching endlessly upward, "if *You* really exist . . . if *You* really are the power Amariah believes in . . . protect my daughter . . . bring her home!"

The bar was crowded with men and women jammed around tables; hovering in alcoves pitting the walls; faces pressed against a few grimy windows provided meager ventilation and not much light. Anxious miners surrounded the old television set in the corner.

Gwelo, eyes blinking against the glare of lights required by a television camera, began to speak--his words halting, laden with the sorrow.

". . . I beseech the citizens of every country to support the efforts of my people. Rally around your black brothers and sisters who suffer oppression at the hands of the whites in South Africa. Their plight is your plight, for as long as one man on earth is in bondage to another, there can be no lasting freedom. Although I am not of their faith, my Jesuit friends, the men who were the instruments of my salvation, assured me this broadcast will reach my native land. I know not how this is to be accomplished because the government of South Africa sealed its borders against my words. They fear my cries for justice! They fear our men, once tribal princes, will have their pride and dignity restored! These men of politics know when a man's self-respect begins to percolate through intimidation and suffering--nothing can ever be taken away from that man again. I call out to my African brothers! Unite! You must band together to resist the propaganda of the white man, for they engage in a desperate war to limit your mind, to repress your spirit. Heed the call of freedom when it comes! Follow the men who will help cast aside the tyranny of thought, which suppresses the person you have the right to be!"

Gwelo's eyes bulged from their sockets; his arteries strained above a homespun shirt and his hands thrashed through the air. The fervor of his words was so intense it seemed as if he were standing in the crowded South African bar exhorting his people to have courage, reminding them of their ability to be strong and vibrant again. "Cling to each other! Unify the power of your thoughts! A white man uses a black man's physical strength to loot our earth of its riches. Turn that might against him! Stand shoulder to shoulder with your neighbor--hold fast to your brother's hand!"

The small television screen faded into blackness as the bar owner switched it off. A silence so heavy it smothered even the most boisterous descended over the gathering. Furtive glances measured the reaction of the next person, each wondering if the other would heed Gwelo's call.

A tall man in the back of the room rose, his movements slow--as if working in the cramped conditions of the mine limited his ability to stand erect. Dark eyes traveled the length and breadth of the bar; he gauged the impact of Gwelo's speech in the attitude of postures, the nervous scuffling of feet, the way breaths were taken as though men were afraid to fill their lungs for fear the next inhalation might be their last. Shoulders bent from hours of working in tunnels began to straighten; hands blistered from holding high- impact drills which tore the earth to shreds, started to flex and strain; heads, whose cap of wiry hair contained the dull gray dust of the diamond mines, lifted.

Father Michael Sorenson's gait was shuffling. He was a Kaffir suffering the indignities foisted upon him by the color of his skin. Every face turned toward him as he shuffled forward, his spine hunched, muscles in his legs shortened by hours of brutal labor in hollow spaces beneath the earth's surface. For one long, anguished moment, his eyes studied the expression of the crowd.

Slowly.

Radiating purpose.

Broadcasting authority.

His voice rang out--the call to freedom assaulting every ear. "In a not-so-distant past, a small brown man experienced the injustice of the white man. He was an attorney, educated at the great English school, Oxford. He spoke the white man's language; he lived according to their customs, yet they shunned him because of the color of his skin. But this man listened to the still, small voice sounding in his ear--a voice which said all men were brothers."

The priest moved toward a man sitting nearby and clapped him on the shoulder. He reached for a small child in the miner's lap and swung the lad into his arms. "This same attorney discovered a Savior, in which the white man believed, preached the brotherhood of man. This Savior, Jesus Christ, counseled forgiveness and implored his followers to put away hatred for others different from themselves. This Jesus counseled men to love their neighbors as much as they loved themselves."

The Jesuit trained miner handed the toddler back to its father, then stood on a chair so people crowded in the hallway and those, who pressed anxious faces against the window, could hear his impassioned plea. "The man, Mahatma Gandhi, studied words of the Prophet Mohammed too, for there was difficulty between the Hindu and Muslim in his native land. Mohammed said all men were one in Allah's sight. Gandhi reasoned if men truly believed the words of their prophets, they would not oppress their neighbor. Here, in South Africa, Gandhi forged the ideals of passive resistance, which eventually brought the government of England to its knees and forced the British out of India."

Sorenson's eyes searched upturned faces. He had to make them understand; it was his mission to unite these simple people; to weld their minds and spirits into the weapons which would bring injustice to an end. His fingers wrapped around rosary beads in the pocket of a cheap pair of cotton trousers as he uttered a silent prayer for guidance.

"Another man, a black man, reminded Americans every person had the right to be free. He marched, he sang, he stood with firm resolve against injustice. In the end, Americans changed the fabric of their social culture-- and black men were begrudgingly given rights white men took for granted."

A sigh lifted his shoulders and his hand thrust deeper into his pockets as he searched for the words to strike the chord of determination in their hearts. "I say to you--to every man, woman and child in South Africa, we can break the yoke of white supremacy through peaceful resistance. Let us join hands in the mines, let us sit in the tunnels and refuse to work! The foremen may kick us, they might beat us, but they cannot make us work! It is the strong back of the black man which creates profit for the white mine owners! Brothers, we will wage a war of attrition. We will raise no hand against them--we will not lash out, nor retaliate with violence. Our refusal to work will break the chains which have bound us to ignorance, poverty, and fear. The world will heed our cries! Others will hear our call for freedom. Each of you will be responsible for setting South Africa in a new direction!"

Several trucks lumbered out of the jungle and ground to a halt in the newly cleared market square. Father Bagaces leaped from the cab and ran to greet the other Jesuit. Embracing warmly, they clapped each other on the back; brothers united after months of separation.

"I counted the days until you got here." Walton Mendez beamed at his long-time friend.

"You were advised of our progress?"

"Nightly. Your coordinates were relayed during my regular transmission. The only thing I didn't know was the hour of your arrival."

Jorge Bagaces brushed the dirt from his cassock. "We made decent time through the jungle. Roads were in better condition than I expected."

A broad smile lighted Father Mendez's features. "Come, tell your men to relax by the well. I will have food and water brought to them. You and I, brother, have much to discuss."

The kerosene lamps flickered against dwindling light and the rectory was bathed in a warm, golden glow. Fathers Jorge Bagaces and Walton Mendez checked their watches, then punched in a sequential series of numbers to link their coordinate locators to the orbiting satellite due to clear the horizon in twenty minutes. They replenished the wine in crude, earthen cups and stepped out onto the porch, prepared to aim at the communications satellite as it passed overhead.

"A modern-day miracle, right my brother?" Mendez stared at the black square of plastic no bigger than a pack of cigarettes.

"Indeed." Father Bagaces took a sip from the cup. It was delightful to allow a bittersweet taste to linger on his tongue. He relished the relaxation accompanying wine after exhaustion filled days spent in a hot, steamy jungle. "The Father General is never out of touch with his men in the field. Ruger has been training Africans in an isolated area of Angola for months. Ryan Evans made deep inroads into China, and if things are going according to plan, Father Sorenson will have penetrated the mines of South Africa by now."

A blip of light appeared on the horizon and both men glanced down at their watches. Following the sweep of the second hand, Mendez counted down the numbers. In unison, the Jesuits aimed their devices at speck of light and depressed zero on the number pad three times in rapid succession. No sound announced the presence of a message, no beam of light traced a path across the atmosphere, but both priests were certain Andrew Simson knew they had made contact--that they were together in Cintalapa.

Communication established, each man slipped his location device into the pocket of his cassock. As if rehearsed, the men returned to the rectory and sat at a table whose bright and shiny planks were evidence of recent repairs. They talked well into the night; it felt good to share their innermost feelings, their triumphs, and tragedies, with someone who understood the purpose of their hardship; the complexities of a mission which elevated them above common men. Mendez talked at length about the earthquake--what a terrible experience it was to deal with the brutal force of nature. Bagaces discussed his exasperation with the bipolar mood swings of Jeraldo Concertas.

The Jesuits laid plans to transport food and clothing to cities whose inhabitants lacked the bare necessities of life. They spoke of what an impact the

Church would have upon simple villagers whose needs were going to be provided by a column of trucks which would soon begin moving south. Like the pillar of clouds which led the Children of Israel across Sinai toward the Promised Land, the people of Central America would depend on the Church to supply their daily manna.

"And weapons?" Bagaces studied his friend over the rim of his cup. "Sealed in plastic--hidden in barrels of flour and sacks of beans and rice."

"We have everything we need to wrest power away from the robber barons who ignore the welfare of the poor, the cries of the starving, the plight of orphans who roam our streets!"

"Everything! M-16's, thousands of rounds of ammunition, LAW rockets, grenades, Claymores."

"Every night I pray for the continued success of the Father General. He is the only real hope the oppressed have."

"Through God, he will unite the world."

They tipped their cups and clasped hands. The new apostles were about to assume the missions for which they had been so carefully prepared.

Stephanov Ivanovo Rubtsovsky held the priest's crucifix in his hand. He turned on the tape recorder and leaned back in the comfortable chair. After years of practice, it was a reflex action to slip into an altered state. Rubtsovsky sensed his fingers growing tingly and his legs no longer felt as if they were part of his body. Training anchored his brain wave at the perfect level of awareness the place he retrieved information from another dimension.

Rubtsovsky took another deep breath, centering his attention on the object in his hand. Images began to take form. He knew the information plucked from this mysterious realm was seldom wrong.

"This man is a soldier. He wages battle with other men. He is a professional--his weapons are mind control, behavior modification, personality imprinting! He assassinates the thoughts of the individual as surely as if he severed the ability to think with a gun or knife. He controls others by subverting their emotions. This man, and forty-three others like him, plan to take command of entire nations. His fellow soldiers are in China, South Africa, America, Ireland, Central America, Mexico . . . and Russia. Their operation hides behind the shield of religion. The leader, a man who wears the robe of a priest, holds the fate of entire continents in his hands. He is blinded by his vision of the future!"

Vassily Kharkov stared at the tape recorder, its wheels still rotating as Rubtsovsky laid the crucifix aside and rubbed his eyes with his knuckles. The scientist twisted his head in a wide arc and flexed his fingers back and forth, as if trying to be rid of an unpleasant sensation.

"What are we going to do?" Vassily's voice was as frantic as it was pleading.

"Let me listen to the tape." Rubtsovsky stabbed the rewind button.

The tape droned out its message and Rubtsovsky toyed with a lock of hair above his ear. His eyes strayed to the floor and lost their focus, as if he were not really hearing his own words.

"Well?" Vassily's expression was a portrait of anxiousness.

"When weeds invade a garden, they must be plucked out. Russia must be rid of this priest."

Vassily rose so suddenly his chair clattered to the floor, the sound bounced off the walls. "What am I to do?"

Rubbing his fingers through the sparse dark hair, the scientist considered the question with the thoughtfulness of a seer. "You are the soldier, I am a man of science! I am not the person to advise you, but I will impart an important secret of the mind. Armed with this knowledge, a way can be found to stop this priest."

Vassily righted the chair and tried to still his raging thoughts, to quiet a body trembling with frustration.

Rubtsovsky tapped the side of his head. "The subconscious mind is a powerful reservoir. Ponder the question you would have answered. The mind will respond--in a day, in a week--but the answer will come. When it does, trust yourself, young Vassily, trust yourself."

"Why do you think Andrew insists on us being present at these dreadful crypt openings? I hate it underground." Anna fidgeted with the strap of her purse, as she surveyed the tunnel stretching into the gloom ahead.

"I think he does it to torment you." The lines around Klaus' eyes softened as he watched Anna's posture stiffen when a rat scurried from its hiding place.

"Frankly, that would not surprise me in the least! He probably stays up nights thinking of ways to torture us--like a Grand Inquisitor! Father Rava, why do you have to suffer these abominable openings?" Anna shuddered as she spoke to the East Indian priest.

"I cannot say I like it here, but the Father General requested I join you. He seems to think this tomb might contain artifacts predating the life of our Savior by many years. We've unearthed documents which indicate there was more interaction between the people of Europe, India and China than we realized."

Anna coughed, and the sound carried down the corridor to the man hidden behind the housing, which controlled the elevator mechanism. A gloved thumb depressed the switch on a hand-held electric tool equipped with a wafer-thin cutting disk. The high-speed rotary head whirred, and the diamond chips embedded on a carborundum disc refracted the weak light cast by the safety lamp on top of the hoist motor.

Other voices drew closer.

"Simson seems to thrive on conflict! Amariah, what do you think?" Leon's tone of voice was good-natured; being in the catacombs felt natural to him. The dank tunnel did not offend his sense of smell and he liked the sensation of being sheltered by Mother Earth.

"My sentiments are with those of Anna and Rava. My flesh creeps the moment I step inside one of the burial chambers. I feel as if the early Christians are calling out from the grave as though they cannot find lasting peace." Amariah quickened her step, they couldn't finish the job soon enough to suit her.

The cutting wheel lowered toward the hydraulic line which carried fluid to the braking system of the elevator. Taking care to penetrate between the diamond shaped network of steel webbing wrapping the rubber hose, a neat slice appeared. Fluid began to weep from the line, it oozed out over the rubber and slid in single droplets along the hose to disappear down the ten-story elevator shaft.

When they reached the elevator landing, Klaus pushed the button that ordered the wire mesh cage to the uppermost level of the catacombs. As they waited, Klaus addressed Anna, "I'm sure a lot of people would feel the way you do about the catacombs." The elevator lumbered to a stop, Klaus unlatched the protective screen and let the others step inside. He noticed the lights on the indicator panel were all illuminated; someone had punched every button. The memory system in the elevator's electronic brain would mandate a stop at each of the ten levels excavated beneath the Vatican. It struck him as odd, but his anxiousness to rush Anna and Amariah back to the surface overpowered the instinctual alarm of warning.

Behind the hoist motor, selector, and crosshead, designed to raise the elevator cage and lower the counterweight, the man with the cutting tool pressed into deep pools of shadow, his concentration focused on the swelling bubble of hydraulic fluid as the wire mesh cage rose to its next stop.

On the next landing, the electronic seal securing the gate released; a metallic clack filled the vertical corridor hollowed into the limestone when the gate slid back--as if moved by an unseen hand. Father Rava's questioning glance darted toward Leon. "Why do you think the elevator is stopping at every level?"

The gate closed on its own and the cage continued its ascent up the solid stone shaft. It seemed as though it was taking longer than usual to go between levels, but the look of distress on Anna's face crowded out Klaus' second alarm warning.

Above, the whine of the hoist motor changed pitch. The sound was low, imperceptible to someone not trained to recognize the onset of mechanical distress, but the man above the shaft smiled when it reached his ears. Each time the braking mechanism was forced to stop the cage, the amount of hydraulic fluid surging through the open gash increased, like the murky water of a reservoir escaping through a crack in a dam.

The elevator stopped and started again, only this time the wooden floorboards shook. When the screen opened again the landing was three feet above their heads. The controls designed to keep the elevator level with the floor of the landing were not in sync. With jolt, the elevator slid down the shaft a little too fast; when the gate drew back, the landing was below them. Klaus felt a drop of moisture splatter against his bare arm. It felt like rain--as he reached to wipe it away a film smeared his skin. He stared at the trail, a rainbow of color reflecting in the elevator light. "Holy Mother of Christ!" The dawn of awakening smashed through Klaus' brain. "Leon, grab Amariah, hold her fast to the cage. This thing is going to drop any second! Rava, hang on to anything you can!"

The instinct to survive, developed in humans when primal ancestors wielded clubs against saber tooth tigers and wooly mammoths, surged through Leon. Throwing himself at Amariah, he forced her against the elevator's wire mesh wall. His fingers dug into diamond shaped metal strands.

Searching for a handhold.

Seeking shelter.

Desperate to survive.

A sickening sensation of nothingness and the upward lurch of his stomach overrode all other feelings as the elevator lost its brakes and careened down the shaft in a free fall through space. Leon clung to the grill with all his strength; stiffening against the impact he knew was coming.

Klaus pulled Anna into his arms. Gripping the handrail at the side of the elevator, he braced against the inevitable. Helpless, he watched with horror as Rava was slammed against the ceiling, distorting his serenity filled features into a grotesque mask.

When the cage crashed against the bottom of the shaft everyone was hurled against the floor. The fall of the elevator pulled the counterweight up the shaft, a missile headed toward the hoist motor. Like a well-aimed rocket, massive steel plates hit the motor and housing, which held the selector and crosshead in place. With one blow, the hoist motor was lifted off its mooring bolts.

A whoosh announced the motor's fall. Klaus sounded the wail of alarm as he fought to make himself heard above the crash of the motor as it hurled against one side of the shaft, then veered into the opposing wall of stone. "Get up against the cage! Move as far away from the center as you can!"

The shriek of steel cables as they whipped over the pulley, pulled by the falling motor, screamed through the shaft. The sound of steel girders buckling under the impact of four hundred pounds of steel added to the cacophony of terror. Although wide and thick, the wood floor planks were no match for the metal frame which collapsed like twigs when the hoist motor hit the cage. On impact, the floor exploded--shooting fragments in all directions like shrapnel from a mortar.

Dust and dirt rained down on the huddled bodies. Small rocks fell through the mesh, larger chunks of limestone crashed against the cage, gouged from the wall by the force of the plunging motor. Finally, silence as heavy as a funeral drape, lowered over the elevator.

Klaus rolled on his back, his eyes turning toward the black steel housing streaked with ugly slashes of red. Lifting his head, Klaus came within inches of Rava's shattered face. Knocked unconscious when the centrifugal force of the plummeting elevator rammed him into the ceiling, Mendicant Rava Prabhupada never heard the hoist motor racing down the shaft. He was unaware of the impact that sent shards of his rib cage spewing like molten magma erupting from a volcano. He didn't know his heart and lungs had been mangled beneath the motor's weight. Sightless eyes dribbled from their sockets, suspended against his cheeks by a still shivering optical cord. The muscle of his tongue protruded through his teeth and hung lifeless against his chin--never to give shape to words of compassion, succor, or joy again. The blood once coursing through the veins of a living, breathing being hung suspended from the wire cage--crimson droplets of death. An obscene path snaked across the floorboards, a river of red, about to engulf the occupants of the elevator.

In shock, Amariah slowly realized her body was pinioned against the cage. Aware she'd survived the fall, an impulse stronger than the current of emotion numbing her brain made Amariah turn her head when a warm, sticky fluid seeped beneath her cheek. The grisly sight, which met her eyes sucked a strangled, garbled sound from her throat. The white of her wimple turned to scarlet as the cloth absorbed the oncoming tide of Rava's blood.

Amariah's thoughts became a maelstrom, eddying and circling between horror and doubt. Certainty bludgeoned her emotions: The elevator had been tampered with--someone had premeditated--plotted--planned--the death of five innocent people.

"Get Anna and Amariah out of here." Shielding her from the ghastly sight with his body, Klaus helped Anna to her feet, checking for signs of injury. As an act of homage, Klaus drew the hood of Rava's habit over his battered face. The specter of death, frozen forever in broken features, was loathsome.

Averting his gaze from the spectacle of human flesh, mashed beyond recognition, Leon lifted Amariah off the floor. Moving as if the nerve endings that commanded her body were traveling through a muddy swamp, she lifted her hand to her cheek to wipe away the blood of human sacrifice.

Anna was crying, she adored the East Indian priest. The accident shredded already frayed emotions beyond repair.

Leon guided Amariah to a wide spot in the landing. Her footsteps were automatic; she followed his direction without question. Her body complied with normal functions despite the thoughts that raged and surged with the fury of a firestorm. Had it not been for Leon's quick reaction to Klaus' warning she would have suffered Rava's fate. Violent trembling consumed her body as the impact of what happened imploded through a disbelieving brain.

Leon held her at arm's length, his eyes searching for injury. A face the color of chalk stared back at him, cheeks stained with blood were hollow, normally cobalt blue eyes turned a color he could only compare to a river polluted with industrial waste. "Amariah, you're in shock--you might be bleeding internally."

Murder. The word surged across synaptic nerve endings and exploded from one neuron pathway to another. *Murderer!* The implication pummeled her emotions with the force of blows from a blacksmith's hammer. The condition of Rava Prabhupada's body took possession of her thoughts. Simson was not a benevolent shepherd. He was ruthless! Truth speared her body and cauterized the bleeding wounds of her soul.

From the darkness, workmen rushed toward the landing. The foreman's face became a grimace as he caught sight of the mangled body. An urge to vomit brought bitter bile up the back of his throat and he struggled against waves of nausea. The smell of blood permeated the landing; the warm, moist, nearly sweet scent of a life that was no more.

Hardened eyes stared across Anna's lowered head as Klaus murmured to Leon. "We'd better hasten our departure."

Leon was amazed by the composure the German displayed. They narrowly escaped death, a close friend had been crushed beneath a motor, yet Klaus had the presence of mind to consider the future! But the frustration taking command of the restoration expert's expression betrayed him. It wasn't fear or shock that raged in waves over his Teutonic features, his eyes revealed a man in spiritual distress--a man in the throes of heart-wrenching agony.

Amariah's eyes were glassy; unseeing. She was face-to-face with naked truth. Life threw her a disastrous surprise; the past was destroyed as surely as if a baseball bat was hurled through the window of her faith.

The fires of Gehenna destroyed doubt and uncertainty. Anger took control as fury percolated up from the deepest layers of her innermost self, transforming her personality in one, swift, all-encompassing blow.

CHAPTER FIFTEEN

Andrew Simson cradled the phone against his shoulder and reached for the note pad on the desk. "I see, Doctor. Thank you for explaining the situation. Get the best pacemaker available. Be assured," his eyes traveled to the window overlooking the garden, now dappled with the last sunlight as the day bled away, "money is no object where Father Murphy's wellbeing is concerned."

As the infirmary doctor droned on about the worsening condition of the priest, the Father General opened the drawer in the center of his desk. His hand rested on the velvet box protecting his prize possession. He drew comfort and a sense of completion from the coin. Currents of energy surged through his body when he caressed it. Lying beside the velvet box was the GPS device. He studied the numeric pad but didn't enter the code, which would connect him to the communication satellite. His fingers lingered on the coin, a feeling of power like a hit of cocaine flooded his body when he rubbed the surface.

"Yes, I see. You estimate two weeks before the pacemaker can be shipped from Bern? Will Father Murphy be all right until then? Good! Order it immediately. Father Murphy has contributed a great deal to this project. I want him to have the best medical care technology has to offer."

Reaching for the crucifix at the center of his chest, the Father General began dragging his thumbnail down the surface. "Doctor, let me repeat, I do not care about cost! The value of human life cannot be reduced to money. Take every precaution you can with this man's health. He deserves the best--he has rendered faithful service to God. Get the new pacemaker to Rome by the fastest means possible!"

Simson replaced the phone in its cradle. He pondered the news for a moment, then reached for the receiver again. He dialed a number and waited for a response.

"This is the Convent of the Strict Observance how may we be of service?"

"Andrew Simson calling. I am checking on the condition of Brother

Julian."

"Ah, Father, Brother Julian was hoping you'd call."

"Oh?" Simson couldn't keep the surprise from his voice. The Cistercian monks practiced a strict vow of silence, it was impossible for Father Julian to express such a desire to the lay monks responsible for tending to the physical welfare of the brothers in the Order.

"Yes," the monk sounded confident, "I have gotten to know Brother Julian's habits. When he needs a word of encouragement from his personal redeemer, he comes to the refectory and places his hands on the phone--as if sending a silent message, he needs your prayers and words of compassion."

"Brother Julian is always in my prayers."

"You are a man of mercy, Father, may God always bless your endeavors."

"When a priest has no time for his brothers, he is not obeying our Lord and Savior. Brother Julian is a lost sheep in this world. His emotional pain is deep, but his immortal soul is worthy of salvation."

"Father, truly, you are one of God's chosen."

"Thank you, Brother. You, too, are on a mission from God. Could you let Brother Julian know I am on the line?"

"Certainly, Father. I'll be right back."

Andrew Simson heard the soft shuffling of sandaled feet against tile as the old monk hurried out of the refectory. The Cistercian monastery was the perfect place to heal a man whose mind was so battered it no longer recognized what was real--and what was imagined. The men who waged shadow wars were foolish not to bring his suffering to an end instead of paving a new avenue of agony in a brain already turned savage. Andrew reminded himself God's ways were mysterious. Father Julian was a child of a just and loving God, and his talents were undeniable.

Footsteps echoed, and the Father General waited for the sound of the receiver being lifted off the desk. Cistercian monks took vows stricter than most; vows that were proving providential. The scar tissue in Father Julian's face and the nearly ruined larynx made it difficult for him to create coherent sound. His face and throat were melted by fire--a fire meant to destroy him--a fire transmuting his iniquity provided the crucible of his salvation.

"Brother."

No words came from the other end of the line.

"God is pleased with you. I pray for you daily, peace be unto the troubled portion of your heart. Your acts atone for the sins of the past. God will accept your penitence."

Silence.

"God has need of you again."

Nothing.

"Meet me in the garden, I will provide you with the instrument of God's will. In one week, at midnight."

Father Gregory Lean put the keys in the ignition of the new Audi. The drive to Monte Cassino would be a welcome diversion after the stress-filled activities of the past few weeks. He was delighted the Father General provided him with a powerful automobile for the vehicle would have to climb through the mountains, up steep grades.

The Franciscan monk tried to put the disturbing events of the past few weeks behind him. Although he felt somewhat guilty, he chose not to discuss this trip with Father Murphy. His friend was enduring a crisis of faith of enormous proportions; it would be an act of cruelty to add to his burden.

Glancing in the rearview mirror, he backed out of the parking lot in front of the L'Observatore Romana, the official newspaper of the Vatican. The Father General was very gracious about his request to spend a few days of research in the library at the Benedictine Monastery of Monte Cassino. Simson made all the arrangements with the Abbot and provided a rental car with an automatic transmission--no need to shift gears as he navigated the mountains on the way to the monastery. The Jesuit Father General provided for all his needs, down to the basket of food on the front seat beside him. Edging the car through the Porta Sant'Anna, Father Lean nosed the Audi into Rome's heavy traffic.

After the emotional turmoil of the elevator accident and Father Prabhupada's funeral, Klaus insisted upon a day of relaxation and sightseeing. They walked from the Vatican to the Castel Sant'Angelo beneath the covered passageway called the *passetto*. Originally built as a mausoleum to provide the Emperor Hadrian with a lasting place of rest, the fortress-like structure turned into a bastion of defense--sequestering popes from the political factions terrorizing Italy after the Roman Empire collapsed. They walked up the spiral ramp to the viewing platform overlaid with a series of additions. Halls and chambers of various kinds were added; then courtyards, storerooms, niches, staircases, and passages, all going in different directions; architectural improvements deemed necessary by each succeeding pope--depending on whether their intention was display or defense. Every direction in which Amariah turned her camera lens provided a magnificent view of Rome as she snapped the shutter, capturing a permanent memory of the city in which she had been laboring for the last two years.

They admired the architecture of the Palazzo de Guistizia, then crossed the Tiber River over the Umberto Bridge. Twisting through narrow streets, they wound their way to the Pantheon, the largest and best-preserved monument of Roman antiquity. A temple was constructed to honor the planetary gods, the enormous dome represented the firmament, with an opening in the center of the ceiling for the sun to penetrate--casting its beneficent rays on the worshippers inside. The Pantheon, a Greek word meaning *most holy*, withstood both the ravages of war and the effects of restoration.

All four friends stepped into bright sunshine and headed toward the monument built to honor Victor Emmanuel II, the first king of a united Italy. White marble columns were topped by a gilded coping on the passageway connecting the twin towers at either end of the monument. Bronze statues rose dramatically, silhouetted against the deep cerulean of the Mediterranean sky. At the front of the building, the King forever rode a bronze horse toward glory. Stairs leading to the main hall were wide and flanked by walls adorned with statues. Gleaming marble and gold trim reflected the sunlight, blinding onlookers. Grand and imposing, the monument served as a silent reminder of what Rome might have been like in the days when it ruled the known world.

They wandered through the gardens and Amariah took pictures of everyone in front of columns which had remained erect for nearly two thousand years astride stone paths laid before Jesus walked the earth; beside the stadium near the Palace of the Flavians, one of the empire's most glorious rulers. They made their way through the traffic to the Coliseum.

A sensation of familiarity swept over Amariah as she walked beneath the massive columns to the interior of the gigantic arena. The roar of an excited crowd thundered in her ears. The stadium she saw, on the screen of her inner mind, boasted a covering of travertine, brick and marble. She walked, as if in a trance, toward the passageway sealed from wandering tourists by iron grillwork.

Wrapping her hands around the metal bars forbidding entry into the area beneath the floor of the Coliseum, she stared down a stairwell she '*knew*' led to changing rooms, the training pits of gladiators, cages for wild beasts and storerooms. As if testing the limits of reality, Amariah looked down--expecting to see her feet clad in sandals and her legs encased in the threadbare robes of a slave. Her fingers gripped the metal grill until the bars pressed deep into her flesh. Amariah felt compelled to journey down the stairs, as if the trip would catapult her into the past and expose the knowledge that hovered at the periphery of consciousness-- beyond the threshold of memory.

"They won't let you down there, Amariah, unless you're an archaeologist whose work has been approved by the government of Italy." Klaus reached for her hand and lifted her fingers away from the gate. "I don't know about you, but I'm hungry. Let's have lunch--we've other important topics to discuss."

Amariah glanced back at the passageway. It beckoned to her. A summons. An acknowledgement of a life lived in ancient Rome. A slave girl who served a gladiator. Klaus led her out of the coliseum slowly, for he sensed she was gripped by a memory she had no way to comprehend.

Sipping a cup of cappuccino, Amariah was glad they decided to stop. As the waiter cleared away the dishes, Leon inched closer and studied Amariah's expression. She was distracted, and her eyes kept flitting in the direction of the Coliseum--almost as if she expected to see someone familiar come strolling down the street. Uncertain of how she was going to react to Klaus' plans for escape, he drew his chair closer, prepared to lend support.

Clearing his throat, Klaus glanced at Anna for a moment. There was nothing easy about bringing the topic of escape into casual conversation. He cleared his throat, then gave sound to the words he'd been rehearsing for days. His eyes searched out Leon; his friend's coiled posture announced readiness. "We wanted to wait until we collected conclusive evidence--but after the incident in the elevator I'm afraid we can't delay any longer."

Apprehension flickered across Anna's expression and emotion made her pupils dilate. "Klaus, are you overreacting?"

"Perhaps you need to tell Anna and Amariah who your source is." Leon toyed with his cup, the coffee laced with whipped cream, cinnamon and chocolate shavings was no longer inviting.

"Balsahov Petrovich." Klaus' voice turned flat and raspy.

"The man you went to see in Leningrad?" Amariah could barely be heard above the roar of the traffic, as if she were afraid to put into words the sense of dread which crept along her spine and wound around the cortex folds of her brain.

"Petrovich is one of the few remaining 'old guard' in Russia." Klaus was trying to decide if Amariah was going to be receptive to what he had to say. The look on her face was nebulous--he couldn't tell what was taking place in the thoughts she held private.

Anna could hardly believe what she was hearing. "Klaus, you're not talking about the Petrovich who won so many honors for the defense of Stalingrad, are you? I thought he'd be dead by now."

"Your historical memory is a credit to you. I am, indeed, referring to the man who engineered the defense of Stalingrad and fought the German army to a standstill. Balsahov Petrovich and I became quite good friends when I worked on the restoration project at the Summer Palace in Leningrad."

"What does all this have to do with the attempt on our lives, Klaus?" Although Amariah's voice was hushed, the words were clipped, they fell from her lips with the brittle harshness of broken glass.

Klaus hovered across the table, almost as if he hoped his body would verify the truth of his statement. Plunging ahead, heart racing, lips dry, he searched for words to convince the nun of impending danger. "Amariah, I want you to withhold judgment until I'm finished. This may sound incredible, but my Russian friend was sincere . . . what's more, I believe him." Taking the last swallow of coffee from his cup, Klaus returned it to the table with a clatter, surprised to find his hand was trembling. "Petrovich told me he's been worried about the activities of a Jesuit priest in Russia. He taped an interview with this priest and had it examined by a scientist who's been working on classified experiments."

"Oh, God." Anna's face blanched white despite the application of warm toned makeup and the lighter flame which refused to connect with the end of her cigarette. Disgusted at the lack of control the sudden rush of adrenaline robbed from her body, she threw the lighter on the table as she uttered words of disbelief. "Don't tell me you've gotten involved with mind control experiments!"

Klaus shielded his eyes from the harshness of the afternoon sun as he turned to stare at Anna. "As a matter of fact, mind control has a great deal to do with what we've discovered. How do you know about it?"

"Klaus, the entire academic community in Europe has been speculating about the Russian's 'psychic' discoveries for years! There are frightening rumors about a doctor by the name of Rubokov, or something like that, who has developed an accurate method of reading another person's mind. A friend of mine attended a seminar in Bonn where this man was lecturing. The doctor put on an unbelievable demonstration."

"Anna, his name is Stephanov Rubtsovsky, and your friend's assessment was accurate--according to Petrovich. Rubtsovsky claims Simson has a cadre of forty-four men positioned in sensitive areas around the world. He's certain the Father General plans to topple governments."

Amariah and Anna exchanged a knowing glance. When Amariah spoke her voice was soft, but its former brittleness turned to wonder. "What would you have us do, Klaus?"

"I've talked to Carole Phillips. She's agreed to take the pictures I need, then I'm going to take the first plane to Leningrad. Petrovich will meet me there and get the four of us new passports. Amariah, Anna . . . we've no time to lose. I've given a lot of thought to this and if the two of you are willing to risk it, I think we can slip past the Father General without incident."

Anna reached to untie the lace of her expensive sandals because her ankles were beginning to swell. She kept her eyes trained on the sidewalk, using the table to shield her face from the others. Mustering all the self-confidence at her disposal, Anna hoped she sounded more courageous than she felt. "Klaus, whatever you need, I'm willing to help."

Amariah nodded. Her eyes were fixed on the German restoration expert's lips. Something primordial sounded in her head; her stomach lurched, her solar plexus knotted--the next words she heard were going to shift her personal axis as surely as if the earth's crust moved.

"After Carole photographs Anna in your veil and habit, Petrovich will alter your passports. Amariah, you'll get your picture taken in Anna's clothing, then, dear lady," he took Anna's hand between his, "you and I will act as decoys to lead Simson away from Leon and Amariah."

Anna's neck arched, and her eyes flashed in the direction of the street. None of the pedestrians seemed to notice the rumbling sensation that shook the earth beneath her chair. They continued to stroll by the restaurant, in casual pursuit of their everyday activities. Anna knew she was going to participate in an event, which would shape the direction of the history for years to come. Her back straightened, her eyes narrowed and the hand reaching for the cigarette lighter was surprisingly calm. "I'm in."

"You want me to travel as Anna Romanov? And Anna will be me?" Disbelief scored deep lines in Amariah's features; how could she be separated from the religious clothing she cherished--had worn every day of her life for the past seven years?

"Sister," Anna tried to sound confident but doubt chased reason across her face in a series of waves, "can you imagine anything more unlikely?"

"I am to give up being a nun?" Amariah's mind refused to accept the implication of what it would mean to her faith to participate in Klaus' plan.

Leon watched the conflicting emotions raging in Amariah's eyes. His tone of voice turned urgent, his body thrust forward as he tried to convince her it was the right thing to do. "It's the only way we could think of to get you safely out of Rome. You can't board an airplane wearing your habit and expect to fly off. Simson won't allow it."

"Why didn't you discuss this with me before?"

"Because we were all afraid of your reaction. For God's sake, Amariah, you believed in the Church so passionately, you defended the institution with each breath you took! You considered the vows of your Order a sacred trust. We were afraid your belief blinded you to what's happening." Leon's hand reached to cover the fingers toying with the rosary beads she'd taken from her pocket.

"I believed in the Church with all my heart. I tried hard to incorporate Christian principles into my everyday life. I prayed for enlightenment, I asked daily to be an instrument of God." A single tear slid down her cheek as she stared at the onyx beads in her hand. "But the foundation of my faith seems to have been destroyed by a fall down an elevator shaft."

Her fingers slid across the beads . . . one by one. How often had the Rosary provided her with comfort? How many times had she found sustenance in the prayers offered to saints and martyrs? The rosary beads were her talisman against injustice, against iniquity, against the dark side of human nature. Quietly, without fanfare or anger, Amariah dropped the string of beads into her lap. The simple crucifix--the mainstay of her faith--fell between the folds of her habit.

"Colonel Petrovich will take care of passports, travel documents and tickets for both you and Leon." Klaus tried hard not to be overwhelmed by the emotions hammering Amariah. The girl's heart poured molten doubt from the crucible of ruined faith. "Petrovich has survived political purges in his country because he is a resourceful man, not because he happens to be lucky. He devised an escape route no one would ever dream you'd take."

Movement out of the corner of his eye caught Leon's attention and he watched in amazement as Amariah dropped her rosary beads into the street. She nodded as Klaus spoke and stared at the beads with indifference when they were crushed beneath the wheels of a passing car.

"Amariah," Klaus' voice offered strength, purpose, conviction, "you and Leon are going to cross Siberia . . . by train."

Andrew Simson waited quietly, his robe devoured by the shadows of the garden. One could not predict the comings and goings of Father Julian. He was like a jaguar that stalked by night; watchful, waiting, more dangerous than any other predator in the jungle.

He was certain Father Julian was out there, slinking along the perimeter of their meeting place. Old habits die hard; espionage was in the man's blood, it dominated the process by which his mind sorted and sifted information. Assassins, betrayers, men who lacked honor, lurked in the crevices of memory encoded into Father Julian's brain.

It required skill to keep the Cistercian monk in check. Although Simson knew the other man revered him; saw him as his Savior; the deliverer from years in a mental institution; the battle for Father Julian's sanity was fought in the trenches of daily existence. Each dawn brought another opportunity for the demons of a ravaged mind; the innate sense guiding other human beings away from the wanton obliteration of their own species was lacking in Father Julian.

He provided Father Julian with a lifeline to salvation, the method of atoning for his sins of the past. He taught a broken mind to pray, gave a savage heart something to believe in, convinced a man who was the scourge of several governments to become a soldier for God. Father Julian had knowledge of lethal technology bordering on genius. The super-powers left him to rot in a drug induced state in the psychiatric ward of one of Europe's prisons. Andrew Simson considered it a sign from God he'd been able to extract the former assassin.

The Father General searched the shadows. There would be almost no moon tonight, no random beam to betray Father Julian's presence. The Jesuit started when the tap on his shoulder came, but he didn't turn. A gloved hand rested on Simson's shoulder for just a moment, an act of homage, a gesture of fealty, before it was withdrawn.

The voice came from behind Simson. Croaked words, the larynx nearly ruined by a fire meant to consign his soul, his talents, his very being, to the furnaces of hell.

"All went as planned with the banker."

"Did you intercept the packet?"

An envelope slid across the Father General's shoulder.

"Brother," Simson heaved a sigh of relief. He only hoped it would be possible to stop such damning information from reaching John Preston's intelligence network, "you've done well. God will find favor in you."

His words were so garbled they were hardly recognizable as human speech. "I live to serve my Savior."

Simson placed the envelope on the bench beside him with caution, his movements slow and deliberate; he'd learned quick gestures brought a deadly response from Father Julian. He reached inside the pocket of his cassock for a thick bundle of lira. "Do you need more?"

"Possibly." The words sounded like an alien struggling with English. "The Electromagnetic Pulse Generator is guarded by a computer defense network."

"I will supply you with whatever you need."

"I know."

Simson only sensed Father Julian disappeared from the garden, but he neither heard not saw him depart. When he was sure, he reached for the envelope. John Preston was an outstanding, even brilliant, operative--but he was no match for someone feared by presidents, dictators, and prime ministers alike. Although he gave Preston credit for the caution he used in collecting the information, the banker underestimated the power of the office of the Father General--and the spiritual terror inspired by the Catholic Church.

Cao Bang rolled over, his hand searching the satin sheets for the warmth of Lily's body. She sat in a chair across the room, observing the man she loathed. He was beginning to rouse from the opium induced torpor. Another pipe, one more sexual release, and Cao would be rendered catatonic for hours. She tamped the bowl of the pipe to pack the opium tightly then reached for a bottle of perfume.

Dousing her body with the scent Cao found erotic, Lily prepared to arouse him again. Once the task was completed, the rest of the day would be hers to do with as she pleased--and she had important plans! Like a general preparing for battle, Lily studied her opponent, gauging the depth of his stupor, giving thought as to how to lift the man from his drug created malaise.

Lily checked to see if there were enough of Cao's favorite chocolates in the box by the bed. His blood-sugar level would need to be elevated rapidly if he was to perform; a certain way to heighten his sense of manliness. How easy it was to manipulate him, how simple to bend him to her will. Cao Bang was a stupid man.

The pipe between her teeth, Lily puffed until the embers in the bowl glowed red. Determined not to end like so many of the unfortunate creatures she knew, she expelled the smoke without taking it into her lungs. Placing the pipe beside the chocolates, Lily went to the window and opened the curtains a crack. A splinter of light pierced the veil of darkness shrouding the room. Cao enjoyed watching her performance in the mirrors above the bed.

Pulling back the satin sheets, Lily dipped a cloth in the warm, scented water she'd placed beside the bed. In a slow, titillating fashion she drew the cloth up the trunk of the sleeping man's body.

Despite the opium, Cao sensed a stirring in his loins. Something was moving across his belly, making the blood surge through his veins like streams of molten lava. It stopped, and the drug-fogged man grew confused; his eyebrows drew together, then relaxed as the sensation began again, and he melted into a state of physical rapture. This time, the warm wetness lingered on each of his nipples for just a moment then traced a path up his neck. His face turned toward the warmth; it smelled heavenly.

Lily inserted her fingers in Cao's mouth. Mashing the chocolate against his teeth, she kissed him, pushing the gooey substance toward the back of his throat with her tongue. The pockmarked man swallowed, the sweetness draining into his stomach. She repeated the process several times and Cao began to stir.

Lifting his head off the pillow, he struggled to open his eyes. Lily placed the cloth in the basin of water and wrung it almost dry before she lowered it over his face. The effect was refreshing, but Cao needed a drink of water. His mouth seemed as dry as the Turpan Depression at the heart of the Gobi Desert. Sensing his need, Lily brought a glass to his lips, and he drank it, greedily.

Cao was so groggy he didn't anticipate the heavy cloud of smoke that enveloped his head as soon as the glass was put aside. Lily blew the opium beneath his nostrils and the smoke, which smelled faintly of new mown grass, hovered over the bed. Cao smiled, and Lily placed the pipe between his teeth. He drew a long, satisfying drag of smoke into his lungs. This woman knew how to please a man. Suddenly, Cao became aware of the rest of his body as Lily slid her leg across his chest in a slow, erotic motion. She started low, near his manhood, drawing her moist, heavenly cleft of flesh upward, along the length of his body. Just inches from his tongue, she stopped. In his desire for her, the frustrated man let the pipe fall against the bed. She retrieved it, then puffed a few times and inserted the stem between his lips again.

"Cao," she whispered silkily in his ear, "this makes you as stiff as a pillar of iron. Use it, then use me."

Taking several more intoxicating hits, his eyes drifted toward the mirrors on the ceiling. Although his vision was blurry, his eyes could still take delight in the beautiful trail of hair flowing down Lily's slender back. His hands reached around her, searching for the firm buttocks he found so enticing. Lily thrust her hips forward, allowing Cao's tongue a moment of glorious passion. She glanced up at the mirror to make certain he was ready.

Slowly, deliberately, Lily extracted herself from Cao's probing tongue and slid back down his body. It would be over in a few quick thrusts if she had gauged his strength correctly. As she lowered herself upon him, a low, almost inhuman moan escaped Cao's throat.

Anything for Lily.

She knew just what to do.

He felt her tiny hands brace against his pelvic bone; she lifted herself then slammed against him--again, and again, and again.

A burst of brilliant red, yellow, green, and orange light was the last thing Cao remembered as he gave in to the pleasures of his body and the numbing effects of opium. His head lolled to one side as his mind crossed to the Elysian Fields where no man, save he, was master.

Lily lifted herself off the inert body. She ran to the bathroom and stood beneath a hot, steaming shower spray. The hot water and soapy lather did little to remove the repulsion she felt for Cao; for the job assigned to her. Still, she washed and washed.

In an extreme hurry, she didn't take time to apply makeup and swept her hair into a simple knot at the nape of her neck. Slipping into a black dress, she reached for her sandals, gloves, and hat, then fled the room.

Stepping from the cab, Lily hurried up the broad flight of stairs leading to the doorway of the church. Overhead, clouds the color of cheap chrome threatened to pound the island with a drenching monsoon rain. A brisk wind churned the water in the harbor to white caps and Lily wished she'd taken time to grab a jacket.

She entered the church and genuflected beside a pew, allowing her eyes to adjust to the dim light cast by the flickering candles of the faithful. The nave was empty, as the church nearly always was at midday. Lily made her way to the confessional and drew back the curtain. She knocked at the grill and the partition slid back.

"Sister, you found favor in God's sight." The unseen priest on the other side of the teak lined box sounded proud--Lily's heart lifted.

"He grows weaker every day."

"Good."

"Father, how much longer must I continue to please him?"

"Just a few more weeks, Sister. Remember, you labor for the Glory of God and the salvation of your brothers and sisters in China. Return to him. Keep him a slave to the effects of opium. I will let you know when everything is in place. You will be released from this sordid responsibility soon."

"Father," her fingers flattened against the metal grill that obscured his features, "it is so difficult!"

"Sister, God asks the most of His chosen. Y our reward will be without limit. Have faith, Sister, have faith."

The camera closed in on the reporter's expression. He stood a short distance from the workers sitting in front of the entrance to the diamond mine. The sun seemed intent upon broiling the earth and the reporter mopped the sweat from his face as the cameraman gave him the cue to begin.

"Hundreds of men sit peacefully, arms--determined arms--linked together. The temperature today is well over one hundred degrees and the breeze offers no relief. Instead, standing here is like being in front of a blast furnace. Sand is hurled with enough force to flail skin to the bone. Conditions on this arid plain serve as a bitter testimony to the fortitude and courage of these workers. They are prepared to endure the punishment of both the elements *and* mine owners."

The reporter glanced at the sun, then gestured toward the chain link fence separating him from the striking workers.

"The world awaits the developments brought on by this group of men, and hundreds of others like them across South Africa who brought the nation's mining industry to a halt. Reports are sketchy at best, but as we understand the situation, there are men blocking the tunnels with their bodies. Hundreds refuse to leave the rolling cars that transport them into the bowels of the earth. This could be the strongest resistance ever brought to bear against an industry. Every mine in South Africa is crippled and mine owners are demanding the government send in troops to clear the tunnels . . . but as one mine owner told us," he glanced down at the note pad in his hand. '. . . We can clear the tunnels, but no one is willing to replace a striking miner. These Kaffirs seem prepared to starve to death! If we don't get back into production soon, mine owners could share the same fate. These mines are heavily mortgaged to pay for mineral exploration and the purchase of new equipment'.

The reporter looked up at the camera. "I interviewed several mine owners and asked them what the demands of the strikers are. They said, and I quote, 'these black men want equality and freedom. They want to be treated like white men, which is as ridiculous as it is preposterous'. The reporter blinked several times as a desert whirlwind eddied around his shoes. A shower of pebbles and dirt sprayed him, and he lifted his arm to shield his eyes. As he did, the notes clutched in his hand scattered before the wind. They blew toward the chain link fence; some got stuck in the metal webbing, other pieces of paper were carried aloft by the wind and floated downward toward the grasping hands of strike supporters. Some notes scudded along the dry, stone laden ground and some were speared by the branches of the thorny bushes clinging to life in the wasted land. The fluttering papers represented the miner's call for freedom.

The newscast reached many ears. Some listeners were sympathetic to the plight of the miners, and others were not. Some would take up arms to help the miners with their cause; others decided the woes of the black man in South Africa were of no concern to them. But the seeds of freedom were maturing in the fertile soil of the miner's hearts. The reporter hoped their harvest would reap equality, rather than the bitterness of lost lives.

The cameraman panned the group of silent men. Strain made the whites of their eyes a startling contrast to the dark, perspiration-laden skin. The grumble of empty stomachs could be heard above the silence hovering over the lifeless plain.

The mournful sound crossed the vast savannahs over which the elephant and giraffe roamed. It traveled over steaming jungles and rose above the roar of Victoria Falls. It lifted over the pyramids and rushed along the Great Wall of China. It left a galling trail throughout the mountain passes of the Pyrenees and Alps. It seeped beneath the doors of Parliament, the White House, and the Kremlin like the fog of Death which delivered the Children of Israel from Egypt. The world heard the cry of angry, silent men who were prepared to die for freedom!

The General stood with his hands on his hips--the fury of a man enraged by incompetence blazing in his eyes. This was not the work of a group of ordinary terrorists. This was the work of someone with the highest priority access codes--someone who knew where the Electromagnetic Pulse Generator was kept and just how to neutralize the electronic defense system protecting the fearsome weapon.

So shrouded in secrecy was this advance in weapon technology, as Base Commander he only had a sketchy idea of its true potential. Yet some son of a bitch managed to waltz through the most sophisticated defense network in the world! No indication of his presence sounded any alarm.

Maybe this would shake up those stupid bastards in Washington! Maybe they'd listen to him now! As the General stood staring at the empty hanger, his fist pounded the hilt of his side arm, a display of impotent rage. When were they going to learn? A hacker could always compromise a computer. It was nothing but a pile of bolts and electric circuits--artificial intelligence, the Army brass called it! God damn it! What did they think the word *artificial* meant? Nothing would ever replace a man trained for combat! Men were the ultimate weapons! Men, by God, men!

The General was consumed with anger, but he knew his rancor was a disguise for fear. Someone was in possession of a mobile weapon that when directed at a target caused all electrical circuitry to fail--all of it! Computers, electric light bulbs, telephones, Holy Mother of Christ, everything!

A trickle of perspiration left a black stain on the back of his uniform. There was nothing he could do to protect his base if the bastard's objective was military. He'd already placed a call requesting support troops. He'd defend the perimeter with men in tanks, with men holding rocket launchers, with foot soldiers, by God! Inside those lines he'd have men in trenches. A secondary line of defense would protect the base--and a third, and if there were time, a fourth!

God, he was waging war like the early Romans. His soldiers would stand shoulder to shoulder, weapon to weapon, shield to shield, to repel the enemy. Trench warfare! He shook his grizzled head. Those stupid sons of bitches at the Pentagon! They wanted the ultimate weapon aimed down Russia's throat. He wondered how they were going to like it when the most fearsome weapon in history was pressed against their own fucking heads!

Sister Magdalene lowered her head in her hands. She was dizzy. Despite the medication the doctor at the infirmary prescribed, her stomach refused to settle. She reached for a box of tissues beside the CRT and blew her nose again. She felt as if she was drowning in the mucous filling her head. The persistent ache behind her eyes refused to go away.

She shifted her frail bones. The effort left her exhausted but there was so much work to be done. The hands that lifted to the keyboard were so unsteady she had to rest. Sister Magdalene clasped her fingers against her chest and said a silent prayer to the Virgin Mary for her health to remain intact a little longer.

Messiah would soon be linked to every other computer in the world via satellite relays; now, it was a simple race against time. The construction crews were finished, the landscapers laid sod and planted bushes--eliminating scars left by heavy equipment and the tread of work boots.

Placing her fingers against the keyboard, Sister Magdalene closed her eyes. The doctors took blood samples to determine whether the virus, which attacked her nervous system when she was a child on the plains of Africa, had sprung to life again. They were at a loss to explain what was happening to her. The braces encasing her legs clanked against the desk. She'd lost so much weight they no longer supported frail bones and muscles wasted to mere cords of tissue covered with folds of sagging flesh.

The Father General ordered a new set of braces manufactured in the United States. He exuded the kindness and compassion of a saint and cared for his flock with the solicitude of the Good Shepherd. Father Simson insisted her blood samples be flown to the Disease Control Center in Atlanta. His goodness and mercy were never ending.

If the virus was no longer dormant, if it was attacking the rest of her body, like it had her legs, Sister Magdalene prayed her brain would be spared until she put the finishing touches on the *Messiah* program. Most of the network was in place, she only had to establish communication with a few mainframes at Langley and several other university sites.

A knock at the door heralded Sister Felicity's entrance into the lab. The Father General issued special instructions to devote her talents to the nourishment of Sister Magdalene's body. The smell of chicken broth filled the lab. Ordinarily, the aroma of fresh baked bread and the pungent smell of chicken broth created epicurean delight. Today, it caused a wave of nausea that left Sister Magdalene's face pinched and drawn.

Laying the tray on the countertop, Sister Felicity fished a bottle of pills from the pocket of her habit. Reaching for a glass, she filled it with water from the cooler. It took a while for the medication to work its healing magic, but the devoted sister soon learned her charge's stomach would settle shortly.

Sister Felicity's heart beat faster every time she thought about the summons to the Father General's office. He held her hand while he explained the seriousness of the situation. Sister Magdalene was a crucial part of God's plan to restore the Church,--and all who served it, to a place of prominence in the hearts of man. Father Simson asked her to study the nutritional requirements of a person with all the symptoms of radiation sickness. Sister Magdalene's body had no reason to manifest such identifying characteristics and the doctors were mystified by her symptoms. Sister Felicity undertook the task of nourishing the weakened nun's body with the zeal of a missionary.

The Father General explained Sister Magdalene also needed a friend. She'd been working so hard since coming to Rome, he feared she overloaded an already weakened body to the point the virus marshaled the strength to attack again.

Sister Felicity vowed to sustain the other nun's body. This was her personal mission from God, this was her part in achieving the new order of things to come, this was how she could serve the Father General.

"Sister?" A tap on the glass drew Amariah's attention away from the computer screen. Jean Paul Deveraux waved, a look of excitement radiating from his thin face. Reaching for the buzzer, Amariah broke the electronic seal. The French archaeologist rushed inside and slammed the door. The room bristled with a static kind of energy as Jean Paul hurried toward her. Amariah depressed the save button on her compute. Whatever had her special friend so excited was going to keep her from work.

"Sister, Sister, Sister!" His hands waved up and down as he pivoted on one foot, turning to the window. "I couldn't get back to Rome fast enough to share my discovery with you!"

"I'm sorry, I didn't realize you were away--I've been distracted lately."

Tossing his briefcase on the counter, the Frenchman dismissed her apology. "I didn't tell anyone I was leaving." Waving a sheaf of papers in her face, the archaeologist rushed on, anticipation making him scattered and vague. "This is going to prove I'm not mad."

"Jean Paul, I never thought you were."

"I know, dear lady, that's why I'm here. There was a look in your eyes when I spoke about Qumram--a transformation in your face when I traced the courtyard of the Essene compound that reminded me of someone longing for home."

Amariah smiled, embarrassed Jean Paul read her feelings so clearly. "There were times when you described the clothing the Essenes wore, their ritual bathing, the strict dietary code, and mysterious temple ceremonies . . . I felt so homesick I wanted to cry. You made me *see* the temple and the rose garden, their living quarters, stables, the patches of cultivated land splashing green against barren hillsides. There were moments I felt as if I was standing in the Essene compound at the heart of the Wilderness of Judah."

"Sister," the Frenchman took a moment to size up the nun before going on, "I think perhaps you did."

Only a year before, Jean Paul's comment would have invoked shock. After her experience with Adamus and the evidence in Carole's vault, Amariah only smiled. "At times, Jean Paul, I've wondered as much myself."

A chill made every hair on his body stand erect as he studied the azure eyes. "Do you remember how intrigued I was by the way vault seventeen was plastered?"

Amariah tore her eyes away from an animal hide covered in Aramaic sentences which called to her with compelling force. "You thought it was possible early Christians knew about the technique the Essenes used to seal the caves to protect their scrolls from moisture."

"Right!" He reached in his pocket and withdrew a round silver object. "A few days ago, I flew to Tel Aviv and drove down to the Dead Sea. Sister," he gestured toward the scroll in front of her, "a recent rainstorm stripped away rocks covering the opening to an unexplored cave." He handed Amariah the round, coin-like object with reverence. "Hold this and tell me what you feel."

A jolt of energy surged up her arm and ran down her body. She turned a coin over in her hand, trying to recall where she'd seen the design. It seemed familiar, but Amariah couldn't decide where she might have run across the symbols. There was something about the way the swords locked together on one side of an ancient coin that tugged at the bank of memory. Her mind sorted and sifted different possibilities, then settled on the box in which she'd found

Adamus' secret treasure. The *same* design was carved in the lid.

"Lady," he handed her another scrap of animal hide, "I am certain the message on this scroll was meant for you."

Amariah's eyes were drawn to a message penned in an ancient time, the words had cadence and order, they ebbed and surged with the rhythm of the tide.

This coin is for a woman called Amariah who has journeyed out of the past.

Fate forged her destiny, now truly, the first shall be the last.

Her calling, the world will know, because five Coins will be placed in her hands.

The second Coin a man of honor holds, he will help her journey across distant lands.

The third Coin will be brought by a man who possesses the wisdom of the ages.

The fourth Coin, guarded by a man at home, will be displayed amid archaic pages.

The Evil One defiles the fifth Coin and do battle with him she must.

Or an age of darkness will consume the world with murder, hatred, and misbegotten lust.

The light of truth must burn bright and clear—it cannot be allowed to falter!

Amariah, woman of destiny, the fate of the world you are here to alter!

Amariah's eyes lifted.

John Paul hovered over her shoulder. "You realize what this means!"

She shook her head, her tongue refused to provide a home for the words surging through her brain.

Jean Paul stabbed at the area beneath his sternum, where the ribs came together as he tried to explain emotions which made a mockery of tradition. "Sister, when I read the contents of this scroll, I knew I finally discovered evidence to support my feelings."

Meeting and holding the man's gaze with the fire of knowing, Amariah fixed the archaeologist with a hypnotic stare. "And what is that, Jean Paul?"

"Amariah, we were both Essenes living in a community at the edge of the Dead Sea during the time of Jesus. When I saw your name on the scroll, I knew my theories are based on experiences in another lifetime."

"Jean Paul, it's only a name."

"No, it's not! Look at the way you fondle the coin! You stroke the scroll as if it were a beloved child! You're holding the coin so fiercely, I feel as though you would die to protect it!" He squinted hard at Amariah, as if peering through darkness. "Your face was rounder," his hand waved through the air over her head, "and your robe was white, not black. But the blue of your eyes is the same!"

Jean Paul jammed his fingers through is hair, the agitation pounding his soul forced him to move. He reached to take Amariah's hand with the same gentleness he lavished on shards of broken pottery. "Lady, this I know. You knew our Lord, Jesus, and *you knew him well!* I do not know how this will transpire but restoring His true message rests in your hands."

"Leon? Got a minute?" Jeff Brown slipped inside the lab, his body lithe and agile.

"For you, Jeff, I've got all the time in the world." Smiling, Leon rose from his desk and shook the other man's hand in welcome.

"I thought I should tell you I'm leaving tomorrow. This is probably good-bye."

"Tomorrow? You're not going to stay until the museum opens?"

"My work here is done. I've trained Simson's people to handle all kinds of analysis. Besides, I don't like it in Rome. To be honest, I'm glad to be going home."

"I can certainly appreciate your feelings."

"I plan to spend a few days with my Mom when I get back. I haven't spent a whole lot of time with her these past few years and . . . she's getting on."

Leon was going to miss Jeff Brown, they'd become good friends. "What will you do after that?"

"I received a good offer from Cal-Poly. I think I'll drive out west and look around. If I like the area I'll stay, if not, I've got some money saved so I can afford to take my time about finding a position."

Clasping the other man's shoulder, Leon found himself growing sentimental. Like soldiers engaged in mortal combat, the team developed strong bonds with one another. They all worked hard, shared each other's discoveries, ate, slept, dreamed . . . together. To realize the closeness was ending brought out emotions Leon hadn't expected. "Let me know when you get settled. I want to keep in touch. Jeff, I count you as a friend."

Jeff Brown slid the toe of his shoe against the tile floor. "I never thought I'd get so attached to some of my fellow researchers. Would you say good-bye to Sister Amariah for me? I'm afraid she might talk me into staying for the opening of the museum and I really think it's time for me to depart."

"I know, once those blue eyes bore into your soul it's almost as if you're powerless to resist! Don't worry, I'll convey your message."

"Thanks, Leon. I knew you'd understand. Well, let's do keep in touch. I'd like to have a drink some day--when the project is behind us, when we can discuss the events which have transpired from a historical perspective!"

"You're on. Name the time and place and I'll be there."

Will Marshall bowed his head as the chaplain of the Senate prayed to the God of the Americans for the proceedings to be blessed. He could hardly believe he was here, taking part in the opening ceremonies of the governmental body that officiated for his country. When the leaders of his party asked him to assume the senate seat vacated by the untimely death of Senator Samuel Fawcett. Will was stunned. A tragic auto accident claimed the Senator's life and the party bosses *picked him* to fill the shoes of someone like Sam!

Will didn't feel confident. How could a working-class man take over the responsibilities of one of the most influential men on the Hill? Senator Fawcett spent years in Washington; he knew where all the skeletons were buried, and everyone owed him political favors.

But Will knew he had to try. He had to find a way to justify the faith of his supporters. Maybe the United States Senate was just a bigger version of his home district. After all, people were people. He'd have to learn to look beyond fancy titles and expensive suits.

The voice on the phone went to great lengths to assure him if he needed anything--information, political support, money--it would be provided. The Jesuits seemed to have a lot more confidence in his ability than he did.

Will looked up at the gallery. His wife was there, radiant in the new coat and dress he insisted she purchase. God, he was such a lucky man. He had friends everywhere, more than most men ever enjoyed over the course of a lifetime. He bowed his head again and prayed to the God he knew ruled the heavens and looked down with benevolence on a miscreant earth. He prayed for help, for divine inspiration. He asked God to help him overcome his insecurity. With his Mama and brothers to support, he'd barely gotten out of grade school. His 'higher' education consisted of fighting it out on the docks, and the assembly line. But life never beat him! He fought for the rights of his people with the cunning and bravery borne of a life in the streets. Will earned the *right* to be proud of his achievements.

A glimmer of hope slowly rose through layers of self-doubt. The Jesuits were men of God. Maybe the Force holding the universe together answered his prayers after all. The men in black had unlimited resources, they knew more about national politics than he did. They could guide him, and they praised his leadership. He could turn to them for help. Will breathed a little deeper. God's mysterious ways were not to be questioned. Suddenly, the future seemed a whole lot brighter.

CHAPTER SIXTEEN

Father Patrick Youghai rapped his hand against a packing crate; the sharp staccato burst drew the attention of everyone gathered in the center of the warehouse. With a wave, he motioned them to take a seat on one of the wooden boxes forming a circle.

A basket in his arms, the Jesuit moved from man to man. The authority blazing in his eyes commanded each of them drop their guns into the wicker container. Weapons collected, he placed the basket on the floor in the center of the circle--every man an equal distance from his Uzzi, Magnum or Sig Saeur. The priest assumed a wide stance, straddling the basket filled with instruments of death. He bowed his head in an attitude of prayer. The men lowered their faces, but no eyes closed; furtive glances darted from one enemy to another. Coiled postures were ready to spring toward their weapons should another's movement betray them.

"Dear God, enter the hearts of every man in this room. Grant mercy upon their souls for the sins of the past and extend them Your loving benevolence for their acts this day. God, we are tired of misery and weary of strife. Lift our spirits and allow us mutual understanding. Let us leave this room as brothers."

Patrick Youghai lifted his chin, meeting, then holding, the glare of nervous men accustomed to intimidating others--the priest stared back until they shifted their gaze. Slowly, he began to stalk the perimeter of the circle, directing his voice, his message, the power of his body, at every man. Candles, lit against the darkness, flickered in the gust of air created by the priest's cassock. The streak of white running through Father Youghai's carrot red hair bristled with static as he confronted members of the IRA, local political leaders, Protestant ministers, factory owners and representatives of the British Army. They had come, each fearful of the uneasy truce; each certain the man across the circle would be the first to violate the rules of accord that governed the clandestine meeting.

"Gentlemen," Father Youghai's voice reverberated from the girders overhead; it resounded against packing crates; it penetrated the heart, mind and soul of the men who listened, "the violence must end. These last weeks cast a pall across the length and breadth of Ireland, which can no longer be endured. The killing must stop! We must settle our differences. We must learn to accept each other, or Ireland will surely perish! All of you know about the frightening immigration statistics. People are fleeing our island by the thousands. If we drive them out, who will be left? For whom will we wage war then? Who will run the factories, who will till the land?" His eyes searched the faces in the circle; he went to each of them. He made a solemn pledge for their safety if they would meet with their enemies in secret. "Do you want your sons and daughters, the generations of the future, to grow up on foreign shores?"

A scuffling of feet, muffled coughs, and quick glances at other faces told Father Youghai he struck a blow using the weapon of nationalism. The priest swelled his lungs with air and drew to his full height, demanding the respect of violent men. He was a large man, a man whose heritage bespoke the strength of peasants who farmed the land. As he moved from man to man, like an avenging prophet, Patrick Youghai thundered the message of an angered God.

"We must stop this senseless slaughter! We must lay down our weapons, we must beat our swords into plowshares, we must come to a peaceful agreement on the future of Ireland . . . or," he drew out the word, ramming home the purpose of the meeting into the consciousness of soldiers, terrorists, industrialists and government officials with force and fury, "we will have no Ireland left to wage war over!" He pointed at the Mayor of Belfast. "Where will be your power then?" He shifted his righteous stare to the Provost Marshall of the British Army in Ireland. "What will be left for you to defend?" He halted before the wealthiest manufacturer in Belfast, the man with the most to lose in an economic sense. "Would you have your factories stand idle?"

The Jesuit paced the circle, his head lowered, his hands clenched behind his back--as if terrified he might lash out at the fools, who violated the commandments of the Savior, afraid he would bring the whip of righteous indignation against these men like Jesus did when he drove the money changers from the temple.

"Every man-jack amongst you is intelligent! We all have sense enough to realize nothing is going to be accomplished by a continuation of this war. We are here tonight as private men, as individuals . . . no one represents his government, his parish, his army unit. We must agree to stop this war of attrition! Your influence, your leadership, will eddy across Ireland like a stone thrown in a pond. Make up your mind to cease the rape of our land and everyone else will follow your example! Begin here . . . begin now! Walk out of this warehouse, your weapons left behind! Look in the eyes of your enemy, the man who sits beside you--realize you are looking at a fellow human being! Join your neighbor to salvage what is left of Ireland while we still have time to save our home!"

A voice called out, anger pierced the air like lightning stepping down from a somber sky. "The IRA was blamed for acts of violence that were not ours! We've lived beneath an edict of death for weeks for an act we did not commit! We demand our oppressors publicly address this wrong!"

The priest pivoted on the balls of his feet with the agility and grace of a dancer. Swinging to face the IRA leader, the Jesuit struck so swiftly his movement seemed supernatural. Youghai grabbed the man by the lapels of his leather jacket in a motion so avenging, so terrifying, no one dared come to the aid of their comrade. His nose inches from the other man's face, the priest spoke in tones so icy the rebel's bone marrow felt quick-frozen. "We *know* who destroyed the apartment buildings. We *know it was not* your organization *and you know that we know*!" The words fell from his lips one at a time, their force and power crucifying the men in the room on the cross of self-righteousness; the priest did not loosen his grip on the man, who begged his patron saint for deliverance from this new and frightening devil.

"Not only will your weapons be left behind tonight, but your bloody egos will also stay imprisoned within these four walls! There will be no public apology. None of us will make known the vow of peace forged in a warehouse turned to a Tabernacle of God by faith and contrition! You," he marched toward the Church of England minister who was observing the proceedings with disdain, "you call yourself a man of God? Will you counsel your congregation to follow your lead? Have you the courage to live as an example of the word you preach? Do you *dare* incorporate the principles of our Lord into the daily actions of your life?" The Jesuit's finger stabbed at the Anglican Bishop, the nails of truth piercing his hands, the spear of hypocrisy thrusting into his side. "Are you a man of God, are you? If I shepherd my flock into peaceful pastures, have you the courage to follow? Will you use the pulpit for the good it was intended? I challenge you, nay, I demand you embody the meaning of the Message, the Life, you say you represent!"

The cleric's breath was hard won, his skin as white as its supporting network of bones. Youghai knew he'd dealt a lethal blow to the man's conscience. "You are the kind of priest Christ repudiated! You are motivated by ego and greed!"

The Jesuit whirled back to the center of the circle, his robes flowing like a desert dervish; slamming his boot against the basket, he spilled guns across the floor. "All of you line your pockets with plunder. You drink from the cup of false pride! You believe others pay you homage, but I warn you," his blue eyes blazed with messianic zeal, "you will all perish and return to dust if you do not put Ireland and her people ahead of personal agendas! Your castles will crumble, and your lands will turn barren. Your factories will grind to a halt and your machinery will rust. Men will not follow you into senseless oblivion! You will cry into the wind, but no one will hear your voice. Unite! Unite . . . here, tonight! Unite and the world will sing your praises. Your names will be shouted from the rooftops, and all shall fall to their knees at your passing. Do not . . ." each man awaited the prophet's pronouncement, afraid to draw breath, to blink their eyes, to shift their weight; they sat in fearful silence anticipating their doom, "and no one will mourn your passing. You will be stripped of power, glory, and riches. You will be consigned to an ignoble, anonymous death. God demands you decide--this night--to which fate your immortal soul will be consigned."

A silence as thick as the moment Death claims the body stole across the warehouse. Men looked from one face to another, as if trying to measure the sincerity in the eyes of avowed enemies. Patrick Youghai stood beside the strewn weapons, his nostrils flared, eyes burning, his arms crossed over his chest, the force of his mission, his faith in God, electrified the room.

Slowly, the Anglican minister shuffled across the circle. He came to a halt in front of the IRA leader and lifted a trembling hand. A man, who spent his entire life hating and fighting the Protestant English in Ireland, stared at the extended palm. The Bishop was shaken, but his hand remained open and was offered in a gesture of friendship. The IRA leader's eyes traveled up the length of the Bishop's sleeve then lingered on his face. There was a struggle going on in the minister's expression, rather like the one he was certain rippled across his own features. Flicking a glance in the Jesuit's direction, the man, who had waged a war with the Brits since he was nine years old, realized the ever-tightening circles of hate and rage, of death and destruction, must be broken. Ireland weighed heavy on his shoulders. In a flash of self-discovery, the Irish freedom fighter recognized he was living on hate. It was a consuming passion, obliterating all else from his consciousness. He was living on hate! The phrase rang through his thoughts. Living on hate. Wasn't life supposed to bring a measure of happiness, a sense of reward? Living on hate!

He reached for, then clasped, the minister's hand. His thoughts were turned inward so deeply, the IRA commander didn't realize Father Youghai was anywhere near. He felt the pressure and warmth of the strong arm, which closed around his shoulders, but his eyes remained fastened on the Protestant minister's face. The tears in the other man's eyes were soon obscured by his own. The knot in his stomach that had been there for as long as he could remember loosened and melted.

The Anglican bishop turned to the Jesuit priest. "Brother, and I gladly call you brother, God has spoken through you this night. I hear His words! My pulpit will amplify the message in sole possession of my heart."

Men turned toward one another, then clapped shoulders and shook hands. The smiles were genuine and the eyes looking down gun sights only days before conveyed warmth, a willingness to forgive . . . and forget.

The Audi took the mountain grades with the ease borne of horsepower and engineering. The drive south to Monte Cassino provided a pleasant outing for Father Lean. The scars and aftermath of war had vanished but the stories about the Benedictine Abbot, who chose to remain at the Abbey during the WWII Allied bombing, were as vivid in his mind today as when he and his brothers gathered around the radio--listening for news of the Abbot's fate. Members of the resistance braved superior forces to get word to the Abbot about the Allied approach. The monks endured terrible hardship and risked their lives to smuggle hundreds of ancient manuscripts and priceless books out of harm's way.

Father Lean didn't understand his urgent need to make the journey to Monte Cassino. Turning on to the road threading up the hillside to the restored monastery, Father Lean felt his heart quicken. He peered through the windshield, anxious to capture a glance of the site selected by St. Benedict in 529 A.D. as the headquarters for the Order. The original Abbey was burned to the ground by the Lombards in 589 A.D. A second building, dedicated by the Benedictine brothers at the direction of St. Willibald in 717 A.D. was erected on the site of the original abbey. This sacred structure was destroyed by the Saracen hoards in 884 A.D. but like a phoenix, the abbey rose from the ashes again in 1066 A.D. rebuilt by Abbot Desiderius. It was Desiderius, who began the collection of documents that made Monte Cassino the seat of learning for centuries to come. In the fourteenth century, the abbey was wrecked by an earthquake, only to be rebuilt anew. So much history, so many events shaping the direction mankind followed for centuries transpired on these hills. His stomach clenched, and a chill caused the hair on his arms stand on end.

The cell and tomb of St. Benedict survived the pulverizing effect of five hundred tons of bombs dropped on the abbey in 1944, as the Allies sought to dislodge the Germans from their control of the road to Rome.

Father Gregory Lean stared at the rebuilt walls, emotion filled tears cast a haze over the fortress. American Catholics donated millions of dollars to help the Benedictines restore their beloved abbey after the war. Monks replanted trees and shrubs on the hillsides to disguise the disfiguring scars of human conflict. He edged the car between the massive wrought iron gates, which sheltered the abbey from stray tourists after dark.

An awaiting monk stood in the parking lot. "Father, the Abbot has cleared his afternoon for you." A kind concerned hand reached to assist the older brother from the car.

Father Lean followed behind the henna-colored robe, through the outer courtyard, up winding staircases, down long hallways. Finally, the Benedictine turned, a smile lighting his weathered face as he paused outside the office door. "Abbot Deconsini will be at his desk."

Gregory Lean stepped into a room of incomparable beauty. A stained-glass window depicting the crucifixion of the Lord splashed a stream of blood-red light across the polished floor. A shaft of afternoon light speared the cruel gash in Christ's side, sending dark red rays along the white stucco walls. The woodwork surrounding windows and doors was carved with intricate patterns. Turning away from a desk crafted by hand, the Abbot smiled. A sagacious man, his bones brittle and joints arthritic, beckoned Father Lean into the sanctuary of his inner office.

Putting aside some papers, the Abbot's voice was dry and raspy. "Andrew told me of your desire to research our humble library. We are honored a man of your stature would journey to Monte Cassino."

"Father," Friar Lean reached for the frail, withered fingers, and drew the ring gracing the Abbot's right hand, to his lips--a gesture of filial respect, "it is I who am humbled by your generosity."

Lids as heavy and lined as those of a lizard lowered over clear eyes as green as a new mown meadow. "Tell me, brother, what is it you seek from our Abbey?"

"I found a document in the Archive which alluded to other manuscripts, believed to be here in your library, which explained the conditions of our Lord and Savior's birth."

"There are many, many records amid our shelves." The lizard lids lifted to reveal eyes, turned as cold and harsh as a disciplinary hand. "Can you be more specific?"

"I understand there are a group of documents, which were not taken from the abbey when the Allies bombed the road. From what I gathered, the manuscripts were of such value the Abbot and a few priests decided to remain behind with them rather than run the risk of moving the scrolls from the monastery."

A wrinkled hand drew across dry, chapped lips. "You seem to know a great deal about the history of Monte Cassino."

"Yes, Abbot, I do. Your monastery has always been a source of inspiration to me. Just after I entered the priesthood, Britain went to war. Along with my Franciscan brothers, I huddled around the radio waiting for news. When the American forces besieged Monte Cassino, we manned the radio day and night. We prayed for the Abbot and were horrified when we learned of the abbey's destruction."

"Indeed, it was a troubled, trying time for us." The Abbot rubbed his eyes, they could no longer spend hours poring over ancient documents; his body was succumbing to the ravages of age.

The tone in the Abbot's voice, the words he used, struck a distant chord of understanding in Father Lean. "Abbot, were you one of the priests who stayed behind to guard the library?"

Eyes, the color of the primeval pools from which life sprang, flashed in the other man's direction. They were filled with surprise the friar made the connection so readily. "Yes, brother, I was."

Gregory Lean dropped to his knees in front of the Abbot and grasped his hand. "Please, Abbot, allow me to see what you guarded so zealously! I know you expected to die," his eyes darted to the window, the bleeding body of Christ a silent testimony to all that was cruel and brutal and savage in mankind. "You planned to shield the documents with your bodies, if it came to that, didn't you?"

Acknowledgement loosened the lines in the Abbot's face for one brief, decision filled moment. "How do you know this?"

"Why else would you have stayed behind? You knew the Allies were prepared to destroy Monte Cassino, it guarded the road through the middle of Italy--the way to Rome! The Allies were prepared to wrest it away from the Germans at all costs. When men stand ready to safeguard knowledge with their lives it had to be important! My faith is being consumed by doubt. I must know, Abbot. I must lay doubt to rest so I can crusade for the Church again!"

The old man leaned back in the chair and closed his eyes. He pondered the friar's plea. Father Lean's cries were an echo of every man, who ever wondered what possible purpose their existence served in a universe so vast it fostered unspeakable loneliness and a sense of desperation in humans. Finally, the Abbot lifted the heavy lids that bespoke the advance of Death. "I will grant you access to the cellar, but remember this, Friar. For centuries men have guarded the secrets of Monte Cassino. The monastery was destroyed many times, but its library always escaped intact--at the cost of many Benedictine lives. The ghosts of these valiant men will rise against you, they will haunt every hour of your day and invade your dreams should you violate our sacred trust."

The Abbot urged his resisting body out of the padded chair. Leaning against his cane, he shuffled toward the wall at the opposite side of the room. "My knees no longer permit me the luxury of going below. You will make this journey of discovery alone as, indeed, must every man on the path of enlightenment." A panel slipped back, revealing stairs chiseled into the mountainside. "Go with God, my son, and always remember your covenant with fallen Benedictines."

The stairs were steep and narrow, they twisted deep into the bowels of the mountain. The muscles in the back of Father Lean's legs burned by the time the stairs ran out. Along three sides of a room chiseled into the mountain, five chests rested on wooden biers.

Walking to the closest one, Friar Lean lifted the lid. A lone document, protected by layers of soft cloth, rested in the sheltering box. With caution, he pulled aside the shielding shroud. The manuscript was spread flat, so it could be read without body oils causing damage. Words shouted at him across a span of time, which felt the tread of Caesar's legions, recorded the Church's rise to greatness, and bore the burden of doubt as man expanded scientific knowledge. The scroll numbed the resisting, fighting, agonizing argument raging in Gregory Lean's mind.

> *"I, Elias, High Priest of the Essenes, have selected this day the man, Joseph, to be the physical vessel by which the Messiah shall come. I have waited. I have preserved the righteous way of living in our community at the Salt Sea since Solomon was King of Judea. I have waited, I have endured, I have protected, for over a thousand years. Also, this day, a young girl in whom the Inner Voice found much favor, has been selected as Joseph's bride. They are clean, free from the many foul diseases that plague our land. They have been chosen to create the body the Messiah will inhabit for his time on earth. They will be joined in union at the appropriate phase of the earth, sun and moon."*

Heart hammering, Gregory Lean rushed to the next chest. This--this information was a direct contradiction of the traditional belief surrounding Jesus' conception!

The documents were probably forgeries. Invalid. Most likely made up. Certainly, did not pre-date the birth of Jesus. Could not possibly have foretold the birth of the Savior.

He threw back the lid and pushed aside the protective layers of cloth.

"This man and woman will create the physical body for the new teacher of the ages, come to earth again. The body prepared for him will need to be strong, free of disease, for the Power he brings with him will be greatly taxing. His soul will not tarry over long, for the Body will not sustain the force of his Spirit for many years."

Gregory Lean felt as if his mind, his body, his very soul, was spinning out of control. He ran to the next chest. Caution gone, he grabbed the shielding cloth as if the hounds of hell pursued him.

"Joseph and Mary will see to his childhood development, they will make certain he grows strong and that he learns the way of the Law. They will prepare him for his teacher, the woman called Amariah. One day, when he is ready, she will take him into Egypt and further East to study with men of great wisdom and learning."

My God! What was he reading? His lungs expanded--yet he felt as if he were drawing in no air. He was being suffocated by these documents; their words drowning what he had been taught, what he had been told was true. The room was turning, he no longer knew top from bottom, right from left. Two chests remained. Had he the courage to lift their lids? Could he facethe message safeguarded by the Benedictines? Stumbling through a saffron colored mist cast by the single electric bulb in the corridor, Gregory Lean shuffled forward--his thoughts raging in his ears.

All the doctrine he had been taught?

Wrong!

Jesus was conceived like any other mortal?

He called himself the son of man, but no one heeded.

He was human, not divine?

He said so often: I am the Son of Man

A virgin birth?

Blaspheme!

Christ was a man?

A mortal--a human being!

Trembling hands lifted the next lid.

"The woman called Amariah will prepare him for his mission. She will teach him to use the Powers of a Mind that is like no other. He will go forth into the world

after many trials and tribulations. He will bring the Message of the Inner Voice to a disbelieving world. He will endeavor to enlighten mankind, to awaken them to the truth of who and what they rightly are. He will tell them of their God-hood, teach them how to use their powers, he will show them the way back to Paradise."

Gregory realized he'd spent his whole life swimming in the abyss of ignorance and confusion. He accepted without question the lies heaped upon him by an organization motivated by politics and economics. The Church sought to manipulate and control its membership through fear; through depression of the spirit; through limitation of the creative process of individual thought!

Lies! All lies!

The warp and woof of Christianity was held together by greed and a lust for power! The tapestry of Christianity contained only a few glimmering threads of Jesus' original teachings. Dare he go on? Could he lift that final cover? Was he prepared to act upon what he found? Friar Lean could not, would not, cease his quest for the truth. Once begun, it was like opening Pandora's Box; the course of action impossible to reverse.

And, again she will come, this woman called Amariah. She will restore the message of the Messiah. Through her, the Second Coming will manifest. She will awaken the hearts of men. For he will not come out of the clouds with the voice of thunder. Rather, he will steal into the heart, slip into the mind. He will come like a thief in the night and call out through the stillness when the heart is quiet and the mind at rest. Some will hear his call and others will not. Some will grasp his glorious vision, others will peer in vain, but they will see it not. Some will feel the warm embrace of truth, but others will turn away--fearing the caress that has the power to transform.

The woman called Amariah will restore His message to an awaiting, pain-stricken world."

Lurching up the stairs, Friar Lean tried to block the messages imploding through a brain turned dysfunctional by shock. How could these documents remain hidden for hundreds of years? It was impossible for the manuscripts to be referring to the slip of a girl who worked so hard on the museum project. Could not be. Impossible; stupid to think such a message was preserved intact for two thousand years. Ridiculous to think a Benedictine nun from America could be the woman in question. Yet a single cloying thought surged through resistance.

Gregory knew, in his heart of hearts, the girl was the one foretold by the High Priest of Melchizedek, Elias. His heart hammer-slammed against his ribs as adrenaline flooded his synapses. The portent was impossible, but the feeling part of his nature told him it was true.

Through a daze of shock and fear the friar lifted a befuddled gaze as he rushed through the doorway, astonished to find the Abbot waiting calmly, his chair turned to face the stairway.

The natural light hurt the friar's eyes and he shielded them against the sun streaming through the window; the red stain of Christ's wound took on a new meaning--Jesus was a flesh and blood man, who learned to take his human abilities to lofty heights. The expression on the Abbot's face burned through the fog of doubt and challenged Father Lean. The expression in the old man's eyes was one of serenity; he had attained absolute peace of mind; he had mastered the cares and concerns of life.

The Abbot knew . . . he knew!

Spitting out words clogging his throat like heavy phlegm, Father Lean searched for a rational way to explain what his tormented brain refused to accept. In anguish, he cried out. "I know this woman! I know this woman called Amariah!"

The Abbot's voice was an understanding whisper. It lingered on the stillness of the room like the last note of a haunting melody. "Brother, we know her too. Our Order protected Elias' message for centuries, awaiting her return. We lived apart from others, and with sad dismay, watched the world deteriorate. But we knew, someday, the time would be right for the lady's blessed return. We knew she would come to restore our Lord and Savior's message. We safeguarded records that will validate her destiny to a world filled with doubt, fear and suffering."

"But, Abbot, this is incredible! To think this girl will be responsible for returning the true meaning of our Savior's words is impossible! Yet--when I think about the look radiating from her eyes, when I remember how passionately she spoke about events that transpired in the days of the Savior, when I recall the zeal she inspired in me . . .." His eyes dropped to the floor, a complex array of emotions rippled across his features. "The message of the scrolls has to be true."

Father Gregory Lean sank to his knees, the sting of aging bones striking the hard, wooden floor went unnoticed. He pulled the crucifix from around his neck and flung it across the room. Searching his pocket for his rosary beads, he hurled them away . . . feeling as though the beads had turned rotten. "We've got to help her! We've got to call a news conference! We've got to announce she's the one we've been seeking to the world! Andrew Simson has nothing to do with restoring the principles of Christianity—it is Sister Amariah!" His voice rose in a crescendo of frustration. "Why are you sitting there? We must do something!"

A worn-out smile graced the wrinkled face. The Abbot laid gnarled, comforting fingers atop the friar's trembling hand. "No, Brother, we can do none of those things."

"Forgive me for saying so, but you are wrong! Perhaps you've never seen this girl. She is slight! She is fragile! She *cannot* challenge the authority of the Church by herself!"

"Brother, God does not compel. The lady must awaken to her destiny without interference. She must accept her burden with joy and thanksgiving. I'm confident she will realize who she is and what it is she has come back to do when the time is right."

Father Gregory's breath caught in his throat, the muscles of his lungs quick frozen. "And . . . if she doesn't?"

"Then I fear the world will be at the mercy of Andrew Simson. An era of darkness will descend over the hearts of mankind, which may take eons to lift."

"I cannot accept there's nothing we can do! Too much is at stake!"

The Abbot's head dipped against his chest as his mind turned inward, searching for a way to explain things to the anguished man at his feet. Finally, eyes that witnessed the invasion of Hitler's arm; hands that fought in the resistance movement against Mussolini; a body bowed to the will of God throughout the course of his life--transfixed the friar with a fervor seldom found in younger men. "Pray for her awakening, Brother, more than this . . . none of us can do."

The car seemed to drive itself out of the courtyard. Although his hands gripped the steering wheel, the friar's mind grappled with problems having nothing to do with the steep grade or winding turns.

He didn't see any of the deep blue pines speeding past the car window. Gregory Lean didn't hear the whine of the radial tires as they worked to hold the line of unbanked curves. He didn't notice the acceleration unaccounted for by the pressure of his foot against the gas pedal.

At a pre-programmed command, the computer chips controlling the disc brakes and acceleration mechanism of the Audi, sent the wrong electrical impulses. The car picked up speed. Acceleration forced Gregory Lean into the cushioned seat, its pressure alerted the stricken priest the car was going much too fast to make the turn. The brake petal refused to respond to the frantic jabs of his foot. The car launched into space as it crashed through the guardrail.

From the hill, a silent monk lowered a pair of binoculars. The hood of his robe sheltered his features from any passers-by, who might have strayed down the mountain seeking the shrines of thanksgiving tucked away in deep ravines. No one was there to notice the smile of satisfaction twisting the muscles in the burn-scarred face as Friar Lean's car burst into a ball of orange flame.

Fuchsine kept well into the shadows cast by tall buildings. The ordinary, loose-fitting trousers and shirt allowed him to blend in with the crowd of curious on-lookers. People jostled one another, vying for a closer inspection of the body sprawled on the pavement. Police shoved the crowd away from the roped off area as the number of shoppers, anxious to witness the gruesome scene, grew larger.

The powerfully built Oriental didn't mind being jostled away from the accident site. He'd seen enough. A grotesquely twisted neck turned Cao Bang's head backward; his face stared up at the building from his back. Blood streamed from distended eyeballs, which stared sightlessly at the sky.

Curtains flapped from the window which opened onto a balcony from which Cao had taken his fatal plunge. The long drop to the street reduced his body to a lumpish sack of broken bones. The form sprawled on the sidewalk looked inhuman; arms and legs once firm and strong, writhed like headless pythons, twisting, and turning—as though boneless--urged by mangled nerve endings to complete the dance of Death.

A hysterical woman burst through the entry way doors of the apartment building, rushed toward an awaiting patrol car by several sympathetic police officers. Distraught, the exquisite lady sobbed and screamed and tried to run to the body of her lover as the ambulance attendants hefted the broken, bloody remains on a gurney. Fuchsine shouldered his way forward. The crowd was pressing closer, delighted to witness the woman's mawkish grief.

Inching close enough to catch a glimpse of Lily's face, Fuchsine was pleased to see a wide track of tears smeared the careful application of makeup. The long black hair coursing down her back was tangled and matted. She was the perfect grieving lover frantic over this catastrophic twist of fate.

A piercing wail split the air as Cao's body was loaded into the ambulance. Lily struggled away from the policeman's hands and ran to the vehicle, pounding against the door as it headed into traffic--away from the accident scene. She fell to the street, her long hair uncombed, her once beautiful satin pajamas now torn and streaked with dirt and blood. Hammering her fists against the pavement, Lily appeared prostrate with grief. The policeman was tender as he lifted her to her feet and led her to an awaiting patrol car.

Swollen, tear-reddened eyes swept across the row of spectators. One brief glance caught sight of Fuchsine. Lily continued to scream, her cries heard above the distressing wail of the police car siren.

A few hours at the police station explaining how she tried to keep the drug besotted man from the balcony and this loathsome task would be over. A few more days in the gilded cage and she could return to her chosen profession. Lily could hardly wait to don the robes and veil of her Order. Soon, very soon, she would spread the word of God in her native land. A new way of thinking would sweep across China. It would surge up rivers, traveling along the mighty waters of the Yangtze, Han, Yellow and Xiang Rivers. It would infuse the rice patties of the lowlands and storm across the mountain barriers, which had protected China since the dawn of time. A distant rumble was calling out to the hearts of her people . . . the Sleeping Dragon was about to awaken.

Amariah zipped up the flame red jumpsuit. Anna was applying the finishing touches to the nun's newly exposed hair. Both women were about the same height, same weight, same coloring; anyone with only a casual description could be fooled since Anna had cut her hair.

"I feel so alien--like a stranger in a strange land." Amariah examined the sleeves and stared down at the expensive leather sandals on her feet. Emotions ranging between anger and despair, fear and frustration, doubt, and disbelief, surged and ebbed across her face like the crosscurrents of a rip tide. The fury she harbored for the institution in which she had so passionately believed burst through her emotional barriers at unguarded moments. The melancholy she felt over lost faith and innocence pulled at her insides and blanketed her mind in suffocating depression. Amariah wondered if she would ever find relief from the burden of distrust again.

"How do you think I feel?" Anna opened her arms, the folds of the habit draped downward to make her look like a hovering seraph with black wings. "How did you get accustomed to this? I'm as wrapped up as a mummy!" It felt ridiculous to be wearing a religious habit. Anna stifled a burst of nervous laughter.

Leon's voice called through the door of the darkroom, "Carole is finished with Klaus and me. Are you ladies ready?"

Feeling his breath catch halfway up his throat as Amariah stepped through the door, a strangled bubble of sound escaped Leon's lips. Amariah was exquisite. Anna had done an expert job of applying just the right touch of makeup and the cap of curls made her look like a fun-loving adventuress. Were it not for the stricken look in her eyes, Amariah's true nature might have succumbed to the cloak of disguise.

Anna loomed behind Amariah's shoulder. Layers of cloth and huge bell-shaped sleeves challenged movement. Her inability to fasten the rosary beads to the belt at her waist drew Anna's features together in frustration. She'd witnessed nuns secure the rope of beads a thousand times, yet she felt trapped, as if she were going to trip over the shroud of fabric or be strangled by the beads.

Klaus laughed at Anna's awkwardness and the utter annoyance in her face. "Anna, if we pull this off it is going to be a miracle as great as Moses parting the Red Sea."

"I don't know if I can perform this charade." Her eyes were trained on the rosary beads refusing to stay in place. "Sister, will you help me?"

Amariah smiled; it was a simple task, one she had performed a million times over the past seven years.

"I guess I should quit calling you Sister." It was disorienting to see Amariah's face without her wimple and veil.

"And I have to stop responding." Crestfallen, Amariah secured the beads and reached to straighten the folds of her once beloved veil. Her cherished habit looked so wrong, so out of place on the other woman.

Klaus searched for a way to break the silence which settled over the makeshift photography studio. "Ladies, did you bring the boxes?"

Amariah hated to part with the box in which she'd found Adamus' scrolls. It represented an invisible connection to Adamus--the voice of the past. It safeguarded the Jesuit's secrets. The box sheltered documents so shocking that when revealed, they contained enough information to destroy existing Christian concepts. Although it would be agonizing to part with the box, Amariah knew Klaus was right. It had to accompany Anna to San Francisco. Custom agents would register it as an item of antiquity leaving Italy, yet no record was ever placed in the museum document log. The discrepancy would ignite the Father General's curiosity . . . a crucial element in their escape. Like a hound following a scent, Andrew Simson would feel compelled to keep the box and the nun under constant surveillance.

Glancing at Carole, Amariah silently thanked the God in which she still believed for such a good friend. The photographer was going to smuggle the most damning of her documents out of Rome in a bag designed to protect undeveloped rolls of film. Special sacks lined with a thin lead shield, protected film canisters from the x-ray device used to scan luggage for weapons and bombs. Custom officials passed her film bags through without inspection because the Seal of the Vatican guaranteed the contents.

Anna handed Amariah the jewelry box she'd given her friend several weeks ago. A false bottom hid the coin and poem--items with which Amariah stubbornly refused to part.

Klaus took the jewelry box and released a hidden spring. "Amariah, give me your coin and the vellum. I'll make sure they don't shift around."

Handing Klaus her precious treasure, Amariah discovered she was reluctant to let the poem and coin leave her hand. "I wish I could keep them in my pocket."

"I think that would be too dangerous." Klaus fondled the tarnished silver.

The coin attracted Leon's attention. Taking it from Klaus, he turned it over in his hand, rubbing away some oxidation. "Amariah . . . where did you get this?"

"Jean Paul brought it to me. He found it in a cave above the Dead Sea."

"As incredible as this may seem, I think it's nearly a duplicate of the coin I found at a dig a little beyond what remains beyond toe ancient walls of Babylon a few years ago." Leon fished in his pocket and withdrew another coin. "Klaus, look at this."

A ripple of cold swept from her head to her feet and every hair on her body stood erect as Amariah drew close to Leon. Even an untrained eye could see the two coins bore the same markings. Mesmerized by the crossed swords lying in Leon's outstretched hand, she whispered, *"The second coin, a man of honor holds, and he will help her journey across distant lands."*

Leon grew alarmed when he noticed Amariah's face had turned as white as a salt flat beneath the sun. He reached for her elbow, steadying her, offering her strength and support. "Amariah?"

"Jean Paul found a poem he believes was written by an Essene high priest buried alongside the coin he gave me." The poem's message was burned into memory and her lips formed the words as she held Leon's astonished gaze.

This coin is for a woman called Amariah who has journeyed out of the past.

Fate forged her destiny, now truly, the first shall be the last.

Her calling, the world will know, because five Coins will be placed in her hands.

The second Coin a man of honor holds, he will help her journey across distant lands.

The third Coin will be brought by a man who possesses the wisdom of the ages.

The fourth Coin, guarded by a man at home, will be displayed amid archaic pages.

The Evil One defiles the fifth Coin and do battle with him she must.

Or an age of darkness will consume the world with murder, hatred, and misbegotten lust.

The light of truth must burn bright and clear—it cannot be allowed to falter!

Amariah, woman of destiny, the fate of the world you are here to alter!

Carole exchanged surprised glances with Anna and Klaus. Amariah searched the shocked expressions of her friends, wondering if she should have recited the poem. If these people didn't know what to make of the ancient message, how were others going to react? What did she expect them to think? She didn't know what to believe herself!

Klaus cleared his throat; the emotional impact of the moment constricted his larynx and he found it difficult to speak. "I guess that puts the entire issue at rest, doesn't it?"

Nodding, Leon turned toward Carole as a low, slow whistle extruded through her teeth. On her part, Anna studied the change in Amariah's face. The nun was struggling against the poem's meaning. On one level, it was obvious the logical side of her brain was trying to dismiss the name as one of those quirky things which sometimes happen. Amariah was searching for a way to rationalize away the implication of the message.

On another level, from a plane of understanding standing in stark contrast to logic, Anna knew she was witnessing the dawn of awakening as it shoved aside the dark threshold of her friend's consciousness. The poem was penned to the present-day Amariah--and it forced her into an uncharted way of thinking.

Klaus found himself stumbling over words rehearsed so often--against the day this situation arose. "Amariah, we've all known you were called by destiny to do something important. We've been waiting for you to realize it. It's difficult to walk up to someone you care about and blurt out . . . by the way, dear lady, did you know you're going to give up everything you now hold sacred and become the messianic leader the world has been awaiting? You've clung to your beliefs with ferocious tenacity--we simply could not decide on a way to approach you. I guess we needn't have worried, fate seems to have snatched the issue from our incompetent, mortal hands."

Smoke billowed around the American photographer's head as Carole Phillips exhaled with sudden force. "You seem to have found the second coin." Her eyes flicked to Leon, then settled on Amariah, measuring the inner strength of the slender girl. Leon and Amariah stared at each other like recently united twins. Each studied the features of the other, searching for something recognizable, a familiar link, a characteristic to explain their mystical union.

Carole shook her head, trying to be rid of the emotion staking a claim on her body. Fearfully, she voiced the thought that rocketed across her brain. "I wonder who has the fifth coin?"

Philipe Laterano didn't bother to knock before bursting into the Father General's office. His stride through the area occupied by Sister Josephina was so rapid she didn't have time to oppose his impertinence. Slamming the door behind him, the priest stopped to take a deep gulp of air.

At the window, Andrew Simson turned toward the door, awaiting the report he was certain would follow the other Jesuit's attempt to regain a calmer frame of mind.

"I've just received word Kaminski and the nun are on a plane headed for London. They passed through customs and the passport numbers in our files correspond to the ones on the passenger manifest. The woman also has an item of antiquity among her possessions. The description of the article, a small wooden box, doesn't match anything logged into the museum's data bank. So far, there's no word on the whereabouts of the Romanov woman or Von Friendberg. We're still doing a computer search on all visas issued out of Italy in the past seventy-two hours."

Simson clasped his hands behind his back and returned his gaze to the window overlooking the museum site. His jaw worked back and forth as he gnashed his teeth, the only demonstration to betray seething anger. The phone rang, Father Laterano reached for it but was waved away.

"Yes? I see. Are you quite certain?" Moody, multi-dimensional eyes studied the face of the young priest across the desk. The hand replacing the telephone in its cradle did not tremor, the grip was firm, in command. "We may need to accelerate the time frame of our plans."

"Father, you have only to give the signal and our men in the field will step up their activities."

"The consequences must be carefully considered."

The look in Andrew Simson's eyes was unreadable although Philipe was accustomed to dealing with his mercurial moods. "Father, what has happened?"

"We may need to undertake more certain measures."

"Your face betrays you. Tell me what is going on!"

"Anna and Klaus just passed through a customs checkpoint. They are in Russia!"

A Cistercian monk slipped into a worn pew. The church of Santa Maria in Aracoeli was off the beaten path and few tourists frequented it. Constructed over the site where the Sibyl prophesied to Augustus Caesar a virgin would bear a divine child, who would overthrow the temples of the pagan gods, the Emperor erected an altar with an inscription, *"Ecce ara primogeniti Dei"*. . .'Behold the altar of the firstborn of God'. Candles flickered beside the railing overlaid with a thin sheet of gold, but the light they shed did nothing to dispel inky shadows cast by tall pillars supporting the barrel vault of the ceiling.

Toward the back of the church, an old Jesuit kneeled on the riser, his head bowed in prayer. His fingers slipped up and down his rosary beads, searching for the comfort promised by unending petitions to God. His knees strained against the maladies of age which had overtaken his body. Having dedicated his life to the service of God, Father Murphy rose and ambled toward an altar covered with gold leaf. He planned to light a few more candles, then enter the confessional.

Thick cotton work gloves shielded the fingers below the coarse cloth sleeves of the Cistercian monk's robe. With one hand, he reached to light a white taper, with the other he withdrew a small black box from the fold of cloth at his waist. The voluminous habit hid the box from view and the monk slowly brought it level with his chest--as if preparing to make the sign of the cross.

Patrick Murphy was so engrossed with the effort it took to keep his mind focused on the Rosary prayers, he didn't notice the arrival of a Cistercian brother. Even if he had, Father Murphy would respect the vows of a man who worshiped God to the exclusion of all aspects of the secular world. Had he given it any thought at all, Father Murphy might have wondered why the monk was in a church at the heart of Rome, so far away from his abbey.

Depressing a button one a plastic box the monk activated numeric coordinates already entered.

Father Murphy felt his heart begin to beat erratically as a jolt of fire traced a searing path down his left arm.

Again! A gloved thumb depressed a relay switch on a wafer-thin electronic circuit board.

This time, pain came in a vice-like grip and it forced all air from his lungs. He couldn't breathe, he couldn't make his chest lift, his body refused to take in air. The pain clamped down on his ribs; his heart fluttered, it strained to keep a rhythmic pace. The air in front of Patrick Murphy's eyes turned dim as he slumped to the floor.

For good measure, the Cistercian jammed his thumb against the button again. Another ten-second burst of electronic impulse would destroy the pacemaker entirely.

The dying priest's hand clawed at his clerical collar in a desperate desire for air. The wall of pain engulfed him with the overriding power of a tropical typhoon. Patrick Murphy clutched at the area around his heart for one lingering moment, then rolled on his back--his hand limp and lifeless.

Glancing around to make certain no one entered the church from the street, the monk kneeled beside the stricken Jesuit. Stripping a glove from his hand, he rested his fingers against the old priest's neck. No blood strained against the artery wall, his heart braved no further contractions; Father Patrick Murphy was dead.

The glove replaced, the Cistercian crossed his arms and jammed his hands inside the bell-shaped sleeves of his drab brown habit. He lowered his head in an attitude of prayer, the deep hood falling over his face. He slipped into funereal shadows and silently disappeared.

Tshikapa rose from his desk and hurried to greet the priest. The smile which broke handsome Nubian features was genuine. He had grown to respect and admire the man who so faithfully honored his Jesuit robes.

"Tshikapa, I knew you would be waiting for a report, so I got here as soon as I could."

The African leader drew two straight-backed chairs beneath the fan's down draft to offer a measure of relief from interminable heat and humidity of the equator. "And?"

"Here is your agreement." The priest withdrew a stack of papers from his briefcase and placed them on the table with care. "Everything is in order. The contract has been reviewed by friends of the Church who are knowledgeable in such matters."

"I see." Tshikapa held the papers at the edge to keep them from being rippled by a current of air stirred by the fan overhead. "This is more than I dared to hope for."

"Once this announcement is made public, you will be hailed as a brilliant leader, my friend. Has a date for the press conference been established?"

"My aides set it for Wednesday next week."

"Good." Ruger Stein made no effort to hide the glow of pride in his eyes. The Father General's plans were following a carefully choreographed timetable.

"You are going to stay on to oversee training?" Tshikapa put the papers aside, adjusted his position to capture more of cooling air and studied the priest hoping his words were more of a statement than question. Many weeks indoors with factory representatives lessened the deep tan earned beneath a torrid African sun, but the Jesuit's hair still looked like oat straw.

"I will remain as long as you need me."

"The men respect you, and they will follow your lead willingly. This is going to be a difficult transition for them. I welcome your help."

"They are good men." Father Stein stared at the rosary beads dangling from his pocket while he composed his thoughts. "I've been considering a plan and I wanted to discuss it with you before I said anything to the captains of industry who will soon be invading your country. I'm quite certain they'll try to discourage me, but I feel it's the wisest thing to do--under the circumstances."

Tshikapa cocked his head forward; Father Stein was a man of many surprises. When a pensive look transformed the priest's face, like now, Tshikapa had learned to listen carefully. His words were always spoken softly, without fanfare, but the pearls of wisdom which fell from the Jesuit's lips were seldom, if ever, wrong.

"I think we should take your strongest warriors and train them to be foremen on the factory floor. They are accustomed to command. By placing them in positions of authority we will be adhering to tribal traditions established by their forefathers. Instead of herding cattle or hunting lions, these men will supervise the welding of automobile parts, but the principles of respect and leadership are the same."

"Can we teach them complicated technology? These men are primitive, most cannot read or write."

"No, but they can see clearly enough. Your men can shoot the eye out of an eagle at a hundred paces. We will show them what to do. Before the printing press people were taught by example. Passing on information through the written, rather than spoken word is a teaching method developed in the last five hundred years. I'm suggesting we train your men the same way your forefathers taught their sons to hunt. It will take a few years to transform a man from a hunter and warrior into a factory foreman, whose territorial imperative is the assembly line, but it can be done."

"Priest, tell me something." Tshikapa's hand fondled the stack of papers which represented hours of negotiation. "Why are you doing this for my people? What is it you expect to gain?"

Ruger Stein clasped his hands behind his head, and he looked toward the ceiling; his eyes wandered along the planes and angles of simple architecture and, finally, settled on the whirling blades churning heavy, humid air. After a long, hesitant moment, Father Stein's gaze lowered to Tshikapa. The words spilling from his lips were filled with conviction--for Father Stein was a man with a mission. "Jesuits want men to be free to worship God as they choose."

"More Catholic missionaries arrive in Africa every day." Tshikapa's middle finger began to stroke the papers making them flutter in whirlpools of air created by the whop-whop of the fan.

"Africa is a large mission. There are thousands of miles to cover and countless people to care for. Our priests are here to undertake the task of educating your people." Bright blue eyes traveled to the window, the sun was lowering over the Dark Continent like a partridge spreading its wings across a nest full of chicks; the priest's mind focused on the job ahead. "Future Catholic churches in your country will have no walls so the Gods of the Rain and Wind will be free to enter. Should the God of Animals care to stroll down the aisle to our altars He will be free to do so because there will be no doors to stop Him. Members in our Church will sing praises to all African gods. Loto said our priests must respect ancestral forms of worship or your people will harden their hearts against the Christian God, and they will shun the men in long black robes who serve that God. Our Lord and Savior, Jesus, came to earth to teach men to open their hearts to all. He taught the heart was large, that it had room enough for everything--different men and women--different ways of thinking--different Gods. Somewhere along the way the white man hardened his heart against those whose values were alien to the Christian way of thinking. But Andrew Simson is a man who talks to our God, and he is here to restore us to salvation."

"You will build many such churches?"

"Yes, Tshikapa. With your blessing, we will build on the plains and in the fields. We will build along the streams and rivers. Our God will seek your people. The Jesuits will adapt to the ways of Africa instead of demanding the African assume Christian customs."

Tshikapa's teeth shone brightly against his perspiration laden, ebony colored skin. It was clear Father Stein wanted what was best for all the people of Africa.

Amariah stared hard at her suitcase, wondering if there was anything else she could put on to ward off the bitter Siberian cold. As soon as darkness fell, the conductor turned off all heat and lights in the railway cars, an economy measure deemed necessary by the Russian Department of Trains. Passengers lay huddled in their bunks, praying for morning to come and with it, some blessed warmth from a winter weakened sun. The discomfort of travel across Siberia did little to allay her fears now that she had little else to occupy her thoughts.

Klaus' Russian friend provided them with flawless connections. They boarded the train with only a glance at their travel papers from soldiers who monitored every passenger. Amariah pressed her face against the window as they pulled out of the Moscow train station enchanted by the panorama. Women in babushkas, round faces smiling and shiny, waved at people departing for Lake Baikal. She watched in fascination as villages, unchanged since the time of the Czars, slipped past the window. One fleeting image represented the timeless bond natives felt with Mother Russia. An old woman in a shapeless coat sat huddled over a large, galvanized washtub. The piece of cloth around her head, washed so often the colors were faded, kept strands of gray hair from falling into her eyes as she labored. Bent with concentration, the woman scrubbed dirt from a pile of beets with majestic determination. For Amariah, this woman was the physical embodiment of what she knew about Russia. Life was bleak by America standards, yet the old woman accepted her role with dedication, conviction, and incredible nobility. The beets were grown by her own hand were produced by the soil of the *Rodina*, the Motherland. The vegetables were as plain as the woman who washed them, and as resolute as the hand immersing them in the tub of water. Such hands, such beets, would sustain the hearths of Russia forever. They labored, they endured, they were the hope of the future. Leon said her description of the old woman was hopelessly romantic. Amariah argued with him for hours, defending herself as a pragmatist. She felt the woman's soul was connected to the earth by the common bond of nurturing--a facet of life difficult for a man to understand because the male genetic code demanded adventure and daring.

Huddled beneath the covers, too cold to sleep, Amariah mulled over her conversations with Leon, which always came with the rising sun. Alone in their compartment, Leon studied Jean Paul's poem. There was no way to explain the wellspring of emotion brought on by holding the coins. Every time Amariah looked at the crossed swords, an image sprang against the screen of her inner mind of brother fighting brother--sisters turned against each other in brutal confrontation--parents and children driven apart by strife. When she reversed the coin and studied the tree, a sense of calm and wellbeing stole through her heart and she felt peaceful, entranced. Why did the coin evoke such powerful emotions? Amariah sensed the key to the past was in her hand; she just didn't know how to useit.

As the train lumbered along the tracks, she stared at the bleak Siberian landscape. Amariah was unprepared for the lack of bathing facilities and feared if she had to wash in the small basin one more day, with water so cold it hurt the skin and took her breath away, she'd give in to the urge to scream. And the food! Amariah prided herself on not being a fussy eater, but that was before the constant supply of vegetables and bread. She felt as though she might murder for a morsel of meat, a single bite of chicken!

There were days, as she and Leon argued the meaning of religion, she thought her brain was going to explode. Where had mankind gone wrong? Amariah found herself thinking about her conversation with Pope Anastasius. Had the Church abandoned the meaning of Christ's mission when its leaders intervened between man and God? Priests taught faithful worshipers to be dependent upon them instead of relying on their own feelings. Mankind descended into an era of despair and loneliness accompanying this separation from God.

People were awakening to the need to find individual pathways back to God, but if Andrew Simson had his way, the Church would assume political, moral, financial, and emotional control over most human beings on earth.

Her strife was so deep, so intense, she felt like she had climbed into a sensory deprivation tank; as though she'd lost the ability to see, hear, feel, taste or smell. It was difficult to perform even simple tasks because so much of her brain was embroiled in emotional turmoil. Had she really lived before? Had she known Jesus? Had she taught him? Why couldn't she remember details of such an important life if she performed these tasks?

Her teachers remarked on how effortlessly she learned the languages of the New Testament. But that proved nothing! And her name could be a simple case of coincidence.

Although she couldn't explain it, Amariah found the lively debates with Leon heartening. He was helping her hammer out a new philosophy. She felt protected as she stripped away layers of past conditioning. No one saw the soul shattering, emotionally naked tears--but Leon. Somehow it didn't matter, because Amariah knew she could trust him with her innermost feelings, her deepest thoughts. He offered comfort, security, and support. Amariah felt like a twig caught in an eddy, her thoughts just kept spinning--around and around and around.

Andrew Simson pressed the phone against his ear. Father Laterano was calling from the office of the Chairman of the Board of Al Italia Airlines. "A man by the name of Leon Kaminski, who matches the description we provided to airline authorities, booked a flight from London to New York. The passport numbers are the same. A woman, dressed in the habit of a Benedictine nun, is traveling with him. Her papers, too, are in order."

"Make certain surveillance remains discrete. We do not want to arouse suspicion. If they realize they're being watched, they might be provoked into making a foolish move. Keep them in sight at all times, but do not let any of our agents approach them."

The phone banged against its cradle. He steepled his fingers over the crucifix and tilted back in his chair. Perhaps the time had come to get Father

Julian into the United States. Deciding it would be better to wait and see what Kaminski and the nun were up to, he returned his attention to the map on his desk. Anna and Klaus were somewhere in Russia. The search for them was like trying to find a needle in a haystack. He banged his fist against the map. Where had they gone? Why had they chosen to flee through Russia?

Malek allowed himself to smile for the first time in many, many seasons. The priest was as good as his word. In the valley below, he watched the progress of the truck caravan threading across the desert floor. His people were going to take possession of a village in the heart of their Palestinian homeland. Father Robert Norton shamed men into putting fears and hatred aside. The Jesuit warned the time had come for Christian, Jew, and Muslim to live together in peace--to live as their prophets counseled throughout the strife filled history of Christian, Arab and Jew.

Father Norton demanded the rabbis, priests and ulemas beat their swords of inflammatory rhetoric into the plowshares of cooperation and brotherhood. He challenged his fellow holy men! He said if they were not willing to discuss volatile situations peacefully, they were unworthy representatives of God. Father Norton chided the others, saying all religious leaders were obligated to lead their flocks away from destruction, to vanquish war, to save precious lives. He reminded the self-righteous ulemas of the proclamation made in the Quran: '*There shall be no compulsion in religion*'. He wagged an admonishing finger in the faces of the turbaned Mullahs and reminded them of the Holy Prophet's words, '*For you, your religion and for me, my religion*'. He reminded the Christian and the Jew that they were commanded to '*love thine neighbor as thyself*'.

It had been a shaky truce, at first. No one trusted anyone else, and tempers flared as often as the cook fires of the Bedouin. Had it not been for the unselfish dedication of Robert Norton, Malek was certain the balm of Gilead would never have been placed upon a wound dating back to the time of Abraham.

The noisy laughter of many children rolled up the wadi on the stillness of the desert air. Women clung to their scant possessions and skipped toward structures of wood and brick which would provide shelter for their families. Men bandied about, chests puffed out, pride filling their voices as they strode up and down the streets . . . determined to remain cautious but hopeful as they laid claim to a newly created Palestine.

The magnificent Arabian's mane and tail wafted on a quickening breeze. The horse snorted and pawed at an unyielding desert floor, anxious to be off. Standing for so long was not to the stallion's liking. He wanted to move, to run atop the sand dunes like an unfettered gust of wind. A firm grip held the reins tight; Malek wasn't ready to turn from the sight just yet.

His people were going about making a new home for themselves, their joy drifted across the rocky ground and floated up to meet him. Malek smiled again. Perhaps the priest was right. Perhaps peace would come to the Holy Land after all.

Klaus opened the door to the suite. The transatlantic flight left them both longing for the comfort of a hot bath, a delicious meal and a secure night's sleep.

Reaching to unfasten the wimple and veil, Anna threw entangling layers of fabric on the table beside the couch. "I am so glad to be rid of this habit!"

"I found you quite fetching." Klaus' expression was filled with wry amusement. "Seriously, Anna, your performance was splendid. You never missed a cue throughout the entire trip. I'm quite certain we'll be safe--I don't think the Father General is prepared to send a squad of men bursting into the suite." He strolled toward one of the bedrooms. "I'll take this room. Why don't you shower? Hot water is guaranteed to wash away jet lag. How does room service sound? Hungry for anything particular?"

Anna called back from the bedroom selected for her. "I don't care as long as it's hot and there's plenty of it! Tell me when the food gets here--I'll be in the tub, soaking away the trappings of my assumed calling!"

Laughing, Klaus lifted the phone receiver. This woman's sense of humor was both delightful and appealing. She was wonderful, and Anna was the only person in the world who didn't know it.

The waiter nodded, then left, after spreading a beautifully appointed table. Champagne was left to chill in the ice bucket and a nearly translucent peach rose rested in a silver vase on a starched, white tablecloth. From beneath the warming cover, the smell of French fries and hamburgers permeated the room.

"Anna?"

The door opened, and Anna stepped from the bedroom clad in a floor-length terry cloth robe provided to patrons of the luxurious hotel. Nuns had no need for hair dryers so the one she owned went with Amariah. The curls around her face were damp. "Oh, Klaus, you shouldn't have gone to such trouble." Anna's rich earth-brown eyes flooded with relief as she jammed a French fry into her mouth. "Don't tell me--you called McDonald's!"

Handing her a fluted glass filled to the brim with champagne, Klaus offered a toast. "To all our tomorrows."

"Wherever they may lead us," Anna responded brightly.

The meal eaten, the remaining champagne poured into their glasses, Klaus and Anna settled in on the couch, comfortable with each other, content and relaxed. Turning on the television, they flipped across several channels, searching for CNN. Klaus scooped Anna's bare feet off the floor and began to massage her instep.

Anna flushed scarlet, embarrassed by Klaus' attentiveness. "That feels divine, but you don't have to go to so much effort, I'm feeling much better."

Pulling her foot further into his lap, Klaus scolded, "I know, but your toes give me something to focus on while I wrestle with a dilemma."

Anna scrunched the couch pillow further beneath her back. Crossing her arms over her stomach, she tried to keep her concentration away from the soothing sensation of Klaus' fingers as he kneaded the flesh around her toes, massaged her arch, and stroked the side of her ankles. "What's on your mind?"

"I've been wondering how more than a billion people are going to react when we blow the whistle on the largest religious scam the world has ever seen. What's going to happen when they find out the institution they believed in deliberately changed concepts they've been taught were inviolate?"

"I hope most will listen to Amariah's message with an open mind. As difficult as it was for me to accept at first, I know she has come from the past. Somehow, someway, locked up in her brain is the truth about what Jesus tried to offer to the people of his day."

Klaus studied the woman beside him. Colored lights from the television set blazed across her skin bathing her in an ethereal glow. Although he'd met queens, princesses, scholars, and women of low moral standing, Klaus didn't think he'd ever beheld a more beautiful sight. "You really believe that don't you?"

"Klaus, I've been trained as a historian. I've learned to accept physical evidence supported by logic. But--as a human, I'm forced to respond to my feelings of 'rightness'. Amariah stirred emotions in me I never knew existed.

When she talks about Jesus it's as if I were sitting on a remote Judean hillside listening to him speak. A sensation comes over me that makes me feel like I reaped the harvest of his message of love and understanding. Certain words attributed to him in the Bible are a far cry from the meaning adopted by modern Christianity. Simple things, like the literal meaning of repentance. *'Turn your mind around'* has far different implications than the hell, fire, and brimstone concept I was taught. Look what we've done to the word *'virgin'*, for heaven sake! In Jesus era, it was a word which meant a body was free from disease. In a day and age where all manner of infections associated with the filth and squalor in which people of the era lived were commonplace, someone whose body was not ravaged by open, weeping sores was a rarity. How and why, we put such emphasis on sex is a mystery to me. Unless, of course, it was a way of controlling diseases transmitted by sexual intimacy. How we got such a simple message so distorted is beyond comprehension. Jesus' teachings were clear: *'Don't look to others for answers. Each of us has the power to turn within to receive all the guidance we will ever need. Love one another. Don't pass harsh judgment on someone else because you don't know what it is they are on earth to learn. He said to have confidence in ourselves because there resided in everyone a spirit of understanding directly linked to God.'* "

Anna's expression was wistful. "I think that's why we got confused about Jesus' divinity. We're not prepared to accept the awesome ability of the human mind, nor do we want to assume the burden of responsibility enlightenment would place on our shoulders."

"I've never heard the essence of Christianity put so eloquently." Klaus took the champagne glass from her hand and sat it on the table. Laying her feet aside, he slid closer. He kissed one eyelid, then the other, and hovered just above Anna's upturned mouth. "I say a prayer of thanksgiving every day you were brought into my life. There were times I thought you would never notice me."

Anna felt her heart leap into her throat. Too much champagne; too little rest. The words on her lips were breathless, soft. "There were?"

"Couldn't you tell how much effort I put into getting the seat beside you during our staff meetings? There were a few occasions when I virtually leaped over the tables before someone else could take the chair next to you."

"You did?" Klaus' breath was warm on her face; his body pressed closer, the radiant heat of strong arms and a heaving chest sent a shudder of pleasure throughout her wilting body. Anna saw the room melt into a kaleidoscope of whirling color as the emotional barriers erected by untold hurt began to thaw beneath the force of Klaus' determination.

"Did you really think the countless trips to your lab revolved around a validation of my findings?" He inched closer and began to run his fingers through her hair.

The electricity generated by the gentle pressure of his fingers seemed to impede all normal brain function. Anna waited, the wild beating of her heart orchestrated by a crescendo of emotion. "They weren't?"

A warm, moist mouth descended on waiting, parted lips. It was hesitating, soothing, comforting. He did not demand, his kiss did not intimidate, Klaus was not seeking ruthless satisfaction for his physical desires. Slowly, softly, he drew his lips across her cheeks, then caressed her face with gently probing fingertips.

"I think I devised this method of escape for my benefit. I don't think I had Amariah and Leon's welfare in mind at all."

Anna pushed herself upright, away from lips that were so inviting, so hypnotic, so filled with promise. "If half what you suspect is true, we are all pawns in a divine plan of destiny. I only hope we're successful."

Pulling her back toward him, Klaus cradled Anna in his arms. He kissed the top of her head, then tipped her chin upward. "We shall be, my love, we shall be successful."

The wall guarding her emotions was being dismantled brick by brick. Klaus laid aside hurt, anger, and bitterness, with each tender kiss. The mortar of resistance crumbled beneath the probe of his longing tongue. Anna's emotional dam ruptured, and she kissed Klaus back--hungry for the affection he offered, lusting for the respect and confidence he inspired.

Klaus slipped his arm beneath her knees and lifted her from the couch. He carried her across the room with deliberate steps--providing her every opportunity to resist; to tell him his advances were unwarranted; to indicate his feelings were not returned. He reached the bedroom door and pushed it open with his foot. Beyond, the bed beckoned, its promise ripe.

Anna stared into eyes the color of cold, hard stone. Behind their normal icy reserve, she detected a flame. It was not the fire of passion, which brought her to this bedroom door, it was not lust, it was not like any emotion she ever encountered. She searched his expression, her mind seeking an answer for the stare holding her prisoner.

The fragile dawn of awakening stole through Anna's thoughts. Gradually, like the coming of the sun, the answer pushed aside the darkness of past despair. Klaus awaited her permission to make her his own. He longed for the pleasure of her body, but something infinitely vaster radiated from his gray eyes.

He wanted her for a partner, someone with whom he could share the joys, the hardships, the suffering, and happiness life offered. Anna suddenly realized where she had seen such an unnerving stare before. Wolves mated for life. They shared responsibility for the litter equally. They saw to the welfare of their mate without question. Their bond was so deep, so intense, it could only be severed by death.

Klaus knew by the change in Anna's expression she finally understood. The woman in his arms comprehended, at last, that he would defend her with his life. He would move heaven and earth to see to her needs, and he coveted guardianship of her emotions. He moved forward, slowly closing the bedroom door.

A Lear jet sat poised on the runway, awaiting a final signal from the tower for take-off. The sole occupant in the passenger cabin hurried aboard at the last moment, darkness obscuring his identity.

The pilot assumed his passenger was a drug lord returning home. He was unlisted on the manifest; the registered purpose of the flight was to pick up a government official in South America and return him to the United States for a conference. It was just as well they didn't acknowledge each other. The pilot didn't want to identify anyone in court--ever! If the plane was searched, the pilot knew it was clean. Drugs were just too risky to move across international borders anymore.

Instructions came from the tower and the pilot set the coordinates. Flights in and out of South America were closely monitored these days. There would be no unscheduled stops, nothing to arouse suspicion. A simple flight plan, filed with the Georgia branch of the FAA denoted the route and time of arrival. From Savannah to San Salvador, from San Salvador to Washington, D.C. He would land the bird in Central America just long enough to refuel and pick up the government official.

He couldn't help gloating a little as he thought about the unexpected windfall. Ten thousand dollars was a lot of cash for transporting an unlisted passenger on a trip he was already scheduled to fly. The guy in the cabin might be a CIA operative or military honcho on a secret mission. Hell, he could be flying the President of the United States for all he knew. If everything worked out well the voice on the phone might use him again.

In the back, the passenger rubbed fingers encased in thin, expensive leather gloves. The animal skin was worked until it was soft and supple, almost like the skin of a human being. Still, when he had to wear gloves for an extended period the scar tissue throbbed. Rope-like, thick flaps of skin encased his fingers, robbing him of dexterity, once a source of pride. Gone forever was the consummate skill it took an X-ray to detect where the neck of an offender was broken. It was useless to lament what would never return. His eyes fixed on the bulkhead, the man concentrated on the future . . . always the future--never the past. He couldn't let his thoughts stray to an assassination attempt gone sour. He couldn't dwell upon the faces of men who had once been his companions, co-workers, and friends. They betrayed him; they were the ones who consigned him to a burning building from which there was no escape.

The man squeezed his eyes shut. He had to stop the terrifying memories. His Savior told him to dwell on the future, never to let thoughts of the past overcome him. Nothing could change the evil inflicted on his mind and body. All he could do now was implement the plans of his rescuer, a man who lifted him from the torment of a drug altered mind; the man who saved him from the wretchedness of an insane asylum in which he did not belong. Now, he would be the instrument by which his Savior controlled the world. Never would those putrefying sops, who ran the Pentagon and Congress, sacrifice another man or woman on the altar of political upheaval. He worked for his Savior with zeal. His Savior would become every man's Savior in a short while.

Winter came late to Georgia. The ground was still soft and bore the marks of several pairs of heavy boots. A local Sheriff was called out of bed to investigate a murder. A boy and his dog, out on an early morning hunting expedition in the woods, stumbled across the body of a black man.

There was a driver's license from the State of Massachusetts, with a security clearance card from the Vatican. The Vatican! What the hell was this guy doing in Georgia? The Sheriff turned as the body bag zipper rend the stillness of the pre-dawn air.

Walking around, the Sheriff took care not to damage any of footprints left on soggy ground. He stood with his hands on his hips, his eyes scanning the countryside. Georgia hills were covered with pine, scrub oak and heavy underbrush. In deep glades, like this one, the evolutionary process seemed like it by-passed this part of the world and its swampy land remained primeval. A creepy feeling oozed up the back of his neck, the Sheriff's finely tuned sense of intuition warned him something far worse than robbery occurred on this backwoods road. It appeared as if the man died of a blow to the head, although it looked like he sustained a severe beating before he finally expired.

The sun pushed against the seam of orange lining the horizon. At least it wouldn't be so damned cold in an hour or two. He stood with his hands jammed into his pockets, his neck tucked into the collar of his coat. The woods began to make awakening sounds--gray squirrels springing from one branch to another, birds calling across the forest to their mates. Yes sir, the world was preparing for yet another day. Too bad this fellow wouldn't witness another sunrise, or sunset, or hear the cries of the jackdaw as it jabbered from a leafy branch.

At the edge of his peripheral vision, a blob of white caught the sun's first challenging rays and something about it demanded closer inspection. The ambulance was pulling away and only the deputy remained--and he was busy taking a leak at the far side of the patrol car. Walking toward the bush, the Sheriff stooped to withdraw an earth-stained pillowcase; blood drained from his face leaving it as white as the bed sheet upon which the pillowcase rested only hours ago. In the center, two holes were cut into the fabric. Jagged, they looked as if the circles were ripped open with a hunting knife. A cold shiver of premonition, honed by countless years in law enforcement, traced a path of apprehension down the overweight man's spine.

The Feds were always looking for an excuse to descend on Georgia and interfere with local authorities. Stuffing the pillowcase in his jacket pocket, the Sheriff stomped back to the clearing. This time, it seemed like he'd forgotten about depressions in the soft Georgia soil as he paced back and forth, mashing the ground with his firm tread.

Maybe he could make it look like another unexplained death of an unidentified black man in the heart of Georgia. The Sheriff hoped the guy wouldn't turn out to be someone important. He wondered if he could make it look like the work of a passing hitchhiker. Money and credit cards could be disposed of in the basement furnace at the courthouse. He could make it appear the motive was robbery.

The Sheriff lumbered into the squad car and slammed the door. Reaching for the gearshift, he shoved the car into reverse. Swearing, he jerked the steering column forward, as though he inadvertently jammed the transmission into the wrong gear. The rear tires spun against the moist earth, finally grabbing purchase. The car lurched forward. Checking his rearview mirror, the Sheriff was satisfied all traces of footprints were obliterated.

Damn those boys! He thought he put the fear of God in them the last time. He was sick and tired of covering for their backwoods, unchanging ways. If this guy turned out to be one of those dandified, educated blacks from up north, the boys just might end up doin' time.

"Really, Cardinal, this surgery is imperative. Look at this." The doctor depressed a button and the videotape which recorded the scoping of his esophagus began to play. His pencil tapped against the screen. "See this area, here?" The eraser rested against the image frozen on the monitor. "For some reason, you've developed a severe blockage where the stomach empties into the gastro-intestinal tract."

Woolsey stared at the screen. The pain in his stomach refused to go away despite increasing amounts of medication. All he saw was a blotchy gray spot on the tiny television. He couldn't make heads or tails of what he was looking at--for all he knew it was the entrails of a sheep or a close-up of a lunar crater!

"What's causing your distress is a buildup of gasses in the stomach. We've got to go in and remove the blockage. Your acute pain is caused by the ballooning effect. Your stomach has been stretched beyond capacity, yet gasses continue to foment. The normal channel out of the stomach has been restricted so there is nowhere for the gas to go. The valve, which admits food into your stomach, only opens one way so you can't release enough gas up the back of your throat to offer any real relief. Cardinal," the doctor's tone turned condescending, "I'm afraid our only alternative is exploratory surgery."

Another spasm of pain rumbled through Woolsey's abdomen. "Good God, man, do you think surgery is an issue with me? All I want is relief from suffering! How it is obtained, what method of quackery you use, is immaterial. Just get on with it! I've swallowed your pills, I've suffered your infernal needles, I've gone through a Medieval torture you call an Upper GI, I've had myself strapped to a table, unable to move, while a machine prodded and probed parts of my body which should only be revealed to God! Despite the mountains of indignity heaped upon me all you can say is you don't know why it's there, but something is causing my stomach to expand! And all you can tell me is you know it's painful! Well, Doctor, I could have told you all that without going through a testing process the likes of which must have been conjured up by someone who wanted to offer human beings a preview of hell! Get me on the table! Cut it out! Do something, but damn it, Doctor, make it stop hurting!"

CHAPTER SEVENTEEN

Kharkov jammed his finger against a button on the recorder. His lips were a taut, thin line. Hands against his hips, the soldier stared at the priest.

Father Stephen Andropov wrestled with surprise. He had to keep his expression impassive at all costs, as if he thought the recording was a bad joke. On his part, Balsahov Petrovich leaned back in his chair, folding his arms across his chest. His eyes were clear, the loving arms of alcohol did not lull him to sleep last night. A soldier went into battle with his mind sharp, his body rested. This day might well prove as important in the defense of the *Rodina* as the battle he waged for Stalingrad.

The priest shifted his weight. On the surface, he appeared calm--indifferent. "Might I know to whom the voice on the tape belongs? Do I have the right to know the identity of my accuser?"

Vassily Kharkov held up a crucifix. The priest's hand went to his chest. The cherished crucifix had been missing for several days. This time, he couldn't keep the amazement from his eyes.

Tossing the crucifix into the Jesuit's lap, Vassily spat corrosive words. "The voice belongs to a man who understands the power of the mind."

Andropov slipped the chain over his head. He adjusted the crucifix several times, using the movement to disguise the time he needed to prepare his defense. "What this man says is absurd!"

Petrovich burst out of his chair and lurched around the desk, lowering his face to within inches of the alarmed Jesuit. "No, priest, all this is true! Our agents know about the activities of Jesuits in South Africa, Ireland, Angola, and Mexico. All have gained prominence among their followers and each one has sworn allegiance to the Father General. I have an ultimatum for you, Andropov . . . one I want you to take back to Rome. Your priests are through in Russia! They will leave quietly, in ones and twos. It would be better for the Father General and our government if no attention is drawn to the expulsion of your fellow priests."

Drawing erect, Petrovich returned to the other side of his desk, but he didn't sit down. Adrenaline stiffened his body, making him feel as young and virile as he was fifty years ago, on the day he knew for certain the Germans had surrounded Stalingrad. He stayed at his post in the mill, he fought the Germans to the last man. He continued to fight long after he'd run out of ammunition; he used his hands as weapons-- instruments of death--and he was still capable of wielding terror.

"I have a message for your Father General." His glance embraced the window. A layer of snow-covered Red Square, Lenin's Tomb, and the filigreed coping on the state-owned department store, GUM, A white mantle draped the domes of St. Basil's. As the brilliant spirals disappeared beneath winter's garment, Petrovich realized how much strength he drew from Red Square. "Tell Andrew Simson I was blinded by my love for the Motherland. Memory of the horrors of Stalingrad clouded my judgment. But tell your Father General I want his priests out of Russia! He will not bring the tactics of the Jesuits into my country. He lengthened the pause between his words, he wanted Andropov to know he understood the methods Jesuits used to convert, "*the end no longer justifies the means.*"

The old colonel's chest swelled with dignity. "I will stand between him and Russia with all the strength left in my body! Your Church will not seduce my country. Rasputin will not enchant the leadership of Russia a second time! I am not the Czarina, priest, I see through the veil of benevolence Simson casts over the eyes of the unsuspecting." Gripping the windowsill until his knuckles turned as white as the snow outside, he lowered his voice until a growl hung in air. "Tell Simson to withdraw his henchmen or I will tell the world of his intentions. Stay out of the *Rodina* and I will remain silent! Remove his Princes of Darkness or I will wage a war he is not prepared to fight."

The hatred radiating from the old soldier distorted his features. Balsahov Petrovich leaned on the desk, supporting his weight with his hands. Like a seething, hissing jackal, he spat words in the priest's face. "I am accustomed to waging war! I faced insurmountable odds and had the courage to stand my ground. I marched through snow and freezing rain with only dedication to sustain me. I buried my face in the mud of the Motherland as shells exploded all around me. I risked my life to protect my country from evil. I starved, I thirsted, I endured hardship and pain! I did not suffer because I was a mindless, obedient slave. No!" His fist slammed against the desktop, once, twice, once again. The metals and ribbons on Petrovich's uniform rattled and clanked as the soldier's ferocity exploded. "I did it because I believe in my country! I bore its ills with resignation and gloried in her achievements--and I will die to protect my homeland!"

The old man stomped back toward the priest, stabbing at the black robe with a stubby, tobacco-stained finger. "Take this message back to your leader, Priest! Tell him I will meet him on the field of battle, and I will repel his army of misguided men. The blood of Cossacks runs in my vein, and I am not too old to fight!"

Turning toward Vassily, he gestured at the younger man. "This fine young soldier, and millions like him, will follow me to war! We will wage a battle the likes of which your Father General cannot imagine." His voice rose like the roar of a lion defending its territory. "Tell Andrew Simson to get out of Russia!"

For more than a week Amariah stared out the train window at the primordial forest of spruce, pine, fir, hemlock, and cedar skirting a windswept plateau. The train passed through stands of trees so dense they held back the light of day--half the forested area of the world was contained in Siberia. Here and there, birch and willow peppered the belt of land known as the *taiga*--a Russian word meaning, "swamp forest". When the snows melted in spring travel was impossible because run-off turned the forest floor turned to slush.

The cities of Kirov, Sverdlovsk, Novosibirsk, and Krasnoyarsk were behind. Another day would see them in Irkutsk. European tourists on the train were there to admire Lake Baikal, by cubic volume the largest lake in the world. A vast body of water, surrounded by a range of mile high mountains, supported fishing villages along its miles of shoreline. Leon was trying to talk Amariah into taking an excursion into Listvyanka along with some other passengers. People, who eked out a life in this remote section of Siberia, were an energetic, pioneering lot. Leon was anxious to visit them and listen to their tales of survival.

Siberia was a wild, untamed land; only the courageous endured a grueling trip across its plains and mountains. As the train trudged through mountains which sequestered Irkutsk and Lake Baikal from the faint of heart, Amariah turned away from the window because their coach car seemed close to tumbling over precipices flanking the track.

Two more days and they would cross the Mongolian border into China--another week of hardship, and they would reach Shanghai, their last port of call before San Francisco.

"A penny for your thoughts."

Amariah turned from the window. Leon smiled, knowing her mind was a million miles away from the Siberian landscape she appeared to be studying.

"I was pondering the Church's future." Sighing, Amariah settled against the compartment couch which unfolded into a bed at night. Cold, she tucked a blanket around her feet. "I wonder if reincarnation can be proven."

Leon slipped a sweater over his head and reached for a jacket; the sun seemed incapable of warming the crisp mountain air even at midday, "I'll never forget the first time I stepped inside a monastery in Tibet. The setting was so familiar, so comfortable, I found it disarming."

"I felt that way when we visited the Coliseum."

Leon glanced in her direction. "Why didn't you say something?"

Amariah turned to peer out the window again. The trees slid past, casting a ripple of shadow across her face. "I didn't know how to express it. The theory of reincarnation is difficult to accept because of my Christian upbringing."

Leon rubbed his chin, it was too painful to shave every day in a tiny basin of freezing water at the far end of the train. "I think most Christians feel the same way. We've all turned a blind eye to subjects which demanded we question accepted tradition."

"Daddy calls the phenomena a *scotoma*--people have the ability to blot out anything that disagrees with their version of the truth. A lot of important people believed they lived before."

Leon's brows shot upward. "Oh?"

"Yes, Carl Jung, Ben Franklin, John McTaggart, Ralph Waldo Emerson, David Henry Thoreau, Louisa May Alcott, and General George Patton, to name a few."

"The same Benjamin Franklin who helped the United States win independence from England?"

"He wrote an epitaph for his tombstone, for some reason I've always remembered it.

'The Body of B. Franklin, Printer,
Like the Covers of an Old Book
Its Contents Torn Out
and
Stripped of its Lettering and Gilding,
Lies here

Food for Worms
But the Work shall not be Lost
For it Will as He Believed
Appear Once More
In a New and more Elegant Edition
Revised and Corrected
by the Author'."

Amariah adjusted the blanket again. No matter how she arranged it, there always seemed to be a spot exposed to a cold draft.

Leaning across the narrow compartment, Leon tucked the corner of the blanket beneath her feet. "Do you suppose Jesus was talking about reincarnation when the disciples asked him, '*Why then say the scribes that Elias must first come? And Jesus answered and said unto them, Elias truly shall first come and restore all things. But I say unto you, that Elias is come already, and they knew him not*'. There's also the passage in the Bible where Jesus asks his followers: '*Who do men say that I, the son of Man, am? And they said, some say that thou art John the Baptist; some Elias; and others, Jeremiah or one of the prophets*'."

Running her fingers through her hair, Amariah toyed with the curls, still not accustomed to being without her veil and wimple. "I can't put my feelings into words, but it's like we're all on an incredible journey. We come to earth to experience, to learn, and cope with all aspects of the human condition. We reacquaint ourselves with people who've been important to us before--good and bad. I'm beginning to wonder if I lived the life of a Medieval priest by the name of Adamus. Perhaps the Vatican evokes memories associated with that lifetime. It might have been my hand which hid the documents in the catacombs and the Secret Archive!"

Leon found himself giving voice to words welling up from a source of knowledge he was powerless to explain. "And what about the Aramaic word Metanaeo: '*Turn your mind around*', or Chata which you said meant to '*Miss the mark.*'

"What?" Amariah was so lost in the complexity of her thoughts she didn't catch the whole of his softly spoken words.

"You said that was the literal meaning of repentance and to sin."

"It is."

Leon scratched at the stubble on his chin. "Do you think Christ was trying to convince people if their minds were consumed by hatred--hateful experiences would follow? Do you think the reason he preached the philosophy of love was because he knew positive thoughts brought beneficial conditions--

not only in the present but possibly in future lives as well?"

She glanced up--awe filled hyacinth-colored eyes. "How could I have been so blind? All the clues were right in front of me--I just ignored them. I've been a victim of my own scotoma! Jesus was talking about the mind! He stressed it all the time! Only the word he used was 'heart'. Ancient Egyptians thought the soul resided in the heart! They preserved the heart and threw the brain away because it was considered a useless organ. Jesus would have used terminology people could relate to--words commonly accepted, analogies shepherds and fishermen readily understood."

Eyes blazing, Leon's voice grew stronger, he sensed they were on the verge of discovery. "That's why Jesus' parables were about weaving, and fishing and harvesting. He used everyday occurrences in the lives of the people of his day to explain his message."

Amariah cast the blanket onto the poorly padded bench. She was no longer cold, her body tingled with a surge of warmth pushed through her bloodstream by the barge of excitement. "We thought Jesus was talking about physical conditions, so we accepted the teachings of the Bible in a literal sense!"

"I think it's logical, after all--we exist in a three-dimensional world. Concepts dealing with the mind can't be seen--they can't be touched, heard, or tasted! We're trapped in a physical environment, Amariah. Human beings try to turn spirituality into something concrete, something with form and substance, because the physical world is the only thing we understand! Mental stuff, like faith and belief are abstract, vague, shrouded in mystery! It's easier to give a priest responsibility for comprehending the incomprehensible. It takes less effort to let another person, in whom you've placed your trust, tell you what to do. If you observe certain rituals, attend a ceremony on a specific day, and offer a predetermined amount of your earnings to the organization providing you with all this information, then you are assured a place in Paradise! We're too worn down from the cares of this world to figure out what is required for salvation all by ourselves. It's simpler to hand over the whole, confusing situation to members of the clergy."

A thought ballooned at the center of Amariah's brain. The medulla portion of the organ, which governed the primitive center assuring survival of the species, sent an idea surging to the surface of her consciousness. This new concept forced its way through layers of tissue; it traveled along unfamiliar synaptic pathways; arcing across previously uncharted, unconnected synaptic channels. It crossed a mental distance so vast it was the equivalent of traveling to the sun and back.

"What are you thinking about? You look terrified." Leon's voice was filled with concern.

"That's what Simson is trying to do." Amariah banged her fist against the windowpane, anger drew her features as taut as the string on an archer's bow. "He wants to make it look as though he's a benevolent father-figure, so people will hand over responsibility for their lives to him. Once they give him that kind of control, it will be easy to manipulate them into complying with anything he deems important. We are passing through a product of that philosophy."

"How so?" Leon sensed it was imperative to keep Amariah talking, she needed to give voice to floundering thoughts.

"Marx and Lenin made their followers believe the government should be responsible for every aspect of their lives. Individualism was stifled. It was forced out of their culture, perceived as the ultimate evil. First the Czars and then the Communist Party denied the Russian people an opportunity to develop along separate lines, to pursue individual endeavors, to honor unique cultures. They were taught to concentrate on the good of the whole. That's a noble concept but you can't take individualism out of the individual--it defies our genetic code! Look at us as a species. The retina of our eyes, the sound of our voice, our fingerprints are completely unique. The good of the whole must come from the individual's development of their highest potential. I'm beginning to wonder if the good of the whole is a by-product of individual effort and achievement."

"Are you saying capitalism is a better way of life than socialism or communism?"

Amariah's eyes reflected the agony of her thoughts. "I don't know--my skill is with languages dead and forgotten. I just have a nagging feeling when you rob a person of the right to do their best--a spark goes out. Think about the Russians we've seen. They are a good people, most of them have been warm, friendly, and compassionate. But there's no glow in their eyes! They're just existing. They go through the routine of their days in a dream-like trance. What have they to look forward to? What enlivens their existence?"

"Jesus warned us of the perils of money."

"Perhaps he was trying to convince us material abundance was the result of striving to be kind, forgiving, loving. Because we are entangled in the physical, we put acquisition ahead of the search within. He said when you value a possession more than you value spiritual development, you snuff out the light, which acts like a beacon on a spiritual journey. There's nothing wrong with tangible objects when you perceive their value correctly. Desire can keep you striving, attaining."

"Like a carrot in front of a donkey?"

"Sort of."

"So where did we get the notion money is evil?"

Amariah drew a long, sucking breath. "I'd be willing to bet the text of the Bible was manipulated to promote the concept."

"Why?" Leon felt his heartbeat quicken, the adrenaline coursing through his veins made him feel like a thoroughbred at the starting gate. He had to keep posing questions to Amariah, he needed to keep her talking; intuition warned him she was about to give voice to thoughts which haunted her and came like a thief in the night to torment and confuse.

"The battle for control of the mind is escalating. Religion, advertising, politics are all engaged in a war of manipulation." Amariah rubbed her forehead. "People don't know--they aren't aware of how much they're being controlled because they are victims of masters of deceit. They don't know where to turn for guidance. People need someone to lead them out of darkness into the light."

What Amariah said made perfect sense. Politicians hired 'image makers' to win elections. Presidential candidates studied acting techniques to convince voters they were deserving of office. Advertising campaigns made people think they couldn't live without a pet rock, a silly looking doll, a certain car, or designer jeans. Religious leaders like Jim Jones and Jim Koresh convinced their flocks to follow them to destruction.

She studied the scene beyond the frost edged window. The day turned gray and dreary. Ugly clouds melted along the Siberian landscape. A steady, dismal drizzle began to fall while she wrestled with her thoughts. Downed trees hung limp, denuded of their protective mantle of white. The realization her viewpoint was potentially explosive came slowly. She fought against a rising tide of panic. She was not a charismatic leader who could exhort entire nations to righteous indignation. She was just an ordinary woman!

A figure wearing the loose-fitting trousers, shirt, cap, and mask required by the hospital pushed his cart against doors opening onto the surgical floor. The technician's cart was filled with vials of blood, empty glass tubes, boxes of bandages, sterile gauze in sealed packets, containers holding needles required for transfusions and IVs, along with several bottles of the orangish-brown solution used to swab skin to reduce the risk of infection. The technician lifted a box from his cart and slipped inside a luxurious private room. He hesitated, making sure the patient was sedated.

Cardinal David Woolsey slept deeply; morphine which dulled the pain rendered him incoherent. He didn't hear the soft pad of feet covered by surgical slippers. He didn't awaken as the technician reached for a bottle of pills on the stand by the bed. The Cardinal was unaware the man replaced the tablets he had been taking for several weeks with a different prescription. If tested, gel caps would reveal a substance which coated the stomach lining and reduced inflammation.

The chemical causing the stomach to swell and seal the natural opening into the upper intestine disappeared into the pocket of the surgical smock. The technician slipped from the room and took his place behind the cart again. He pushed it down the corridor toward the elevator at a leisurely pace; a bored staff member making rounds at two o'clock in the morning.

Damning evidence was on its way to the hospital basement. Capsules containing aluminum flakes, which turned the acid in the Cardinal's stomach into hydrogen gas, would soon be eliminated forever.

Nurses at the station turned to watch the technician as he walked by. They noticed how far the surgical cap was drawn down on his forehead and how protectively the mask was secured over his face. They assumed he just left the room housing the AIDS patient around the corner. He'd protected his hands from the deadly virus by wearing latex gloves.

They went back to talking as soon as he passed. They didn't see him store the cart in the supply room, nor did they notice him disappear into the stairwell. The medication Cardinal Woolsey took so faithfully in hope of finding relief was on its way to the incinerator. The hospital disposed of as much contaminated waste as they could in the furnace. Fire was one sure way to kill the demons of infection which plagued mankind.

Opening the furnace door, a gloved hand tossed the plastic container into the fire. Immediately, the vial containing the capsules filled with aluminum flakes melted, then burst into a short-lived flame. The technician stripped off his gloves, consigning them to a fiery oblivion.

Heavy scars on his fingers made untying the strings of his surgical mask a chore. Finally, they loosened, and he tossed the remainder of the hospital clothing into the furnace.

He reached for his habit and pulled the hood far out over his face. Satisfied everything was reduced to ashes, he closed the furnace door and headed back to the stairs.

Andrew Simson stopped the tape recorder. He steepled his fingers over his chest and closed his eyes, as if in deep conversation with the Almighty, while he considered all possibilities before returning his attention to Andropov. When, at last, he concluded his inspirational mediation, he fixed Father Andropov with a rapacious stare.

"Certainly, this information will force me to act sooner than I anticipated."

The young priest thrust forward, anxiety written on his features. "I thought it best to bring the tape to you, so I caught the first flight out of Moscow."

"No one else has heard this, I trust?"

"No."

Reaching for his crucifix, Andrew Simson began to toy with the cross. "The Russians obviously discovered something new. I would like to meet this Stephanov Rubtsovsky. He may have stumbled across a technique to unlock the secrets of the mind. We might be able to put his technique to excellent use."

Pupils dilated with nervousness, the other Jesuit twisted his rosary beads in a tight spiral. "Father, do you really think it possible this man has the power to read minds? Or was it the result of clever detective work? Granted, Rubtsovsky seemed to know a great deal about our plans, but I can't believe the information was gathered with the method described by Balsahov Petrovich."

The thumbnail began to scrape back and forth, softly, caressingly. "The Russians devoted countless hours to studying what we call 'psychic phenomena'. It seems like they are not as blinded by the three-dimensional world as we in the west. If Rubtsovsky obtained these details by holding your crucifix, then he is a man we need to include in our plans. Think what power we could wield over the rest of the world, Father Andropov! How much easier it would be to convince the faithful we are acting on direct authority from God if we invade a man's thoughts and tell him his inner most secrets! The implications are staggering."

The priest cocked his head, there was a tone in the Father General's voice he hadn't heard before and a new expression took possession of Andropov's face. "I allowed the fear of failure to obscure the positive potential of the situation. I hadn't considered the possibility we might use Rubtsovsky's methods for our own purposes."

"Stephen, you're not thinking like a Jesuit!" Andrew Simson smiled at the young man, letting him know his words were not intended as criticism, rather, they were meant to offer paternal counsel. "Go back to the Kremlin. Tell Petrovich and Kharkov we will meet their demands. Present him with a timetable for extracting our priests from Russia."

"But Father," the young man jumped to his feet, his arms churned the air with agitation, "how can we turn away from what we've begun? Our work is going so well. People are flocking back to the Church! Surely, we cannot stop now!"

"We'll lull the Russians into a false sense of security to give me enough time to put a contingency plan in motion. I need you to stall a few days. Send three of the brothers back to Rome for a period of rest and renewal. Inform these priests they are to participate in a retreat to renew their vows and strengthen their commitment. Try to ascertain whether Kharkov and Petrovich said anything about expelling the Church to their colleagues in the Ministry."

"What can you do to change their minds? Petrovich is like a rabid dog. He will stop at nothing to eliminate the presence of the Church."

"Perhaps I will send a brother, who excels in the art of persuasion, to reason with our Russian friends. And, remember Stephen, to a Jesuit, the end always justifies the means."

An ambulance siren warned traffic clogging a major conduit through Rome it was on an emergency mission. Inside, a paramedic adjusted monitors tracking the nun's respiration rate and heartbeat, then increased the flow of saline through the needle piercing the vein inside her elbow. Thin and weak, Sister Magdalene's heartbeat was shallow. Keeping a close eye on one of the monitors, he hoped the woman's vital signs were strong enough to survive the trip to the hospital.

He stripped off the nun's wimple and veil, surprised to find her head devoid of hair. It appeared as if she recently lost several teeth, and her gums were red and swollen. He reached for a basin as the sister's chest began to heave and gently turned her on her side. The poor woman had been vomiting continuously since they found her slumped over the computer in her lab.

She was so fragile, so pitiful, the paramedic felt compelled to hold her hand. Eyes, large and out of proportion, stared at him from a face whose skin shrank against the skull until it resembled a death mask.

Sister Magdalene tried to smile, to return the gentle pressure of the young man's hand. She appreciated his kindness, his sympathy for the condition of her body as he reached to wipe away the spittle laced with acid lingering at the corner of her mouth.

A prayer of thanksgiving kept floating through her pain muddled thoughts. She'd put the finishing touches on "*Messiah*" before she passed out at the computer. God gave her the strength to continue, to finish the program that would be at the vanguard of the one-world government. Nothing else mattered. She was ready to die. She could go home now.

The paramedic's face grew dim. From somewhere off to her right a radiant light flooded her senses. She tried to turn her head, to see the point of origin, but she was too tired, so very tired. Perhaps if she rested a few moments she would gather enough strength. Yes. That was it. She would close her eyes and rest before concentrating on the light again.

A voice called to her from a lighted mist hovering near the edge of her peripheral vision. Surprised, she summoned the energy to turn her head . . . or so it seemed. The light was closer now. It was beautiful; sparks of blue, yellow, and green chased along an arch resembling a rainbow. The voice came again. Pain pummeling her head melted as the mist drew closer. Her mouth didn't hurt anymore, and she no longer had the urge to vomit. She was comfortable, as if in a familiar bed with covers tucked beneath her chin. Sister Magdalene felt happy and secure. She no longer heard the wail of the siren, the roar of traffic; her body found surcease from its pain, and the technician's face faded although she stared in his direction.

The voice called out again. This time, it was sharp. Demanding. "Chacha! Chacha Zawi!" This voiced used her African name, the name she had before taking the sacred vows of her Order, and it was growing insistent. Sister Magdalene tried hard to concentrate. Who would know her by that name now?

A figure walked out of the light.

She wasn't thinking right anymore. It was probably the boy who held her hand. Sister Magdalene was certain she was still in the ambulance, headed to a hospital.

But this--no, this was a woman! An old woman, with a blanket draped over her shoulder. Her hand clutched a walking stick, and she pounded the earth with it as she marched forward. There was a necklace of bones around her wrinkled neck, and she carried herself with the pride and dignity of a Zulu warrior.

Suddenly, Sister Magdalene knew who the woman was.

"Grandmother!"

"Chacha, I've come to take you home." The voice dismantled the barriers of what was left of Sister Magdalene's conscious mind.

"Are we going to the village? Will Zotho, Mindahabe and Tawata be there?"

"No, not yet. They will meet us later. First, we go to the hut beside the river."

"Oh!" A smile split lips as dry and cracked as a desert riverbed. Sister Magdalene spent the happiest days of her life in the little thatch hut at the river's edge. Her grandmother carried her down to the water every day. She taught the frail girl how to kick her feet in the river's current. The water's natural buoyancy made it easier for the child to exercise legs twisted by the ravages of illness. Those were happy days, wonderful days; days of freedom and abandonment known only to a child. Her grandmother taught her to make blowing sounds, which frightened the mighty hippopotamus. Oh, how she laughed as huge beasts turned in horror at the gurgle. To think she had the power to make hippos flee gave her a feeling of confidence. Her grandmother instilled courage in a crippled little girl. She said nothing was impossible. If fierce hippos feared her then Chacha had the power to overcome any difficulties that might arise throughout her life!

Quite suddenly, Sister Magdalene found herself standing at the hut, her grandmother at her side. Only now . . . she wasn't a little girl and her legs bore her weight without the help of metal braces. Testing newfound strength, she walked a few steps away from the hut--free of pain.

"Chacha, you will be happy here. Your legs will not hurt anymore."

Thrilled, Sister Magdalene's attention was drawn to the hut as a tall black man with a bushy beard stepped from behind the curtain of tanned animal hide sheltering the occupants from a fierce midday sun. His eyes were deep set and penetrating, the smile that broke the somber countenance of his deeply lined face was reinforced by luminous, understanding eyes. There was an air of compassion radiating from him and instinct announced he meant her no harm. Sister Magdalene wondered who he was. She turned to ask, but her grandmother was at the river filling the pots with water in a chore as old as the river itself. Women of the tribe always carried crudely formed earthen jugs back to the village on their shoulders. This time, Sister Magdalene was confident she could help with a task she was incapable of performing before.

"Sister Magdalene."

Turning back, Sister Magdalene was surprised to find the man had moved away from the doorway. He walked to her side, but she didn't hear his approach. "How do you know my name? I don't remember you."

A warm, lilting voice floated across the clear air of the high savanna, it was a caressing sound--a sound to soothe away any troubles she might have, a voice which soothed with tenderness, a voice echoing a feeling of limitless love. "*Know me not, Sister?*"

Sister Magdalene stared hard at rocky ground while she searched her memory. "I don't believe I know you, I am certain I would have remembered a man of your stature."

"*I am the One to whom you prayed throughout your sojourn on earth.*"

Pressing her hands against her mouth to stifle instant disbelief, Sister Magdalene felt her eyes fill with tears at the tenderness in the man's voice. "But! But your skin is black . . . like mine! My Lord and Savior had light skin!"

"*I AM the same. I come in many guises, I use many voices, many faces. People hear me through the sound of their own thoughts, others sense my presence in the wind caressing their skin, in the balm of a summer's eve. I came only to welcome you home, to tell you your life was well lived. Your constant struggle to overcome the adversities you chose to endure when you returned to earth were managed well. You never lost your faith--your belief in the Force which guides this Universe. You have done well, Sister, very well indeed. I've come to take you home.*"

The smile brightening the fragile nun's face shocked the paramedic. Monitors began to screech an electronic alarm as the heart to which they were attached spluttered a few last, feeble beats. A green line indicating brain wave activity jerked upward, then flattened. The pulsating, rhythmic sound normally emitted from the compact equipment turned to a dull, monotonous tone--a sound indicating life, as it was known on earth, had ended.

Reaching for the hypodermic filled with adrenaline, the paramedic stopped--just short of plunging it into the woman's median basilic vein. Adrenaline might start her heart again, but the look on the old woman's face stopped the hand holding the needle from performing an action he had consummated a thousand times. The sister was at peace. A look of serenity, which transformed the haggard, illness ravaged face into one of contented beauty, shook the medic. The face looking back at him from the mirror every morning was filled with despair and anguish, for he was a deeply troubled man. Would he ever find the peace evident in this Sister's face?

What would her life be like if he forced her to return? His hand trembled. He wasn't supposed to make this kind of decision. His job was to prolong life, no matter what the cost. The needle clattered against the ambulance floor. The wail of the siren turned to a stiletto pitch which pierced his heart. He couldn't, wouldn't, bring her back . . . even if it cost him his job. Wherever the sister was now--was where she belonged. And, where he desperately wanted to be.

He drew the sheet over the nun's face as the ambulance turned into the driveway leading to the emergency room. Maybe he'd go to church again. He'd heard a lot about a new breed of Jesuits preaching around Rome. He'd heard they didn't talk a lot of mumbo-jumbo like the priests he remembered from childhood. A friend invited him to go to church; he said he knew peace of mind for the first time in his long, weary life. He said a Jesuit restored his faith in a Higher Power and taught him how to believe again.

The paramedic pulled the sheet away from the nun's face for one last look. Dead, the nun was stone cold dead, yet her face was so radiant, so jubilant, so filled with wonder, it brought tears to his eyes. He wanted to feel her happiness, he wanted to know her joy. Maybe the Church had something to offer him after all. He turned toward the doors of the ambulance as they opened.

Richard Weatherby brought the big, black SUV to a stop and reached for the dog's leash. Damascus cocked his ears forward as he caught sight of people in the distance; jogging, walking, bicycling around pathways hugging the edge of Lake Merced.

Fog hung low over the water, ghosts of moisture drifted aloft, trailing rags of cloud behind them as they traveled toward the sea. The lake looked as if it belonged in the highlands of Scotland rather than on the fringes of a cosmopolitan city like San Francisco.

The dog growled; a low, rumbling sound so characteristic of his breed. The Rott stood with his back straight, the stub of his tail at a right angle to his spine, his chest out--ready to defend his master from anyone foolish enough to draw near.

"Easy boy. "They're clear across the lake."

A warning snarl echoed through the predawn stillness. "Let's go." The dog sprang from the SUV and rushed to shrubbery clinging to the shoreline. Quickly and efficiently, he marked every bush, tree, and blade of grass with his powerful scent. Any dog happening by would recognize the odor of a superior, alpha male.

Richard's thoughts refused to settle on any specific topic for the past week. He hoped a walk with the dog would help clear his mind. Perhaps when the sun burned away the heavy mist--doubt, fear, anxiety, and apprehension--would lift as well.

A call alerted him to their coming. Dread over her daughter's danger was etched into the lines around Elizabeth's eyes, it melted into the network of creases around her mouth, drawing them downward, but his wife could be counted on to perform a flawless charade. She would greet the stranger at the airport as if it were her only daughter, come home at last, for the benefit of anyone who might be watching.

The dog lifted his square head and sniffed the air. A snort of challenge carried across the lake. Several joggers turned, aware of danger.

As if time had frozen, hands of the clock marking its passage refused to move forward for Richard Weatherby. He had twenty-four hours to endure before he could talk with the people who knew where his daughter was--and why she chose to flee Rome with a man his dead friend said could be trusted.

Twenty-four hours. Twenty-four more hours. Where was Amariah now? Was she safe with Kaminski? Did Andrew Simson know her whereabouts?

The dog swung around, inspecting his master. He watched the expression on Richard's face for a few moments, then crossed the short distance between them in a few loping strides. The Rott stood on his hind feet, his front paws braced on the shoulders of a worried human being. Richard tried to break the brute of the habit because their friends found it disconcerting to look eye to eye with a dog whose jaws were capable of pulverizing bone. A huge pink tongue lolled from the side of his mouth and his eyes radiated an intelligence Richard Weatherby found unnerving.

A lonely, primeval howl burst from deep inside a massive rib cage. Reaching to stroke the expanse of skull between Damascus' ears, Richard spoke softly. "Are you telling me Amariah is all right?" Lids lowered over large brown eyes which could convey the emotions of a human being. It was almost as if the dog was using his body to communicate--a shorthand of sorts--which substituted for verbal language.

"Do you know, Damascus? Has that brain of yours connected with Amariah? Do you know where she is?"

The dog dropped on all fours. He tugged against the leash, urging Richard back to the SUV. Leaping inside the moment the tail gate was dropped, he paced back and forth conveying an urgent need to return home.

The hand working to place the keys in the ignition trembled so hard it took Richard three tries to spark the car to life. The Rott barked in his ear, making his head ring.

"Damascus! Stop! You'll make me deaf!"

The dog rooted beneath his arm, muscles in his head and neck forced Richard's arm toward the gearshift.

"All right! All right! We're on our way. Sit down! I can't see with you in the way. For Christ's sake--move!"

Satisfied he compelled his owner to hurry, Damascus lowered on his haunches, but his eyes never left Richard's face as the SUV broached the line of oncoming cars speeding down the road bordering the lake.

The newscaster shuffled papers in front of him and twisted his head a few times. His Adam's Apple went up and down as he swallowed against the tie and starched shirt collar.

A voice called from the darkness behind the lights used to illuminate the studio. "Four seconds, Jerry."

"Is my tie straight?"

"You're fine. Three...two...one...on air!"

"Good evening ladies and gentlemen. Sources inside the Kremlin reported on what may be the most severe scientific accident of modern times. The launch site of Russian Federation spacecraft in Western Siberia was the scene of a massive explosion today. A rocket loaded with complex equipment designed to test the atmosphere of Mars exploded on lift off, about six hours ago. Western experts speculate a fuel leak, combined with a trajectory error, may have led to the mishap which resulted in the deaths of many high-ranking officials. A geo-stationary satellite, which monitors all Russian space launches, recorded a near perfect lift off. A flame near the first stage fuel cell became evident prior to second stage ignition. Then, for reasons that have experts baffled, the rocket tilted--nose downward--and hurtled into the bunker which allows technicians and government officials to observe lift off. We switch you now to Houston and the Chairman of the National Aeronautical Space Administration, Frank Jones."

The television screen split, and the newscaster turned to his right. To the viewing audience it appeared he was speaking directly to the Chairman when, in fact, he was only repeating carefully rehearsed questions. The Chairman's responses would be piped into his ear through a miniature microphone.

"Mr. Jones, can you give us your opinion as to what might have happened at the Russian test site?"

"Well, Jerry, bearing in mind our satellite's orbit is about five hundred miles above the earth, I've reviewed the tapes as carefully as possible. Using computer enhancement techniques, we detected a flame bursting through the outer skin of the fuel cell. This alone could have caused the rocket to explode in mid-air. What we do not have a clear answer for is why the trajectory changed. The nose did a complete one hundred and eighty-degree turn and plunged into the space center. The rocket appeared to be responding to a pre-determined course change. Under ordinary circumstances, a fire like the one that broke out in the first stage pod would not have caused this kind of malfunction. We estimate the rocket was several thousand feet above the Siberian plain when it turned. The test site location is remote, and the resulting shower of fuel and rocket parts would do minor damage on the ground if it exploded in mid-air."

The newscaster stole a glance at the monitor which contained the face of the most experienced man at NASA. Mr. Jones, would you hazard a guess as to what happened to the trajectory?"

Rubbing the area beneath his nose—the newscaster's expression reflected genuine bewilderment. "Jerry, we've been reviewing video tapes of similar failures the United States experienced over the years, along with what we have available on Russian space exploration. We've never seen anything like this explosion. The rocket turned smoothly--it wasn't forced out of its trajectory--it moved like it was following a pre-programmed change of direction."

"Thank you, Mr. Jones." The newscaster squared up in his seat and faced the camera directly. "We now go to our Washington studios and Brian McConnell at the State Department."

The camera closed in on a slightly balding, gray-haired man. Working to keep heavy glasses on his short, bulbous nose, his face had a pinched, pained expression as the director signaled they were going live. The television studio was not the Washington bureaucrat's normal domain, and he was uncomfortable in front of a camera.

"Mr. McConnell," the newscaster's voice crossed the airways, "you have a reputation for being the State Department's leading analyst of Russian intelligence. Will you give us an overview of what you think the loss of so many

Soviet statesmen and military commanders is going to do to party leadership?"

The nervous man pushed his glasses against his face and blinked at the bright lights a few seconds while he formulated a response. "Jerry, there is absolutely no way to predict what course of action Russia will take now. According to our sources, about half of the country's most prominent leaders died in this explosion. Members of the Politoboro, military leaders, TASS representatives, and some top men in the KGB were killed. With this turn of events, all the Russian minorities might push for complete autonomy."

"Was the President on hand for the launch?" The newscaster found his throat turning as dry and parched as the Mojave Desert. The State Department analyst's nervousness seemed to reach him like a hot desert wind.

"No, that much we've been able to determine. Unfortunately for the President, some of his leading supporters were at the launch site." A bead of perspiration rolled down the side of Brian McConnell's face and his glasses slipped further down his nose. He prayed this ordeal would end soon so he could go back to the hallowed halls of his office building, where a thousand sheets of paper awaited analysis.

"Do you think the political accord recently reached between the United States and the Russian Federation will be upset? In another day and age this accident might have been perceived as providential . . . however, the new President has been working to increase disarmament and improve relations with the United States along with the rest of the western world."

"Jerry, it's going to take months to assess the full impact of this tragedy. How the Russians will react, who moves up to fill the vacancies created by so many deaths, we simply can't predict what this situation is going to do to world-wide relations. In my opinion, the Russian Federation, as we know it, has been effectively destroyed. The glue holding the old guard together perished in that fire."

"Do you know the identities of those who were killed?"

"Not completely. We do, of course, monitor the comings and goings of many top officials." Brian McConnell reached into his jacket pocket and pulled out a piece of paper turned limp with perspiration. "This list is unofficial, but we have every reason to believe the following men died on the plains of Siberia:

> Donetsk Millerovo, Chief of the Combined Departments of the Military.
> Ivanovo Arzamas, highest ranking KGB officer in the Soviet Union; Balsahov Petrovich, a hero of the Soviet Army and one of the top

military advisors for defense.
Vassily Kharkov, an aide to Colonel Petrovich.
Vladimir Vlasov, the head of the Politoboro.
Nobokov Voinovich, Minister of Soviet Economic Restructure.
Nikolai Aksyonov, Chief Minister of the Department of Agricultural Development."

Amariah wished she knew what was so special about the travel papers Klaus' Russian friend provided. Crossing the border into China at Erenhot was suspiciously smooth. In fact, they were being treated like royalty. Assigned a soft berth compartment, they would be required to share their quarters with only two other passengers, at some point during the journey. For now, the conductor explained, the cubical, which was both a bedroom and sitting room, was for them alone. Any means of conveyance was always crowded in China. So many people journeying so many places.

The conductor smiled, folding the wide expanse of his flat, round face into crevasses as deep as the Himalayan passes in which his ancestors originated. He bowed respectfully and pointed in the direction of the dining car. Their travels would take them south to Datong and Beijing. From the nation's capital, they would pass through the Shandong province to Nanjing, then on to the coast toward their destination of Shanghai.

She dropped her bag against the lower berth and smiled at the little man who continued to bow and gesture toward the dining car reserved for foreign visitors and high-ranking government officials. In the passenger cars behind them, Amariah caught a glimpse of how an average Chinese citizen was transported across the length and breadth of their vast country. The hard seat section consisted of doorless compartments with six poorly padded bunks in three tiers. To the Chinese, lack of privacy was common. On the train, which carried its load of passengers toward the port city of Shanghai, privacy was impossible. Even the small room at the end of each car containing a sink, a mirror, and a hole in the floor over which passengers relieved themselves, didn't have a curtain.

Outside, a vendor tapped the window. Leon raised dirt-streaked glass and asked the price of freshly baked bread through hand gestures. Weeks of travel across Siberia taught them to purchase whatever they could from vendors who eked out a subsistence along the train's route. They stockpiled breads, fruits, and vegetables in their compartment to ward off the hunger which was the inevitable companion of travel through primitive areas.

With a final flourish, Leon concluded negotiations and smiled at a teenage girl. She handed him a dozen round, fist sized loaves of golden bread. Still warm, the aroma filled the compartment and memories of her mother's homemade bread lifted Amariah's spirits.

They watched with fascination as a cart mounted on bicycle wheels rolled up beside the train. Huge blocks of ice were lifted into a car Amariah assumed housed the kitchen serving first-class passengers. Poorer excursionists, they discovered, carried their meals with them or purchased what they could afford from the trackside vendors.

Amariah found Leon's camaraderie with the Chinese fascinating. He moved through the 'coach' section with complete assurance. Stopping to hold squirming children, chatting with the elderly, teasing the young, he became best friends with everyone on the train. Leon made it a practice to discover who among the travelers were the poorest and made certain they always had something to eat.

Perhaps it was his friendly manner which made the rigors of travel less difficult than the papers in his pocket. Always ready with a smile and a helping hand, he eased the burden of old women trying to board the train. At one point in their trip through Siberia he purchased tickets for two stranded musicians who ran out of money. Like most Buddhists, Leon believed goodness returned tenfold to the provider of alms.

"Hungry?" Leon handed Amariah a loaf of bread.

"I wasn't, but the smell reminds me of home." Taking the bread, she bit into it. "All I need is some butter and honey."

"Maybe if I go to the dining car I can find some."

"Don't be silly. This is fine." Amariah settled against the berth as the engine began to build pressure and clouds of steam obscured the track.

"The Chinese are the last of a dying breed." He pressed his face against the window, excited by the sight. "China is the only country in the world still using steam to power their trains."

Amariah smiled. Leon delighted her with information, which made the journey across the frozen tundra and primeval forest interesting, if not comfortable. She learned a lot about the history of the forbidding landscape during the ten days it took to span the breadth of Siberia. She loved to listen to Leon describe how the Tartar's lived, how they tamed wild Mogul ponies, how they marched across the steppes; conquering, wenching, leaving an indelible mark on history. He knew a great deal about the folklore of people who inhabited this brooding, haunting land. He related stories about descendants of those first, wild Tartars and the pioneers struggling to tame virgin land. Both tourists and Russians listened with rapt attention as he pointed out landmarks. Genghis Khan was the undisputed master of the steppes again in the imagination of passengers on the train. At times Amariah felt as if she might catch sight of a caravan of camels laden with spices and silks which brought fame and fortune to Marco Polo.

Although he stood head and shoulders taller than anyone else on the train and his sandy hair, fair skin and blue eyes made him a spectacle in the milling crowd, Leon socialized with the Chinese so effortlessly it seemed as if he'd lived in Mongolia his entire life.

The train began to pull away from the station. They were a week away from Shanghai, the port city on the Yellow Sea. A few hours on an airplane would see them in San Francisco and facing the uncertain future which lay ahead. Gone were the trappings of a way of life she embraced with all her heart. No longer could she look forward to a teaching position at St. Anne's. What was she going to do? Her goals had been so firm, so fixed, a change of direction never envisioned. Her unease grew intense as the village of Erenhot slipped away and the train headed into the heartland of China.

Leon chatted with other passengers in the dining car about the wonders of Datong and translated their conversation for Amariah. "The old man by the window says the Great Wall at Fengzhen, just beyond Datong, was critical to the Ming Dynasty because it defended a major Mongol entry route from the northwest. Behind the wall lay vast fortified garrisons and soldiers were assigned rotating tours of duty at the front-line forts. Some emperors granted them land around garrisons and they were encouraged to marry, raise a family, and spend their lives as soldier-farmers at these outposts. There were beacon towers atop every bluff. From them, sentries signaled the appearance of hostile troops by firing guns and burning a mixture of Sulphur, saltpeter, and wolf dung. The alarm, relayed from tower to tower, could reach the Forbidden City in Peking in a matter of hours!"

Amariah nodded at the old man, indicating she understood the story and was pleased he shared information about his country with her. During their long ride through Siberia, Leon spoke of the importance of body language. A genuine smile, a light in the eyes, a respectful bow could smooth their passage better than ruble or yen.

At Datong, an old man in a saffron robe boarded the train. A wispy mustache drooped toward a goatee comprised of a few gray hairs. His mustache framed a mouth that was only a slash through layers of wrinkled flesh. The monk's demeanor was so reproving men and women fortunate enough to be traveling in the soft berth section were quick to let him pass. If they wondered why a Shaolin monk, as ancient as his monastery, was traveling with privileged Chinese and western tourists, but none dared question him. The glowering spark in eyes half-hidden by scraggly brows and folds of skin stood as a tribute to the passage of years and silenced curiosity about his status.

The monk didn't reach for a ticket nor glance at the compartment number as he slid the door aside to enter the tiny room. Leon bowed, acknowledging the crimson robes and superiority of age.

Amariah stared at the scene slipping past the window, her face averted from the corridor. The monk settled himself on the berth opposite Amariah. She was so absorbed by an orchard of apple trees and rows of grain stalks, which cut an emerald swath through the deep brown loess soil of a fertile plateau, she didn't hear the compartment door open and close.

Leon started to engage in conversation, but the old man raised his hand--a command to remain silent.

Resting her chin in her hand, Amariah was making a valiant effort to digest the grandeur and beauty of a land which defied the absorption of western values for centuries. A farmer walked to his field carrying a spade crafted from branches; a willow basket swung back and forth, suspended from its handle. A thick quilted jacket, like the one his ancestors had worn since the Ming and Tang Dynasties ruled China, provided protection from the wind howling out of Mongolia.

Leon could hardly suppress his excitement. He was overjoyed at an unbelievable turn of luck to be sharing the compartment with a Shaolin monk. The old man seemed intent on not breaking Amariah's mood, but it was difficult to stifle questions which harried Leon's inquisitive mind.

Amariah felt relaxed, at home in China. Gone was the sensation of misgiving, which often accompanied the unfamiliar. She felt as if she had been in this part of China before. Suddenly, the presence of another person registered, and she turned from the window.

The old man had tucked his feet beneath crossed legs and his hands were pushed deep into the folds of a scarlet robe. His eyes were closed but he was not asleep; his body posture conveyed a sense of alertness totally misunderstood by the western world.

Amariah drew her hands together, placed them beneath her chin and bowed her head in homage. She spoke a single word. "*Sannyasi.*"

Feeling as if his heart had dropped out of his chest, Leon wondered where Amariah learned the word which meant *leader, master, exalted teacher*, in Sanskrit--the language of the enlightened ones in the ancient world. Leon gaped at Amariah. Her eyes were closed, her head still bowed. A bridge of understanding, a recognition so strong it was almost palpable, formed a link between the old man and the girl at the other side of the compartment. Holding his breath, Leon feared the slightest sound, the faintest movement might disturb what instinct announced was a moment of reunion.

As if by unspoken cue, both Amariah and the monk opened their eyes and gazed at each other with recognition reserved for a beloved friend.

"Young man," the monk addressed Leon in flawless English, "could you bring an old man a cup of tea?" He withdrew a packet of folded paper from inside his robe. "Use this, it was grown inside our monastery near Longmen. Bring each of us a cup. It will restore vigor to these old bones and reduce the stress travel has placed upon your bodies these past weeks."

The monk dropped the packet into Leon's outstretched hand, and he rushed from the compartment down the hallway toward the dining car.

"*Sannyasi*." Amariah formed the unfamiliar vowels and consonants with her lips as easily as those demanded by her native tongue.

"Daughter, knew you not that I would find you in your darkest hour? Has it not always been so?"

"Yes, Sannyasi, I knew you'd come." The words leaked from a chamber deep in her mind. Amariah knew this man--just as she knew Leon--from another place and time.

"Daughter, I am here to restore knowledge which has been hidden beneath layers of present memory. The gateway to the past must be reopened."

A tap at the door announced Leon's return. Amariah slid the door back and reached to take the cups of steaming water from his hands.

The monk stirred his tea, then sipped it cautiously. The interlude provided him with an opportunity to focus his thoughts. Taking a long draught, he swirled bits of leaf around the bottom of the cup. He seemed absorbed by the pattern created by the tea leaves. There was so much to tell. His job was to fit the key into the lock. It was the girl's responsibility to open the gate of memory. A hopeful sigh preceded words that found their way to his lips as he began the message to serve as a beacon to humanity. "The holy scriptures of the Hindus are called the Vedas and the Upanishads. Krishna, believed by the Hindus to be the reincarnation of Vishnu, the God of Supreme Spirit, recorded his message in the Bhagavad-Gita. 'When goodness grows weak, when evil increases, I make myself a body. In every age, I come back to deliver the holy, to destroy the sins of the sinner, to establish righteousness'."

The monk paused, and he scratched at a few straggly hairs in his goatee, his motion as strained as his desire to make Amariah understand.

"Twelve hundred years prior to the return of Lord Jesus, Moses led the Hebrews out of Egypt into the Promised Land. He gave his people the Ten Commandments and the Mosaic Code. Even though blessed with Hinduism and Judaism, the world continued to suffer the horror of war. Within a few years, some of the greatest minds in recorded history came to earth to stem the tide of ignorance, fear, and superstition. Within fifty-three years of each other, Lao-tse, Zoroaster, Buddha and Confucius were born."

The Shaolin monk watched Amariah, trying to determine if the importance of his message was registering. She leaned forward, listening, but the veil of uncertainty clouded her eyes. She hadn't grasped her spiritual identity, nor did she comprehend the role she was destined to play.

The old man continued, resolve dominated his tone of voice. "Lao-se founded the Taoist religion in China. This philosophy is based on living in harmony with the Impersonal Power controlling the Universe. Zoroaster was a Persian prophet, who centered his teachings around the one and only God. Lord Buddha taught universal good will was expressed from a heart of love. He counseled his followers to experience no anger, so they would suffer no ill. He understood lack, limitation, disease, and death are situations imposed upon existence by the human mind. Confucius believed the use of ethical ideas would help mankind put in practice the harmony and justice of the Universe."

The Shaolin priest bent forward, closing the space separating him from Amariah. His eyes conveyed urgency, his body expressed desperation; he had to make her understand! "The next great teacher was our Lord, Jesus. Like other religions developed around the ideology of an enlightened Master, his teachings soon shattered into a spectrum of different beliefs. Five hundred years after Jesus died, the world passed through an age of spiritual darkness. Wars, turbulence, invasions, plague, the break between the Western and Eastern Christian Churches resulted in the Crusades. Mohammed came to such an era. To stem the tide of human cruelty and barbarianism, he banned war and violence! But the hearts of the Muslin today are filled with anger! They twist the Prophet's words to inflame the minds of the oppressed."

Glancing at Leon, the monk decided the boy was well acquainted with the history of religion. Leon nodded his head in agreement, his eyes bright, his mind ready to pounce on unfamiliar information. The monk swirled his tea, then hurried on. "Between the fifteenth and eighteenth century, the Western world experienced four major occurrences. Trade was established between nations and commerce expanded. As the influence of the Catholic Church spread advances in art, literature and science were taken back to Europe when priests returned from foreign lands. This era boasted souls such as Leonardo da Vinci, Michelangelo, Rembrandt, Voltaire, Rousseau, Bacon, Shakespeare, Milton, Galileo, Newton and Copernicus!"

The sun was preparing to set, and it hung low against the sky--a reflecting temple of wisdom and knowledge. The retreating sphere cast a glow over Amariah's face. Her features appeared gilded. Amariah was special; he must awaken her gently so as not to sever the fragile grip her mind had on reality; he had to part the shroud of an unremembered past with care lest the girl slip from the physical. He'd witnessed the soul vacate the body before--a danger if too much was given too fast. "You may wonder what such a review of history has to do with you, my dear."

Amariah bobbed her head but found her voice incapable of a response.

"I recite this information only to illustrate how far away from the Source the world has traveled. We paid a serious price for experience, children, a serious price. But, at last, many long to return to our original state. People are not willing to endure the limitation demanded by our physical senses. We want to go home! We want to claim our birthright! We want to know who we are and why we are here!"

Leon couldn't contain his excitement any longer, he had to interrupt. Sensing the old man had the answer to questions which baffled him for years, he broke into the conversation. "Sannyasi, are you saying all great religions stem from the same source? Do you think all important religious leaders came to earth to bring a message of enlightenment to separate cultures when it was most needed?"

"I am saying that and more! One enlightened Mind channeled itself through different souls!"

Leon cupped his hands behind his head while he pondered the message. "Sannyasi, it is difficult to cast aside what I've been taught to believe all my life."

"Lady," a hand reached toward Amariah and intertwined her fingers between earthen colored, care-worn palms, "you came back to assume responsibilities of tremendous importance."

The chill ravaging her body as the old man's touch set off a firestorm of reaction. Amariah opened her mouth to protest, but the monk held up an admonishing hand--demanding silence--commanding obedience. "Hear me out! I have awaited your coming all my life. It falls to me, you see, to convince you of your identity."

Amariah could refrain no longer. The argument going on inside ruptured, the magma of doubt melted the barriers of resistance. "But--I am nothing! I am a woman of common intelligence. I have no mystical talents, no inspiring virtues! Why me?" Amariah's eyes were pleading, the desperation filling her expression softened the monk's heart. He squeezed her hand, trying to assure her, pouring the balm of enlightenment on a troubled heart.

"You have only to turn inward and listen to the voice that speaks within, the sound you hear at the center of your heart. It will answer your question. You must follow the dictates of that inner voice. You know what must be done. This is my message—never turn back! Have courage! Do what you know is right!"

A subtle feeling stole through Leon's consciousness; it slipped down his spine and wrapped its way around his solar plexus--Amariah and the monk needed to be alone. He left the compartment and headed toward the dining car to replenish their cups with hot water for more tea.

Eyes as dark as a cave beneath the sea glowed with intensity, the inner fire of conviction and purpose. Wispy hairs, which fell from the old man's chin, trembled as he studied Amariah. He placed his fingertips in the center of her forehead.

Images, like movie trailers, flashed through Amariah's mind. A woman, a midwife, holding a screaming infant in the air; the umbilical cord still pulsating. A woman leaving the man she loved--a prince. A parting filled with anguish. A woman traveling across an immense, uninhabited desert, her heart filled with grief at leaving everything familiar. The haunting sound of camel bells echoing off the hard, rocky ground, pounded in her hears. A man, a teacher, imparting wisdom as she sat beside the banks of a wide, wide river. A boy stands alone amid scorning elders. His back is straight, his stance rigid, challenging the priests who berate him. The boy is ready now. Their journey must begin.

Whirling, scenes shifted rapidly, too swift for comprehension. An old woman alone, her hand shielding her eyes from the desert sun. He needed her now--more than ever. A storm, black clouds, hail hurled against the ground. Gone. Her beloved student, gone.

Amariah stared out the window; a full moon hovered above the horizon, streamers of cold, reflective light tipped the earth's fragile crust. Flooded rice paddies mirrored a thousand different moons. A water buffalo pulled the cart of its master homeward, toward a group of huts further down the road. She stared at the land, felt its benevolence, and was stirred by the people who called it home.

"Here we are." The door slid back, and Leon bustled into the room. "Amariah, where's the monk?"

Amariah turned a questioning gaze to Leon. "I don't know."

"I'll find him. Perhaps he went to the dining car, or maybe he's looking for the commode."

Moments later, Leon burst into the compartment. "He's not on the train!"

"That's impossible. He's probably in the hard berth section."

"I looked. Amariah, he's not on this train!"

"But--we haven't made any stops. He must be somewhere."

"An old man wearing a scarlet robe would be pretty hard to miss in this crowd. We haven't made any stops since he boarded, nor does the schedule call for any other stops for the next several hours."

Her words were quietly spoken but her voice conveyed anguish. "An ancient monk comes out of nowhere, tells me I'm going to be involved something I don't understand, conjures incredible visions I have no way to explain, then disappears?" Tears of frustration filled her eyes as she searched for an answer to events that seemed dream-like, out of sequence, haunting-- yet incredibly familiar.

"Amariah," Leon put his arm around her shoulders, "I don't have an explanation either. The monk said, 'there are far more things in this world than mankind can presently understand'. Maybe his disappearance is a message. Maybe he wants us to have faith in the unseen, the unexplainable."

The moon crawled over the treetops, filling the tiny compartment with silver light and pendant shadows. From the corner of his eye, Leon saw something lying on the padded cot, where the old man had been sitting. Perhaps he'd forgotten it and would return.

Leon reached for it. A hiss of surprise escaped his lips as his thoughts slid into a realm where logic and reason had no value. "I don't believe it!"

"What?" Amariah reached to take the object from Leon's hand. Emotion roiled through her consciousness, then stopped with the suddenness of a Wagnerian crescendo terminating in one last, thunderous note. A coin, an exact match to the two in her possession, rested in the palm of her hand. The coin felt warm. The coin was warm! It had been carried by a human being whose blood coursed through arteries and veins, whose chest expanded and contracted with air. The monk was not an illusion! He was a flesh and blood man, not an apparition. The words of the poem took unchallenged ownership of her thoughts.

'*The third coin will be brought by a man who possess the wisdom of the ages*'.

If the Shaolin monk's message were true, mankind was on a collision course with a whole new way of thinking. She was frightened and confused. She could no longer rely on the foundation of a faith that was firm, unchanging, ever guiding. If the monk was right, history would have to be rewritten and schools of thought, which had existed for thousands of years, abandoned. Withdrawing the folded scrap of leather from beneath the velvet padding at the bottom of her wooden box, Amariah reread the poem for the thousandth time.

This coin is for a woman called Amariah who has journeyed out of the past.

Fate forged her destiny, now truly, the first shall be the last.

Her calling, the world will know, because five Coins will be placed in her hands.

The second Coin a man of honor holds, he will help her journey across distant lands.

The third Coin will be brought by a man who possesses the wisdom of the ages.

The fourth Coin, guarded by a man at home, will be displayed amid archaic pages.

The Evil One defiles the fifth Coin and do battle with him she must.

Or an age of darkness will consume the world with murder, hatred, and misbegotten lust.

The light of truth must burn bright and clear—it cannot be allowed to falter!

Amariah, woman of destiny, the fate of the world you are here to alter!

Three coins lay in her hand. She was guided to the first one by the spirit of the Medieval Jesuit, Adamus. Leon discovered the second coin on an archaeological dig near the ancient city of Bagdad and carried it in his pocket for years. The third coin, left by a Shaolin monk, who disappeared from a train crossing the heartland of China, forced her to suspend belief in everything she thought was true.

CHAPTER EIGHTEEN

The wing of the museum built for *Messiah*, laboratories and restoration rooms had been vacant for hours. Main frames containing magnetically encoded historical documentation, research material, and articles written by the archaeological team, were silent. A gloved hand inserted a key into the lock on the outside door. No alarm sounded in the command post, no television camera tracked him as he made his way through shadow draped hallways.

He inserted another key in the door to Sister Magdalene's lab. Moving swiftly, he unscrewed cables connecting a video display screen to the hard drive. Just as quickly, he reattached different cables to the nun's monitor.

No one would ever know an exchange was made. After screwing a plate imprinted with the monitor's serial number assigned to Sister Magdalene's lab, the man stood back, satisfied with his handiwork. He slid the monitor back into position and glanced around the lab again.

Everything was in order. If anyone investigated the Sister's death, they would find nothing out of place. No one could trace the plutonium coated electrostatic deflection plates in the monitor. Agitated electrons bounced against these deflector plates and bathed Sister Magdalene in radiation as she worked at her computer. Long hours caused her to succumb more quickly than he anticipated, but fortunately, the nun completed the *Messiah* program, which would allow the Father General to feed or eliminate information to virtually every databank in the world. Locking the door behind him, the man with a monk's cowl pulled over his face slipped through shadows to a car parked outside the Porta Sant'Anna.

Dumpsters and trash bins throughout the city would soon contain bits and pieces of plutonium coated plates. No dumpster or garbage can would contain enough radiation to attract notice. Father Julian survived the CIA by being cautious. He left no telltale signs, no traceable clues, nothing to lead to Andrew Simson, his Savior and salvation.

"Your story boggles my mind!" Richard Weatherby sagged against a kitchen chair. He stared out the window overlooking a bank of hydrangeas Liz tended with loving care. Beyond, vibrant green grass stretched toward a stand of pines, whose boughs drooped with the grace of an angel's wing. He glanced up at his wife, observing the kindness he took for granted after thirty years of marriage as she replenished his coffee, cream, and sugar. "I just can't believe it!" A silver spoon clattered against the rim of a china saucer as he grappled with his thoughts.

"Dr. Weatherby," Klaus searched for a way to explain the sequence of events so astonishing it shook the foundation of Richard Weatherby's structured world.

"Please--call me Dick. This is hardly the time for formalities," Richard interrupted.

"All right, Dick. We've spoken to Carole Phillips. She's on her way here from New York. She stopped at her publisher's office to pick-up some negatives she smuggled out of Rome. Amariah suspected someone was tampering with the translated manuscripts, so Carole took the precaution of photographing various documents in their original state."

"And Amariah will be here within the week?" Richard Weatherby's eyes searched Klaus' face. He trusted the German, but sought physical clues, which might betray him--eyes straying in the wrong direction, hands revealing nervous tension, a tongue which tripped over simple syllables, if he were not a man of his word.

"If everything went as planned. Balsahov Petrovich was certain they would pass through Russia and China without incident because of the travel papers he prepared for them."

Unable to contain his frustration, Richard struck the table with the flat of his hand. "For God's sake--why Russia! Why China? Why didn't Amariah just get on a plane and head for San Francisco?"

"Dr. Weatherby, we hoped it was the last thing Simson would expect. Your daughter has information with the potential to challenge Simson's plans." Klaus rubbed his forehead. He couldn't rid himself of an unspeakable apprehension which made his head pound and his stomach churn. When he heard Petrovich's name on the list of Russians, who died in the accident at the space center in Siberia, an unnerving feeling one of Simson's Jesuits was behind the catastrophe dogged his thoughts.

"John Preston suspected Amariah's work in the Archive might reveal startling information. But why on earth would Amariah's work play a part in his plan for world domination? It seems farfetched."

Her coffeepot crashed into the sink despite Elizabeth's attempt to catch it. The sound of breaking glass shattered her attempt to remain calm as surely as if a speeding bullet destroyed the carafe. She turned toward the table, eyes blazing, the light from the kitchen window magnifying tears, which could no longer be suppressed by will. "Because she's special, that's why!" Elizabeth's shoulders squared as she confronted her husband with a truth he didn't want to accept. "From the moment she opened her eyes, I knew she was here for a purpose. I knew it the second she was placed in my arms." Tears of anger and fear brimmed, then rolled unchecked down Elizabeth's cheeks as she picked up shards of glass.

Richard got up, his eyes trained on his wife's heaving shoulders. He encircled her waist and she turned, pressing her face into his chest. "Liz, we'll put our heads together and find a solution."

"That's why we're here, Dr. Weatherby . . . uh, Dick." Anna tilted the coffee cup, sloshing its remains back and forth. "The poem said Amariah would find the fourth coin at home—that has to mean it's somewhere in San Francisco."

"We don't have any items of antiquity." Elizabeth dried her tears with the hand towel she removed from the oven handle.

She extracted a tissue from a box on the counter, blew her nose, then dabbed at continuing tears with another. The days ahead were going to require clear thinking, her emotions needed to be controlled if she was going to be of any value to her daughter. "All of you can stay with us. We have plenty of room and besides, you'll be safe here. I just hope Carole reaches us without incident."

"You needn't worry." Klaus smiled, happy to turn the conversation away from his concerns over Amariah's safety. "Carole Phillips made a name for herself during Viet Nam. The woman is incredible--she parachuted into hot zones with Airborne Rangers. She's weapons qualified and carries a Sig Saeur!"

"Still," Richard's eye sought the window again, his expression apprehensive. "I took the precaution of alerting the Chief of Police, who happens to be a friend of mine. I told him prowlers might be in our neighborhood again. After the last incident, I had an alarm system installed that's wired into the police station. Between the electronic surveillance and our dog, we're pretty secure."

Damascus lifted his head, surveying the strangers at the table, then rose and crossed the floor to Anna. She began to rub a sensitive spot between his ears. "Amariah said you liked to be scratched right here." Baleful eyes lifted toward the dark-haired woman. A whine like whale song filled the kitchen. "She'll be here soon, don't worry."

The dog stalked to the door, his shoulders and hips swinging one way, his mid-section the other. Anyone attempting to enter the house would have to pass him first; the genetic code of his breed impelled the dog to stand guard and protect his family. Muscle and sinew in his legs and shoulders rippled beneath a coat of slick black fur. His ears were cocked forward listening for sounds alien to his environment.

Klaus scooted his chair sideways to admire the dog. "Has Damascus had special training?"

Richard reached for the box of tissues and blew his nose. His eyes watered and his sinus cavities poured mucus down the back of his throat, but it wasn't a reaction to pollen, it was pure, raw emotion; fear his daughter was in trouble and there was nothing he could do to prevent it. "It's his heritage. Roman soldiers trained his ancestors to fight with them."

"Rottweilers were bred in a village not far from where I grew up in Germany.

"Oh?" Elizabeth finished brewing another pot of coffee and she poured everyone a fresh cup.

"According to legend," Klaus scooped a spoonful of sugar into his cup and began to stir, "Romans brought the dogs with them when they crossed the Alps to conquer the Visigoths. These powerful animals not only herded cattle, which supplied the soldiers with their food, but they were war dogs. It would be intimidating to meet upraised swords, shields and a pack of snarling, snapping jaws! Rottweilers remained an important part of the cattle industry in the valley of Rott for generations. When Germany suffered a severe economic depression right after World War I the breed almost died out."

"I didn't know that!" Richard looked at Damascus with concern. To think the proud, determined beast might have been lost to succeeding generations was a sobering thought.

"I always wanted one, but I traveled so much it didn't seem fair to have a dog and be away from home for long stretches. Now that I have plans to settle down, maybe I'll get one." Klaus took Anna's hand, admiration transformed his normally inscrutable expression into something soft and sensitive as his glance settled on the woman he adored.

Elizabeth saw the look that passed between them. Her mood turned melancholy as she wondered whether Amariah would ever know such happiness--or if her daughter's life was going to be one of shouldering such immense responsibility it precluded the simple joys of life: a loving husband, children of her own.

Damascus lifted his head; nostrils flared, ultra-sensitive olfactory receptors scanned the air wafting up the driveway. His growl interrupted the conversation. Richard went to the door, looked out, but saw nothing. Patting the Rottweiler's head, he tried to sound confident. "She's on her way home Damascus, she'll be here soon . . . very soon."

A man dressed in blue coveralls stepped out of a telephone company van. The Air Italia jumbo jet was in line for take-off at the Leonardo Di Vinci Airport, across the field from where a generic looking van was parked. Thick leather gloves protected his hands from rough cables telephone repairmen handled and sheathed the fingers opening the van's rear doors. Leaping inside, the man took a seat at a computer console. His face, redefined by many surgeries, contained cold gray eyes which scanned blinking lights and digital read-outs on all the electronic equipment lining one side of the cargo bay. Punching in a set of coordinates, one of the screens started to display cascading numbers. The roof slid back, and a disc lifted through the opening. As the sun began to set, a crimson glow spread throughout the darkened interior—making the van look cancerous.

Settling deeper, Paul Grant adjusted his weight, preparing for the force of gravity which would press him against a luxurious first-class seat as the plane took off. He smiled at the flight attendant fastening her seat belt, in the hope he would be the first one served a welcoming cocktail when the plane reached cruising altitude. Once relaxed, he would catch a few hours of sleep--his wife had a round of appointments all set up with various real estate agents anxious to be of service to an up-and-coming executive at Microsoft. He winked at the girl and smiled. Rome had been fruitful.

As the jet rolled into take-off position, the digital display rolled numbers downward, and the disc aligned with the jet's path down the runway. The man watched the aircraft's progress on television screens in the console. Slowly, deliberately, the disc adjusted its position by a few degrees, then dipped. A metal arm protruding from the disc's center took aim at the cockpit as the plane gathered the momentum required to sever the restraining bond of gravity.

Acceleration matched Paul Grant's excitement as he thought about his new position and the status it would provide. His wife wanted a house overlooking the country club golf course, but Paul thought what she described in a more exclusive section of town was more prestigious.

Giant tires drew into the cavity of the jetliner's body to eliminate drag. At the crucial moment, the point when pilots know there is no possibility of a safe return to earth, all electronic circuitry in the jumbo jet stopped functioning.

There was also the matter of what kind of car to drive. He needed to purchase something to exude status yet not be ostentatious. He had to enter the corporate world cautiously, he couldn't afford to tread too hard, too fast. The co-pilot and pilot exchanged disbelieving glances as the on-board computer system, programmed to judge air speed, rate of climb, the velocity of thrust provided by four massive Rolls Royce engines, the weight of the plane, its cargo, and passengers, stopped feeding information to the instrument panel. Every dial, each digital read-out, all gages dropped to zero. No controls responded, landing wheels were frozen midway into the cavity, the rudder was dead, wing flaps, which were fully extended to promote lift, demanded the plane return to earth. The flying boat, which was a marvel of circuitry and design, fell to the ground like a twenty-ton rock.

Feeling the lurch, Grant's eyes flew to the face of the stewardess--seeking assurance instinct warned him wouldn't be there. Her eyes widened, and she threw her body forward; arms covering her head in a survival posture ingrained through countless hours of training. Eyes open, Paul Grant had no time to close them against the searing wall of orange, which turned his vision liquid as his corneas melted in the heat. There was no time to release the seat belt trapping him against a nylon seat cover so hot it burned through his jacket and fused into his skin. The jet fuel explosion dissolved the tissue in his lungs as he made a last, desperate scream of anguish against what almost was; a horrifying cry against the certainty he was going to die in an incinerator; a furious wail signifying he would never enjoy the goodness of the life ahead.

The man stepped outside the van, seeking a better view of the crash than a small black and white screen provided. Impact came with a shudder as tarmac resisted the aircraft's assault. Using the back door of the van as a shield, the man protected himself from flying objects hurled through the air. Pieces of red-hot metal, parts of human bodies, bits of luggage and drops of burning fuel rained down from the sky when the plane belly-flopped on the runway and exploded. He shielded the scars on his face from searing heat, as high-octane fuel sent black, mushrooming clouds with underbellies of red, soaring above the runway.

He watched flames devour the plane and smiled as smoke billowed skyward in a gigantic funnel. Sirens screaming, rescue equipment raced toward the burning coffin. It was time to leave--his work was done.

Walking to the front of the van, he slipped a note beneath the windshield wiper. A crude red outline of a hand made the crash appear as if Italy's extreme terrorist group, the Red Brigade, claimed responsibility for this tragedy and the theft of the Electromagnetic Pulse Generator. One glance assured him everyone on board was dead. If any passengers or crew hadn't died on impact, flames would rapidly consume any unlucky survivors.

When the public learned a stolen military weapon caused the failure of the jet's computer system, a cry of outrage was certain to be heard around the world. Deadly instruments, used as weapons against a civilian population, had been the topic of debate since terrorists began to turn impotent rage against the innocent. Liberals and conservatives alike would inflame the press with rhetoric over loss of civilian life.

A twisted smile drew the corners of a ravaged face into a grimace as he walked toward the awaiting car. Paul Grant's end was swift and merciless. Andrew Simson's secret was safeguarded forever by an avenging ball of flame.

"Ah, Dr. Rubtsovsky, thank you for coming to Rome." Andrew Simson extended his hand toward the Russian.

Rubtsovsky took his hand and held it a moment longer than necessary. "I wasn't aware it was an invitation. Being removed from my lab by government officials seemed more like a summon."

Peeling back taut lips, Andrew Simson forced a weak smile. "We have a lot to talk about. Together, we can achieve social transformation."

The parapsychologist was not picking up good feelings; Simson was surrounded by darkness. A single spark of light came from the coin-like object the priest stroked with a lover's caress.

"I've heard of your discoveries and would like to know more. With the disturbance that has taken place in Russia these past few weeks, I thought it prudent to extract you. If the method was harsh, you have my sincere apology."

Rubtsovsky's eyebrows arched. "I wasn't aware the Vatican worked with those who manage our internal affairs."

Returning to his desk, Andrew Simson sat down and waved the

scientist into the other chair. "The Church has many well-placed friends throughout the world."

"Your detractors are certainly diminishing."

The Father General took a hard look at the Russian. Although small, Rubtsovsky carried himself with an air of confidence and inner security seldom found in shorter men. "God moves in mysterious ways. Tell me, Stephanov, do you believe in a Higher Power, a Force that guides the destiny of mankind?"

"I do." The statement was simple, spoken softly and without hesitation.

"In a political environment which has done its best to smother a belief in God?"

Rubtsovsky settled back. He kept his fingers flared and let them drop ahead of the arms of his chair; testing, checking, sorting impulses and feelings drifting across the desk. "I dedicated my life to the workings of the human mind. In pursuit of understanding, I studied all great religious philosophies--Muslim, Hindu, Christianity, Judaism, Confucianism, even the Born-Again movement. I also examined traditions left behind by the mystery schools in Egypt, Greece, and Tibet. These ancient schools led me to investigate cases of modern-day 'psychic' phenomenon reported by people all over the globe."

Interrupting, Andrew Simson could hardly contain his impatience. "And, what do these extensive studies lead you to believe?"

"There is a force, a power, an intelligence, governing the action and reaction of each part and particle of our universe."

"You speak in riddles!"

Stormy eyes swept across a body sequestered behind strained ambivalence. He studied the expression on Andrew Simson's face. The Father General was acting, playing a part on the world stage. Receptors in the right side of his brain screamed an alarm. Simson was not to be trusted!

Simson rolled the coin between his fingers, seeking solace, comfort. Random thoughts turned cohesive when he held it tight. Ideas which were only pinpoints the moment before focused like a laser beam when the coin rested in his hand. Rubtsovsky was far more than he expected, the Father General sensed he was playing a game of mental chess with a man who was a master. One slip, one word out of character, and the imaginary chessboard between them would be tipped--pieces of logic hopelessly scattered. The game must be played with caution or Rubtsovsky would not reveal the secrets he alone possessed. "Your words paint a cloudy picture."

Rubbing his goatee with the palm of his hand, Rubtsovsky spread his fingers wide. His hand aligned with the Father General's face, but it appeared as if the gesture was a response to an annoying itch. He didn't like the sensation clawing at his stomach--the path of warning snaked across his chest and radiated down his arm. Cautiously, carefully, the Russian lowered his hands to his lap. He had gathered all the information he needed. Glancing about the room, he began to search for an avenue of escape. "The mind is far more complex than the brain."

Scorn deepened the ravines lining the area around the Father General's mouth. "Pray, tell me, how is it men of science have overlooked such an obvious fact?"

Rubtsovsky smiled, he was accustomed to dealing with doubters, scoffers, men of science blinded by the limitations of the physical. "As the Ancient Egyptians believed: You have a brain, you are a mind!"

Drawing up sharply, Simson checked his sudden outburst. He had to make this man trust him, he had to get Rubtsovsky to teach him the skills it took to unlock secrets hidden away in folds of the cerebral cortex. "Perhaps I will come to an understanding after we've had more opportunity to talk. Father Andropov tells me you can sense things through your hands--that you can pick up an object and decipher information about the person who owns it."

"As can anyone trained to recognize individual signals." Rubtsovsky's eyes flitted about the room, examining windows, wondering where the hallway led, considering his chances of survival should he bolt from the chair.

"Can you explain how such a miracle is possible?" The Father General relaxed deep into his chair and clasped his hands behind his head--a motion meant to portray confidence and interest.

Escape was impossible. Perhaps he could use his power of persuasion to convince the Father General his concept for the future was misguided. Turning thoughtful, Rubtsovsky allowed his eyes to drift downward. He seemed to study wooden planks, and molding covering the angle where the wall joined the floor. He searched his memory for the words to use to convince Simson he was on the wrong, very wrong, path. "Our true potential has lain untapped since the dawn of recorded time. Instead, science concentrated on our physical world. True power cannot be measured or monitored. The degree of consistency science seeks when searching for a way to control the human mind will never be discovered! We must develop new methods of exploring our potential. The mind is as individual as a fingerprint and no two impressions, glimpses into unseen dimensions beyond the physical, will ever be the same."

"Are you suggesting science cannot develop a statistical pattern to psychic phenomenon?"

Rubtsovsky sat straight up in the chair. Casting aside his initial feelings about the Father General, the scientist was delighted Simson grasped his meaning. Perhaps there was hope. "Yes! That's exactly what I'm saying. Answers to questions, which seem beyond knowing, are readily at hand. But, you see, the mind communicates in symbols!"

"Turn your words into something real, something I can relate to, something I've seen or heard before." Simson studied the other man's face. There was a light in his eyes that hadn't been there moments before. Interest in a subject, which earned the Russian the scorn of his peers, would allay Rubtsovsky's fears; it would lower his shield of resistance. "Gathering information is as simple as understanding the impressions conjured up by the mind?"

"As simple and as difficult! Learning to de-code the message is often a frustrating task. Much self-examination must be undertaken before you can truly understand what the right side of the brain is trying to convey."

"So," the Father General reached to pick up the old coin lying on the desk between them, "you think everyone's brain can provide them with unlimited information about any subject?"

"Everyone has potential once they understand how their brain processes information."

"Tell me what this coin reveals." He pitched the coin at Rubtsovsky.

Catching it deftly, the scientist examined the markings. "This is very old."

"We have every reason to think it might have been minted around the time of Christ."

"Yes." Clasping the coin between the palm of his hands, Rubtsovsky breathed deeply then slowed his intake of air, slower, then slower again. "This coin has passed through many hands, many times. It was not used for monetary purposes; rather, it was an important symbol. An organization, a group of people, used this object for identification. To possess it meant you were one of the elect, one of the chosen. I sense the crossed daggers represent the group of zealots who were active in Jesus' time—the Sacari. The other side undoubtedly represents the Tree of Life, which would have represented Jesus and his mission.

He fell silent; his face registered a change of inner vision and his expression contorted as he struggled to analyze incoming information. Tapping his head, the Russian appeared to listen to some distant, interior sound. Finally, he smiled. "Ah, it is clear now. I did not understand the image, nor the sensation in the bottom of my stomach. I beheld a woman dressed in white. This woman was Jesus' teacher."

Andrew Simson felt like someone of immense strength squeezed the air from his lungs. As his diaphragm lurched upward, his elbows struck the desktop with such force the sound echoed through the room, but Rubtsovsky didn't seem to notice.

Rubtsovsky spoke again, words tumbling from him like a stream rushing over a precipice. A woman has returned to earth many times. She helped steer mankind in positive directions through other ages. Jesus was not the only student she prepared to teach the world, she . . ." The scientist stopped in mid-sentence, his face assumed a pinched, drawn expression as he wrestled with a message that could neither be seen, nor heard, nor felt by anyone other than himself. He shuddered, his chest rising and falling rapidly as the enormity of what he sensed settled across a resisting mind. "She's here now!"

Jumping up, Rubtsovsky paced the room, unable to contain his passion. His thoughts hammered the content of an unexpressed prayer into dust before it could be spoken; his mouth went dry, and words clung to his parched lips and tongue like a man searching for water in the desert. He whirled, stabbing an admonishing finger at the Father General. "This girl saved mankind from iniquity in other ages, and she will do so again!" His eyes swept the room as he searched how to describe the visceral feeling tearing his guts apart. "With the Ancients and again in Judea." The shadow of retribution glimmered in his eyes, like a prophet of old commanded his thoughts, "You sought to slay Him, to destroy Him before He came to power."

Andrew Simson felt a veil lower across his vision. He could no longer tell night from day. A dam broke on some dark interior level and rage consumed him. He leaped around the desk, snatching the coin from the Russian's hand. His motions fueled by fury, his strength that of a hundred men. He grabbed Rubtsovsky by the front of his coat and slapped him . . . again and again.

The Father General's ring smashed delicate flesh against teeth turned to weapons; a sudden gush of blood stained his knuckles. Another slap knocked the glasses from the scientist's head, but Rubtsovsky locked his knees and stood steadfast against raining blows.

Emotion flooded the Russian's body; a surreal calm pervaded his senses. He knew Simson intended to kill him. "Do to me what you will but the power of righteousness flows in this woman!"

As if looking thru a window of nightmare and illusion, Andrew Simson watched his fingers close around Stephanov Rubtsovsky's thin neck. It was easy to apply a pressure that crushed, destroyed, that was something beyond human. The Russian's face turned a sickly gray, his eyes bulged out of their sockets and his tongue lolled grotesquely against the side of his mouth. The warm, pink color of life retreated. In its wake, the sickly pallor morticians worked to disguise claimed his skin. The film of death lowered over Rubtsovsky's eyes, reducing once sparkling orbs to flat, dull spheres. A living, breathing, thinking man was reduced to flesh, blood and bone--a mere container for the departed soul. And like a sack stripped of its contents, the body lost its form.

The shroud of anger clouding Andrew Simson's mind lifted, and he let go of the Russian scientist. Running his hands through his hair, the Father General's glance darted around the room. Darkness pressed against the windows, Simson's thoughts focused on a different direction as he realized he would have to get rid of the scientist's body. Shadows looming from every bush and building would conceal his entrance into the catacombs. Slinging the small man over his shoulder without ceremony or compassion, Simson rushed down a stairwell. He paused at the outer doors, checking to make certain none of the Swiss Guards were close. Deciding no one was around to observe his flight, Simson rushed across the courtyard to the gate separating him from the entrance to the catacombs.

Time passed as if in a slow-moving dream. After what seemed like hours of twisting and turning through the maze of corridors which honeycombed the earth, he stopped before an empty crypt. Strength provided by fury and fear enabled him to stuff Rubtsovsky's body inside a gravesite prepared for some anonymous early Christian. Placing his shoulder against a large slab of stone, which once sealed the chamber from the corridor, he shoved it across a narrow opening. Tomorrow, he would give instructions for the tunnel to be sealed. All traces of the Russian would be consigned to the earth from whence Christians believed they would rise again. With Rubtsovsky's death, the secrets of the mind, which could have changed the destiny of humanity, were lost. But, he had protected his mission, his calling--and that was all that mattered.

Damascus rooted his nose beneath Elizabeth's arm and gave her a nudge. Awake, she looked at the clock. It was half past two. The dog was being assertive, but not aggressive. Elizabeth decided he wanted to go outside to relieve himself. Over the years she learned the various nuances of the dog's nearly human behavior. Tossing back her covers, she swung her legs to the floor. The Rottweiler pressed against the back of her knee, urging her to hurry. He padded down the hall as she slipped on her robe. Waiting impatiently, he stood beside the front door. Strange, she thought, the backyard was more his territorial domain.

Pursing her lips, Elizabeth made a few soft, clucking sounds to coax him into the kitchen. Ears cocked square, chest thrust forward, feet spread in the solid fashion unique to his breed—the dog's eyes never strayed from the door facing the street. It was as if he could see through the thick oak planks--he seemed to be watching something beyond.

Elizabeth quietly opened the front door. She paused to watch the Rott instead of returning to bed. He did not stop to sniff at any of the bushes or trees in the yard. He marched straight to the wrought iron gate shielding the Weatherby property from street traffic. Standing at full alert, Damascus' attention was fixed on the road.

Beyond the penumbra cast by the porch light, interlocking shadows of pine trees wove a pattern of shifting darkness. Lawn and shrubs were lost to a blanket of fog, which rolled in from the ocean during the night. She could barely make out the stub of the dog's tail. It was extended skyward, his hind legs planted, prepared to launch his massive body forward. He always stood by the gate and watched the street when he sensed Amariah was on her way home.

Elizabeth felt her heart hammer-slam. They'd had no word, no telegram to alert them. Yet Damascus peered into the fog as if responding to a telepathic summon. Slipping outside, she clutched the robe beneath her chin. Damp fingers of ghost-like fog invaded the marrow of her bones.

The dog's ears flicked, the only sign he sensed Elizabeth walking up behind him. Straining to see down the street, she peered through the iron bars of the gate. Quaint streetlights cast halos through the mist.

Damascus' tail began to switch. Searching, Elizabeth tried hard to detect movement, sound, something to alert her to what the dog sensed. Suddenly, the animal stood erect, using the gate as a brace for his forepaws. Nearly as tall as his mistress, the Rott quivered; he emitted a haunting whine. Out of the fog two figures emerged. They trudged up the steep hill, their footsteps weary. Damascus pawed at the gate, anxious to have the restraining barrier pushed aside. Elizabeth could see the figures plainly now. A man and a woman approached carrying suitcases. The Rott turned toward Elizabeth, his liquid brown eyes pleading with her to open the gate.

As she lifted the latch Damascus bounded into the street. He gave vent to a deep-throated rumble, Elizabeth saw the smaller figure lower the suitcase and drop to her knees. The most welcome sound she ever heard reached Elizabeth's ears as her daughter's voice greeted the excited Rottweiler.

"Damascus! Oh, Damascus--how I've missed you!"

Elizabeth sped down the street--arms open wide.

Richard Weatherby reached across the table and squeezed his daughter's hand for the hundredth time that morning. Anna and his wife were busy clearing away the remains of an early morning breakfast. Klaus was outside smoking his pipe. He and Leon sat on the patio--the Rottweiler between them. As Richard stared out the bay window at the two men, he decided John Preston was right--his daughter had been in capable hands.

Damascus leaned against Leon, his enormous head taking up most of the young man's lap; a portrait of pleasure with closed eyes, the dog reflected his joy at being scratched. Carole and Amariah were busy examining the black and white prints the photographer extracted from her briefcase. Richard glanced up as Leon and Klaus returned to the kitchen. With the table cleared and the dishwasher running, it was time to address an uncertain future.

A few hours of sleep in her own bed with her dog at her side renewed Amariah. Her mind was clear, her body pulsated with a kind of static energy; she was ready to face the events ahead. Now that the evidence was in one place, spread across her mother's kitchen table, the portent was alarming. Photographs of centuries old documents silently demanded she right the wrongs of history. The tissue of lies had been torn, exposing the naked reality of a truth which lay beneath a thick layer of deceit.

"I've been thinking about this whole situation for the past several days." Klaus put his arm around the back of Anna's chair, and she inched closer, drawn into the shelter he provided against a world of hurt and rejection. "Simon's use of the press is unprecedented. No one, not even your President Kennedy, ever wielded a more subtle or formidable campaign to win public opinion."

Anna reached for a picture, her nails were short and no longer brightly polished. "He fooled a lot of us. I, for one, took pride in my ability to spot a charlatan. In my younger years, I was seduced by every lothario in Europe, who wanted access to my father's money. Andrew Simson reeled me in--but it's still hard to accept a leader of the Catholic Church has world domination on his agenda."

"But Anna," Leon absently gathered the few stray crumbs lying on the tablecloth and dropped them into the saucer beneath his coffee cup, "the Church is the perfect blind! What better way to mask your true intentions than to make it seem like you have the welfare of mankind at heart? Stir in aid to disaster victims, temper your audience with emotional interviews, which make you seem paternal, and a society that's desperate for leadership will endorse a man they've been convinced is the new 'Good Shepherd' of the ages!"

Shifting sheets of photographic paper back and forth, Carole interrupted. "Anna, you weren't taken in any more than the rest of us. We all got involved with Simson's madness. If it hadn't been for Amariah, I would never have examined what was taking place behind his charade."

To lift the mood, which settled over the emotions of everyone at the table, Elizabeth spoke softly as she refilled the cups with coffee. "I think self-recrimination should be put to rest. It would be far more productive if everyone turns their energies toward deciding what to do next."

Richard wiped the corners of his mouth and tossed the napkin on the table. His wife never ceased to amaze him; she had an uncanny ability to bring events into focus with a few well-chosen words. "Liz, you're right! Anyone got any thoughts? Simson has quite a head start on public opinion, but people are basically smart! They'll recognize fraud when evidence is presented. We just need to decide how to take the story public."

Klaus rested his chin in his hand, thoughtfulness elongated his features and rings of weariness created bruised crescents beneath his eyes. "If we can interest *The Chronicle* the story will get picked up by the international news wire. I'm certain the information Amariah has will generate its own momentum once it's out in the open."

"How so?" Carole was no stranger to journalism, but she didn't share Klaus' certainty about the results.

"Think about this situation from an emotional perspective. Won't most people be interested in finding out the institution they put their faith and trust in for hundreds of years is not what it claimed to be? Imagine the reaction of a billion and a half Christians when they discover the Catholic Church suppressed information and systematically changed doctrine to suit its political ends for the past fifteen hundred years! Dick, you said it yourself. The ground swell against organized religion has gained impetuous for the past decade. It's human nature to want to believe in something, yet religious leaders have consistently betrayed our sacred trust. Religion offered expiation of guilt--a soothing rationalization for which people were willing to pay enormous sums of money. Televangelists play on deep seated human emotions. Corrupt men turned a philosophy designed to relieve suffering into a burden of conscience too difficult for most people to bear! Amariah is in possession of proof that clarifies Jesus' message. He said to turn within--not to place faith in someone or something else. Jesus counseled his followers not to depend on others to provide information they could gather for themselves. I hope modern society is ready to be rid of the concepts He railed against two thousand years ago. The faithful were told they couldn't purchase salvation by supporting priests in their fancy palaces of worship. He took people out into the fields and preached beneath the sun and stars to prove his point. Jesus was a huge threat to the religious and political structure of the time--that's why He was killed. He was turning people away from the temples. The influence of the priesthood was diminishing, and they weren't about to relinquish their privileges or social status. Yet, a mere three hundred and fifty years after Jesus' death, advocates of His message created the same kind of religious/political structure He fought against."

Anna felt her heartbeat quicken and she thought she would burst with the adoration she felt for the man at her side. "Klaus, you've made order out of chaos! Why didn't anybody ever realize it before? Why have we blindly followed a religious tradition filled with error and fraud?"

"That's easy to answer!" Richard Weatherby disappeared into the den, but his voice carried down the hallway like the blare of a warning trumpet. "From a psychological standpoint, the human brain has an amazing capacity to sort and sift incoming information. It disregards what's irrelevant at an amazing rate of speed. The reticular activating net at the base of the brain screens out information, which conflicts with our preconceived beliefs and attitudes. Information is discarded before we can examine it. We see and hear what we want to see and hear!" He returned with a large book on Ancient Egypt in his hands.

A wave of expectancy bore down on Carole. She was a journalist and photographer--psychology was not her area of expertise but she knew as sure as she was sitting in the kitchen of the Weatherby home something was coming; something for which she had no frame of reference; something that was going to shift everything she thought was true. "I didn't understand a single word of what you just said!"

A grin spread over Amariah's face. "Don't mind Dad, Carole, he discovered this years ago and delights in using the information to make people confront the incredible power of the human brain."

Richard thumbed through the large picture book. "All right, Carole, you're a photographer, one accustomed to detail--tell me what you see." The psychiatrist pushed the book in her direction.

Glancing at the caption below the pictures, Carole's glance flitted over the text. The statues in the photos were fashioned from limestone and clay. They portrayed the lifestyles of noblemen and overseers of the 18th Dynasty of Egypt.

"What do you see?" Richard prodded.

"Well," Carole studied the images, "the artist captured their clothing in incredible detail. Linen pleats in the noblewoman's gown hug every curve in her body."

"Look at her hair. What does it look like to you?"

"Corn rows."

"And the man, what does his hair look like?"

"I guess you'd describe it as an Afro."

"Okay. Now look at the skin tones painted on the statues. Howwould you describe those?"

"Dark. Very dark."

"Examine the features . . . the lips and the eyes." Richard studied the change in the photographers' expression as she huddled over the picture; her natural eye for detail picking out information he knew she'd seen a million times before never allowed to penetrate her conscious mind.

"The lips are full, the nostrils wide on all three of these statues."

What race of people would you say these pictures portray?"

The photographer's eyes lifted, astonishment widening the set of her mouth and deepened lines chiseled into her face by years of extreme experience. Before she spoke, she looked at the pictures again as if trying to make certain her brain had drawn the correct conclusion; a conclusion she'd been taught to overlook since childhood. "They're Black. The noblewoman and Pharaoh in this picture, as well as the overseer, are Black."

"Obvious, isn't it?"

Carole nodded her head, then began to flip the pages, examining other pictures. Pharaoh's tomb depicted slaves with helmet-like hairstyles. The skin tone was dark in every picture. A photograph of Tutankhamen's statue in the Cairo Museum was carved from ebony; arms, legs, face, body torso were as black as a sharp-edged shadow. Finally, she glanced up at Richard Weatherby. "Why did I think the Pharaoh's were white?"

"Because the Church, Michelangelo and Cecil B. DeMille created images based on what the white man looks like."

Klaus exploded with laughter. "Oh my God it's true!"

Turning toward his friend, Leon's expression reflected Carole's mystification. A note of frustration crystallized in his voice as he spoke. "Carole, I'm with you on this one! The information Richard is presenting is the opposite of everything I learned."

"Daddy used ask me how a Semitic child could have been accepted as a Negro baby. My faith in the Bible was so absolute I dismissed the evidence. If the Bible said Moses passed for a son in the royal house of Pharaoh, then it had to be true! Now," her humorous mood collapsed, and her expression turned somber, "I realize there are many such incidents in the Bible which need to be understood metaphorically--not taken literally. We have been so blind, so ignorant."

"Amariah, I can support your father's theory with historical evidence." Anna spoke softly, knowing her words had the power to dismantle one of Christianity and Judaism's most treasured stories. "The Moses legend was brought from Babylon with the Jews after their years in captivity. Its originator was Sargon of Agade, who lived from 1728 to 1686 B.C. A well-preserved tablet was unearthed several years ago, and I happened to be one of the people who verified the tablet's authenticity.

> '*My mother was of lowly birth; my father I knew not; the brother of my father is a mountain dweller; and my city, Azupiranu, lies on the bank of the Euphrates. My lowly mother conceived and bore me in secrecy; placed me in a basket of rushes; sealed it with bitumen, and set me in the river, which, however, did not engulf me. The river bore me up. And it carried me to Akku, the irrigator, who took me from the river, raised me as his son, made of me a gardener: and while I was a gardener, the goddess Ishtar loved me. Then I ruled the kingdom*'.

"Moses typifies the birth of the "Hero" theme found in early civilizations from Mesopotamia to Polynesia. One of the most interesting facets of the Moses legend is the Bible indicates Moses' mother sealed his basket of rushes with bitumen. There's not a tree in the whole of Egypt, nor any of its neighboring countries, capable of producing the tar-like resin." Anna studied Amariah's bowed head, her folded hands, the lost expression on her face. "The Jews borrowed the story of Sargon from Babylonian mythology and adapted it to suit their religion."

Amariah continued to study her hands. She couldn't face her friends. Doubt held her voice captive as she asked, "Do you think Moses ever existed?"

Klaus broke in, "I think a man, who exhibited extraordinary courage, challenged Rameses. More than likely, he was instrumental in leading a sizable portion of the Israelites out of Egypt. His acts of moral leadership probably seemed god-like to peasants, farmers, and merchants. These uneducated people needed an explanation for behavior they had no way to understand. The solution was to make Moses a demi-god, capable of performing miracles and defeating evil. If he studied in the Egyptian Mystery Schools, he would have possessed skills and knowledge far above the average person."

Slamming the oversized book shut, Carole sympathized with the anguished look chiseled into Amariah's porcelain features. "I now know what happened to Christianity over the centuries but what are we going to do to set things straight? How can we make people aware of what really happened to Christ's philosophy?"

A chilling light blazed in Richard Weatherby's eyes. "A close friend of mine owns the *San Francisco Chronicle.* Klaus is right, if his paper runs a series of articles with some of Carole's pictures, other papers around the country will pick-up the story too. From there, television interviews and feature articles will be a natural progression." Richard turned to look at Amariah; her panicked expression left no room for further discussion; blind fear took command of her face. "Sweetie, that's what lies ahead of you if you're determined to bring this information to light."

Amariah's body went rigid, and her fingers gripped the tabletop like it was the only thing she could hold on to in a rapidly shifting world. "Daddy, I can't do that! I will not become the object of world-wide attention."

Richard sought his daughter's hand. Tension and misery made them tremble so hard she tried to hide them in her lap. "Let's see if we can arrange an appointment with Sam Jordan. He's got a world of experience in these matters. Maybe there's another way."

Shock, panic, fear registered in Amariah's eyes. When she spoke, her voice assumed a subdued tone, like she addressed a bereaved family congregated around a casket. "My life has been spent in study, I do not have the talent nor the ambition it takes to sway public opinion. If that's what it takes to bring this information to the attention of the world, then Simson will have his way."

The surgeon nodded at the nurse after a quick glance at the anesthesiologist confirmed the patient was properly sedated. The nurse, whose job it was to place the correct instrument in the surgeon's hand the moment it was needed, passed him a high-tech laser, which recently replaced the scalpel.

Surgical methods abreast of the times were potent weapons in the surgeon's medical arsenal. The laser produced an opening in the patient, which was quick to heal, the intense heat from the beam of light sealing blood vessels as it passed through the patient's flesh.

The surgeon's movements over his influential patient exuded caution. The Vatican paid his exorbitant fees quickly and without question. A patient referred to him by a physician at St. Peter's infirmary was as good as cash in the bank. And, after all, medicine was big business. His cash flow and investments were zealously guarded, and the Cardinal represented an unexpected windfall.

The laser beam sliced through a thin layer of skin swiftly, cleanly. More skill would be required to get to the stomach because of the layer of fat, but it was nothing out of the ordinary for the surgeon. The team of technicians held their collective breaths when the distended stomach was exposed. It was no wonder the Cardinal complained about pain. The digestive sack was about to rupture.

One glance from the surgeon silenced the team and they returned their attention to supplying his needs. After a moment of study and some suction to withdraw body fluids beginning to seep around the incision, his hand moved toward the lower end of the stomach--closer to what caused the mystifying blockage. The only way to determine what was wrong with the Cardinal was to slice open the distended area.

With a hand that did not tremor, the surgeon lowered the laser-scalpel. There was a faint hissing sound as the beam of light seared across tissue connecting the stomach to the upper intestine. The instant the laser beam pierced the muscle wall hydrogen gas, created by the combination of aluminum flakes in the stomach's natural acid, escaped through the microscopic fissure under tremendous pressure. Heat generated by the laser ignited the gas and a ball of fire erupted from the Cardinal's stomach.

None of the operating team had time to react. Shock froze their muscles and held them in place as surely as a sudden ice storm. No hands lifted to protect, there was no time to shield their faces from the wreckageof violent death. Blood, intestines, bits of flesh, a substantial portion of the liver, a coagulation of rotting food splattered across the bodies of those huddled over the operating table.

The surgeon screamed as a ball of flame engulfed his hand. The nurse let out a piercing wail as a large piece of the Cardinal's gastro-intestinal tract slowly slid down her cheek, leaving a trail of sour blood. The anesthesiologist was protected from the worst of the explosion because he had leaned down to adjust the rate of sodium pentathlon flowing through a plastic tube into the Cardinal's vein. Everything happened so fast he was still staring at the instruments, whose needles flopped wildly, then fell inert. He looked up. Disbelief clouded his eyes as he surveyed the bloody carnage--his mind refused to process the scene splattered against the walls; dripping down the operating table; seeping across the white tile floor.

The stain of blood was everywhere. The ceiling, the floor, the walls looked as if someone sprayed the operating room with crimson-colored paint. The surgeon was screaming, his nurse was screaming, three technicians, who normally assisted the surgeon with complicated procedures, seemed quick frozen--their instruments still poised over the Cardinal's body. The entire room appeared suspended in time, punctuated only by the primordial howls filling the air.

Doors to the surgery room burst open. Men and women in various forms of hospital garb poured into the sterile environment. For one terror filled moment, the hospital staff was incapable of action--the shock of seeing a gaping body cavity on the operating table riveted everyone's attention. It looked as though a bomb had exploded inside the Cardinal's abdominal cavity. Intestines writhed across the floor like seething, pulsing serpents. Splinters of bone turned to shrapnel lacerated one technician's face; hunks of flesh laced with gobs of yellowish fat hung from another's glasses.

Slowly, people in the room became aware of why the surgeon was screaming. The plastic glove meant to protect the patient from bacteria had melted on his hand--the hand needed to perform delicate surgery. An emergency room doctor galvanized himself into action and jammed a hypodermic filled with morphine into the surgeon's shoulder. The pain began to recede, but the surgeon screamed . . . and screamed . . . and screamed.

More people spilled into the room, some led the shocked, frantic members of the surgical team away from the grizzly scene. No one thought to disconnect the pump, which forced oxygen into the Cardinal's lungs. His chest continued to rise and fall as what was left of his internal bellows filled with air, which quickly escaped into the room with a frightening hiss.

After a brief meeting, the Hospital Board decided to allow the Cardinal to be buried with dignity--no autopsy would be performed. So little was left of David Woolsey's body, it hardly mattered anyway. If the press got wind of the gruesome incident, they would make a circus of the story and cast a pall of sensationalism over the hospital's reputation. The surgeon, detested by many medical professionals because of his unfailing arrogance, was consumed by the fear he might never have the dexterity in his hands--required by complicated surgery--and most of the hospital staff didn't care.

Andrew Simson conducted a solemn Requiem Mass for the Dead in St. Peter's. Church officials from all over the world flew in to attend the Cardinal's funeral. He was laid to rest with all the pomp and ceremony accorded a Prince of the Church. The entire Vatican mourned the tragic, untimely death of Cardinal David Woolsey.

The office of Samuel Jordan was large, very large; it bespoke the wealth of a family who dominated the San Francisco political scene. As the Managing Director of the Chronicle, Jordan was probably the most influential man in the Bay area; he knew it and took for granted the benefits accorded wealth and power.

Seven people occupied the chairs and couch in his office. His friend since college, Richard Weatherby, twisted against a chair at the other side of his desk; Klaus Von Friendberg occupied the matching chair. On the long leather couch stretching down the side of his office wall, Leon Kaminski sat between Richard's wife and a gorgeous woman, Anna Romanov. Another woman, plain by comparison, but whose work he knew well, Carole Phillips, occupied the far end of the couch.

A striking girl, Richard's daughter, stood at the window staring at the city which stretched to the rim of the bay and blanketed the steep hillsides of San Francisco. She seemed unaware of the heated conversation taking place as her father and friends explained the documents lying on his desk.

Even now, shed of religious trappings, the girl reminded him of a nun. Her movements were circumspect, as if the group of people spoke about someone else--someone she didn't know, a person to whom she couldn't relate. If half of the documents on his desk proved accurate . . . the girl might well destroy Andrew Simson, the Catholic Church, and alter the role Christianity played in succeeding generations. Doctrine would have to undergo serious reevaluation due to the evidence beneath his hand.

Picking up a sheaf of photographs, Sam Jordan shuffled through them--pausing every now and again to give one or another closer inspection. From the corner of his eye, he kept track of the girl as she wandered about his office. There was something fascinating about the tilt of her head, how she carried herself, the way she seemed to glide rather than walk. Sam tried to concentrate on the German's recounting of her incredible story, but the girl continued to draw his attention away from both documents and photographs.

Would anyone believe she discovered evidence which would compromise the foundation of Christianity?

Richard's daughter wandered toward the bookcase at the far end of his office. She withdrew random volumes, scanned their contents, and replaced them with a loving care. Amariah's eye wandered over leather spines, many of which were lettered in expensive gold leaf. Classics were there, along with popular novels, mysteries, a sprinkling of poetry lined the shelves, but most volumes were works of reference. Her father's friend possessed an interesting collection of Bibles, many of them antiquated and worth a fortune. The passion she felt for these Bibles made her withdraw one from its place on the shelf. Turning the pages carefully, Amariah paused to admire artwork in the margins. Penmanship was old, perhaps dating back to the medieval era. Engrossed by the antique Bible, Amariah didn't hear Sam Jordan walk up behind her. She started when he spoke.

"This particular Bible happens to be a favorite of mine and probably the most expensive item in my collection."

Lifting eyes so blue they sparkled like chips of polished cerulean, Amariah whispered. "It's beautiful. You're fortunate to possess such a book. I saw several in the Vatican library that may have been somewhat older, but they weren't in such good condition."

"If you're intrigued by this Bible, you might enjoy another item I prize. I've had it appraised and it isn't terribly valuable except for its age, but for some reason I felt compelled to purchase it." Jordan opened a drawer and withdrew a box.

Shock took immediate possession of Amariah's face. Her mouth went dry as she tried to break the hold imposed on her vocal cords by the weight of emotion. Like the hollow roll of distant thunder, Amariah finally gave sound to thoughts awash in a rising tide of awe. "It's the fourth coin."

The room exploded in a blur of motion as everyone rushed to Amariah's side. The coin was a perfect match to the three she withdrew from her pocket. Her lips moved woodenly; her voice little more than the sough of wind through trees as she recited the verse. "*The fourth coin, guarded by a man at home, will be displayed amid archaic pages.*"

Of the four coins, Sam Jordan's was the best preserved. Its imprints were clear, as if this coin had not passed through a thousand different hands. Sam's tone of voice echoed the astonishment everyone felt. It was impossible to believe someone, centuries before, knew this coin would end up in his bookcase, surrounded by other centuries old books! "Where did these coins come from and what do they represent?"

"Amariah, show him your poem." Leon felt as if he was being drawn into a vortex so powerful there was no avenue of escape.

Strangely, Sam Jordan's eyes misted with tears as Amariah read the verse. In a voice which seemed familiar, yet foreboding, recited the ancient message.

"*This coin is for a woman called Amariah who has journeyed out of the past.*

Fate has forged her destiny, now truly, the first shall be the last.

Her calling the world will know because five Coins will be placed in her hands.

The second Coin a man of honor holds, he will help her journey across distant lands.

The third Coin will be brought to her by a man who possess the wisdom of the ages.

The fourth Coin, guarded by a man at home, will be displayed amid archaic pages.

The Evil One defiles the Fifth Coin and do battle with him she must.

Or an age of darkness will consume the world with murder, hatred, and misbegotten lust.

The light of truth must burn bright and clear--it cannot be allowed to falter!

Amariah, woman of Destiny, the fate of the world you here to alter!"

A powerful sensation swept through Sam Jordan's body. He felt every nerve tingle with an electric shock. Wave after wave of cold ran from his cerebral cortex to the soles of his feet. What remained fixed and firm in a room spinning in darkness were the blue eyes beholding him. Everything about the girl's face seemed to change, the office in which they stood was lost to mist . . . but her eyes remained in focus. They exuded a power, a force, something to which he could, should, must cling!

The eerie feeling passed, and Sam shook his head, seven people stared at him--awaiting a response, but no one seemed to notice his world just altered. Clearing his throat, hoping he staked a claim on normalcy, Sam Jordan spoke, his tone cold with resolve. "Let's sit down and decide how to segment this story so it can be run as aseries."

Richard Weatherby clapped his friend on the shoulder. "Sam, you realize what a storm of controversy this is going to brew, don't you?"

"Dick, I've been in the newspaper industry all my life. I'm probably more aware of what this is going to do to the Christian world than any of you." He demanded each person return his unflinching glare. Commitment shone in every face, each was prepared to offer Amariah every ounce of strength at their command. "Let's get busy!"

Hours passed. Lunch was sent for and consumed; wrappers and plastic containers were shoved to one end of the conference table. The publisher's legal pad was filled with notes as each person added their perspective to the story. The huge oak tabletop was littered with Carole's pictures, copies of documents, the scribe's journal Amariah smuggled out of the Archive, manuscripts torn and tattered, lay like the bleached bones of an extinct species--evidence of what once was.

Sam ran a hand over his eyes, he couldn't remember ever feeling this tired. "Okay, I think I've got enough to get started. If I have questions I'll get one of you on the phone."

A collective sigh escaped the tired group as everyone took a moment to relax. Carole began to gather up her photographs and put them in order. "You know, there's still one thing that bothers me."

Klaus stretched his hands above his head to relieve the taut muscles in his back and neck. "What's that?"

"We've gone over these documents in detail, but there's an area we've all sort of danced around. It's as though we don't want to recognize it for fear we'll unleash some primitive superstition."

Anna pressed against the table, her heart rumble-thumping. A feeling as strong as the instinct for survival warned her Carole was about to give voice to the thought which had been buzzing inside her own head these past few hours.

"Carole, what are you talking about?" Sam was exhausted and confused. He knew his background in theology was limited, but he was a trained journalist. The story was well structured. Flaws had been whittled down, what was outlined on his legal pad was clear and concise . . . an excellent example of expert reporting.

"If we accept the message of this verse, and it has proven correct so far, whoever holds the fifth coin must represent a terrifying force."

Carole's words hung over the table like an exotic perfume. They lingered in the air, suspended in each person's thoughts--unwanted; unbidden; refusing to go away.

A tremor of awareness pulsated through Amariah. She felt as though the emotional side of her nature had been set aside and she found herself peering through a veil, which suddenly made the events of the past few months turn crystal clear. "I know who has it."

Mute, frightened stares turned in her direction, but Amariah was oblivious of the cascade of emotions transforming their faces. "Carole, hand me those pictures."

Obedient, Carole Phillips pushed the stack of black and white photographs across the table. Amariah sorted through them quickly, she knew what she was looking for; it simply did not register until now. Withdrawing one from the stack, she handed it back to Carole. "Remember when you took this?"

Carole stared down at the photograph. "I'm not likely to forget!" The image of Andrew Simson as he stood in the center of vault seventeen was as unsettling to her now as it had been the day she developed it. A spectral glow around his head, the way light streamed in from the corridor; the way his robe was absorbed by the dark chamber walls made her skin crawl.

"Carole," Amariah said without emotion, "look at what's in his hand." Returning her attention to the piece of paper, Carole reached for the magnifying glass on the conference table to examine the photo. "Jesus, Holy Christ! Why didn't I notice this before?" The photographer's face turned bone-white, as shock and fear forced the blood from her skin. "I saw him pick something up off the table and right after that he rushed out of the crypt! I just didn't put the two actions together. Dear God in heaven—Andrew Simson has the fifth coin!"

The conference room seemed to detonate with the sound of scraping chairs, hastily expelled breath filled the air as everyone rushed around the table for a better look at the picture. The black and white glossy passed from hand to hand, the magnifying glass enlarging the eye of the examiner.

Across the table, Carole studied the complex transformation going on inside a young woman she considered a friend. Changes were subtle. The former nun's jaw hardened; it assumed a more inflexible line than moments before. Something was shifting in Amariah's eyes. Slowly, reaching for the camera beside her with caution, Carole brought the recording instrument to her eye. She wanted to capture this moment and prayed the film would chronicle a fraction of what she sensed taking place in the woman seated across the table.

Amariah didn't hear the debate going on between Klaus and Leon as they discussed Andrew Simson with Amariah's father and his friend. She didn't realize Anna had taken Elizabeth's hand; they were sharing a moment of emotion, each sensing a dreadful scenario lay ahead for their friend and daughter.

Amariah was aware of only one thing . . . she was filled with a sudden sense of understanding. "I'm going back."

A silence as oppressive as the heat and humidity of summer in Alabama filled the room. Propelled by the overpowering love he felt for his only child, Richard Weatherby yelled, "You can't be serious! When Simson finds out you're taking this evidence public, he'll do anything to stop you." He pounded the conference table relying on anger to make Amariah retreat from an insane course of action. "You are not going back to Rome!"

The shriek of the telephone bell underscored everyone's tension. Amariah lifted a preoccupied gaze to find her father's expression contorted, distraught. "No one can stop him but me, I know that now. I have to confront him. "

Klaus lifted the receiver, anxious to stop the incessant ringing which seemed to electrify every nerve ending in his body. He listened quietly, then laid the phone aside. Mastering complex emotions, Klaus cleared his throat, knowing he could not soften the coming blow. "Jean Paul has been trying to track us down. Father Lean was killed in an automobile accident as he left the Benedictine Abbey at Monte Cassino. Father Murphy died of a heart attack before his new pacemaker arrived from Bern. The plane carrying Paul Grant to New York exploded on the runway in Rome. Police blame the Red Brigade. And" his eyes shifted to Leon, he hated to be the bearer of such sad news, "Jeff Brown was found murdered on a deserted road not far from his mother's home in Georgia. I don't think these deaths were accidental or coincidental."

Amariah fought to hold back the waves of emotion which raged like an ocean beset by a hurricane. Good men had been lost. Men of vision. Men of learning. "Don't you see? If the Father General is responsible for the deaths of our friends and colleagues. It's up to me to stop him."

Leon joined the chorus of anguished pleas. "What can you do? Your battle can best be waged through the press, Amariah. You're tired, you're overwrought, you aren't thinking clearly. Let's go back to your house and get some sleep. In the morning, we'll talk about this again--we'll come up with another way to stop him."

Amariah shoved her chair away from the table. "I'm going to the airport. I'll take the first plane to Rome. I have to stop him--before it's too late."

Klaus nodded, the dismal look taking possession of his features startled everyone. "She's right--Amariah is the only one who can stop him!"

Running his fingers through his hair, Leon felt an emotion akin to blind panic assume control of his thoughts. Amariah's stance announced she was not going to change her mind; her knees were locked, her feet planted, as if prepared for a blow.

· No amount of logic, no passionate words of persuasion would change the course of her direction. Leon felt acid besiege his stomach. "I'm going with you."

Father Philipe Laterano burst through the door into Andrew Simson's office. "She just got off the plane."

Black eyebrows flared like the hood of a cobra over expressionless eyes. "Oh?"

"Yes!" Breathless from running, sentences came in rapid-fire order--a machine gun of sound blasting all tranquility. "A customs officer called me. Kaminski is with her, they're both under surveillance. Sister Amariah is not wearing her habit. They're in a taxi right now and they appear to be heading here.

"To the Vatican?" Eyes as dark and unwelcoming as the bottom of a grave registered surprise the girl had shed the religious trappings so meaningful to her only weeks before.

"Yes!"

Leaning back in his chair, the Father General turned his mind inward. He hadn't thought her courageous enough to leave San Francisco. He assumed she would wage war against him from the fortress-like environment of her childhood home. This turn of events was unexpected . . . very unexpected. He reached for the telephone receiver. "Get me the Cistercian Convent of the Strict Observance."

CHAPTER NINETEEN

Amariah stared out the taxi window. Cypress trees lining the roadway to Rome passed unseen. Hills beyond lost the riotous colors of summer and faded into shades of dull, flat green--barely discernable from the brown color which announced the arrival of winter. A low ceiling of clouds turned the sky slate gray and moisture cast gloom over the countryside.

No birds sang to Amariah, no flowers bobbed blossomed heads in welcome, the land itself seemed to reflect the bleakness which took ownership of her heart.

Leon studied the features of the woman sitting quietly beside him. Folded hands cupped the coins. She appeared to be drawing the courage to confront Simson from them. Lines of weariness scored furrows around her mouth and eyes, but Amariah seemed to be feeding on nervous energy connected to a mysterious source of supply. Leon's concept of reality had undergone an undeniable shift since becoming involved with the girl at his side.

He was a different person than the man he'd been on his first journey to Rome. Glancing at Amariah again changes in her were also visible. An alteration of character had taken place. Gone was the adoring young girl with an uncompromising faith in the Church. In her stead, came a woman who shed the false skin of religious belief. A mythopoeic power charged the atmosphere around her now. The luminosity in her eyes could not be explained by logic.

Andrew Simson slipped a key into the lock. A fireproof metal door, which protected the *Messiah* operations center, swung open. The room was dimly lit--technicians had departed for home, dinner, and an evening with their families. Slipping inside, he reached for the cord on louvered blinds, turning them flat against the window, on the chance a security guard might be making rounds. He did not want to be interrupted.

A few quick steps led him to the workstation housing an isolated PC. He punched a few keys, typed in a source code and the video display terminal glowed with phosphorescent light as the hard drive whirred to life. From the pocket inside his cassock, Andrew Simson withdrew a flash drive. Inserting it into the USB port, he loaded Paul Grant's deadly program into *Messiah.*

The monitor dissolved into a rainbow of colors as he moved through the program screens. Tapping keys in the order of the prompt, electronic circuitry was activated to 'ready'; explosive charges beneath the museum awaited his command.

The taxi stopped at the Porta Sant'Anna, an opening in the Leonine wall outside the Swiss Guard barracks. Amariah studied the Vatican Bank, offices of the L'Observatore Romana, the Post Office and tapestry workshop. Fear--it savaged her senses, it turned air sucked into her lungs to molten lava, it consigned rational thought to a bottomless abyss of despair. She hesitated, welcoming an opportunity to rein in an imagination threatening to run wild as Leon thrust a fist full of torn and crumpled lira into the taxi driver's hand.

Leon turned toward the gate; his heart sank when he saw the naked terror in her eyes. He would have given anything to take the burden crushing her spirit. Offering his hand, he said, "Ready?"

"As ready as I'll ever be." Amariah took a ragged breath and stepped inside the gate--into the lair of the dragon. What would she say to Andrew Simson? How could she stop someone consumed by such a distorted view of destiny? Could she reason with a man who was mad with power, drunk on ego; a brilliant mind consumed by his concept of the future? Amariah's footfalls sounded with the hard clack of resoluteness as she walked past the Apostolic Palace. There was a light burning in the Pope's bedroom window. The gentle man still clung to life. Perhaps when this was over she would be able to talk to him again, listen to his advice and wisdom--how she longed for his counsel now. She trudged between buildings which housed the library, past the Corridor of Bramante, the Museo Pio-Clementino and marched toward massive buildings in which the Museo Gregoriano de Profano, Museo Pio Cristano and Pontifico Museo Missionario-Etnologico resided. In happier times, she wandered blissfully through the maze-like corridors of these museums, awed by the collection of masterpieces. The Pinacoteca loomed ahead, its salmon-colored walls a stark contrast to other, more weathered museum buildings. The sweat of a believing poor, who were told the road to salvation was paved by their financial support of an institution more political than spiritual, paid the staggering cost of the new museum. Like a creature from a nightmare, the windows of the Pinacoteca became eyes of a monster, its doorways jaws of terror. A wave of emotion bore down on Amariah.

Leon held the Pinacoteca door open. Rushing forward, Amariah hurried up its steps as if momentum alone could successfully propel her though the events which lay ahead. To keep up with her super-human burst of energy, Leon assaulted the stairs two and three at a time--Amariah would not confront Simson alone if he could help it.

Cautious, he opened the outer door to the Father General's office. Sister Josephina was already gone. File folders were stacked in separate piles--the next day's order of priority. A flash of foreknowing surged across Leon's consciousness, stair-stepping through his mind like a bolt of lightning: There would be no tomorrow.

A faint, scuttling, rustling sound inside Simson's private office drew Leon's attention away from his thoughts. Pressing a finger against his lips to ensure Amariah's silence, he motioned her behind him with his other hand. Praying the floorboards did not betray their presence, they crept forward.

Leon pushed the door ajar, mercifully, time-worn hinges did not announce their entrance. Philipe Laterano stood at a file cabinet tucked into the corner, huddled over a manila folder. After a quick survey of its contents, he slapped it shut. Other files were consigned to a briefcase at his feet--a few lay on top of the cabinet.

"Going somewhere?" Leon couldn't quell the rage which crept into his voice; the hardness was not only threatening, it was blacker, stranger, far more terrifying.

Whirling, file folders fell from the cabinet, dislodged by Father Laterano's elbow. The flapping, sliding sound of paper and cardboard careening to the floor reached Amariah out of sequence, as if she were watching a movie in slow-motion, whose soundtrack didn't match the action.

Laterano pressed his body against the file cabinet seeking shelter which was impossible to find when Leon lunged forward. Grabbing the priest by the front of his cassock, Leon's rage began to vent--fury spilling onto its hapless victim. "What did you plan to do--remove proof of what's happening around the world? Were you going to consign evidence to oblivion? Evidence to substantiate the Jesuit Order's role in murder, political interference and religious domination?" The fear in Philipe Laterano's eyes verified feelings Leon had hoped would remain unfounded. "Where's Simson?"

The Jesuit's jaw clamped shut. Betrayal would never come from him.

Rage provided the strength to lock his arm beneath the other man's chin. A strangling, gagging sound ruptured from the Jesuit as Leon applied pressure.

The voice in his ears was so icy it quick-froze blood, bone, and tissue. "Where is he?" The sound was so foreign it took Leon a moment to realize he was the one speaking.

From the corner, Amariah cocked her head, listening to a silent, interior sound. "I know where Father Simson is."

Leon eased the pressure on the Jesuit's throat, but his gaze never wavered from Laterano's face.

Her words were simple, clearly spoken, but they roared like the wind announcing a tsunami rushing across the ocean. "Keep Father Laterano here until I return."

Before Leon could protest, Amariah shot through the door.

Leon released his grip on the priest so suddenly Laterano collapsed on the floor. Eyes glassy, Leon hissed at the Jesuit sprawled at his feet. "If any harm comes to Amariah, I'll claw the skin from your body. I will peel the flesh from your bones! I will kill you inch by inch because that woman is the only hope mankind has!"

The sky turned a ghastly shade of crimson. A huge, blood-red sun hung suspended in the cloud layer settling across Rome. The fiery disk appeared to hesitate on the horizon--seemingly reluctant to leave the earth and its inhabitants unprotected and vulnerable to darkness. Birds tucked their bills beneath their wings earlier than usual, as if a violent storm were brewing. Cats scurried across the courtyard, and a silence, not of this earth, settled over the Vatican.

Amariah kept her eyes fixed on the walkway; she didn't dare look at the steel and glass building ahead for fear common sense would deter her.

The Jesuit Father General was in the computer control room on the top floor of the museum. Amariah didn't know how she knew--but something warned her she was on a collision course with destiny. Trying to ignore feelings coming from all directions, Amariah attempted to steady her breathing. With a shove, she pushed open the outer door. It banged against the marble casing; steel striking stone echoed through the foyer designed to hold several hundred tourists while they listened to museum guides extol the building's virtues.

The soles of her shoes rang against marble as she stormed across the lobby; a precise, military sound, the footfall of an advancing army. A crystal chandelier three stories above cast rainbows against walls of polished stone. Her eyes swept the lobby; searching; seeking; finally coming to rest on a doorway marked "No Admittance" in several languages.

Testing the doorknob, whomever passed this way had not locked the hallway entrance door which ran behind public display rooms. A sense of urgency propelled her through the door into the corridor.

Turning, twisting, running up several flights of metal stairs, Amariah was drawn to the room which contained the massive *Messiah* computers. She placed her hand against the entrance door which shielded tons of hardware and sensitive software from the outside world. Simson was in there, she felt his presence in a way that registered on a purely instinctual level. Asking for help and guidance from a force she had no way to explain, Amariah stepped onto the field of conflict.

"Ah, Sister." Andrew Simson turned from the terminal displaying letters which questioned 'go?' "I've been expecting you." He glanced at the monitor and tapped in a few keystrokes. An image dissolved--the lobby, a succession of corridors, stairwells she took to *Messiah's* command center flashed across the monitor as Simson gave electronic commands to rotate surveillance cameras. Resignation settled across her face as Amariah realized the Father General watched her path through the gardens as she headed for the Pinacoteca.

"We have much to talk about . . ." His voice challenged Amariah, seeking a crack in her resolve. He kicked a chair in her direction. "You may as well be comfortable while we discuss our dilemma."

Easing into the chair, Amariah kept her attention trained on the priest as he hovered over the console displaying blinking lights and digital readouts.

Simson drew a keyboard, connected to its PC by a spiral umbilical cord, closer. As he continued to depress a series of keys, a clacking, plastic sound filled the room. On the panel, lights shifted from red to yellow ad numbers on the counters began to register downward.

"I hope after this little chat our talents will be united." Glittery eyes beheld Amariah in a hypnotic stare. Blue jeans and a silk blouse hugged a woman's figure. "I didn't expect you to shed the trappings of your vocation so quickly."

His eyes crawled along her body; Amariah felt exposed beneath the

Father General's stare, as if she were suddenly naked. "False skin is easily shed."

A primitive, superstitious look rose in Simson's eyes; anger, then awe, battled for supremacy as the realization Amariah was going to be a powerful adversary took command of his thoughts. "Why, Sister, I detect a note of harshness in your voice."

"Truth is often harsh."

"Indeed." Simson reached for the crucifix and began to toy with it. "We need to speak plainly--the time for truth is at hand."

Amariah felt as if she were watching a snake coil, drawing its long, writhing body into striking position. The Father General's eyes assumed a lidless, unblinking stare as he spoke.

"A time for truth, my lady." Shifting, assuming an authoritative stance, Simson challenged his opponent. "I've known about you for quite some time. When I was assigned to the Vatican, as a young Jesuit just out of seminary, I was put in charge of cataloguing all the documents in the Secret Archive. Important manuscripts came to light--doctrines consigned to oblivion by early Church authorities." He sighed, as if the enormity of the burden he'd carried for so many years lay heavy on his shoulders. "You see, dear lady, I discovered the dogma I'd been taught to believe without question was filled with inaccuracy and error. What was I to do?" Simson raised his hand as if pleading with a higher power to provide him with an answer. "Oh, my lady, how I prayed! I pleaded with God to show me the way. I had documents in my hands which would destroy the institution in which I placed my faith,my absolute trust."

Appearing anguished by the memory, the network of lines around Andrew Simson's eyes deepened. Perhaps he had endured a crisis of faith. Remaining silent, Amariah waited for Simson to go on. If she did not contribute to the conversation the Father General would be forced to keep talking--to fill the silence. She wanted to understand. She wanted to know what convoluted part of his psyche compelled him to destroy--to murder. Amariah wanted to get inside his skin, to follow the labyrinth of his thoughts, to decide if he could be turned from darkness, in the hope there was something left to salvage of his soul.

Simson surveyed the folded hands, the bowed head, the serene expression which settled across the girl's face with the delicacy of a bird in flight. She didn't fear him! There was a look of compassion in her eyes conveying pity. Pity! Anger surged through his body with such force it left him lightheaded. If she would not join him, she would be eliminated--like all the others. Nothing was going to stop him, God chose him for this mission! God spoke to him through his thoughts and in his dreams! God ordained him!

Hoping to appear overcome by emotional memories, the Father General cleared his throat, as if struggling to free himself from the twin juggernauts of doubt and shattered faith. "As I wrestled with my troubled thoughts, I discovered a document which led me to believe an awesome truth lay buried in the monastery at Monte Cassino. Many Benedictine monks went to great lengths to protect their library despite catastrophes suffered by the abbey throughout the centuries."

Amariah nodded her head, aware of historical details about the Order founded by St. Benedict.

"My curiosity was ignited, so I journeyed to the abbey, where I was finally granted permission to see documents protected by the monks since Visigoth raiders swept across the Alps. I pleaded with the Holy Father to relocate the manuscripts to the Vatican, where they would receive proper care and better protection. Pope Anastasius thought it important for the scrolls remain with the Benedictines because they were part of the Order's spiritual treasure. He knew of their content, of course, the Pope knows a great deal more than he cares to reveal." Andrew Simson checked his thoughts. He could not allow fury to make him say too much. The former nun was no longer naive. She had the fire of mind, an ability to take abstract, intuitive threads and weave them into a tapestry of logic.

Confusion chased fear from Amariah and curiosity gained the upper hand. None of the documents she translated indicated there was a treasure buried at Monte Cassino.

Simson noticed doubt flitting through the girl's eyes. "I removed all the evidence about Monte Cassino from the Archive," his tone of voice turned polar. It was intended to freeze her very spirit. "I was expecting you, you see. I knew someday we would be brought together to change the course of history. I spent the next ten years searching for you."

The suggestion hit Amariah like the strike of a snake. Its deadly force pressed her back into the armless chair. Apprehension clawed at her solar plexus and forced its way up the back of her throat with the acid burn of bile. Join Simson? Never! At the cost of her life, Amariah knew she had to resist this man: the hypnotic spell cast by his lightless eyes and tone of voice, so adept at lulling the unwary into a false sense of security. Paternal body movements fueled the need to belong--a desire to believe in a better world; a greater humankind; a yearning for spiritual comfort. Amariah stiffened, as if seeing a ledger upon whose surface resided the formula for the salvation of the world.

Simson studied the girl, waiting for a reaction to betray the content of her thoughts. "I passed those years by gaining influence in the Jesuit Order. I bided my time, moving slowly, cautiously, with one goal ever present in mind, but I never lost sight of my God-given purpose. I had to find you, to determine what kind of woman you were, and . . . I had to strengthen the political framework through which we could influence nations!"

A mercurial smile appeared, and just as quickly faded, replaced by the unmistakable glimmer of an ego beyond imagining. Emotional turmoil was evident in his voice as he tried to convince Amariah of his divine calling. "God provided me with the answer, you see. I was thrust into the Office of Father General of the Jesuit Order, and He allowed me to discover what was hidden below the Vatican. I was thrust into a position to sway world opinion! I had the vehicle by which to accomplish a task ordained by destiny! God granted me the means with which to build the museum--and the direction leading me to you! During my search for a scholar of ancient languages, one of my brothers at Loyola submitted your name. He told me you possessed an eerie command of the languages spoken at the time of Jesus--almost as if you had stepped out of the past." Simson leaned forward, his body radiating strength, force, the power of conviction.

'Her name is Amariah,' my Jesuit brother said, 'She understands scripture in a way that makes me feel as if the shroud of time has been ripped away, as if I am standing beside the Master as he spoke to the multitudes on the hillsides of Galilee.'

“Don't you see?" Simson's eyes were blinking wildly--logic, reason, conscience consigned to an inaccessible region of his brain. "God led me to you! It was as if He put a pointer in my hand. And--you were already a nun! I didn't have to convince you of the message of our Lord and Savior! Your name, your vocation, your gift of language--everything about you was foretold by the documents at Monte Cassino! You have come from out of the past!"

Amariah recoiled; images flashed before her eyes, obscuring *Messiah* and Andrew Simson. She blinked, trying to clear her vision--instinct warned her not to divert her gaze from the Father General. She could not allow memories pounding at the door of consciousness to distract her from what was going on in this room. She had to remain clear-headed!

Andrew Simson wanted to rise, rampant energy compelled him to pace back and forth across the room, he needed to gesture . . . to vent the passion he felt; but he couldn't move from the keyboard resting at the edge of the console. He had to be able to jam his finger against the 'g' sending an electrical impulse along wires put in place by Father Julian; the order to commence the destruction of everything he created. He had to convince Amariah to unite with him, to sway her, he had to make her understand how his vision of the future would relieve the world of its suffering and bring them back to God. "You and I must ease the Christian world into an acceptance of this new concept."

"Like the way the early Popes handled the information presented by Galileo and Newton?" Her voice was strained, and darkness seeped beneath the periphery of her vision as the impact of Simson's statement registered in her brain.

"Yes!" The word was an elongated hiss, a venting from the super-heated crater of Andrew Simson's mind. "Our discoveries must be managed and directed through the Holy Mother Church instead of against it! The Church is a potent weapon, it represented authority in the mind of man for centuries! Why not use it? Why destroy a structure which is already in place, one wielding so much presence?" As Andrew Simson swelled his lungs with air the black robe expanded; a cobra flaring its hood. "Through you, Amariah, the Second Coming will happen--your destiny was foretold by the documents at Monte Cassino." Andrew Simson drew upon memory to recite the words preserved by the Benedictines.

'. . . *And again, she will come, this woman called Amariah. She will restore the message of the Messiah. She will usher in the Second Coming, the awakening of the heart of man. For He will not come out of the clouds with the voice of thunder. Rather, He will steal into the heart, slip into the mind. He will come like a thief in the night and call out in the stillness when the heart is quiet and the mind at rest. Some will hear him, and others will not. The woman called Amariah will deliver His message to a pain-stricken world!*'

"I do not know how this will happen--but through you, the Savior will return!"

The air thickened with an unknown power, the room blackened and swirled--as if a storm swept across the landscape of electronic apparatus and the whirling magnetic discs which contained the *Messiah* program. Pumice colored clouds obscured the space between Amariah and Andrew Simson. A current welled up from inside and her mind released the floodgates of memory. An emotion so compelling, so gripping, so firm in resolve, she could no longer repress it burst through her consciousness. The Amariah who lived in the twentieth century ceased to exist; she rose from the chair with such momentum it tipped over. "I will not be used."

"Amariah, don't you see? Together we can be an invincible force! The importance of the role you are here to play has been predicted for centuries. There are over a billion Christians in the world--each of whom would be eager to follow the person whose destiny has been foretold by our prophets across the millennia! Through you the Second Coming! Through you, Amariah! I set the stage: Governments have been swept away, entire cultures prepared to accept the Church. I have priests located in every corner of the globe." He withdrew a box from the pocket of his cassock and held out the cross suspended from the chain around his neck. "When I insert my crucifix into this box, a message will be broadcast via satellite and all my men will go into action. You have only to assume your role! The world awaits a Redeemer!"

"Do you think," Amariah's voice was low, flat, ironclad with determination, "anyone has the right to dominate the world?" Amariah took a step forward, the light in her eyes so fierce the Jesuit drew his hand across his face, a shield against the authority the woman radiated. "You cannot control me, nor what happens. God does not speak through you . . . God grants mankind the freedom to choose whom they will follow. You cannot compel others to accept your vision of the future! Man is here to make his own choices. No, Andrew, your hand will not be on the helm that guides and directs the world."

A spasm of anger spread across Andrew Simson's face, drawing it into a grotesque mask; anger turned his skin a mottled shade of red. "What I cannot control, I destroy!"

From the doorway behind Amariah, a gloved hand slid around the heat resistant metal designed to protect *Messiah's* hardware from fire. His fingers stretched, forcing flexibility into scarred muscles. Clutching two wooden pins connected by a strand of wire, the hooded figure moved forward, silence his most potent weapon.

Simson's eyes flicked away, and Amariah sensed someone's approach. She whirled; the wire glimmering in the phosphorescent light cast by the fluorescent fixtures overhead descended so quickly its motion was reduced to a blur.

An instinct born before the dawn of time, an intelligence beyond normal levels of awareness, demanded Amariah stretch forth her hand. She touched her assailant's arm a fraction of a second before the wire plunged over her head. Words defying logic gave clarity to the emotions suffered by a tortured man. "I cast out the demons which haunt you. Turn not your hand against me . . . I bring you love, brother, and peace of mind."

The force of lambent blue eyes froze the killer, his arms extended over her head. Amariah pressed her hand into the cowl concealing his deformed face. At her touch, the hounds of Satan which tore at his mind with such fury, loosened their grip. The hatred he harbored since that fateful day vanished; gone was anger, dread, and the agonizing pain which controlled his life.

Gentle pressure from the woman's hand created a fire storm of response. The overload on Father Julian's nervous system began a systematic shut down of his brain's circuitry and caused the equivalent of a massive stroke. Too many simultaneous impulses made Father Julian collapse on the floor in a heap.

Philipe Laterano studied the other man. Kaminski's eyes flitted to the window, following the nun's direction. He had to get to the command center; to be with the Father General. Logic told him the girl would be no match for Father Simson, but emotion warned him his hero and mentor was on the verge of destruction.

When the other man's gaze shifted toward the window again, Philipe bolted from the chair. In his peripheral vision, Leon caught a blur of movement as Laterano lunged for the door. Leon flung himself against the priest's back. The weight of both men falling against the door forced it open with a loud crack. Thrashing arms and legs locked in combat, the two men rolled across the reception room. Philipe rammed his knee into Leon's abdomen, forcing breath from his lungs. Leon reached to pull himself up by grasping the edge of Sister Josephina's desk.

Regaining his feet, a fraction of a second quicker, the priest, who survived childhood in a rough neighborhood bouncing drunks and cleaning tables in a local bar, balled his fists. He slammed clenched hands against the back of Kaminski's neck.

A mushroom cloud of blue-white light exploded in his head. Fighting to retain consciousness, he gripped the front of the Jesuit's cassock with all the strength at his disposal, a strength which seemed to ebb and flow like the rhythm of the tide. Father Laterano fought to get clear of the reception room; desperate to be rid of the parasitic burden clinging to him with such passion. Eager to break free, the Jesuit hammered at Leon's face and head, using his fists to bludgeon, breaking the thin line of cartilage giving shape to the other man's nose. Blood gushed from Leon's face and turned his shirt scarlet.

The blue-white light faded into a velvety midnight-blue, then burst to life again. The illuminating flash robbed Leon of coherent thought. He was unaware of the coppery taste of blood filling his mouth as his lips split and his flesh bruised beneath the Jesuit's merciless pounding. Physical sensors which warned through pain were paralyzed by raining blows striking his head and ears. All Leon knew was he had to hang on. He had to keep his grip on the Jesuit's cassock. It was the only thing he could do to protect Amariah.

At the head of the marble stairs, Father Laterano tore at his tormentor's hands. He bent his head to bite at Leon's fingers, knowing the mandible could exert greater pressure than anything else at his disposal.

A boiling fog which numbed Leon's mind parted. He saw the Jesuit lower his head, his teeth exposed like those of a scavenging jackal, his eyes ablaze with animal savageness. A sound akin to the blare of trumpets rang in Leon's ears--disaster would follow if he didn't summon the strength to fight back. A veil of crimson seeped across his line of sight as the flesh above his eyebrow split beneath the punishing impact of another blow.

The Jesuit's legs turned to pillars of fire; they delivered torturous blows to Leon's shins, ankles, and knees. Drawing energy from an unknowable source, Leon struggled to his feet and launched his body against Laterano.

Toppling backwards, the two men crashed down the lobby stairs; their bodies twisting and turning over one another as they rolled, careening and thrashing, from landing to landing, unable to stop the forward momentum of their fall.

As they rolled into to the lobby Leon's head struck the last step. The blue-white light which had been his salvation deserted his thoughts, replaced by blackness as cold and unyielding as the grave. His fingers opened, unconsciousness relaxed the grip on the Jesuit's cassock.

For a moment Philipe lay still, all breath battered from his lungs as they crashed against the floor. His head throbbed, his vision brightened by a thousand colored stars; it seemed like he'd struck his skull a million times as they thudded down the staircase. It took him a minute to realize Leon was lying on top of him, fingers loose, body inert.

A tentative push, followed by a forceful shove revealed Leon was unconscious. Philipe struggled against two-hundred pounds of dead weight. Pushing Kaminski to one side, he reached for the handrail and pulled himself to his feet. A wave of red engulfed him, followed just as quickly by a curtain of black. He lurched, cursing an equilibrium refusing to stabilize. When his vision cleared, he prodded Kaminski with his foot. A stream of blood seeped from beneath the Polish scholar's head. One eye was rapidly swelling; contusive colors of blue and purple already beginning to rise. Leon's neck was marked with angry red welts and his hands bled from numerous cuts. Blood oozed from the gash on his lip--it joined the stream of blood from the cut above his eye and spread across his face. Leon's nose was swollen, blue-black flesh left no doubt it was broken. Kaminski wouldn't bother him again.

Swallowing hard, trying to slow the rapid hammering of his heart, working to moisten a throat turned parched and rancid by a desperate need for air, Philipe Laterano knew he had to reach the Father General. His steps were uncertain, his movements awkward as he pushed open the Pinacoteca's outer door.

In a last-ditch effort make Amariah see reason, Andrew Simson broke the silence with a hard edge to his voice, then changed his tone to cajoling tenderness. "I will raise you up above kings and princes! The earth's populace will bow at your passing! I can do that, Amariah! I am the Lamb who will open the Seal . . . I have the power to manipulate the future with *Messiah*! I will make you the ruler of our world--join me!" He extended one hand toward the woman huddled over the Cistercian monk, her fingertips against his artery, checking a dangerously reedy pulse.

Rising slowly, Amariah turned to face Simson; when she spoke the bitterness in her voice was corrosive. "Those are your desires, not mine. You have been seduced by pride and ego. The political framework you created to govern the world has its points of brilliance. You encouraged the ideal of peace and global brotherhood in millions. If your motives were not self-serving, if you really had the good of mankind at heart, you might have succeeded. Andrew, don't you realize you are the Beast? Don't you know it is Satan who speaks through your mind? Don't you understand it was the Dragon who gave you the authority of office? Andrew, you do not speak with the Almighty!"

Amariah pointed at the Father General, her hard expression melded with compassion then slid downward into sorrow. "Will you cleanse yourself of pride and arrogance? Will you put personal aims of glory behind the good of others? Will you take my hand? Will you listen to the Voice within counseling you to ease human suffering, to teach people to love one another, to be compassionate, caring individuals--like our Lord Jesus?"

The thin thread of sanity snapped. He would not be pitied! It was his destiny to rule the world! His genius, his vision, his guidance returned the Church to its rightful position of authority. Simson's voice made a strangling, gasping sound as the words spilled from lips stretched over clenched teeth. "I will not be rebuked by a woman!"

His finger stabbed the 'g' key. The southwest museum wing seemed to lift off the ground as an explosion ripped through footings designed to support the museum for a thousand years. No amount of concrete, nor tons of reinforcing steel, could withstand the force of the C-4 explosive which buckled support beams. Like a dying leviathan, the enormous building shuddered, its girders screaming in protest. The crash of marble, rain of shattered glass, the scream of tortured wood were the pallbearers accompanying the death of the structure.

It took Amariah a moment to make the connection between the horrid cacophony of sound, a wall of flame which seemed to grope at the dark night air, and the Father General's movement. She turned from the scene of devastation, her voice rising to an inhuman shriek. "What are you doing?" The wing of the building devoted to priceless manuscripts lay ravaged, its graceful architecture obscured by an onslaught of flame.

Simson's eyes filled with hatred, as if he were scrolling backward through an accumulation of corrupted memories. "What I have created, I have the power to destroy. The angel's trumpets that herald disaster blow their sirens song at my command!"

Phantoms of firelight reflected on the walls, throwing ghastly shadows across the room like cavorting demons. Amariah screamed, "You're mad! You must stop this senseless destruction. You cannot deprive future generations of what we've discovered!"

"Oh, but I can!" He depressed his finger against the computer 'g' key again and another explosion ruptured the air with the ear-splitting sound of chaos. Simson reached beneath his cassock and withdrew a revolver; the barrel reflected the fire outside--mirroring his intent. From his cassock pocket, Andrew Simson extracted an ancient coin which never left his person. He flashed it in Amariah's direction. "You will not destroy me, I am too powerful. If you do not join me, then you will be consigned to the everlasting fires of hell! God speaks through me!"

Amariah tipped her chin, hostility stiffened her slender body and turned her voice to ice. "God might have spoken to you, once. Now you listen to the dictates of your own mind--a mind turned malignant by pride and self-righteousness. The sinfulness pervading your soul rules your actions, but the Almighty awaits your awakening to the truth!"

The door burst open, and Philipe Laterano lunged into the room. "Father," his eyes fastened on the gun, then traveled the direction in which the barrel pointed, but his mind was compelled to finish the pointless sentence already on his lips, "there's been an explosion. The museum is on fire!"

Time froze action to slow-motion. Philipe's glance returned to Andrew Simson, then followed the Father General's other arm down to his hand, to the index finger pressed against the computer's keyboard; a coin held securely against his palm by his thumb. His brain sorted through hundred different possibilities before selecting a conclusion--but Philipe continued to search for an answer he wanted to believe. Mesmerized, he found it difficult to tear his eyes away from the gun. With extreme effort, he lifted a terrified gaze to the Father General's face. The man he trusted implicitly, followed, worshipped--wasn't there anymore. At this moment, his mentor was only a shell of a man; the physical body abandoned and a fearsome, alien force replaced his human soul. The eyes staring back at him were not those of Andrew Simson--the compassionate, the knight of truth, a champion of Christianity. They were the eyes of a common madman. Still in the grip of agonizingly slow movement, Philipe's eyes returned to the barrel of the gun then jerked in Amariah's direction. The passionate light of truth radiated from the woman's clear blue eyes. No malice, no evil resided in her expression. She possessed extraordinary virtue. A warning shiver, announcing precognition, tracked his spine as he stared at her. She was the one! She would save the world--not Andrew Simson. In a flash of super-human deductive reasoning, Philipe Laterano was filled with a certainty of purpose which propelled him across the room toward the Father General.

The computer room filled with a deafening roar as Andrew Simson fired the gun at the woman who waited with such mocking patience. Philipe Laterano was one instant quicker, one fraction of a second ahead of the Father General's intent. Philipe threw himself in front of the Father General, taking the bullet at point blank range through his heart. His life force evacuated in an instant, as blood, bone, muscle, and sinew spewed across the room when the bullet which entered his chest exploded through his spine. A spray of red covered Amariah's face. Pieces of muscle lay quivering on the floor, shards of bone slashed through tender flesh, to lay like spines of coral in a sea of blood. In the last instant of his life, Philipe Laterano grabbed the gun and took it with him to the floor.

Simson stood above the mound of tissue which once had been his faithful vassal, his companion, the man to whom the mantle of responsibility would have fallen when his own days on earth were at an end. A recriminating expression in Philipe's eyes was forever fixed in the mask of Death. In them, in the warm pools of brown, which followed his orders so faithfully, Andrew Simson saw the naked truth. Philipe, his beloved disciple, deserted him as surely as Peter denied his relationship with Jesus. The accusing looks in the dead man's eyes speared him; Philipe pierced his side with the sword of betrayal.

In anger, the Father General lashed out at the traitor's face with his foot, smashing a once proud Roman nose against his cheek, splattering liquid from the eyes which beheld him with unequivocal truth. Rage blotted out the last remaining shred of logic. He pounded the 'g' key again, commanding *Messiah* to continue its sequence of destruction.

An old, undocumented gas main ruptured as the earth shifted beneath the pressure of another C-4 explosion. Miles of corridors beneath the Vatican began to fill with lethal fumes as a ruptured valve spilled its never-ending contents into the catacombs intended as places of lasting rest for early Christians. A noxious cloud rolled through empty passages, it hovered close to the ground, an avenging seraph awaiting the unwary.

In the museum lobby, ornate wooden copings covered with shiny lacquer provided instant fodder for encroaching fire. Paintings, hundreds of years old, burst into flames--adding to the inferno which devoured Andrew Simson's monument. An errant line of flames licked the sheath of insulation covering electrical cables which lowered an elevator to the lowest level of the catacombs. Rolling downward, flames headed toward the layer of gas as if pulled by a magnetic force.

Suddenly, a computer room window overlooking the southwest wing of the museum exploded inward, hurling fragments of glass into equipment, desks, walls, and unprotected flesh. Endless sheets of paper filled the air and plastic reels strung yards of magnetic tape ahead of the flames taking command of the room. The force of the natural gas explosion hurled Amariah against metal framework housing *Messiah*. Her head recoiled, then smashed against the door casing as she fell to the floor, unconscious. Banks of hardware toppled over as the ground beneath the building lifted, then settled lower as tunnels beneath the museum began to collapse. File storage bins, main frame cabinets and workstations toppled, burying Amariah.

Another explosion hurled the Father General against the floor, ripping his fingers from the console. Instinct forged from pure survival surged through his dementia. A gas line, laid to service the kitchens of the sampietrini, must have gone undetected. Not only was the new museum going to be destroyed, but the entire hill of the Vatican was also in peril. The portion of his brain dedicated to self-preservation forced him to his feet, but each new blast rumbling beneath the earth buffeted his body. He would leave Amariah to die in the flames. The misbegotten bodies of his enemies would be consumed by the fires of hell--Father Laterano, the betrayer; Father Julian, the coward; and the woman called Amariah, would be turned to ash in the crematorium of Justice. A primordial force, which sought to save him from his own destruction, propelled Andrew Simson out of the room as the museum shuddered beneath the impact of another explosion.

Escape--a plan for salvation percolated through layers of his rapidly degenerating thoughts. He would carry the Pope to the papal heliport. They could escape the burning city. The world would applaud him as the true Redeemer, the Savior of mankind, risen again.

Yes! It was a workable--he would convince the press. He would blame the destruction of the Vatican on a group of zealots. Muslims. Shiites or Sunnis. These groups were considered raving lunatics who would happily destroy the heart of Christianity. He would make it appear as if the destruction of the museum was perpetrated by a wild, radical sect. Their motive painted as fear of Christianity's growing influence. He could turn what seemed like failure into the instrument of his salvation. Andrew Simson knew he could convince the world.

More C-4 crumbled what remained standing of the museum's southwest wing. A cannonade deep in the earth rolled along the corridor beneath the ancient buildings housing the Museo Gregoriano de Profano, Galleria degli Razz, and Galleria dei Candelbri. The enormous metal pinecone, which adorned the Cortile della Pigna for hundreds of years, toppled off its base. A gaping fissure collapsed the Nicchione del Belvedere as its foundation began to crumble. Exquisite buildings of the Casino, the splendid retreat of Pius IV, disintegrated as its marble columns fell like straws before the wind. The fountain of sporting dolphins shot skyward propelled by a torrent of flaming gas. Children, who had guided the dolphin's activities for the past five hundred years toppled on their sides; sightless, stone eyes stared skyward as if yearning for the God which freed them from their thankless task.

Leon lifted his head. The pounding in his ears demanded he remain on the floor as red waves surged across a field of black when he opened his eyes. He tried to remember where he was and what caused the hammering pummeling his skull. As the memory of his fall down the stairs swam to the surface of his thoughts, Leon became aware of a sensation more threatening than the one inside his head. The floor was rising like an incoming tide. He'd been in earthquakes before and this one was severe. The chandelier's crystal tear drops tinkled as the light fixture swayed from side to side. He had to get out of the lobby before restraining bolts securing it to the ceiling worked free from the plaster.

Forcing himself to his knees, he waited for the room to stop heaving, then scrambled out the door. Seconds behind his stumble into the garden a ball of flame spewed from the ground, consuming the Pinacoteca and its priceless contents. Shock and fear freeze framed events going on around him. He turned his head, unable to comprehend the incredible devastation. Library walls had collapsed, and the building containing the Secret Archive was engulfed in flame.

Another tremor directed Leon's attention toward the new museum. Amariah was in the museum! He had to reach her--he had to! Pushing himself off the walkway, Leon demanded his motor skills respond with urgency. A dizzying sensation threatened to force him back against the walkway, but anxiety over Amariah's safety suppressed the wave of darkness.

The handle on the museum's outer door was hot. Leon wondered if he would be swallowed by a wall of fire if he opened it. Deciding there was only one way to find out, he ripped off his jacket and wrapped it around the metal handle. Cautious at first, then angry, he threw the door aside. The foyer was engulfed in smoke but there was no evidence of fire. Dropping to his knees, he scuttled along the floor, where dense smoke pushed breathable oxygen.

Leon forced himself to think, to keep panic under control, to push aside the pain in his head and ignore the swelling which closed his eye. Where would Amariah be?"

The computer control room.

Leon allowed one brief, amazed thought to dwell on the voice ringing so clearly in his ear. It seemed to be guiding him, telling him where to go and what to do. Galvanized into action, he scrambled to the staircase and vaulted the steps three at a time.

On the top landing, Leon looked around, a desperate glance searching for the door to take him to the command center. Smoke billowed down the hallway; he coughed and dropped to his hands and knees again. The display rooms were in flames. He had to be in time . . . he had to reach her!

After what seemed an eternity, Leon found a door marked "Authorized Personnel Only". It was cool beneath his probing fingers. Perhaps the sprinkler system had contained the fire on the other side--but sprinkler system wasn't working anywhere else. No metal doors sealed hallways leading to the display rooms, no warning alarm brought fire fighters running to the scene. Yet the fire detection system was one of the museum features about which Andrew Simson had boasted. *Messiah* failed beneath this first, punishing test. The voice in his ear provided the answer.

Messiah had been turned off, deliberately.

Fear he would be unable to rescue Amariah urged him through the door into a tiled hallway amazingly free of smoke. Using the wall for support, he stood up cautiously, wondering which way to turn. The corridor stretched in both directions for what seemed like a thousand miles.

An inner compass compelled him to turn right; urgency demanded he break into a run. The hallway snaked behind hundreds of display rooms, doors loomed on both the left and right. He passed them quickly, inwardly knowing none of them led to Amariah! Finally, a metal door with a narrow window cross-hatched by reinforcing metal strings blocked his progress. He pressed his face against the window, searching the room: *Messiah* was inside, and his heart responded with the anxious timpani of a kettle drum. Enormous computer discs were still rotating; they continued their predetermined circles as if all were normal, as though the world had not shifted from its axis, forcing mankind in a new direction. Amariah was in the room, he could feel her presence, but--it was faint. Fire raged at the far end of the room, and he eased the door open, afraid a sudden flood of oxygen would further fuel the flames. Once inside, he realized his fears were groundless. Windows facing the museum were blown out and a vicious wind created by the blaze howled through the room.

He scanned banks of overturned equipment, piles of scattered papers, desk, and chairs. A shocked and frightened gaze settled on Philipe Laterano's body, lying in a pool of thickening blood. Another body, one he didn't recognize, was slumped at the base of the *Messiah* console. Where was she? Fear, anger, panic, lifted his senses above the veil of waking consciousness. His head pounded, blood dripped from open wounds, he felt the floor pitch and yaw like he stood on the deck of a heaving ship. God in Heaven, help me find her!

A sound came from beneath a pile debris near the shattered window. Leon hurried to the whimper. Amariah lay beneath a mound of ledgers holding data produced by *Messiah*'s artificial brain. Hurling aside plastic binders, Leon rushed to free a woman he suddenly knew he loved.

Pulling her into his arms, he whispered, "Amariah?"

Slowly, her eyelids lifted away from powder-blue irises and an unfocused gaze met his urging voice. Leon knew he had get her to her feet. "Amariah, we've got to get out of here."

Spirit blazed into her eyes as recognition of where she was and memory of what happened returned. Leon's bruised, bloodied, and battered face came into focus. "Leon?"

"I'm here. The way out might still be clear, but we've got to hurry! Can you stand? Do you think anything is broken?"

Leon helped Amariah to her feet as she challenged her limbs to respond. Rubbing the bump on her head, she nodded. "I'm okay. Nothing feels out of place." Her glance settled on the figure of the monk. Stepping across scattered mounds of now worthless information, she knelt beside his body and placed her fingertips against his aorta. No life force pulsated through a network of vessels which once carried his blood. She lifted his eyelid, but the pupil did not dilate in response to changing light. His tortured mind and body had endured too much. She drew the cowl of his habit over the scared face. There was a look of peace in the monk's expression, as if he were grateful the end had come at last.

Another explosion rocked the building. Leon pulled on Amariah's arm and rushed her into the hallway. Just as they reached the first turn, the metal door designed to protect the command center exploded outward--filling the hallway with shards of red-hot metal and clouds of deadly fumes. Leon shoved Amariah into a crouch, and they inched along the corridor, desperately seeking shelter and safety. The door to the foyer was still cool, but Leon's inner sense urged caution as he opened it. He pushed Amariah onto her stomach, and they slid forward, bumping down marble steps toward the lobby on the ground floor.

Amariah gagged, trying not to inhale dense smoke forcing its way into her lungs with every strangled breath. Leon jerked his tee-shirt over his head. "Put this over your mouth," his voice a scream above flames roaring all around them. He motioned her behind him, his eyes watered, he was nearly blinded by the smoke clawing at cornea, pupil, and iris like a many fingered beasts. "Come on! We've only got a few more feet to go!"

Hoping they were headed in the right direction, Amariah followed the retreating pattern on the soles of Leon's tennis shoes.

Leon's heart sank as they neared the door which opened into the garden--the foyer was engulfed in flame. Behind them, the marble staircase collapsed beneath the onslaught of another explosion heralding the steady advance of Death. Clutching Amariah to him, Leon fought against the panic possessing his thoughts. Fire prevented escape into the garden and the only other avenue out of the burning building was reduced to smoldering rubble. Fragments of crystal began to rain on the landing as the chandelier worked loose from its moorings. They would be roasted alive if they remained in the lobby much longer.

The voice, which provided so many answers, sounded in his ear again.

Go through the door, roll past the fire. Put fear behind you, trust in Me.

Leon stabbed at the tears in his eyes. He studied the door; a gust of wind parted the flames, and he could see beyond into the garden. If they could get through the fire fast enough, perhaps they would survive.

He took Amariah in his arms. The look of trust, the faith in his actions, filled Leon with a burst of courageous energy. "Put your head against my shoulder--we're going through!"

Leon coiled his body around Amariah and rolled out the door through the barrier of flame blanketing the outside of the building. He kept rolling, tucking Amariah beneath the shelter of his arms, chest, and head as they careened down the stairs. He kept rolling until he felt the cool moisture of grass beneath his back, then he rolled further into the garden--away from heat and flames. Grass blanketed with dew soothed singed skin. He lay silent for a moment, heart pounding; only the heavy pant of his breathing registered in his ears as he kept Amariah's head pressed against his chest. When he opened his eyes, Amariah's blouse was smoldering in several places. Leon smothered flames which had not been extinguished by the drop and roll technique learned in grade school.

He examined Amariah. "Are you okay?" He tilted her chin, searching for burns. Although her cheeks were streaked with smoke and she coughed up black phlegm, Leon was satisfied Amariah sustained no serious physical damage. The emotional impact would be harder to determine.

On her part, Amariah stared at the man who cradled her so protectively. His hair was scorched--a blackened halo framed an anxious face. One eye was completely swollen shut, the cut above it sagged open, and a stream of blood followed a jagged path down the side of his face. A greasy film of smoke covered his shoulders and he'd lost his eyebrows to the fire. She wanted to inspect his back for burns. "I think I'm better than you are. Turn around."

He turned; obedient; his mind was denied the will to resist as the miracle of their escape overtook his thoughts.

"Your back is burned, but I think it's superficial in most places."

Their physical condition assured, Leon pulled Amariah further away from the burning building into the safety offered by the garden. He rushed her toward the Casino of Pius IV. His emotions plummeted when he discovered the chaplet would provide no shelter. Its graceful buildings, which once framed the beautiful courtyard, looked as if they had been ravaged by war. He urged her forward, toward the section of garden behind St. Peter's. No smoke billowed skyward from that area, no flames engulfed the trees; perhaps they could find safe haven there. One arm firmly around Amariah, the other pressed against ribs which had begun to ache without mercy, Leon plunged ahead.

They sank to the ground in a fireless sanctuary. A few draughts of smoke free air restored Amariah's ability to think. Despair took unchallenged ownership of her emotions, and all hope she had clung to with such ferocity collapsed when she looked at the old museums. Most of the buildings had collapsed; the skeletal outer shells of a few others remained standing despite the explosions. Horror overtook her when she realized the fire was headed straight toward the Apostolic Palace. "The Pope! We've got to reach the Pope! He'll be trapped--he's too weak to escape." Amariah struggled to her feet. Leon reached to restrain her, to try to make her see reason, to convince her to stay in this sheltered area of the garden, but it was too late; she escaped his frantic grasp. Amariah stumbled toward the courtyard separating the library and museums from the papal apartments.

At the entrance to the Cortile della Sentinella, Amariah's nervous system stopped, flash frozen by the terror suddenly welling up inside her. The black cassock of the Jesuit Father General slipped from the shadows into a doorway leading to the Sistine Chapel. The thought penetrating her brain struck with the force of a canon fusillade. Of course! Simson would try to reach the Pope, to make it look as if he were attempting to rescue the man held dear by the Catholic world.

A distant rumble warned of another explosion. Its blast threw Amariah to the ground. Inches away, the force pushed Leon against the marble tiles. In a mad, scrambling motion, he scurried across the heaving courtyard on his stomach and grabbed Amariah's ankle, his hold becoming a panicky clutch. The air turned as dense as molten iron, a blunt wind fanned by relentless flames, grew sharp. Fear became rage, and Leon felt the tempo of his heartbeat accelerate beyond the point of being human.

"Amariah!" He had to scream above the fusillade of bricks raining down around them. "Stop! You can't help the Pope! We've got to save ourselves!"

Cupping her hand over Leon's iron clad grip, Amariah's steady voice seemed to settle the sediment of fear which muddied his emotions. "I have to go."

There was a light in her eyes that couldn't be accounted for by the flames. They broadcast an eerie incandescence, which made Leon feel as if she knew what was going to happen. She was calm, dangerously calm, the sort of composure displayed by soldiers and policemen, who knew they were already dead, and performed acts of courage beyond the understanding of other men and women.

On her part, Amariah sensed Leon's panic over her safety had subsided. Pointing to the window three stories above, Amariah gave Leon rushed directions. "Get to the Pope. Head straight through this series of courtyards. When you reach the Cortile del Maresciallo take the second doorway. That flight of stairs will take you directly to the Pope's bedroom. Simson is in the Sistine Chapel--I've got to find him. I will meet you in St. Peter's Square when this is over."

Leon didn't argue. He had to hurry. Sprinting across the courtyard, he raced toward the doorway, each inhalation hard won, each furious squeeze of his heart leading him toward the edge of an uncertain destiny.

Amariah slipped inside the hallway; the walls seemed to cave inward, distorted by leaping shadows whipped by flames. Overhead, heavy beams designed to support Pope Julius' private chapel billowed a dense cloud of smoke as tongues of fire raced across their ancient surface. She opened the door a crack and pressed her eye against a narrow slit. Simson stumbled toward the grille in front of Michelangelo's *Last Judgment.* He halted beneath the upraised hand of Jesus as He cast sinners into eternal hell. Confusion and lunatic madness receded, making room for logic as he realized there was only one exit from the chapel, and it was across the room from where he stood.

Turning, he sought to retrace his steps. A mysterious power clotted the air and preternatural sensitivity warned him he was not alone. A woman barred his retreat from the burning room! She stood in front of ornate wooden doors at the chapel entrance, unnerving directness radiating from unnaturally blue eyes.

Amariah stepped forward: Obeisant shadows seemed to bow at her passing as she challenged the man in black with the voice of an avenging prophet. "You will not harm the Pope!" Relentlessly, with stubborn purpose, she closed the gap between them, her movements deliberate.

There was something in her countenance which rang an alarm of doom in Simson's brain. He shrank back, shielding his face with his hands. The woman radiated the power of a Sibyl; she seemed guided by a spiritual force. She was not afraid . . . not ofhim, nor the fire raging around them.

Yea, though I walk through the Valley of the Shadow of Death, I will fear no Evil, for Thou art with me.

The Bible's promise surged in Amariah's ears. It drowned out the hiss of flames, the scream of tortured wood, a softer tinkling rain of thousands of pieces of fresco loosened by heat generated expansion of the ceiling, and the roar of continued explosions outside the chapel. Amariah stalked the Prince of Darkness, predatory ferocity taking up residency in her eyes.

With every step she took forward, Simson stumbled backward, repelled by the power of righteousness exuding from a woman who moved as though Moses and Elijah walked beside her.

Leon battled fatigue, heat, and smoke as he lunged up the final series of stairs wondering why the Papal apartments weren't located on the ground floor. The door was exactly where Amariah described it, and he burst into the room. No nurses stared out flame shrouded windows, no attendants lingered beside the stricken man. Anastasius turned his head, cognizant of what was happening around him.

Three strides took him to the Pope's bedside, "Amariah sent me."

A faint smile lifted the old man's withered lips. "Unhook me." He gestured weakly at the tubes of life sustaining liquids pouring into the back of his hands and the cavity in his chest. "They will do me no more good--but I shall live until I behold her face once more!" The Pope's voice was soft, like the dry rustle of wind over a barren desert, but Leon understood. Anastasius wanted to see Amariah again--he wanted to gaze at her face, to hear her voice, to touch her hand, to bequeath a final blessing.

Wincing, Leon pulled the needles from Pope Anastasius' body; it hurt him to think he caused the gentle old man more pain. Lifting the Pope from the bed, Leon paused, then grabbed a piece of cloth from a nearby table. Gently tucking the fabric over the Pope's face, he hoped it would offer a measure of protection from the smoke through which they had yet to pass. It was the only thing he could think of to ease Anastasius' discomfort.

"Holy Father, tuck your face toward my shoulder. I will protect you the best I can--and pray for us, Father, pray as you have never prayed before."

Leon ran from the papal apartments as fast as his burden allowed, hoping against hope fire had not blocked their only avenue of escape. Squinting his eyes against the caustic smoke, gritting his teeth against the pain of agonized muscles, he asked the Benevolent Force in which he believed so firmly to sustain him.

Amariah stormed forward, her pointed finger accusing, demanding. Another blast shattered the windows near the ceiling, spraying the chapel with shards of glass. Only vaguely aware of the stiletto edges that stabbed her hands and face, Amariah's gaze never strayed from Andrew Simson's terrified expression. Jabbing at the air in front of her, she marched across the distance between them, her voice filled with retribution, her wrath as fiery as the spits of flame racing across the ceiling consuming plaster and paint.

"*You* are solely responsible for this senseless destruction! The darkness in your soul caused malignant currents to eddy across the world. You manipulated our Master's words to rally mankind behind your evil banner. Had your heart remained with the Almighty you might have succeeded. *But you forgot God!* You turned away from truth and began to listen to the Servants of Darkness--Greed, Ego, and the Lust for power!"

The Jesuit Father General backed toward the altar. Some dazed, frazzled part of his brain hoped he could shield himself from the power of righteousness radiating from the woman. He feared her; he feared her as he had never feared anything before; he feared her because he sensed she had the power to cast him into eternal hell.

A hiss filled the chapel, the floor ripped apart, a yawing crevice opened, which looked like the sucking orifice of an awaiting demon. The earth spewed tongues of flame--propelled toward the heavens by the explosive force of the gas trapped in the catacombs beneath St. Peter's. The ceiling creaked, then sagged as timbers weakened by time loosened from their supporting biers. Andrew Simson was impervious to the scream of splitting wood; he didn't feel the caldron of heat which seared the hair from his hands and face; he seemed blind to the ravaging destruction of the priceless monument to Christendom. The only sensation of which he was aware was the horror inspired by the glowing light in the woman's eyes. She drew closer, a seraph bent on vengeance, intent upon sealing the doom of Orcas and Hades and Erebus and Minos and Satan.

Simson backed away, terror crumbling the once proud face, a whine of entreaty on his lips. "Get away from me!" A trail of saliva dribbled from the corner of a mouth twisted into a pitiful grimace. "I represent God on earth--not you! You can't . . . you're only a woman!" His eyes were glassy, and his glance flitted from one side of the room to the other, as if he expected the hand of salvation to rescue him from his self-created hell.

Enormous beams, which had supported the vault of the Sistine Chapel for the last five hundred years, ripped from their buttresses as an explosion erupted somewhere deep in the heart of the earth. Amariah tumbled backward as a huge black cloud of smoke and gas belched from a newly opened fissure in the chapel floor. The sound of rafters tearing away from brackets; the sickening thud of massive timbers crashing against the marble floor; the brittle sound of the fresco as it burst apart and sprayed down on the chapel, echoed in her ears. The grille in front of the altar was cloaked by a veil of oily black smoke.

Struggling to her feet, Amariah lunged across shifting tiles as larger portions of Michelangelo's fresco fell to the floor, vaporized into dust by the impact. The Sistine Chapel turned into a horrifying conflagration, the very place tortured souls in the *Last Judgment* sought so desperately to escape. Piercing screams of wood being twisted and torn, an overpowering hiss and spit of fire, belching steam and noxious gas filled the chapel.

The Father General glanced away from the blaze of the woman's blue eyes, which had been so transfixing, as a deafening whoosh announced an enormous section of ceiling was plummeting toward him. The face of God, His arm extended to imbue life into an awaiting Adam, hurled earthward. A scream halfway up Simson's throat was silenced by the blade-like sharpness of splintered timbers which once supported the panel in which God reached toward Adam. The hand of God plunged through the Father General's chest, pinioning him to the floor. His crushed heart faltered, then offered one last feeble beat which sent blood spewing through severed arteries across the outstretched arm of Adam.

Flames shot toward a gaping hole in the ancient ceiling, fanned to gigantic heights by the sudden draught of air. Smoke billowed through the chapel obscuring Amariah's vision. A gust of searing steam momentarily cleared away the smoke, revealing Simson's mangled neck. His head was ten feet away from his body; the rest of the heavy timber beam brutally crushed his ribs. The hand of God in the fresco reduced flesh, blood, and bone to a mass of bloody tissue. Sightless, distended eyes stared at the upraised hand of Christ as the *Last Judgment* was consumed by a sheet of Pentecostal fire. Simson's claw-like fingers splayed open--the fifth coin lay in the palm of his blackened hand.

A feeling. A sense of preservation. Certainty her life was not to end here and now drew Amariah through the wall of flame. She snatched the coin from the Father General's outstretched hand, then paused to stare at his severed head, an unrepentant expression etched on Simson's tortured face. Slowly, she tugged at the golden chain holding his crucifix, sliding it past the tide of red, mangled tissue, and open arteries which once carried the lifeblood of Andrew Simson. Shoving against the ceiling beam with all her might, she only moved the wood a few inches, but it was enough. His cassock was saturated with warm, moist blood and bones stood at sharp angles through the cloth of his cassock. Slipping her hand into his soggy pants pocket, she extracted the frequency locator. She knew it was the key. Fatigue, shock, and anger diverted logic. She could not figure out what to do with the crucifix! Running her thumb down the side of the cross like she'd seen Simson do a thousand times, Amariah was rewarded with the expulsion of four small prongs. The religious symbol suddenly took on a frightening new meaning. It plugged into the black box, but how? Leon. His name imploded through her brain. Leon would know what to do!

She glanced back at the severed head, a sympathy so deep it defied the boundaries of human emotion welled up inside. Amariah felt sorry for the Father General; sorry he'd lost his faith in God; sorry he hardened his heart against what he knew to be right; sorry he consigned his soul to another, perhaps more painful, existence.

A supernatural power pulled her away from the dismembered body, it guided her from the burning chapel, along hallways cluttered with broken marble and ruined frescoes, through chaos, out of hell, into the relative calm of St. Peter's Square.

She stabbed at her eyes, they were raw from smoke and fire; her head was clogged with the dust of centuries liberated by countless explosions. Thick mucus drained down the back of her throat turning her stomach sour. Leon crouched in the shelter of the still standing base of the obelisk, the Pope cradled in his arms. Amariah rushed forward, tears of relief and thanksgiving rolled down her face unchallenged, leaving wide tracks through the smoke and grime.

From a cloud of smoke, Leon saw Amariah emerge into the square. She hurried toward him, something clutched in her outstretched hand, weariness making her movements slow and awkward. But--there was a glow in her eyes, a bright burning fire, clearly discernable despite the darkness, despite an obscuring blanket of smoke, despite the distance between them.

Kneeling beside the Pope, Amariah handed the box and crucifix to Leon. She placed one hand on Anastasius' shoulder, the other caressed shrunken flesh which clung to the skull of the dying Prince of the Church.

The Pope's eyes flickered open. Pain savaged his senses but the flood of emotion that filled him as he beheld Amariah's tear-stained face gave him the strength to speak. "Lady, we are proud of you. You have done well. We leave the earth to you now." He tried to lift his hand in benediction, but his strength vanished. A withered forearm fell against the supporting circle of Leon's arms. His wrist fell limp, his hand loose, his fingers lifeless.

Statues of popes and saints encircling the attic of Bernini's colonnade, peered down on the man and woman huddled at the base of the obelisk. Marble eyes, which witnessed the passing of generations, seemed to flare with life for one brief, time-altering moment. As if echoing the last words of the dying Pope, statues began to topple into the square, as if their work on earth was done, as if they could now be released from their duty to guard and protect mankind, as if they could now return to the dust and ashes from whence they had been created.

With tender love and greater reverence, Leon lowered the old man's body against the paving stones of St. Peter's Square. The Pope's hand was extended toward Amariah, his finger pointed in her direction, as though willing her the last vestige of his strength. Leon began to tremble, the shock of these last hours, the head injuries, and burns took command of his nervous system. On a deeper, inner plane of awareness, he sensed physical pain was not what caused him to shake. The Pope's finger stretched toward Amariah . . . like Michelangelo's painting of God reaching toward Adam to bequeath the gift of life. Leon lifted his gaze to Amariah. She stared at the old man as though she understood his final message.

Testing the muscles in his legs, Leon rose to a shaky stance. He drew Amariah to him and cradled her head against his shoulder, offering his strength, his courage, and the reservoir of an unexpressed love. Glancing at the crucifix, he noticed thin wires protruding from it. "What's this?"

"Simson said it would stop *Messiah's* destructive sequence. Perhaps the program is the Anti-Christ foretold by the prophets. This crucifix fits into the black box somehow."

Leon turned it over in his palm, inspecting the shape, indentations, and screws holding it together. He tested a crease in the side with his thumb. A lid slid back, revealing a port. Leon inserted the crucifix prongs into a receptacle. The box pulsated with a thin, electronic feel.

Taking it from Leon, Amariah studied two buttons on the opposite side. One might destroy the planet, the other could provide its salvation. Knowledge, which came from a region of the brain she couldn't begin to explain, made her depress the button on the right. A series of red dots began to scroll across the display. Individual letters traveled across the screen one at a time. T-E-R-M-I-N-I-A-T-E -D.

A final explosion sounded the Vatican's death knell--the symbol of Christianity, which had withstood the scourge of invading armies, the plunder of barbarian hordes, and the scheming manipulation of man. The dome of St. Peter's trembled. Layers of travertine split apart, then fell to the ground in a roar. Inside St. Peter's massive slabs of marble crushed the golden altar. One by one, the gigantic bronze pillars of the Baldacchino leaned forward, then toppled to the floor. Priceless tombs of early popes, gilded copings on frescoed ceilings fractured and fell.

A pillar of fire shot into the air, illuminating the dying structure. Never again would man be humbled before this monument; never again would a single soul be intimidated by its grandeur.

Leon sensed he was witnessing the collapse of organized religion--its fearful grip over humanity cauterized by cleansing fire. He glanced down, sensing a change in Amariah.

Amariah's shoulders squared. The voice which reached Leon's ears through the chaos of destruction knew no fear, it was calm, self-reliant. "I know who I am now, why I'm here, and I'm ready to face the future."

EPILOGUE

That night, as fire consumed the Vatican, a new star crested the horizon. The scientist, who operated the deep space telescope at Greenwich, jammed his eye against a plastic fitting which allowed him to view the heavens without the glare of artificial light created by humans inhabiting the planet. He turned a dial, focusing in on a light which had not been in this quadrant of the universe, home to the constellation of Orion, only the night before! It was brighter than Polaris!

With trembling hands, he dialed an overseas operator, placing a call to the Lowell Observatory at Kitt Peak in Arizona. A warbling voice called out the vector to the Palomar Observatory in central California, and the newly built observatory in the clear, unpolluted air of the outback in Australia. Although Australia's giant telescope was below the equator, the light was so intense the astronomer thought perhaps its glow might be seen all the way to the Southern Hemisphere.

Giant lenses around the world scanning the night sky were quickly set to track the unfamiliar star as earth rotated toward another promised sunrise. Men of science awakened others who dedicated their lives to the study of the universe. Cars raced down darkened highways toward remote observatories built on high mountain tops as anxious men hurried to look at the *new light* shining down on the earth from the heavens.

www.ingramcontent.com/pod-product-compliance
Lightning Source LLC
Chambersburg PA
CBHW022235020726
47496CB00004B/918